A Matter of Honor

VOLUME TWO OF THE
HORSTBERG SAGA

Books by Elizabeth D. Michaels

Horstberg Saga
Behind the Mask (Volume One)
A Matter of Honor (Volume Two)

A Matter of Honor

VOLUME TWO OF THE
HORSTBERG SAGA

Bestselling author Anita Stansfield writing as

Elizabeth D. Michaels

WHITE
STAR
PRESS

This is a work of fiction, and the views expressed herein are the sole responsibility of the author. Likewise, certain characters, places, and incidents are the product of the author's imagination, and any resemblance to actual persons, living or dead, or actual events or locales, is entirely coincidental.

A Matter of Honor: Volume Two of the Horstberg Saga

Published by White Star Press
P.O. Box 353
American Fork, Utah 84003

Sword and scarf painting copyright © 2014 Anna C. Stansfield
Cover and interior design by ePpubMasters

ISBN: 978-1-939203-36-6
Printed in the United States of America
Year of first printing: 2014

For Lorelle Victoria.

Abbi du Woernig came awake abruptly, gasping for breath. In the darkness she felt her husband's arms come around her and she clung to him, grateful to have Cameron near while she attempted to calm down and think rationally.

"A dream?" he asked close to her ear. He was well aware of her gift of dreams. Throughout her life she'd occasionally experienced dreams that had, without question, been premonitory, as their content had come to pass at some subsequent time. In fact, a dream had led her to Cameron and had put her in a position to help guide him to the determination he needed to take back the country he ruled from hands that were destroying it. To the people of Horstberg, these happenings were practically legend, even if they knew nothing about the dreams that had prompted such miraculous events. For Abbi, they were tender and personal memories, and one of many reasons she had learned to respect the messages of her dreams.

"Yes," she said, "but I've never had such a . . . *horrible* dream. It was a nightmare, in truth."

"A nightmare?" Cameron asked, his voice low and husky. "Just a bad dream, or does it have meaning, Abbi? How did it make you feel?"

She groaned in response to the question and clung to him more tightly. "I feel as if it will come to pass. I've never felt it any more strongly than I do now."

"Tell me," he prodded gently. "You'll feel better if you talk about it."

"I saw a woman . . . murdered," she said and heard Cameron draw a sharp breath.

"There hasn't been a murder in Horstberg since my first wife was killed," he said, his astonishment evident.

"I know," she said sadly.

"Did you see who it was? Who did it?"

"No. I could only see the victim, and her face was obscured." Tears came with her clarification. "She was dressed simply, like a common woman. As a woman would dress who worked at a pub, perhaps, except that she had a white silk scarf around her neck; a very lovely scarf that did not go at all with her attire. Her hair was dark blond and curly. She was . . . near my age, I would guess, perhaps just a little older—early to mid-twenties. She was stabbed through the heart with a dagger; the dagger had a carved, ivory handle. And that's all I saw."

Cameron pressed his lips into her hair and muttered gently, "It's going to be all right, Abbi."

"How can it be all right for a woman to be murdered? Is this meant to be some kind of warning? Am I expected to protect a woman that I can't even identify?"

Cameron leaned up on one elbow and remained thoughtfully silent. Abbi could feel his compassion and concern, but she knew he didn't have the answers any more than she did. She touched his dark hair and then his face. He put a hand over hers, holding it there a long moment. He then touched her face in return, saying, "Abbi . . . I believe that sometimes . . . there are things that simply happen, and there's nothing we can do to prevent them, however tragic they may be. Perhaps your dream is more for the purpose of being prepared."

Abbi had to admit that felt right, but it didn't erase her anxiety. She had to ask, "For who to be prepared, Cameron? And how?"

"I don't know, Abbi. We just have to go on and be aware, and perhaps the answers will come."

Abbi knew he was right, but she had trouble going back to sleep, and when she did the dream recurred. She rose early and went to the window, looking out over the valley below. She wondered what unsuspecting woman might be destined for this horrible fate. The sun was barely showing itself when Abbi noticed a sleigh being harnessed in the courtyard below. Elsa would be leaving soon and the thought darkened Abbi's mood further. Elsa was her lady's maid and dearest friend, and Abbi wasn't certain how she would manage without Elsa while she traveled far to care for an ailing aunt. They had exchanged farewells before going to bed, but she felt an added sadness as she watched Elsa attempting to say goodbye to her husband before she finally got into the sleigh and it disappeared through the castle gate.

Abbi stood as she was until the sun came up, and she couldn't deny that it was a beautiful day. It had been snowing almost nonstop for days, but now the sun had appeared and the world was brilliantly white. If only she could free herself from her heavy thoughts. Thinking it through, she knew that she *had* to free herself of them in order to do all that was required of her. If she went about her day melancholy and distracted, people would be concerned and question her. And she had no desire to discuss her feelings with anyone except her husband.

Abbi went to the wardrobe to find an appropriate dress. What she needed was a distraction, and getting started on her Christmas shopping seemed the perfect way to go about it.

Chapter One

DAMSEL IN DISTRESS

Sunlight peered tenuously over the snow-covered peaks standing to the east of Castle Horstberg. The sky was brilliantly clear, a stark contrast to the heavy clouds that had steadily dumped snow for the last three days. Georg Heinrich eased his wife a little closer to his side and walked sullenly across the castle courtyard toward the waiting sleigh, harnessed to four bays. Georg and Elsa stood silently facing each other while servants tightened down the baggage and rechecked the harnessing to be certain all was in order. Georg became lost in Elsa's eyes until an officer's voice startled him.

"I believe we're ready to go, sir."

"Thank you, Lieutenant," he said absently. Then to Elsa, "I've been dreading this moment."

"So have I," she said and gave him a lingering kiss. "But the time will go quickly. You'll see. I'll be back before Christmas. I promise."

"Yes, well. Christmas is more than seven weeks away. It seems like an eternity, in my opinion."

Elsa managed a smile, but he saw her chin quiver and knew she was trying to be brave. He knew she didn't really want to go, but her aunt needed her. They weren't close, but this woman was Elsa's only remaining relative. She strongly valued the family tie and felt compelled to answer the plea. This aunt had close friends who were caring for her through a lengthy illness, but they had some other pressing matters to attend to and had written to ask if Elsa could come and stay just long enough to give them the time they needed. Georg had wanted desperately to go with her, but working as the duke's highest advisor was especially demanding at the moment, and he simply couldn't get away. He'd made every possible arrangement to see that she would be well cared for, but he still couldn't help being concerned. And oh, how he was going to miss her!

"You've got that worried look again," Elsa said. "Now stop that. Gertie will keep me company, and the lieutenant will take very good care of us."

Georg glanced briefly to Lieutenant Joerger standing nearby. He was competent and trustworthy, and Georg knew he was the perfect escort for Elsa and her friend. But he just hated the thought of being away from her at all. The Black Forest seemed terribly far away.

When it became evident that everyone was ready and waiting discreetly for him to complete his goodbyes, Georg took Elsa's delicate shoulders into his hands, though he could barely feel them through her heavy cloak. He pressed his mouth over hers as if he might never have the chance again, oblivious to being observed.

"I love you," he murmured, trying not to think that he'd never been away from her for more than a day or two since they'd been married nearly four years ago.

"And I love you," she replied in a shaky voice. He saw tears brim in her eyes, but she smiled them away—at least for the moment. He knew she'd be crying once the sleigh pulled away, and so would he. "You take good care of Han, now. Tell him every day that I love him and I miss him."

"I will," he promised and kissed her once more before he forced himself to help her into the waiting sleigh next to Gertie, who was already seated beneath a heavy quilt. She eased a portion of it over Elsa's lap just as the lieutenant took a seat next to the driver and the sleigh moved forward. Elsa turned back, pressing a gloved hand over her lips and waving. Georg returned the gesture and stood in the cold until the sleigh had disappeared through the high castle gate and slipped down the hill.

He glanced skyward and pushed back his emotion as the biting cold forced him to return quickly to his apartment in the servants' housing to one side of the courtyard. He hurried inside and up the stairs where he found three-year-old Han still sleeping soundly. He paused a few minutes just to watch his son and ponder how good their life was together. Then he gently woke him, holding him until he became coherent enough to get dressed. Once Han was bundled up for the cold, Georg carried him across the courtyard and through the main entrance of the castle. Even though Han's mother was gone, the routine was familiar. Each day, while Elsa assisted the duchess as a lady's maid and Georg worked with the duke, Han played in the nursery with Erich, who was younger than Han by only a matter of months, and destined to be the next Duke of Horstberg.

They had only been in the nursery a few minutes when the duke and duchess arrived with their young son, who would be turning three in a few months. Little Erich and Han were playing together as quickly as Erich's father set him down.

"Good morning, Georg," Abbi du Woernig said brightly, pressing the standard kiss to his cheek. They'd been friends since childhood, and their relationship now was warm and comfortable.

"Good morning, Your Grace," he replied and Abbi laughed softly.

"We're in the nursery, Georg. Formalities are really not necessary."

Georg managed a faint smile then became distracted by his thoughts until Cameron du Woernig slapped him lightly on the shoulder. "I take it Elsa's on her way," he said, "unless there's some other reason you've got that pathetic look on your face."

"How perceptive you are," Georg said with subtle sarcasm. "I'd wager you'd look a whole lot worse if Abbi were off for nearly two months."

Cameron glanced toward his wife, then back to Georg. "You've got me there, my friend. A day without Abbi is difficult to bear."

Abbi tossed her husband a warm smile, saying, "Then you'd do well to be empathetic, my dear. I already miss Elsa myself. I'm certain the weeks will drag for Georg."

Again Georg managed a weak smile, and he was grateful when Cameron shifted the conversation by bringing up a matter of business that would be on the day's agenda.

While Abbi watched her young son playing with Han, her mind was drawn against her will to the horrid images of her dreams. She forced her thoughts elsewhere by focusing on the boys playing and their fathers sitting close together, talking comfortably. Han was a childlike miniature of his father, with fluffy blond hair and gentle features. Erich too was the spitting image of his father, except that he had inherited Abbi's red, curly hair as opposed to his father's, which was dark and wavy. Abbi's thoughts guided her eyes to Cameron. Her husband typically wore his hair combed back off his face and it hung to the bottom of his neck. He had an innate regal air about him that could not be diminished by the way he often dressed so casually and behaved, with no effort at all, like a common man. He just looked like a duke without even trying, which Abbi found intriguing simply for the fact that she had known him for so long before she'd realized that noble blood flowed in his veins.

Breakfast was brought into the nursery for the children and Abbi watched how naturally Cameron and Georg helped their sons with the meal while they continued to visit intermittently. Cameron had once declared that he would keep his country strong by keeping his family first, and she loved him all the more for the way he had held to that promise. The citizens of Horstberg would likely be surprised to see their ruler cutting his son's food into bite-sized pieces while the nanny waited nearby for any order he might give her. But Cameron valued purposeful interaction with his son at every possible oppor- tunity, and even though he was a very busy man, he took his time in the nursery very seriously. He talked with Erich for a few minutes while the child ate, then he and Georg stood side by side, continuing their conversation while the boys giggled and tried to kick each other under the table. The nanny just observed and smiled. Abbi did the same, loving the way that Erich and Han were being raised together, especially in light of the close relationship shared by their fathers. The two men together were a striking contrast in coloring and features but similar in build and stature—tall and thoroughly masculine—and kindred spirits to the core. Their strengths and weaknesses balanced each other richly, and they were well practiced at translating their unified strength into the running of a country.

Georg and Cameron stayed in the nursery until their sons had eaten breakfast and were off playing together as if they were brothers. Abbi was visiting with the nanny when Cameron interrupted their conversation to kiss his wife.

"You take care now, my love," he said, briefly setting a hand to her well-rounded belly. The baby was due a few weeks after Christmas.

"I hope your day goes well," she said and kissed Cameron again before he and Georg left the room to get an hour's work in before breakfast was served for the adults.

After breakfast Abbi sat in front of her mirror while Bruna put the finishing touches on her hair. Caring for the duchess's rich, red curly hair was an envied task among the servants, and it was usually Elsa who saw to it. But in Elsa's absence, Bruna always proved capable and pleasant.

"That looks very fine," Abbi declared once she was finished. She pinned a hat into place that went well with the rust-colored dress she wore, and hurried down the stairs, knocking lightly at the door of the duke's office.

"You're looking as lovely as ever, Your Grace," one of the officers flanking the door remarked.

"You're too kind," she said just before Cameron's voice called for her to enter. The officer smiled and opened the door for Abbi, but it was evident when she stepped in that she had interrupted something. "Oh, I'm sorry," she murmured, glancing quickly at each of the men seated in the room. Along with Cameron and Georg, there was Lance Dukerk, who was the Captain of the Guard. Also present were three of his highest officers. She focused her attention on her husband as he came to his feet and she added, "I just wanted to tell you that I'm going into town now and—"

"What for?" Cameron asked, moving around the desk to take her hand, oblivious to anyone else in the room.

"I need to get some Christmas gifts. I—"

"Christmas is more than seven weeks away," Cameron protested gently.

"Don't I know it," Georg said in a surly voice.

Captain Dukerk laughed and spoke in his deep voice. "If he's going to be in this kind of a mood until his wife returns, we should all be praying the time goes quickly, indeed."

Cameron glanced wryly toward the captain then turned his focus back to Abbi. "I know when Christmas is," she said in response to his comment. "And I can assure you that I will not feel like going anywhere at all long before it arrives. At the moment, I feel great and the weather is good. And I'm going shopping."

"Yes, Your Grace," Cameron said facetiously, then he turned more toward the men and added, "I know better than to stand in Her Grace's way when she's set her mind to something."

"Indeed," the captain sniggered.

"Who are you going with?" Cameron asked his wife. "If Elsa's not here, then . . ."

"I'm perfectly capable of managing just fine. The carriage is waiting and—"

"I'm not having you go into town alone," Cameron insisted.

"I won't be alone. The driver and—"

"And is the driver actually going *shopping* with you, or—"

"I think I can manage fine on my own."

"You're seven months pregnant. And I'm not letting you go *anywhere* alone."

"Are you offering to come along?" she asked with a teasing smile, knowing there was far too much work for him and Georg to justify time off for shopping. She could also understand Cameron's concern, since Erich's birth had come with some complications that had nearly cost Abbi her life. They were both thrilled with the prospect of having another child, but neither of them dared admit aloud that the ordeal ahead was frightening.

"I wish I could," he said, and she knew he meant it. "But the captain won't be needed here for quite some time," he added as if he were discussing some great military maneuver. "He would be happy to escort you, I'm certain."

Lance Dukerk looked up from some papers he was studying that were spread out on the table. "What was that?" he asked.

"We can finish here," Cameron said. "I'd like you to escort Her Grace into town. See that she doesn't overdo it."

Abbi opened her mouth to protest, but the captain grinned and spouted with enthusiasm, "I'd love to."

"Really, Captain," Abbi said, "I don't think that you should worry about . . . Surely you have more important things to do and . . ."

"Nothing so important," Lance said, offering his arm. He winked at her and nodded toward the duke. "A pleasant duty, Your Grace."

"Not too pleasant, I trust," Cameron said with a little smirk. He gave Abbi a brief kiss then pointed a finger at the captain. "Mind your manners, Captain, or I'll have you sweeping out cells in the keep."

"Yes, Your Grace," Lance said with mock fear before escorting Abbi from the room.

"And how are you feeling?" Lance asked Abbi as they moved down the long hall toward the main entrance.

"Very well, thank you. And you?"

"I'm fine as always. Thank you, Your Grace."

Abbi smiled up at him as he helped her with her cloak and they stepped out into the cold. It was highly common for Captain Dukerk to escort the duchess whenever such a thing was necessary. The duke trusted him implicitly, which trust had been proven in the past through incidents that had drawn them all close together, almost like family. In fact, Lance's sister, Gwen, had been Cameron du Woernig's first wife. Several years earlier, she'd been murdered by Cameron's younger brother, Nikolaus, who had attempted to frame Cameron for the crime. Cameron had gone into hiding for a period of four years, and the circumstances which had proven Nikolaus's guilt and restored the throne of Horstberg to Cameron had deeply involved Abbi, as well as Georg—and Lance Dukerk. The story of how it had all come together was well known among the people of Horstberg, but Lance Dukerk was one of the few people who fully understood what they had gone through to get where they were now. Neither of them could ever forget that they had come within a breath of being married to each other, and if Cameron had not survived the precarious game that had given him back his country, Abbi would this day be *Mrs.* Lance Dukerk.

In the carriage, Abbi turned away from the window to notice Lance watching her, an almost dreamy gaze in his eyes. Even though his features and coloring could be called average, he had a smile that glowed and a commanding presence that suited his position. Abbi turned back to the window, saying curtly, "If you don't stop looking at me that way, Captain, I'll find someone else to escort me."

He cleared his throat loudly and turned away, embarrassed. "Forgive me, Your Grace," he said. "It's just that . . . you seem to grow more beautiful every year."

"I'm quite pregnant, if you hadn't noticed. I've rarely felt less beautiful."

"That's a matter of opinion, I suppose."

"Well, your compliment is appreciated, but I think you should be paying them to other ladies—*unmarried* ladies."

Again he seemed embarrassed. "I didn't mean anything inappropriate, Abbi," he said. It wasn't unusual for them to be less formal when they weren't in public.

"I know that," she replied. "And Cameron knows it too, or he wouldn't be sending you to look out for me."

"Why *does* he send me?" Lance asked.

"You know the answer to that question more than anyone."

"I was just wondering if the answer had changed."

Abbi looked directly at him and fought the urge to give some witty response that might lighten the mood. His question was intently serious. It deserved an equivalent answer. "He knows you would defend me with your life if it became necessary."

"Gladly," he said.

"Then it seems the answer hasn't changed."

"But I'm not so sure that most men wouldn't. You just have a way of making people adore you . . . without even trying."

"Now you're flattering me, Captain."

"I don't use flattery and you know it. I'm well aware of the way people regard you. I'm just one of many who would lay down in the mud to prevent you from getting your feet dirty."

"So you tell me." She laughed softly. "But I'm not certain I believe it." A moment later she said, "You're looking at me that way again."

"What way?"

"The way you used to look at me when we were engaged to be married."

Lance laughed softly. "There's no need for concern, Your Grace. I'm well aware that Cameron's love for you is something I could never compete with, and the vows you share with him are not something I take lightly, I can assure you. It's just that . . . I'm envious."

Abbi shifted uncomfortably, wondering how they'd gotten into this conversation. "Lance, you really shouldn't be saying such things; not after all this time. Not when—"

"No, you misunderstand me. I can assure you that I'm feeling nothing inappropriate, Abbi. It's just that . . . I'm envious of the way Cameron feels about you. I want to feel that way about a woman."

Abbi relaxed. "There have been many women vying for your attention these last few years."

"Yes," he said with a sour voice, "women who are enchanted by my uniform and my position. Shallow, flighty women, all of them."

"There's got to be someone out there who could find a way into your heart."

"Do you really believe that, Abbi? Is there really a special someone for everyone?"

"I'd like to believe that. You're a good man, Lance. You deserve to be happy."

The carriage halted at the edge of the square and Lance helped Abbi step out. He gave the driver instructions and escorted the duchess into the square where she eagerly began her search for the perfect gifts for those she loved and cared for. An hour into their shopping, they sat together on a bench at the edge of the square so that Abbi could rest her back. Lance relinquished his armload of packages and sat beside her.

Abbi hated the way she found herself searching in the crowds for women who fit the profile she had seen in her dream. She wanted to find every woman with dark blond hair and look into their eyes and tell them to be careful. When anxiety began to overtake her, she forced a distraction into her mind.

"Don't you find it a little demeaning for the Captain of the Guard to be carrying about the duchess's packages?" Abbi asked.

Lance laughed. "Not in the slightest. I can assure you I get plenty of opportunities to explore other more masculine aspects of my calling. Such things as this are a pleasure."

"So," Abbi asked, "what is it you're looking for in a woman?"

"I want someone who needs me—I mean, really needs me."

"A damsel in distress, then?"

"Perhaps," he laughed, "but . . . not necessarily. I mean . . . I just want someone who will allow me to care for her, and will do the same for me. I want a woman who loves me for who I am, not what I am. No pretenses. And . . . well, I just want to feel the way I know Cameron feels when you walk into a room."

"Have you ever felt that way?"

"No, I don't believe so. But when I feel it, I'm certain I'll know."

Abbi smiled. "I'm certain you will. And when you find this great lady, I expect to be one of the first to know."

"Oh, you will be," he said and came to his feet. They bought some lunch from one of the vendors and took it back to the carriage to share with the driver, who was waiting with a good book. After eating, they shopped a while longer, then set out for the castle, the seats piled with packages.

"A successful endeavor," Lance commented, eying all that Abbi had acquired.

"Yes, I believe so," she said. They talked casually of the happenings of Horstberg, which Abbi kept well versed on. She knew every political maneuver taking place, and was well aware of the problems and struggles of their little country.

The moment Lance stepped down from the carriage, an officer approached him, clearly agitated. "Good, you're here," he said. "I was about to send someone to get you."

"Has war been declared or something?" Lance asked, knowing his men were trained well enough to handle practically anything without him.

"No, sir. It's . . . a woman, sir."

"A woman?" Lance laughed as he helped Abbi step down.

"Yes, sir," the officer continued, seeming even more flustered. "She arrived a couple of hours ago, insisting that she see the duke personally."

Lance exchanged a comical glance with Abbi. "And surely you told her that no one sees the duke personally under such circumstances."

"Yes, sir, I did."

"Then why is she still here?"

"Well, she has nowhere to go, sir. She just arrived in Horstberg and . . . well, I think you should talk to her yourself. Then you'll understand."

"Very well," Lance said and turned to tell the duchess goodbye. But she firmly said, "I'm coming with you."

"Very well, Your Grace. Perhaps this calls for a lady's touch."

"Perhaps it does," she said, and they followed the officer into the area of the keep where the captain's offices were located. The officer opened the door of a small room used for interrogation where a woman came immediately to her feet, along with a young girl who appeared to be about four or five years old.

"This is Captain Dukerk, madame," the officer said. "You may address your problem with him."

"Thank you," the woman said and the officer slipped out of the room, closing the door behind him.

Abbi managed to keep from gasping when she saw this woman. She told herself not to overreact. Simply because she had the same type of hair that Abbi had seen in her dream did not necessarily mean a thing. She forced her heart to slow down and allowed Lance to do his business.

Lance took a moment to absorb this woman, while the woman absorbed Abbi du Woernig, who was standing at his side. She had a typical awe-struck expression that came over most people when they first got a good look at the Duchess of Horstberg. Abbi just had a way of affecting people that was difficult to describe.

The woman and child were both dressed poorly, especially considering the weather. Their faces were pinched with stark evidence of cold and hunger. The woman looked to be in her middle twenties. Her hair appeared to be dark blond and curly, although most of it was covered with a gray, wool scarf that had obviously been through some difficult times. The child had dark hair and brows, a stark contrast to her pale skin. Lance didn't know what the problem was exactly, but he asked the first thing that came to mind. "Have they given you anything to eat?"

The woman looked surprised but answered in a quiet voice, "Yes, thank you. We just enjoyed a fine meal while we were waiting."

"Good. It would seem my men actually know what they're doing occasionally. Now, what can I help you with?"

"I need to see the duke, right away."

"I'm afraid that's not possible, Mrs. . . . uh . . . I didn't get your name."

"Rader," she stated. "Nadine Rader."

"Well, Mrs. Rader, I'm afraid that seeing the duke is not possible. But if you would like to discuss the problem with me, I am able to act on his behalf and I'm certain we can take care of whatever—"

"No," she snapped, "you don't understand. I have come many miles to see him. I must talk to the duke . . . personally!"

Lance exchanged a discreet glance with Abbi before he said gently, "Mrs. Rader, if you will tell me what the problem is, I will determine whether or not it warrants the duke's personal attention. He is a very busy man and—"

"He will see *me,*" she said firmly.

"And how is that?" Lance was firm but kind.

A long minute of silence passed while Lance's frustration became undermined by a certain intrigue. It was easy to feel sorry for her, not to mention, curious. When she didn't answer, Lance stated the established policy, "If you would like to write down your name and request, I can see about getting you an appointment sometime next week and—"

"No," she interrupted again, but this time her voice cracked. "That's impossible."

"And why is that?" Lance asked.

Again only silence responded until Abbi stepped forward and urged the woman to sit down. "Mrs. Rader," Abbi said, sitting close beside her, "we can't help you if we don't know the problem. Please . . . just tell us why it's impossible."

Nadine Rader looked into Abbi's compassionate eyes and her voice broke as she said, "We have nowhere to go. We have nothing. What little we had was sold or stolen through the journey. We barely made it here alive. If I could just see the duke, everything would be all right."

Abbi glanced toward Lance who asked, "And why is that, Mrs. Rader?" When she didn't answer, he stated, "We can provide you with some food and clothing and a place to stay until other arrangements can be made. But seeing His Grace is not so easy. And until you tell me *why* you want to see him, I'm not even going to consider it an option."

Lance and Abbi both waited while Mrs. Rader was clearly gathering her courage. She came to her feet and drew back her shoulders. With a shaky voice she muttered quietly, "I need to see His Grace because . . . this is his child."

Lance shot his eyes toward Abbi and they exchanged a silent understanding. *Oh, not another one,* he could almost hear her saying. But they kept quiet and turned toward Mrs. Rader, attempting to handle this with compassion.

"Captain," Abbi said firmly, "I think it would be a good idea for Mrs. Rader to see the duke, right away. I'm certain I can arrange it."

"Yes, of course," Lance said as Abbi turned to leave the room.

"Who is that?" Mrs. Rader asked the captain.

"That would be the Duchess of Horstberg." At her questioning gaze he clarified, "The duke's wife."

Mrs. Rader gasped just before she fainted, falling into the captain's arms.

Chapter Two

SHATTERED ILLUSIONS

adine came awake to the sound of her daughter's frightened whimpering. Her next awareness was the captain's face looming above her as he murmured in his deep, gentle voice, "Mrs. Rader? Are you all right?" She felt his hand on her face and forced herself into coherency, if only to avoid further embarrassment. She sat up and opened her arms for Dulsie; the child ran to her and immediately stopped crying.

It took Nadine a minute to recall what had led up to the moment when everything had gone black. As the conversation came back, a sick dread tightened in the deepest part of her. Something was horribly wrong. Of course, she had known for a long time that something *must* be wrong, or she wouldn't have been in the circumstances she'd been left to. Still, in her heart she had clung to the tiniest hope that arriving in Horstberg would set everything right. But it was obvious now that *nothing* was right.

"Are you all right?" the captain asked again and she turned toward him, startled from her thoughts.

"I'm fine, thank you," she insisted, coming carefully to her feet. "I believe you were going to let me speak with the duke."

"Just follow Her Grace." The captain motioned toward the door, where the kind woman she had spoken to was waiting, her expression filled with compassion. There were a thousand questions Nadine wanted to hurl at this woman, but she knew it would accomplish nothing, and she'd likely be put out on the streets without further argument. So she kept her thoughts to herself and took Dulsie's little hand. They followed the duchess outside, with the captain coming close beside her. They walked across the courtyard and into the main entrance of the castle, and she found it ironic to realize that in spite of her connections, she'd never been here before. The enormity and elegance of the place left her in awe, and it was apparent that little Dulsie was having similar thoughts.

Nadine kept her concentration on following the woman ahead of her, fighting off a lingering lightheadedness. Dulsie began to drag behind and whimper with exhaustion. She couldn't recall the last time that either of them had actually enjoyed a good night's sleep. Nadine stopped to pick Dulsie up and carry her, grateful that she was light for a five-year-old. But she'd only taken a few steps when the captain stopped her with his hand on her arm. "May I?" he asked, holding out his arms.

Nadine asked her daughter softly, "Is it all right if the captain carries you? I'll be right here with you. I promise."

Dulsie nodded and went easily into his arms, laying her head against the red fabric of his uniform that covered his shoulder. The hallway seemed to go on forever, and Nadine noticed that Dulsie was sound asleep long before they reached a door where two officers of the Guard seemed to be waiting for orders, looking rather bored until they came to immediate attention.

"Is His Grace in a meeting?" the duchess asked them.

"No, Your Grace. He's with Mr. Heinrich."

"Thank you," she said and went into the room, closing the door behind her.

Nadine felt the officers discreetly observing her, their curiosity evident. The captain paced slowly back and forth, as if holding a sleeping child were a natural part of his routine. Nadine leaned against the wall, her arms folded tightly around her middle. The anticipation and hope she had expected to feel at this moment had turned to dread and disbelief. How could he have married another woman? Why hadn't he sent for her? Why had he ignored her every letter? What had gone wrong? And where would all of this leave her? Well, at least she knew the answer to that last one. Out in the cold. No matter what the circumstances might be, she had obviously been left out in the cold. But *why*?

Nadine's heart nearly beat right out of her when the door came open and a man's voice called, "You may come in now."

"Mrs. Rader," the captain said. With a quick nod he indicated that she go ahead of him into the room. She heard the door close behind her as she glanced quickly at the woman she had followed here and also a tall, important looking man with blond hair who was watching her with subtly skeptical eyes. But her attention was drawn to the man seated behind the desk as he said in a firm voice, "You wanted to see me?"

It only took a long moment for Nadine to absorb his appearance. His clothing was fine but simple, and his hair was almost black and combed neatly off his face. His modest appearance was contrasted starkly by the undeniable power in his eyes. But one thing was certain. She'd never seen this man before.

"Well?" he bellowed when she only stood in dazed silence.

Nadine forced her voice. "I . . . well . . . I don't understand. You're not . . ." She didn't know how to say it.

"Nikolaus?" he said, and just hearing the name spoken aloud brought back that lightheadedness. She teetered slightly but managed to maintain her composure and remain standing.

"No," she said in a shaky voice, "you're not Nikolaus."

"Which means, I am glad to say," the duke said firmly, "that I am not the father of this child."

Nadine looked at the floor and shook her head slowly, not knowing how to ask what had happened, not daring to ponder what her future might be like from this point. She was grateful now to have her daughter sleeping, if only to be spared this conversation.

"Perhaps you should sit down," she heard the captain say, and she felt herself being eased into a chair.

"Thank you," she murmured then forced herself to her senses. This might be the only chance she'd get to at least have some questions answered. She could fall apart later. She cleared her throat tensely and looked up with trepidation. "I . . . don't understand. Where is he? What happened?"

"My brother . . ." the duke said carefully and Nadine's surprise deepened. She hadn't even known that Nikolaus had a brother, ". . . was killed a little over three years ago. I'm not certain why you didn't know that or—"

"I sent letters," she said. "He didn't answer or . . ." The reason began to settle in even before the duke went on.

"We've received letters from a woman—letters with no return address, which left us with no means to notify you."

Nadine nodded, attempting to put all of this information in order. "He . . . knew where I was, and . . . asked that I keep my whereabouts from anyone else."

Silence settled uncomfortably over the room until the duke said in a kind voice, "I apologize, Mrs. Rader, for the misunderstanding. I will see that your needs are taken care of until you can find the means to provide for yourself and your daughter." He added with only a trace of bitterness, "I'm quite accustomed to caring for my brother's illegitimate children."

Nadine shot her head up as every defense inside of her became alert. "But Dulsie is not illegitimate. Nikolaus and I were married. There were political problems, complications that prevented him from . . ."

Nadine hesitated when she saw a stern glance pass between the duke and the captain. The duke turned back toward her and finished her thought all too easily. ". . . That prevented him from making the marriage public. He sent you away with a large sum of money when you became pregnant, wanting to keep you and the child safe until things settled down. He didn't want you to use his name for reasons he couldn't divulge. When the money ran out he was difficult to find and so you were working just to survive, certain he would send for you any day."

Nadine could only stare at him in stunned silence, wondering how he could know the situation so accurately. When she said nothing he answered the question she couldn't put a voice to. "I've heard the story four times now, Mrs. Rader. I'd wager you have no living relatives in Horstberg who might have complicated matters. And you have a marriage certificate."

Nadine's voice squeaked with one last thread of hope. "I *do* have a certificate."

She pulled the carefully folded parchment from inside her bodice and held it out toward the duke. He unfolded and glanced at it briefly before handing it to the other man in the room. He looked it over and said in a grave voice, "It's the same signature."

"As what?" Nadine demanded.

"The first time this came up," the duke said, "we did a thorough investigation. The man who *married* the two of you is now serving time in prison for a number of colorful crimes, including fraud. He's a thief and a con artist. Performing mock marriages was one of his specialties. The document is not legal, madame. And I wish I didn't have to be the one to tell you that Nikolaus du Woernig was also a thief and a con artist. There's one count he didn't lie to you about. Things here were very complicated, indeed. He was trying to run a country that he had acquired through murder and blackmail, and he was trying to keep his betrothal to the Baron Von Bindorf's daughter from interfering with his numerous affairs. He would do just about anything to get a woman into his bed. Pretending to marry her was apparently one of his favorites. He was known for severely punishing anyone who attempted to make him do the right thing by his illegitimate children and their dishonored mothers. But it all came undone around him in the end."

Nadine absorbed the information as it crept through a shroud of numb shock that seemed to be protecting her emotions. With a fairly steady voice she asked, "How did he die?"

Again Nadine caught a glance that passed between the captain and the duke before the duke cleared his throat and said in a tight voice, "One of my officers killed him while he was holding a gun to my wife's head, after he'd dragged her out of her bed in the middle of the night."

The silence that followed threatened to penetrate the shock protecting Nadine. She was surprised when the duke pulled a chair in front of her and sat down. He leaned his forearms on his thighs and looked directly at her. While she was wondering what else he might tell her, she reminded herself that this was a man so important that most people had to make an appointment weeks in advance to see him—if they got to see him at all.

"Mrs. Rader," he said in a voice completely kind and gentle, "I want to—"

"It's Miss Rader," she interrupted.

The duke heaved a sigh laced with regret before he continued, "I want to say that . . . I'm truly sorry for the hurt my brother brought into your life. What he has done to you, and to others like you, is not only criminal, it's immoral, it's base and contemptible. I have spent the last three and a half years attempting to pick up the pieces that my brother left behind. But nothing has been so difficult for me as the broken hearts and shattered illusions of the women he claimed to love."

Nadine found it impossible now to hold back her tears as she looked into the eyes of this great man and saw so clearly his perfect compassion and sincerity. Her surprise deepened when he took her hand and pressed a kiss to her fingers, saying in a soft voice, "I wish you every happiness as you put your life back into place, *Mrs.* Rader. No one beyond those in this room will ever know that you are not a widow, who has come here to make a fresh start. I hope that you will be able to find happiness and peace here in Horstberg, in spite of all that has happened."

Nadine nodded, attempting to express her appreciation, fearing she'd fall completely apart if she so much as uttered a sound.

The duke stood and his voice returned to its previous imposing tone. "Captain," he said, "make the usual arrangements. Have one of your men see that she has what she needs."

"Yes, Your Grace, of course."

Nadine forced herself to her feet when she realized that she was expected to leave now. As she turned toward the door, the duchess took hold of her hand. With a tender smile and a hint of tears in her eyes, she said softly, "I wish you every happiness, Mrs. Rader."

Nadine could only nod before she hurried toward the open door, fearing she'd erupt with emotion. As the captain walked beside her down the long hall, still carrying Dulsie, she forced her tears back, knowing there was business to be taken care of. She could fall apart later.

By the time they had returned to the captain's office, she was able to find a steady voice. "What did he mean by *the usual arrangements*? Were there so many like me that—"

"No, Mrs. Rader. He simply meant seeing to your needs. We have a program set up to care for those in need, whatever the reason might be. We'll simply see that you have what you need and help you find work."

"I see," she said as they entered his office. "I am truly grateful. I don't know what we would have done."

"I'm just glad you got here." Then to an officer obviously waiting for any order he might be given, he said, "Get me a blanket, please."

He added to Nadine, "Please, sit down. We just need to fill out some papers, and then we'll go into town."

The officer returned with the blanket and Nadine watched as the captain gently laid Dulsie on it and covered her legs. The child snuggled into it and slept on, oblivious to the horror going on inside her mother as everything she'd believed throughout these years shattered around her. But Nadine forced back the reality and concentrated on the moment. *She could fall apart later.*

The captain sat down behind his huge uncluttered desk, saying to the lieutenant, "Get me the usual forms for the relief program."

"Yes sir," the officer said and returned with them only a moment later. "Would you like me to see to it, sir?"

"No, thank you. I'll take care of it myself."

Nadine noticed the officer looking distressed. "Sir?"

"I know it's not how we usually do it, Lieutenant. But I'm taking care of this one myself. I'm certain you can see that everything runs smoothly while I do this."

"Yes, sir. Of course."

"Thank you, Lieutenant. That will be all."

Nadine didn't know why the captain had taken a personal interest in helping her, but she was glad that he had. She felt comfortable with him for reasons she couldn't explain. Observing him discreetly while he kept busy writing, she felt compelled to say, "You seem familiar. Have we met before?"

The captain glanced up and smiled, showing nearly perfect teeth. His neatly styled hair was more blond than brown and had a soft wave to it, and his blue eyes had a meekness in them that was an intriguing contrast to his overall aura. He was obviously a very important man, and quite accustomed to having his word adhered, as she had seen in the behavior of his men.

"I was thinking exactly the same thing," he said. "Since you lived in Horstberg at one time, it stands to reason that our paths crossed somewhere. But I don't remember exactly. Although," his smile took on a hint of mischief, "I think I should have."

He turned his attention back to what he was writing before she had a chance to read anything into his meaning. He asked her some simple questions about herself and wrote down her answers. When he had all the personal information he needed, he asked, "So, what work experience do you have, Mrs. Rader? I assume you've been supporting yourself for—"

"Yes, I have," she interrupted quietly. She told him how she'd worked serving meals and drinks at an inn more than once. She'd assisted a seamstress and a cobbler, and even a doctor for a short time.

"And do you read and write?" he asked.

"Of course," she insisted. "When my father was alive, I kept books for his mill."

The captain made a noise to indicate that he was impressed while he jotted down notes. A minute later he set aside his pen and came to his feet. "That should be all here," he said. "I'll take you into town where we can get some things you'll need, then we'll get you settled at the inn. Tomorrow we'll see about finding you some work."

"Thank you," Nadine said, also coming to her feet.

She watched the captain take up his cloak and fling it carelessly around his shoulders, and the effect took her breath away. It was black and heavy, made of rich, fine fabric, trimmed with red and gold to compliment the uniform—obviously designed as a military accessory. And the captain looked as striking in it as he did the red and black uniform he wore, adorned with more gold trim than the other officers she had seen. He picked up the papers he'd been filling out, and she noticed a hat on his desk, similar to those worn by the other officers, but he left it there. She glanced toward Dulsie, who was still sleeping, just as the captain said, "If you'll hold these, I'll carry her."

"Thank you," she said, taking the papers from him.

He picked the child up along with the blanket and wrapped her securely in it. She followed him outside, noting the way his cloak billowed behind him. A carriage was waiting, and he situated Dulsie on one of the seats before taking Nadine's hand to help her inside. She heard him give instructions to the driver, and then he talked with one of his men for a minute before he climbed up on the box seat beside the driver and the carriage moved out of the castle courtyard.

By the time the carriage pulled up in front of a little shop on Horstberg's main street, Dulsie was coming awake. Nadine held her close and quickly explained what was happening, which soothed the child's anxious expression. The captain helped them down from the carriage and led them into the cluttered little shop.

"Good afternoon, Captain." A woman not much older than Nadine greeted him warmly.

"Good afternoon," the captain replied, and Nadine noticed that he was oblivious to this woman's fascination with him. It occurred to Nadine that the captain was undeniably handsome, although he was all the more attractive by his apparent ignorance to his own good looks. She briefly thought of Nikolaus and his vanity and arrogance. When she had first fallen for him, she'd found it endearing. But knowing what she knew now, the thought sickened her. Thinking of Nikolaus tightened the knot inside of her that she was attempting to ignore. She pushed her thoughts away and concentrated on the moment.

Captain Dukerk handed the shopkeeper a piece of paper, saying, "Would you please see that Mrs. Rader and her daughter have what they need. I'll be back for them in half an hour."

"Yes, of course, Captain," she said, then she smiled warmly at Nadine. "It will be a pleasure."

Half an hour later, the captain returned to haul Nadine's packages out to the carriage. She left equipped with more than adequate clothing, warm cloaks, and even shoes, for both her and Dulsie. And she didn't feel the least bit looked down upon by this woman who had helped them.

They were then taken to the Horstberg Inn where they left the packages in the carriage and the captain took her and Dulsie inside. They stood for a minute just inside the door of a large common room with many tables, but the crowd was sparse this time of day.

"Hello, Drew," the captain said casually when a middle-aged man with very little hair and a bright smile approached them.

"Captain," the man who was Drew replied with enthusiasm. "You're a bit early, aren't you?"

"Well, this is business," the captain said, handing Drew a paper. "Would you please see that Mrs. Rader and her daughter have a room and plenty to eat?"

"Why, of course," Drew said, smiling at Nadine. Then he glanced at the paper and added, "No problem. My wife Gerda is just now cleaning up a room that should be perfect. Why don't you sit down and make yourselves comfortable in the meantime."

"Thank you," Nadine said quietly and sat on a smooth bench next to a table. Dulsie sidled up next to her.

"Can I get you something?" Drew asked Nadine, showing a broad smile. "Are you hungry or—"

"No, thank you. We're fine for now."

Drew smiled again and excused himself to check on something in the kitchen. Following a long minute of silence, the captain cleared his throat and moved toward the door. "I'll just . . . uh, get your packages and . . ." He left the sentence unfinished and disappeared before Nadine could offer to help.

Before the captain returned, Drew appeared again with his wife, a thin woman with carrot-colored hair and an equally cheery smile. "This is Gerda," he announced as if she were royalty, and Nadine wondered how it would feel to be loved and cared for in such a way.

"Pleasure to meet you, Mrs. . . . uh . . ."

"Rader," Nadine provided.

"And this would be?" Gerda asked in a tone of voice that caught Dulsie's attention.

"This is Dulsie," Nadine said.

"Hello, Dulsie," Gerda said. "I would bet you're about five years old. Would that be right?" Dulsie nodded. "I thought so. I've got a little grandson about your age, but he lives far away. Would you like to come upstairs with me and see the room where you can stay?"

Again Dulsie nodded and Gerda motioned for them to follow her. Dulsie held tightly to her mother's hand as they went up a narrow staircase and past three other doors before Gerda opened one and they followed her into a room. It was small with a slanted ceiling on one side, and a fireplace already ablaze with warmth on the other. The furnishings were minimal but adequate. Beyond the bed there was a bureau, a washstand, a small sofa and a little table with two chairs. The green and ivory quilt on the bed was color-coordinated with the simple curtains at the window and the little framed painting of a forest scene on the wall. A braided rug in the same tones covered the majority of the polished wood floor.

Before Nadine had a chance to fully absorb her surroundings, Drew and the captain entered the room, their arms loaded with packages which they deposited on the bed.

"Thank you," she said, thinking it sounded trite.

While the captain chatted comfortably with Drew and Gerda, Nadine paused to digest the reality. Tears of a different breed crept into her eyes to think of actually sleeping someplace warm and safe, with adequate clean clothing and plenty to eat. In contrast to the way they had been living, she could hardly comprehend the difference. It was a miracle.

Remembering that she was not alone, she turned her attention to the conversation just as Drew asked the captain, "Will Mrs. Rader be looking for work?"

"Yes, actually," the captain said, briefly glancing her way. "Do you know of anything?"

"Something temporary, at least," he said and Nadine perked her interest. She felt anxious to take responsibility for herself and her daughter, and knew she was capable of handling almost anything.

"You see," Gerda explained, "Wilma, one of our girls that works here doing the evening shift, is coming near her time; she's expecting a baby, you see. She's just not able to put in her hours. And Cornelia, who helps on the breakfast and lunch shifts, is out of town. We could sure use a little extra help."

"It would be serving food and drink downstairs," Drew went on, "and some help in the kitchen. Maybe cleaning some in the rooms. What would you say, Mrs. Rader?"

"Oh, that would be fine," she said with enthusiasm. She noticed the captain seemed equally enthused, and she wondered if he was anxious to have her problems solved and be done with her. But then, if that were the case, why hadn't he just assigned her to one of his officers?

"Perhaps by the time Wilma is able to return, we can find you something more permanent," the captain said and Nadine nodded, suddenly feeling very tired. The reality of why she was here crept into her mind, but she pushed it away as suddenly as she could slam a door. *She could fall apart later.*

Chapter Three
HEAVY WITH GRIEF

Gerda and Drew made a gracious exit, promising to go over details the next day. Gerda said she would put some water on to heat so they could get cleaned up, and she would send Drew up with it. Nadine thanked them again before they left, then she turned to see Captain Dukerk, seemingly hesitant to leave. When he said nothing and seemed nervous, she cleared her throat and muttered a quiet, "Thank you. I don't know what we would have done."

"We're glad to help," he said. "If there's anything else I can do . . . anything at all . . . just tell Drew or Gerda. They know how to contact me."

"Thank you," she said once more, wondering if he was impressed by her diverse vocabulary.

Once the captain left and the door was closed, Nadine leaned against it and let out a long, loud sigh. She closed her eyes and took a deep breath, as if she could inhale the security surrounding her. Dulsie moved toward the fireplace and Nadine felt inclined to do the same. She couldn't remember the last time she'd been completely warm and wondered if her daughter even knew what warm meant.

"Are we going to stay here forever?" Dulsie asked, as if the idea were magical.

Nadine reminded herself to be optimistic. The present circumstances helped strengthen her resolve. With the first real hope she'd felt in years, she admitted readily, "Staying here at the inn is only temporary, but we'll find someplace just as nice, where we will always be warm and safe, and there will always be plenty to eat." Dulsie smiled and eased closer to the fire, holding her hands out toward it eagerly.

Thoughts of Nikolaus smuggled their way into Nadine's head, but again she quickly slammed them into the darkest recesses of her mind where they wouldn't be felt. While she was opening packages and putting their new things away in the bureau drawers, she marveled that used clothing could be so fine. She couldn't remember the last time she'd had something new for Dulsie, let alone herself. And used or not, the things they'd been given made her feel like royalty. The thought touched a sore spot and she forced it away just as a knock came at the door. Drew was on the other side holding two large buckets of steaming water. Nadine opened the door wider and he set them near the little galvanized tub.

"Come down for supper whenever you're ready," he said.

"Thank you," Nadine said and he hurried away.

By the time she and Dulsie were cleaned up and wearing new clothes, Nadine felt better than she had in months, maybe years—in spite of the reality of her circumstances, which she was fighting to ignore.

Going downstairs, she found the common room more crowded now, but the food that Drew put before them tasted better than anything she'd eaten since her father had died nearly six years ago. The heartache she was in the habit of feeling on her daughter's behalf began to dissipate as she watched Dulsie, wearing a red striped dress, eating her meal eagerly, intermittently laughing. They were nearly finished with their apple pie when Nadine looked up to see Captain Dukerk.

"Forgive me for intruding," he said, "but I—"

"Oh, you're not intruding at all," Nadine said. "Please, join us."

"Thank you," he said, sitting across from her. "I simply wondered if you have everything you need."

"Oh, yes, and more. Thank you."

He seemed hesitant to leave, but he said nothing more. In an effort to make conversation, Nadine said, "Forgive me if it's none of my business, but I've felt so overwhelmed with generosity today. I can't help wondering where the funding comes for such things."

"Well, as I understand it, many people make regular donations of second-hand shoes and clothing and such. The shop we went to specializes in gathering such things, cleaning them and making sure they are in good repair. The government pays for the items that are used for people in need. The government also works a deal with Drew for the rooms and meals."

"But couldn't people take unfair advantage of such a thing?" Nadine asked.

"People are only allowed to use the program for short periods of time and with limitations. Needs and circumstances are carefully examined and followed. Long-term help is only available for cases such as physical disabilities that make it impossible for a person to work at all, or for the elderly who have no family to care for them."

Feeling almost guilty for being the recipient of so much generosity, she felt compelled to say, "May I ask where the money comes from?"

The captain gave a warm chuckle. "You're a curious creature."

"Forgive me," she said, glancing away. "I suppose I am, but . . . I'm simply so grateful that I can't help feeling—"

"It's all right," he said. "It's not any great national secret or anything, even though it's not common knowledge that the duke funds the majority of the program from his personal income. The rest comes from taxes."

Nadine was surprised and wondered why. The duke had certainly been generous with her. Perhaps it was everything she'd learned about Nikolaus today that made the idea of generosity from the duke seem so incongruous. The thought tempted her raw emotions to come out and be felt. But she shoved them back once again, concentrating instead on how very blessed they had been this day.

"Well," she said, "you must express my gratitude to the duke once again."

"I'll do that."

"And I must thank you as well," she said. "You've been very kind."

When he made no comment she glanced up to see him watching her intently. She was beginning to wonder why when she realized that she was watching him as well. They both laughed uncomfortably in the same moment and turned away.

"You are quite welcome," he said and excused himself. She noticed that he sat down across the room to share a meal with another officer. From the corner of her eye she couldn't help feeling that he was aware of her, but the implication of his interest was something she simply felt too numb to consider.

As Nadine turned her attention fully to her last bite of pie, Dulsie asked with perfect innocence, "Is he my father?"

Nadine was so stunned that she found it impossible to come up with a reply that carried any kind of astute explanation. "No," she said tonelessly. Knowing her daughter deserved some kind of acknowledgment, she added, "Hurry and finish your pie. We'll talk when we get to our room."

"I like our room, Mama," Dulsie said as they returned and Nadine stoked the fire. While Dulsie hovered near its warmth, Nadine made up a bed for her daughter on the little sofa with some extra bedding that Gerda had provided. Together they changed into new nightclothes, cleaned their teeth, and washed their faces. After kneeling by the sofa to pray, Nadine tucked Dulsie into her makeshift bed. She almost felt moved to tears just to see her daughter clean and warm and secure.

As Nadine kissed Dulsie's little face, the child said, "Tell me now, Mama."

"Tell you what?" she asked, tucking the blankets tightly around her.

"Where is my father?" she asked and Nadine's heart sunk. "You said we would come here and find him."

"Well, we did find him, Dulsie, in a way." She quickly considered exactly what to tell her. Under the circumstances, she realized that Nikolaus's death could be an advantage. "He was killed, sweetheart."

"He's dead?" Dulsie asked, more astonished than upset.

"Yes, I'm afraid he is."

"But who will take care of us?"

"I will take care of us," Nadine said with confidence. "Now that we are here, and these kind people have helped us, I will be able to work for what we need, and we will never go without again. I promise."

"Are you sad about my father?"

"Yes, darling. I'm very sad." She didn't clarify that her sadness was more due to Nikolaus's betrayal than his death. "But you and I have each other, and now we are going to have everything we need, and we'll be all right. Get some sleep now."

Nadine doused the lamp and crawled between the crisp, clean sheets of her own bed. The luxury soothed her heartache long enough for Dulsie to fall asleep. But as the night closed in and sleep eluded her, the reality of her shattered illusions settled like a knife in her heart. And with them came a torrent of tears. For years she had held onto and treasured her memories of the seemingly magical times she had spent with Nikolaus, always believing that the love they'd shared would last a lifetime. How clearly she recalled his promises, his tender words, and the adoration she had seen in his eyes. And now she had to accept that it had been a farce. She wondered now if any piece of her experience with him had been genuine at all. Had he felt any degree of love for her? Or had his every word and action toward her simply been some kind of playacting to get her into his bed and keep her there until the pregnancy created an inconvenience? The very idea was so horrifying that Nadine sobbed without control into her pillow, praying she would not wake Dulsie and upset her.

With Nadine's emotion came unfathomable anger—at Nikolaus for being so completely evil, and at herself for being so naive and gullible. The bitterness became so intense, so consuming, that she had to force her mind to prayer in order to cope. Attempting to focus on positive thoughts, she could not deny the miracles of this day. In spite of her deepest hopes and dreams being dashed, she was safe and warm, clean and full. And so was little Dulsie. She thanked God for all they had been blessed with and the many kind people she had encountered. With that thought she finally slept. She woke before dawn and watched the room gradually fill with light, while her disillusionment settled in more fully. She could not deny that in spite of all she'd learned about Nikolaus since her arrival in Horstberg, she had truly loved him. And in spite of many nagging doubts, she had spent years trying to convince herself that he'd loved her, too. But whatever she might have felt made no difference now. Her love for Nikolaus had turned into something ugly and bitter, but she knew better than to think that harboring such feelings would do her any good. Nikolaus was dead, and no amount of anger would have any effect on him. She simply had to let go and press forward. She had a second chance to begin her life again. She had her daughter to consider, and she would make the most of what she had, for Dulsie's sake, if not her own.

Lance was stirred from a fitful sleep by a loud knocking. When he became coherent enough to realize that it was still dark and someone was pounding at the front door of his apartment, he pulled on some breeches and felt his way down the stairs. His heart quickened as he considered what might constitute such a disturbance.

"What is it?" he demanded, pulling the door open.

"Forgive me, Captain," a young officer said, "but you are needed at once."

Lance's heart quickened with dread. "What's happened?"

"I'm not certain, sir. I was simply sent to get you."

"All right. Tell them I'll be there in ten minutes."

Lance hurriedly donned his uniform and pushed a comb through his hair. He stepped out of his apartment in the castle compound and hurried across the courtyard to where his office was located. An officer met him halfway and walked with him. His grave countenance heightened Lance's uneasiness.

"What's happened?" he demanded.

"It's Lieutenant Reusch, sir," he said.

"What about him?"

"He was apprehending a thief when . . ."

Lance stopped walking when the severity of this man's voice—and his inability to go on—became impossible to ignore. The officer stopped as well and Lance asked quietly, "Is Lieutenant Reusch all right?"

"No, sir. He's been killed."

Lance sucked in his breath and reminded himself to maintain his professionalism. But it was difficult when the man facing him looked as if he were barely managing to keep his own emotion in check. There was little so difficult for these men—or himself—as losing one of their own in the line of duty. Lance swallowed carefully and said, "He was a friend of yours."

"Yes, sir."

Lance put a hand to his shoulder. "Then maybe you should take some time off and—"

"Perhaps later, sir. I would like to volunteer to accompany you to inform his family, sir."

"Of course," Lance said. "Why don't you go take a few minutes to get some composure, and we'll leave when you're ready."

"Thank you, sir," the officer said and walked away.

Lance sighed and looked down at the stone courtyard beneath his booted feet, then he looked heavenward and squeezed his eyes shut. There was only one thing he'd ever had to do in the line of duty that was more difficult than losing one of his men. Thankfully he'd not had to see to this responsibility frequently, but still far too much.

Lance forced back his emotion and hurried to his office to find Lieutenant Brueger, the man in charge on the night shift, waiting for him.

"Please tell me we have the man responsible behind bars," Lance said.

"We do," the lieutenant said with an edge to his voice that made it clear he'd like to personally see to his execution this very minute.

"Good," Lance said. "That will save me from sending out the entire force to comb the country this very moment."

"I would have already sent them out, were that the case, sir."

"Yes, I know you would have," Lance said.

"Do you wish to see the prisoner now or—"

"No, I'll save that chore for later. I want a trial right away." Lance couldn't keep the anger out of his tone. "I want him executed before the funeral if it's at all possible."

"Yes, sir. I'll arrange it as soon as morning comes. Should I wake His Grace?"

"No, let him sleep. I'll speak with him soon enough."

Lance, along with three officers, were soon on their way to inform the Reusch family of this tragedy. He had done this before, and he wasn't surprised by the grief and emotion that came in response to the news he had to deliver. But he was taken aback by the way the undeniable anguish in the eyes of the young Mrs. Reusch reminded him of Nadine Rader. He was riding back into the castle courtyard before it occurred to him that she too had been faced with the death of someone she loved. But far worse, she had been faced with his betrayal. Lance found his heart aching for this woman he barely knew, and he tried to convince himself that it was the issue of grief that had brought her to his mind. But truthfully he'd been thinking about her almost continually throughout the day and into the night. She was the reason for his difficulty sleeping, and the reason he found it a challenge to focus on the business at hand.

As soon as the sun was up Lance went into the main entrance

of the castle and directly to the duke's bedroom. He knocked lightly at the door, hoping they weren't still sound asleep.

"It's open," he heard Cameron call.

Lance peered into the room to see Abbi sitting on the edge of the bed, brushing through her hair, while Cameron sat in a chair nearby, his bare feet peering out from beneath his breeches, reading a newspaper.

"Good morning," Abbi said brightly.

"Good morning, Your Grace," he said, unable to smile at her.

"Captain," Cameron said. "Come in. What can we . . ." He tipped his paper to look at Lance and hesitated, his countenance darkening. "What's happened?" he demanded.

"An officer was killed very early this morning."

"No!" Abbi insisted as Cameron hung his head and sighed. "How?"

"Apprehending a thief; caught in the act, apparently. A typical case of robbery gone wrong. The culprit is behind bars. The trial will be this afternoon. The family has been informed and are being cared for. Funeral arrangements are underway."

Cameron looked up at Lance and sighed again. "It's not even time for breakfast, Captain. How did you manage?"

"I didn't. I have good men who do their jobs well."

"Indeed," Cameron said. He closed his eyes and shook his head. "I always feel responsible."

"Yes, I know what you mean," Lance said.

Following a long moment of silence, Abbi said, "I'll go and visit the family today and see what we might do."

"Thank you, my dear," Cameron said with an adoration in his eyes that Lance longed to feel. His thoughts rushed to Nadine and he was startled by the way his heart quickened.

The remainder of the morning was chaotic for Lance, while a dark pall hung over him and those he worked with. His thoughts repeated over and over the report he'd been given of the lieutenant's death, intermixed with his memories of Mrs. Reusch's response to the news. Shortly past noon it occurred to him that he'd eaten nothing since the previous evening. He informed his officers that he was taking a break for lunch. En route to his most frequented place to dine, his heart quickened again unexpectedly. Nadine would be there. And with any luck he would actually see her, or better yet, be able to talk with her. The very idea put a tiny bright spot in an otherwise horrific day.

Nadine drifted back to sleep and was awakened by Dulsie to a room filled with sunlight. She knew immediately that the temperatures outside were extremely low by the excessive chill in the room. She silently thanked God for shelter and warmth as she stoked the fire and added wood from the ample pile left at her disposal.

She and Dulsie arrived in the dining room for breakfast just as the last of the crowd was finishing up. After eating a fine meal, Nadine set to work in the kitchen helping Gerda. She didn't even bother asking what she might do. She just rolled up her sleeves and began scrubbing the pile of dirty pots. Gerda was obviously pleased with her efforts, and they chatted comfortably as they worked. Dulsie was drawn to a little table and cupboard in the corner of the kitchen, and Gerda took a break to show Dulsie the toys stored there.

"This is where my little ones played while I worked many years back," she said kindly to Dulsie. "And now and again my little grandchildren come to visit and play. You are welcome to play with anything here, so long as you keep the toys here in the corner and put them away when you're finished."

Dulsie nodded eagerly and pulled out a couple of rag dolls and a tiny set of dishes. Gerda offered a grandmotherly smile and returned to the stew she was hovering over for the lunch crowd. When the pots were all washed, Nadine asked, "What else might I do to help?"

"The main thing would be serving the guests when they come in. The captain mentioned you had some experience with that."

"I do, yes," Nadine said, feeling a quiver inside of her as the captain was mentioned. "But lunch won't be served for a while yet. What might I do in the meantime?"

Gerda looked pleasantly surprised by Nadine's insistence. "Well, it would be mighty helpful if you could check the two guest rooms that were used last night and see that they're clean and tidy. There's a checklist there by the door." She motioned toward it and Nadine stepped closer to look it over.

"I should be able to handle that."

Gerda informed her that one of the rooms had guests leaving, and the other had a guest that would be staying over. The rest of the rooms available were empty and ready for guests. Nadine reminded Dulsie to be a good girl before she went upstairs and set to work. Hearing guests arriving downstairs, she washed up and went down to help serve in the dining room. She felt gratified with the work and tried not to think about the reasons she had lost her last two jobs before coming to Horstberg.

Nadine wasn't certain what to make of the way her heart quickened when she saw Captain Dukerk come in and seat himself once he'd removed his cloak and hung it near the door. She attempted to be nonchalant as she moved past his table to serve drinks nearby, but she couldn't help noticing how Drew approached him immediately, saying in a compassionate voice, "I heard what happened. I'm so sorry. I suspect you've had a pretty rough day. And a long one."

"I have, yes. Thank you. But my day is not nearly so rough as it is for others. I barely knew him personally."

Nadine had no choice but to move away unless she wanted to appear to be eavesdropping. Through the next few minutes she kept busy while her thoughts remained with what she'd overheard, and she couldn't help noticing from a few discreet glances in his direction that the captain appeared especially somber.

Drew handed Nadine a tray with stew, bread, and ale, saying, "For the captain. Be quick about it."

"Of course," Nadine said and hurried to his table.

"Hello," she said, setting the food in front of him.

He looked up, apparently startled from deep thought. Then a smile broke through his grave countenance. "Hello," he replied. He glanced at the food in front of him. "Thank you." He looked back up at her with a gaze that was almost hypnotizing. "I see they're keeping you busy."

"Yes," she said, "for which I'm grateful. If I can at least earn our room and board, then . . ." She became distracted once again by his eyes and completely lost the rest of her sentence. She cleared her throat and glanced away, saying quickly, "Enjoy your meal, Captain."

She hurried away and kept busy while he ate. For a while she remained aware of him as she bustled back and forth across the dining room, then she became so engrossed that she was startled to realize the inn had become almost empty and she'd lost track of him. She turned to see that he was still sitting alone, and Gerda had obviously cleared away his dishes. His elbows rested on the table and his clasped knuckles were pressed to his lips. His brow was furrowed in deep thought, his expression heavy with grief. A wave of compassion urged her to approach him. The quickening of her heart as she did so made her wonder if it was a bad idea.

"Forgive me," she said as her compassion overruled. He looked up, pleasantly startled. "I couldn't help overhearing earlier . . . but not enough to know what exactly happened—something tragic, apparently." She watched his expression darken and glanced around to see that nothing needed her attention at the moment. "May I?" she added, motioning to the chair across from him.

"Of course," he said so eagerly that she was almost flustered.

"If it's none of my business, just say so," she said. "I was just . . . concerned. Your grief is evident."

He chuckled tensely and leaned back in his chair. "Now I know why I could never get away with fibbing to my father when I was a child." He became more serious and added, "Your concern is appreciated, Mrs. Rader. One of my men was killed in the line of duty early this morning."

"I'm so sorry," she said and he forced a quick smile.

She watched his face tighten further as he added, "I had the honor of knocking at his wife's door to tell her why he wouldn't be coming home." He glanced away and swallowed carefully. "I fear such things have a way of clinging to my mind."

"I have that problem too," she said gently.

"What problem?" he asked in the same tone.

"Difficult moments . . . memories . . . are hesitant to relent."

Nadine watched his lips part as if to speak, but he only drew a deep breath. She felt indelibly tempted to start spilling all of those difficult memories into his lap, right here and now, but knew such an idea was preposterous. She was stunned to realize how they were openly gazing at each other while neither of them had anything to say. Was his shameless gaze an indication that she stirred him the way he stirred her? Or was he just another black-hearted cad like

Nikolaus du Woernig who could skillfully draw a woman into his web by playing on her emotions?

Nadine broke her gaze and looked away, telling herself that Captain Dukerk did not deserve her mistrust. "Is there anything I can do?" she asked, glancing toward him again.

"No, but thank you," he said. She stood to leave and he added, "Do you have everything you need?"

"Amply so, yes. Thank you," she said and hurried away. Coming into the safety of the kitchen, she realized that she was downright afraid of the compelling need she felt to simply be in the presence of this man. But how could that be possible when her heart was so heavy with grief over Nikolaus's betrayal? She wasn't certain her heart could ever trust again, and she felt certain that expecting it to do so now would only see her a fool once again.

Chapter Four
FROM A DISTANCE

Over the next few days Nadine and Dulsie settled comfortably into their new life. Nadine told Drew that she wanted to work for her room and board and not have the government paying for it. He agreed, but told her the amount of work she was doing would warrant more than simply room and board. She considered being able to put some extra cash away to be a good thing. Drew reminded her that Cornelia would be returning to work and they would only be needing evening help, which would cover the room and board, but Nadine would do well to start looking for some daytime work elsewhere. She made it a matter of prayer and decided to deal with that when it came. As long as they had shelter and food, they would be all right for the time being.

Dulsie quickly thrived on her new surroundings and began behaving like a child again for the first time in many months. Drew and Gerda took to Dulsie and gave her a great deal of attention. And Gerda often commented on how well behaved and polite Dulsie was. Nadine found it a comfort to realize the child had not inherited her father's malicious tendencies.

On Sunday the inn was closed, and Nadine and Dulsie went to church with Drew and Gerda. After their horrific journey to get to Horstberg, with no opportunity for worship along the way, to be back in a church felt deeply comforting. People were friendly and welcoming for the most part, although she grew tired of answering polite inquires about her deceased husband, especially when her answers weren't true. She wondered more than once what these people would think if she said, "Nikolaus du Woernig swindled me into his bed and abandoned me." She chose to stick with the lie that she'd left Horstberg to marry a man who had soon thereafter been killed in an accident at a lumber mill. She was grateful to be living and working at the opposite side of the valley from the mill her father had owned, and where she had lived and worked prior to his death and to leaving Horstberg. The country was well populated, and she had known very few people during the few years she and her father had lived in Horstberg, but she preferred to avoid any connections to the past. It occurred to her that perhaps she should have chosen a false name, since anyone who had known her father would know that Rader was her maiden name. But it was too late for that, and she doubted that it would ever become an issue.

As the inn opened again with the new week, Nadine couldn't help taking notice of Captain Dukerk's habits. He always came in for supper, and occasionally at an earlier time of the day for another meal. He was often alone, sometimes with one or more other officers. He was never with a woman. She marveled that a man so attractive and virile would be unattached, then it occurred to her that perhaps he had a wife at home somewhere. The idea didn't fit with his behavior, or the fact that he ate supper at an inn every evening. Still, she was ridiculously relieved to overhear his men teasing him about being the most coveted bachelor in Horstberg. Her relief was quickly followed by a stark realization: women like her did not win the most coveted bachelor. Especially considering that he knew her sordid past. Nadine considered where her thoughts were headed and scolded herself for even allowing them to take such a direction. The very idea was foolish in so many different ways that she didn't even care to start counting. Still, she couldn't deny that, as far as she could tell, Captain Dukerk was a kind and generous man. It was easy to see him as the figurative knight on a white horse who had come to her rescue, but she had to consider that his concern for her was not necessarily personal. Surely he would have done the same for any damsel in distress.

Five days beyond her arrival, Nadine was surprised, as she removed her apron at the end of the day, to hear Drew say, "We'll not be open for lunch tomorrow. We'll be closing down right after breakfast is served, and opening back up for supper."

"Why is that?"

"The funeral, of course," Gerda said. "I suspect the entire country will be lining the streets to pay respects. It would be disrespectful to keep a business open during such an event."

"Of course," Nadine said and wondered what role Captain Dukerk might have in relation to this event. Her heart ached for his grief, and her thoughts were with him far too much. Still, she reasoned, better to have her thoughts with him than with Nikolaus du Woernig. At least the captain kept her distracted.

The following day, Nadine and Dulsie dressed in appropriately dark clothing and walked a short distance with Drew and Gerda to where people were lining the streets for the funeral procession. As always, Nadine enjoyed listening to the chatter between Drew and Gerda as they gossiped about their friends and customers in a pleasant, caring kind of way. As they settled into a place on the street to wait for the procession, Drew commented on the crowds.

"Much more than the last time we did this," Gerda commented. "Of course, quite a few came out anyway, if only to be assured that he was really dead."

"That wasn't the last time we did this," Drew corrected. "There was that officer killed in that accident last year."

"Oh, that's right," Gerda said. "But I missed the funeral—down sick, remember?"

"I remember now," he said. "Well, in that case, I suspect there'll be a great deal more people out today than there were the last time *you* did this. And we won't have anybody tempted to be dancing in the streets over this one. Tragic, this is."

"Indeed," Gerda added.

Nadine felt a subtle uneasiness over their conversation without understanding why. She felt compelled to ask, "Forgive me, but whose funeral are you discussing? The one with . . . what did you say? Dancing in the streets?"

"Nikolaus du Woernig, of course," Drew said, as if it should have been obvious. And maybe it should have been, Nadine thought as her stomach tightened and her throat went dry. She simply hadn't bothered to connect Nikolaus's death to a funeral procession.

"In spite of its tragedy," Gerda said, breaking into Nadine's thoughts, "his death was something he brought on himself."

"Yeah," Drew gave a sardonic chuckle, "after he'd brought years of misery on the rest of us. It was difficult to mourn, even though we all tried to follow His Grace's example and pay the proper respects."

"A good man, His Grace," Gerda said. "Imagine, him giving his brother a respectful burial after all he'd put him through."

Nadine was relieved to hear a distant drum cadence that distracted her hosts from their conversation. She didn't feel at all like hearing details of what Nikolaus du Woernig had put his brother through. She had once believed that she would be a practical and literal part of the du Woernig family. And while living her life as royalty didn't necessarily seem suited to her, at least in the conventional way, she couldn't deny that living among the walls of Castle Horstberg and being treated like a queen certainly had its appeal.

As the drum cadence drew closer, a hushed reverence fell over the crowd. Nadine watched the procession approaching, like a red and black serpent in the distance, winding its way through town and toward the cathedral. The solemnity of the occasion penetrated her heart; she was even overtaken by tears. And she hadn't even known the man. But then, most of these people hadn't. Still, his death represented something to them. His life had been given protecting the peace of Horstberg.

The procession began with standard bearers, carrying tall flags of different shapes and designs that Nadine felt certain represented something significant for Horstberg. And with them were several drummers, in uniform, beating out a slow, sullen cadence. Behind the flags came a regiment of officers of the Guard, marching in perfect precision with somber faces. The usual black and red uniforms were a simpler version of what Nadine had seen the captain wear. Of course, she'd seen officers everywhere since her arrival—on the streets, at the inn—but she realized today they wore a subtly different style, perhaps dress uniforms for such an occasion. And each man wore a significant black armband as a symbol of mourning. Seeing the force together this way was breathtaking. Their exactitude betrayed an enormous amount of drilling practice, and she couldn't help but feel impressed and somehow safe to think of this country being watched over by such men.

Following the regiment were two open coaches draped with black and pulled at a slow pace by caparisoned horses. Nadine easily recognized the young widow, enveloped in black with a veiled face, sitting between two small children. Along with her, what appeared to be other family members and closes friends filled the coaches. More foot soldiers marched before and to the sides of the hearse, which was draped with the ducal colors of gold, red, and black. And following the hearse was another large regiment of officers.

Nadine became so caught up in the beauty and solemnity of the procession that she was startled to see that it ended with several uniformed men on horseback, and among the three in the lead, closest to her side of the street, was Captain Dukerk. The other two were the Duke of Horstberg, and Mr. Heinrich who had been in the office with him. The duke wore a uniform more elaborately adorned than any other, with a red robe attached to his shoulders that flowed down over the back of his mount. He wore a simple, conservative crown on his head. She couldn't help noting his attire because she recalled once seeing Nikolaus dressed the same way. The irony was startling. Beside him, Mr. Heinrich and Captain Dukerk were dressed in a more formal version of the military cloak she had seen the captain wear on previous days, the black fabric flowing over their horses, similar to the duke's robe. The only difference between Captain Dukerk and Mr. Heinrich's uniforms were the numerous medals and distinctions on Lance's, and she wondered what they all symbolized. Seeing the captain this way, it was difficult to imagine the tenderness with which he'd handled her situation and made certain she had everything she needed. She felt intrigued by the contrast as she took in his perfect assurance and dignity. He had a presence about him that was breathtaking. She thought of his compelling gaze and candid words to her, and her stomach was seized with a swarm of butterflies. But her very personal feelings for this man were intruded upon by the reality of the distance between them. The evidence of his position made her feel small and insignificant. She reminded herself that his kindness in the past was no indication that she would ever catch his eye the way he'd caught hers. A quick glance around herself made it clear that the entire crowd was focused on these incredible men who served their country with such majesty and forbearance.

While Nadine was distracted by her own thoughts, she was startled to hear Dulsie call out, "Captain!" Grateful that the sound of the drums and the horses' hooves on the cobblestone didn't allow her outburst to be too obvious, she quickly and quietly reprimanded Dulsie, telling her that such a thing was not appropriate. Then she looked up to see Captain Dukerk give a subtle wave to Dulsie. Nadine met his eyes, offering an embarrassed smile, a slight wave, and a shrug of her shoulders. He nodded discreetly toward her and she was surprised at how long he held her gaze. When he'd moved on enough that it would have been awkward to keep looking at her, he finally looked ahead. But she noticed that he tossed a discreet glance over his shoulder as the procession pressed forward.

Long after the drum cadence could no longer be heard in the distance, much of the crowd hovered silently as they were. It was as if the vision they'd just beheld had left such an impression that they felt hesitant to break the spell and return to their homes. Nadine heard many sniffles and even some audible sobbing that hadn't been noticeable when the sound of the procession had been close by.

When Drew and Gerda finally turned away to walk back to the inn, Nadine reluctantly followed. Contemplating what she'd seen and felt, she found her thoughts mostly focused on Captain Dukerk. She was struck again by the distance between their worlds—the same distance that had existed between her world and Nikolaus's. She felt certain she should have known better than to believe that a man in such a position would ever be serious about a woman like her.

As they moved further from the hovering aura of the procession, Drew and Gerda became more talkative. She heard them say that the thief responsible for the officer's death would be executed the following morning. It had been initially scheduled for this morning, but the officer's family had requested that the execution not be the same day as the funeral. Thinking of the captain, Nadine wondered what role he played in such events. She felt an unexpected surge of compassion for him, certain that such things must surely be difficult, especially since she'd seen evidence that he was a sensitive man.

All of Nadine's thoughts came to a grinding halt when she caught a brief glimpse of a familiar face in the crowd. A face that brought terror to her heart, and a deep dread in wondering if Albert Crider really would have managed to follow her here. She hurriedly looked away, not wanting to stare or make eye contact, and when she looked back, he was nowhere to be seen. She thought she had been so careful to elude him in her travels. Had he followed her through the entire journey? Would he continue hounding her for attention as he had before? The thought sickened and frightened her. But all she could do was keep an eye out for him and be careful. She decided then that if he so much as attempted to approach her, she would report his behavior to the captain. The very idea that she had such an option available eased her nerves and left her comforted.

Nadine hoped to see the captain that evening for supper, but he didn't come. It was easy to imagine that his day was complicated, but she found herself hoping that he got a decent meal. She went to bed that night with a prayer that his heart would be comforted, and a prayer for herself that Captain Dukerk would not end up breaking *her* heart.

Long after his shift should have ended, Lance found himself sitting at his desk, staring at the wall. His mind flew through the memories of recent events, culminating with today's burial of a good man. Interspersed with the events of losing an officer, trying his killer, and overseeing a military funeral, were tender memories of a woman who had only brushed up against his life, but had left a deep impression. His glimpse of her and her daughter in the midst of the funeral procession had soothed his heart like balm on an open wound. Her simple wave, her embarrassed smile, the sparkle in her eyes that seemed to send him a silent message—a sparkle that somehow penetrated past the deep grief of loss and hardship that was engraved in her countenance.

As Lance realized how thoroughly exhausted he was, his thoughts reluctantly led him to the reality of what he had to face tomorrow at sunrise. Executions, however right and justified, were simply distasteful. And he dreaded it.

A light knock at the door broke into his thoughts. "Yes?" he called and couldn't help chuckling when Abbi entered, carrying a tray with a white cloth draped over it.

"And what is this?" he asked.

"I just had a feeling that you would be here and hungry."

"Are you psychic? Did you foresee my hunger in a dream?"

Abbi pushed away the thoughts that were triggered by his mention of a dream. "Neither," she laughed. "It was just a . . . hunch."

"A very good one," he said. "I didn't even realize I was hungry until you said it, but I don't think I've eaten since breakfast."

Abbi set the tray in front of him and lifted off the cloth with aplomb. "You are amazing," he said.

"Well, I didn't cook it," she said, "so don't go groveling too much."

"You're still amazing," he said. "How many men get personal service from the Duchess of Horstberg?"

"Beyond the Duke of Horstberg?" She laughed. "Not many. My father, perhaps."

"Georg," he said.

"Yes, Georg is like a brother to me."

Lance began to eat, glad that she sat down across the desk to visit with him.

"And me?" he asked. "To what do *I* owe this privilege?"

"You, my dear captain, are my protector and defender. You are the man who has carried me across muddy streets, helped me graciously mount horses that are far too big for me, and toted my packages on many shopping sprees." Her voice became more serious. "You are the man who would lay down his life for me at the snap of my fingers. You have quite literally saved my life. And what you endured to do that is something I know plagues you still, even if you won't admit it." Lance stopped eating and leaned back in his chair as she went on. "You once pledged your very heart and soul to me even though I had clearly given my heart and soul to another." Her voice lightened as she added, "Bringing you supper once every year or two is a small price to pay for such devotion, Captain."

Lance swallowed carefully and couldn't keep himself from admitting, "I love you, Abbi du Woernig. Maybe I shouldn't say that. Most people wouldn't understand, but I know that you know what I mean."

"Yes, Lance. I know what you mean. And I love you; not as I love anyone else. You are my brother, my friend, my knight in shining armor. And I'm glad you said it, because after all this time it should be said. I think we've both felt it for a long time. It's like . . . we share a love that's perfectly noble, and not remotely romantic."

Lance sighed deeply. "I've spent years trying to find words to explain it, and you just did it perfectly in one sentence." He leaned his elbows on the desk. "How long?"

"How long what?"

"How long have we felt it?"

"Well, I don't know when you felt it, but I felt it when you looked into my eyes and I realized that you were risking your life to keep me safe, even while you knew I was secretly married to a fugitive." She sighed. "And there was a moment, Lance, when I believed that if Cameron hadn't made it, we could have been very happy together."

"I'm grateful he made it, Abbi."

"Yes, you and me and every resident of Horstberg." She motioned toward his food. "Eat before it gets cold."

"Yes, Your Grace," he said and proceeded with his meal. "Does your husband know where you are? That you're consorting with the Captain of the Guard and exchanging tender feelings?"

"Yes," she laughed, "he knows where I am. And he is putting Erich to bed, like any good duke would do. I'm not sure if he knows we're exchanging tender feelings, but he's heard it all before, and he'll probably hear it again a little later. It will be a good topic for tonight's pillow chat."

"Pillow chat?" he chuckled.

"Of course. That perfect little window of time when he's not the duke, he's not chief judge and prosecutor, he's not even a father, or my husband, or my lover. He's just my best friend. And we talk. We share our day. We count our blessings. And we kiss goodnight."

Lance found his mind wandering to an image that filled him with perfect contentment. He could only imagine what it would be like to share such a relationship with a woman. And while he'd spent years with his dreams of the future Mrs. Dukerk being vague and obscure, they suddenly included a very clear and real image. But he hardly knew the woman. Was he out of his mind?

"Where are you?" Abbi asked, startling him.

"Just . . . a long day," he said.

"Yes, it certainly has been. And tomorrow doesn't look too promising."

"No," he sighed, "tomorrow isn't very appealing at this point."

"So, let's change the subject."

"All right, Your Grace. What would you like to talk about?"

"Well, as much as I love you, Lance, my consistency in bringing you supper isn't very impressive. When are you going to find someone who will serve you supper every evening so that I can be freed of the responsibility?"

Lance smiled and looked away until he heard Abbi chuckling.

"What?" he demanded.

"That's what I'd like to know." She leaned her elbows on the desk and her eyes became eager. "For years I've been asking you when you were going to find someone and your answer has always been some light, witty remark. And now you completely ravage your own predictability by getting a dreamy look in your eyes and *blushing.*"

"Blushing?" he echoed, sounding insulted. "I accept dreamy eyes, but blushing? I was not blushing."

"You were!" she protested strongly.

"I was not!"

"You can't even see yourself. How could you possibly know whether or not you were blushing? I saw you. You were blushing."

Lance chuckled then forced a stern voice. "The Captain of the Guard does *not* blush."

"I won't tell your men you were blushing, Captain. But if you don't tell *me* why you're blushing, I will tell Cameron that you tried to kiss me and I had to slap your face."

"You wouldn't!" he said, genuinely astonished until he realized she was teasing.

"Of course I wouldn't. And even if I did he would know I was lying. You are positively the most honorable man either of us have ever known. But you will tell me why you were blushing, won't you?"

Lance chuckled and looked away. She laughed and said, "You're doing it again."

"All right. All right," he said and looked directly at her. His voice deepened as he admitted, "I can't say if I've met that certain someone. I've not known her long enough to have any idea if that's a possibility. I do know that she preoccupies my thoughts, and just seeing her stirs me in a way I've never felt before."

Abbi's voice took on an ethereal whisper. "Just as you described the other day in the carriage."

"Yes," he said firmly, "it is."

Abbi smiled widely and reached across the desk, taking his hand into hers. "Tell me about her. When do I get to meet her? Is she—"

"One question at a time," he chuckled. "She's incredible and you already have."

"Have what?"

"Met her."

"I have?" She looked thoughtful and confused for a full minute while he forged ahead with his meal, wondering if she would figure it out. He saw enlightenment fill her countenance and laughed just before she said with conviction, "Mrs. Rader."

"You're a shrewd woman, Abbi. I'd swear you *are* psychic."

Abbi was suddenly thrown from the conversation into a heart-pounding terror. She would never consider herself psychic, but how could she not wonder if Nadine Rader was the woman she'd seen in her dream? She certainly fit the description. And now Lance, one of her truest and dearest friends, was falling in love with her. She had felt that the dream's purpose was to prepare. Was it to help this good man through a possible horrific loss? She wondered if she should tell him of her dream. Would that help him be prepared? Could it help him protect her? Not feeling any distinct answers, she knew that now was not the time. It needed careful thought and consideration. Now, she would just let him glow with his newfound feelings.

"Abbi, are you all right?" Lance asked, breaking into her thoughts.

"I'm fine," she insisted with a smile. "Just felt a little lightheaded there for a second. I'm fine."

"You're sure?"

"Of course, yes. You were accusing me of being psychic. I'm *not* psychic," she said boastfully. "Just . . . insightful." She leaned forward even further. "Tell me," she insisted eagerly. "Tell me everything."

It took Lance more than an hour to finish his meal as he told Abbi everything he was feeling, and every detail of their every minimal encounter. But he didn't mind the food being cold, and he didn't mind the exhaustion he was feeling. He just thoroughly enjoyed this pleasant respite. When he'd finished eating and there was no more to tell her, he said, "It's getting late. You'd better get home or you'll miss your pillow chat."

"He'll wait for me," she said. "After all, I usually wait for him. He's always got something to discuss with Georg."

She stood and picked up the tray. Lance stood as well and doused the lamp just before he picked up his cloak and threw it around his shoulders. "Let me walk you back," he said and took the tray from her.

"So gallant," she said and put her hand over his arm as they walked slowly across the courtyard to the main castle entrance. At the door she pressed her hand to one side of his face, and her lips to the other. "Goodnight, Captain," she said and took the tray.

"Goodnight, Your Grace," he replied and pressed a kiss to her brow. "And thank you."

"It was a pleasure," she said and went inside.

Lance slept surprisingly well and credited it to Abbi's soothing effect on him. But at sunrise he was standing in the courtyard, with Cameron and Georg on the balcony above him. The prisoner was brought out, the order given, and the execution carried out. He almost believed that he had gotten through it without the usual troubling emotions, then he walked into his office to hear one of his lieutenants say, "So, the execution is complete. I'm glad that's over."

"Me too," Lance muttered and attempted to focus on his work, but an hour later he felt so deeply troubled that he had to excuse himself and leave his work in the hands of his men. He rushed discreetly to the castle chapel, seeking a solace that he prayed would soothe the deepest parts of his soul. But the words in his head went there with him, pounding over and over, *The execution is complete.* He stayed there a long while and left feeling more calm but still deeply troubled. Hunger prompted him into town to at least eat a good breakfast. His meals had been so sporadic the last couple of days that he was almost feeling sick. Or was the sickness a result of his inner turmoil; a turmoil that had been lured to the surface by this morning's event?

Through his brief ride to the inn, Lance was not surprised to have Nadine Rader appear in his thoughts. She had come to be there so often that he was becoming comfortable with having her there. He was surprised, however, by the yearning he felt to just be in her presence, as if she could somehow soothe this ache in him. He certainly didn't know her well enough to spill his deepest thoughts and concerns, and he felt certain she had no desire to hear them. He simply felt the need to see her and soak in her presence; a need that felt suddenly tangible, as surely as he might thirst and long for water.

Lance was relieved when he arrived to realize that he'd missed the breakfast rush, then he panicked, wondering if she might not be there at all if there were no customers to be served. He stepped inside and felt warmth bathe him just to see her on the far side of the empty dining room, wiping off tables with a wet rag. She wore her hair the way she always did, pulled back into a loose knot at the back of her head that didn't at all disguise its curliness. Stray curls framed her face and teased the back of her neck. Hearing the door she turned toward him and for a long moment the world around him seemed to freeze. He wondered if it was his imagination that she felt as drawn to him as he did to her. He was trying to convince himself that was the case when she tossed the rag onto a table and walked toward him without breaking eye contact.

"I've been worried about you," she said.

"I'm all right," he said, trying to be noble.

Nadine looked into his eyes and attempted to discern this power he had over her. Was it for good or ill? Instinctively she believed it was for good, but her instincts were something that still needed examination in light of what Nikolaus du Woernig had done to her life. At the moment, however, she felt no need or desire to analyze anything. She could only see the pain in his eyes. She could only feel a deeply innate desire to ease it.

"Have you eaten?" she asked.

"No, I . . ."

"Here," she said, unfastening his cloak, hoping he wouldn't consider her too bold or presumptuous, "let me take this for you and I'll get you something."

"Thank you," Lance said and watched her fumble momentarily with the clasp before their eyes met again.

"You must be half frozen," she said.

"It is cold out there," he commented while she motioned for his gloves. He removed them and set them into her hands.

Their fingers briefly made contact and she looked startled as she grabbed one of his hands, declaring, "You *are* freezing; even inside your gloves. Go sit by the fire. I'll only be a few minutes. Drew and Gerda have gone to the bank and the butcher's. They've taken Dulsie with them and left me in charge, but I think I can manage. There's still plenty left that I can heat up."

"Thank you," he said again and watched her leave the room. Finding her here completely alone seemed too good to be true. Or perhaps it was the answer to his prayers. He certainly hadn't prayed to find her alone, but he had prayed for the means to find some peace with what he was feeling. And just being in her presence seemed a good place to start.

Lance sat near the fire and held his hands close to the flames, squeezing his eyes shut as he heard the words in his mind, *The execution is complete.*

"Here you are," Nadine said, bringing him out of his disturbing thoughts. She set a meal down on a nearby table and he moved closer to eat it.

"Thank you. It looks wonderful."

"Well, I didn't cook it," she said in a way that perfectly mimicked the way Abbi had said those same words just last night. For a moment she reminded him so much of Abbi that he felt chilled from the inside out. Or maybe it was his feelings for her that reminded him of Abbi. "I *can* cook," she continued, "but not nearly so well as Drew. The customers would surely notice if somebody else started doing it. And he can cook for a small army. I'm accustomed to cooking for two."

"Well, thank you for your wonderful service, Mrs. Rader. Perhaps one day I will enjoy the pleasure of your cooking."

"Perhaps," she said with a smile, as if he would be incredibly privileged to do so. He silently agreed.

Lance feared she would excuse herself to get to work, when he so wanted to just have her near. Simply being with her soothed a formless ache in him and he wanted to beg her to stay. He was just wondering how he might do that appropriately when she said, "Would I be imposing to sit with you? I ate long ago, but . . . company is nice."

"Yes, company is nice," he said.

"Unless you're in the mood to be alone," she added. "And if that's the case, I understand and I would be happy to just—"

"No, please sit down. I would very much enjoy your company."

They talked pleasantly of trivial matters and asked polite questions of each other's preferences and upbringing while Lance finished his meal. When he was done she took his dishes to the kitchen.

"Thank you again," he called. "You'll see that the amount gets put on my bill."

"Of course," she called back, tossing a smile over her shoulder.

Chapter Five
PRACTICALLY STRANGERS

Nadine returned a few minutes later and he said, "If I wouldn't be imposing, I'd like to stay a while. The peacefulness here is a nice reprieve from . . ."

"From what?" she asked. He looked into her eyes but didn't answer. "Your thoughts are with you wherever you go, Captain. Will you find reprieve here from them as well?"

Lance marveled at her gentle boldness, which made it easy for him to say, "Perhaps."

She moved a chair in order to sit beside him and said, "It's been my experience that the only way to truly find reprieve from one's thoughts is to be free of them."

"And how does one go about doing that?"

"Two possibilities," she said. "You can write it down, or you can tell someone. Personally, I keep a journal. I've rarely had anyone to talk to that cared to truly listen, so the writing works better."

"I have a friend who keeps a journal; more than one friend who does actually. I've been encouraged to do so, but I've never taken to it."

"Perhaps you should," she said.

"Perhaps," he said and they both laughed, realizing how many times that word had come up.

"In the meantime," she said, "you could talk to me. We're practically strangers. I'm not biased. And I'm very good at keeping confidences."

Lance watched her closely, as if to size up her invitation. He had to admit, "Your offer is tempting, Mrs. Rader. But I'm not certain I want to weigh you down with my burdens."

"It won't weigh me down. I'm just listening. Besides, you've done so much for me. Allow me to return the favor." While he wondered where to begin, she said in a voice that was alluringly tender, "Just tell me what's troubling you, Captain. What's on your mind?"

"Well, I must admit that . . . the events of late have stirred things up in my memory—difficult things."

"I'm listening," she said.

Lance was surprised at how easy it was to say, "I . . . uh . . . once had to kill a man. I mean . . . in my line of work, I've had to kill many times, in truth, but . . . well, it was part of my training. My job is to ensure peace for the people of Horstberg. When people threaten that peace, it sometimes comes down to life-or-death situations. Horstberg has not seen war for many years, but circumstances have arisen where I've been forced to defend myself, or my men, or the well-being of a citizen, and I've had no choice but to take a man's life."

Her voice was tender as she said, "But one time was different. Is that what you're saying?"

"Yes," his voice became heavy, "it was different."

"Tell me," she urged.

"It's not a pleasant story, Mrs. Rader. I don't want to burden your mind with images that have haunted mine."

"My father was a solider for many years. He grew up far from here and was forced to fight in many battles. He minced no words when sharing his experiences, especially when he'd had a little too much to drink. I dare say I can handle whatever it is you need to say. Perhaps talking about it might help."

Lance felt suddenly uncomfortable, but he couldn't figure if it was his concern for her, or his reluctance to say what had resounded in his head for years. He suspected it was more the latter. He glanced around and asked, "Am I keeping you from your work? I don't want Drew and Gerda to be upset with me for—"

"It's all right. Cornelia has come back, actually. She's cleaning upstairs and will help through the lunch rush. I'm without a job until this evening."

"I see," he said, feeling profoundly relieved until she gently urged, "Talk to me, Captain."

At his hesitance she added, "You don't have to tell me if you don't want to. Forgive me. At times I can be a little overbearing and . . ."

"No, it's not that. I just . . ." A moment of thought made him realize that he instinctively wanted to talk about it, and he'd be a fool to pass up such an opportunity. She didn't know him or the situation well enough to care one way or the other. "Well, as you said, there was one time that was different. I was . . ." Lance stopped abruptly and looked up at her. He felt stunned to realize that she *did* have cause to care. The words he needed to say were related to the man who had deceived her into a mock marriage. He'd abandoned her and left her with his child. And now she was begging him to talk about his own troubling memories of Nikolaus du Woernig. And that's what he needed to do, he decided. He couldn't back down now, but she didn't have to know who he was talking about. He quickly fixed a method in his mind and forged ahead.

"There was a man, you see, who was guilty of many crimes. We were in the process of trying to bring him to justice; in fact we had the witness in custody who could testify against this man and—"

"Forgive me, but who is *we?*"

"Oh, uh . . . there was Cameron." She looked confused and he clarified, "Forgive me, His Grace. And Georg, whom you met in the office."

"Mr. Heinrich."

"That's right. And there were more than a dozen officers—besides the one who had actually assisted this . . . criminal. Anyway, it was night; a dark night. We were in the forest and this man felt . . . threatened. The walls were closing in on his crimes, and he knew it. He took a hostage . . . he had a gun to this person's head . . . made some terribly ugly threats and then . . . the witness stepped forward and just . . . stated what he knew. And then this man was really cornered, and really desperate, and it became evident that if somebody didn't do something the unthinkable would happen. I managed to get behind him and I just . . . stabbed him in the back."

Nadine watched his eyes darken further. Her heart quickened as she could almost feel his anguish. "But you had to," she said gently.

"Yes, I had to," he said, but he didn't seem convinced. "He went to his knees and the hostage got out of his reach and I moved in front of him just in time to keep him from falling forward. He was still very much alive when I looked into his eyes and told him that the witness had spoken, the jury was present, the verdict was guilty.

And then I . . . just . . . pushed that knife into his heart while I told him that . . . the execution was complete. I lowered him down to the ground, and I saw the blood on my hand and something inside of me died right along with him."

Nadine could feel his pain, and she sensed his grief. Still, she had to admit, "I don't understand, Captain. It was in the line of duty."

He looked into her eyes with a severity that chilled her. "He was my friend, Mrs. Rader," he said and she gasped. "He was my playmate from the nursery. We took lessons together. We rode and played and worked together all our lives, side by side. He'd always had a difficult side to him. Arrogant, harsh at times. But I knew how to handle him. Then something changed. His circumstances changed, and he allowed his circumstances to change him. I'd watched him deteriorate into some kind of evil impersonator of the man I'd once known. And then when I was standing there, watching him threaten someone I cared for with their life, several puzzle pieces came together when that witness stepped forward and cleared up a very big misunderstanding that I'd struggled with for many years."

"What was that?" she urged when he hesitated.

Lance looked hard into her eyes again. "This *friend* of mine . . ." She watched him squeeze his eyes shut and heard his breathing sharpen. "He'd killed my sister." Nadine sucked in her breath and held it. "He'd stabbed her through the heart because she'd threatened to expose his treasonous actions. So I did the same to him. And I know it was necessary, and I know that even if I'd been able to set the hostage free without violence, he would have gone before a firing squad within the next few days. Still, the memories plague me. And every time I'm confronted with death, it comes back to me, haunting me. And this morning . . . after the execution, one of my men said, 'The execution is complete.' And that did it. The memories were so clear . . . too clear. And I just can't seem to shake them."

"Do you feel guilty? There's no need to."

"No," he said easily. "I don't feel guilty. He got what he deserved. It was necessary. I know that."

"Sorrow, then?"

"Yes, definitely. But there's more. Something more that I don't understand."

"So what do you feel, Captain? What makes you hold onto this?"

"I don't know," he admitted. "But I think it would be good if I figured it out. I don't want to spend the rest of my life having this come up over and over."

"Well, when you figure it out, you must share what you learn with me."

They exchanged a smile and a sudden tension descended, as if the conversation had nowhere to go. He was relieved when she spoke, even though he wasn't terribly fond of the topic. "So, the thief was executed this morning. I dare say his burial will be quite a contrast to that of yesterday."

"Indeed," Lance said.

Thoughtfully she added, "Do you suppose his loved ones mourn him any less than the officer whose death urged an entire country to mourn?"

"One man's death was honorable, the other a disgrace."

"That's true, but to the women who loved these men, their absence could well be the same. Of course, we don't know what their private lives were like. An officer could go home and beat his wife; a thief could treat her like a queen. What we see on the surface is not necessarily the reality of life behind closed doors. A widow's grief is more related to the way a man treated her in private. For her, that is the true measure of honor . . . or disgrace."

Lance watched this woman closely, in awe of her amazing insight and wisdom. In that respect he couldn't help comparing her once again to Abbi. And yet she was so different, so perfectly unique, so unlike any woman he'd ever known. Contemplating her words again, he asked, "Where did you learn to be so wise?"

"Me? Wise?" She laughed softly. "No, Captain, I simply know from experience that it's just as easy to fall in love with a scoundrel as it is a hero, especially when the scoundrel goes to so much trouble to paint the illusion of a perfect life around you."

Her words struck Lance deeply as he perceived the thoughts between them. He felt constrained to clarify, "You're talking about Nikolaus."

Nadine glanced down abruptly and her lips tightened. "Yes," she said with a tight voice, "I'm talking about Nikolaus." He could see her thoughts shift before she said, "You knew him . . . personally." It wasn't a question. "You don't call the duke by his given name without knowing him well."

Lance was so struck by the irony of the conversation that his insides started to tremble. While a part of him wanted to say, *Yes, I knew him. He was my friend and I killed him,* he settled instead for saying, "I am the Captain of the Guard, Mrs. Rader. I worked with Nikolaus as I work with Cameron. I also grew up close to the du Woernig family. I speak of them, and to them, formally in public. But I know them well enough that their given names slip when I am relaxed."

Nadine wondered if that meant he felt relaxed with her. She hoped so. He certainly seemed to be. "Of course," she said and glanced down.

Lance recalled Cameron telling her how Nikolaus had been killed, and he wondered now if she might put the pieces together and figure out that it was he who had committed the deed. He wasn't certain why he didn't want her to know, not yet at least. He simply hoped that by the time she figured it out her heart would have healed more in regard to Nikolaus, and perhaps she would have come to know him well enough not to hold Nikolaus's death against him. As much as Nikolaus had hurt and betrayed her, Lance suspected that she'd loved him. Nikolaus had always been able to make women love him—until they discovered his true character. Then they had *hated* him. But it was difficult to tell exactly where this woman's feelings for Nikolaus were, and until Lance knew for certain, he preferred to omit particular details of the situation.

Lance found himself staring at her again and wondered why he didn't feel embarrassed by his overt attention. Perhaps it was the way she stared back. Reminding himself that they were practically strangers, he looked away and cleared his throat. "Your time on my behalf is appreciated, Mrs. Rader, as well as your compassion." He came to his feet, finding some measure of comfort in her apparent disappointment. "I should be getting to work, however, and I'm certain you have better things to do with your day."

"Not necessarily," she said and he briefly searched her eyes, wondering over her motives. What he felt, and sensed, was so unfamiliar that he hardly knew what to think.

Nadine watched his apparent hesitancy to leave and erupted with a quiver inside as she considered his possible reasons. She was pleasantly surprised when he took her hand and pressed a kiss to the back of her fingers, allowing his lips to linger there a long moment.

"Good day, Mrs. Rader."

"Captain," she said and watched him walk toward the door, taking up his cloak and gloves on his way.

"Heaven help me," she muttered into the empty room once he had gone. A little voice inside her head demanded to know how she could be foolish enough to even consider opening her heart to a man again after what had happened. And another voice countered it with the justification that Captain Dukerk was nothing like Nikolaus du Woernig. Looking back, Nadine could see that her instincts had encouraged her to be suspicious and wary with Nikolaus, but his charm and charisma had squelched those instincts as he'd enchanted her into an irrevocable trap. Nadine had spent years attempting to justify and rationalize feelings of uneasiness and doubt, trying to talk herself into the belief that Nikolaus truly did love her. Being confronted with the truth upon her arrival in Horstberg had done nothing but validate everything she had tried to ignore all along. And what she felt in the presence of Captain Dukerk was completely different. She sensed a genuineness about him and a marked sensitivity and honesty that almost seemed incongruent with a man of his position. She was drawn to him, stirred by him. And she couldn't deny the evidence she'd seen that, at the very least, he was drawn to her. But she reminded herself that her heart had been badly abused, and she wondered if she could ever fully trust any man with it again. She couldn't help feeling lonely and longing for companionship in her life. She'd not actually spent any time with Nikolaus since she'd discovered that she was pregnant. That was when he'd sent her away with a large sum of money, promising to send more and to come for her at the first possibility. He'd responded to her first few letters, and then he'd written to say that political difficulties were intensifying, and even his mail was being closely watched. He'd asked her to be patient and not lose hope. And she had certainly done that. But gradually her hopes had dwindled and then been dashed while she had given birth and raised a child completely on her own. With Dulsie constantly needing her, she'd never been alone, but she had continually been lonely. And having a man like Captain Dukerk gaze at her with silent meaning in his eyes, she could almost believe that he was as lonely as she, and that maybe, just maybe, they could ease that loneliness for each other. Still, she had to keep perspective. The hints of intrigue she'd seen in his eyes did not necessarily mean that anything would ever come of this attraction she felt. She'd drawn the attention of one man in a position of prestige and power, but she'd come to realize his attraction to her was more due to her uncomplicated circumstances and gullible nature. Well, she'd gotten past being gullible, but she was still vulnerable in the sense that she had no family beyond a dependent child, no brother or father to look out for her, and no money or power in her background to withstand the dallying of a man with money and power.

Nadine pushed away her musings over the captain and set to work gathering dirty laundry and heating water to wash it. For the hundredth time since she'd come to Horstberg, she prayed that she would be able to come to terms with what Nikolaus had done to her and move on with her life. She recounted her blessings, which were many, and considered among them the presence of Captain Dukerk in her life. Whether he became any more a part of her life or not, his kindness and willingness to be open with her had restored a degree of faith in the goodness of mankind. She prayed that her instinctive belief that he was, indeed, a good man, would not see her undone.

Lance rode away from the inn realizing he actually felt better, at least as far as his troubling thoughts regarding this morning's execution. But his deep and tender conversation with Mrs. Rader had derisively deepened the lonely ache inside of him that he usually managed to keep at a tolerable level. It took great willpower not to turn around and go back and get down on his knees to beg for the opportunity to be in her presence every possible moment. He found himself wondering what it would be like to kiss her and hold her, and his insides shivered at the very idea. He'd not kissed any woman since he'd been betrothed to Abbi du Woernig. He'd not found a single woman worth kissing since. But what he'd shared with Abbi had been reserved and completely respectable. While he'd certainly enjoyed kissing her, he looked back on it now as a brotherly kind of affection. It was not at all how he imagined kissing Nadine Rader.

Struck by the cold air and the slow pace he was taking, Lance reminded himself that he had work to do, and daydreaming over a woman was not conducive to getting it done. He heeled the stallion into a gallop and headed up the castle hill, unable to keep from wondering when he might see Nadine again.

Lance arrived at the castle and was met by a lieutenant. "His Grace asked to see you as soon as you returned."

"I'm on my way," Lance said, leaving the horse with him.

He pulled off his gloves and tucked them into his belt as he walked across the courtyard to the main entrance of the castle. A maid took his cloak as he flung it off his shoulders. "Thank you, Berta," he said. "Don't work too hard now."

"Nor you, Captain," she said with a smile.

Lance hurried down the long hall to the ducal office. The two men in uniform hovering casually at the door went to attention at his appearance. "Good day, gentlemen," he said. "I trust all is well."

"Yes, Captain," they said together.

"At ease," he said and pushed open the door.

"Ah, Captain," Cameron said, removing his glasses and tossing them to the desk. "Come in. Sit down."

"Forgive me for being unavailable earlier," Lance said, taking a chair next to Georg. "I had a late breakfast after the . . ."

"I figured as much," Cameron said. "It's not a problem. Personally, I think you work too much."

"No more than you do, sir," Lance said.

"That's disputable," Georg interjected before they got down to business.

More than two hours later, Cameron leaned back in his chair and said, "All right. I think that's enough for today. I've got that blasted advisory committee meeting in half an hour and I need a break."

"Have you heard how Mrs. Rader is doing?" Georg asked and Lance's heart quickened like a guilty child caught stealing. It took him a moment to realize that his only crime was the fact that he'd spent a great deal of time being aware of how Mrs. Rader was doing.

"Doing well, I believe," he said, "beyond having a broken heart, I suppose."

"How *did* he manage to break so many hearts?" Cameron asked with disgust.

"It's beyond me," Lance said. "I guess he knew how to say what a woman wanted to hear."

"Apparently," Cameron said.

"So, is she working?" Georg asked.

"Some. Drew had need for someone to fill in at the inn temporarily, so that's worked out conveniently. But one of the girls has come back, so they only need her evenings now, as I understand it. Why?" Lance asked, hoping it hadn't sounded defensive. He almost feared that these men could see into his heart and realize how preoccupied he'd become with the object of their conversation.

"Well," Georg went on, "I was looking through our records of women in need of employment, since we have a temporary position that needs to be filled. Apparently she's literate and has some bookkeeping skills."

"I believe so," Lance said, trying to sound indifferent while something inside of him rejoiced to think of her working here at Castle Horstberg. And if Georg was looking at bookkeeping skills, then it wouldn't be menial labor. He realized then that he had an aversion to having her serve and clean up after others. "And what is this position?" he asked nonchalantly. "I wasn't aware of anything."

"Well, it just opened up," Georg said.

"Replacing who?" Lance asked.

Georg sighed. "Elsa." Lance felt his own intrigue deepen, even while he sensed Georg's ongoing dismay over his wife's temporary absence. He went on to explain, "Abbi mentioned to me last night that when Elsa had left she'd not considered the time of year. She's accustomed to having Elsa help organize the Christmas festivities and the usual charity projects. There are invitations and menus and . . . oh, good heavens. I don't know what there is. I only know Abbi was going on and on about it. And with her pregnancy progressing, she's likely to become rather limited very soon. I sensed that Mrs. Rader is a good woman, and if she has those skills, perhaps she would be interested. And by the time Elsa returns, we can find something else for her to do."

"I think it's a great idea," Cameron said. "Of course, Georg always has great ideas. He's the brains here, you know. Abbi always goes to him with her problems."

"As I recall," Georg said to Cameron, "you were present when the conversation came up."

"Yes, well . . . I didn't know what to do about it. So, I'm glad you had a great idea."

Georg chuckled and Lance smiled. He was tempted to ask Cameron if the topic had come up later during the usual pillow chat, but he decided to save that for another time when he was more in a mood to tease him.

"Well," Cameron said to Georg, "why don't you send a message to the inn and—"

"Actually," Lance said, "I usually go there for supper. I'd be happy to talk to her about it."

"That's perfect," Georg said. "If she's interested, she could come for an interview tomorrow morning, say at ten. If that's a problem let me know. I'll tell Abbi."

"Very good," Lance said.

The three men chatted a few more minutes before Lance excused himself to go to his own office and go over duty rosters, among other tedious chores. The remainder of the afternoon dragged, while Lance looked at the clock every ten minutes. He ended up staying later than usual when unexpected challenges arose, including a problem with one of the prisoners being held in the keep. But as he rode toward the inn, he thought being late could be better. He preferred to avoid the rush anyway, but adding his incentive to talk with Nadine Rader, he didn't want to arrive when she was too busy to sit down for a few minutes. His heart quickened at the thought as he tethered his horse near the inn and went inside, tucking his gloves into his belt. He hung his cloak near the door and quickly surveyed the dining room. Only a few scattered guests remained, and Gerda was refilling glasses of ale from a pitcher. Nadine was nowhere to be seen. Lance took a seat where he could see the door to the kitchen. Gerda greeted him with a smile. "I'll have your dinner in a moment, Captain," she said. "Drew made his bratwurst today."

"Sounds wonderful, thank you," Lance said.

By the time Lance was nearly finished with his meal, the dining room had completely emptied of guests except for a small group that was drinking and laughing in the corner. Gerda had wiped clean all of the tables, and Lance hadn't seen Nadine. His heart sunk at the thought, and he wondered how he could get up and leave without even catching a glimpse of her. At the moment it seemed more than he could bear.

Chapter Six

HOLDING HANDS

When Gerda came to clear his dishes away, Lance recalled that he had a legitimate reason to talk with Nadine. "Is Mrs. Rader here?" he asked. "I have a message for her regarding some potential employment."

"She's in the kitchen," Gerda said. "I'll go and get her."

"Thank you," Lance said, trying to sound indifferent. But he couldn't help smiling when she emerged from the kitchen, drying her hands on her apron.

"Hello," she said.

"Hello." He stood to greet her.

"I, uh . . . volunteered for kitchen duty to be close to Dulsie while she plays. She's been somewhat . . . clingy and whiny today."

"I see," he said. "Well, I have a message for you."

"You do?" Her surprise was blatant. "Gerda just said you wanted to see me, and . . ."

"Do you have a few minutes?" he asked, motioning her to a chair.

"I think I've earned a break," she said and sat across from him. For a moment he felt a deep tension between them that made their heartfelt conversations earlier difficult to imagine. The problem was bridged somewhat when she added, "You seem better this evening; not so dark."

Lance smiled. "Yes, I believe I'm doing better. You were right. Talking about it did help, I believe. Thank you again."

"A pleasure, Captain," she said, smiling.

"And you still smile at me," he said, "even after hearing my darkest confessions."

"Were those your darkest?" she asked.

He chuckled. "Perhaps."

Dulsie came running from the kitchen, seeming panicked. She clung to Nadine, pressing her face into the folds of her mother's skirts.

"It's all right, Dulsie. I'm here. You remember the captain? Remember how kind he was to us when he brought us here?"

The child looked up at Lance, looking more pleased than concerned.

"Hello, Dulsie," he said and was struck by something he hadn't noticed before.

"Hello," she said quietly.

Nadine said to the child, "I'm not leaving this spot right here. You go back and help Gerda while I talk privately with the captain."

The child obediently went back to the kitchen. Nadine said, "She had a little incident in town today that set her off."

"What happened?" Lance asked, concerned.

"Nothing really. She went with Drew and Gerda on some errands and was separated from them for just a couple of minutes. But she panicked. And with what we've been through the last few months, it just . . . set her off."

Lance looked at her directly in a way that was becoming comfortable. With that in mind he hoped she wouldn't be set off when he commented, "She looks like Nikolaus."

"Yes," she sighed, "Dulsie is a beautiful child."

"With a beautiful mother," Lance said, wondering where this sudden ability to say such things had come from.

Nadine looked pleasantly alarmed by the comment before she glanced down and said, "Apparently not beautiful enough."

"According to who?" he asked. "If you're talking again about Nikolaus du Woernig, the man was a fiend and a crook."

He said it with such vehemence that Nadine was taken aback. His voice softened as he added, "Whatever Nikolaus was attracted to had little to do with what really makes a woman beautiful . . . in my opinion. Forgive me if saying so is inappropriate for our brief acquaintance."

Nadine couldn't hold back a little chuckle. She found his formality and perfect graciousness thoroughly endearing. "You're very kind, Captain, but that's not what you came here to talk about."

Following a long moment of silence he asked, "What *have* you been through the last few months?"

Nadine absorbed his compassion and felt her heart momentarily leap for joy. But it was quickly squelched as she considered answering the question. She glanced away and said, "I'd rather not talk about that right now. I fear it would take far more time than I've got at the moment."

"When will you have time?" he asked.

Nadine considered the question while fear battled with hope in her head. "I'm not certain," she said and struggled for an avenue to change the subject. "You said you had a message for me."

"Georg Heinrich asked me to tell you that he knows of an opening for a temporary position. His wife is out of the country helping an aunt, I believe, and they need someone to cover for her."

"What would it entail?" Nadine asked, feeling afraid. She needed the work, and she wanted to take care of herself and Dulsie, but she always felt leery of the unknown. And her deepest concern was what to do with Dulsie while she worked. If she couldn't have Dulsie nearby, or cared for properly, what would she do?

"It's mostly secretarial type work, I believe. An assistant, you might say."

"To who?"

"The duchess," he said as if it were nothing.

"Her Grace?" Nadine countered, wishing it hadn't sounded so astonished. She thought of the beautiful, red-haired woman who had been so kind to her. She thought of how they should have been sisters-in-law, of how she held the position that Nadine had believed she would one day hold, and she felt incredibly sad. She reminded herself that she needed work and such a position would likely pay better than anything else she could get. Even if it was temporary, working at the castle could very well bring other opportunities. And she couldn't deny a certain intrigue at the thought of working with the duchess. Nadine had been impressed with her character, and she'd felt instinctively drawn to her.

"Yes, Her Grace," he said with a smile. "She's really a very gracious woman, and easy to work with." He leaned toward her. "And in my personal opinion, you are far more suited to such things, as opposed to waiting tables. And I'm certain the pay is better, as well."

"Well, thank you for your opinion, Captain. But the amount of money I make and the means in which I make it are less important to me than whether or not an occupation allows me to be close to my daughter. I am definitely interested in the job, but I need to know if—"

"There is a nursery at the castle for the children, with wonderful nannies. I don't know details of such things, but if you're interested, you may come to the castle in the morning for an interview, and you can see for yourself if it's something you would be comfortable with."

Nadine thought for a moment and said, "I would appreciate the opportunity for an interview. What time?"

"Ten o'clock."

"All right," she said, "but . . . I have no transportation, Captain. I have earned some cash. Is it possible to hire a carriage or—"

"No need," he said, "I will send one for you at quarter to the hour."

"That's really not necessary, Captain. I can—"

"I insist. It's not a problem."

Nadine told herself to be gracious. "Thank you," she said. "You're very kind. I hope that you're not just . . ."

Gerda appeared from the kitchen, saying, "Dulsie is awfully tired. She's in her nightgown and had her teeth cleaned. Would you like me to put her to bed for you, dear, or—"

"Oh, thank you, Gerda. Here I should be working and you're taking care of my daughter. Forgive me. I—"

"It's fine," Gerda said with a little laugh as Dulsie ran into the room. "It's a joy to help with Dulsie, and you've already put in far too many hours today. You just go ahead and visit and I'll—"

Dulsie climbed onto Nadine's lap and clung to her. "Thank you, Gerda," Nadine said. "She's fine. I'll take her up to bed in a few minutes."

"Good night then," Gerda said and moved away.

"Thank you for supper, Gerda," the captain called and she turned back. "It was magnificent, as always. Tell Drew his cooking keeps getting better."

"I'll tell him," she said with a little laugh. "You have a pleasant night, Captain."

"And you," he said, then he focused on Nadine. "I should let you get Dulsie to bed. I'm certain you have things to do."

"Apparently I have the rest of the evening off," she said with a little laugh. "But don't let me keep you."

"I have the rest of the evening off as well," he said, hoping he wasn't being too presumptuous. Her smile eased his concerns.

"Will you rub my hands, Mama?" Dulsie asked

"Yes, of course," Nadine said. "Run upstairs and get the cream."

Lance watched the child run up the stairs, and he couldn't help thinking what a good mother Nadine seemed to be. "She keeps you busy," he said when the silence grew too long.

"She does indeed," Nadine said, but it was evident that the child also kept her happy.

Dulsie returned with a jar of hand cream that Nadine opened and set on the table within reach. She took out a small amount and began rubbing it into one of Dulsie's hands with practiced efficiency, massaging every part with detailed care. As she did so, Nadine explained, "My mother did the same for me. She had the belief that every nerve in the body came together in the hands, that they were almost like a map of the rest of the body, and this kind of massage could ease a great deal of pain and stress."

"Do you hold to that belief?" he asked, intrigued.

"Perhaps. I do know that it has a soothing effect for Dulsie."

"Indeed," Lance said, seeing that the child was almost asleep. He watched as Nadine repeated the ritual with the child's other hand, so mesmerized that no conversation seemed necessary. He liked the way he could just *be* with this woman and not feel the need to make constant clever discourse.

By the time she was finished with the second hand, Dulsie was sleeping soundly. Nadine kissed Dulsie's head and held her close, overtly relishing her nearness. "She is such a joy to me," Nadine said, although that was already evident from the relationship he'd observed between them.

"So, she is living proof that good things come out of affliction," he said.

Nadine looked momentarily startled, then she gave a subtle smile. "Yes, she certainly is."

"Would you like me to carry her upstairs for you?" he offered.

"That would be nice, thank you. She is getting too big for me to carry."

Nadine shifted Dulsie into the captain's arms before picking up the jar of cream and leading the way up the stairs. She hurried to light a lamp and motioned him to the little sofa that had become Dulsie's bed. She watched him tuck her in and press a tender hand briefly over her hair.

"You've had experience with children?" she asked softly.

"No," he chuckled. "Well, a little here and there with the children of some friends, but nothing significant."

"You have no nieces or nephews? No one?"

"No, actually. I only had one sibling, a sister, and she—"

"Oh, of course. You told me that she'd been killed. I'm truly sorry."

"Thank you, but . . . it's been a long time. Truthfully, we were never terribly close. We just seemed to look at life through entirely different eyes."

"How is that?" she asked and he glanced around, as if standing in her bedroom was not the time or place to answer a complicated question.

"Perhaps I should save that for another time and leave you to get some rest, Mrs. Rader. I'm certain that—"

"Oh, I won't be able to sleep for a long while yet. This is my quiet time of the day, and I tend to hold out going to bed as long as possible. Would you like to sit? Or if you need to go, of course don't let me keep you."

Nadine moved a chair close to the fireplace while he seemed to be considering a response, then she squatted down to stoke the fire. "Here, let me do that," he offered and took the poker from her. She moved the other chair next to the first and sat to watch him stir the coals and add a few small logs, strategically arranging them so they would burn well.

"You're very good at that," she said as he straightened his back and brushed his hands together.

"Practice," he said with a little chuckle before he took a seat.

They sat staring into the flames and saying nothing. Nadine noted that he seemed tense, perhaps anxious, and the horrifying thought struck her that perhaps he thought her invitation to stay was somehow leading toward him staying the night. Nikolaus du Woernig certainly would have made such an assumption. But then, Nikolaus would have been trying to lure her to the bed long before now. Her mind wandered as she considered how firmly she had stood her ground, insisting that she would not be giving in to such things until they were married. And when he'd declared that they *would* be married, she had believed that she'd won. But he had won in reality, and had left her and her daughter out in the cold.

The flames crackled and brought her back to the present. The captain turned to look at her, that anxiousness still in his eyes. She thought of the in-depth conversations they'd shared and determined there was no reason they couldn't get beyond this silence. Addressing the problem head on, she said, "You seem tense. Are you all right?"

"I'm fine, really. Just . . ."

"Tense," she said and he felt touched by her perception and her willingness to address it, even if he wasn't quite sure how to respond.

"Perhaps," he chuckled. "The last few days have been . . . a challenge."

"Well, you need to relax," she said in a tone much like the duke would have ordered him to gather his men for an emergency.

"Yes, I should. But I don't know if I'm very good at that. My life has been my work for so many years that . . . well, relaxing is not one of my stronger qualities." He glanced at Dulsie sleeping as she made sweet noises and turned over. "Perhaps I need one of your famous hand massages," he said lightly.

"What an excellent idea," she said, coming to her feet.

"No, no," he laughed. "I was joking. You don't have to . . . do that."

She ignored him and turned her chair to face him, setting the open jar of balm on her lap.

"You really don't have to do this," he said, embarrassed for even bringing it up.

"I know," she said, "and if I didn't want to, I wouldn't have offered." She held out her hand. "It's relaxing for me as well. Come on, give me your hand."

Lance held out his hand and wasn't surprised by the spark he felt from her touch. He watched her face as she methodically rubbed every part of his hand with a firm gentleness that was intoxicating.

"So," he said, and she turned her eyes from his hand to his face, "what *have* you been through the last few months?" She looked taken aback and he added, "You said earlier you didn't have time to answer the question. I bet you could answer it before you get done with the other hand."

"Very well," she said. "But first I have to go back. I left Horstberg when I was about five months pregnant. Nikolaus gave me some money and told me where I should go. He promised to send more money, and to send for me when he got just a few things ironed out. The money he gave us didn't hold out terribly long considering I was too ill to work through the pregnancy, and then I had to pay for a doctor to attend me, and for some help with the baby until I got back on my feet. By the time she was a few months old, I was down to very little. He did send more, but not much. I was able to find work where I could keep her with me, and we managed. I did bookkeeping for a store half of the day, and filled the rest of my time working as a seamstress. We managed well enough, and I was even able to put some money away. Then about a year ago Dulsie became ill, and then I came down with the same thing. Our savings were quickly eaten up, but I was able to get back to work and we got by, but then . . ." She stopped rubbing his hand and he realized she was trying to say something difficult. "Then . . . there was a man who . . . took excessive interest in me." She started rubbing again absently as she spoke with distant eyes. "I'd known him for as long as I'd been there; we were vaguely acquainted, but he suddenly seemed to . . . fall for me. He wasn't old, but definitely too old for me. He made me uneasy and I was very clear with him that I was not interested in his attention. I told him that I was married and waiting for my husband to send for me. At that point, a part of me had completely given up on Nikolaus—while another part of me could never stop hoping. But it was a good cover for keeping Mr. Crider at bay. He believed I was lying, but with time I told him that as far as he was concerned, it didn't matter whether I had a husband or not, I wasn't interested. However, I assured him I was not lying. To put it simply, he caused so much trouble for me that I ended up losing my job because of him. And the same thing happened twice more. And that's when . . ."

She looked directly at him and let his hand slip out of hers. "Are you a praying man, Captain?"

"I am," he said immediately.

"Then you will understand what I mean when I say that after much fervent prayer I felt an urgency to return to Horstberg. I considered many possibilities of Nikolaus's abandonment; honestly, death never occurred to me. Although, it's evident that his death had little to do with my circumstances. Still, I thought that if I could only get here and see him, that he would surely do something to help me. I was likely wrong in that respect, but . . . I just felt that if I got to Horstberg, everything would be all right."

"And it was," Lance said, "even though it didn't turn out as you'd expected."

"That's right," she said, wondering if she should tell him that she believed she had seen Mr. Crider since her arrival in Horstberg. She told herself that one possible sighting was not a cause for concern. Surely it was just someone who had a similar appearance, and it had sparked her paranoia. She smiled and motioned for him to give her his other hand.

He sighed as she began the ritual again. "That is very nice," he said.

"Relaxing?"

"Indeed."

"So," she continued her story as she maneuvered the cream into every crevice of his hand, "I sold everything I could and set out. The last segment of our journey was rather hellish, to be quite frank. Most of what we had was stolen, and there were a couple of times that I truly feared we would not survive." Lance thought of the way they had looked when they'd arrived, and he considered that a testament to what she was saying. "So, that's it, really," she concluded.

"What did you have stolen?" he asked and she looked surprised. "I'm sorry. You don't have to tell me. I've handled more robberies than I could possibly count, and I'm always amazed at what people will steal. I just wondered if you lost anything of real value to you."

"Yes, actually. No monetary value, but . . . my journals were taken. And a Bible. The rest was just some clothing and such. I'm certain the journals were just thrown away; at least I'm hoping they were. I hate the thought of a stranger reading my deepest feelings.

And the Bible . . . well it was old and falling apart, but I miss reading from it." She forced a smile. "But we're safe and well, and I'm just grateful to be here."

"I share your gratitude on that count," he said and they exchanged a long gaze, as if she could find the true meaning of his words in his eyes.

"I truly am grateful, Captain. Still, this is not how I imagined my life to be. All I ever wanted was a simple life, to be a wife and mother, to care for a home and cook the meals and raise a family with peace and security."

"But you fell in love with the Duke of Horstberg. If your marriage had been legal, your life would have been anything but simple."

"That's true. Like every woman, I think there was a part of me that longed to live in a castle, to be treated like a queen. But truthfully, I was never comfortable with the thought of filling that role. I feel a certain relief that it didn't work out. I think a part of me knew all along that it wouldn't, in spite of the things he said to me."

She shrugged her shoulders and sighed. Lance said with fervor, "You would have made a fine duchess. You have a natural grace and dignity that many women do not possess."

"You're flattering me, Captain."

"I'm not a flattering man, Mrs. Rader. I can assure you that if I say something, I mean it."

She looked into his eyes and instinctively believed that he was telling her the truth. Graciously she said, "You're very kind then."

Lance watched her closely while she concentrated on his hand in hers. Her convictions stirred him, especially as he considered all of the women he'd encountered through his bachelorhood who only wanted to socialize and collect belongings that represented opulence; they wanted servants and fine clothing and jewelry. And that's why he had long ago stopped any attempt to court at all.

Nadine finished her massaging and took both his hands into hers. "Soft, hmm? The ladies will be impressed."

"Ladies?" he asked, almost wondering if she could read his mind.

"Surely there are many ladies you encounter in your associations, ladies who are vying for your attention."

He made a scoffing noise. "The ladies I encounter in my

associations are drawn to me by two things: my uniform and the amount of my payroll."

Nadine smiled slightly. "It is a fine uniform, and you do look dashing in it. But perhaps if you set it aside more often, you might find more opportunities to experience life as a man, rather than a captain."

Lance searched her eyes, marveling at her insight and depth. "Perhaps," he said, feeling for the first time in years some incentive to actually find a life beyond his work.

"So," she went on, still holding his hands, "you must be a wealthy man, if the ladies are drawn to your payroll."

"I don't keep track, truthfully. I have little to spend it on. I live in an apartment at the castle, which is one of many benefits of my job. So the money accumulates in the bank, while starry-eyed women imagine the lavish gowns and jewels I could buy for them with it."

In his mind Lance saw himself going down on his knees, here and now, and pledging himself to her eternally. He wanted to build her a home and grant her every wish and devote himself to her happiness for as long as he lived. But the power of what he felt for her was subdued by his proper nature and the need to progress appropriately. They were little more than strangers, even if it didn't feel that way.

Silence descended around them again and he wondered if he should leave. Not wanting to, he dipped his fingers into the jar of balm on her lap and took her hand into his. "Now it's my turn," he said. "I don't have the practice that you do, but I'll never get good at it without some experience."

She smiled warmly and he thoroughly enjoyed methodically rubbing every part of her delicate hand. He was amazed at how slender and small they looked in contrast to his own. She made a pleasurable noise and said, "You're very good at that, actually. You can practice on me anytime."

"We must make a habit of it, then."

"What a pleasant thought," she said. He smiled and she added, "So, I have an interview with the duchess in the morning. If I think too hard about that, I could be decidedly nervous."

"No need for that," he said. "Abbi du Woernig is a kind and gracious woman."

"You know her well, I take it . . . from the way she was with you when we first met."

"Yes, I know her well," he said.

"Would it be impertinent of me to ask you about her, then? I confess to being somewhat curious by nature, and my encounter with her left me . . . intrigued."

"Ask whatever you like," he said. "I'm certain she's a popular topic of gossip. She is revered more as a goddess than a queen by the people, and yet she interacts with them so naturally on their level."

Having met the duchess, Nadine didn't find the comment surprising—simply because she had sensed the commanding presence of this woman as well as her genuine compassion. But she noted aloud, "That's quite a reputation for one so young; she can't be more than twenty."

"Twenty-one, I believe," Lance said. "But she is wise far beyond her years. She is fine and extraordinary."

"And well admired," Nadine observed from his resolute description.

"Abbi du Woernig is a legend in her own time," he said with no defensiveness or arrogance. He seemed to simply be stating a well-known fact.

"And she is much younger than her husband," Nadine added.

"More than twelve years, I believe. Yet the love and mutual admiration they share is likely one of the largest factors in the people's admiration for them. They are both amazingly modest, in spite of their well-proven abilities to rule a nation appropriately."

Nadine smiled at the comment then said, "So, I don't need to be nervous?"

"Not at all," he said and their eyes met with a recently familiar magnetism that lasted for several minutes of silence.

"So," she said, while he was working on her second hand, "tell me how you are different from your sister."

He took a minute to think about it then said, "She was very much like the ladies I was just describing. Our association with the royal family to me was simply a matter of bonds and friendship just as it would be with a family of farmers or shopkeepers. But she saw it as an opportunity for gain. She married well, but her actions were not always ethical, and I believe they contributed to her tragic end."

"She was killed," she clarified softly, "by your friend . . . who was involved in treasonous activities."

"That's right," he said, his eyes darkening.

Nadine attempted to lighten the mood without diverting the topic. "Who did she marry?"

"The duke," he said.

"Nikolaus?" she asked, surprised.

"No, Cameron. He is the elder brother. Nikolaus only became the duke when . . ." He hesitated and said, "I think I should like to save such a conversation for another time. Talk of Nikolaus du Woernig just seems to ruin an otherwise perfect moment."

"Agreed," she said warmly. "But I must clarify . . . Cameron was married to your sister then, before she was killed. The present duchess is his second wife."

"That's right," he said and her curiosity seemed appeased.

Finished with his massaging, Lance impulsively took both her hands and held them to his face. "Soft, indeed," he said

While she expected, even wanted, him to kiss her, she feared where a kiss might lead in light of all that she was feeling. She felt a marked relief when he rose to his feet, saying firmly, "I must be going, Mrs. Rader. It's been a thoroughly pleasant evening, and I thank you."

"No, thank *you,*" she said, rising to walk him toward the door.

He hesitated for a long moment and she felt his reluctance to go; a reluctance she shared. She was surprised to feel his lips come against her brow with a lingering kiss. "Good night," he murmured and opened the door.

"Will I see you tomorrow?" she asked, pleased to see the positive response in his eyes before they narrowed with disappointment.

"I don't know. Tomorrow I have many obligations with His Grace, and the following morning I will be leaving the country for a few days."

"Business?"

"Yes, just routine. We regularly take different regiments out for periods of intense training, just to keep them well-tuned and ready for any emergency that might arise."

"I see," she said, unable to hide her disappointment. "You will be careful?"

"Of course," he said. "I'll send a carriage tomorrow morning, as we discussed."

"Thank you," she said and watched him walk down the hall before she closed the door and leaned against it. The room seemed empty and lonely in his absence, but the memory of his being here put an added glow inside of her, and she went to bed feeling the security of his presence surround her like a warm blanket. She prayed that the warmth would last forever.

Chapter Seven

INTERVIEW WITH THE DUCHESS

Nadine felt decidedly nervous as the time for her interview at the castle approached. The carriage arrived right on time, a fine vehicle pulled by four bays and driven by a man wearing castle livery. Another man dressed the same opened the door for Nadine and helped her step into the lush interior. She attempted to quell her nerves through the brief drive, but her thoughts were drawn to the difficulty she'd had trudging up the castle hill in the bitter cold with her daughter, not so many days ago. She focused on her gratitude of the present, rather than the heartache of the past, as she stepped out into the castle courtyard. The man who had helped her said, "Go through that door there." He pointed. "And Berta will take you to Her Grace's office. We will see that you're delivered safely home when you're finished."

"Thank you very much," Nadine said and hurried toward the appointed entrance. Berta was very kind and Nadine was struck, once again, by the incredible beauty of the castle as she followed the maid down a long hall, up an elaborate staircase, and down another hall. They stepped through the open door of a lovely room that had many places to sit comfortably, two desks of different sizes, and a table surrounded by chairs. She could easily imagine the duchess here having tea with her friends or breakfast with her husband, or writing letters, just as she appeared to be doing at the moment. Her red, curly hair was hanging down her back, and she wore a dark green dressing gown. A boy of about three with hair like his mother's was sitting on the floor, surrounded by an odd array of toys.

"Mrs. Rader, Your Grace," Berta said and the duchess looked up.

"Oh, wonderful. Come in. Thank you, Berta." The maid left and closed the door.

Abbi took a moment to gather her thoughts. She was startled to see this woman dressed so much like the woman in her dream. A simple, dark dress; same hair, same build, same age. And she didn't even want to think of how she'd felt when she'd learned that Mrs. Rader was now working at an inn. She didn't know why that seemed significant, but it did.

When Abbi had mentioned to Cameron and Georg that she needed some extra help in Elsa's absence, she hadn't even considered that her first interview would be with this woman Lance was falling for. If they were indeed going to end up working together, the implications of the dream kept getting closer to home.

Abbi forced her thoughts away and focused on the moment. "How are you doing, Mrs. Rader?" the duchess asked, as if she genuinely wanted to know.

"Well, thank you. And you?"

"Oh, well enough," she said. "I'll be better when I get this baby out of me. You know how that is."

"Yes, of course."

The duchess motioned her to one of the little sofas where they sat close together. Nadine noticed how the most important lady in Horstberg kicked off her slippers and tucked her feet up beneath her.

"And how is your daughter?" the duchess asked.

"She's doing well. It's been an adjustment, but a positive one for the most part."

"You didn't bring her?" she said as if she were disappointed.

"I didn't know that it would be appropriate. Drew and Gerda are watching her, at the inn where I'm staying."

"Ah yes, good people. Drew is one of the finest cooks in the country."

"I believe so," Nadine said.

"Well, next time you come, you must bring your daughter," the duchess said. "She could play with Erich. And the nursery here is marvelous. Erich loves it there with the nannies and the other children. We have a private nursery for certain times of the day, but my husband and I both feel it's important for him to interact with the others and learn to get along and share. Overall, I prefer to keep him with me as much as possible."

Nadine felt her hope of the situation deepen. She appreciated this woman's attitude about her child, and felt certain she would understand Nadine's need to keep Dulsie close. She was intrigued to know that little Erich, the royal heir, played in the nurseries with the servants' children. Then it occurred to her that Erich was Dulsie's cousin—not legally, but by blood. The thought was startling. She was grateful when the duchess went on to say, "You're welcome to bring your daughter with you if we decide the position will work out. The nursery service comes with the job, or if you prefer to keep her with you, that's fine as long as we're able to accomplish what we need to."

"Of course," Nadine said. "I'm grateful for your insight. I do want to be close to Dulsie. She's well behaved and quiet. I'm certain it wouldn't be a problem."

"Well then, shall we move on?" The duchess asked Nadine a number of questions about her work experience and basic etiquette. Interspersed with those were many questions regarding Nadine's personal life and past, but she felt that the duchess was more trying to get to know her and be friendly, as opposed to searching for inadequacies. She asked Nadine to sit at the desk and pen a thank-you note as she dictated, then she commented, "Oh, you have lovely penmanship."

They chatted a short while longer about children and pregnancy and the horribly cold weather they'd been having, then the duchess told Nadine she could have the job if she wanted it. She asked if Nadine could work each day except Sundays from ten in the morning until two or three in the afternoon. The hours suited Nadine well, since she would be left to work evenings at the inn for as long as she was needed. Nadine eagerly accepted her offer, and then the duchess mentioned what the pay would be and Nadine had to fight to keep from choking. In the six weeks left until Christmas, when Elsa returned to take her job back, Nadine would be making more money than she'd made in six months as a seamstress. She considered this a huge blessing as it would give her some money to put away for an emergency fund while she found another job. Nadine wondered for a moment what she might do when the time came but decided such concerns could wait.

She was surprised when the duchess invited her to share an early lunch before she returned home. A servant brought a tray to the room where they were visiting, and Nadine marveled at how comfortable and easy it was to be with the duchess. Apparently the captain had been right about her in that respect.

As Nadine returned to the inn, she felt deeply gratified with the prospect of working with the duchess. If her work days were to be as pleasant as this morning had been, it would be a job from heaven. As the carriage let her out, she wondered what the captain was doing, and *how* he was doing. She recalled their time together last evening, and how it had felt to have her hands in his—and against his face. Her insides quivered and her heart quickened at the thought. She marveled at the intensity of her feelings when, in most respects, he was a stranger to her. Still, they'd had deep conversations that had stirred and warmed her. She couldn't recall ever talking about much of anything with Nikolaus.

Once inside the door, Dulsie ran to greet her with laughter and a tight embrace. She was in good spirits, which relieved Nadine after yesterday's clinging and whining. Nadine talked for a few minutes with Dulsie then went into the kitchen to help Gerda clean up from the lunch crowd.

"Oh, you don't need to do that," Gerda said as Nadine rolled her sleeves up and starting washing the pots.

"I'm happy to," she said.

"Well, I'd appreciate the company as much as the help," Gerda said. "Drew's gone to help a friend for a few hours."

"Did you have a good crowd today?" Nadine asked.

"Fair," she answered. "I think the cold keeps people closer to home."

"It would seem so."

"And how did the interview go with Her Grace?" Gerda asked excitedly.

"Very well, actually. I start tomorrow."

"Oh, that's wonderful," Gerda said.

"And I'll still be able to cover the evening shift until Wilma returns."

"That'll be perfect for all of us, then," Gerda said. "It would seem the good Lord is looking after you."

"It would seem so," Nadine said.

"Her Grace is a fine woman. Though I've not had the chance to meet her personally, she's brought a great deal of good to this country."

Nadine listened to her go on for several minutes about Abbi du Woernig's fine qualities until Dulsie interrupted, needing help with something. When Nadine returned to her work, Gerda was apparently finished with what she had to say. Nadine's thoughts naturally went to Captain Dukerk and she wondered if this might not be a good opportunity to glean some information.

"Might I ask," Nadine said, "what you know of the captain?"

"What? Captain Dukerk?" She laughed softly. "A fine man if there ever was one." She smiled conspiratorially. "Would you be having an interest in the captain? I've noticed the two of you visiting a few times, so you must have some interest, eh?"

Nadine forced a straight face. "I doubt there's a woman in the whole of Horstberg who hasn't turned her head to look at him and wonder."

"That would be for sure," Gerda said. "It's a wonder he's not found a good woman years ago, but then . . . a broken heart can be hard to heal."

"A broken heart?" she asked, attempting to keep her voice from betraying the depth of her interest.

Gerda lowered her voice, as if it were too tragic to speak of in a normal tone. "He was left at the altar, my dear, by a woman that I believe he loved very much. Of course, any man would love such a woman, I believe, but no man would get over such a thing easily. But then it was . . ."

"Gerda!" Drew called as he returned home and she hurried away, saying over her shoulder, "We'll have to finish this conversation another time."

Nadine felt anxious to hear what else Gerda might know, but it didn't come back up, and Nadine didn't want to pry too much. In the midst of the evening rush, her heart skipped a beat to see Captain Dukerk come into the dining room. He caught her eye and smiled at her as he removed his cloak, then she realized that he was with three other men. She recognized two of them as the duke and Mr. Heinrich. The other was an officer in uniform, who had the adornment of a lieutenant. The four men sat down together at a table, talking and laughing amongst themselves. Nadine approached, saying, "Good evening, gentlemen, Your Grace," she nodded toward the duke, "what will you be drinking?"

They each told her then Mr. Heinrich said, "How are you doing, Mrs. Rader?"

"Very well, thank you."

The duke then said, "I understand you'll be working with my wife, starting tomorrow I believe."

"That's right," she said and didn't miss the pleasure in the captain's eyes.

"The interview went well, I take it," he said.

"Yes. She's a fine woman."

"Hear, hear," all four men said with enthusiasm.

"Well, congratulations," the captain said.

"Thank you," Nadine said. "Will you all be eating tonight or—"

"Yes," they all said and she hurried to the kitchen to dish up tonight's menu item and pour their drinks. She returned a few minutes later to serve them, feeling disheartened to think that the captain wouldn't likely be available for any conversation with her this evening. As she set their drinks on the table, the other three men were talking to each other, but the captain turned his attention to her and she asked quietly, "So, you're leaving in the morning?"

"That's right," he said, his regret evident, which appeased her emotion somewhat. She was amazed to note how thoroughly she didn't want him to go. "But I was hoping when I return that we could hold hands again."

Nadine smiled and hoped she wasn't blushing. He smiled in return and she said, "I'll look forward to it."

While Nadine served meals and cleared tables, she was discreetly aware of the captain and his coworkers, although they seemed much more like friends. In spite of her own relationship at one time with the Duke of Horstberg, she found it difficult to imagine being on such comfortable, congenial terms with such important men. Of course, Nikolaus had never been seen in public with her. And then she considered that Captain Dukerk was not simply comfortable with these important men, he was one of them. Preoccupied as she was with him, she couldn't help feeling pleased to note that he was discreetly aware of her, as well. Three different times she glanced his way to find him watching her, and they exchanged a conservative smile.

Nadine was disappointed to return to the dining room after several minutes in the kitchen and realize that the captain had left with the others. The remainder of the evening dragged as she considered what the previous evening had been like. She went to bed early and rose feeling a certain excitement to embark upon her new job. Drew and Gerda had eagerly told her that she could drive their trap to the castle for the time being, since they rarely used it. Nadine bundled up Dulsie and harnessed the trap herself before they set out for Castle Horstberg. She arrived early enough that she could go to the nursery with Dulsie and help her get acquainted. Dulsie took to one of the nannies quickly and when Nadine left to get to work, Dulsie hardly noticed. She was already involved with another girl near her age and a shelf filled with lovely picture books.

Over the next few days, Nadine quickly became comfortable with the duchess, and she thoroughly enjoyed her work. Dulsie loved the nursery and was always anxious to go back. Nadine enjoyed having lunch with a group of servants in one of the kitchens each day, after which she'd check on Dulsie before returning to work. Nadine's thoughts were often with the captain, wondering how he was faring in his efforts to keep Horstberg safe. She wondered if he was keeping warm, and if he was looking forward to *holding hands* again, as she was. She often pondered what Gerda had told her, and wondered if it were true. Of course, what Gerda knew likely amounted to local gossip. Thinking the matter through, Nadine decided to try a different approach to satisfy her curiosity. While she was going over lists with the duchess, she ventured to say, "Forgive me, Your Grace, if I'm out of line, but . . . I can't help being curious about . . . the captain." The duchess smiled in a way that made it easy for Nadine to go on. "He's been so very kind to me, and sometimes he seems so . . . sad. I've only heard bits and pieces of gossip, and I thought that you might know what *really* happened."

Her Grace leaned back in her chair and took a deep breath, as if she was somehow startled or concerned. When she said nothing for a couple of minutes, Nadine asked, "Did I say something wrong? If it's inappropriate for me to—"

"Oh no, it's not that. You may ask me anything you like. Of course, I wouldn't break a confidence, but . . . well, I guess I just never considered what the perception of gossip might be in relation to . . . what happened." She looked directly at Nadine and asked, "What *do* the people say about Captain Dukerk?"

"I've heard very little except that . . . he has a broken heart; that he was left at the altar by a woman he loved very much."

Nadine felt concerned when the duchess's countenance became grave. She stood abruptly and moved to the window. Nadine's curiosity overrode all else as she pressed gently, "You know what happened then?"

"Yes, I know what happened," she said.

"So, it's true."

"Yes and no," she said, sounding more composed. She turned to face Nadine and said, "I can't help feeling that your interest is some-what . . . personal." Nadine looked down abruptly and the duchess laughed softly. "There's no need to be embarrassed to admit that you have an interest in him."

"Me and every other woman under thirty in Horstberg."

The duchess laughed again and sat back down. She put a gentle hand over Nadine's and said, "Tell me."

Nadine looked into her eyes and found no reason not to trust this woman. And it felt so good to have a woman near her age to talk to. "Well, yes . . . my interest is personal. I even sense that he has the same interest in me, but . . . I know so little about him in some respects. I couldn't help thinking that . . . well, if there had been another woman, and she left him . . ." Nadine felt suddenly nervous and wrung her hands tensely. "Truthfully, Your Grace, after what happened with Nikolaus, I have difficulty believing that any man could be as good as he seems. If there's a woman out there who knew enough about him to leave him at the altar, I can't help wishing I could talk to her. I know it sounds silly, and I wouldn't really venture to track her down and do such a thing, but . . . I was hoping that knowing him as you do, that you might know what had happened." She chuckled tensely. "I'm sounding crazy now."

"No, not crazy," the duchess said gently, "just in love."

Nadine felt startled. "In love? No, I don't think that . . . I mean, intrigued, yes. But . . . in love? I hardly know him. I . . ."

"Nadine," the duchess said, "from one woman to another, I know well what it's like to be thoroughly smitten with a man who has a past; a past that you desperately want to know if only so you can reach into his heart and truly understand him. You have good reason to be afraid, my dear, after what you've been through. You also have just cause to want to be happy. Whether or not anything comes of you and the captain, he is having an impact on your life, and your curiosity is natural. I would far prefer that the gossip be cleared up. Perhaps we should send out a proclamation or something and straighten out the story."

"You know the story then?"

"Quite well."

"Will you tell me?"

"With pleasure. You see, Lance grew to—"

"Lance?"

"Captain Dukerk."

"Oh, of course. I'd never heard his given name. Lance," she repeated, deciding she liked it; it suited him.

"Yes, well. Lance grew to care for a young woman who was terribly naive and gullible. And at the same time, Nikolaus du Woernig set his sights on her."

Nadine caught her breath. She hadn't expected this story to have *him* in it. The duchess met her eyes with compassion and kept on. "This young woman was actually the great niece of Lance's stepmother; that's how they met. Eventually she discovered that Nikolaus's intentions were not honorable, and she came to see that Lance's motives were *completely* honorable. But an incredible thing happened. She was lost in a blizzard, and for an entire winter Lance believed she was dead. He told me later that he'd been heartbroken over the loss, but when spring came she returned home, none the worse for wear, having been taken in by a man living in a secluded mountain lodge who had discovered her in the storm and saved her life."

"Is this true?" Nadine asked, thinking it sounded more like a legend.

"It is," she said with a little smile, as if she were thoroughly enjoying herself. "It turned out that the man she had been snowed in with was a fugitive from the law, and Lance was the Captain of the Guard. She had married this man secretly and was expecting his baby, waiting for him to put his life in order and come for her. When Lance proposed marriage, she was actually already married. But she told him she would marry him, being completely honest with him regarding her previous marriage and her pregnancy. She told him she believed her husband was dead, but she didn't know for certain, and she needed a father for her child, a man who would care for them. She promised nothing of her heart, but she did pledge her willingness to be a good wife. They were at the altar when her husband arrived, alive and well, and stopped the marriage."

"How horrible that must have been for him!" Nadine said.

"Yes, I'm certain it was. Sometimes I wonder if it was more difficult for him than he let on. There have been many times that my heart has ached for him."

"So what they say *is* true. He is a man with a broken heart and—"

"A broken heart?" Lance's voice startled them both and they looked up to see him sauntering into the room. Nadine's heart threatened to pound out of her chest, and she blatantly avoided eye contact as she felt herself turning warm. But her pleasure at just seeing him again quickly overruled her embarrassment.

"Forgive me, ladies," he said. "I couldn't help overhearing, and when I realized I was the topic of conversation, I couldn't resist the temptation to listen."

"You're truly wicked," the duchess said with laughter.

He laughed as well and took her hand, kissing it while their eyes met with a strong gaze; a gaze that tempted Nadine to jealousy.

"When did you get back?" the duchess asked as if she were as glad to see him as Nadine.

"Not an hour ago," he said.

"Ooh," the duchess said, "that explains why your hands are so cold."

"They'll get warm, eventually," he said with the subtlest sly glance in Nadine's direction. "Now what were you saying? Me? Wicked?" He laughed again as he took Nadine's hand and kissed it in much the same way, looking into her eyes with an equally compelling gaze. "I'm not the one sitting around gossiping." He sat down in a vacant chair and crossed his ankle over his knee as if he'd spent many comfortable hours in this room.

"It's not gossip if it's true," the duchess said.

"But apparently they say I have a broken heart. Whoever *they* might be, I'm afraid they've got it wrong."

Nadine watched him turn toward her with purpose, as if to imply some hidden meaning in his penetrating gaze. She wondered if his masculine pride would balk at having a reputation for being broken-hearted, and he would deny it even if it were true.

Spurred by an apparent challenge in his eyes, she said quietly, "Well then, Captain, perhaps you could set the record straight."

"I would love to," he said. "I was never broken-hearted. Disappointed, yes; for a while. But never broken-hearted. What I felt was . . . grateful to have been able to call her mine, however briefly. And honored to have been a part of the greatest event this country has ever seen."

Nadine felt terribly confused as she admitted, "I don't understand."

"It was complicated at best, Mrs. Rader. But I can tell you this. I knew days before I went to the altar that the wedding was a charade; it was a ruse, the means for a public political forum—and I was in on it. Public hearsay has little to do with what actually happened. My place at the altar was simply playing my part in making it possible for an exiled king to come back from the dead and reclaim the country that so desperately needed him—and the wife who so desperately loved him. She was a woman who had answered a nation's prayers, a legend in her own time, and she was not to be mine. No, I was not broken-hearted."

"Perhaps not," the duchess said, "but you sure left in a hurry."

"It was somewhat embarrassing," he said in a light voice that seemed almost teasing. "I mean I *was* left at the altar. That part is true."

"Yes, it's true. But when you left, you missed the best part."

"Yes, I did," he admitted. Nadine was about to demand that she be told the missing pieces when he turned to her and said in a voice that was nearly reverent, "My almost bride was crowned Duchess of Horstberg that day, soon after I left the cathedral."

Nadine gasped and watched the two of them exchange a sly glance and a warm smile before he turned to look at her with that penetrating gaze she was coming to know so well.

"You?" she said breathlessly to the duchess.

"Yes, it was me," she said.

Nadine quickly recounted the conversation in her mind and admitted, "I am terribly embarrassed. I should learn to keep my thoughts to myself and—"

"There's no need for that," the duchess said. "Your questions were perfectly appropriate, and there was no way you could have known."

"Well," Nadine said, "I must admit that it's an incredible story."

"Yes, it is," the captain said.

"I'm still a bit lost on certain details, however. Why was His Grace a fugitive and—"

"I can clear that up rather succinctly," the captain said. "His first wife was killed, murdered. He was framed for the crime, thrown in prison and told by his brother that he would not be getting a fair trial."

"His brother," Nadine said. "You mean Nikolaus."

"Yes, I mean Nikolaus, who was so eager to take over the country that he managed to implicate his brother for the crime. Cameron escaped from prison and was believed dead, while in truth he was only in hiding. Abbi was led to him by a series of miracles that would only be her privilege to tell. They were wed secretly while he struggled to prove his innocence. My proposing to Abbi gave them an excuse to have a great many important people gathered in the cathedral to witness his return and to hear him declare his innocence, which was later proven."

"Incredible," Nadine said. Silence settled around them while Nadine absorbed what she'd been told, and the others seemed sensitive to her need to do so.

The duchess finally said, "So, Captain, did you have a reason for coming here? Or was it simply to invade our private conversations?"

"Both," he said proudly, as if he might have known they would be talking about him.

"Yes, out with it," the duchess said with a mock authority that made the captain chuckle.

"Of course, Your Grace," he said, and rose abruptly to his feet. "His Grace wished to inform you that dignitaries from Kohenswald have sent word that they will be arriving the day after tomorrow, midmorning, to confer on the ever-present challenge of borderland disputes. The baroness will be accompanying her husband, as well as other family members. A full social observance will be put into place, and he wished for you to be prepared." Abbi groaned and he added, "And before you make some witty remark about the difficult duties assigned to me, I would like you to bear in mind that I am not merely a messenger, but the bearer of bad tidings. His Grace informed me that it would take great courage to inform you of the baroness's visit."

"Indeed," Abbi laughed. She then turned to Nadine and said, "I have an idea. You can be the duchess the day after tomorrow, and I shall hide away in my rooms with a headache and a good book."

Nadine was too stunned to respond, wondering what to make of such a remark, even though it was obviously said in jest. The captain said with enthusiasm, "I think that's a brilliant idea, Your Grace." He again took Nadine's hand to kiss it, saying with a little smile, "She would make an excellent queen."

The captain left the room, leaving a hovering warmth in his wake. Nadine watched him go and was startled when the duchess said with a little laugh, "Did you see the way he looked at you?"

Nadine attempted to appear astonished, while in truth she'd been keenly aware of the way he'd been looking at her for several days now. "Good heavens," the duchess added, laughing again. "I have seen Lance Dukerk come face-to-face with many women from all walks of life, and I have never seen his eyes light up the way they just did."

"You're exaggerating, surely," Nadine said.

"No, my dear, I am not. And as I recall, that last conversation began with your admitting to the intrigue you feel for him." She leaned forward eagerly. "We must talk."

"But, Your Grace, I . . ."

"Please, just call me Abbi, and I shall call you Nadine. If it turns out that you're the woman to win Lance's heart, we shall practically be sisters."

Nadine put a hand over her heart, overwhelmed and thrilled and terrified with such an idea. *Winning Lance's heart?* Could it be possible? While she'd indulged in the intrigue that was so apparent between them, she'd not allowed herself to even consider what the future might bring.

"Whatever is wrong?" Abbi asked. "You look . . . terrified."

"Perhaps I am," Nadine admitted. "I . . . may I speak candidly, Your Grace?"

"Of course," she said, "and my name is Abbi. As long as you and I are alone, please forego the formalities."

"Abbi," Nadine said, liking the idea of being friends with this woman. "Well, Abbi, I must confess that after what happened with Nikolaus, I find it difficult to really believe that any man could be as good as he seems. I *want* to believe it. He's been so kind, and what I feel is . . ."

"So you do feel something," Abbi said.

"Yes, I do."

"Well, let me tell you something, Nadine, there is not a more honorable man in all of Horstberg as Lance Dukerk."

"You really mean that," she said, struck by the intensity in the duchess's voice and expression.

"I do. He's a good man."

Nadine inhaled deeply and wondered how many hours would pass before she saw the captain again.

Chapter Eight
MOVING FURNITURE

The women returned to their work, and when Nadine was ready to leave, Abbi said, "On your way out, could you please take this message to the captain?"

Nadine wanted to accuse her of conspiring, but she said nothing since Abbi's attitude implied there was no connection to the errand and their previous conversation. Nadine felt curious about the note Abbi was writing, but she sealed it up before she handed it to Nadine. "I believe he's in the duke's office. If not, try his office near the keep. If he's not there, just leave it for him. His men will see that he gets it."

"Of course," Nadine said. "I'll see you the day after tomorrow then." Abbi had informed her that she would be busy elsewhere tomorrow and Nadine had the day off.

Nadine got Dulsie from the nursery and went to the duke's office, but the men standing at the door informed her that the captain wasn't there. She walked across the courtyard to the keep and asked the officer at the door, "Is Captain Dukerk available? I have a message from Her Grace."

"He is," the officer said and motioned her inside. He stepped into Lance's office ahead of her, saying, "A message from Her Grace."

"Thank you, Lieutenant," he said without looking up from his paperwork for another twenty seconds. When he did, his eyes filled with light and he smiled widely. She noticed that he seemed less somber than when he'd left a few days earlier. Perhaps his grave mood associated with the funeral and execution had dissipated.

"Such a pleasant messenger," he said and Nadine nudged Dulsie, who was holding the important envelope.

"Why, thank you, Dulsie." He squatted down and took it from her. "You're looking lovely today. And you know what? If you reach in this pocket right here, I think you'll find something for yourself."

Dulsie tossed her mother an excited glance before she reached into the pocket of the captain's red coat. She laughed as she pulled out a tiny brown sack. She looked inside to find a few pieces of candy. "Now, don't eat it without asking your mother first."

"You may have one piece now," Nadine said, "and you can save the rest until after supper."

"And will I see *you* after supper?" Lance asked Nadine.

"I hope so," she said, her heart racing. She took Dulsie's hand and left his office, anticipating this evening immensely.

On the way home she stopped at a little shop on the corner of the square in a way that had quickly become a habit. They sold some of the best pastries Nadine had ever tasted, and with the money Nadine was making, she considered it a treat to let Dulsie pick one out each day and they would share it before returning to the inn. Leaving the shop, Nadine's heart threatened to stop when she saw Albert Crider across the street. Her glimpse of him was brief before a carriage rolled past, but she knew it was him. When the carriage had gone by, he was no longer there. But she had no doubt that it had been him, if only by the familiar way he'd been staring at her.

"What's wrong, Mama?" Dulsie asked.

"Nothing, darling," she insisted, and they hurried home. She did well at covering her nerves for Dulsie's sake, but she felt decidedly concerned.

While Nadine worked through her shift at the inn, she forced her thoughts away from Albert Crider and contemplated all she had learned this day about Lance Dukerk. Putting pieces together from things he had told her previously, she was struck again by the tragedy of his sister's death. In truth, she realized there was a tragic edge to his life, and yet he was a man of such dignity and graciousness. Oh, how she prayed that he was as Abbi had said—an honorable man. If not, she was lost.

As soon as Nadine and Dulsie left, Lance broke the seal to read what Abbi had written. *I believe you could use some romantic counsel, and I'm in the mood to rearrange the furniture in the library. Moving heavy objects is high on your list of duties, is it not?*

Lance chuckled and tucked the note in his pocket. He went to the duke's office to go over a few things, then he reported as he stood, "I am now off to the library to meet your wife."

"Moving furniture again?" Cameron asked. "Praise heaven I'm not a blind man. With the way she wants furniture moved, I'd never know where I stand."

"Oh, you love it," Georg said to him. "Variety. Abbi gives your life variety."

"Oh, Abbi gives my life much more than that," Cameron said with a defined warmth in his voice. Not so long ago, Lance would have envied such feelings. Now, he understood them.

"Indeed," Lance said. "Well, I am here to serve, and my greatest allegiance is to the Lady of Horstberg. You know where to find me."

"Have a good time," Cameron called.

Lance found Abbi in the library with her feet up on the sofa where she sat, reading a book, one hand methodically rubbing her pregnant belly.

"Oh, hello," she said, peeking over the top of the book.

"Your Grace," he said, going down on one knee beside her and putting a fist over his chest. "Your wish is my command."

She laughed and said, "I think I want this sofa turned that way." She motioned with her hand.

Lance immediately stood and pushed the sofa abruptly while she was still on it, which provoked a flourish of girlish laughter. "Not with me on it, silly."

"I am not silly!" he insisted, pretending to be insulted. He pushed it a little farther and asked, "There, how's that?"

"Good, I like it."

"And what else?" he asked.

"Nothing. We'll just say we moved it and put it back."

"Your husband will know better."

"Yes, he will. But he knows I love him best. Sit. Talk to me."

"Is that an order?"

"Yes it is, Captain. Be quick about it."

He plopped onto the other end of the sofa, making it briefly bounce and provoking another giggle.

"What is your wish, Your Grace?"

"I wish to consult with you about a certain *woman* in your life. By the way your eyes lit up when you saw her today, I assume you're still feeling as you felt when we last spoke."

"No," Lance said quite seriously, then he smiled. "Actually my feelings grow deeper by the day. And to be truthful, I was glad for your message because I was intending to hunt you down and beg for advice. I don't know how to do this. I've spent a fair amount of time with her, and I sense that she has feelings for me as well, but . . . where do I go from here? You're the only woman I actually *courted* and I don't think I was very good at it."

"You were gallant and perfectly proper."

"Well," he drawled, "maybe I should be . . . fun, or . . . exciting, or . . . dashing."

"There's not a problem with dashing; you've got that mastered," she said. "And as far as anything else goes, I think you have to be yourself. You *are* fun and exciting, but perhaps that doesn't come through in formal conversation or when you're nervous. You just need to get her in a setting where you can have some fun. Of course, I don't know how much of an expert I am on courting. The only man who ever courted me was you. Cameron and I were snowed in together. It wasn't courting. It was more like surviving."

"Still, you know what a woman wants, how a woman feels."

"Yes, I certainly know that," she said.

"So, help me."

"All right. Well . . . let me think." He watched her for a moment, praying she would be more inspired than he was. He smiled when her face brightened. "I think I'm onto something, my dear captain. And the timing is perfect."

"Yes?" he drawled when she hesitated.

"Tomorrow is the annual winter festival," she said as if she'd announced the Second Coming.

"The one to raise money for the hospital?"

"That's right. You know we always have to make an appearance at these things. It's too cold to stay out for long, but . . . they just want our money, anyway. So . . ." She became lost in thought as if she were trying to put the pieces together in her mind, then she said firmly, "Here is what you're going to do. Nadine already has tomorrow off, because I told her we would be doing other things. So, first of all, you need to arrive this evening bearing gifts for her and Dulsie. Do you think you can afford it?" she asked and laughed.

"Yes, Abbi, I can afford it. But what do I buy?"

"Patience. We'll get to that. Now, there will be a lot of silly things going on at the festival, but you need to do something to just . . . have fun with her. Like . . . sledding."

He snorted a chuckle. "I haven't done that for years. It's a child's sport."

"Many adults do it and you know it. Are you not capable of sledding, Captain?"

"Of course I'm capable."

"Yes, well . . . you also said that you don't blush."

He smirked and otherwise ignored the comment. "And how do I know that Nadine would enjoy such a thing?"

Abbi smiled. "With your strong arms around her? Trust me, she'll enjoy it. And Dulsie will too."

Lance felt doubtful—or perhaps nervous. "Are you sure Nadine will—"

"She's starry-eyed, Captain. She'd do almost anything just to be with you."

"What makes you think so?" he demanded.

"I saw the two of you together today. And how do you think that conversation we were having got started? She was curious, asking questions. I think she's in love, and I think you are too."

Lance took a deep breath. "I hope so," he said. "Because if this isn't love, I'm losing my mind."

Abbi laughed and then they talked through the details of the plan. As far as gifts were concerned, Abbi suggested, "Something useful but still a little bit frivolous. That way you appeal to her obvious practical nature, but you make her feel special."

Lance was feeling pretty good about the gifts and the festival, but he had to admit, "Sometimes I fear I'm being too presumptuous. I think I hold back from saying and doing what I want because I'm afraid I'll offend her."

"Lance," she leaned toward him, "I don't think it's possible for you to offend another human being, especially one that you care about. Trust me when I tell you that you've come far enough with her to get beyond being cautious. She likes you. She likes you a lot. But women like to know where they stand. So just . . . follow your instincts."

Lance nodded, wishing he didn't feel so nervous about the whole thing. She gave him a few suggestions until her attention was drawn toward the door when Cameron entered. "So there you are," he said, pretending to be astonished, "consorting with this riffraff."

"You consort with him," Abbi said, "why shouldn't I?"

"The furniture looks the same," Cameron said, glancing around.

"No, this sofa is going this way instead of that way," Abbi said. "As far as the rest, we moved it and then we put it back. I like it this way."

"We?" Lance countered. "You were ordering me about, as I recall."

"Yes, of course," Abbi said as Cameron caught her gaze. Lance watched the way their eyes connected and held, as if tangible matter bound them together. It wasn't a dramatic thing—rather simple in truth—but undeniable nevertheless. Cameron crossed the room and took Abbi's hand, helping her to her feet before he pulled her into his arms. He gave her a lengthy kiss and made a pleasurable noise.

Lance cleared his throat loudly. "I'm still here," he said.

"Yes, we know," Cameron said. "Why is that?"

Lance chuckled. "Because you haven't ordered me to leave, Your Grace."

"What are you doing here so early?" Abbi asked her husband.

"I thought I deserved a few extra hours with my wife," he said.

"How pleasant," Abbi said with drama.

"I guess that makes me a crowd," Lance said with exaggerated disappointment.

"What you need," Cameron said, apparently done greeting his wife, "is a woman of your own."

Abbi tossed Lance a sly smile that was missed by the duke. "You say that at least once a week," Lance said. "I'm working on it."

"Yes, I've seen the way you work on getting a woman. At this rate you'll wait until I'm dead and marry Abbi."

"I love Abbi terribly," Lance said, "but I don't think I want to hold out another thirty or forty years. I think I'll just find a woman of my own."

"When?" Cameron demanded, however lightly.

"I'll tell you what, Your Grace, if I bring a woman to the winter festival tomorrow, I may be excused from entertaining the baron and his family."

"Done!" Cameron said immediately and Abbi laughed. "What's so funny?" he demanded.

"Nothing, my dear." She forced a sober face. "If I bring someone to the winter festival, may I be excused as well?"

"You're taking *me* to the festival," Cameron said, "and *no* you may not be excused. The baroness loves your company."

"The baroness is an old cow with more jewelry than brains," Abbi said and the men both laughed heartily.

"This is all very delightful," Lance said, "but I must be on my way."

"Where are you going?" Cameron asked.

"Well, I'd better start combing the streets for a woman. With any luck she won't be too ghastly."

Abbi laughed again as Lance kissed her hand in the usual way, then he slapped Cameron's shoulder lightly, saying, "Good day, Your Grace. Have a pleasant evening with one of the two most beautiful women in the world."

Cameron looked momentarily astonished as Lance turned to leave. Just before the door closed behind him, he heard Cameron say to Abbi, "He's already got a date, doesn't he! He's in love." Abbi laughed again and the door closed. Lance headed down the hall, chuckling to himself. With any luck his shopping would go well, and Abbi's instincts were as keen as he hoped.

When the last customer of the evening had left the inn, Nadine felt suddenly depressed. A memory caught her off guard of a night when Nikolaus had promised he would come to see her, and he'd never shown up. The next day he'd had some flimsy excuse, and soon afterward he had sent her away. She thought of how Nikolaus had never taken her into public, his excuse being that he was a political figure and his life was complicated. But Nadine felt that he was likely embarrassed by her. She had been nothing more than a concubine to him, a woman to be hidden away and looked down upon.

As her thoughts gained momentum, Nadine almost began to feel angry with Lance. On a logical level she knew that her own mistrust was the biggest problem, but then . . . he had told her he would come for supper.

Nadine finished clearing all the tables but one and went into the kitchen for a clean tray. With Drew banging pots and pans, she was startled to return to the dining room and find Lance standing near the door, removing his gloves. "Am I too late?" he asked. "Do you think Drew will feed me?"

She couldn't keep from smiling, even though her thoughts were still muddled with doubts and concerns. And intermixed with them all was an ever-present realization that Albert Crider had followed her to Horstberg. "I'm sure he will. I think for you he would get up in the middle of the night."

"Nonsense," he said, hanging up his cloak. "Just tell him I'll have the usual, and tell him there's a bonus if I can have a particular beautiful woman keep me company while I eat."

Nadine smiled again. "I'll tell him."

"Wait," he said, taking her arm. "Is something wrong?"

The sincere concern she saw in his eyes quickly assuaged her doubts regarding his intentions. But she couldn't deny the opportunity to share something with him that she felt certain he should know. "Yes, actually, there is something wrong."

She saw his brows furrow. "What is it?" he asked, guiding her to the chair across from him.

"Well," she said tensely, "I believe it's more business than personal."

"I'm listening," he urged.

"I told you about Albert Crider, the man who caused so much trouble for me . . . before I came here."

"Yes," he drawled.

"I saw him today," she said and the concern in his expression deepened. "I thought I had seen him once before, the day of the funeral, but I wasn't certain. Today I was certain."

"Where?" he asked.

"Across the street from Mrs. Backer's Bakery. He was just standing there when we came out. A carriage went past and he was gone. I don't know what to do, Captain. I don't want him causing any trouble for Drew and Gerda, just because I'm working here. They've been so good to me."

"I don't want him causing trouble for you, either," he said, then went on in a voice that was calming and confident. "This is what we're going to do. I am going to file an official report, so that if trouble occurs, his presence will already be on record. You will not go anywhere when it's dark unless you are with another adult, and you must keep the door to your room locked, all the time. If you see him again I want to know exactly when and where. Stalking is against the law, Mrs. Rader. You have a right to live without fear. Is that clear?"

She nodded and smiled, grateful for his validation, if not his attitude that made her feel safer already. "Thank you," she said. "I'll be careful."

"Is there anything else?" he asked in a way that made her feel as if she could pour out her heart to him for hours over matters that were either business or personal.

"No, thank you, Captain. I'll tell Drew that you're here." She went to the kitchen and repeated the captain's message while Drew dished up a plate from what was left on the stove. Drew and Gerda exchanged a conspiratorial grin.

"I do believe the captain's got his sights set on you," Drew said.

"You just take your time and enjoy yourself," Gerda added.

Nadine returned to the dining room with a tray and stopped in her tracks to see a stack of packages, wrapped in brown paper, in the center of the table where he was sitting.

"What is this?" she asked, setting his food and drink in front of him.

"I come bearing gifts, my lady," he said. "Where is Dulsie?"

"She's changing into her nightgown," Nadine said, feeling a skeptical excitement.

"Well, perhaps she'd like to open hers before she goes to sleep."

"She'll come down. She won't go to bed without my tucking her in."

Lance smiled. "Perhaps you'd like to open yours now."

"Oh," she pressed her hands down her apron, suddenly flustered, "you really didn't have to do such a—"

"I know I didn't have to," he said. "I wanted to. Simple as that. Are you going to open them or stand there?"

He took a bite of his supper and motioned her toward the chair. Nadine tried to remember the last time she'd been given a gift. Even Nikolaus had never given her a gift. She felt close to tears for reasons she couldn't explain as he handed her a small package. She unwrapped the paper and opened a long, flat box. She folded back the tissue paper to see a beautiful pair of ladies leather gloves, lined with fur. "To keep your hands soft and warm," he said.

"They're beautiful," she muttered, pulling them onto her hands. "I've never owned anything so lovely. Thank you."

While she was still admiring her gloves, he pushed another package in her direction. "Keep going. We haven't got all night," he said lightly.

She laughed and set the gloves reverently on the table in order to open the next package, which was wide and deep. She gasped when the fur muff appeared. She pulled it out as if it might break, then slid her hands into it as if she were tasting chocolate for the first time. "Oh," she said, "you must be terribly concerned about my hands."

"Indeed, I am," he said. "After experiencing their marvelous capabilities, we want to take very good care of them." He handed her another, not-so-large box.

She looked at him sideways and hesitantly took it. "Why are you doing this?" she asked.

"I'll tell you later," he said. "Just open it." She pulled away the paper but as she moved to lift the lid, he reached a hand over to stop her. "Wait," he said, "before you open it, perhaps I should explain. There is a party tomorrow. It's an annual event to raise funds for the hospital. I would like you and Dulsie to go with me."

Nadine looked at him long and hard, slowly closing her mouth. She wanted to shout, *What? You want to be seen with me in public?* But she only said, "It would be a pleasure, Captain."

He smiled and said, "You'd better open the gift."

She hesitantly lifted the lid and folded back the tissue, smiling as she lifted the finely woven, soft wool muffler. The red and black reminded her of the ducal uniform he wore. She pressed it to her face and said, "You must want me to stay warm."

"I do indeed. It's an outdoor party; a winter festival, they call it."

"It sounds marvelous," she said with enthusiasm.

Dulsie appeared and her eyes widened at the sight of the gifts, but she was distracted when Lance said to her, "You haven't checked my pocket yet."

She giggled and reached in to pull out a little bag of candy, which made her giggle again.

"You'll spoil her terribly," Nadine said, but she said it with a smile.

"Someone needs to," he said and pulled her onto his lap. "And this," he said, handing her a small package, "is for you."

"A gift?" Dulsie asked as if she had no comprehension of such a thing.

"Three, actually," Lance said and laughed.

Nadine found it difficult to keep from crying as she watched Dulsie open gloves, a hand muff, and a muffler to go around her neck, all very much like her mother's. The child's excitement was something she'd rarely seen.

Lance finished his supper while Nadine and Dulsie gathered their packages and headed toward the stairs. He was about to say that he'd be waiting for her to come back, when she turned and said, "Will you come up when you're finished?"

"I'll be there in a few minutes," he said and they exchanged a smile.

When Lance had finished, he gathered his dishes and carried them to the kitchen where he could hear Drew and Gerda talking and laughing as they worked.

"Oh," Gerda said when he appeared, "you didn't have to do that. But thank you."

"Thank you," Lance said as she took them. "The meal was wonderful, as always. And I appreciate getting special service at odd hours."

"You're our best customer," Gerda said and Lance chuckled.

"And how is business?" Lance asked.

"Going well in spite of the cold," Drew said, "as far as meals being served, that is. Most of the rooms are empty, but that's typical this time of year. People don't travel in this kind of weather so much. But it will pick up in the summer. All in all, it's going well."

"I'm glad to hear it," Lance said. "I left my trap in your stable. I hope you don't mind. I unharnessed the horses, since I think I'll be staying a while."

They both smiled at him and Drew said, "You quite like our little Nadine."

"I do, yes. And I promise to be a perfect gentleman."

"No worries there," Gerda said and winked at him.

"Good night then," Lance said and went up the stairs.

He knocked lightly at the door and heard Nadine call, "Come in."

He stepped inside to see Nadine curled up on the little sofa that was Dulsie's bed, with the child half in her lap while Nadine rubbed one of her hands. "Have a seat," she said as he closed the door. He noticed the room was terribly warm just before she said, "I'm afraid I built up the fire a little too much earlier. You might want to remove your coat."

"Thank you," he said. "I think I will."

Nadine discreetly watched him as he set aside the sword and pistol he always carried at each side and efficiently unfastened the hooks down the front of the red coat of his uniform. She realized then that she'd never seen him without it. Beneath the coat he wore a high-collared white shirt and black braces over his shoulders. He slid his arms out of the sleeves and hung the coat over the back of a chair. As he made himself comfortable on the rug in front of the fire, she felt stirred just to watch him. He leaned back on his hands and stretched out his long legs, crossing his booted ankles. She couldn't help thinking how nice it was to simply be in the presence of a man and to feel the security of his nearness.

When Dulsie was asleep, Nadine tucked her in and moved across the room to stand near Lance. He looked up at her and she asked, "Don't you want a chair?"

"No, thank you. This is fine. Would you like me to get you one?"

"No, thank you," she said and was surprised when he reached up and took her hand.

She expected him to urge her down to sit beside him, but he only fondled her fingers almost intimately, looking at them as he did so. "I missed your hands while I was away," he said, and the tears she had fought back in the dining room threatened once more. Feeling subtly weak, she knelt beside him, keeping her hand in his. Her heart quickened as he pressed her hand to his face, squeezing his eyes shut as if it were an experience to be savored. She watched as he turned his lips into her palm and kissed her there, then he pressed a kiss to her wrist before he looked up at her, saying, "You have beautiful hands, Nadine. May I call you Nadine?"

"Yes, Lance," she said, "you may call me Nadine."

"Sit beside me," he said, urging her close as he turned to face her, nearly encircling her with his long legs without hardly touching her. The ethereal quality of the moment deepened when he reached up to touch her face, absorbing it with his fingers as if it were a rare work of art. "I've wanted to do this for so long," he admitted.

"How long?" she asked.

"The day I met you," he said. "No woman has ever stirred me the way you do, Nadine." The sincerity in his voice and the severity in his eyes reached into Nadine's heart and she found it impossible to hold back the tears any longer.

"You're crying," he said, sounding alarmed. "Did I say something wrong? Did I—"

"No," she said, pressing her fingers to his lips, "you say everything right." She instinctively pressed her face to his shoulder and relished feeling his arms come around her, urging her closer. "Just hold me," she said and pushed her arms around him, pressing her hands to his back.

Lance sighed and squeezed his eyes closed, marveling that such a moment was even occurring in his life. He pressed a kiss into her hair and tightened his arms around her.

Nadine moved her hands over the fabric of his shirt, and the braces that crossed in the center of his back. She nuzzled subtly closer, inhaling his masculinity. He smelled of horses and leather and the vaguest hint of shaving lotion. Impulsively she tilted her head back to look at his face, and reached a hand up to touch his stubbled cheek. She had forgotten what it was like to have a man in her life, but even then, it had never been like this. He looked into her eyes and she felt certain he would kiss her. Their faces were so close that it would have been easy. She hated the way her mind went back to Nikolaus's first kiss. Would he never cease to plague her thoughts?

But how clearly she recalled the moment. She had wanted desperately for him to kiss her, but once he did, something changed between them. It was as if his kiss had unleashed the full breadth of his passion, and she'd had to become continually vigilant at protecting her virtue. And while she desperately wanted Lance Dukerk to kiss her now, she didn't want the serenity of being with him this way to change.

"You are so beautiful," Lance murmured, gliding a hand over her cheek. His lips pressed against her brow and his embrace tightened. She felt so touched by his apparent contentment in simply being with her that tears came again to her eyes. She was grateful he couldn't see her face, but when she sniffled he asked, "Is something wrong?"

"No. Everything is perfect. I just can't remember the last time I felt so . . . secure, so safe."

"You deserve to feel safe and secure, Nadine."

"Whether or not I deserve to, it's not happened since my father died."

"That's going to change now, if I have any say in the matter." He felt her relax more deeply into his arms, and his thoughts wandered through what he knew of the life she'd lived, most specifically her relationship with Nikolaus. And he wondered if it was in his power to somehow free her of the scars that Nikolaus du Woernig had left behind.

Chapter Nine

FAMILY CONNECTIONS

"What are you thinking?" Nadine asked, breaking into Lance's thoughts.

"Well, if I answer that question honestly, it might not be conducive to the mood. So it might be better if just say 'nothing.' "

"No, tell me," she said, pressing a hand gently up and down his arm. "I want to know."

"Well, I can't help thinking of Nikolaus . . . of the way he hurt you. I knew he was up to such things, or at least I found out eventually, and I've often considered the heartache he was passing around. But . . . in getting to know you, it's become more . . . personal. I often find myself thinking about what he did, and I wish I could just . . . somehow erase all of that pain from your life."

"Your wish is very gallant, Captain, but I'm glad that you can't. There are many good things that have come out of these experiences for me, and I would not want to erase all that I've learned and gained."

"Like Dulsie," he said.

"Most especially Dulsie," she said. "How can I regret her existence? She's a human being, real and full of life and love, with no comprehension of the means that brought her into the world. I'm grateful for her in my life, and I've never once, even for a moment, wished that she hadn't been conceived."

"Well, I can certainly agree with that. So I guess I'll just have to say that I'm grateful your connection to Nikolaus brought you back here. Horstberg will surely benefit from your presence."

"I don't know about that," she laughed softly, "but I'm certainly glad to be here. Life has not been this good to me in many years—perhaps ever." She eased closer. "I've never felt less lonely. Even as a child, I always felt lonely. But I don't feel lonely now."

"I could agree with that, as well."

Lance held her close until she nearly fell asleep in his arms, then he carried her to the bed and tucked her in. "You're leaving?" she asked, disappointed.

"I must," he said, pressing a kiss to her brow. "But I'll be here to get the two of you at ten in the morning."

"I can't wait," she said with a smile.

"Sleep well, my love," he said and slipped out of the room, locking the door behind him. But it wasn't until Nadine woke after dawn that she realized what he'd said.

"He called me his love," she whispered into the security he'd left surrounding her. She let out a contented sigh and lay in bed indulging in her memories of the time she'd spent with him and her anticipation of the day ahead.

Dulsie came awake with immediate excitement, and they were both eagerly ready to go when Lance arrived at the inn. His smile alone warmed Nadine through, and she couldn't recall the last time she'd felt so happy. She felt him absorb her with adoring eyes and uttered a silent prayer that this dream he was pulling her into would never end. Nadine forced her eyes away from his intrepid gaze and realized that he wasn't wearing his uniform. His attire was common with a refined edge that suited him so well. She couldn't help thinking that while his uniform was definitely dashing, he could certainly shine without it. In fact, she found his dark coat and breeches downright compelling and couldn't resist saying, "You look very nice today, Captain. Setting aside the uniform suits you well."

"How refreshing," he said and kissed her hand.

"How is that?"

"There are many women in Horstberg who would find my only appeal being the fact that I wear that uniform. Apparently it carries some kind of prestige." He said it with a little twitch of his lips, as if he had no idea of the prestige he held.

Lance watched her closely for a reaction. He'd never felt that her apparent attraction to him had anything to do with his position, but he couldn't help being touched by the sincerity in her eyes as she said, "I dare say if you were a farmer or a butcher, you would still hold the same appeal."

He smiled. "I considered a change of profession at one time."

"Really?" she said. "What did you consider becoming?"

"I have no idea," he chuckled. "I'm only good at one thing."

"Then it's likely good you stuck with it."

"Shall we go?" he asked, holding out his arm.

"I'm ready!" Dulsie said eagerly and he let out a delighted laugh.

As they stepped outside Nadine was struck by the beauty of the day. The air was crisp and cold, as it has been since her arrival in Horstberg, and the skies were brilliantly blue and cloudless. Then her eyes caught the elegant sleigh harnessed to two beautiful bays. She caught her breath then laughed. "A sleigh?"

"Where we are going," he said, "the snow is not so packed down as it is here."

He helped Nadine and Dulsie in and took his seat beside them. The furs that had been left on the seat were arranged over their laps, then he took the reins and urged the bays forward. During the drive to the far side of the valley, they talked and laughed. Lance thoroughly enjoyed Dulsie's excitement and the way Nadine held to his arm with her gloved hands.

Nadine felt so perfectly content that she didn't even notice the cold. The beauty of the countryside combined with the magnitude of Lance Dukerk's presence seemed, in that moment, all that she could ever need. When they arrived at the scene of the party, Nadine realized that it was being held on a private estate, and the admission money charged for each person would be donated to the hospital to help those who needed medical care but couldn't afford it. Vendors were set up where a path had been cleared in the snow, selling hot cocoa and cider, warm soups, breads, pastries, and other delights. The profits from these items would also go to the hospital fund. There were several fires burning in different places and benches surrounding them where people could warm up. Many games and activities were taking place, but Dulsie was quickly drawn to observing the way people, children and adults alike, were sledding down a hill with two significant bumps that apparently created a great thrill by the way people were laughing as they came down.

"Do you want to try it?" Lance asked Dulsie and she nodded eagerly.

He went down the hill with her twice, laughing at the way she giggled, and not unaware of Nadine's laughter as she observed. Then he told Dulsie to stay in a certain spot before he took Nadine's hand, saying, "Now it's your turn."

"Oh, I don't think that—"

"No arguments," he said with laughter.

"But . . . it looks a little . . . scary."

"Then you shall have to hold onto me very tightly," he said with a little smirk. She realized then that she'd not seen his subtle sense of humor come through before now, and she reasoned that recreation was a good thing for both of them.

Lance held Nadine's hand as they trudged together up the hill. Her occasional laughter for no apparent reason led him to the conclusion that she wasn't entirely against this activity. Sliding down the hill with his arms tightly around Nadine, Lance absorbed her laughter and felt certain Abbi *was* psychic. Of course, she would just call it woman's intuition. Either way, it was working.

After sledding with both Nadine and Dulsie for better than an hour, they moved to one of the fires to warm up. While they were sitting there, Lance bought hot cocoa and a pastry for each of them. Then they wandered around, observing other activities and participating in some.

Nadine couldn't help being aware of the discreet glances being tossed toward her and Lance, mostly by women of marriageable age. Women were intrigued by him, and yet he was completely oblivious to it. She recalled having noticed that very thing about him the first day they'd met, but it had slipped her mind. She also felt more than a few women judiciously sizing her up, as if to gauge what kind of woman the captain would be consorting with. But then, according to things Abbi had told her, he'd not been seen in public with a woman for a very long time. She couldn't help feeling delighted to be the woman who was with him, but her pleasure had little to do with his position and prestige.

"Cameron and Abbi have arrived," he said, nodding toward them as they moved toward a bench while they greeted many people who seemed to want to get close to them. Once they were seated, with a couple of officers standing at ease nearby, Lance urged Nadine to the same bench.

While Nadine and Abbi were chatting, Lance moved to the other side of Cameron and sat down. "Hello, Your Grace," he said.

"Captain," Cameron said in a tone of mock anger. "You sly dog. You already had a date for this when you made that bet with me, didn't you."

"No," Lance laughed, "but I had a woman in mind that I felt relatively certain would say yes."

"Well, it's just not fair that you don't have to deal with the baron."

"Sure it is," Lance said. "You're the duke. You get paid more than I do."

Cameron laughed. "That's true."

"Besides, I'll stay for the luncheon and the meetings. I'm just bowing out of the evening activities." He raised his brows. "I have something much better to do with my time."

Cameron glanced toward the women talking close by and added in a whisper, "She's a beauty, Captain. Is this serious, then?"

"I'm hoping it gets serious. It will if I have any say in the matter. She's an incredible woman."

"You're in love then?" Cameron asked with no hint of humor.

Lance met his eyes, saying firmly, "Quite."

Cameron just smiled.

Lance took Dulsie and Nadine to get warmed up again, then they had some soup and bread and more hot cocoa before they went sledding a little longer. Dulsie was reluctant to leave but eager to climb beneath the furs in the sleigh where she could be warm. She fell asleep within just a few minutes. Nadine put her head to Lance's shoulder and relished the way he moved the reins to one hand and put his arm around her.

"I know it's cold," she said, "but I don't want to go back. It's so wonderful just to be with you."

"Amen," he said, pressing a kiss into her hair. "Where would you like to go?"

Nadine thought about it a minute and said, "I would like to see the cathedral where the duke and duchess were married. Abbi's told me the story in more detail. And I vaguely remember the cathedral, but I've not seen it since I returned."

"Your wish is my command," he said and she laughed softly.

Lance pulled the sleigh up beside the huge cathedral and Nadine looked up. "It's bigger than I'd remembered. It's magnificent, really."

"Yes, it is. Would you like to go inside?"

"Oh, I would," she said.

He helped her down and then eased Dulsie into his arms. She woke for a second before settling against his shoulder and going back to sleep. They went up the many wide, stone steps to a huge set of double doors. In spite of their size, one of them swung open easily when Lance pushed against it with his shoulder.

"Oh, it's beautiful," Nadine whispered as the door closed behind her. Many candles were burning at the opposite end, near the altar, and a few people were praying, scattered among the many pews. "And it's huge."

"Yes, it is," he said. "I like it best when the sun is shining through the east windows." He motioned to the high windows on either side, and she admired the view before looking again at the wide, stone aisle that led to the altar.

"So, this is where you almost married Abbi."

"That's right."

"Were there many people here?"

"As many as could possibly fit."

She smiled at him and said, "I'm glad you didn't marry her." He attempted to discern if she had some implication behind the comment, then she added lightly, "It would have been terribly inappropriate for you to take me sledding today if you were married."

"Yes, it would have." He smirked and took her back outside.

She was stepping into the sleigh when she glanced toward the nearby graveyard and commented, "Oh, what a beautiful cemetery." She stepped back down and asked, "May we walk for just a few minutes? Is Dulsie too heavy for you?"

He chuckled. "Dulsie is fine. Take your time."

He followed her into the graveyard and watched her read many of the stones, as if she found fascination in the names and dates of people who meant nothing to her. As they approached an area in the center, partitioned by a high wrought-iron fence, she asked, "What is that?"

Lance commented easily, "That is where members of the royal family are buried."

She stopped walking abruptly and he was two steps ahead before he did the same and turned back to look at her. "Nikolaus," she said.

"Yes, Nikolaus."

She looked at him, as if seeking approval, or perhaps support. "May we?" she asked.

"Of course," he said with compassion.

Lance led her directly to the grave, marked by an ornate marble stone. When Nadine saw Nikolaus's name engraved there with the dates of his birth and death, she was surprised to feel her heart tighten, and tears came to her eyes.

"Are you all right?" Lance asked and she glanced toward him.

"I . . . don't know. Forgive me." She pulled off her glove to wipe her tears quickly away. "I wasn't really prepared to feel anything at all. I'm not certain where the tears came from."

"You loved him?" he asked, as if it were something he deeply needed to know.

"Yes," she said, touching his name with her fingers before she put her glove back on. In a whisper she said, "Dulsie's father."

Lance instinctively tightened his arms around Dulsie while she continued to sleep. He could never explain the deep gratitude he felt in that moment that Nikolaus du Woernig would never be a part of this child's life. Lance had seen firsthand the results of Nikolaus's evil ways, and he was grateful to know that Nadine and Dulsie would never have to face him again.

"You love him still?" Lance asked when she continued to stare at the gravestone, seeming stunned.

Nadine turned to look at him and said firmly, "No. I suppose I was simply struck by the tragedy of the whole situation." She tried to recall what she'd been told by the duke about Nikolaus's death, and she honestly couldn't. She only remembered that he'd come to a senseless and violent end. "I'm sure he brought his end upon himself, and he likely got what he deserved, but . . . there was a time when he was everything to me. I suppose there is grief for all that was lost between us."

Lance forced away his feelings about Nikolaus's death. He wondered if she had put the pieces together and knew that he'd actually been the one to kill him. He sensed that she hadn't, but this certainly wasn't the time to tell her. And perhaps it was better that she simply didn't know. He was trying to put all of that behind him, and she was doing the same. He forced his mind to the moment and said gently, "Your grief is understandable. I believe that we must grieve any time we have loss in our life of any kind. I too have grieved for Nikolaus. But not necessarily when he died. His behavior had been so completely atrocious that his death was nothing but a relief. Still, I struggled with it. And I realized that I was grieving for the loss of the friendship we'd once shared, before he had changed. And I grieved for the tragedy of his coming to such an end. But time truly does have a way of softening such things."

She smiled at him and said, "It's awfully cold. We should be getting back, I suppose."

"I suppose," he said, and they walked away until Nadine's eye caught something on one of the other large headstones nearby, and she stopped abruptly. She glanced toward Lance and found his expression unreadable. She looked back to the name that had caught her eye, and read it aloud. "Gwendolyn Dukerk du Woernig. Your sister."

"That's right," he said.

It only took her a moment to recall what he'd told her. She'd been killed; murdered by a friend of his that he'd eventually had to kill or jeopardize the life of a hostage. But what else had he told her? She couldn't quite recall.

"She was married to His Grace," she said, if only to make sense of it in her mind.

"That's right," he said solemnly.

"You and His Grace share a great deal of history. Much of it tragic."

"Very true."

"You said the two of you were friends, but you also have family associations. I hadn't made the connection that the two of you were actually brothers-in-law."

"Well, we were at one time. But truthfully, we get along much better now than we did then. I wasn't serving as the captain at the time. I was a lieutenant. His marriage to Gwen was not a good one. I eventually realized that she was a difficult person, but there were times when she did well at convincing me that Cameron was completely to blame for the problems. The process of putting Cameron back on the throne opened my eyes to many things, and I'm grateful. My association with him has taught me a great deal about judging others unfairly. Things are not always how they appear to the public eye."

"I can certainly agree there," she said and they returned to the sleigh.

Little was said through the drive back to the inn. Dulsie came awake as they arrived, but he carried her inside anyway. Nadine didn't want to say goodbye, but Drew and Gerda were counting on her to help with the evening shift. She was relieved beyond words when he said, "I'll come back for a late supper. Perhaps I could see you when your work is finished. Unless you prefer that I—"

"No, that would be wonderful. I'd love to see you."

"Until later then," he said and hurried away after kissing her hand in the usual manner.

Nadine quickly became busy with the supper rush, and she was forced to take a break before the last customers had left and help Dulsie to bed. In spite of her nap, the child was apparently worn out from awaking early and all that sledding. Once Dulsie was tucked in, Nadine returned to the dining room to find only an older couple remaining. And no Captain Dukerk. She finished clearing tables and wiping them down, then she set to work washing dishes in the kitchen while Drew and Gerda worked on preparations for the next day's meals. She'd only been there a few minutes when Gerda said, "The captain is here. I'll dish up some supper for him and tell him to find you here when he's finished."

"Thank you," Nadine said and hurried along, wanting to be done with her chore before he finished eating. Looking at the piles of dishes, she doubted that would happen. But she knew Drew and Gerda had let her off easy many times so that she could be with Dulsie or spend time with the captain, and she was determined to see the dishes through this evening, if only to show her gratitude for all they'd done for her.

She was surprised to look up and see Lance standing in the kitchen doorway a few minutes later, holding his empty dishes. "Oh, you didn't have to do that," Gerda said, taking them from him. Nadine glanced toward him and felt momentarily breathless. He was still dressed in the common clothes he'd worn earlier, except that now he was minus the long, heavy coat he'd worn over them. His narrow dark breeches and tall boots were flattering to his lean form. And the striped shirt he wore, topped by dark braces, showed the muscles of his shoulders and chest more clearly than she'd ever been able to see. He was positively the most handsome man she'd ever known. Of course, there had been a time when she'd felt that way about Nikolaus. But she'd long ago lost such feelings as they had slowly drowned in the reality of his abandonment. And now she could only feel grateful to be the woman who had gained favor with the captain.

"It's not a problem," he said to Gerda. "You don't have to serve me meals when I come in at odd times, but you do. I'd likely starve if you didn't."

"It's a pleasure, Captain," she said. Then to Nadine, "There's no need for you to finish all of those, my dear. If you—"

"It's all right," Nadine said. "I don't mind. It's a small price to pay for having a roof over our heads and plenty to eat." She met Lance's eyes and added softly, "If you don't mind waiting a few minutes, I can—"

"It's not a problem," he said again, but the next thing she knew he was standing beside her, his sleeves rolled up. He stuck his hands into the sink full of hot rinse water and started rinsing off the dishes piling up there.

"What are you doing?" Nadine laughed.

"Cleaning the dishes is what I believe they call it," he said as if it were a serious matter of state.

"You really don't have to—"

"I know I don't have to," he said, meeting her eyes briefly, "but I want to."

He rinsed dishes and set them aside to drain, then he took up a clean towel and began drying them, intermittently rinsing more as Nadine washed them.

"This is a rare privilege," Drew said. "I wonder how many people in this country have had the good captain in their kitchen helping clean the dishes."

"None that I recall," Lance said lightly.

"Well, you're very good at it," Gerda said. "If you weren't already well employed, we'd have to hire you."

They all chuckled and Lance said, "I had once considered a change in profession, but I do think I prefer the one I've got. Still, it doesn't hurt a man to spend a little time in the kitchen here and there."

"Where did you hear that?" Nadine asked.

It took Lance a moment to recall, then he said, "Her Grace has said that more than once, I believe. Apparently His Grace is rather competent in the kitchen when he needs to be."

"And when would he need to be," Drew asked with a scoffing noise, "with a castle full of servants as he has?"

"Ah, yes," Lance said, "but you forget that His Grace was completely on his own for a number of years during his exile before he was able to prove his innocence. As I understand it, he was entirely alone until Her Grace was snowed in with him—about three years, I believe. He saw to his own needs in every respect."

"I'd never thought of it that way," Gerda said. "We've all heard the stories of his exile, but I guess I just always imagined that he had *someone* to take care of him."

"He's got more to him than meets the eye, then," Drew said.

Lance smirked toward Nadine and said, "Yes, I believe he does."

When Nadine was finished washing, she dried her hands on her apron and started putting away the dishes that Lance was drying. When they were finished, she removed her apron and Lance rolled down his sleeves.

"Thank you," she said. "I shall have to record in my journal that I washed dishes with the Captain of the Guard."

"You do that," he said, "but don't be showing it to anybody. I wouldn't want my men to think I'd gone soft. Well, not too soft, anyway. I think they already know I have some soft spots."

"Thank you, Captain," Drew said.

"A pleasure," Lance replied. "Good night then."

"Good night," Drew and Gerda said together, and Lance escorted Nadine from the room with a hand at her back. Nadine felt warmth from his touch and wished that it wasn't so late and they could share more time together. The day had been wonderful, but they both had to return to work tomorrow and their time would be more limited. Knowing how long it had taken them to clean the dishes, she wondered if he felt pressed to return home and get some sleep.

"Can you stay a while?" she asked at the foot of the stairs. She realized then that her feelings for him had continued to grow every hour since she'd met him, and at the moment she felt so completely drawn to him that she just wanted to press herself into his arms and beg him to kiss her. Trying to maintain reason, she added, "Or are you—"

"I'd like to stay a while, if that's all right," he said. "I don't want to intrude on your evening if you're tired or—"

"I'm really not," she interrupted gently, although she couldn't bring herself to look at him. Would he read in her eyes what she was feeling? Would he think she was wanton and forward if he knew her thoughts, taking into account the trouble she had gotten herself into with Nikolaus du Woernig?

"You're not?" he said, and the hope in his voice soothed her fears somewhat.

"It would be nice to have you stay," she admitted. "It's so nice to have someone to talk to and . . . and just to . . . be with."

"I couldn't agree more," he said and followed her up the stairs.

Chapter Ten

THE CAPTAIN'S REPUTATION

Once in her room Lance built up the fire while Nadine checked on Dulsie to be assured that she was sleeping peacefully. He sat on the rug when he was finished and she sat beside him. Recalling how pleasant it had been to sit with him this way the previous evening, she felt grateful to have the opportunity again.

As if he'd read her thoughts, he said, "We should make a habit of this."

"I wouldn't complain," she said with a smile that quickly sobered as he looked deeply into her eyes. Nadine's heart quickened and her mouth went dry, as if he'd never looked at her that way before. And yet he'd been looking at her with that avid, unabashed gaze almost right from the start. Her heart quickened further when he reached up a hand to touch her face. It wasn't the first time he'd done it, but her senses reacted in a way that was completely unfamiliar. There was something different in his gaze, his touch. Without a word spoken, she felt the thinning of a boundary between them. In her mind she could nearly see him taking her hand to lead her across a bridge that could never be crossed back. Yet, she felt no concern for her virtue, no need to be troubled over his intentions. Her every instinct knew that this man would treat her like a lady; he always had, and she felt certain he always would. She felt her breathing sharpen as he pressed a thumb over her lips, exploring them with purpose, while his eyes never broke their overpowering gaze. She wasn't certain if he kissed her or she kissed him. She only knew that their lips came together as if by some force beyond their ability to control. She heard him gasp and felt his breath quicken, as if the experience had affected him as deeply as it had her. "Nadine," he muttered against her lips before he kissed her again. For a moment Nadine nearly expected his kiss to overwhelm her physically, as it was doing emotionally. She felt passion creep into it and held her breath, praying the moment would not be marred by that passion burning out of control. For a moment she wondered if she might have misjudged him and she *did* have reason to be concerned. And then he eased back, smiling at her as his eyes came languidly open.

"Oh," he said, touching her face again, "I've wanted to do that for so long."

"You have?" she asked in a soft voice that didn't detract from the mood. "How long?"

He chuckled warmly and put distance between them. "I think it was somewhere between your demanding to see the duke, and your fainting into my arms."

"Really?" she said with a lilt. "Then I must say you are a very disciplined man."

"Patient," he said, lifting his brows in a mischievous way that made her laugh. "I wanted it to be perfect."

"I think it was," she said dreamily.

"Really?" he said just as she'd said it a moment ago.

"Were you worried?" she asked lightly.

"Maybe," he smirked. "I don't have much experience in kissing."

"How many women *have* you kissed?"

"By women, I suppose that would exclude what little opportunity I had in my youth. So, as an adult . . . two or three."

"And one of them was the duchess."

"Well, yes. But she wasn't the duchess at the time."

"I'm glad for that," she laughed.

"She was rather reserved, however. Of course, she was actually married to Cameron at the time. I think she was just being polite."

Their eyes met again as she said, "Well, for so little practice, it was . . . perfect."

For a full minute Nadine wondered if he would kiss her again. She could feel the intensity of how badly he wanted to, and she couldn't deny that she felt the same way. But he cleared his throat and looked away abruptly before he stretched out on the rug, laying his head back into his hands and crossing his booted ankles. She couldn't help noticing how tall he looked. Of course, she knew he was tall, but stretched out on the rug like that, he seemed to be the epitome of everything virile and masculine. And she was hopelessly in love with him. Any minuscule thought she might have had along the way to keep her heart protected was simply hopeless. Her heart was lost, and she could only pray that he kept it safe.

Noting the way he closed his eyes, she said softly, "You look tired."

Dulsie made some noise in her sleep and they both glanced toward her.

"I'll be right back," she said and went to Dulsie's side. She put another blanket over her in case she was cold and watched her until she settled quickly back into a deep sleep. She returned to Lance's side to find that he was sleeping as soundly as Dulsie.

"Oh, my love," she murmured and lightly pushed his hair back from his face. She wondered briefly if she should wake him and concluded that there was no harm to his spending the night on her floor. She hurried downstairs with the intention of going out to the stable to see that his horse was unsaddled and fed for the night. She found Drew and Gerda sitting by the fire in the common room and thought it would be well to inform them of what might otherwise appear scandalous.

"Since you're up," she said, "I thought you should know that the captain fell asleep on the rug by the fire. I'm not going to disturb him."

They both chuckled. "Ah, that'll give him a reputation he's never had before," Gerda said. "Bless his soul. He works so hard, he must be exhausted."

"I'll see to his horse," Drew said as if it would be a pleasure.

"Thank you," Nadine said.

Drew chuckled on his way out. "At least he won't have to go far for breakfast."

Nadine returned to her room and locked the door. She checked again on Dulsie, then she just watched Lance sleeping for several minutes, amazed at what she felt for him. She covered him with a blanket and slid a pillow carefully beneath his head without disturbing him, then she went to bed herself, loving the sense of security she felt just having him in the same room.

Lance came awake and felt briefly disoriented. Squinting against the early morning light, it took him a minute to recall where he was, then he sat up abruptly, realizing he'd just spent the night in a woman's room—however innocent. Then he looked up to see Nadine standing above him, smiling warmly.

"Good morning," she said as he jumped to his feet.

"Good morning," he replied. "Forgive me. I just . . ."

"You must have been very tired."

"I confess that I was, but . . . still . . ."

"It's all right. If you must know, it was very comforting not to be alone." She said it with a severity that made him wonder if something frightened her. Before he could think how to ask, a thought occurred to him that made him panic.

"What time is it?" he asked.

"Half past seven," she said.

"Good heavens," he rushed toward the door, "I'm supposed to be in a meeting this very minute."

"Wait," she said and he turned back, "I think . . . you should comb your hair first."

Lance chuckled and pushed a hand through it self-consciously. "I probably should. Thank you."

Nadine motioned toward a basin of warm water with a comb and brush sitting nearby. Lance splashed water on his face and over his hair. He dried his hands and face with the towel she handed to him, then he pressed the comb through his hair. He took her hand and kissed it quickly, feeling an unexpected surge of excitement as he met her eyes. Something delightfully warm sparkled in them, and he felt briefly frozen and oblivious to the time.

"I must go," he said, forcing himself to the present.

"Will you come back?" she asked eagerly.

"As soon as my work is done," he promised, "I'll be back."

"I'll be waiting."

He eased toward the door, but she didn't let go of his hand. He turned back to her, wondering what he might have forgotten. Her hesitancy in wanting to let him go tugged at his heart and impulsively he touched her face. "Nadine," he murmured, and without a second thought, he gave in to the urge to kiss her, but not as he'd kissed her last night. Instantly everything changed inside of him. He'd kissed women before, but it had always been controlled and confined, stemming from a source of logic and reasoning. Even last night's kiss had been thoughtful and premeditated. But this! This made him feel as if his entire heart and soul had just come to life for the first time. He knew now that until this moment he had never felt what it was truly like to be alive. He'd never known passion or vulnerability or joy or fear or ecstasy. Or love. Until now. In the breadth of a long moment, *everything* changed. He felt completely out of his senses, almost oblivious to his own actions as he took her shoulders into his hands and kissed her as if he might never breathe again without her. Her response was sweet and warm, contributing to a sensation he'd never dreamed existed. When his head was swimming and his knees weak, he forced himself to ease back, fearing he'd collapse otherwise.

"Nadine," he murmured again, slowly opening his eyes, as if he'd emerged from a sweet, magnificent dream. He couldn't help smiling when her expression mirrored everything he was feeling.

While he was gazing into her eyes, attempting to come up with the words to tell her all he was feeling, she smiled tentatively and said, "Your meeting?"

"Oh, good heavens!" He stepped back and attempted to clear his head. "I'll be back . . . as soon as I can."

"I know," she said with a sweet little laugh and opened the door for him.

Lance hurried down the stairs and out to the stable, where he had to stop and lean his head against the wall to steady himself. He laughed aloud and then mounted his horse bareback and hurried toward the castle. He could already hear the jibes he'd get when he arrived significantly late for the first time in his life. He was at least grateful that there would be no visiting dignitaries to apologize to.

Lance ran down the castle hall and stopped a moment to catch his breath outside the office door.

"Is everything all right, sir?" one of the men guarding the door asked him.

"Fine, thank you," he said and went in. He was glad to see only Cameron and Georg. If it had been a more extensive meeting with the advisors and officers, that would be all the more people he'd have staring at him right now. He saw Cameron and Georg exchange a glance that made him wonder if they were going to burst into laughter. Cameron slid his glasses down his nose and looked at Lance over the top of them as if he'd never seen him before.

"Forgive me," Lance said, taking his usual seat. "What did I miss?" He was hoping to get right to business and draw attention away from his tardiness. Then he realized that he wasn't wearing his uniform. He'd *never* attended to anything related to his work without being in uniform, but there was nothing he could do about it now.

"Not much," Georg said and leaned back in his chair. He was also looking at Lance as if he'd suddenly turned green or something. "We sent someone to your apartment, but you weren't there."

"No, I wasn't," Lance stated in a straight voice.

Cameron looked again at Georg and said, "It's just as I suspected."

"Yes, I think you're right. In fact there's no question about it."

"About what?" Lance asked, hoping that this was their attempt to get back to whatever they'd been discussing.

"It's a woman," Cameron said.

Lance sighed and looked away, but he knew he was doomed when something completely out of his control bubbled from deep inside him, emerging in a grin that consumed his entire face. He pressed a hand discreetly over his mouth, attempting to hide it, but Cameron and Georg both chuckled.

Lance cleared his throat and forced a straight face. "What makes you think so?" he asked in the most casual voice he could manage.

"Well," Cameron drawled, "you've seemed distracted for a couple of weeks now. Then yesterday you appear in public with a woman—for social reasons—for the first time in months. And this morning you're *late*—and out of uniform, no less. You've never been late anywhere in your entire life. Have you? Not anywhere that I've been. I'd wager that even Abbi never made you late for a meeting." Cameron chuckled again. "She must be something, eh?"

Lance subdued a spurt of irrepressible laughter with a stilted chuckle. "Yes, she certainly is. Now, can we get down to business?"

"This *is* business," Cameron insisted lightly. "So, did you have an early morning picnic, or what?"

"Not exactly."

"Don't tell me you spent the night with her!" He sounded appalled, but the teasing element was still evident in his voice.

"No, I did not!" Lance said, wishing it hadn't sounded so defensive.

"But you weren't home this morning, so—"

"What are you now? My father, all of a sudden?"

"You've got a lot of room to talk," Georg said to Cameron. "Don't forget where you were spending *your* nights when Abbi was—"

"We were married!" Cameron interrupted firmly, acting far more insulted than he actually was.

"Not that anybody else knew," Georg said, remaining calm. "Maybe Lance is really married and—"

"I'm not married, and I did absolutely nothing inappropriate; not that it's any business of yours," Lance insisted. "I fell asleep on the rug while we were talking. Now, can we get on with the day, please?"

Cameron and Georg each looked at him, then at each other. "Yes, he's got it bad," Georg said with a sigh.

"And it's about time, too," Cameron added. Then more to Lance, "Can't wait to get back to her, can you."

Lance chuckled and shook his head. "No, I can't, if you must know. Now can we—"

"Did you kiss her?" Cameron leaned over his desk like a naughty school boy. "Was it good?"

Lance could only laugh, but he could feel himself turning warm. Recalling Abbi's insistence that he'd been blushing, he felt completely doomed. And his hope that it would go unnoticed was vanquished when Cameron and Georg both broke into hysterical laughter.

"Face it, Captain," Georg said with a chuckle, "your reputation is at stake."

"My reputation?" he asked, not certain what he meant.

"All those eligible women in Horstberg will be crying into their pillows when they realize that you're in love, and your men will be teasing you mercilessly."

Lance could only chuckle and hope they would get on with the meeting. He knew that by afternoon every one of his men would know what was going on in his life. It had been a running joke for years that he was an eternal bachelor, and almost marrying the woman who was now the duchess had given him a reputation for being too difficult to please. His lack of promiscuity was often a source of teasing from his men, and most of the time he took it in stride. But he could well imagine the fodder for gossip that had been spurred. Still, considering the reason for it, he couldn't help feeling that it was well worth any amount of teasing. He felt relatively certain that Nadine Rader was going to be the best thing that ever happened to him.

When Nadine didn't find the duchess in her office or sitting room, she walked into the nearby bedroom to find her visibly flustered as she rummaged through a jewelry chest.

"Oh, good. You're here," Abbi said. "The baron and his family will be arriving within the hour, and Bruna had to take her mother to an appointment. She managed to get my hair tolerable before she had to leave, and she'll be back to help me later this afternoon. And for some reason every other maid is absent or busy elsewhere. That's what happens when dignitaries come to visit; the whole place turns upside down. You must help me find something to wear and . . . oh, where is that other earring?"

Nadine put a hand on her arm. "Let's decide what you're going to wear, and I'll look for the earring."

Abbi took a deep breath then smiled. "Forgive me," she said as they went into the duchess's dressing room where her wardrobe was kept. "I always get this way when I have to entertain the baroness. She really is an annoying, difficult woman."

"All for the sake of political peace," Nadine said lightly.

"Indeed," Abbi scowled. "I can tell you one thing. Such duties never crossed my mind when I was falling in love."

"Is it worth it?" Nadine asked.

"No question there," Abbi said, smiling again.

Together they picked out an appropriate day dress that Abbi hadn't worn in the presence of these particular dignitaries before, and it was full enough with a high waist that it would accommodate her pregnancy. Nadine helped her get dressed, and while Abbi was finding the right shoes, Nadine found the missing earring.

"There now," Nadine said, handing it to her. "You look lovely, Your Grace."

"Thanks to you," Abbi said.

"What would you like me to do while you're at the luncheon with—"

"Oh, no you don't," Abbi chuckled. "You're not getting out of this."

"What?" Nadine couldn't help her astonished tone.

"You're coming with me, my dear."

"I can't do that," she protested. "I'm not dressed for any such occasion, and I don't know the first thing about the protocol or—"

"You're dressed just fine to do what needs to be done, and there is no protocol beyond just being close by if I need you."

Nadine sighed, wishing she could think of a suitable protest. She reminded herself that she worked for this woman and she was being well paid. She'd do well to do what was asked of her.

"What is it exactly that I'm supposed to do?" she asked, resigned.

"Just . . . stay close by me and I'll tell you what to do. Don't speak to anyone unless they speak to you first. Then be polite. That's it."

Nadine sighed again. "Very well. I'll do my best."

"Thank you," Abbi said triumphantly. "Come along. They'll be arriving any minute."

Nadine followed Abbi down the stairs into the primary hallway, past the ducal offices, and toward the main entrance. She saw a cluster of men in uniform hovering near the door, and a chorus of masculine laughter floated down the hall as they approached. Her heart quickened just before she realized that Lance was among them. Her reluctance shifted eagerly at the prospect of seeing him here. She thought of his kiss just before he'd left this morning and she tingled from the inside out.

Cameron was the first to notice their approach. He turned and smiled toward his wife, reaching a hand toward her as he said, "Well, isn't this a pretty sight."

The other men turned as well, and Nadine felt Lance catch her eye. The pleasant surprise in his expression was priceless. Cameron greeted Abbi with a kiss, then he turned toward Nadine and said, "Good day, Mrs. Rader. So, you're the lucky one who gets to stand beside the duchess and pretend to be enjoying yourself."

"Indeed, Your Grace," she said.

"It's a pleasure to see you, Mrs. Rader," Georg Heinrich said, "but I must confess that I would prefer to see Her Grace with the usual companion."

"He's talking about his wife," Cameron said easily to Nadine. "She's out of the country until Christmas, and he's been absolutely intolerable without her."

"Poor Georg," Abbi said, stepping toward him. She put a hand to one side of his face and a kiss to the other. "Are you missing Elsa?"

"Yes, I am," he said indignantly.

"Well, so am I," she said. "But Christmas will be here before we know it."

"In the meantime," Lance said, "I dare say Mrs. Rader makes a fine addition to your entourage, Your Grace."

"Indeed, she does," Abbi said with a little smirk as she slipped her hand into his. "And how are you today, Captain?"

"I'm well. And you?" He kissed her hand in greeting.

"Beyond getting kicked from the inside out, I'm quite well," she said, making the men chuckle.

Lance then turned to Nadine and greeted her the same, by kissing her hand. "Good morning, Mrs. Rader. It's been too long."

Cameron snorted a laugh. Lance chuckled but otherwise ignored the implication. He looked into Nadine's eyes with a silent meaning that tempted her to melt into the floor. Then an officer opened the door and announced, "They have arrived, Your Grace."

"Thank you, Lieutenant," Cameron said and blew out a long breath.

Nadine watched as the men all stepped easily into a line, with Abbi standing at her husband's shoulder. She discreetly pointed behind her and to the left, where Nadine took her place. While they were waiting, she noticed Lance lean back slightly and smile toward her, winking as he did. She smiled in return and their attention was drawn to the arrival of the Baron and Baroness Von Bindorf of the neighboring country of Kohenswald. Nadine enjoyed observing the matters of echelon unfold, even though she quickly recognized her place as a servant when she was not introduced or acknowledged by their guests. But Nadine realized she was completely fine with that. In fact, observing the effort Abbi put into being diplomatic and appropriate, Nadine felt sure she would loathe such responsibilities.

Following an elaborate luncheon, the men divided from the women, and Nadine followed Abbi through another two hours of entertaining the baroness, along with her homely and arrogant daughter. When the guests were finally shown to their rooms in order to rest and freshen up for the evening's events, Nadine felt as relieved as Abbi appeared. Knowing this was the time of day that she usually left, she began to say her farewells when the duchess said, "Oh, no you don't. You're not leaving yet."

"But I . . ."

"Forgive me, Nadine, for being presumptuous, but I promise you'll get a generous bonus for enduring this day. I've already sent word to Drew and Gerda, and they've responded. The girl who works the lunch shift will be covering for you this evening at the inn, and you will be spending the evening with me. Dulsie will be well cared for."

While Nadine was attempting to come up with something reasonable to say, the duchess took her arm, "Now come along. I think Elsa is near your size. We must find you something to wear."

"I thought you said that what I had on was fine."

"It was fine for a lady-in-waiting," Abbi said with a conspiratorial grin. "Tonight you will be the lady."

Lance leaned back in a chair in the duke's office, feeling the relief of having the baron and his advisors absent. There had been tension in the air since they'd arrived, if only due to the constant effort to be perfectly poised and diplomatic. But now their guests had gone to their rooms to rest, and Lance was counting the minutes until he could escape, and perhaps he would even be able to see Nadine before she began her shift at the inn this evening.

A knock at the door preceded Abbi entering the room. "Hello," she said, and she smiled at him and Georg before she greeted Cameron with the usual kiss.

"To what do we owe this pleasure?" Cameron asked.

"Well," she said, tossing a conspiratorial look toward Lance, "I was thinking how it irritates you to think that the good captain won't be forced to endure this evening's event, and I thought you might like to know that he will likely be attending, anyway."

"I beg your pardon?" Lance said, wishing it hadn't sounded so upset. "I have no intention of—"

"You see," Abbi spoke to Cameron as if Lance were not present, "I've come up with the perfect way to manipulate him into being there."

"Really?" Cameron said, smirking toward Lance as if he were thoroughly enjoying this. "And how is that, my dear?"

"Bait," she said, and Georg laughed, apparently onto where she was headed while Cameron and Lance were oblivious.

"Bait?" Lance echoed, momentarily regretting all of the simple practical jokes he'd initiated with Cameron in the past.

"That's right," Abbi said. "Bait." She laughed and walked back toward the door, saying simply, "Nadine will be there. And she will be dining *with* us. You should see her in that gown. But then," she pinched Lance's cheek like the proverbial aunt, "you will see her, won't you. I'm certain you wouldn't want to miss such an opportunity."

Abbi walked out of the room. Cameron and Georg burst into laughter. Lance shook his head but couldn't keep from laughing himself. "Blast that woman," he said.

"She got you this time," Georg said.

"Yes," Lance admitted, "she certainly did."

Cameron moved toward the door, still chuckling as he said, "I'll see you this evening, Captain."

Lance hurried to his office to make certain that all was in order before he returned to his apartment to get cleaned up and change into his dress uniform. He'd barely come through the door, however, when a thought occurred to him. He glanced at the clock and thought he might actually have time to follow through with an idea that he hoped would be appropriate. Through his errand—which proved to be successful—and returning to his apartment, he caught himself laughing out loud a number of times as he considered what the evening might bring. He had endured countless diplomatic socials, escorting shallow or homely women to dinner and sharing obligatory dances, all for the sake of international relations. Being the consummate bachelor of Horstberg, it had become his unofficial duty to keep young ladies from neighboring countries entertained at such gatherings. But tonight would be different. Tonight he would be very much attached. He blessed Abbi for her insightful conspiring, and thanked God for blessing his life so abundantly. And then he started counting the minutes.

Chapter Eleven

CONFESSIONS

Nadine spent the remainder of the afternoon caught up in a frenzy. She was pleased to realize that Abbi had been right in the respect that Elsa was very near the same size. Abbi felt confident that Elsa wouldn't mind having her things borrowed. "If she were here, she'd be making the offer herself. I can't wait for you to meet her."

Nadine looked forward to that as well, except that when Elsa returned, she would be out of a job. For the moment, however, Nadine felt as if she were caught up in some delightful dream, and she was determined to enjoy every minute of it. After trying on a few of Elsa's gowns, it became evident that they were very close to the same height, but Nadine's figure was somewhat fuller. Still, Elsa's clothes were not made to fit terribly close, so it worked well enough. Nadine had a difficult time deciding which gown to use until she tried on a royal blue with tiny puffed sleeves that dropped off the shoulders. The skirt was heavily gathered into a high waistline, and swept down to hang slightly longer in the back. Looking at her reflection, she felt more beautiful than she ever had in her life. She wondered for a moment why Abbi's lady's maid would own such clothes, and then she recalled that Elsa was also married to the duke's highest advisor. Surely she was required to attend many socials in that regard. Then it occurred to Nadine that Abbi's reason for conspiring for her to attend this social had very much to do with Lance Dukerk. She hardly dared entertain the thought that they could one day end up together permanently. She pushed such thoughts away and focused on appreciating this opportunity while it lasted.

Elsa's shoes proved to be more of a problem, since they were a bit large on Nadine. And the shoes Nadine had with her would be completely inappropriate. They finally solved the problem by carefully stuffing the toes with pieces of rag, and Nadine was actually able to walk in them and not feel clumsy.

Bruna returned from helping her mother in time to do Abbi's hair, and she still had time to do Nadine's as well. With less than twenty minutes until they needed to go downstairs, Nadine was assaulted with nerves. Abbi distracted her by telling early experiences with being the duchess and how out of place she had felt. She briefly explained what to expect, and Nadine was relieved to recall how her father had taught her to dance in her youth. She hoped that it would come back to her without too much difficulty.

At ten minutes to the hour, a knock came at the door.

"Yes," Abbi called.

Berta entered and curtsied slightly, holding out a small box, tied with a white ribbon. "Your Grace," she said, "the captain sent this for Mrs. Rader."

Nadine gasped and Abbi chuckled, taking the box from Berta. "Thank you," Abbi said and Berta left the room.

Abbi handed the box to Nadine, wearing a smile. Nadine hurried to sit down, feeling a bit lightheaded. Abbi sat beside her, expectant.

"Did you put him up to this?" Nadine asked and the duchess's expression alone proved her innocence.

"Honestly, I did not. I admit to some conspiring, but I've not actually spoken to him since he realized you would be here this evening."

Nadine took a deep breath and opened the long, black velvet box. She sucked in her breath and couldn't let it go as the diamond necklace and earrings came into view. She was as struck by their beauty and value as she was by the fact that they had just been given to her as a gift. *Her!* She was startled by the emotion that jumped out of her throat, and the next thing she knew she was sobbing with her head on Abbi's shoulder.

"It's all right," Abbi said softly. "I understand."

"You do?" Nadine muttered. "I'm not sure I do."

"I think you do," Abbi said.

"He treats me like a queen." Nadine sniffled and tried to get hold of herself.

"As he should," Abbi said, handing her a clean handkerchief. "Come now. It's time to go."

Abbi provided Nadine with some powder to smooth over the redness around her eyes and helped her put on the jewelry when she couldn't pick it up because of the way her hands trembled. Nadine took another long look at herself in the mirror, certain it was somebody else looking back at her. Then she took a deep breath and followed Abbi into the hall. They met Cameron and Georg at the top of an elaborate staircase that Nadine realized descended into the ballroom.

"You run along with Georg," Abbi said to Nadine. "I'm afraid I have to make a rather grand entrance. You can arrive more discreetly."

"I'm glad for that," Nadine said, pressing a hand over her quivering stomach.

"I'll see you in a few minutes," Abbi said and winked.

As they moved down the hall, Georg offered his arm, saying, "Lovely dress, Mrs. Rader. I do believe I bought it."

Nadine hurried to say, "Her Grace told me it would be all right if I borrowed it. I hope you don't mind that I—"

"It's more than all right," he said with a smile. "I'm certain you'll have the captain swooning."

Nadine laughed tensely. "Oh, I hope so," she admitted, deciding she liked Georg. Still, she had difficulty believing that she was socializing with such incredible and prestigious people. She had to admit that she was far more impressed with their character and goodness than she was their social distinction. But given the chance to live a fairy tale—if only for one evening—was not something she would sniff at.

They went down a different staircase and to the main door of the ballroom where Nadine knew there would be socializing until the dinner hour. Stepping into the room, she was struck by the overall effect of the polished floor, the brilliant decor, and the string ensemble playing lively music. The room was already crowded with people, and among them were many red and black uniforms.

"Now, to find the captain," Georg said.

"There's no need for you to tend me, Mr. Heinrich," she said. "I'm sure you have better things to do than—"

"On the contrary," he said. "Seeing Lance Dukerk's eyes when he gets a look at you will be the highlight of my evening, I can assure you."

Nadine smiled at him and ventured to use this opportunity to her advantage. "You know the captain well."

"I do yes, very well. I've known him for many years—most of my life, in truth."

"Forgive me if I'm being too bold," she said, "but if you were my father or brother, what advice would you give me in regard to the captain's interest?"

The penetrating gaze he gave her was so startling that for a moment she feared he would reprimand her for asking such questions. But he said in a voice that was firm and gentle, "I would tell you that Lance Dukerk is one of the finest, most honorable men I have ever known. He is everything that Nikolaus du Woernig was not. You could do no better."

Nadine smiled while her heart quickened in response to the validation she'd just been given. She absently touched the diamonds at her throat, a tangible reminder that Lance Dukerk's interest in her was no small thing. "Thank you," she said and glanced around the room, searching for him. "Perhaps he is late."

Georg chuckled and guided her further into the room. "The captain is *never* late," he said. He laughed more loudly. "Well, he was this morning, but that was the first time—ever."

Nadine laughed softly, recalling the reason he'd been late to this morning's meeting.

"Oh, there he is," Georg said and Nadine turned to see where Georg was looking. She caught sight of Lance while he was talking with a man in a blue uniform who was obviously not from Horstberg. She was grateful to have a moment to soak him in before he saw her. As at the funeral, she noted the differences in the dress uniform, from the added adornment on the coat, to the highly polished boots that were much finer than those he wore daily. Just seeing him took her breath away, and when she paused to consider that this was a man who had held her, kissed her, courted her publicly, and had given her diamonds, her heart threatened to burst with joy.

Just when Nadine felt she could bear no more, Lance turned to glance around the room. His gaze abruptly stopped when he saw her. She watched him say something else to the man at his side, who nodded and moved away to visit elsewhere. Lance turned back to look at her, and the sparkle in his eyes seemed to outshine the diamonds she was wearing as the world froze and every sound in the room became distant and obscure. She was grateful for the way Georg guided her toward him as she doubted she could have moved of her own accord. When they were standing face-to-face, Georg took her hand from over his arm and placed it into Lance's outstretched hand. The two men exchanged a long glance, as if the moment had some meaning that she didn't understand. They both chuckled in the same instant, sharing some private joke. She was about to question it, when Georg said to Lance, "I think that could be justified as a moment of nostalgia."

"Indeed," Lance chuckled again, as his eyes turned back to Nadine, filled with blatant adoration. "Thank you, Georg," he said. "I have a feeling this will work out better for me than last time."

"I should hope," Georg said with a chuckle. "Have a wonderful evening, both of you."

"Thank you," Lance and Nadine said at the same time, absorbed with looking at each other.

"You're staring at me, Captain," she said.

She perhaps expected some clever quip in response, but he said with severity, "How can I do otherwise when I've never seen anything so beautiful in my entire life?"

"Surely you're exaggerating, Captain."

"No," he said abruptly and pressed her hand to his lips.

"Thank you . . . for the gift." She touched the diamonds around her throat. "I've never imagined anything so lovely."

"A pleasure," he said. "You look even more beautiful wearing them than I could have possibly imagined."

Nadine was certain they would end up standing there, gazing at each other, for the entire evening, when the music stopped and a loud voice announced the arrival of the duke and duchess. Lance pressed her hand over his arm as they turned to see Cameron and Abbi descending a huge staircase. "Now, watch," Lance whispered. "About halfway down he will turn and look at her, and they'll smile at each other. Notice the look in his eyes. Even from across the room, there's no missing it."

Nadine laughed softly when Cameron and Abbi did exactly as

he'd predicted. With her opportunity to have gotten to know Abbi personally, she marveled freshly at her regal presence that was such a stark contrast to her youth and her petite frame. She felt equally intrigued to see Cameron's obvious adoration of his wife. He was more than a decade older than her, raised to be a king, but he was clearly in awe of the woman at his side. She took notice of Cameron's expression and felt deeply touched as it reminded her of something. She turned to look at Lance, saying, "He looks at her the way you look at me."

"Precisely," he said and smiled as if she'd just announced that the world was not flat. "I used to envy the way he looked at her, and she at him. I longed to feel that way about a woman, and wondered what it might be like when it happened. Sometimes I feared it would *never* happen." Nadine absorbed the deeper meaning in his words that was echoed by the praise in his eyes. "Now I understand the way he looks at her; now I know how he feels."

Nadine didn't know whether to be elated or terrified at the implication. She simply smiled and said, "Yes, I believe I understand, as well."

A servant approached with a tray of champagne glasses. Lance handed one to her and took one himself before the servant moved on. "To a perfect evening," he said, touching his glass to hers. Nadine smiled at him and took a careful sip. She couldn't remember the last time she'd had champagne, but she did remember how it affected her.

"So, tell me what Mr. Heinrich meant . . . about the nostalgia," she said and he chuckled.

"You already know that story," he said, "most of it anyway. When I nearly married Abbi, Georg gave the bride away. He placed her hand into mine, just as he did yours." He chuckled again. "It was an odd sensation, I must admit." He smiled toward her and added, "Perhaps it's some kind of presage."

"Perhaps," she said and he kissed her hand while she tingled from the implication.

For nearly an hour Lance introduced her to many people whose names she couldn't recall as soon as they'd walked away. The importance of his position began to sink in more fully as she met royalty and nobility and many people highly successful in business—from

Horstberg as well as its neighboring countries—all who knew Lance well and were highly interested to see him with a woman. Nadine was especially aware of the way he was regarded by eligible women, and his apparent oblivion to them. It seemed he only had eyes for her, and she marveled at the reality of such a concept.

When there was a break between curious guests, he asked, "Are you doing all right?"

"I don't know. You tell me. I keep fearing I'll embarrass myself, or you."

"No worries there," he said. "I was just wondering if you're enjoying yourself. It can all be rather tedious, in my opinion."

"I'm enjoying being with you," she said and he smiled. "I can see that this kind of thing could get old after a while. I prefer a simpler life, myself. But this could be nice occasionally."

"My thoughts exactly," he said. "Or at least . . . it could be nice occasionally with you beside me."

"Amen," she said and they shared one of those heart-stopping gazes.

He then took notice of her full champagne glass. He'd long since emptied his and set it aside. "Not thirsty?" he asked, taking it from her to take a sip. "Or you don't like champagne?"

"It's all right," she said. "I just know it will go straight to my head and then I *will* embarrass myself *and* you." He chuckled and she added, "And I don't want my senses dulled. I want to enjoy every minute and be able to remember it all in the morning."

"Very wise," he said and handed her glass to a butler as he passed by. "If you don't mind," he said, "I think I could use a little break before dinner. We should have a while yet."

"Very well," she said, wondering if he would leave her here, but he took her arm and guided her toward some tall glass doors at the back of the ballroom. They stepped outside onto a terrace, and beyond it was a vast expanse of gardens stretching into the darkness, completely submerged in deep snow.

"Oh, it's beautiful," she said, and she hardly had a chance to notice the cold before he lifted her into his arms and took a dozen steps through the snow and set her down on another terrace, where he opened a different set of glass doors, not quite so elaborate as those in the ballroom. They stepped into a dimly lit parlor-type room and he closed the doors. The sound of music playing could still be heard. "How quaint," she said, looking around herself. Her gaze came back to him and she heard her pulse beating in her ears as the intensity in his eyes took her breath away. Then with no warning he closed the space between them and took her shoulders into his hands and kissed her, just as he'd done this morning—except that it was better than she'd remembered, if such a thing was possible.

Lance fully absorbed the experience, allowing it to soak into him like water to a man in the desert. "Oh, I've missed you," he murmured close to her face and kissed her again. He marveled at the way she melted into his arms, almost becoming a part of him. He felt her hand at the back of his neck, and then in his hair, and he wondered if anything in life could be as good as this.

Remembering who he was and where they were, Lance eased back slightly and looked into her eyes, warmed by her smile. "Forgive me," he said quietly.

"For what?"

"For getting so carried away."

"Were you getting carried away?" she asked with a whisper of a laugh.

"Oh, yes," he muttered and kissed her again.

"I forgive you," she said and kissed him back.

"I've never held a woman this close before," he said, if only to explain the behavior in himself that was so unfamiliar.

"Never?" Nadine asked, looking into his eyes. He certainly seemed sincere, although such a thing was difficult to imagine—that a man this handsome and virile, of thirty years, could be so pure.

"Never," he said gently and kissed her brow. Nadine pushed away the memory of Nikolaus du Woernig saying that very thing. This was not Nikolaus, she reminded herself, and she urged him to kiss her again. She felt his breathing become sharp as he urged her more fully into his arms. While she succumbed to the pleasure of the moment, she hypocritically prayed that she would not be forced to defend her virtue.

"Oh, Nadine," he muttered and stepped back abruptly. He blew out a long slow breath while he looked at the floor. He glanced back up at her then turned his back as if just looking at her had suddenly become difficult.

"What?" she asked quietly, wondering if she'd inadvertently done something to offend him.

"May I speak candidly?" he asked, turning back to face her.

"Of course," she said, praying that whatever he had to say would not dampen the mood, or worse, leave her heartbroken.

"Nadine," he spoke her name tenderly, "I must confess that I am sorely inexperienced with women. In fact, the men I work with are continually badgering me about my . . . naivety."

Nadine watched the genuine embarrassment invade his countenance and realized that he'd been telling her the truth. There was something starkly different in his confessions, as opposed to the lies that Nikolaus had told her. She wished she could tell him what it meant to her to know that he truly never had held a woman as close as he'd held her. His innocence was brilliantly refreshing and gave her only one regret. She only wished that she was equally innocent. She couldn't help feeling that the prospect of a future with him would leave him cheated, somehow. But she could not regret Dulsie's existence, and she knew in her heart that there was no good to be found in regret.

She watched Lance draw courage to look at her directly as he went on to say, "Forgive me for being so bold, Nadine, but there's no other way to say what I feel needs to be said."

"It's all right," she said.

"I always made a point of *not* being promiscuous. I was raised on the Bible and instinctively believed that living by its precepts would be the best way to live, even though many people I've been close to have not agreed. My sister was promiscuous and many of my friends were—most especially Nikolaus. The thing is . . . it was never difficult for me to remain chaste. I never felt even remotely tempted to cross those lines . . . until now." His voice softened and his eyes sparkled. "Now I wonder if I truly have the self-discipline to do what's right . . . for both of us."

Nadine sighed and felt compelled to admit, "I think that's the sweetest thing anyone has ever said to me."

"Sweet?" he asked, surprised. "Why?"

"Being a common woman as I am, with the need I've had to work at many different occupations to simply survive, I've encountered many men who seem to think that a pub is no different from a brothel. Unfortunately I have a great deal of experience in keeping men at bay. Before you, there was only one man who didn't make me feel like a cheap commodity, but in the end, that is exactly how he made me feel. Your respect for me is touching, Captain. I only wish that I had the same innocence to offer you."

"It doesn't matter, Nadine," he said with vehemence, though his tone remained gentle. "You believed you were married to him. I consider you a widow in every respect."

"You're very kind, Lance. But what if I had—"

"And if you had willfully become involved with him, without the ceremony, it's in the past. It doesn't matter."

Nadine attempted to fight back the tears forming in her eyes without success. "You're crying," he said, stepping toward her, as if he would do anything to spare her grief or pain. "Did I say something to hurt you? Did—"

"No, of course not," she said. "You say everything just right. At moments I fear that all of this is just . . . too good to be true."

"Oh, it is true, Nadine," he said. "At least it's true for me. It's more true than anything I've ever felt."

Nadine took in the intensity of his sincerity and pressed her lips to his. He responded eagerly and drew her into his arms. Their kiss turned warm and moist, going on and on until he looked down to break contact, chuckling as he did. "I should be more careful."

"You are being careful," she said. "If you weren't, we'd be on the sofa by now." He chuckled again, grateful for her openness. "Don't worry," she said. "I'll tell you what I told Nikolaus."

"What's that?"

"I told him I would never be giving any man any more than a kiss until he had first given me his name and I had the certificate in my hands to prove it. He came through with the certificate. I didn't ever get the name." She looked down. "You know the end of that story."

"I'm truly sorry for what he did to you, Nadine. I witnessed a great deal of grief as a result of his indiscretions, but very little has pained me more deeply than what he did to you."

She smiled. "Perhaps you are biased in that regard. There are other women out there who share my plight."

"Yes, there are. Quite a number of them, actually. Although there weren't many who held out for the wedding, as you did. I've met several of them, but none were as beautiful as you."

"So you are biased," she said.

"Yes, I am," he said proudly. "You are the one that I love."

Nadine soaked his confession into herself, looking into his eyes. "You really mean that," she said. It wasn't a question.

"I really do," he said and kissed her again. The music in the next room came to a halt and he glanced that direction. "Dinner is served," he said and elaborately offered her his arm.

They left the room by going into a dimly lit hallway, through a library, and into another hall that was lit more brightly and led into the ballroom. They moved easily into the mass of people that flowed into the huge dining room off the ballroom. Many long tables were set elegantly, and servants lined the walls. Nadine marveled at the experience as Lance helped her with her chair and sat beside her. Noting the variety of silverware in front of her, she whispered, "I've not done anything like this in my life. I have no idea what to do."

"You eat," he whispered back and chuckled. "Just watch. You'll do fine. You're a perfect lady without even trying." She gave him a skeptical glance and he added, "I once knew a young woman who dressed in calico and blatantly refused to wear her hair up, even for such grand occasions as this. She was quite defiant about adhering to society's silly rules. But even then she had a natural grace and dignity that came through brilliantly. You remind me of her in that regard."

"Whatever happened to her? I should like to meet her."

Lance pointed to the head of the table and Nadine turned to see Abbi pointing back at him, smiling wickedly. She didn't realize the incident was connected to his comment until he added, "I'm afraid that won't be possible. You're already working for her."

"Her Grace?" Nadine said. "Calico?"

"You'd better believe it."

Nadine thoroughly enjoyed the meal and didn't feel the least bit nervous. She visited easily with the people surrounding them. On one side was a lieutenant and his wife, a very sweet woman who lived a simple life beyond her occasional visit to Castle Horstberg. On the other side of her and Lance was a princess from Kohenswald, the daughter of the baron, who was here with her husband. She was polite and Nadine found her somewhat fascinating, but she had an arrogance about her that was a stark contrast to Abbi du Woernig, whose position was even more prestigious than what this woman held in her own country.

When dinner was over, the crowd moved back into the ballroom where the music began again, and within minutes several couples were dancing. Nadine became so preoccupied just watching them float effortlessly over the floor that she was startled to see a hand come in front of her. But the face she met was not Lance's.

"Mrs. Rader," the duke said, "may I have the honor?"

Nadine felt so flustered she couldn't speak. She glanced to Lance, who smiled and nodded his encouragement. "I haven't danced for years, Your Grace," she said, curtsying slightly. "I fear I will—"

"There is nothing to fear," he said with a smile. "You must understand that this is an opportunity I've been anticipating for a long time."

"What is that?" she asked, finally slipping her hand into his.

"The captain will explain it to you later," he said, smirking toward Lance as they walked to the center of the dance floor. Nadine was aware of all eyes on them, and she could only pray that she would be able to dance reasonably well without tripping over her own feet. She was grateful that the duke seemed sensitive to her nervousness and he started out slowly, actually counting the steps for her. He led her easily and she quickly got a feel for it. "Very good," he said with a little laugh before he gained momentum. When they were dancing as fluidly as the other couples on the floor, he said to her, "So, you must be an amazing woman."

"Why do you say that?" she asked.

"Well, first of all, my wife has told me nothing but good about you. She enjoys working with you very much."

"I'm glad to hear it," she said. "I've enjoyed my work with her, as well."

"I have a feeling the two of you will become very good friends."

"I do hope so," Nadine said, doubtful that such a thing would ever happen once her temporary position ended.

"And . . ." the duke drawled, "that's not the only reason that I've concluded how amazing you are."

"Yes?" she asked, certain he was teasing her.

"I've seen countless women bend over backward trying to get his attention, and he's never taken a second glance. How did you do it?"

"I have no idea," she laughed and he did the same.

"Well, whatever you're doing, keep doing it. I've never seen him so happy."

Nadine felt warmed from the inside out over the comment. "That would make two of us," she said. "I too have never been so happy."

"Good then," he said. "You deserve to be happy."

"I only wish that every woman who shared my losses could be so happy," she said.

She saw him look briefly into her eyes with a penetrating gaze that made it easy to see his ability to rule a country. "I wish it as well," he said, his voice edged with sadness.

Attempting to lighten the mood, she said, "You dance very well, Your Grace. Well enough to compensate for my lack of ability."

"It was one of many things I had to endure learning. Apparently somebody believes you have to dance well in order to be a good duke."

"Well, considering the present circumstances, I can see why," she said. "Perhaps these people wouldn't respect you enough to negotiate if they didn't see that you could hold your own on the dance floor."

He laughed and Nadine decided that the more she got to know this man, the more she liked him.

Chapter Twelve

The Stalker

Once Nadine was on the dance floor with Cameron, Lance had no choice but to even out the odds. "Your Grace," he said to Abbi, "I believe you need to dance."

She laughed. "I'm too big and fat to dance."

"Nonsense," he said, "I'll take very good care of you."

As he eased her into an easy waltz, he said, "It's not very easy to get close to you, however, with that baby inside of you."

"Cameron would be pleased to hear that," she said and he laughed.

"I want to thank you," he said with a sincerity that perked her attention.

"For what?" she asked, as if she had no idea what he was talking about.

"For conspiring to allow her to be here tonight. It's the most pleasurable social that I've ever attended here, if you must know. And I think she's having a good time, as well."

"That's good, then. The diamonds were a nice touch. She accused me of putting you up to it, but I set her straight. Although, you know that when a man gives a woman diamonds, he's implying long-term commitment?"

"Really?" he said with a smile. "How delightful. I must have been inspired."

When the dance was nearly finished, they moved close to Cameron and Nadine. Cameron pretended to be insulted when he saw them, saying to Lance, "I was trying to get even. How can I get even while you're at it again?"

"I'm getting even for your getting even," Lance said and Cameron laughed.

They took one more turn around the room before Lance moved close to them again and gracefully eased Abbi toward Cameron as he took Nadine's hand and urged her into his arms.

"How clever you are," Abbi said, and Lance swept Nadine across the floor.

"Oh, this is nice," Nadine said when they were waltzing comfortably. "The duke is very kind and a pleasure to dance with, but I definitely prefer *your* company."

"I could say the same about the duchess," he said.

They danced through a number of songs until Nadine was breathless and hot. Suddenly overwhelmed with the closeness of the room, she asked, "Could we go elsewhere for a breath of fresh air?"

"Of course," he said. "It's awfully cold outside, but we could—"

"Anywhere would be fine," she said and he ushered her into a long, wide hall, lit only by a few wall sconces. She immediately felt better as the cooler air struck her. Lance put an arm around her shoulders and they walked slowly in peaceable silence until he asked gently, "What are you thinking about?"

"Well," she laughed softly and glanced down, "as you once said, if I answer that question honestly, it might not be conducive to the mood. So it might be better if I just say 'nothing.' "

"And as I recall, you made me tell you anyway." He shrugged his shoulders and smirked. "Fair is fair. I'm willing to risk the mood."

"Very well," she said. "I was comparing you to Nikolaus. Perhaps it's not fair to make such comparisons. Fair to you, I mean."

"That depends on how good it makes me look," he said lightly and she laughed. She loved it when his sense of humor came through.

"Oh, it makes you look really good."

"Then compare away," he said.

More seriously, Nadine said, "Nikolaus was an active part of my life for several months. And not once did he allow me to even get close to this side of his world. Of course, he had all kinds of reasons why the secrecy was important, and I believed him. But knowing what I know now, I realize that if I had dared to step foot into Castle Horstberg, and especially into one of these social events, he would have been mortified. He would have denounced me and claimed to have never known me. He never gave me a gift, never. No tangible tokens; nothing with any value, sentimental or otherwise." Nadine turned to look at Lance. The sadness in her eyes faded to a defined sparkle. "Already in the short time we have known each other, you have made me feel more . . . valuable, more adored than he ever ventured to do in all our months together. He always managed to say the right things, but looking back, I realize that I was often left feeling empty and hollow and scared. I simply wasn't willing to take those feelings out and look at them for what they were." She stopped walking and touched his face with her fingertips. "So, thank you . . . for making up somewhat for what he did to me. I've seen the way eligible ladies look at you and vie for your attention."

"Do they?" he asked, his tone bored.

"They do," she said, "and you know they do."

"They're all a bunch of mindless and impertinent cows," he said so severely that she couldn't help laughing.

"I will consider that a compliment."

"As you should," he said.

"It is compliment enough that you would have me on your arm and keep me at your side. Your acceptance heals something in me. So . . . thank you."

Lance took her fingers and kissed them. "A pleasure indeed, my lady. It is I who am blessed to have you beside me," he added and she smiled. "And let me make something very clear," he went on, "you are *not* a common woman, at least not to me." She smiled again.

He noticed her shiver and said, "I take it you've cooled off."

"I have, yes," she said. "These hallways don't ever get very warm, do they."

"No, they don't," he said, unfastening the hooks of his coat.

"Oh, you don't need to—"

"There," he said, putting the fine, red coat over her shoulders. "A uniform of the Guard has never looked better."

"I wouldn't say that," she said with a little smirk. "But thank you."

As they walked back toward the ballroom, Nadine wondered how many women would sell their souls to be wearing the coat of the Captain of the Guard, offered as a gallant gesture. She considered herself terribly blessed and left it at that.

"Oh, by the way," she said as the sounds of the music became closer. She tugged on his arm to urge him to stop so that she could face him. "I love you as well, Captain Dukerk."

He smiled brilliantly. "Then life is good," he said.

"Yes," she said, "life is good."

He smiled again and kissed her.

The following day Lance was glad to see the visiting dignitaries set out early for their home country. His work kept him busy, going in and out of the ducal offices. He couldn't help hoping that he might see Nadine, knowing that she was working with the duchess. But he didn't. It was a big castle, and he came up with no legitimate excuses to interrupt his work and find a reason to intrude upon them.

He returned to his office following a meeting with the advisory committee to find Lieutenant Kepler waiting for him. "We've had a crisis, Captain," he said.

"What's happened?" Lance demanded.

"A suicide, sir," he said and Lance heaved a harsh sigh. "The victim is a twenty-three year old male. He shot himself in the head. He was found by his younger sister, who heard the shot."

"Merciful heaven," Lance said. "Is she all right?"

"She's here, sir, with her mother. I've sent three officers to do a more thorough report of the scene and to see that the body was properly cared for. But I felt you should talk to the family before we close the report."

"Thank you, Lieutenant. I just have to know . . . do we have any reason to believe that it *wasn't* a suicide?"

"No, sir. We spoke with a neighbor who told us the sister asked him for help because the door was locked from the inside, and the neighbor broke the door open. The two of them, along with the mother, all heard the shot. There is no other possibility."

Lance nodded, feeling some relief. As horrible as this was, the idea of a murder investigation would have been far worse. "I'm grateful for your efficiency, Lieutenant. I would appreciate it if you'd join me."

"Of course," the lieutenant said. Lance took a deep breath and followed him down the hall, into one of the interrogation rooms. As the door was opened, Lance's attention was drawn to the two women holding each other's hands tightly, their faces etched with grief. They looked up as the lieutenant closed the door, saying, "This is Captain Dukerk. He'd like to speak with you for a few minutes, and then a carriage will be ready to take you home."

Lance leaned against the edge of the table, saying gently, "I'm so sorry to hear of your loss. I know how difficult this must be, and you must be anxious to be on your way. I simply need to know, for the official report, if you feel there was some reason he would have done this."

The two women exchanged a glance that made it clear the mother wanted her daughter to do the talking. The daughter turned to Lance and said in a shaky voice, "He simply had taken all he could bear, feeling outcast the way he did." She went on to tell of her brother being spurned one too many times by women who wanted nothing to do with him and whose families had openly condemned him. She spoke of this young man's entire life being a string of ridicule and degradation. As Lance listened, he could well imagine the hopelessness of such a life, and he found it easy to understand why this man would have wanted to put an end to such madness. But he was unclear on one point, and gently asked, "Forgive me, but . . . I must have missed something. Was there a reason for all of this ridicule and degradation?"

The young woman looked to her mother, who was crying vehemently now. She turned back to Lance and said quietly, "He was born before Mother married, you see. Everyone knew he was a bastard. My mother learned to deal with the disgrace, but he just . . . couldn't live with it any longer."

"I see," Lance said, feeling unexplainably angry on behalf of this family. It didn't matter what choices this woman may or may not have made to bring her son into the world under such circumstances; there was no excuse for people to be so cruel. He offered words of compassion and reassurance to the best of his ability before Lieutenant Kepler escorted the women to the carriage that would see them safely home.

As with many of his duties that proved to be disturbing, Lance contemplated the tragedy for several minutes and then put it out of his mind. If he became emotionally involved with every case he encountered, he would lose his sanity. He forced himself to finish the necessary work and turned his thoughts to the anticipation of seeing Nadine.

Late afternoon he finally got away, hoping to get to the inn before the crowds began filling it up. He felt an indescribable relief to enter the dining room and find it completely empty—except for Nadine, who was wiping off tables in preparation for the supper rush. When she heard the door, she looked up to see him and her smile alone completely erased the cold he'd endured to get here. The hours since he'd seen her the previous night suddenly seemed like days. His heart quickened, and a rush of butterflies made him feel like a giddy school boy.

"Hello," she said, absently wiping her hands on her apron.

Lance smiled and crossed the room. Without a word spoken, he took her into his arms and kissed her as he'd been wanting to all day. "Oh, Nadine," he muttered and kissed her again, marveling at how the experience could be so thoroughly blissful each time. She melted into his arms and pressed her fingers into his hair, fully succumbing to him with complete, unspoken trust.

Lance finally forced himself to stop, feeling what little control he had of his senses slipping away. "How long do you have to work?" he asked close to her face. He hated the fact that she had to work at all. He wanted to take care of her and Dulsie, but he knew that he had to let their relationship take its proper course. He knew she took pride in being able to care for herself and her daughter, and he didn't want to take that away from her until it was proper.

"The usual," she said. Then she looked deeply into his eyes and asked, "Is something wrong?" He glanced quickly away as he realized his thoughts had strayed to the drama he'd encountered this afternoon. "Something *is* wrong," she said, and he marveled at her perception.

"Just . . . another tragedy in Horstberg: a suicide. A young man. I can't help feeling affected when such things happen."

"Oh," she said, touching his face, "dealing with such things must be a difficult aspect of your work."

"Indeed," he said, putting his hand over hers, grateful for her compassion.

"Do you know why he did it?" she asked. "Was he in trouble or—"

"He was apparently tired of living with the brunt of being a bastard."

He was completely taken aback when she said, "Like Dulsie."

"No," he retorted, angry, "not like Dulsie! People need never know the truth about—"

"*We* know the truth," she said. "Do you honestly think that she can live out her entire life without ever knowing? Without people around her knowing?"

"I pray to God that she can," he said with vehemence. "It's no fault of hers, or yours, but people can be so cruel."

"Yes, they can," she said and seemed to want to drop the subject. He was eager to do the same and felt relieved when a customer came in the door. "Where *is* Dulsie?" he asked, forcing normalcy into his voice.

"In the kitchen with Gerda." She smiled and seemed to have let go of the tension that had been between them. "You don't have more candy for her, do you?"

"I most certainly do," he said proudly. "And I was wondering if I might take her with me while you work. Only if she wants to go, of course."

"I don't know," she said, smiling still. "Why don't you ask her?"

Nadine went to get her, and Dulsie eagerly begged to go with the captain, even while she was digging into his pocket for the expected candy. "Of course you can go," Nadine said. "Just remember to behave yourself."

"I'm sure she'll be a perfect lady," Lance said and she ran to get her coat and gloves.

"It will be good for her to get out of that kitchen," Nadine said. "Thank you."

"The pleasure is mine," Lance said, stealing a quick kiss. "I'll take very good care of her, I promise."

"I know you will," she said and rushed away to begin her work.

Lance thoroughly enjoyed his time with Dulsie. He took her to some shops that stayed open into the evening along the edge of the square, and they went for a walk along the river while she kept her hand securely in his.

Nadine barely caught a glimpse of Lance and Dulsie returning, their arms loaded with packages. She saw them glance her way as they slipped up the stairs, and there was a definite conspiratorial glimmer in their eyes. When Nadine was finally finished with her work, she went up to her room to find Dulsie all ready for bed and Lance reading to her from a beautiful picture book that he'd purchased for her. She jumped up from the rug where they were sitting when Nadine entered the room and locked the door. "Mama, Mama," she said excitedly, "Lance bought me two books and we went for a walk and I had something to eat that I've never had before. It was wonderful. And we saved some for you, and you and Lance can have a picnic just like we did a while ago, right here on the rug."

"How perfectly delightful," Nadine said, smiling at Lance. "I take it you're now on a first-name basis."

"Of course we are," Lance said. "We're best friends."

While Nadine rubbed Dulsie's hands, Lance continued to read aloud from the storybook until the child drifted to sleep. Lance removed her from Nadine's lap and tucked her in, pressing a kiss to her little forehead.

"You spoil us terribly," she said as he sat down on the rug beside her.

"After what you've been through, I dare say you could both use some spoiling."

They shared their picnic on the rug as they discussed events of their separate days, then he insisted that she massage his hands while they continued to talk.

"Tell me about your parents," she said. "You've talked of your sister, but never your parents."

"My parents," he said with pleasant nostalgia. "My mother died when I was young, but my memories of her are good. She was kind and tender and very beautiful. With my mother gone, my father raised me and Gwen, in spite of his busy career. He married again, but not until we were practically on our own. My stepmother lives in Horstberg; I should like for you to meet her. But back to my father . . . He was not necessarily warm, but he was a good man. He had a strong sense of integrity; he was responsible and hard working. I knew that he loved me, even if he was somewhat lacking in affection. We had a strong, stable relationship. Looking back, I realize more and more that my perspective of life is strongly rooted in the upbringing he gave me. It's an honor to have such a man as a father."

"And what was your father's busy career?" she asked.

Lance smiled subtly. "He was the Captain of the Guard, and a very good friend to the duke, Cameron's father."

"Oh, I see." She smiled as well. "So, did he press you to have a military career, then?"

"Not at all. But I was always drawn to it, and he encouraged me to go after it zealously. He let me know that he believed I could succeed at whatever I put my heart into. He died of illness long before I ever came into this position, but I believe he would have been pleased." She smiled at him as she switched hands and continued her chore. "Now it's your turn. Tell me about your parents."

Nadine sighed. "I also lost my mother very young," she said. "And my father was a very good man that . . ." She paused and sighed again. "I have to clarify that. As far as my relationship with him, he was a good man. He was sensitive and kind, and he always made me feel confident and capable. However, I strongly suspected that he was not entirely ethical in his business dealings."

"That must have been difficult," he said with compassion.

"It was, yes," she admitted. "I quickly learned that there was no good in confronting him. He would simply deny it and lie to me, but there were far too many suspicious incidents for me to believe he was innocent. It was disturbing, but there was nothing I could do about it beyond remaining honest myself. So I just learned to turn the other way."

"And what sort of business was he in?" Lance asked.

"He owned a mill, along with a partner who worked with him very closely."

"And what happened?" he asked, noting a cloudiness in her eyes.

"Well, his partner was caught involved in some kind of treasonous activities. He was executed and his property confiscated."

Lance couldn't help wondering if this was during Nikolaus's reign. Most likely, from what he knew of her history. He was well aware that many had been tricked or framed into such circumstances so that Nikolaus could be rid of people he didn't like and confiscate their property.

"And how did your father die?" he asked.

"I fear his end was equally tragic," she said. "He was robbed and shot one night on his way home from town. After his death he was implicated as being involved with his partner's crimes, and his property was confiscated according to the law." She drew a ragged breath and stopped her massaging as her eyes became distant, but she held tightly to his hand with both of hers. "I had discovered my pregnancy not long before his death. Nikolaus was very compassionate about the whole thing, and my father's death was part of his excuse for sending me away. He always managed to say the right things and be sensitive to me even though I had suspected that his dealings were not ethical either." She chuckled without humor. "Perhaps that's why he got along so well with my father."

"So, your father was alive when you married Nik?" he asked, surprised. "Most of the women he took advantage of were without family."

"I recall His Grace saying that," she said, "but . . . yes, my father was alive. In fact, my father introduced me to Nikolaus. They were involved in some kind of business venture together; they wouldn't tell me what."

Lance quickly searched his conscience and felt he had to say, "Nadine, it likely doesn't matter anymore, but you should know that . . . well, I didn't learn about such things until after his death, but it quickly became evident that Nikolaus had illegally managed to have many people convicted of treason, only so he could confiscate their property."

Nadine gasped and her eyes grew distant once again. "Good heavens," she said and sighed loudly. She was deep in thought for a few minutes before she shook her head and said, "I'm grateful he's dead, Lance." She met his eyes and added, "I simply don't know how I would cope with all that he did to me if he weren't."

"Yes, I know what you mean," he said gently, holding her close for a long moment. In an effort to distract her, he began massaging her hands. "Talk about something else," he urged.

Nadine looked up at him and quickly became lost in his eyes. "I've meant to ask you about your aversion to hats," she said and he chuckled.

"You noticed," he said.

"Every officer either has a hat on his head or tucked beneath his arm . . . except you."

"Fortunately, being the captain has certain privileges. I don't have to wear a hat if I don't want to . . . except on rare occasions, when weather or protocol require it."

"Why would you want to cover up this?" she said, touching his hair with her free hand. She loved the thick waves and found them irresistible. She smiled timidly and added, "So, exactly how *did* you get to be the Captain of the Guard?"

Lance looked at her hand as he continued rubbing cream into it. "When Nikolaus took over the duchy at the same time Cameron was believed dead—and believed guilty of murder—the captain serving at the time took an early retirement. He didn't want to work with Nikolaus, and he was only a few years from retirement age. I was serving as a lieutenant at the time, and Nikolaus offered me the position. Of course, I knew he was biased; we'd been friends for years. As I said, my father had served at one time as the Captain of the Guard, but he had taken the position at a much older age. I'd grown up with military training and I felt I could handle the position, but I was troubled over whether or not to take it. I didn't want the men serving under me to feel that I was in the position out of favoritism. They needed to respect me or I could never do my job effectively."

"So, what made you decide to take it?" she asked.

"A lieutenant that I had worked with, who I trusted very much, he . . . well, he was much older than I was—a good man. And he pulled me aside and told me that there was talk among the men that they were hoping I would accept because they knew I had the integrity and backbone to represent them well with a ruler like Nikolaus. They all knew he was erratic at best, and their hope was that the friendship I shared with Nikolaus would keep some balance in his power. So I took the position, and I'm grateful I did because I know I did make a difference. It didn't feel like it much of the time—he was difficult to work with and became more difficult as time went by— but I did stand up to him as far as it was possible without aggravating him against me. And I was quietly able to have some counteracting influence over things he tried to do that simply were not ethical. Still, I realized after he was gone that I had not been aware of half the trouble he'd stirred up."

"And once again our conversation comes back to Nikolaus," she said sadly, looking away.

"Nadine," he said, touching her chin to lift her face to his view, "he's gone; it's in the past, and he's not going to hurt you ever again. A day will come when we won't need to talk about him anymore, but healing takes times." He pressed a kiss to her lips and felt her respond immediately. "Oh, how I love you," he muttered and kissed her again.

She was smiling when he drew back to look into her eyes. In silence he finished massaging her hands, then he helped her tidy the room before he left for the night, kissing her at the door. Nothing more was said about the suicide or Dulsie's illegitimacy. And that was fine with him. He was glad to put that conversation in the past.

Nadine went to bed feeling perfectly content as long as she forced any thought of Nikolaus out of her head. As Lance had said, it was in the past and he wouldn't hurt her anymore.

Through the following days Nadine found her life blissful. Having received her first pay allotment from Abbi, she went into town and ordered some new clothes that would be more suitable for working with the duchess and being courted by the Captain of the Guard. On Sunday, Lance came for her and Dulsie and they attended church with him in the castle chapel. Afterward, they shared Sunday dinner with Cameron and Abbi and their young son, Erich. Georg and his little son, Han, also joined them, since Elsa was out of the country. Although, Nadine learned that Georg and his family often shared meals with them; they were *all* like family. And Erich and Han, being close in age, were often together and got along rather well. Dulsie enjoyed playing with the little boys, and she was just enough older that she enjoyed mothering them and seeing that they didn't get into things they shouldn't. Nadine thoroughly enjoyed the day, in awe of the friends she had found here who were common and ordinary when it came to chatting by the fire on a Sunday afternoon. But she was more in awe of the way Captain Dukerk kept her hand possessively in his. His love for her was evident every time he looked at her, and she felt perfectly happy.

As a new week began, temperatures dropped even further and it was difficult to stay warm. Nadine and Abbi huddled close to the fire as they went about their work. Nadine couldn't help feeling an excited anticipation as they planned menus and activities for the

Christmas parties that would be hosted by the royal family. Nadine addressed invitations and listened as Abbi recounted her plans.

The first party would be two days before Christmas, and it would involve the royal family and their close friends as well as the high-ranking officers, advisors, and their families. Nadine was amazed at the size of the guest list and the different activities that would be hosted for children of all ages, as well as the adults. The following day, on Christmas Eve at midday, there would be another celebration for all of the servants and lower-ranking officers which would give them time off after covering for the previous day's celebrations. It would be equally elaborate with huge amounts of food, activities, and gifts for all.

Along with the parties, Abbi had taken it upon herself in the few years that she had been duchess to oversee a number of different charity projects. Some were in effect year round, but through the Christmas season she used many different avenues to give an added outpouring to those in need. As Nadine listened to her plans and helped oversee the ordering and gathering of goods, she felt overwhelmed at the quiet generosity of this woman she had the privilege of working with. She found an honor in the friendship they shared and how easily they could talk and laugh, as if they had been childhood companions.

In working so closely with Abbi, Nadine wondered occasionally what it might have been like if she had married Nikolaus and ended up the duchess. Quite frankly, she couldn't even imagine. It simply didn't suit her, and now that her life had come where it was, she couldn't help feeling grateful that everything had worked out as it had.

Again Nadine saw Albert Crider waiting outside the bakery, just after she'd picked up new clothes she'd ordered the week before. She realized the bakery had become a daily stop she made, and he had obviously picked up on her habits. She told Lance about it that evening and admitted to being severely unnerved. The very fact that he hadn't approached her almost made her more afraid. The following day Nadine wondered whether or not she should go to the bakery, but just having to ask herself that question made her angry. She told herself that she shouldn't have to change her habits just because of this creep. So she went anyway. And when she came out, an officer of the Guard was patrolling the very spot where Albert

Crider had been standing previously. Nadine smiled and returned to the inn feeling decidedly safe. She wondered if the captain would take such precautions for *any* woman, or if she was getting special treatment. She didn't wonder too long over it; she just thanked God for bringing this man into her life.

Lance felt a magnifying of the joy in his life as his relationship with Nadine quickly deepened. And added to his joy was the growing love he felt for Dulsie. He made a point to take her now and then for an hour or two, and he thoroughly enjoyed their time together. She was bright for her age, and he often marveled at how well they could converse. Still, he was surprised when she said one evening, "Did you know that we're the same?"

"The same, how?" he asked.

"I don't know," she said. "I can't explain it. I just feel it. We're the same. We're like best friends because we are the same kind of people." Lance just nodded and smiled. She added firmly, "And that's why I love you, Lance."

He smiled again. "I love you too, Dulsie."

Every evening while Dulsie was sleeping, Nadine and Lance would take turns massaging the other's hands while they talked of their days, their pasts, their dreams. Nadine marveled that they had known each other so short a time when being with him felt as natural as breathing. She only prayed that it could last forever, while she simply refused to wonder if he would ever break her heart as Nikolaus had.

On a day that was actually a little warmer than it had been, Nadine was addressing invitations while Abbi checked over some lists. They both looked up at the sound of a man clearing his throat. Lance was leaning in the doorway, his arms folded over his chest.

"Well hello," Abbi said and Lance crossed the room to take the duchess's hand.

"Good morning, Your Grace," he said, kissing her fingers and looking into her eyes. Nadine told herself there was no reason to feel envious of his attention to the duchess, but she couldn't deny a certain amount of uneasiness, even if she couldn't quite pinpoint why.

"And who do we have here?" he asked, turning toward Nadine as if he'd never seen her before. Her thoughts of envy fled at the blatant adoration in his eyes.

"This is Mrs. Rader," Abbi said, going along. "She's my new secretary; when Elsa comes back we shall have to find something else for her to do."

"No need for that," Lance said, kissing Nadine's hand as well, then her wrist and her arm. "I think I shall sweep her away to some faraway land and never bring her back. You'll have to get somebody else to address your silly little envelopes."

"I beg your pardon," Abbi said, pretending to be insulted while Nadine giggled.

"I rather like addressing silly little envelopes," Nadine said.

Lance picked one up and said, "You are very good at it, I confess."

"What are you doing here, anyway?" Abbi asked.

"I was thinking what a lovely day it is and how blessed I am to actually have a few hours free. I was thinking the best thing I could possibly do with said hours is to take the two most beautiful ladies in Horstberg into town and show them off; it's market day, after all."

"So it is," Abbi said. "But I am far too tired and pregnant to go into town. I can certainly spare Nadine, however, and I insist that she go with you."

"Are you certain?" Nadine asked, trying to subdue her excitement.

"Of course," Abbi said. "You work so fast that we're always ahead, anyway. I'll check on Dulsie when I check on Erich. You go and have a marvelous time." To Lance she added, "Buy her something frivolous and beautiful. That's an order, Captain."

"Yes, Your Grace," he said with a smirk. "I might even buy her two or three things that are frivolous and beautiful."

Nadine laughed and put her hand over his arm. Since Abbi had declined going, Lance insisted that they go by horseback. They barely stepped into the cavalry stable when an officer put the reins of a saddled horse into the captain's hand.

"Thank you," Lance said.

"Would you be liking another mount for the lady?" the officer asked.

"No, this is fine," he said with a wink toward Nadine.

"Very good, sir," the officer said and moved away.

"Did they know you were coming?" she asked.

"No," Lance said, patting the animal in some kind of greeting. "They keep at least a few horses saddled constantly so they will be ready at any given moment. The horses take turns being on alert. Consequently, I rarely ride the same horse twice in a week. So," he drawled and looked closely at the horse, "it's good to take a moment to get acquainted."

When the greetings were apparently finished, Lance helped Nadine into the saddle while she laughed nervously, admitting that she'd not been on a horse in many years. He climbed into the saddle behind her and took the reins in one hand while he put the other arm around her waist. She found the experience of galloping down the castle hill with his chest firmly against her back completely exhilarating. When they arrived at the square, he dismounted and tethered the horse before he helped her down. While they perused the open markets and maneuvered through the crowds, he kept his arm securely around her or held tightly to her hand. The pride he seemed to hold in just being with her was more healing to her heart than any amount of flowery words or gifts could have ever been. Although he did keep his promise to Abbi when he insisted on buying Nadine an expensive bottle of perfume. They smelled several and tried them on her wrists until they found the one they both felt suited her best. The storekeeper wrapped it carefully, and Lance placed it in one of the deep pockets of his uniform where he often kept candy for Dulsie. With Dulsie in mind, he also bought a good supply of candy to be kept on hand. While they were waiting for the candy to be bagged, Nadine's attention was drawn to a woman nearby who was arguing with a fabric vendor. Her crass behavior and rudeness startled Nadine, especially as she noticed a young boy near Dulsie's age holding to the woman's skirts. She couldn't help wondering if his mother treated him as she was treating the vendor. Then the child turned toward Nadine and she gasped.

"What is it?" Lance asked. She loved his sensitivity to her.

"Look at that child," she whispered discreetly, grateful the mother was still preoccupied.

Lance turned slightly to see the young boy, and he gasped himself. The child was a miniature replica of Nikolaus du Woernig. "Good heavens!" he muttered, glancing unobtrusively at the mother.

"It's incredible," he murmured to Nadine, forcing his eyes away. He didn't admit to the difficult memories that were being stirred, but one look at Nadine made it clear that she too was plagued with the same.

"A woman who shares my plight," Nadine said quietly.

Lance took notice of the woman's ongoing rudeness to the vendor and replied in a whisper, "She'd do well to follow your example and handle her *plight* with a little more dignity and graciousness."

Nadine looked into his eyes, absorbing the meaning of his words. By the time she was able to tear her gaze from his, the mother and child were gone, but they hovered in her mind.

Lance tucked the bag of candy into the pocket that wasn't holding the perfume, and they walked on to the next vender which brought them to a beautiful assortment of silk scarves. Lance picked out a very expensive white one and draped it around Nadine's throat while he admired her with his eyes.

"I love you," he said quietly.

"And I love you," she replied, longing to be alone with him and to feel his lips over hers.

They went to a pub that was delightfully noisy and ate lunch together. She noticed many officers there, drinking and laughing, and she couldn't help feeling that he had brought her there to show her off. A stark contrast to Nikolaus du Woernig hiding her away from the world.

As they wandered back across the square to where they had left the horse, Nadine noted that the crowds had thickened. She became aware now as she had been earlier of how women regarded Lance, which only deepened her gratitude for being on his arm.

In a place where it was terribly crowded, Nadine lightly said, "How many people are in this country?"

Lance systematically responded, "27,842, last I checked."

Nadine laughed. "I was joking."

"Oh," he chuckled sheepishly, "so you were. Well," he shrugged, "now you know."

"Yes, now I know," she said and was relieved when they reached a spot where the crowd thinned a bit. But a moment later she distinctly saw Albert Crider and gasped.

"What?" Lance demanded, stopping.

"I just saw him," she said, trying to appear nonchalant.

"The stalker?" he asked quietly, and she nodded. "Where?"

"To your left. In a dark cloak with the hood up."

Lance looked around, trying to be subtle. "There are a dozen people wearing dark cloaks with hoods," he said, frustrated.

Nadine looked around and admitted, "He's gone."

Lance turned to look again himself, straining to see anything or anyone who looked suspicious. He finally turned back to Nadine and asked quietly, "Are you all right?"

"Yes, of course. It's just . . . unnerving. Do you suppose he's been following us around all this time?"

Lance said nothing. He felt decidedly uneasy but didn't want to alarm her. He simply said, "Just keep doing what I told you to do. Be careful, not afraid, all right?"

She nodded and he kissed her brow before he escorted her back to the horse, and they returned to the castle. She noted how quickly an officer took his horse and led it away. As he walked her back to where Abbi would likely be, she said, "I can't stop thinking about that woman we saw, and the child."

"Nikolaus's child."

"That's right. I'm certain there are many women who share my plight. And I wonder if we couldn't somehow help each other. I just keep thinking that I should like to come in contact with other women like me. Do you think it's possible? Or is it silly?"

"Well, I don't think it's silly. I know, for instance, of a group of young widows who meet together regularly. They give each other help and support, and they share friendships."

"But how would I ever find such women? I can't just go scouring the streets for children who look like Nikolaus."

"You could," he chuckled. "However, I believe there are records kept. You'd have to get permission to access them. Talk to Abbi and see what she thinks."

"I believe I will."

Lance left Nadine with a kiss and returned to work. She folded the scarf and tucked it into her coat pocket, knowing it didn't go well with her dress. Nadine discussed her idea with Abbi, and Abbi also thought it was a good one. Abbi told Nadine she trusted her to handle approaching these women with appropriate discretion. While Nadine worked on her addressing project, Abbi went to talk to Cameron and Georg about Nadine's idea, not wanting to do something that could bring unforeseen problems. With their permission, Abbi took Nadine to an office on the main floor and introduced her to Mr. Gutendorf, one of the duke's many secretaries. She explained to him that Nadine was helping her with a project, and she wanted to see the files for illegitimate children. Abbi left Nadine in his care and said, "I'll see you tomorrow, dear. Good luck."

Mr. Gutendorf exchanged friendly chatter as he led her into a room where the walls were lined with drawers from floor to ceiling. A ladder hooked to a rail near the ceiling could be moved around the perimeter of the room to reach the higher drawers.

"Incredible," Nadine muttered. "How do you keep track?"

"It's more organized than it looks. Everything is indexed. But what you're looking for is right over . . ." He turned and pointed a finger before he moved the ladder to that point and went up a few steps. He opened one drawer then closed it, then another and said, "Ah, this is it." He pulled out a thick stack of papers with both hands, shoved the drawer closed with his elbow, and came down the steps. He set the papers into a nearby wooden box with handles cut into each end, and she realized there were several empty boxes, obviously for the purpose of carrying about large sets of records when necessary. "There you are, my dear. If the duchess trusts you, so do I. Just return them in at least as good of order as you found them, and I'll need them back in a week or less."

"Of course," she said, feeling a little nervous. She planned to get them back much sooner than that. "Thank you very much," she said and took the box.

Chapter Thirteen

BURIED SECRETS

"What is that?" Lance asked when Nadine met him in his office a few minutes later with the box in her hands.

"Her Grace gave me access to the records."

"What records?"

"See here," she pointed to a tab on a heavy piece of paper at the top of the stack that said *Illegitimate Children*.

"Good heavens," he said, recalling now what they'd been talking about earlier. "It's awfully thick. Do you really think there are that many?"

"I'm certain they don't *all* belong to Nikolaus," she said and Lance laughed, grateful to see that she could say something like that with a smile. "And actually, I think some of these are very old. No one has probably opened these for decades except to add new records. Look at these pages at the front of the file; they're yellow and cracking."

"True," he said, becoming distracted by his desire to kiss her.

"So, what brings you here?" he asked, once he'd kissed her thoroughly.

"Just wanted to see you for a minute before I start home."

"I might be finished early, and I could take you."

"Thank you, but . . . I have to get the trap home anyway. So, maybe I'll see you before supper tonight?"

"Perhaps," he said and kissed her again.

When Nadine arrived back at the inn, she felt anxious to dig into those papers, but she knew if she didn't do some laundry, she and Dulsie would have no clean underclothing the following day.

She visited comfortably with Drew and Gerda in the huge kitchen while she scrubbed clothing in the laundry tub, just as she'd done many times previously. In a large pantry area behind the kitchen was strung a clothesline that Gerda used during months when it was too cold to hang the wash outside. Nadine was hanging the last of her clean laundry when she heard a deep voice say, "You are a woman of many talents."

Nadine turned to see Lance leaning in the doorway, and she laughed softly, "Laundry is hardly a talent, Captain."

"Well, *I* don't know how to do it," he said, stepping closer. "Cameron has bragged about being able to do laundry and cooking. I think he's the only man I work with who is capable of completely surviving on his own, and he's the one with the most servants."

"Ironic," she said and put the last clothes peg in place just before he kissed her.

"Do we have a little time before you have to work?" he asked.

"An hour or so," she said.

"Good. How about an early supper together?"

"Sounds marvelous," she said and he motioned her ahead of him to leave the room. She noticed then that he was keeping one hand behind his back and she asked, "What have you got back there?"

"I'll show you once you sit down," he said with a little laugh.

They were sitting by the fire in the empty common room before he brought a wrapped package out from behind his back. "Not another gift!" she said. "You shower me with gifts. Surely I'm not deserving of such—"

"Hush," he said, pressing a finger over her lips. "You *are* deserving . . . of the best that life can give you. It's from the heart. Just open it."

Nadine sighed and pulled the paper away, realizing it was a large book, but only when she turned it over did she see that it was a Bible. "Oh, Lance," she gasped, "it's beautiful."

Lance watched her touch the cover reverently and thumb through the pages as if they were priceless. She looked up at him with tears swelling in her eyes. "I've never owned anything so dear," she said.

"Not even diamonds?" he asked and was gratified with her answer.

"No, not even diamonds . . . although they are very precious to me." She touched the cover of the book again. "Thank you," she said. "You can't know what this means to me. I've so much missed being able to read from its pages."

"I know well what you mean," he said. "You're welcome."

Nadine put her Bible in her room before she had supper with Lance and Dulsie. After they'd eaten, he took Dulsie for a walk and Nadine got to work in the kitchen. When her shift was completed she was grateful that Lance had gotten Dulsie tucked into bed.

"Thank you," she said, entering the room to find Dulsie asleep and Lance reading a book.

"I'm glad to help," he said. "You work too hard."

"I've worked much harder," she admitted, leaning over to kiss him in greeting.

She said it as if it were nothing, but Lance couldn't help thinking of the women he'd encountered in his life, women vying for his attention who considered themselves above any work beyond overseeing the menu. He took Nadine's hand and kissed it, saying warmly, "I want you to know how much I admire that."

"What?"

"The way you know how to work. But personally . . . I would prefer that you didn't have to work at all."

Nadine wanted to ask if that was meant to be some kind of implication, but he just kissed her hand again and returned his attention to his book, saying, "Let me finish this page and—"

"No, that's all right," she said. "Actually . . . I need to go through these papers so I can get them back."

While Lance read, Nadine dug into the papers that had her name on them—beginning with the newest. She became so absorbed that she was surprised at how time had passed when Lance took a break to stretch and said, "Forgive my ignorance, but I've never been aware that such records were kept. Exactly how do they record illegitimate children?"

"Well, most of them are the result of a mother coming to the government for help, and apparently there are times when the fathers have taken responsibility indirectly by using the government as a mediator to provide the funds so that anonymity could be maintained."

"It's incredible," he said, looking at the stack of papers on the table. "I had no idea that people were so promiscuous."

"Well, as I said, many of these are very old. It's likely not as bad as it looks. Still, promiscuity is as old as the world; there's plenty of it in the Bible."

"True," he said, and his voice turned sad. "I was just thinking of the heartache and struggle represented in those papers. It's difficult to imagine. And there are likely many who were never reported because they never came to us for help."

"I'm sure you're right," she said and Lance went back to his book.

Nadine finally gave her project up to visit with Lance before he had to leave. While they sat together in comfortable silence, a thought occurred to her that had troubled her a number of times, and she wondered if she dared bring it up. She had learned from her association with Nikolaus that ignoring her instincts on things that left her uneasy had set her up for a great fall. Of course, Lance was different. She believed she could actually address something uncomfortable and he would acknowledge her and help her understand. Nikolaus never would have. As for Lance, she would never know if she didn't try.

"May I say something that's . . . troubled me somewhat?"

He looked concerned and said easily, "Of course. What is it?"

"And you won't be angry?"

"No," he said with a little chuckle. "Tell me."

"Well," she said, not looking at him, "I must confess I am surprised to see the way you flirt with Her Grace."

"Flirt?" he laughed, but not in a way that felt critical. "No, that's not it, I can assure you."

"Then what exactly is it?"

"Well . . . Her Grace and I are very good friends. And I do not behave any differently with her in or out of her husband's presence."

"You blatantly adore her."

"Yes, I do," he said firmly. "Me and every other citizen of Horstberg. I'm simply privileged enough to be her friend and to have the assignment of often personally seeing to her well-being in the duke's absence."

"And he trusts you to care for his wife?"

Lance felt mildly put on trial and said, "I don't know. Why don't you ask him?"

Nadine sensed his terseness, however subtle—something she was quite unfamiliar with. She paused to consider the reasons and had to say, "Forgive me. I know this has more to do with me than you."

"If my attention to Abbi makes you uncomfortable, then we need to talk about it. You're the most important thing to me. It's never bothered Cameron because he knows me well enough to know that he can trust me completely, and I would never be alone with Abbi in a situation that was even remotely inappropriate. He also knows, as I do, that the love they share, and the way they work at keeping that love alive, is not something that would allow for mistrust. He's confident that he gives her everything she needs, and she would have no need to turn elsewhere. Cameron and Abbi know me well enough to know they can trust me. I understand that you haven't had time to know me that well, but I swear to you, Nadine, you are first and foremost to me in everything I do."

"I'm sorry," she said. "It's just that . . . I can't compete with that."

"Compete with what?"

"With a woman like the duchess. With the feelings you have for her."

Lance laughed again, and this time she wondered if he *was* laughing at her. "Oh, my dear. There is no competition." Nadine steeled herself to hear how no woman could compete with the duchess and it was something she had to live with. But she wondered for a moment if she was hearing him wrong when he said, "What I feel for you, Nadine, far surpassed what I felt for Abbi du Woernig in about twenty minutes. I love her. I honor her. My work is pledged to protect her. But what I feel for her is . . . perfectly noble and not remotely romantic. What I feel for you is . . . inexpressibly deep. It has consumed my thoughts, my heart, my soul with feelings that I had only stood back and observed in others until then. I envied the love that Cameron and Abbi shared, but I never once envied what Cameron had."

Nadine sighed and eased into his arms, admitting softly, "Oh, I love you."

"And I love you," he said, pressing his lips into her hair. "I will love you always."

"I'm glad we got that cleared up," she said.

"Me too," he added with exaggerated relief.

Lance reluctantly went home, sharing a long, warm kiss with her at the door. Once he was gone, Nadine opted to continue her project rather than going to bed. It wasn't terribly difficult to find the pages with Nikolaus du Woernig's name as the claimed father. And on every one of them that carried his name, it was written: *Father contacted. Paternity denied. Assistance to child denied.* The very idea made Nadine sick. She wrote down the names and contact information for each of the women who shared her plight and was disappointed by those that stated they had left the country. Before she went to bed, she had a list of nine women who still lived in Horstberg at the time the records were last accessed on their behalf. The following evening after work, she approached the stack again with the purpose of organizing the forms more thoroughly before she returned them. She was almost grateful that Lance had been needed at some late meetings so that she could get through them and be done with it. Once they were returned to their rightful place, she would feel more at ease. Going through the older records, Nadine concentrated mostly on the dates, wanting to be sure they were in chronological order. The oldest forms were about fifty years old, and she wondered if that was when this process had begun or if records prior to that time had been destroyed. Or perhaps they were kept elsewhere. She wondered for a moment how someone tracing their genealogy might find their ancestors when an illegitimate birth took place. Of course, there were likely family records, even if state records weren't accessible.

Nadine was struck by the name "du Woernig" on a couple of the really old forms, and realized the father of these children would be Cameron and Nikolaus's grandfather. There were two other du Woernig names, which she figured must have belonged to Cameron's great uncles. She wondered if royalty was simply prone to being promiscuous, but then she didn't have any reason to believe that Cameron wasn't loyal to Abbi. Moving forward through the years, another two du Woernig names came up as fathers of illegitimate children. One was obviously the duke—Cameron's father—and the other the duke's brother. Nadine was especially intrigued with the records relating to Cameron and Nikolaus's father. She wondered if Cameron knew he had illegitimate half-siblings. And she wondered if those half-siblings were aware of the blood connection—a connection that could never be acknowledged publicly, for many reasons.

But Nadine found an interesting contrast in the records of Nikolaus's father as opposed to Nikolaus. There were three forms, for three different children, and on each of them was written: *Paternity volunteered and verified. Assistance given.* Whatever Ferdinand du Woernig may or may not have been, he had taken accountability for his children.

Nadine barely glanced over the names of the women and children tied to the du Woernig family, wondering about their stories. Had these women loved the duke? Had he loved them? Or had their affairs simply been sordid and a convenient distraction for the ruler of a country? Nadine felt a distinct heartache for these women and children, wondering what they might have made of their lives. And then she found herself looking at a name that jumped into her heart. *Katarina Dukerk.* She held her breath, convincing herself that it had to be a coincidence. Surely there were many Dukerks in this country. She forced her eyes down the page, then she started breathing so hard she feared she would pass out. It took several minutes to get hold of herself and to be convinced that what she saw was real. Through a sleepless night she wondered: Did he know? Did *anybody* know? And now that she knew, what was she supposed to do about it? Through much prayer and consideration, she came to a conclusion and was determined to see to it as soon as she arrived at the castle.

She purposely arrived early, and once Dulsie was safely in the nursery, she first took the box of records back to where they belonged, except for the page in question. Then she steeled herself and pondered once more if this was the right course to take. And in her heart she knew it was.

Nadine approached the officers at the door of the ducal office, hoping that in spite of the personal association she'd developed with the duke, he would not deem this an inappropriate move. "Is His Grace available?" she asked one of the men in uniform.

"One moment," he said and knocked at the door before he pushed it open. "Mrs. Rader would like a moment," he said. "Should I tell her to come back when—"

"No, no," she heard Cameron say, "send her in. Thank you."

Nadine stepped into the room, relieved to see only Georg there with him. She knew enough of the workings of the country, as well as the friendship shared by these two men, to know that there were no secrets between them. And, according to Abbi, Cameron would go to Georg for advice in any matter. The men both came to their feet as the door was closed behind her.

"How are you today, Mrs. Rader?" Cameron asked.

"I'm well, and you?"

"Very well, thank you."

"Have a seat," Georg said, motioning her toward a chair.

They were all seated before Nadine forced out her memorized preamble. "I understand that Her Grace spoke with you about my wanting to find women who shared my circumstances, so that we could perhaps help each other."

"She did, yes," Cameron said. "An excellent plan, I think. Let me know how it goes."

"I will, thank you. The thing is . . . the records I was given went back many years, and they were terribly disorganized. I took it upon myself to put them in better order before I returned them, and now I'm wishing that I hadn't." She watched the duke's countenance darken. He and Georg exchanged a concerned glance. "I'm afraid I discovered something that I shouldn't have, and yet, considering my . . . involvement, I have to wonder if perhaps . . . I was meant to. I wondered what to do, who to talk to, and . . . I felt you should know, and you can decide what—if anything—should be done."

Cameron glanced at the yellowed paper in her hand and said, "Let me see what you have there."

Nadine slid the paper across the desk while her heart beat painfully hard. She watched Cameron slowly put on his glasses. He looked at her almost fearfully over the top of them before he focused his eyes on the paper in his hands. Nadine wasn't surprised by the way he sucked in his breath, nor his astonished expression. But she hadn't expected him to press a hand over his mouth while a hint of moisture appeared on the rims of his eyes.

"Heaven be merciful," he muttered and tossed the paper scorn-fully to the desk. His glasses followed, and he erupted from his chair, turning his back abruptly. She felt almost afraid as he leaned his hands on the windowsill and hung his head. She could hear his breathing turn sharp and watched his shoulders rise and fall. Nadine glanced toward Georg, startled to see him visibly upset. He had always been so calm, so controlled.

The duke's reaction spurred Nadine's emotion and she couldn't keep from crying as she said, "Was I wrong to tell you, Your Grace? I didn't know what to do. I just . . ."

"No, you weren't wrong, Nadine," he said in a voice that was barely steady, and she couldn't recall his ever using her given name before. "Such secrets should not be kept, in my opinion. I just don't know what the hell to do about it."

Nadine sensed Georg's curiosity, as well as his concern, but he said nothing, as if he would allow Cameron to determine how and when he should know. Following minutes of grueling silence, Cameron finally said, "Georg."

"Yes, Your Grace," he said as if they weren't the very best of friends.

"Would you go and get Abbi please, and postpone this morning's meeting; put it back an hour."

"Of course," Georg said and quickly left the room.

When the silence persisted, Nadine said, "I . . . don't know what to say, Your Grace. I . . ."

"I don't know what to say, either. I just . . . can't believe it. I can't even get my thoughts to come together. But Abbi will know what to do. She has a way of seeing things that I can never quite grasp."

He said nothing more, but he did finally turn away from the window and sit back down. He put his glasses on and looked at the paper again, shaking his head in disbelief. They were both startled when the door came open.

"What is it?" Abbi said, rushing to her husband's side as Georg closed the door and leaned against it. Cameron rose to take her in his arms, holding her tightly for a long moment. He drew back to meet her eyes and she asked, "What's happened? Georg said you were upset."

"Yes, I am," he said. "You'd better sit down." They were all seated in chairs around the desk, except for Cameron, who sat on the edge of the desk and folded his arms over his chest. "It would seem," he said in a voice of reasoned sovereignty, "that my father, the former Duke of Horstberg, had a significant affair with a woman named Katarina Dukerk." Nadine sensed Georg and Abbi holding their breath. "Lance Dukerk is the result."

Abbi gasped and put a hand to her heart. Georg muttered a stunned, "Unbelievable!"

"Does he know?" Abbi asked.

"No, I'm certain he doesn't," Cameron said. "The question is *should* he know?"

Nadine watched Cameron turn to his wife, clearly expecting her to spout off some glorious words of wisdom, but she only stared back at him, visibly dumbfounded. "I honestly don't know," she said and Cameron sighed. "I would think he *should,* and yet his knowing could be so . . . difficult, especially considering . . . well, just considering the kind of man he is. I don't believe he would take such news well."

"Whatever the outcome," Nadine said, "I feel that I must step back and have no further involvement. I can be there to support him through whatever comes of this, but we're talking about a situation involving the royal family. I will say nothing more about this until he chooses to come to me concerning the matter, if that ever happens."

Abbi looked hard at Nadine, then she turned to Cameron. "Forgive me if I'm being presumptuous here, but I know that Nadine's relationship with Lance is progressing quickly. If they do end up together permanently, could we possibly expect a woman to spend the rest of her life knowing something like that about her husband and not feeling at liberty to discuss it? I think such a thing would be maddening, perhaps even destructive to what they share. I think it would be better for him to know, but . . . I'm not sure the best way to go about it."

"Perhaps we just need to give the matter some time," Georg suggested. "Some prayer wouldn't hurt, either."

"Indeed." Cameron sighed and shook his head. "I can't believe it. I just can't believe it."

Nadine was overtaken by a fresh surge of emotion that she found impossible to hold back. Tears came as she admitted, "I should have just . . . minded my own business, and we all could have gone on with our lives as they are, and no one would have ever known."

Georg said gently, "Didn't I hear you mention that considering the situation, perhaps you were *meant* to find this? As difficult as this is, I have a deep belief in divine providence. It seems a little too coincidental to me that *you* of all people would uncover this."

"I agree," Cameron said. "And I agree that we just need to give the matter some time." He rose and reached out a hand toward Nadine.

She slipped hers into his and he said, "Thank you for bringing the matter to my attention. We will handle it discreetly, I assure you."

"Thank you, Your Grace," she said and came to her feet. "I should get . . . to work." She nodded toward Abbi. "I'll see you upstairs whenever you're ready, Your Grace."

"I'll be along shortly," Abbi said, and Nadine left the room. Once she was past sight of the officers waiting for orders in the hall, she slipped into a little-used room and cried. When she felt that she could go about her duties and not be conspicuously upset, she went upstairs and found no one there. She got to work without Abbi and was managing to keep herself distracted until the duchess walked into the room and closed the door, which she usually left open. Their eyes met and there was no denying the reflection she saw there of her own emotion.

"I can't believe it," Abbi said, crossing the room.

"Neither can I," Nadine said. "I've heard him talk about his upbringing, the stability he found from his father in spite of certain challenges. I can't even imagine how he'll adjust to something like this."

"Nor can I," Abbi said. They talked it through for a long while, and Nadine felt better in having someone who shared her secret and also shared her love and concern for Lance. One of Nadine's greatest concerns was wondering if she had been wrong to go snooping through the records to begin with, but looking back she knew that her feelings had been strong about doing so. Abbi validated her feelings when she said that she strongly believed it had happened that way for a reason, and there was no room for regret.

Lance came in a few minutes before noon and Nadine was grateful for Abbi's example of showing him a normally bright smile, as if nothing in the world were wrong.

"Hey," he said, "the duke invited me to join him for lunch. I was hoping you ladies would be there."

"I'm going to be there," Abbi said. "How about you, Nadine?"

"If I'm invited, I'll certainly be there."

"*You* are with *me,*" he said, putting her hand over his arm.

Nadine enjoyed lunch very much, in spite of the fact that everyone sitting at the table knew something about Lance that he didn't know. She sensed the subtle gravity in their eyes, but was grateful that Lance didn't seem to sense it.

The evening went well in spite of her heavy heart. Lance took Dulsie for a while and read her stories again while Nadine finished her work. They talked until late, and when he sensed her somber mood, she just insisted that she was tired. She thought about what Abbi had said, however, and had to agree. Her deepest hope was that she and Lance would be together forever. And she could never spend her entire life married to a man, knowing such a thing about him and not being able to discuss it.

The following day Abbi sent a note to the inn rather early, stating that she would be with her husband for the day, accompanying him on some ducal business, and that Nadine should take the day off. Nadine decided it would be a perfect day to search out the women on her list. Dulsie was disappointed about not going to the castle nursery to play with her friends, so Nadine opted to take her there anyway since it might not be good to take her along on her quest. She had no idea what to expect.

The day ended up being a success and a failure. Of the nine women on her list, she found out that three of them had moved, and as far as neighbors knew, they had left the country. Nadine could understand why it would be difficult to raise one of Nikolaus's children in this country. She was grateful that in spite of Dulsie favoring her father's looks, it was not nearly so obvious as it had been with the boy she'd seen in town.

Three of the women were reported by family to be at work or out, but she was invited to try back. By the end of the day she made contact with all six. Two of them were cool and guarded but didn't seem upset by her visit. She wrote down her name and where to find her if they changed their mind and wanted to talk to her. One woman was angry and slammed the door in her face. The remaining three actually invited her in, eager to talk and seemingly grateful for her visit. One of those three was by far the most bitter and angry person Nadine had ever encountered. The child she had conceived through Nikolaus had been sent to live with relatives in another country because, as she had put it, "She couldn't bear to look at him." Her age and appearance actually reminded Nadine of herself. Beyond stark differences in their facial features, she was amazed at the similarities, and she had to wonder if Nikolaus had been attracted to a certain type of woman. Another stark difference was the fact that this woman's entire aura was as dark as her home began to feel while Nadine listened to her acrid diatribe. She listened and attempted to validate the woman's feelings and give her some direction toward coming to terms with it and being able to let go. But the woman wouldn't hear of it. She considered it her right and privilege to hate Nikolaus du Woernig, and she would die doing so. Nadine was relieved to be out of her home and on her way.

Of the remaining two that invited Nadine in, one was very kind and even fed Nadine lunch while they visited. But this woman was so different from Nadine that she simply couldn't relate to her. She seemed to be well adjusted and happy, however, and that was good.

The best visit of all ended up being her last stop. This woman was warm and friendly and very open with her past experiences, making it clear that she had healed from Nikolaus's betrayal and had put the past behind her. This woman had also been the victim of a mock marriage and had believed that he loved her and would eventually make her the queen of Horstberg. But she had now forgiven Nikolaus. She was married to a farmer who treated her well. And she was happy. Nadine found that she admired this woman and felt grateful for the feelings that had spurred her to this meeting. They shared a hug when Nadine was leaving, and they promised to keep in touch. Nadine didn't know if that would ever happen, but she was grateful for the example she'd seen today of what forgiveness could do to a woman, as opposed to holding onto bitterness and anger. She knew which kind of woman she wanted to be.

On the way home, Nadine realized that the woman she'd seen in town had not been among those she'd met today. Of course, Nikolaus likely had spread himself among many women who'd had no need to go to the government for help. But she felt content in her search and returned to the inn with a light heart.

That evening she told Lance all about her adventure and he seemed pleased. The following day she repeated it all again to Abbi and they had a long, wonderful visit about the glory of forgiveness.

The next day Nadine was approached at breakfast by Gerda. "I wanted to talk with you," she said. "I know you're enjoying your work with the duchess, and I know she can afford to pay you better than we can. We've had a girl that used to work here come back and asking for some hours; she's come upon some hard times. Would you feel all right about cutting back on your hours? You're still welcome to use the room as long as you need."

"That would be fine," Nadine said. "I can afford to give you some money for room and board. In truth, I would like to have more time to spend with the captain."

"As you should," Gerda said. "I'll let you know how we'll schedule it then."

Nadine actually felt some relief. She didn't want to leave Drew and Gerda in a bind, but she was finding her evening shift tiresome. She sensed that Lance would prefer she wasn't working, but he likely would not ask her to make such changes under the circumstances.

A few minutes after Gerda returned to the kitchen, a message arrived for Nadine from Castle Horstberg. She was again not required to go into work because the duchess would be doing other things. Lance got wind of her time off and was able to find some free hours himself. Nadine wore the new scarf Lance had given her, liking the way it went well with a black and white striped jacket she had been given the day she arrived in Horstberg. He picked up her and Dulsie and took them into town. After several hours, he asked Dulsie if she would like to go play at the castle since he'd remembered he needed to check on something. Nadine took Dulsie to the nursery while Lance went to his office, and then she went back to meet him there. She waited only a few minutes for Lance to finish up, then they walked out into the courtyard and he asked, "Since I have you here with time on your hands, would you like to see where I live?"

"Oh, I would," she said with enthusiasm. He'd told her it was an apartment in the castle compound. She knew the castle was like a small community in itself, but when he led her to where the apartments were located, she was surprised to see two long, open-air corridors moving off of the central courtyard. The corridors divided the rows of apartments like miniature streets. She was also surprised by the size of the apartments as they walked to the one where he lived. She'd imagined it to be something small and adequate for a military bachelor, but when he opened the front door and motioned for her to enter, she was taken aback.

"Oh, it's lovely," she said with enthusiasm, and he seemed pleased.

To one side of the entry hall was a spacious parlor, to the other a small library behind glass French doors, and in front of her was an elegant staircase. He showed her around the main floor, through the kitchen, the breakfast room, and the formal dining room. When she commented on it being so tidy, he told her that he paid a woman to come in regularly and keep it clean, although he admitted that he was rarely at home so it didn't require much maintenance beyond keeping the dust from gathering.

"And do you ever eat here?" she asked.

"Not much," he admitted with a chuckle. "There's some minimal food kept on hand that won't spoil easily; enough that I could dig up a meal or two and not starve to death. I'm not capable of cooking much, but I can make a decent pot of coffee."

He took her up the stairs and showed her two guest bedrooms that were furnished minimally and never used. There was also a sitting room with a lovely view of the forest below the east side of the castle. The last room he showed her was his own bedroom, the only room that truly looked lived in. It wasn't messy, but the bed, though made, looked rumpled as if he'd sat there to pull on his boots. Books were scattered on the bedside tables, a couple of empty glasses were lying about, and the wardrobe had been left open to reveal his clothing hanging there. She was surprised, though she realized she shouldn't have been, to see that he had several uniforms and that some were more formal than others. She briefly recalled events where she had seen him wearing dress uniform.

She turned to fully absorb the room and how it represented his personality, from the paintings on the walls to the dark colors in the draperies and rugs. Again she said, "Oh, it's lovely."

"You like it then?" he asked, kissing her hand.

"I do!"

"Well," he glanced around, "I like it too. I've considered having a home built in the country somewhere. And while I sometimes wish for a yard and a garden, I fear I would not be able to do much with either at this time of my life. Being here I can be available if I'm needed and still be home. If I had a family, it might be different."

Lance waited for a reaction, but she just continued looking around herself, as if the room was thoroughly fascinating. He couldn't see the appeal, personally. Still watching her, he added, "If you would prefer a home in the country, it wouldn't be a problem."

This time she reacted. She turned to look at him abruptly, her eyes filled with question.

"What are you saying?" she asked, sounding more defensive than pleased.

Lance took a deep breath and said softly, "We need to talk, Nadine."

"I'm listening," she said in the same tone.

Lance took both her hands into his, hoping that what he had to say would soften her. Either way, he knew he had to forge ahead. He simply couldn't go on without letting her know exactly where he stood. "I've never felt this way before, Nadine. Something powerful and overwhelming has taken control of me, and there's only one thing I can do."

The hope that lit her eyes was undeniable, but her voice still rang with skepticism. Considering her past, he couldn't blame her. "And what is that?" she asked.

"I want to take care of you, Nadine. I want to give you a home where you can live in peace and security. I want to provide your every need and to be a father to Dulsie. I want to be the only man in your life for the rest of your life."

Nadine took a step back, attempting to take in what he was saying. His sincerity was evident. But so was his message. She turned her back abruptly, unable to help the curt tone when she said, "I've been told more than once that a woman in my position can't expect anything better than to be set up by a man who can afford to do such things, but it's not in me to settle for such an arrangement. I'm sorry to disappoint you but—"

"Nadine!" His voice nearly squeaked as he perceived what she was saying. "You can't possibly think that I would . . ." Not knowing how to put it, he took hold of her arm and touched her chin, forcing her to look at him. "I'm asking you to marry me, Nadine. Nothing less would ever do."

Nadine looked up at him, feeling moisture burn into her eyes. He pressed a hand over her face, murmuring softly, "You're a good woman, Nadine. You deserve the best this life can give you. And I intend to prove it."

Still seeing a measure of doubt in her eyes, Lance quickly analyzed where it might be coming from and sought to alleviate it. "And we will have the biggest wedding this country has seen since Cameron married Abbi. I want to marry you in the cathedral, for the whole world to see that you are mine, and I am yours." Tears in her eyes urged him to add, "No secrets, Nadine. No room for you to have to wonder if it's real. We will have a wedding bound by holy authority and sanctioned by God. Nothing less would ever do."

Nadine absorbed the sincerity of his words that so vividly matched the honesty in his eyes. Her own eyes filled with mist just before he dropped to one knee, pressing a fist over his heart and taking her hand into his. "Marry me, Nadine. And I will devote my life to your happiness and security, and I will make Dulsie my own."

"Yes, of course. Yes," she said tearfully. He laughed and stood to take her into his arms, lifting her off the floor as he turned around quickly and they laughed together. She'd never felt so happy, not even when Nikolaus du Woernig had told her he would marry her. There was no comparison.

Chapter Fourteen
MANIFESTATION OF A DREAM

"I want to be married soon," Lance said, setting her down. "Well, I know we need a little time, because I want you to have a wedding fit for a queen, but . . . I was thinking about Christmas coming. Through all the holiday celebrations I usually spend time with my stepmother and her sister, and Cameron and Abbi are always gracious about including me, but it's not the same as having a family of my own. I was thinking how nice it would be for us to be married before Christmas and to have our own celebrations—you, me, and Dulsie. What do you think?"

"I think it sounds wonderful," she laughed, "but I don't know the first thing about planning a wedding."

"I think we both know someone who does," he said and took her by the hand. "Come along. I think Abbi should be the first to know. She should be back from her appointment by now, because Cameron should be in a meeting."

Nadine laughed again as he urged her down the stairs, outside, and across the courtyard. Just inside the main castle entrance, he glanced both ways to be assured they were alone before he kissed her long and hard. "You've made me the happiest man alive," he said and kissed her again before they hurried up the stairs.

They found Abbi at her desk in her office. Lance knocked on the open door and she looked up, "Good day, Your Grace. How have you fared without us?"

Abbi stood to greet them in the same moment she noticed the white scarf around Nadine's neck. She tried to tell herself to keep a straight face and not let on to her thoughts, but she was so deeply struck by the image that her chest tightened and she suddenly found it difficult to breathe. She reached for the back of the chair and gasped for breath, vaguely aware of Lance rushing to her side.

"Abbi, what is it?" he demanded, pushing his arms around her.

She leaned gratefully against him, muttering breathlessly, "It's nothing. I just . . . stood up too fast, I suppose. I'll be fine."

Lance lifted her into his arms and put her carefully on one of the sofas, while Nadine put a pillow beneath her head. "Will you be all right?" Nadine asked.

"Oh, of course I will," she said, embarrassed by their attention.

"What's wrong?" Lance demanded. "It looked like more than just getting a little lightheaded. Tell me what happened. Should I send for the doctor?"

"No, of course not," she insisted. "I'm fine."

"Then tell me what happened, or I will not only send for him, I'll tell your husband that you've been—"

"There's no need to tell him anything, and there's no need for you to be concerned," she insisted. To Nadine she said, "Could you get me some water please, dear?"

"Of course," Nadine said and went into the next room to get it.

"Not now," Abbi said to him in a whisper. "I need to talk to you, but not now."

"Did something upset you?" he asked just as quietly.

She nodded just as Nadine returned with the water and Lance was left feeling frustrated and helpless, wondering what on earth could have spurred such a reaction in Abbi—that she didn't want to discuss in front of Nadine.

"Thank you," Abbi said and sat up with Lance's help to drink it. "I'm fine now, really." She reached up a hand to touch the white scarf hanging around her neck. "It's beautiful. Wherever did you get it?"

"I took your advice and bought her gifts the other day," Lance said and tried to ignore the vague alarm in Abbi's eyes.

"What else did you buy her?" Abbi asked and Nadine reached into her handbag for the perfume. The women both smelled it and fussed over its lovely fragrance. Abbi put some on Lance's face and said, "Your men will know you've been consorting with a woman."

"They already do," he laughed. "Besides, I don't need gossip. I intend to tell the world this afternoon that I am officially unavailable."

"Really?" Abbi looked pleasantly distracted from whatever had been troubling her. "Do tell."

Lance nodded toward Nadine, who grinned at Abbi and said, "The captain has asked me to marry him."

Abbi smiled, but when she turned to look at him, there was something bordering on tragic in her eyes. "How marvelous," she said as if she truly meant it. She threw her arms around his neck. "Oh, it's wonderful. You so deserve to be happy." She touched Nadine's face then hugged her as well. "Both of you."

They talked with Abbi about wanting to be married soon, and she helped them come up with a feasible plan. It was Abbi's idea to use the party two days before Christmas to double as a wedding celebration. They could be married in the morning and simply add a receiving line in the midst of the other activities through the afternoon and evening. She pointed out that everyone there would likely be on Lance's guest list anyway, and either of them were welcome to add names to that list. They both liked the idea, which would prevent them from having to be busy with elaborate wedding plans, and since Nadine knew practically no one, she was thrilled to have it work out this way. The wedding was still over a month away, but at least they would be married before Christmas, as Lance had wished.

When they had talked everything through, Lance left the ladies to get some work done before Nadine had to leave.

"Where are you going?" Nadine asked.

"I may not know much about planning weddings, but I do know how to post a proclamation, and this one will be all over town before sunset if I have my way."

Nadine laughed and watched him leave the room. She turned to Abbi and said, "I'm just so perfectly happy."

Abbi's smile didn't seem completely genuine, but Nadine credited it to her not feeling well. "As you should be," Abbi said. "You could not have won the love of a finer man."

As soon as Lance had the official proclamation written up and put into the hands of those who would copy and post it about town, he returned to Abbi's rooms and found the two women still visiting. He joined them for a short while, then he and Nadine went to get Dulsie from the nursery, and he took the two of them home. Claiming that some things had come up he needed to see to, he left and returned to the castle and immediately sought out Abbi in her sitting room. He quietly entered the open door to find her sitting on the sofa with her feet up, staring at nothing, her countenance troubled.

"How about now?" he asked, startling her.

She said nothing, but her expression betrayed that she knew well what he meant—and she didn't want to talk about it. He sat down at the other end of the sofa and added, "What is it you need to tell me that you couldn't tell me in front of Nadine? I'm assuming it's the same something that upset you so badly that you could hardly breathe. And you were fine until we walked in the door. Talk to me, Your Grace."

The anxiety he was trying to talk himself out of rushed forward with fury when Abbi hung her head and quietly sobbed. "Abbi, what is it?" he asked, moving closer and pulling her into his arms, where she cried against his shoulder. "Talk to me."

"I had a dream," she said and Lance sucked in his breath. Having once been betrothed to Abbi, he was one of few people who knew the significance of her dreams and how they had guided her to Cameron and to his reclaiming of the duchy. In the time since, Abbi had shared some of her dreams with him, and he'd been astounded by her gift. But now, putting together what little he knew in relation to a dream made him heartsick.

Attempting to remain calm and not jump to conclusions, he asked, "Who was the dream about, Abbi?"

"I don't know. The face was obscure, but . . . everything else about her fits Nadine perfectly. And in the dream she was . . . wearing a scarf, a white silk scarf—exactly like the one Nadine is wearing now."

Lance felt his breathing sharpen but he kept his voice steady as he said, "Tell me the rest."

"I don't want to," she said, "but I fear if I don't she could be even more vulnerable. Why would I be given such a dream if it wasn't to warn us? Or is it simply meant to prepare us for something that will inevitably happen and would be impossible to prevent? I don't understand," she said and sobbed so hard she couldn't speak.

"Abbi, you're scaring me."

"Well, I'm scared too!" she shouted.

He took her face into his hands and demanded quietly, "Tell me, Abbi. I have to know."

She visibly made an effort to calm down, but she squeezed her eyes closed as she spoke, as if she couldn't face him. "I saw a woman," she began, her voice trembling, "her face was obscure but in every way she is the same as Nadine—her age, her coloring, the way she was dressed. *That white scarf.* I told you to buy her a gift, and with everything you could have bought, it would be *that* gift. I don't understand."

"Tell me, Abbi. What happened to the woman in the dream?"

Abbi hung her head. "She was murdered, Lance," she said and he couldn't breathe. "She was stabbed through the heart with a dagger—a dagger with a carved ivory handle." She sobbed again and Lance just held her, trembling from the inside out. In his mind he tried to discredit the dream, but he couldn't. He couldn't suddenly stop respecting something he'd always respected simply because it didn't suit him. Abbi obviously couldn't discredit it, or she wouldn't be falling apart.

"When did you have this dream, Abbi?" he asked, unbelievably calm on the surface while his insides roiled.

"Several times," she said, "but the first was . . . the night before Nadine arrived in Horstberg."

He sighed and squeezed his eyes closed while she continued to cry.

"What's wrong?" a deep voice startled them and Cameron entered the room, but Abbi made no effort to retract from Lance's embrace. Cameron squatted beside them and met Lance's eyes with concern.

"Did you just *know* something was wrong, or what?" Lance asked him.

"Yes, actually. I think I did," Cameron said. "I just . . . felt like you needed me," he added more to Abbi, pressing a hand over her face. "What is it, my love?"

Abbi didn't answer; she just cried harder. Cameron looked to Lance, who was forced to answer his question. "She just told me about the dream she's been having."

"Oh, I see," Cameron said and sat down on the sofa, on the other side of Abbi. "Come here," he said, easing her away from Lance and into his own arms. "There's nothing you can do about it, my darling. You can't let it get to you this way. You'll make yourself sick." He pressed a kiss into her hair and held her closer.

"Then why?" she asked through her tears.

"I don't know," Cameron said. "I don't know."

"The scarf," she said. "Nadine has the scarf."

"The white one?" Cameron asked and Lance's stomach tightened. Why white? His only thought when he'd bought it was that it seemed to enhance her natural glow.

Abbi nodded and Lance considered what he knew that they didn't know. He only had to wonder for a moment if he should tell them. If Abbi ever found out that he'd known such a thing and not told her, she would be furious. And given the widening scope of the situation, Cameron needed to be aware as well. He was the ruler of this country. They were partnered in trying to keep it strong and safe.

"Um . . ." Lance cleared his throat. "There's something you need to know."

"What?" Abbi sat up and turned toward him, keeping a tight hold on Cameron's arm. They both looked to him with expectancy.

"Nadine is being stalked." Abbi gasped. Cameron's eyes widened and became angry. "Apparently he set his sights on her a long time ago and caused problems for her when she spurned him. When she came to Horstberg, she had felt confident that she'd been careful enough that he hadn't followed her. But she has seen him a number of times since her arrival here."

"Oh, good heavens," Abbi said. "You have to find this man."

"I'm going to do everything I can to find him, Abbi. But there are a lot of people in this country. A lot of places to hide. And someone like that is going to be very careful and clever. I will do everything in my power. That's all I can do."

Lance came to his feet and Abbi asked, "Where are you going?"

"I've got a criminal to track down," he said. "I pray to God that we can find him before he does something unspeakable."

Lance hurried from the room and to his office while questions pounded through his head. Would he truly lose Nadine to this horror? Were Abbi's dreams meant to prepare him? What could he do beyond everything in his power to protect her? Not get too emotionally involved? He already was! He'd fallen in love with her almost immediately. To think of holding back was ludicrous. Could he protect her enough to see that this didn't happen? Not without putting her under continual lock and key. But there were things he *could* do, and for that reason he considered his position a blessing.

He called together the lieutenants on duty and stated firmly, "We have a stalker, and we have good reason to believe that he's capable of murder." He felt good about the way he'd put that. He doubted they'd be interested in hearing about premonitory dreams. He pointed at each of them as he delegated orders. "You will come with me to get a full report and description from the woman he's following. You will set up twenty-four watch for this woman. You will see that the description and circumstances are passed accurately to every shift."

"Who is this woman?" one of them asked.

"Nadine Rader," he said.

"The woman you've been seeing?" another one interjected, appalled and compassionate.

"Yes," Lance said. "More accurately, the woman I'm going to marry."

They offered congratulations and assured him they would get on their assignments before Lance left with Lieutenant Brueger to go to the inn. They entered to find only a couple of customers since the rush hadn't yet begun. Nadine smiled when she saw him. He tried to smile back, and he could see that she sensed his concern. He sent the lieutenant to the kitchen to inform them that they needed to speak with Nadine for a few minutes. Gerda came back with him and said quietly, "Is something wrong?"

"Yes. I'll explain after we talk with Mrs. Rader. If you'd cover for her, it shouldn't take long."

"Of course," Gerda said.

Nadine watched Lance approach her with an officer at his shoulder, and she knew something was wrong. "This is business," he muttered when he was close enough for her to hear. "Would you sit for a few minutes?"

"Of course," she said and the three of them sat at a table.

The lieutenant pulled out a pad and pencil as Lance said, "Would you please tell us, as close as you can, what Mr. Crider looks like."

"Uh . . ." Nadine tried to ignore the severity in Lance's eyes and treat this for what it was; they were trying to help her. "He's a little taller than average, but not too much. Not quite as tall as you." She nodded at Lance. "He's in his middle to late forties, I would guess. His hair is . . . brown, dark brown. And wiry. He has a bald spot on top of his head, and the rest of his hair is just kind of a little too long and . . . wiry. His eyes are . . . brown as well. He's thin. He's built like . . . the perfume vendor. His chin is wide—kind of square. His nose is long and narrow. His brows thick and dark."

"That's a very impressive description," Lieutenant Brueger said.

"His face haunts me," she said, shuddering visibly.

"All right," Lance said, "now we need to know exactly when and where each of your sightings were."

Nadine repeated everything while the lieutenant took notes. By the time they were finished, the dining room was filling up. As they all stood, Nadine said quietly to Lance, "What's going on?"

"We just want to get this guy," Lance said. "We'll talk later. In the meantime, do not leave here. At all."

"I won't," she said. "You'll be back later?"

"Of course," he said and kissed her hand.

Lance took a minute with Drew and Gerda in the kitchen to warn them to keep doors and windows locked and to keep an eye on Nadine. They agreed to take every precaution and to assist the officers that would be on duty.

Lance sent Lieutenant Brueger back to the castle to get the information officially recorded and distributed to every officer. He found himself wandering around outside of the inn, examining the situation. He was relieved to see that there was no easy access to Nadine's window, no trees or outcropping of roof that could leave her room vulnerable. When he went back around to the front of the inn, he was pleased to see an officer casually ambling back and forth.

"Good evening," Lance said.

"Captain," he replied eagerly, going to attention.

"At ease. What were your orders?" he asked, if only to ascertain that the situation was being taken care of as he'd intended.

"To patrol the inn, inside and out, at regular intervals. And if

Mrs. Rader leaves, I shall accompany her safely to her destination and back again."

"Very good," Lance said. "I hope you're bundled up well."

"Indeed, I am, sir. Thank you."

Lance went inside and had his supper while the last of the crowd slowly filtered away. His thoughts became freshly consumed by the reality of what he was facing. While he anticipated Nadine being done with her shift so that he could be with her, he dreaded having to tell her what she had to know. It seemed forever before Dulsie was finally asleep and they were sitting together by the fire. He was wondering how to approach the subject when she said, "Why the new precautions, Lance? Drew told me there would be an officer on duty at all times."

"That's right. Drew and Gerda will be giving him a key so that he can go in and out as he needs during the hours that the inn is closed. I'm only putting my best men on this. They have been given orders that you will not be going anywhere without being accompanied. They will escort you to the castle and back. They will go shopping with you if I am not available. There will be no exceptions. Do you understand?"

Nadine felt startled and afraid to see his intensity. "I understand, and I'm grateful, but . . . why? Do you really think he's that dangerous? I mean . . . it's unnerving to have him stalking me. I don't want him to cause any trouble, but . . . dangerous?"

"Nadine," he said gently, taking both her hands into his, "what I am going to tell you may sound strange, but . . . hear me out."

"All right."

"Abbi has this . . . gift. The gift of dreams. Many times in her life she has been given dreams that were premonitory. In fact, a dream led her to Cameron when he was hidden in a mountain lodge in exile. You must hear her tell you herself of those experiences. I only know that I'm convinced the gift is real, and I have a deep respect for it."

Nadine let his explanation settle into her before she asked, "Are you trying to tell me that Abbi had a dream . . . related to this . . . situation?"

"I don't know if it's related or not, but it's too much coincidence for me."

"What did she dream? Was it me?"

"She said the face was obscure, but in every other way, it was you. And in the dream, this woman had a white silk scarf around her neck."

Nadine gasped. "Is that why she became so upset today . . . when she saw us?"

"That's why," he said. "Nadine, she had this dream the night before you arrived in Horstberg, and many times since. I don't know what it means, but I'm going to do everything in my power to see that you are safe."

"Tell me," she said, her voice trembling.

"The woman . . . in her dream was . . . murdered." Lance felt her hands trembling in his. He hurried to add, "We are going to keep you safe, Nadine, at all costs. Just do as I ask, and pay attention to your instincts, and we can prevent this from happening."

She nodded but he wondered if she believed him. He pulled her tightly into his arms, muttering with fervor, "I will not lose you to this, Nadine. I will not!" She nodded again but nothing was said for several minutes.

Lance finally lifted her chin with his finger and kissed her long and hard, if only for the sake of distraction. She responded eagerly and he found the distraction was working for him as well.

"Hey," he said, smiling at her, "I told my stepmother I was going to ask you to marry me, and she wants to meet you. We're invited to dinner tomorrow evening. Do you think you could get the evening off? I know it's difficult for Drew and Gerda, but—"

"Actually," she said, realizing she'd forgotten to tell him, "I'll be cutting back my hours. I won't be needing to work every evening since there's a girl who needs the work more than me. And I'm fine with that, so . . . we'll have more time together."

"Really?" he said, grinning widely. "I like that idea very much."

"Yes, so do I," she said and he kissed her again. Nadine felt certain if he kissed her enough, she might actually forget that she had somehow become a candidate for murder.

Nadine received a message the following morning that Abbi would be coming for her with a carriage and that they needed to go into town and do some shopping. A couple of officers escorted them continually, but Nadine enjoyed the excursion nevertheless, grateful for the distraction. Some of their errands were related to the work Nadine had been hired to do for Abbi, but the bulk of their time out was spent ordering a wedding gown for Nadine, as well as a few other dresses that Abbi insisted she order. They also ordered a dress for Dulsie for the wedding.

"Your fiancé can afford it," Abbi said, "I assure you. If he didn't have to attend all those insipid socials, you wouldn't need such fine clothing. So, it's his fault you need these gowns, and he'll be glad to pay for them."

Nadine couldn't help feeling delighted as she was pampered and fussed over by the dressmaker, and it was evident that gossip was spreading about the captain's forthcoming marriage.

Following their shopping, Nadine had very little time to freshen up before Lance came for her and Dulsie. She thoroughly enjoyed her evening with Lance's stepmother, Ramona Dukerk, and Ramona's sister, Salina. They were both English women, and in fact were aunts to Abbi's deceased mother, which was how Lance and Abbi had met. Nadine was fascinated to realize that their home was once owned by Abbi's grandfather and was where Abbi had been living prior to her marriage to the duke. In fact, Abbi's father, Gerhard Albrecht, also lived there, and at one time Georg had worked for the Albrechts before he'd joined the duke as his highest advisor. Nadine now understood that Georg and Abbi had been friends for many years since he had been the stablemaster on this estate where she'd grown up.

On their way back to town in the carriage, Lance asked, "Did you have a good time?"

"Oh, I did. They were delightful. All of them."

"They certainly loved you; that was evident."

"Was it?" she asked.

"Oh, yes. But it's not a surprise. I certainly love you," he said and kissed her.

"I love you too, Captain," she said and put her head on his shoulder. Only then did it occur to her that if Ramona was Lance's stepmother, perhaps she knew something about the affair between her husband's first wife and the duke. She put her arms more tightly

ing forward to it. But she loved him and he loved her, and together they would get through anything.

The following evening, Nadine worked at the inn while Lance was needed in meetings and she didn't see him at all. Near the end of her shift, Drew handed her a note.

"What is this?" she asked.

"I don't know. A customer handed it to me, asked me to give it to you. A woman."

Nadine opened the little paper to read an address not far away with eleven o'clock written below it. She felt certain it had to be from one of the women she'd invited to contact her. She never would have considered going out except that she knew an officer was outside the door, and he would accompany her.

Nadine asked Gerda to be aware of Dulsie while she went out, then she stepped outside and said to the officer waiting there, "Would you walk with me, please?"

"A pleasure, madame," he said.

They chatted comfortably while she found the address. It was a home she'd not been to before, but perhaps this woman might have preferred being contacted at the home of a friend or relative. The home was situated only a short distance from the inn, and next to an alley. She knocked at the door several times and got no answer. She peered down the alley, wondering if there might be a side or back door, but she had no desire to go down there, even with her escort. She could see a light on in the little home and felt hesitant to leave for reasons she couldn't explain. She tried the doorknob and it turned in her hand. "Wait right here," she said to the officer. "If I don't come out in two minutes, come and get me."

"Very good, madame," he said and she slipped inside. She peeked into the parlor and kitchen and noted that the other rooms were dark. "Is anybody home?" she called and got no answer, so she slipped back outside and returned to the inn with the officer, feeling odd about the situation. She wondered if perhaps this woman was in trouble and needed some help, but she'd not been able to meet the appointment.

Once safely back in her room with the door locked, Nadine hoped that whoever this woman was, she would be all right. And if Nadine could help her, she hoped that she would be able to contact her again. With that she went to sleep, completely ignoring the possibility that a murderer was on the loose.

Chapter Fifteen
RECOLLECTIONS

Lance was awakened in the middle of the night by an urgent pounding at his door. The last time it had happened an officer had been killed. He wondered what horrible situation he might be called upon to face now. Abbi's dream came to mind as he pulled open the door, buttoning his shirt as he did. But he told himself to be rational and not let his thoughts get the better of him.

"You're needed, sir," an officer said and hurried away.

"Blast!" Lance muttered and hurried to pull on his coat and boots. He threw his cloak over his shoulders on his way out the door and pulled his gloves onto his hands. Before he got to his office he was met by three officers and four saddled horses.

"What's happened?" Lance demanded as he mounted.

"There's been a murder, sir," the lieutenant said and Lance felt his insides turn to hard knots.

Galloping toward the scene of the crime, Lance told himself over and over that it was coincidence—that it would have nothing to do with Nadine or Abbi's dream. He felt sick just to think of something like this happening in his country. It brought back ugly memories of losing his sister, which was the last time a murder had taken place in Horstberg. Under any circumstances this would be horrible and unspeakable. But knowing what he knew, he felt tangibly ill. He told himself that Nadine was safely tucked away at the inn and an officer was guarding her. Then he imagined the officer dead on the ground and Nadine dragged from her bed. And he realized he'd never been so afraid in his life.

The lieutenant led them to an alley a short distance from the inn.

He could see some officers with a lantern in the alley, and a lifeless form on the ground that was covered with a sheet. An officer met him at the head of the alley.

"What happened?" he demanded, fighting to remain the captain while he needed to be.

"Young couple out walking," the officer said, motioning to a young man and woman leaning against the wall. They both looked visibly shaken; the woman looked nauseated. She was crying. "They found the body," the officer added.

Lance approached the body as if his feet had turned to lead. He squeezed his eyes shut and prayed with every fiber of his being before he nodded toward the officer squatting close by. He pulled back the sheet and Lance found it difficult to breathe. *It was her,* he thought with certainty, even though he could only see her from behind. Curly dark blond hair. Simple dark dress. And the white silk scarf wrapped around her throat. "Oh, God help me," he muttered, his voice trembling. He drew every ounce of courage from the deepest recesses of his soul to step around the body and see the woman's face. And while the sickness inside him smoldered more intensely, his relief was indescribable. It *wasn't* her! His eye was drawn to the dagger sticking out of her heart—with a carved ivory handle.

"All right," he said to his men, "you know what to do. Get on it."

He'd never been more grateful to know that they were well trained and could handle anything without him. The protocol of having him see the crime scene before it was disturbed had been met, and now he could leave it in their hands.

Lance mounted his horse and galloped the short distance to the inn, relieved to see an officer pacing back and forth. "Sir?" He was evidently surprised.

"There's been a murder, up the street. You stay right where you are. Give me the key."

Lance unlocked the door and handed the key back to the officer before he felt his way up the stairs in the dark and knocked at Nadine's door. He knocked three times before he heard her call in a loud whisper, "Who is it?"

"It's me, Lance. Open the door."

She pulled it open, and by the light of a candle's glow, he saw for himself that she was alive and well. "Oh, thank you, God," he said, pulling her into his arms. He kissed her over and over and held her as tight as humanly possible.

"What is it, Lance?" she asked softly.

"It happened," he said, suddenly weak. He sunk onto a chair while she closed the door and locked it. "Just as she described it." He looked up at her. "I thought it was you. It looked like you from behind. And that scarf. She was wearing the same kind of scarf."

"Good heavens," Nadine said as she finally became coherent enough to digest what he was saying. "You're talking about the murder. There was a murder?"

He nodded and pulled her onto his lap, holding to her tightly, desperately. "I thought it was you," he muttered again. "I wanted to die."

Nadine sought for words to comfort him, but she felt so deeply troubled herself that she couldn't even think what to say. Her uneasiness was profound, yet difficult to pinpoint. So she just held to him, concentrating on her gratitude to have him in her life. She found herself wishing he would stay, even while knowing it wasn't a good idea. With the way they felt about each other, spending time together in the middle of the night with such fear and desperation between them would be foolish at best. She was both disappointed and relieved when he said, "I must go. It's my responsibility to tell His Grace." He eased her off of his lap and came to his feet.

"And *Her* Grace?"

"Yes."

"I'm so sorry," she murmured and gave him a lengthy kiss.

"I'm just grateful to know you're all right."

"And it's over now."

He looked startled. "It's not over until the man stalking you is behind bars."

"Do you think there's a connection?" she asked, astonished.

He wanted to tell her that his gut instinct *knew* there was a connection. Not wanting to frighten her any more than she already was, he simply said, "It's possible. And we're not taking any chances. Please be careful, very careful."

"Of course," she said. "And you."

He kissed her again then left, waiting until he'd heard her lock the door before he rushed down the stairs. Galloping the distance to Castle Horstberg, Lance was struck repeatedly with the image of seeing that woman from behind, and how much it had looked like Nadine.

In the courtyard an officer appeared to take his horse. As he dismounted, Lance ordered, "I want a second man at the Horstberg Inn—one inside, one out. They can take hourly intervals to stay warm."

"Yes, sir. I'll send someone within the hour."

"Thank you," Lance said and rushed toward the main entrance of the castle. Hurrying down the main hall, he was grateful that certain areas of the castle were left dimly lit at all times. He took the stairs three at a time then hesitated on the landing. He really didn't want to do this. But it was protocol that the duke be alerted—no matter the hour—when something such as this occurred.

Lance lifted his hand to knock and took a deep breath. He waited and knocked again, knowing it would take some time for them to become coherent. "What is it?" he heard Cameron call, but the door came open before he could answer. He was wearing a long dressing gown that he was tying around his waist. His expression clearly showed his concern at being awakened in the middle of the night.

"Is Her Grace awake?" Lance asked. "She needs to hear this as well, and I would prefer not having to repeat it."

"Yes, I'm awake," she said, appearing at Cameron's side with a lamp in her hand. She too wore a long dressing gown. "What is it?" She motioned him into the room, and Cameron closed the door as she set the lamp aside.

Lance turned to face them and stated, "It's happened. There has been a murder."

Abbi gasped then demanded, "Is Nadine—"

"Nadine is fine, but you should know . . . it was exactly as you described it."

"Good heavens," Cameron said, putting his arm around Abbi. She just turned her face toward Cameron's chest and started to cry. Lance told them all he knew while his instincts smoldered. In the deepest part of him, he knew it wasn't over.

Through the following days, Lance kept busy every minute doing everything within his knowledge and power to get to the bottom of this crime and to prevent it from happening again. Some of the duke's advisors questioned his concern on that count, seeing no logical reason why one murder would turn into two. But a woman was being stalked with the same description as the woman who had been murdered, and he'd done enough study of crime through history to see a connection. In direct verification of his beliefs, Abbi reported to him that she'd had another dream. Same murder, different woman; still the face was obscure.

While he dreaded what might yet happen, he learned that the murder victim was a twenty-one-year-old woman who had been working at a pub as well as in her father's millinery. She was the oldest of four children, leaving behind one sister and two brothers. She was well-liked and had many friends. The loss was devastating. For Lance it wasn't personal, but it still pierced him deeply.

Lance oversaw the posting of a detailed description of Albert Crider throughout the entire country and a thorough combing of inns and pubs. His officers questioned people and questioned them again. The suspect had been seen many times, reported as being quiet and keeping to himself but not causing any trouble. But he seemed to have disappeared. Lance knew he had to be sleeping someplace warm, and he had to eat, but they had no leads as to where and how he was doing that.

The most difficult piece of evidence Lance received was a report from the scarf vendor. He had reportedly sold five white silk scarves to a single customer.

"Did he get a good look at him?" Lance asked the officer who had questioned the vendor, aching for a connection to the suspect.

"It wasn't a him, sir. It was a woman."

"What?"

"It was a woman who bought the scarves, but it was late in the day, kind of dusky," he said, "and her head and most of her face was covered with a wool scarf."

Lance stewed and stewed over that one. A woman? Could it be coincidence? But then, there was only one vendor in town with that particular type of scarf available—the same that had been on the murder victim, and the same that he had purchased for Nadine. Had the stalker seen him buy that scarf for her? Was that the connection? But why would a woman have purchased them—the only white ones sold since he'd bought the one for Nadine? The only possible solution was that the murderer had gotten a woman to do this seemingly simple errand for him. But who? And where was she? Where was *he*? The very idea of this perverse criminal lurking about Horstberg made him sick to his stomach. And it was evident that Cameron, Georg, and many others shared the same opinion.

Lance saw Nadine and Dulsie as much as he could between his long hours. He felt better knowing that she was being looked out for by some of his best and most trusted men. But he knew better than to think that any such precaution was a guarantee. Anything could go wrong. Anything. And he simply didn't know what else to do.

Lance dreaded attending the funeral of the victim, but he knew he needed to be there. Cameron and Abbi had personally visited the victim's family, and the government would be paying for the woman's burial, which would avoid putting a strain on the family. Beyond that, there was nothing to be done except attend the funeral in order to show respect and keep working to track down the man responsible.

Attending the funeral was made easier when Nadine asked if she could go with him. He'd not wanted to ask her, certain it would be difficult, but she insisted that she wanted to be there. Having her on his arm was a great boon to him, while her continual silent weeping clearly expressed his own heart. He could only pray that they would be guided to this man before he broke any more hearts.

Setting out for the castle the morning following the funeral, Nadine found she was almost getting to like her continual escort of an officer of the Guard. The man on duty would drive her to the castle and see her safely inside, and another officer would be waiting for her when she was finished with her work. She particularly liked the young man, Officer Kamm, who accompanied her home that afternoon, and they talked of how terribly cold it was. He went with her on a couple of errands in town, waiting just outside the shop doors while she went inside and did her business.

Lance came that evening and they shared a quiet supper in her room, then he read stories to Dulsie until she slept. Nadine massaged his hands while he kissed her frequently, and then he did the same for her. They talked of the future they would share, the children they would have, and the traveling they would do with all of the vacation time Lance had saved up from working more hours than anyone else on the force. Nadine appreciated his positive attitude, as if this elusive threat were not hanging over her.

The following evening Nadine was again escorted home by Officer Kamm. She enjoyed his company but was disappointed when he gave her a message from the captain that he would not be able to see her that evening. Nadine helped in the dining room, and was surprised to be handed a note by a woman in a dark, hooded cloak as she headed toward the door. The crowds had been heavy and she wasn't certain if it was a woman she had served or not. The woman hurried away before Nadine could even think to stop her and see who it was. She opened the note to read, in the same handwriting as the note she'd received previously, a different address and the time eleven o'clock. Certain that whoever had tried to meet with her before was making another attempt, she checked to see that Dulsie was sleeping soundly and asked Gerda to be aware of her, glad to have an officer patrolling nearby. She asked Officer Kamm if he would walk with her, and they chatted comfortably as she found the address. She was surprised to find that it was the home of the woman she had visited earlier—the one who had been so bitter and angry. She knocked repeatedly and got no answer, hating the uneasiness she was feeling. Everything inside of her seemed to scream that this woman was in trouble. Was her husband abusing her? Or someone else, perhaps? Or was she simply so depressed that she felt despair and needed a sound listening ear? Just as before, Nadine asked the officer to wait by the door while she peeked into the house. "If I'm not back in two minutes, come and find me," she said and he smiled. This time Nadine searched the house more thoroughly but found no one. She went back outside, frustrated and feeling helpless, even scared. Convinced that there was nothing more she could do, she returned to the inn with the officer at her side.

Nadine found Dulsie sleeping soundly, but it was difficult for her to do the same. She felt decidedly uneasy but wasn't certain what to do about it. She finally drifted off but was plagued with troubled dreams, although she couldn't recall their content when morning came.

Nadine dressed quietly while Dulsie continued to sleep. She was brushing through her hair when a light knock came at the door. She rose to answer, grateful to see that Dulsie had not even stirred in her sleep.

"It's me," she heard Lance say softly and she pulled the door open. His eyes looked pained, his expression more troubled than she had ever seen it.

"What is it?" she asked in a whisper, motioning him inside. "Please don't tell me it happened again," she said as he stepped in and she closed the door.

"It *did* happen again," he said, his voice shaking. He wrapped her in his arms and she realized that *he* was shaking.

"Exactly the same?" she asked, fighting to keep her own composure, if only to avoid upsetting him further.

He held to her for long moments, saying nothing, pressing his lips into her hair, nuzzling against her throat. "No," he finally muttered, "I mean . . . yes."

"Which?" she asked, looking into his eyes. She felt him teeter slightly and eased him to the edge of the bed.

When they were sitting side by side, he said, "Last time she was in an alley. This time she was in her home. Apparently a friend is in the habit of stopping for her early in the mornings; they walk together to work . . . at a pub. She noticed the front door open and went in and . . . found her. Everything else was the same." He squeezed his eyes closed, as if he could block out the image. "Except for the face it could have been you," he said, pulling her into his arms again. Nadine felt herself tremble from the inside out, trying to make sense of what this had to do with her.

"A scarf?" she asked and felt him nod.

"Yes, and . . . the same kind of dagger, through the heart; a carved ivory handle and—"

"What?" she asked abruptly, pulling back to look at him. "You didn't tell me that before . . . about the dagger."

"I didn't know it was relevant," he said, looking confused and even more upset.

Nadine erupted to her feet and started pacing as several pieces of knowledge attempted to fit together in her mind and make sense. "Oh, help," she muttered, wringing her hands. "Oh, heaven help me. I had no idea . . . I never would have dreamed . . . I . . . I . . ."

"Nadine," Lance said, noting that she'd gone pale, "you're scaring me. What are you talking about?" When she apparently didn't hear him, he stood and took hold of her shoulders to stop her pacing. When their eyes met, the terror he saw there further tightened every knot inside of him.

"Mama?" Dulsie called and they both turned toward her. Lance watched Nadine visibly put a calm mask onto her face before she went to Dulsie's side. He greeted her with an equally pleasant exterior, waited while Nadine helped her get dressed and then sent her downstairs to where she knew Gerda would get her some breakfast.

"Now, talk to me," he said, alarmed by the immediate shock that returned to her face once Dulsie was gone.

She moved unsteadily to the edge of the bed and he noticed her hands shaking. In a voice that quavered she said, "It *is* about me, Lance. It's *all* about me. There's no other possibility. But it's far worse than I ever imagined."

"Tell me," he said urgently.

Nadine looked up at him standing before her and huge tears trailed down her cheeks. "Where I lived . . . before I came here . . . it was in the newspaper, and . . . people were talking about it, horrified and frightened. There were five women killed." Lance sucked in his breath and held it. "I avoided listening to the talk because it scared me so. I don't know anything about those women except that . . ." She began to cry so hard she could barely speak. "They were all . . . blond and . . . the dagger; it was always a dagger . . . through the heart . . . with a carved ivory handle." She pressed her trembling hands to her face and looked up at him again. "What have I done?" she sobbed. "I brought him here! It's me he's after. But why? *Why?*"

Lance sat beside her and pulled her into his arms, unwilling to let himself feel what he'd just learned. He attempted to take it in as the Captain of the Guard, not as the man who loved her. Doing the latter would leave him completely incapable of functioning.

"It's not your fault, Nadine," he said. "You mustn't blame yourself. We are going to find him. Do you hear me? And you are going to be safe." He drew back and looked into her troubled eyes. "Perhaps you and Dulsie should move to the castle. Abbi mentioned it last night. You can stay in a room in the north wing until the wedding. With another killing, and with what we know . . .

I think we would all feel better if you were there. It would be easier to protect you."

He expected to have to talk her into it, but she nodded immediately. "I'll pack our things. Would you tell Drew and Gerda? I can't . . . talk to them right now."

"I will," he said. "I must go. I need to talk with the committee about what you told me. We'll send someone to talk with officials about the previous murders. We'll do everything we can. I'll come back for you this afternoon . . . with a carriage, and I'll let Abbi know that you're packing."

"Thank you," she said, holding to him tightly. "What would I ever do without you?"

"I'm not prepared to *ever* do without *you*, Nadine. I love you. I love you more than life."

"And I love you," she said, pressing a hand over his face. He kissed her long and hard before she wiped her tears and they walked downstairs together to find Dulsie eating her breakfast. Nadine sat down beside her, aware that Lance was in the kitchen speaking with Drew and Gerda before he left. As soon as they had eaten, they went upstairs to start gathering their things.

Nadine emptied the contents of her drawers onto the bed, determining that some of their clothing could go back to the second-hand store. She had now purchased clothing that was more to her liking—for herself and for Dulsie—and the clothing she'd been given was still in good shape. She set those things aside, realizing she had no trunk to pack her belongings in. When they'd come to Horstberg, they'd come with nothing so one hadn't been needed. She contemplated a trip to town to buy a trunk, or perhaps asking Drew and Gerda if they had something she could borrow. As she contemplated how dramatically her life had been altered, she found a folded paper beneath a pile of neatly folded underclothing. Its familiarity caught her off guard, when looking at it now seemed so strange with all that had changed since she'd last put it away.

Nadine unfolded her mock marriage certificate, even as she glanced toward the fire, certain that burning it would be the best thing. She had found a new life, a new love. And in spite of the horrible circumstances facing her, with her very life in danger, the love she shared with Lance was her deepest comfort.

Looking over the certificate, Nadine felt a distinct heartache. But she was able to see the perspective of lessons learned, and all that she had been blessed with, in spite of Nikolaus's betrayal. She moved toward the fireplace then stopped abruptly, turning cold from the inside out, as if her heart had immediately transformed to ice, freezing the blood that flowed through her every vein.

"No," she gasped and wilted onto the rug as her legs turned to jelly beneath her. She was grateful that Dulsie had gone downstairs when she found it difficult to breathe. Her labored breathing turned to anguished sobbing until she found herself numbly staring at the paper in her hands, so filled with shock and betrayal she couldn't even fathom how she would ever get to her feet, let alone go on living. She considered the countless times she had talked herself into trusting and opening her heart. And for what?

Nadine found the strength to stand as her hurt turned to bitterness, and both fed an anger beyond her understanding. She paced the room, fuming and cursing under her breath, even while she felt her heart breaking into thousands of pieces. She was startled when Dulsie burst into the room, and she looked up to see Lance enter behind her and hesitate at the door. She watched his eyes take her in, then his brow furrowed in concern. There was so much she wanted to say to him that she didn't know where to begin. The hurt began to overtake her anger and she quickly turned her back to him, knowing that only her anger could keep her from falling apart.

Lance absorbed the aura permeating from Nadine and panic gripped him. This was not the frightened and troubled woman he'd left a few hours ago. She was visibly angry. He could almost see her seething, even with her back turned.

"You seem upset," he said, closing the door behind him. "What's happened?"

"I'm upset all right," she snarled.

"So, let's talk about it."

"You bet we will," she said and grabbed a piece of paper from the bureau. "Do you recognize this, *Captain?*"

Lance hated the sick knot forming in his stomach as it became evident that she was upset with *him.* Her formal approach only deepened his dread. But he forced himself to stay calm and just looked at what she held. "It looks like your wedding certificate."

"Very good," she drawled with sarcasm. "My *fraudulent* wedding certificate. And do you recognize *this*, Captain?" She pointed to a specific place in the corner.

Lance felt something die inside him as an obscure memory filtered into his mind, making a connection to the piece of paper in her hand. When he said nothing, she added bitterly, "Is that or is it not your signature?"

Lance swallowed. Then he sighed. "Yes, it is," he stated, and before he could get out another syllable, she slapped him hard across the face. He closed his eyes, feeling the sting settle in.

"Damn you!" she snarled. "I was really beginning to think that you were everything you said you were. I was beginning to believe that you were different from other men. But oh, how wrong I was! You're all alike when it comes right down to it. You, of all people, signed your name as a witness to something that destroyed my life, something criminal and immoral. You were *there* and you *condoned* it. You have a lot of nerve to be—"

"Nadine," he interrupted, figuring she'd ranted long enough, "listen to me. I can explain. I was—"

"There's nothing to explain, Captain. It's all very clear in black and white as far as I can see. Now get out. I don't ever want to see your face again."

His heart dropped to a deep pit in his stomach. Everything inside of him screamed in protest. He was so stunned he could hardly put together a coherent thought. "Nadine," he pleaded, his voice shaking, "you can't just . . . you must know that I—"

"Get out!" she screamed.

"No!" Dulsie cried, reminding them both that she was there, that she had observed their exchange. She ran across the room, grabbing onto Lance's leg. "No! You can't leave! No!"

"Dulsie, stop it!" her mother insisted, attempting to drag her away from him.

"However angry you might be," Lance said, "you must come to the castle where you'll be safe. You can't stay here when—"

"I have plenty of protection right here. I'm not going anywhere," she insisted. "Now get out!"

Lance forced out a long, slow breath, attempting to be convinced that they could talk away from Dulsie once Nadine calmed down.

For the child's sake he forced himself to ignore what had just been hurled at him. He knelt beside Dulsie and took her shoulders into his hands. "Everything will be all right," he said. "You must stay with your mother. But I'll be back, I promise."

"No, you won't!" Nadine snapped and Dulsie held to Lance, whimpering.

"I'll be back to see Dulsie," he said firmly. "Whatever might be wrong between you and me has nothing to do with her, and I will not break my promises to her just because you're too angry to listen to what I have to say." He looked into the child's eyes again. "I'll be back. I promise."

He eased the child away in spite of her protests, and Nadine grabbed onto her. Lance forced himself to leave, while Dulsie's cries and Nadine's angry words thundered through his mind. By the time he arrived at the castle, the full impact of what had just happened had crept to his every nerve. He felt as if he'd turned to stone as he dismounted and left the stallion with an officer. He felt the need to be alone, but he was immediately assaulted with problems that needed to be solved, and then he was needed at a meeting in the duke's office. He went through the motions of his responsibilities while he felt tangibly ill and so completely stunned that he couldn't even fathom how he was even managing to put one foot in front of the other. He couldn't believe it. He just couldn't believe it. He felt an anger toward Nikolaus roiling inside of him so intensely that he clenched his fists over and over beneath the table where he was sitting. And if he looked past the anger, he found his heart breaking. He didn't know how he could possibly go on if Nadine wouldn't be convinced of his innocence. He just *couldn't* go on. He couldn't.

Chapter Sixteen

THE ESTRANGEMENT

When the meeting was over, Lance felt compelled to talk to Cameron, if only to vent all of these heated emotions that had nowhere to go. He stood close to the desk and waited for the other men to leave the office.

"Might I have a few minutes alone?" he asked Cameron quietly as the door closed behind the last man and only Georg and Cameron remained.

"Of course," Cameron said, his brow furrowed. "Is something..."

The door flew open abruptly and Nadine rushed into the room with the officers who had been at the door standing behind her, looking apologetic and flustered.

"Yes, madame?" Cameron said in that ducal voice that made it easy to wonder if he had some measure of dictator in him.

"Forgive the intrusion, Your Grace," she said as if she didn't mean it. She glared at Lance then slapped the marriage certificate down on the desk. "But I felt it should come to your attention that your honorable Captain of the Guard is guilty of misrepresentation."

Lance squeezed his eyes closed for a long moment and opened them to see Cameron lifting the document to look at it closely. Then he turned to look at Lance over the top of his glasses, his expression filled with disbelief.

"I can explain, Your Grace," he said.

"Yes, I'm certain you can. And you will."

Cameron turned to look at Nadine. "I'm certain there is a reasonable explanation, Mrs. Rader. If you—"

"Yes, I'm certain there is," she said with sarcasm, "but whatever lies he may tell you, his signature is there in black and white. That's all I have to say."

She left the office as quickly as she had entered, slamming the door behind her. Lance tried to ignore the inner trembling that threatened to make him crumble as he turned to look at the faces of these men he worked with, men with whom he'd shared years of mutual respect.

"Are you all right?" Georg asked, breaking the silence.

"No," Lance admitted.

"I think I can guess why your signature is on this," Cameron said, "but for the record, would you please tell us. Now."

Lance sighed and looked at the floor. Then he looked directly into Cameron's eyes as he said, "Yes, of course, Your Grace. I had every reason to believe that the marriage ceremony was real. There are far too many clergymen in Horstberg for me to have known that the man performing this marriage wasn't one of them. Nikolaus spent an entire evening telling me how incredible this woman was, how he intended to marry her secretly, and at some future date, when things were not so touchy, he would call off his betrothal. I had my concerns, but I saw a Nikolaus that I had believed was in love with a woman who could have softened him." He sighed and repeated, "I thought it was real. It was several weeks later that I realized nothing had changed. He was with a different woman every night, and then he asked me to do it again. That's when he told me it had been a mock ceremony. I demanded to have the certificate back so I could destroy it. He assured me that it already had been."

"So, you remember Mrs. Rader then, from that incident?"

"Quite frankly, no. I wasn't feeling well that evening. The home where the marriage was performed was not well lit. It was the middle of the night. I don't think I even got a good look at her face. That's it. There's nothing more to tell except that . . ." His voice faltered. He swallowed hard and cleared his throat. "The woman I love believes I am the same kind of liar and cheat as Nikolaus was. And she simply refuses to listen long enough for me to tell her what I just told you."

Cameron and Georg both sighed, as if they shared his grief but had no answers.

"Your brother," Lance snarled, "had better be rotting in hell."

"He might be my brother," Cameron countered, "but he was *your* friend."

"Yes," Lance laughed with bitter sarcasm, "my *friend*. He lied to me, manipulated me. He used me more than I ever knew at the time. And now that he's gone, his ghost continues to follow me around like some kind of plague intent on destroying me."

"Well, you can't let him," Georg said. "It's as simple as that."

"Is that *simple?*" Lance growled.

"Not easy, but simple," Cameron said. "What are your options?"

"I'm not sure that I have any."

"Do you think you can live without her?"

"No!" Lance snapped.

"Well then, you know what you have to do."

"She kicked me out, Cameron. She told me she never wanted to see me again."

"Then you're going to have to fight to convince her otherwise."

"And how exactly do I go about that if she won't talk to me?"

"I don't have all the answers, Lance. But I have learned a thing or two about women since Abbi came into my life."

"Like what?" Lance asked, a glimmer of intrigue pushing past his hurt and anger.

Lance sat down and listened as Cameron told of how Abbi had given him hope when he'd been alone in exile for over three years, and how she had taught him that circumstances were not going to magically change just because he wanted them to, but that he had to fight for what he wanted.

"Abbi made it clear that if I wanted a life with her, I had to fight for that as well. She wouldn't put up with having me wallow in my pride and fear, and I had to prove that my love for her was more important than those fears. And you have to fight for Nadine," Cameron went on. "She wouldn't be so angry if she didn't care for you, Lance, and you have a right to tell your side of the story."

"Give it a little time," Georg suggested. "I'm certain when she gets past the anger, she'll be more willing to listen."

"I can hope," Lance said, but memories of the fury in her eyes left him doubtful.

Lance left Cameron's office, telling himself to be patient and give the matter some time. He desperately wanted to talk with Abbi, knowing she could give him a woman's perspective, but he knew Nadine would be with her. He returned to his office and attempted to focus on his work without success until he knew that Nadine would have gone back to the inn. He found Abbi in her sitting room.

"Captain," she said as he entered the open door, "is something wrong?"

Lance nodded, then added quickly, "It can wait if you're busy."

"No, it's all right. Come in," Abbi said, her concern evident.

Lance ambled slowly to a chair and sank into it.

"What's happened?" Abbi asked, sounding panicked.

"It's personal."

"I see," she said and waited for him to go on.

"Nadine threw me out."

"What?" she shrieked.

"She said nothing to you?" he asked. "You were with her all day."

"No, nothing. She seemed . . . upset, troubled, but I assumed it was related to the murders and she said she didn't want to talk about it. She threw you out? What in heaven's name would—"

"Dulsie was screaming to come with me," he went on. "Nadine was screaming at me to get out. It was ugly."

Abbi asked forthright, "So what did you do to upset her?"

"I didn't *do* anything," Lance snapped. "At least I . . . well, I guess I did. But it was so long ago, and . . ."

"Just get to it," Abbi insisted.

"You remember that marriage certificate?" he asked.

"I remember."

"Guess who signed it as a witness?"

"You?" Abbi said, her astonishment evident. He nodded and she sighed loudly, wincing visibly. "Ouch."

He told her what he had told Cameron and Georg. She listened with compassion, then repeated some of the same advice that she'd already given via Cameron, adding firmly, "If you've truly found the woman for you, I don't want to see you lose her to misunderstanding. You're a good man, Lance. One of the best. And time will prove that to her. She could knock on every door in Horstberg and not find a single person who could discredit you."

"Well, I'll see if I can get her to do that," he said with sarcasm.

They talked for a while longer and again he felt as if he just needed to give Nadine some time to cool off. In the meantime, he felt that he needed to at least try and see Dulsie. Her screaming for him not to go kept ringing in his ears. He prayed that such an undertaking might be possible. He arrived at the inn to find it empty of customers and Dulsie sitting in the dining room with the officer on duty. She was showing him a picture she had drawn. Nadine was nowhere to be seen. Perhaps his prayers were being heard. He had no desire to repeat this morning's episode with her.

"Lance!" Dulsie said when she saw him and ran into his arms. He squatted down and eagerly accepted her tight hug around his neck.

"Oh, I missed you," he said.

"I missed you, too," she said. "Can I go stay at the castle with you? I don't want to be here. Mama's just crying all the time."

Lance briefly closed his eyes against the image. In a tender voice he said, "No, Dulsie, I'm afraid you can't come with me. I know this is difficult, but your mother needs you. She won't let me be there to watch out for her, so I need you to do that for me. Can you be brave and do that?"

She thought about it then nodded reluctantly. Lance sat down and pulled her onto his knee. They talked quietly for a short while. He did his best to explain the problem in terms she could understand, and he told her he would do everything he could to help her mother understand how sorry he was for what he'd done. She was asking again if she could come and stay with him when Nadine appeared in the doorway to the dining room, her eyes red and swollen, her expression angry.

"Come along, Dulsie," she said, holding out a hand.

"Go with your mother," he said gently, urging her along.

He watched Dulsie reluctantly leave with Nadine, who wouldn't even make eye contact with him. He forced himself to eat the supper that Gerda offered him before he returned to the castle, feeling more empty, more alone, more afraid than he ever had in his life. Not only had she shunned him and shut him out personally, but she would not allow him to bring her where she would be most safe. Thankfully she didn't seem to have a problem with the officers posted to look after her. Oh, how he envied them. He wondered what she might do if he assigned himself to that post for a shift, but he feared she would just tell him she would rather be vulnerable to murder than have him anywhere nearby.

Following a sleepless night, Lance was in his office early,

attempting to distract himself from his broken heart by digging into his ongoing efforts to find the criminal at large. When he realized that Nadine would be arriving soon, he went into the castle, determined to talk to her, praying that it wouldn't be a complete disaster. He waited discreetly around the corner of a cross-section of hallway near the nursery. When she came out after leaving Dulsie there, he stepped in front of her.

"What are you doing?" she demanded angrily.

"I just need to talk to you," he said. "Could you at least have the decency to give me a minute of your time?"

"I have work to do."

"It can wait a few minutes. Abbi will understand."

She attempted to step around him, but he moved to block her. She turned to go the other way and he grabbed her arm, forcing her to face him. There was venom in her eyes when she looked up at him, but he did his best to ignore it. "Nadine, listen to me. What I did was done in innocence."

"How can you say that about something that destroyed my life?"

"Your life is not destroyed, Nadine, unless you choose to make it that way. You have a good life at your fingertips, unless you choose to throw it away because you're too proud and afraid to see what's really going on here. This isn't just your life, Nadine. What you're doing is hurting me, and it's hurting Dulsie. You must believe me when I tell you that—"

"Believe you?" she interrupted. "How can I believe anything you tell me, knowing what I know? I can't. It's as simple as that. Now let go of me. I have to get to work." She wormed from his grasp and huffed away, and he felt no motivation to try and stop her. It was evident that she would hear nothing he had to say. Her mind was too clouded with anger to even listen.

Getting through the remainder of the day was more difficult than Lance had ever recalled. He had to forcefully keep moving from one responsibility to another, praying continually in his heart that this nightmare would end and he could be reunited with Nadine and Dulsie.

Late afternoon he looked up from his desk to see Abbi standing in the door frame.

"Your Grace," he said. "What a pleasant reprieve."

She showed a wan smile and closed the door. He noticed how she moved slowly and with some difficulty to a chair; the pregnancy was quickly overtaking her petite body. It had obviously taken significant effort for her to get here.

"You could have sent a message," he said. "You didn't have to come all the way down here to—"

"I needed some exercise," she protested. "Besides, I didn't think you would be up to moving furniture today."

Lance chuckled but could feel no humor. "What can I do for you?" he asked.

"Well, I've been pondering your situation a great deal. I trust she still won't talk to you?"

"No. It's as if her mind is so clouded by anger, my words won't even penetrate. Has she said anything to you?"

"Not a word. But I've had a thought. I don't know if it's the answer or not, but it couldn't hurt. In such situations, when I am plagued with thoughts and feelings that have nowhere to go, I like to write them down. Sometimes in my journal, sometimes in a letter. I was thinking if you write Nadine a letter, then you can carefully ponder what you need to say, and say it exactly as you want to. She will have your words in black and white in front of her. She can read them over and over if she chooses."

Lance sighed. "I think it's a good idea. I only pray that she can get past her anger enough that she will at least read it and be open to what it has to say."

"Write the letter," she said. "Write it from the heart. You can't control her response or the outcome. You can only do what you are capable of doing. You must put the matter in God's hands." She reached across the desk and took his hand, squeezing it tightly. "Do you want to know what I think?"

"Of course."

"I truly believe that the two of you are meant to be together. It may take some time for her to work through this and get beyond it, but I believe she will. You just need to be patient and keep doing all you can to let her know you love her."

"I will," he said, actually feeling a tiny glimmer of hope for the first time since Nadine had slapped him. "Thank you, Your Grace. You are such a treasure to me."

"The feeling is mutual, Captain. Take care now."

Lance walked her back to the castle entrance before he went to his apartment and sat down to write Nadine a long, heartfelt letter. It was more difficult than he'd anticipated to put his feelings into written words and he ended up doing several drafts. Far past midnight he finally finished a letter that he felt truly said what he wanted to say. He read it over once more, praying that his words would find their way into her heart. He began by expressing the powerful feelings he'd had for her, right from the start, and his heartache over what Nikolaus had done to her. He explained his own feelings toward Nikolaus, the hurt and betrayal that *he* had endured through their supposed friendship, which illustrated that he knew how she felt to some degree. He told her his account of the incident in question, repeating in detail the anger he'd felt toward Nikolaus at the time when he'd discovered that the marriage had been a charade. He finished by again expressing his love for her, his commitment to care for her and Dulsie, and he begged her forgiveness for this transgression that had hurt her so deeply.

Lance signed the letter and sealed it up, writing her name on the outside. He managed to get a few hours of sleep, then he went to the inn early and knocked at her door, his heart pounding back and forth between dread and hope. She pulled the door open and the anger in her eyes was immediately evident. Beyond that, she looked horrible. It was evident she'd not been sleeping well, and she'd been doing a lot of crying. If nothing else, he felt some relief to know that she wasn't taking this any more easily than he was.

He hurried to speak before she could. "Before you say anything, I just want you to read this." He held out the letter. "I deserve the opportunity to have my side of the story heard, Nadine. Please just . . . read it. And try to do so with an open mind."

"I'll try," she said, snatching the letter from him. "Thank you," she added forcefully, as if it were a great strain to be polite. Then she closed the door. Lance left the inn with a heavy heart, but at least he knew he had done all that he could for the time being.

Nadine sat down on the edge of the bed and opened the envelope with trembling fingers. Fresh tears came to her eyes, blurring her vision, and she wondered over their source. She'd never cried so much in her life. When her vision finally cleared, she focused on the first sentence. *My dear Nadine, My effort in writing this letter is not to try and excuse my actions, but rather to offer an explanation so that you might understand the intent of my heart.* He went on with expressions of love that should have melted her, but she felt inexplicably cold from the inside out, and she found it impossible to truly believe what he was saying.

Nadine read the letter through twice, then she tucked it away and forced herself to press forward with her day, not certain what she should do. By the time she got to the castle, she knew she needed to talk to him, but it wasn't likely to be a pleasant experience. Hoping she would have an opportunity to see him, she took Dulsie to the nursery and hurried to begin her work.

"Good morning," Abbi said when she entered the room.

"Good morning," Nadine replied, wondering what Lance had told her.

As if in direct response to her thought, Abbi added, "There's no need for you to pretend that everything is all right." Nadine said nothing and she went on, "You've said nothing about this estrangement between you and Lance. Have we not become friends enough that you would share such things with me?"

"I assumed that he would tell you everything. There's nothing more to say."

"So, you're shutting me out as well," Abbi said and Nadine forced back her frustration.

"Forgive me, Your Grace, but you and Lance have been friends for a very long time. I'm well aware of the way you feel about each other, and I know well which of us you would side with. It would be ridiculous of me to believe that after working together for only a few weeks, your loyalty to me would be more so than to him."

Nadine felt almost afraid as she clearly saw the duchess come into Abbi's countenance. Still, her voice was soft as she said, "Let me tell you something, Nadine. I am not here to *side* with anyone. This is not about taking sides or having loyalties. This is about truth and right. No problem can be solved effectively without first learning the truth, and then doing what is right and good with that truth. But I wonder if you're ready to hear the truth, Nadine. Apparently not."

"With all due respect, Your Grace, the matter is extremely complicated from my perspective. I would prefer that we keep personal matters out of our working relationship, considering what has happened. If you would prefer that I not work for you any further, I'll start looking for something else."

"You need this job and I need you," Abbi said. "I'm certain we can manage."

Nadine dug into her work, grateful that Abbi's mood was tolerable, and she would apparently not allow this to put a strain on their time together. She found it difficult to focus while she wondered how she might find Lance alone and talk with him, if only to be done with it. She'd only been there an hour when she looked up to see him standing in the doorway.

"Hello, Captain," Abbi said brightly. "How may we help you?"

Lance stepped into the room while Nadine continued to work, trying to ignore him. This was hardly the time or place to say what needed to be said.

"His Grace asked me to tell you that the luncheon with the preservation committee has been postponed to another day, and it will be lunch as usual."

"Oh, what divine news," Abbi said. "I can eat my lunch without having to be diplomatic and cheerful."

"And I thought you were *always* diplomatic and cheerful," Lance said, wishing Nadine would even look at him. Had she read the letter? He had hoped for some softening—even just a little bit.

"Not necessarily," Abbi said. "Of course, it's easier to be that way around people I like being with. The preservation committee is not high on that list." She pointed a finger at him. "Don't you ever repeat that I said such a thing."

"My lips are sealed, Your Grace," he said, then told himself he should leave.

He was just wondering how to go about it when Abbi stood, saying, "Forgive me for being blunt, but I'm going to give the two of you some time alone. And for heaven's sake, talk to each other." She went into the next room and closed the door.

Nadine stopped writing and put down her pen. She looked up at him with trepidation as he closed the door to the hall as well. "You read the letter," he said, almost hoping she hadn't. If she had read his words and still looked that upset, he doubted he could ever get through to her.

"I did," she said and he looked down, biting his lip in an attempt to keep his emotion under control.

"And?" he pressed without looking back up.

"It certainly helped me understand a great deal about you and Nikolaus, and I am glad to know what happened from your perspective."

"And?" he said again, looking up at her, his heart pounding.

"And what? Is that supposed to magically erase what's happened?"

"My involvement was innocent, Nadine. Why would I do something like that when it goes against every grain of my character?"

"That's what I'd like to know," she snapped. "That's the very question that haunts me."

"Nadine, you're not hearing me. Yesterday it was as if you were ready to put me in front of a firing squad without a trial, now you're as good as telling me that the trial proved me innocent but you're going to shoot me through the heart anyway." She looked away but said nothing. "Why will you not believe me?" he pressed. Still she said nothing and his frustration mounted. "How can you hold one innocent mistake against me like this?"

"How do I know it's innocent?" she insisted. "How can I believe that you're telling me the truth?"

"Because that's the kind of man that I am!" he said firmly. "Because that is the way I have always lived my life—always. Maybe you should just go through the entire country, and ask all 27,842 people if they can come up with something to discredit me."

She looked at him hard and he felt as if he truly were facing an executioner. She had the power to give him life or death in that moment, and he felt the inevitable horror of her belief that he was guilty, in spite of any proof that could be found in his favor.

"Forgive me, Lance. Perhaps I'm not being fair. As I said, the letter did help me understand a great deal. It also brought some difficult emotions to the surface for me, especially in regard to Nikolaus. I realize that I have much further to go in healing than I had realized."

"Perhaps we can work on that together," he said, certain the same applied to him. "I want to marry you, Nadine. I want to help you face life's problems, not be shut out from them."

Nadine's expression hardened further and he felt the axe about to fall. "I don't know if I can marry you, Lance. Whether this is your fault, or my fault, or nobody's fault, I simply don't know if I can ever trust a man again—any man."

"So, what are you saying?" he demanded, hearing anger creep into his voice. "Because of this you will lock yourself away from the world and spend the rest of your life alone?"

"Perhaps," she said, looking at the floor.

"That's not what you want and I know it. And you know it. If you allow such a thing to happen, then Nikolaus continues to have power over you, even from the grave." He took a step toward her and she stepped back, alarmed by his intensity. "You know what, Nadine? You're scared, plain and simple. And you're using what I did as an excuse to lock your heart away so you don't ever have to worry about getting hurt again. No, you'll just hold onto the old hurts and let them eat you alive for the rest of your life. You'll turn into a bitter and hateful old woman. Well guess what, my love. Trust and risk are a part of love, a part of giving your heart. I learned that. I took a risk. I trusted you with *my* heart, and look where it got me. But I'm still willing to stand here and tell you that it was worth it, that I'd do it all again. What are *you* willing to do?"

She looked as if she'd like to hurl a thousand angry words at him, but in a controlled voice she stated, "I can't marry you, Lance. What Nikolaus did is just . . . too deep."

"Yes, what Nikolaus did runs deep, all right," he snarled. "But what you don't seem to understand is that he did it to me, as well. He was my best friend, Nadine. He cheated me, manipulated me, betrayed me more deeply than even *you* realize."

She looked momentarily curious, and he wondered if she would ask, but she only turned away. His anger took hold completely and he felt a hatred toward Nikolaus that he'd not felt since the moment he'd realized that the man had killed his sister. In a voice of controlled fury, he growled, "It is incredible to see what that man has put me through. Even in death he seems to follow me around, attempting to undo me. I swear by heaven and earth if he were still alive, I'd kill him again."

Lance heard her gasp and turned to look at her just as he realized what he'd said.

Nadine felt the words come into her like a bullet while a story she'd heard in bits and pieces suddenly fell together in her mind, making perfect sense. "It was you," she said breathlessly. "You're the one who . . . killed him."

Lance was nearly grateful for the anger he felt that kept her words from penetrating the parts of his soul that were plagued by that very fact.

"Why didn't you tell me?" she demanded.

"I didn't tell you because you were grieving, Nadine, and I didn't think you needed to share in *my* burdens. Yes, I killed him. And beyond the prospect of losing you, it was the most difficult thing I have ever done in my life."

"But . . . but . . ." she stammered, assaulted with a composite of emotions all at once. "He's Dulsie's father, and . . . I loved him, and . . . I gave him everything I had."

"You think I don't know that? You think I don't look at Dulsie without thinking of him? I loved him, too, Nadine. He was my *friend*. I grew up with him. We were playmates from the nursery. I worked by his side for years, believed in him, trusted him. But he betrayed me. He lied to me, used me, manipulated me. Don't go passing judgment on me until you know what you're talking about. Killing Nikolaus du Woernig was the hardest thing I've ever done in my life, but it was far more justified than you can possibly imagine. And I, more than anyone, had the right to do it. He killed my sister, Nadine. He stood beside me, time and time again, and called me his friend, all the while knowing that he had killed her. And more than once he threatened to put *me* in front of a firing squad if I didn't carry out his orders. Yes, I killed him, Nadine, and you know how and why. He had a gun to Abbi's head, and he was guilty of murder among countless other crimes. I killed him and I'd do it again, in spite of the memories I have had to live with, because it was the right thing to do!"

Nadine felt such a turmoil of emotions that she could hardly think straight. She could blatantly see Lance's integrity, his strength, his honor. But at the same time, her own fear and mistrust whirled together with what she'd just learned, adding upon what she'd read on her marriage certificate. She felt as if the floor would fall out from beneath her. The anger in his eyes was evident, but she didn't know how to respond to it. Knowing in her heart that she was at the root of that anger, his expectant gaze left her helpless and frightened. In that moment she felt as if she might turn to stone if she looked at him another second. She turned her back abruptly and felt her chest tighten further as their conversation settled more deeply into her.

"Forgive me," she said, "I need to be alone." She hurried to the side door and opened it, saying abruptly, "Forgive me, Your Grace, but . . . I need a break. I'll return and work as late as you need." She glanced at Lance once more and rushed past him, running from the room as quickly as she could manage. She quickly found an unoccupied room where she sobbed helplessly, muffling the sound into her hands in order to avoid being found.

Chapter Seventeen
MISSING

Lance watched Nadine leave the room and stood staring after her, while something inside him turned cold. He heard a sound and turned to see Abbi standing beside him. "Please tell me you heard all of that," he said, "so I don't have to repeat it."

"Yes, I heard," she said. "The walls are thick but the doorframes are drafty."

Just looking into her compassionate eyes melted his anger into the raw fear and hurt at its source. He felt his legs go weak and was grateful when she took his arm, guiding him to the little sofa. "Sit down," she said. "You don't look like you're doing very well."

"Imagine that," he said, pressing his head into his hands. "My life used to be so measured, so controlled. Now look at me. I'm a mess, Abbi. I'm falling apart. I'm barely managing to do my duties. I can't sleep. I have no appetite. How can I go on like this?"

"Bear in mind that you *are* managing to function. That's a good sign. Sometimes I think we just have to keep putting one foot in front of the other until solutions present themselves. You just need to give the matter some time . . . and some prayer."

"I've never prayed so hard in my life as I have the past several days. I was terrified that she'd end up getting killed; I still am. But now this. I just . . . don't understand."

"I think there's a reason for that."

"What do you mean?" he asked.

"Lance," she took his hand, "I really believe that this is more about her than you. She as much as admitted it." He felt more confused until she clarified, "She admitted that she had more healing to do. I believe it has more to do with her inability to trust a man than her questioning whether or not you are trustworthy. I don't know if she can fully admit that, but I would bet that in her heart she knows that it's more about her than you. And perhaps time will heal her."

"And perhaps it won't," he said.

Abbi sighed. "That's a possibility you're going to have to accept."

Lance pressed a hand absently over his chest where a tangible pain tightened at the very idea. Her voice was gentle as she went on to say, "There was a time when I had to accept that as much as I loved Cameron, and as much as I believed we were meant to be together, if he chose to stay rooted in his pride and fear and not allow me into his heart, there was nothing I could do. It was out of my hands. Gratefully, he came around, but if he hadn't, our lives may have taken much different courses."

Lance felt tears bubble out of him as she spoke, and the next thing he knew, he had his face buried in what was left of her lap beyond the space occupied by the baby. He couldn't even entertain the thought of life without Nadine. He just didn't know how he could go on.

"Lance," Abbi muttered when he had calmed down, "I know this is difficult for you. I wish there was more I could do."

"What you do, Your Grace, is priceless." He kissed her hand, realizing his tears had given way to a complete shock that had blanketed his entire being with a fixed numbness.

"I should go," he said, sitting up abruptly as it occurred to him that Nadine would be returning. The last thing he wanted was to have her find him bawling like a baby.

"You know where to find me if you need to talk," she said.

"Yes, I do. Thank you." He kissed her cheek and hurried from the room, going the opposite direction from where he felt sure Nadine might come. If he saw her now he wasn't sure he could avoid causing a scene, and he'd already had enough drama in the past several days to last a lifetime.

When Nadine returned to her work after lunch, Abbi said nothing about Lance. She recognized the duchess's effort to be cheerful and make polite conversation, but the strain between them was evident.

A short while before she was scheduled to leave, Nadine was surprised to have one of the maids bring word that His Grace wanted to see her. Nadine couldn't help feeling concerned, and Abbi was quick to notice. "Don't worry, my dear," she said lightly, "his bark is much worse than his bite."

Abbi laughed as if it were terribly funny, but Nadine didn't feel amused. When her work was completed, she went to the duke's office before going to get Dulsie. The officer at the door let her in and closed the door behind her.

"You wanted to see me," Nadine said, standing at the edge of the duke's desk.

"Sit down please," he said and she did. She noticed Georg in the room, as he always was. He nodded and smiled toward her in greeting. But there was a definite formality in the air that didn't ring of their social encounters. She turned her attention to the duke and waited for what he might say.

"In response to the issue you brought to my attention regarding the captain, I want you to know that we have thoroughly questioned him and examined the situation, and we are convinced that his participation was completely in innocence. Nikolaus was very good at manipulating people, especially those he was closest to. You, of all people, should understand that."

"Yes, the captain explained everything to me."

"And?"

"It's all very well and good, and . . . I know he never meant to do me harm, but I'm just not certain I can go on with the relationship."

Cameron leaned his forearms on the desk. "Nadine," he said gently, his royal manner less evident, "speaking as a friend, I hope that you will not let this ruin the love that you and Lance have come to share. Trust me when I tell you that there is little in life worth living for without having that kind of love."

Nadine swallowed carefully and told herself he meant well. "Thank you for your concern, Your Grace. It's complicated. I just don't know if it's possible to mend this. I'm certain the problem has more to do with me than him, but I can't help how I feel."

Cameron looked frustrated and concerned, and she wondered

what else he might say. He only motioned toward the door, saying, "Very well then. Thank you for your time. That's all I have to say."

"Thank you, Your Grace," she said and hurried from the room, wishing she knew how to change the way she felt.

For the next two days Lance managed to go through the motions of living while he felt empty and hollow inside. His highlights were the opportunities he found to sneak into the castle nursery and see Dulsie. He only hoped her mother wouldn't find out about it and tell the nannies he was forbidden to be there.

Putting in long hours at work, Lance continued pushing every officer on the force to find the man responsible for these murders and for stalking Nadine. Collaborating with the law in the country where Nadine and Albert Crider had both migrated from, they were able to determine that the crimes were indeed identical—beyond the addition of the white scarf on the two victims in Horstberg.

Lance awoke three days after he'd last seen Nadine and wondered if she would ever take him back, and if she didn't, he wondered if his heart would ever heal. He forced himself to face the day, knowing he had a meeting to attend where the current status of the investigation would be thoroughly covered.

Through the course of the meeting, Lance felt mostly bored and terribly frustrated. He'd heard most of this before, over and over. They believed the stalker and the killer were the same man and that the daggers had been purchased before his coming here. He had come to Horstberg within hours of Mrs. Rader's arrival. They had tracked three different inns where he had stayed, and many places where he had eaten and purchased insignificant items. But he had not been sighted at all since the murders had begun, which made them suspect that he'd actually rented or purchased a place to live, but a thorough investigation of such transactions had turned up nothing. They suspected that he had a female accomplice, since the scarves had been purchased by a woman. And a neighbor of the second victim had seen a woman enter the victim's home, quite late, on the night of the murder.

A criminal analyst was present, a Mr. Fruberg, who was

employed full-time by the government to help solve crimes, as well as to help criminals reform their behavior when appropriate. Lance was beginning to wonder what they paid this guy for when he rattled on and on with theories that Lance had figured out on his own long ago. He went into a tedious oration on the patterns of serial killers that he had studied through the course of gaining his university education. It was Mr. Fruberg's opinion that Mr. Crider's obsession with Mrs. Rader was being projected onto the victims who had similar profiles as her. He believed that the suspect was acting out violently with these other women in response to the rejection he'd gotten from Mrs. Rader. Lance listened with growing repulsion, his heart aching more each time he heard her name. And all the while he wanted to scream at Mr. Fruberg and tell him, *I already knew that. Tell me something I don't know.* But he bit his tongue and listened, pretending to take notes while his mind wandered. Mr. Fruberg finally said something that Lance could appreciate when he mentioned that Mrs. Rader might not actually be targeted for murder since she was the original object of the suspect's desire, and he would not want to harm her.

When Mr. Fruberg's turn at speaking had finally ended, Lance was so relieved he wanted to jump up and dance on the table. The time was then turned over to Lieutenant Kepler, one of Lance's highest officers. He was bright and thorough and had been put in charge of gathering and organizing all of the information related to the case.

"Thank you," the lieutenant said, "I will try to be brief. We have a new development." He looked to Lance and added, "It came in just before the meeting, Captain, and I didn't have a chance to discuss it with you."

"Go on, please," Lance encouraged. He could do with a new development.

"An officer was given an anonymous tip this morning regarding the identity of the woman who was seen going into the second victim's home the night of the murder, and that she was also seen at the home of the first victim on the night of that murder. We don't have a name but we have enough information that we believe we can find her with some effort. If we can search her home and find any evidence at all linking her to the crime, then she can surely lead us to the suspect." He went over some details of their plans to search this woman out, while Lance listened with half an ear.

"Forgive the intrusion," Mr. Fruberg said, "but how do we know this woman is not actually the killer? In spite of all the theories we've discussed, we have to consider every possible scenario."

Lance sighed, knowing instinctively that such a theory was simply irrelevant. One of the duke's advisor's said, "Let's follow through on this lead and go from there. If we can find one or the other of them, then we can at least have a trial and get some answers."

"Agreed," several men said

"So get on it," Lance said, hoping this meant the meeting would be over, but it still dragged on with hashing out and revisiting several other facts that he already knew by heart. When the meeting was finally adjourned, Lance was the first to leave the room. He almost felt as if he'd suffocate if he didn't get away from discussing the topic of *Mrs. Rader,* and the danger she could be in. The remainder of the day was long and difficult as he saw to other matters of business while those assigned to the murder investigation kept busy following their leads. He could only pray that the waiting would soon end in regard to Mrs. Rader—both personally and professionally.

Nadine crawled into bed once again feeling lost, alone, and more depressed than she ever had in her life. She had managed to keep going in order to do her work and care for her daughter, but she knew Dulsie wasn't very happy with her, and she thought it was pathetic to have so much strain between a mother and daughter—especially when the child was only five.

Nadine woke at dawn and wondered how she would get through another day, loving a man that she couldn't trust and running from a man who was trying to kill her. She sat up in bed and glanced habitually toward where Dulsie was sleeping, only to have her heart jump into her throat. The little bed was empty. Telling herself that she likely just woke early and went down to the dining room, Nadine grabbed her robe and flew into the hall, noting the door to her room wasn't locked. But then, it could only be locked from the inside. An officer was sitting in a chair near the bottom of the stairs.

"Good morning," he said.

"My daughter is gone. Have you seen her? Did she—"

"No, madame," he said with alarm, coming to his feet. "I've been right here for more than an hour, and I haven't seen her."

Nadine grabbed onto the stair rail, fearing she would pass out otherwise. She told herself not to panic. She told herself there had to be a logical explanation. But under the circumstances, it was difficult not to think of the fact that there was a very sick man on the loose who was after her. Would he use Dulsie to get to her? Had he been so clever as to elude the officers as they moved back and forth in and around the building?

Through the next half an hour Nadine's dread tightened inside of her, exploding into an unfathomable fear. Neither officer had seen Dulsie. She was nowhere inside or around the inn. The doors were all locked—but Nadine's key to the outside door was missing. And while she was certain she'd left the key on her bedside table, she knew she hadn't used it for at least a couple of days because she hadn't left when the outside door would have been locked. An officer pointed out that someone could have slipped into her room and stolen the key during business hours when she and Dulsie were downstairs and the room would have likely been left unlocked. While Nadine was amazed that in all of their efforts to stay protected, they could overlook such a simple thing, and she was beside herself with despair in trying to accept that Dulsie was missing. She cried and shook and screamed while Gerda attempted to keep her calm. Once it was established that Dulsie was absolutely not on the premises, one officer stayed to watch over the inn while the other went to Castle Horstberg to sound the call for a thorough search. He had assured Nadine that they would do everything they possibly could, but the dread inside of her was difficult to dispel. In her heart she had to wonder if she would ever see her little Dulsie alive again.

Lance was crossing the castle courtyard, almost to his office, when a man in uniform galloped in and dismounted as if the devil were at his back.

"Captain!" he called.

"What is it?" Lance demanded, approaching him.

"Sir," he said breathlessly, "Mrs. Rader's—"

"Is she all right?" he demanded while everything inside of him turned to knots.

"She's fine, sir, but her daughter is missing."

"Missing?" Lance echoed and those knots tightened painfully. He listened to the officer give a brief report before he bellowed, "You know what to do. I want every man called in and I want this country torn apart. And I want it done now."

With orders given, Lance got on his horse and galloped to the inn while a deep dread smoldered inside of him. He analyzed what they had overlooked and felt sick. A missing key. Could it have been stolen from her room as the officer suggested? The thought made his insides seethe. The officers would not have been watching the outside doors continuously, because they were locked. And if Dulsie ended up coming to harm—or worse—because of a stupid oversight, he wasn't sure if he could ever live with that. He prayed with all the energy of his soul that she would be spared any harm and that she would quickly be reunited with her mother.

Lance tethered his horse at the inn and hurried inside, not caring if Nadine wanted to see him or not. "Where is she?" he demanded of the officer near the door.

"In her room with Gerda," he reported.

Lance took the steps three at a time and knocked at the door. "Come in," he heard Gerda call.

He entered to see Nadine crying in Gerda's arms. Lance's heart skipped a beat just to see her. Both women looked up to see who their visitor might be. Gerda looked relieved. With Nadine, it was impossible to tell. "Did you find her?" Nadine asked.

"No, but we're doing everything we can. I've had every officer called in to comb the country. We won't stop until she's found." Nadine nodded and visibly tried to compose herself. Lance added, "Gerda, would you give us a few minutes alone?"

"Of course, Captain," she said and hurried from the room.

"Does everyone in this country move so quickly to follow your orders?" Nadine asked as if she resented such an idea.

"Is that question relevant to the problem at hand?" he countered.

"Is your visit personal or business?" she demanded, wiping at her face with a handkerchief.

"Both," he said curtly. "If you were any woman in Horstberg with a missing child, I can assure you that the captain would be paying you a visit unless he were indisposed or out of the country, in which case the highest lieutenant on duty would see to it. But don't pretend to be surprised that my interest is *extremely* personal. I love Dulsie, and I love you. Whether you want to acknowledge that fact is up to you, but I will move heaven and earth to get her back."

"But there is no guarantee," she said.

"No, Nadine. I'm the captain, not God. There is no guarantee. I can only do the best I can do."

"I appreciate your concern," she said and seemed to mean it, "and your help. Is there anything I can do?"

"You can answer a few questions for me. I don't have to go over the usual 'what was your routine' questions. I'm well aware of that. But I have to know . . . was Dulsie upset when she went to bed? Did she give any indication of being . . . concerned, or . . . angry?"

"What are you implying?" she demanded, fully defensive.

"These are standard questions, Mrs. Rader. With any missing child we have to consider the possibility that they might have run away, and they're simply lost or hiding."

"Clearly she was abducted," Nadine insisted. "With a stalker on my tail, how can you even think that—"

"Just answer the questions, please."

Nadine looked as if she'd rather die than do so, and when she spoke he understood why. "I wouldn't say she was upset, but she wasn't very happy with me."

"Why is that?" he asked, already suspecting what the answer might be.

"Is that relevant?"

"Perhaps."

"She's unhappy with me because I sent you away. She's too young to understand."

"I'm twenty-five years older than her, and I don't understand," he said and began to wander through the room.

"Just stick to the pertinent questions, Captain."

"Of course," he said absently as he opened the door and

squatted down to examine the lock. He looked at it from both sides and locked and unlocked it twice. He closed the door again and walked the perimeter of the room, examining the details closely with a thorough gaze.

"Did you hear anything in the night? Anything at all?" he asked.

"No. I slept soundly, once I got to sleep."

"And when was that?" he asked.

"Probably after three, I'm guessing."

He wanted to ask why she was having trouble sleeping, but he knew she'd remind him once again to stick to the pertinent questions.

Lance noticed something that didn't seem right. He looked down at the floor, over his shoulder, then at the bed. He looked all three places again, then he opened the wardrobe.

"What?" she demanded.

He picked up her nightgown from the foot of her little bed and held it up. "Her shoes and coat are gone," he said. "So is her red dress; that's her favorite, isn't it?" He looked at her directly. "Would an abductor wait for her to get dressed?"

"I don't know!" she snapped.

"I have a feeling she's not very far away," he said and turned toward the door. He hesitated and looked at her severely, trying not to think of how he wanted to take her in his arms and kiss her—even as angry as he felt. "I'll keep you informed," he said and hurried from the room and down the stairs. As he rushed from the foot of the stairs toward the door, Gerda bustled from the kitchen with a drink in each hand. They collided and the liquid spilled down the front of Lance's uniform. While Gerda gushed and apologized profusely, Lance assured her it was not a problem, and that he had another uniform at his apartment. He hurried back to the castle, telling the officer on duty at the main door to the keep that he wanted the search concentrated on the area between the inn and Castle Horstberg.

"May I ask why, sir?"

"Because I have a suspicion that she wasn't abducted. I think she ran away, and this is where she comes every day to play. Her mother didn't go to sleep until after three, so she couldn't have gotten terribly far before sunrise when someone would have seen her."

"I'll get right on it, sir," the officer said and Lance hurried to his apartment to change his uniform. He left his cloak at the door, grateful that it had escaped the spill, and went straight up to his bedroom while he unhooked the red coat. He tossed it on the floor of his bedroom and pulled his braces over his shoulders, since his shirt was wet as well. He was buttoning a clean, white shirt when he heard a strange sound that made him freeze. He turned abruptly and relief engulfed him. Dulsie was sound asleep on top of his bed, wrapped in the quilt that was usually folded over the footboard.

"Good heavens," he muttered and squeezed his eyes shut, silently thanking God for keeping her safe. He had to wonder if his little accident that necessitated a change of uniform wasn't perhaps God's way of guiding him to her. He wondered how many hours it would have been before he'd found her here, otherwise.

Pulling on the clean coat, Lance went downstairs and walked out into the courtyard far enough to get an officer's attention. "You, and you . . . come here!" he called and two men came running.

They followed him through the door of his apartment and up the stairs while one of them asked, "What is it, sir?"

"I want you to see something. I spilled something on my uniform and came home to change." He motioned them into his bedroom and then toward the bed.

"Well, if that isn't amazing!" one of them said.

"I left very early this morning," Lance said. "It was still dark. I'm not sure how she got through the gate without being seen. I'm going to let her sleep and then we'll ask her some questions. I want you to spread the word that she has been found and she's safe and to call off the search. Where and how she was found is not to be repeated."

"Yes, sir," they both said together.

"Inform Mrs. Rader of the same," Lance said. "Tell her the child is being questioned and she'll be returned later today."

"And should we tell her that—"

"Don't tell her any more than you tell anybody else. The fact that she ran away will be a sensitive issue for Mrs. Rader. I wanted you to see where she was found, should any concerns arise in the future. That will be all."

The officers left and Lance sat down on the edge of the bed to watch Dulsie sleep. Oh, how he'd missed her! He thought of her leaving in the night and making her way here and he felt terrified on her behalf as he considered all that could have happened to her.

While she slept, he made himself comfortable with a book. He'd not felt this relaxed since that first murder had occurred, and then he had been confronted with losing Nadine. But right now, Dulsie was in his care, and she needed someone to watch after her while she slept. There was no duty more important for him right now.

Nadine was pacing her room with the door open when she heard booted footsteps bounding up the stairs. She stepped into the hall and met the eager face of an officer. "She's been found," he said and Nadine nearly collapsed, leaning against the wall. "She's safe and well and she'll be returned to you after she's been questioned."

"Oh, thank God," she muttered. "Where did they find her? Was she—"

"I know no more than that, Mrs. Rader."

"Very well. Thank you." She went into her room and closed the door, weeping with a relief that was as intense as her grief and worry had been only a while ago. When time passed she wished she would have asked the officer more specific questions on when to expect Dulsie's return. The officers on duty at the inn knew nothing. The routine of the day quickly settled back to normal at the inn, and Nadine felt restless. She'd sent word to the castle earlier to let Abbi know the situation and that she wouldn't be coming to work. Of course, Abbi would know by now that Dulsie was safe. Would she be expecting her to come in now that the drama was over? But how could Nadine leave until she saw for herself the evidence that Dulsie was safe and well?

Nadine hovered in the dining room once the breakfast customers had cleared out, but she became tense with the presence of the officer on duty who seemed to want to ease her nerves by making clever conversation. It was too cold to wait outside, so she returned to her room, keeping the door open so that she could hear any approach. Hearing footsteps on the stairs she rushed into the hall in time to see Lance appear at the other end of the hall, with Dulsie in his arms. She had no thought beyond the joy of seeing that Dulsie was safe. Lance set her down and she ran as Nadine went to her knees and they shared a tight embrace.

"Oh, my darling. You're all right."

"Why are you crying, Mama? I'm back now."

"I know. And I'm so happy that you're back. Are you hurt?"

"No," Dulsie looked confused, "I'm fine."

Nadine stood, keeping her arm around Dulsie. "Thank you," she said to Lance. "I don't know what you did to find her so quickly, but I'm grateful."

"Well, I think God was with us," he said. She nodded and hugged Dulsie, who was holding to her skirts.

"I hope whoever is responsible will be severely punished. I want—"

"Perhaps we should talk about that," he said. "I don't really think that putting Dulsie in prison would accomplish much, do you?"

Lance couldn't help chuckling in response to Nadine's dumbfounded expression. "Are you trying to tell me that she . . ." She couldn't seem to finish.

Lance motioned toward her room. "Perhaps we should talk . . . privately. I think there are some things Dulsie needs to tell you."

Nadine moved hesitantly into the room and watched Lance take a chair. Dulsie climbed eagerly onto his lap and clung to him. Nadine closed the door and took the other chair, already knowing she wasn't going to like this.

"Tell your mother what you did," Lance urged. Dulsie looked at him hesitantly and he added, "You promised me that you would tell your mother everything."

She still said nothing and Nadine asked Lance, "Where was she found?"

"She was asleep in my apartment," he said. Nadine sighed and looked away, more embarrassed than anything. She recalled her indignant words to him when he'd implied that she had run away, and she wanted to just disappear. As if the situation between them weren't already bad enough.

He went on to explain, "I bumped into Gerda in the dining room and my uniform was soaked from the spill. I went home to change; if not for that, I wouldn't have gone home for hours. There's not much there in the way of food, but certainly enough for a little girl to get by on for a day or so. It could have been many hours before we found her." Lance nudged Dulsie and added, "Come on. You need to tell your mother what you did."

Dulsie looked timidly toward her mother and said, "I . . . woke up in the night and couldn't go back to sleep. I didn't want to stay here so I got dressed very quiet and I took the key so that I could lock the door when I left so that you would be safe. I was careful to sneak past the officers when they were looking somewhere else. I walked for a long way, then I saw the milk wagon at somebody's house and I knew it would go to the castle because I've seen it there sometimes in the mornings. I got in the back and when it stopped at the castle I got out and went into Lance's house when nobody was looking."

Nadine sighed loudly but said nothing. She was too happy to have Dulsie safe to be very upset. And she knew she couldn't take out her embarrassment by getting angry with the child. Still, she wanted Dulsie to understand the seriousness of what she had done. Then it became evident that she already did.

"Keep going," Lance said firmly to Dulsie.

Dulsie sighed and got tears in her eyes as she turned to her mother and said, "I'm sorry that I worried you so badly. Lance told me how wrong it was for me to do that. He told me about all the people who were worried. And he told me about all of his officers that were out looking for me. He said that you were worried more than anybody, and that I needed to tell you I was sorry. I am sorry, Mama. And I'll never go anywhere again without telling you where I am."

Nadine met Lance's eyes and wished she could find the words to tell him how grateful she was, then she turned abruptly away. While a part of her wanted to blame him for this, she knew that such a course would be completely unfair and ridiculous. He had done nothing but show love to Dulsie since their arrival in Horstberg, and he had brought her safely home and well taught concerning the situation. She reminded herself that this changed nothing between them, but she was grateful for all he had done.

"Thank you," she said before she became too emotional to speak. She opened her arms for Dulsie and she came running. While they were embracing and crying together, Lance got up and left the room.

Chapter Eighteen

VICTIMS

Nadine eased Dulsie aside and went after him. "Wait," she said in the hall, and he turned back to look at her. The hope in his eyes broke her heart when she knew it wasn't in her to answer that hope. She wasn't sure what was wrong with her, that she would feel so compelled to keep this distance between them. And now that he was looking at her, she didn't know what to say.

"Is there something else you needed, Mrs. Rader?" His formality bit at her, but she couldn't blame him.

"No, I just wanted to . . . thank you. I apologize for the trouble that was caused for you and your men."

"We're glad to be of service, madame, and equally glad that we had a favorable outcome."

"Yes, of course."

Lance watched her standing there, wanting with everything he had to just have her run into his arms, the way Dulsie had run into hers. But he'd come beyond begging. Now, all he could do was let her know that he was there if she needed him, and pray that eventually she would come around. He cleared his throat and said, "If you need any other assistance, you know where to find me."

"Yes, of course," she said again. "Once more, thank you."

Lance nodded and hurried away, wondering if this ache inside of him would ever go away.

Later that day, Nadine was in the dining room with Dulsie when three officers came in, obviously on business. They spoke with Drew and Gerda in the kitchen for a few minutes, then went upstairs. Gerda said quietly to Nadine, "They're searching the rooms. I can't imagine what for."

"Nor can I," Nadine said, a little unnerved to think of them in *her* room. She was glad she'd left it tidy. She noticed that they were up there for quite some time, and were still there when she decided to go for a little walk into town with Dulsie. They took an officer with them, according to the standard procedure, and returned to find that the officers were gone. Her room looked a little disheveled, but everything was where it was supposed to be. They had obviously done a thorough search but had not disturbed any of her belongings as far as she could tell. She wondered what they had been looking for and if it had anything to do with the murder investigation.

Feeling the exhaustion of many sleepless nights and a great deal of emotional strain, Nadine went to bed early, grateful to have her daughter safely with her and to know that in spite of the estrangement between her and Lance, all was well.

Once Dulsie was safely reunited with her mother, Lance returned to the castle, feeling more exhausted than he'd ever felt in his life. He almost felt sick, which was something he'd rarely encountered. He considered how many days he'd gone with very little sleep, and how poorly he'd been eating, and it wasn't difficult to imagine why he felt the way he did. After eating a good lunch in the castle kitchen with some of the servants he was well acquainted with, he told his men he wasn't feeling well and he was taking the rest of the day off.

"If anything comes up," he said, "either take care of it or it can wait until morning. You know what constitutes enough of an emergency to wake me. Anything less will put me in a very foul mood."

The men chuckled. He knew that he was not reputed for having foul moods, so they considered it a joke. But they didn't know the half of what was going on in his life. He'd been in a foul mood since Nadine had kicked him out, and he found himself more and more hard-pressed to keep it from flowing into his work.

Lance went to sleep early in the afternoon and slept through the night, coming awake just before dawn. He bathed and got dressed before he went into town for an early breakfast at a pub he went to on occasion. He didn't have to wonder why he was avoiding the inn, even though their food was by far the best, in his opinion.

Lance returned to the castle and went straight to his office. He entered to find three of his men waiting for him, including Lieutenant Kepler.

"Good morning, gentlemen," Lance said. "I trust you have something worth telling me."

"We do," Kepler said. "This turned up yesterday afternoon through the course of searching out the leads we'd been given. We had our analysts look over the materials we confiscated, but we didn't want to disturb you. We figured half a day wouldn't make much difference."

"I appreciate that," Lance said.

"You're feeling better then?" Kepler asked.

Lance answered honestly, "I feel much more rested, thank you." He noticed one of the men holding the standard canvas bag that was used to gather evidence. "Show me what you've got," he said.

He was astonished to see three white silk scarves and three identical daggers with carved ivory handles, laid out on his desk. "Where did you find this?" he demanded.

"In a woman's room," Kepler said. "The scarves were in one drawer, beneath clothing. The daggers in another, the same way. And we found this." He set a leather-bound book on the desk. "It's a journal of sorts, sir, with some very disturbing details of how the crimes were premeditated and committed."

Lance thumbed through the pages, not wanting to read what was written there. He noted that the handwriting looked very feminine and precise. But he felt confused. "Are you saying then that this woman is guilty of the murders?" In his mind it didn't make sense. His instincts didn't agree, but the evidence before him was not to be taken lightly.

"It appears that way, sir," Kepler said. "We also found these in the same room." He set out two small pieces of paper with handwriting on them. "You'll notice they are written in the same hand as the journal."

"What's the significance?" Lance asked.

"The addresses of where the murders occurred."

"Good heavens," Lance said. "So what are you waiting for? You should have arrested this woman yesterday. Did you need my approval for *this?*" He saw the men exchange wary glances. "Well?" he demanded.

"Yes, sir," Kepler said, seeming nervous. "I mean . . . we don't need your approval, Captain. But we felt it was best that you were adequately informed before the arrest was made."

"I don't understand," Lance said.

Kepler cleared his throat and stated firmly, "The woman in question is Nadine Rader, sir."

Lance took a sharp breath, certain he'd heard wrong. He was so completely stunned he couldn't even put together a cohesive response. He resisted the urge to argue and get defensive, not wanting to make himself look like a fool. He swallowed carefully and asked, "Are you sure?"

"Yes, sir," Kepler said.

"Isn't it possible these things were planted to implicate her?" he asked.

"It's possible, sir," Kepler said, his voice maintaining compassion, "but that's not for us to decide. The standard protocol states that—"

"I know what it states, Lieutenant," Lance said, and for a full minute he said nothing more. He had believed that this situation could get no worse. Never in his wildest imaginings could he have fathomed something like this.

"Forgive me, sir," Kepler said, "I understand how difficult this is for you, but if it were any other woman, you would have had her arrested for much less than this."

Lance swallowed hard. He leaned his hands on the edge of the desk and hung his head. "Yes, you're right, Lieutenant. Forgive me." He sighed. "Bring her in," he said, "but please . . . handle the situation . . . carefully."

"Of course, sir," the lieutenant said with compassion.

The moment they left Lance hurried into the castle, desperately needing the support of the only friends he truly had. He was grateful to find Cameron, Abbi, and Georg all just finishing their breakfast.

"Good morning, Captain," Cameron said. "Won't you join us? We can—"

"No, thank you. I've eaten."

"What's wrong?" Abbi asked as he took a seat across from her.

All eyes turned to him with obvious concern. He cleared his throat and said, "I'm glad you're all here. That will spare me from having to say this more than once."

"What is it?" Cameron asked. "What's happened? Please don't tell us that Nadine has been hurt or—"

"Nadine is at this moment being arrested," he said.

"What in the name of heaven for?" Cameron demanded.

"She is where the evidence led my men," he said. "She is being implicated as the killer."

"That's impossible!" Abbi said.

"I know that!" Lance insisted. "It doesn't take a lot of brains to see that whoever is behind this has been stalking her and now he's playing some sick joke on her by setting her up. But the evidence against her is . . . startling, to be truthful." He sighed and absorbed the silence that clearly indicated nobody could think of anything to say that would have any meaning. He cleared his throat and said, "I have to believe that when all is said and done, her innocence will be proven. For the moment, my greatest concern is for Dulsie. I must see that she's cared for, and—"

"You must bring her here," Abbi said. "She's comfortable here; she'll be safe. And we can watch out for her while you're working, and she can even share Erich's room and be close to us. You can see her as much as possible."

"I confess that I had hoped for that very thing. I don't know that Nadine will want me associating with the child, but . . . quite frankly, I'm not certain I care what Nadine wants. I love Dulsie. She loves me. Whatever estrangement there is between me and her mother has nothing to do with her." He sighed and added, "Forgive me, but . . . this is difficult and . . ." He sighed and forced back his emotion. "Will the two of you . . ." he nodded toward Cameron and Georg, "be going to the office or . . ."

"Yes, we are. Did you want to stay with us until you know she's been brought in?" Cameron asked with compassion.

"I was hoping for that very thing, yes. Thank you," Lance said.

"I can't believe it," Abbi muttered. "I just can't believe it."

"Well, I have to agree there," Lance said, going to his feet.

With sarcasm he added, "Life just keeps getting more unbelievable every day."

Nadine sent Dulsie downstairs to wait while she finished with her hair. Having missed work the previous day, she knew there would be much to catch up on and she was hoping to get there early. She was startled by a knock at the door, and opened it to see two officers standing in the hall. "What is it?" she asked, wondering if they had some news concerning the investigation.

"Mrs. Rader," one of them said gravely, "I'm afraid we are here to arrest you."

"What?" She actually laughed, certain it had to be some kind of joke.

"Significant evidence has been found to connect you to the recent murders, and we have orders to bring you in. Your hands, please."

Nadine was so stunned she couldn't move, couldn't speak. When the officer took her hands and put them into handcuffs, an unfathomable fear overtook her. "What evidence?" she muttered. "I don't understand. I . . . I . . . ." Realizing she was about to cry, she stopped talking and forced back her emotion, determined to go with dignity. Surely once she had a chance to speak for herself, they would realize this was all just a terrible misunderstanding.

With her hands bound, they led her down the stairs, one officer in front of her and the other holding tightly to her right arm. At the foot of the stairs was another officer who had obviously informed Drew and Gerda of what was happening. Their stunned expressions said it all, and Gerda was holding tightly to Dulsie, who looked more confused than upset. She had come to trust the officers who were looking out for them.

"We'll watch out for her," Gerda said. "You mustn't worry."

"Thank you," Nadine said, then she squatted down to face Dulsie. "Can Mama have a hug?" she asked. Dulsie looked skeptically at her bound hands and threw her arms around Nadine's neck. "I'll be back as soon as I can. You be a good girl."

Dulsie nodded and was eased away by one of the officers before

Nadine was led outside. She kept telling herself that this was just a misunderstanding and it would be easily cleared up. Arriving at the castle, she was taken into a room not far from Lance's office. The irony was horrible. She wondered where he was right now, and what he had to do with this. If these men had been given *orders* to arrest her, where else would those orders have come from? While it seemed completely out of character for him, she couldn't help wondering if his anger toward her might have contributed to this situation.

Nadine was asked to sit beside a long table while one of the officers stood at the door, his hands behind his back. Another sat in the corner, crossing his ankle over his knee, and the one who had done all the talking stood directly across from her. He reached for a long, shallow box at the other end of the table and set it directly in front of her. Nadine gasped to see three white scarves and three daggers, just like what Lance had described related to the murders. There was also a leather-bound book. "These," the officer said, "were all found in your room at the inn."

"What?" she gasped. "I've never seen these things before in my life."

The officers exchanged a glance that clearly said they'd heard such things before and they didn't believe her. The officer opened the book and pointed to the handwriting on one of the pages. "Is this not your handwriting? It matches samples of your work that we acquired from the duchess."

Nadine attempted to keep her voice steady as she looked this man in the eye and said firmly, "It looks like my handwriting, but I did not write this. I have never seen this book before."

"And what about these, Mrs. Rader? These are evidently in your handwriting, as well. Have you seen these before?"

The officer set in front of her the two little pieces of paper she'd been given with addresses on them. She gasped to note that the handwriting *did* look like that in the journal, and it *did* look like her own handwriting. She'd not even thought of it before, simply because she'd known she hadn't written them.

"Have you seen these before, Mrs. Rader?"

"Yes, I have," she said. "They were given to me. One by a woman in a cloak at the inn, as she was leaving. I didn't see her face. The other was given to me by Drew, at the inn. He said it had been given to him by a customer. That's all I know."

"You were seen at these addresses. In fact, the officers that escorted you have both told us you were there, and that you went inside each of these homes alone."

"That's right," she said, "but only for a couple of minutes, just to see if anyone was home."

"Are you aware, Mrs. Rader, that these are the locations where the murders occurred?" Nadine sucked in her breath and couldn't find the means to let it out. "Are you also aware that your visits to these homes occurred within the parameter of time that we know the crimes took place?"

Nadine's chest began to burn for want of air. She gasped for breath and willed herself to stay calm. She couldn't believe this. It was a nightmare! In her mind she put pieces together. The first home she'd never been to, but the second she had. And the woman who lived there had borne a strong likeness to her in build and coloring. Was that who the second victim had been? The woman she had visited with not so many days ago? Had she led the killer to this woman? And now the killer was deliberately framing her for his crimes. It was too horrible to believe.

"Mrs. Rader," the officer said in a voice that lacked compassion or kindness. She reminded herself that he was accustomed to dealing with criminals, and the evidence had put her into that category. She also reminded herself of her innocence and she looked at him directly.

"No, I was not aware," she said and went on to explain her reasons for visiting the women that she'd gone to see previously, and her reasons for going to the addresses, believing that these women wanted to talk to her. She didn't hesitate to share with them what she knew of the man stalking her, and that it was evident he'd been tracking her and that he'd clearly set her up. They listened carefully, but the officer in charge admitted, "We've heard most of this information before, Mrs. Rader. It doesn't change what the evidence tells us. How do you explain the journal in your handwriting? This book goes through the careful planning and carrying out of these crimes, with details that only the law has been aware of. Do you have any explanation for that, Mrs. Rader?"

"No, I don't," she said firmly while everything inside of her wanted to melt into the floor and die. "I know that I had some things stolen before I came to Horstberg, and among them were my journals. Perhaps someone duplicated my handwriting."

The officers exchanged a skeptical glance before she was taken by the arm and urged to her feet. "Come along, Mrs. Rader. I'm afraid you're staying."

Nadine felt raw, unbridled terror bubbling inside of her and feared she would start crying like a baby before she could be alone. She fought with everything inside of her to hold herself together, certain her dignity was the only thing she had left. She was taken to a small, stone room with no windows, where the handcuffs were removed and a lantern was left on a hook. The heavy metal door was slammed behind her, making her wince. She turned to take in her bleak surroundings. There was a narrow bunk in the corner, with some blankets folded at one end and no pillow. There was a small table and a single chair. A bucket on the table had water in it. Another bucket was in the corner on the floor. The reality descended harshly, and the fear and anguish inside of her refused to be held back. She curled up on the bunk and muffled her sobbing by pressing her face into her skirts. She couldn't believe it. Her life was over. And at the moment, being murdered by Albert Crider seemed preferable.

Looking down into the courtyard from the window of the ducal office, Lance felt a smoldering sickness in the pit of his stomach as he watched Nadine being taken into the keep, her hands bound.

"I can't believe it," he muttered to Cameron and Georg, who were sitting nearby, offering silent support. How grateful he was to know that these men he worked with were willing to be his truest friends when difficulties arose. "This is like some kind of nightmare."

"Well said," Cameron muttered. "I think I can imagine how she must be feeling." Lance turned to look at him as he added, "When I found Gwen dead on the floor, I felt so . . . shocked, and . . . sick. I couldn't believe it. Our marriage hadn't been good, but I never would have wanted something so horrible to happen, and then I turned around and realized I was being arrested. It was a nightmare, plain and simple. Thankfully it ended . . . eventually."

Lance didn't even want to talk about how long it had taken for Cameron's nightmare to end. Now that he knew Nadine was in the keep, he could see to his next order of business. "Thank you for keeping a vigil with me, gentlemen. I need to get Dulsie so that I know she's safe. Her Grace offered to go with me."

"Good plan," Cameron said. "Please keep us posted. And if there's anything we can do . . ."

"Thank you again," Lance said and hurried to find Abbi.

Little was said between them through the brief carriage ride to the inn. It seemed they were both in shock. But Lance felt grateful for the numbness coating his emotions. Without it he felt as if he would disintegrate into nothingness.

He was glad to arrive and find the inn devoid of customers prior to lunch being served. Abbi helped Dulsie pack her things while Lance talked with Drew and Gerda, explaining what he knew. They offered to care for Dulsie, but Abbi insisted that they had plenty to keep them busy with running the inn. "She loves the nursery at the castle," Abbi said, "and she's comfortable there. We can look out for her, and little Erich loves to play with her."

Abbi also assured Drew and Gerda that she would see the rent was paid on the room so that it could be available with Nadine's things in place when this misunderstanding was cleared up and she returned. Abbi also packed some things for Nadine that she felt sure she could use.

"They do allow prisoners a change of clothing and common necessaries, do they not?" Abbi asked Lance.

"Of course," he said, not liking the subtle bite in her voice. He knew she wasn't blaming him. She was just angry over the circumstances, as he was.

Through the carriage ride back to the castle, Lance and Abbi answered Dulsie's questions and did their best to explain what was going on without giving Dulsie cause to get upset. The child was quiet but seemed to understand and accept the situation as a temporary misunderstanding. Lance prayed that's all it would turn out to be.

Lance went with Dulsie to the castle nursery and actually ate lunch with her and the other children. In spite of how much he hated what was happening, he couldn't help being happy to be with Dulsie and have her in his care. Dulsie seemed comfortable and glad to be with him, and he told her he would be back to see her this evening, and that Her Grace would see that she had everything she needed.

Walking back to the keep, Lance was glad that at least he could stop worrying about Albert Crider getting hold of either one of them. Although, it seemed that indirectly he had certainly gotten hold of Nadine. Lance couldn't even fathom what kind of sick mind this man had, and he greatly looked forward to the day when they caught up with him. He went to his office, knowing that the standard interrogation of the new prisoner would be long over. Lieutenant Kepler came in to give him a report of the results of the interrogation, and the sickness inside of him deepened. It would take a miracle to prove her innocent.

Nadine was grateful to be fed a decent meal, and at least she concluded that prisoners here were not deprived and mistreated. She could credit a good duke and a good captain for having something to do with that. Still, just being here was more horrible than anything she had ever endured. She felt certain it was only a matter of time before the captain himself came to see her, and the very idea made her sick. She didn't even want to think about it.

Through the afternoon she paced the little room, praying that Dulsie would be all right and that she wouldn't be upset by this. She felt as if she'd go mad with the close quarters and nothing to do with her time, and she wondered how long she would truly end up being here. Late afternoon she heard footsteps in the hall and the key groaned in the lock. Dreading the moment she had to face Lance, she felt certain this would be that moment. She was surprised, instead, to see Abbi.

"I'll be back in five minutes, Your Grace," the officer said.

"Thank you," she said, and the door was closed and locked. Their eyes met for a long moment while Nadine wondered what to say. Abbi finally asked, "Do you have what you need?"

"Relatively speaking," she said.

"Well, I've brought a few of your things," she added, drawing attention to the basket on her arm. "They searched it thoroughly, so I'm afraid there are no weapons or tools to pick the locks."

"Too bad," Nadine said with sarcasm and Abbi chuckled.

Nadine was grateful to hear even a bit of humor in the midst of this blackness.

Abbi set the basket on the table and removed its contents. "Here is a change of clothes—one of everything you need. No nightgown. I think you'd do well to sleep in your clothes. You never know when they might want to question you. I understand they will wash your clothes and return them so that you can stay clean, and they'll bring fresh water each morning and evening for you to wash."

"That's good to know," she said, wondering again how long she would be here.

"Apparently the captain doesn't like his prison smelly," Abbi said lightly, but Nadine could find no humor in that particular comment.

"I've also brought your hairbrush, and the toiletries that were in your room."

"Thank you," she said. "You don't know what this means to me."

"Well, it's the least I can do," Abbi said. "And," she pulled something out of the basket, "your Bible."

Nadine sighed deeply as she took it, feeling a deep irony as she recalled Lance giving it to her. "Thank you," she said again, holding it tightly against her. Nadine felt compelled to add, "You must be so disappointed in me."

"Disappointed? Why?"

"Well, I know you're not happy about the estrangement between me and Lance, and this . . . this is just so . . ."

"Listen to me, Nadine. Whatever may become of you and Lance, I am in no position to judge your heart. I will always be your friend. And this . . . well, this is just a ridiculous misunderstanding, and we can only pray that it gets cleared up, and soon. In the meantime," Abbi lifted from the basket a small box, ink and pen, "you can keep busy by continuing your work. I need these addressed, and you need to stay busy."

"Oh, what a blessing!" Nadine said. "I feared I would go mad."

"I had a hunch on that," Abbi said. "I don't know that they'll let me in very often, but I can have more delivered and these picked up."

"They won't let *you* in?"

"I have to adhere to the rules like everyone else, my dear. In the keep, there are no designations. My position got me in to begin with, but time and frequency of visits are very strict."

Nadine felt touched by her efforts and downhearted by her statement. If Abbi had no power here, then who did? What would become of her if even her connections to the royal family meant nothing?

They heard the officer in the hall, then the key in the lock. "Thank you," Nadine hurried to say.

Abbi hugged her tightly. "We will be praying for you, my dear," she said and hurried away. Only when the door was locked behind her did Nadine realize that she'd forgotten to ask about Dulsie, but then she was likely with Drew and Gerda. And that was fine. She only hoped that she would stay safe while they were so busy with their work.

Nadine looked through her belongings and the work Abbi had brought for her to do. She felt comforted at having her own things with her and knowing that she wouldn't be wearing the same clothes indefinitely. But the simple reality of being here seemed more than she could bear. She could only pray that it didn't go on too long.

Chapter Nineteen

INTERROGATION

Lance saw to his business, doing his best to stay busy and not think about the situation. He went to the inn for supper, hating the memories but somehow feeling drawn to them. The very absence of the officers patrolling the place made him heartsick as he considered the reason. He returned to the castle and spent some time with Dulsie before she was taken to bed, along with little Erich. Lance appreciated Abbi's tenderness with Dulsie, and he was grateful for her willingness to care for the child.

He returned to his office and sat there, mostly staring at the wall, as the hour became very late. He knew he needed to see Nadine, but he didn't want to. It was standard procedure for the captain to make contact with every new prisoner and assess the situation, and it was hours overdue. While he couldn't help feeling sorrow and compassion for her, he felt angered by knowing that she wanted nothing to do with him. He finally steeled himself to be the Captain of the Guard as he walked slowly down the long, stone hallway to her cell. He took a deep breath and turned the key in the lock. He pushed open the door and turned up the wick on the lantern hanging nearby in order to see her sitting on the bunk, her back pressed into the corner, her arms wrapped around her knees. Her eyes were filled with a stark fear that tore at his heart. He saw her recognize him before he pulled the door closed and tucked the keys into his pocket. She looked abruptly away, just as she had the last time he'd seen her. The gesture taunted his anger and lured it to the surface.

Nadine felt her trembling increase as she realized that having him here under the circumstances was far worse than she'd imagined.

There were no words to describe the humiliation and degradation overtaking her. She stole a glance at his face, wondering what he might say, and she was startled to see a hard, unyielding man she'd never seen before. In that moment it was easier to see him as the Captain of the Guard than it ever had been. She'd always had some difficulty imagining him in command of hundreds of men when the man she had come to know was so tender and sensitive. But the side of Lance Dukerk she had become comfortable with was nowhere to be seen in that expression. The power and dignity of his presence was not unfamiliar, but it had taken on a new level of supremacy.

"So," he said in a voice that was hard and unmerciful, "this is certainly an interesting twist. One can only imagine what the gossip mongers would say about this. His first fiancée left him at the altar, and the second left him for a life of crime. The Captain of the Guard and a murderer certainly aren't very compatible."

"You must hate me for that."

"For what?" he asked as if he wanted to be exactly clear on his reasons for hating her.

"For . . . what people will say."

"I don't give a damn what people say, Nadine, and I'm not going to stand here and pretend that you are like any other prisoner in this keep."

"Except that you gave the order for me to be arrested," she guessed with some degree of certainty.

"Don't make it sound as if it were easy. What I had to do today is one of the hardest things I've *ever* had to do. You know what the other one was. What I do is dictated by the law, and the law dictated that there was too much evidence against you."

"So, you did it to save face."

"I did it," he actually shouted, "because it was the right thing to do! And sometimes the right thing is the hardest thing. And you can't condemn me for that."

Nadine looked away. "Please tell me that Dulsie is being cared for."

"Of course she is. Did you think I would leave her unattended for even an hour? Gerda offered to care for her, but they're far too busy. She's with Abbi."

"Bless her heart," Nadine said. "She brought me some things, but she can't be very happy with me."

"She thinks this is all a horrible mistake, but even *she* is bound by the law. You might get some compassion from Cameron. He once spent time in here, accused of a crime he didn't commit. But even *he* is powerless to do anything when evidence stands. He's not like his brother who ran this country according to his whims and fancies until there was no order at all. His Grace is a man of honor, and I would have dishonored him to do anything different than what I did today."

Silence followed his harsh words until Nadine asked, "What will they do to me?"

"I don't know," he said. "There will be a trial . . . eventually. What they really want now is information, and I am not even going to tell you what they will do to get information out of criminals."

"But I don't have any information," she said frantically. "They already know what I know. I had nothing to do with this, Lance. You must believe me."

"I *do* believe you," he said, his voice still harsh, his persona rigid. "But it doesn't matter what I believe. I will be viewed as biased in this matter, and my opinion will carry little weight in regard to the technicality of the law."

"What do they do . . . to get information?"

"Well, it's . . . humane as far as my not allowing any physical harm or torture. It wasn't always the way it is now. You can thank God your deceased *husband* isn't in charge."

He saw her press a hand over her mouth, as if to hold back her emotion, but a whimper escaped nevertheless. He squeezed his eyes closed as her anguish ripped at his heart. He wanted more than anything to just take her in his arms, to hold her through this, to give her the love and encouragement he felt for her. But she had put a wall between them and he didn't know how to break past it. Certain he couldn't bear being in her presence any longer, he asked, "Is there anything you need that I can legally get for you?"

Nadine watched him through the mist that spread into her eyes, while all of her fear and anguish over the situation rushed unchecked to the surface. "I need to get out of here," she cried. "I need to be a mother to my child! I need to *live!*" She sobbed without control, and Lance couldn't keep the distance between them any longer.

He went to his knees beside her and took her shoulders into his hands. Her sobbing relented to a quiet whimpering while she appeared terrified of him. "Listen to me, Nadine, I would do anything in my power to get you out of here, but it is not in my power to do so. But you cannot let this undo you. You cannot! Do you understand me? You've got to be brave and strong and trust in God to get you through this and see justice met. Are you hearing me?"

She whimpered and nodded. His voice softened to a harsh whisper. "I want to be here for you, Nadine, to give you strength and support. I want to be the man who loves you. But you've made it very clear that I can only be the Captain of the Guard to you, and as the captain my hands are tied."

"I need you, Lance," she murmured tearfully. "I'm so scared. Before I came here, I knew he was stalking me, but I'd never dreamed the murders were connected until . . . and then . . ." She moaned as if she was experiencing physical pain. "I was so afraid that I'd be the next victim, and of how that would affect Dulsie. But now . . . oh, heaven help me! How could this have happened? What did I do to deserve this? What if I end up facing a firing squad? How can I—"

"Listen to me, Nadine. You didn't *do* anything. Sometimes things just . . . happen. There are wicked and evil people out there who do awful things that take choices away from the rest of us. You just have to ride the storm and have some faith, and pray to God that it doesn't come to that."

She nodded again but didn't seem convinced. Lance looked into her eyes and wanted desperately to kiss her. But he couldn't. He just couldn't. So he forced himself to his feet and stepped backward. "I must go," he said, and while he wanted to say he'd see her tomorrow, he wasn't certain he could handle it. Instead he muttered, "I'll return when I can."

He turned his back and moved to the door, fumbling for the keys in his pocket. "Stay with me tonight," she said. "Don't leave me alone. I need you."

Lance stopped and squeezed his eyes closed, forcing reason past his own raw emotions. Recounting the state of their relationship prior to this event, his anger resurfaced. His voice was caustic as he said, "You need me?" He turned to face her. "Knowing that you see me as a liar and a fraud, a villain in disguise, I have to assume your *need* is spurred by desperation. You weren't desperate enough to need me when you knew a murdering stalker was on your tail and I wanted you to come to the castle. Whatever needs you might have, Mrs. Rader, you can take them up with the captain. The man you claim to need is not available. And the captain would never stay in a woman's cell alone for more than ten minutes. It's against protocol."

"I never imagined that you could be so bitter," she said, more sad than anything else.

"I never would have imagined it, myself," he said in a tone that only further validated her accusation. "But maybe you should be grateful I am. If I spent the night in here, however innocent, you would have a reputation by morning. Do you want them to think you're a tramp? That you were seeking special favors from the captain with the hope of getting better treatment? There is an officer down the hall who knows exactly where I am and he's counting the minutes. You've already got enough to rise above, I think. You'd do well to spend the night alone."

She said nothing and he hurried to unlock the door before any more hurtful words came out of his mouth. The door closing between them cracked his heart in two and he felt as if a volcanic eruption would spew from the chasm. Lance hurried as quickly as he could manage to his apartment and locked the door, as if the horror of his encounter with Nadine might catch up and smother him. All the emotion that he had suppressed through the day was suddenly spurred to the surface. The first sob erupted from his throat as he tore his cloak off and tossed it. The second came as he lumbered up the stairs in the dark. By the time he fell to his knees beside the bed, he was heaving with unleashed emotion that threatened to devour him. He cried himself into prayer, and prayed himself to sleep, curled up on top of the bed, still wearing his uniform and boots. He woke up freezing but couldn't find the motivation to build a fire, or even pull a blanket over himself.

The cold finally won and he got up to build a fire. He lay on the rug close to its warmth but couldn't go back to sleep. When morning finally arrived, he went to the private nursery in the castle, where he knew Cameron and Abbi usually were this time of day with Erich. And today Dulsie would be there, too.

"Good morning," Abbi said when he entered.

"You look terrible," Cameron interjected.

"It's nice to see you as well, Your Grace," Lance said with sarcasm, then Dulsie saw him and came running into his arms. He laughed and held her close, grateful for this one bright spot in his life. While Cameron played quietly with Erich and Abbi sat close by, Lance read a story to Dulsie. When the nanny arrived to take over, Lance left with Cameron and Abbi.

Ambling slowly down the hall toward the stairs, Cameron asked, "Any new evidence?"

"Not as of midnight last night," Lance said.

"There has to be a solution, Captain. There just has to be."

"That's what I'm praying for," Lance sighed and put his hands behind his back as he walked.

"You know," Cameron went on, "when I look back over my being in a similar situation, I have no doubt whatsoever that God's hand was present in proving my innocence. It wasn't easy, but it came together miraculously in the end."

"Yes, and it only took four years," Lance said, unable to avoid sounding cynical.

"Well," Cameron countered, "that was only because Abbi could hardly win me over at the age of fifteen."

"And," Abbi inserted, "you needed more humbling than that."

"Indeed, I did," Cameron chuckled and hugged Abbi.

Lance bid them good day and attempted to focus on his work. His heart felt heavy, and his soul weary, but he was determined to keep going, just as he'd told Nadine to do. But Lance's day took a turn for the worse when he was informed that the committee of national security would be convening to question the suspect. Being a member of that committee, he had sat through many such meetings. But this one would be hell. He knew what these men were like. They were all good men in their own right, and good at their jobs, but their opinions on how certain matters should be handled varied greatly. And some of them could be ruthless. When it came to dealing with genuine criminals who were a menace to society, such ruthlessness was warranted. But the thought of Nadine, an innocent victim, facing this committee, just made him want to break something. And he had to be there to watch it happen.

Nadine had just finished her breakfast and was sitting down to do the work Abbi had brought when an officer came to her cell to get the dishes from her meal and to inform her that she would be taken before a committee in less than an hour to be questioned. Nadine felt sick at the thought. She didn't have to wonder *who* was on that committee. She reminded herself that she just had to tell the truth and maintain her dignity, but as difficult as all of this was for her, she had serious doubts in regard to the latter.

When the officer returned to get her, he bound her hands in front of her with handcuffs. "Standard protocol," he explained, "whenever a prisoner is taken out of their cell."

"Of course," she said, pretending not to be humiliated.

She was led down the long hall of the keep, with an officer at each side holding her arms, past the section where the offices and interrogation rooms were. Rather than going out into the courtyard, they continued on down the hall and through a door that led into a different section of the castle. They were standing in a huge foyer that had an entirely different feel from the cold practicality of the keep. Nadine noticed some huge double doors that were open. As they walked past, she realized it was an enormous courtroom. She prayed that she never ended up in there, at least under the present circumstances. She was led further down a corridor to an open doorway where she could hear the low rumble of men conversing. She was escorted into the room to find herself facing a long table, and seated behind it were twelve men. Some wore uniforms. Some wore fine suits. All had a distinct authoritative presence that intimidated her. Among them was the duke, Georg Heinrich, and Captain Dukerk—who was the only one in the room not looking at her. She was guided to a chair that faced the long table. She was seated and the officers stood at her sides in an at-ease position.

"Good morning, Mrs. Rader," the duke said and she was grateful for the undeniable compassion—even apology—in his eyes.

"Good morning," she said.

"You know, of course," he went on, "that we are dealing with a terribly serious matter in relation to these murders that have taken place."

"Of course," she said.

"We need to get as much information as possible and do everything we can to see that these crimes are stopped and the culprit punished."

"Of course," she said, knowing from their eyes that at least half of the men in the room already considered her to be that culprit.

"This is not a trial, Mrs. Rader. We are not here to determine your guilt or innocence. Our purpose for this gathering is to uncover the truth. We ask you to be completely honest with your answers, and to understand that while this will likely be an unpleasant experience, the outcome of this meeting does not determine your future in relation to the charges against you."

"I understand," she said while her mind remained on that word "unpleasant."

The questions were simple to begin with, as she was asked to tell her reasons for coming to Horstberg, her background, her past experiences with Albert Crider. Different men asked her questions with no particular order about the details of the crimes and the evidence they had found. One particular man, introduced as Mr. Fruberg, asked especially difficult questions related to her feelings on life and death, her theories on crime and punishment, her attitudes about herself and about men, women, religion, and politics. Interspersed with ongoing questions about the crimes, Mr. Fruberg assaulted her with question after question, often repeating certain questions over and over. When she commented, "I already answered that question twice now," she was told to just answer the question. She realized then that he was trying to trip her up, likely attempting to discern if she was lying as he focused on the consistency of her repeated answers.

It seemed hours that questions continued to be hurled at her like bullets. She became hungry and her back ached, and she wondered when it would end. And she couldn't help noticing that the only man who didn't speak at all was Lance. He wouldn't even look at her. She could well imagine his humiliation in having been associated with her at all, and she had to wonder what course he might have taken with their relationship in light of all this, if she had not already severed the ties between them.

Just when Nadine thought this nightmare might end, the question was asked, "Could you please tell us about your association with Nikolaus du Woernig?"

Nadine gasped, completely unprepared to have this come into the situation. She was startled to see Lance's reaction, when his expression had been completely unreadable through the entire session. He straightened his back and met her eyes with blatant alarm showing. He then snapped with that voice of firm authority, "I would like to know what relevance that has to any of this. The evidence against her does not require her entire personal life to suddenly become public knowledge."

Nadine wished she could tell him what that meant to her. The very fact that he would defend her so hotly reminded her of why she had grown to love him.

"The knowledge of this committee is not *public,*" another man countered, just as hotly. "Considering that one of the victims had also been one of Nikolaus's whores—and for all we know, the other one may have been, as well; I'd swear he'd bedded half the women in this country—I would say that Mrs. Rader's *personal life* could very well have bearing on this case."

Nadine saw Lance become visibly angry so fast that for a moment she feared he would jump out of his chair and do the man bodily harm. She saw him fight for composure and toss her an apologetic glance just before hot tears pressed into her eyes and blurred her vision. She didn't have to wonder over the source of those tears. She'd just been slapped neatly into the category of "one of Nikolaus's whores."

"Just answer the question, Mrs. Rader," she heard the duke say, but she distinctly heard compassion and apology come through in the firmness of his voice.

Nadine swallowed hard and attempted to wipe at her tears with little success, having her hands bound. She searched for the right place to start, and stated firmly the heart of the issue. "I was one of many women who were victim to Nikolaus du Woernig's game of mock marriages. He pretended to marry me with a fraudulent clergymen, then sent me away when I got pregnant with the promise that he would send for me. He never did."

The next comment Nadine heard was a skeptical voice saying, "It must be terribly degrading for you to be in such a position, Mrs. Rader. But it's not *Mrs.*, is it."

"Yes, it is degrading," she said, "but it's in the past."

"Still," the same man said, and she wished she could remember his name, if only so she could hurl it back to him in the same cynical tone he'd used for hers. "There must be a certain degree of anger and jealousy toward the *other* women in his life. It's not difficult to understand how such jealousy could overtake someone when you had been so hurt and degraded."

"I object," Lance said firmly as it became evident where this was headed.

"Given your personal bias in this situation, Captain, I think you would do well to let the case be presented."

Lance erupted to his feet. "You're grasping at straws, Mr. Hertz. This is not a trial and you are overstepping your bounds. I don't care what personal interest I may have in *Mrs.* Rader, any suspect sitting in that chair who was a prisoner in my care would not be subjected to coarse speculation that has *nothing* to do with the evidence at hand. If you must speculate, do it on your own time."

Lance held his breath and was relieved beyond words when Cameron said, "The captain is right. You will hold your speculations for another forum, Mr. Hertz, and—"

Mr. Hertz interrupted. "This woman is clearly responsible for the deaths of two other women and I will not—"

"Mr. Hertz," the duke said, coming to his feet as well. "This is not a democracy. You would do well to remember who you are talking to. As the captain mentioned, this is not a trial. If you ever speak to me that way again, I will have you expelled from this committee."

"Forgive me, Your Grace," Mr. Hertz said sheepishly, but with anger in his eyes.

Cameron looked at Nadine and added, "I think Mrs. Rader has endured enough of this for one day. I caution each of you that the information you heard today will go no further. If certain topics end up as common gossip, I will know where to start bringing up charges of aspersion and slander. This meeting is adjourned."

Nadine was grateful beyond description to be taken back to her cell where at least she could feel humiliated in private. She cried for an hour before somebody seemed to realize that she'd missed lunch and finally brought her something to eat. Soon after she'd finished her meal, the key turned in the lock. She expected someone to take her tray until she heard a familiar voice say, "Thank you, Lieutenant. Leave us alone, please."

"Your Grace," Nadine came to her feet as the door was closed behind Cameron.

"Sit down, please," he said and she sat on the edge of the bed as he moved the chair closer and sat on it.

When he said nothing, she attempted to ease the tension. "I doubt this is standard protocol."

"No," he said.

"To what do I owe this honor, then?" she asked, wondering if he had come to advise her against talking about his brother, or perhaps to keep his captain out of whatever might happen.

"Well," he said, "considering that you and I have shared a dance and you've eaten in my private dining room, I would consider you among a rather small group of people that I call friends. Abbi has grown to care very much for you, and we are concerned for your well-being in this matter."

Nadine fought back a surge of tears and muttered, "You're very kind, sir."

Cameron scooted his chair closer and leaned forward. He took her hand into his and she wondered if his personal attention had anything to do with Lance. Had Lance requested this visit? Or did the duke's attention stem more from his concern for Lance and Lance's worry for her? While he seemed to be gathering his words, Nadine noticed more closely the ring he wore on his right hand. She'd noticed before that he wore one, but she'd never been in a position to note the detail. It was simple and tasteful but beautiful: gold with the image of a red lion on it. She recalled seeing a red lion on the flags outside the castle and in the funeral procession, and the red lion was a common symbol through the decor in the castle. She wondered what it meant.

"You're a good woman, Nadine," Cameron said gently, drawing her attention to his face. She was reminded of the day she'd come to Horstberg, and he'd sat close to her in his office, apologizing for his brother's bad behavior. "I hate to see you going through this, and I can't begin to know what the outcome will be. I want you to know that I've been where you are." He glanced around himself and sighed. "One minute I was the ruler of a prosperous nation, and the next I was locked in a cell, wondering if I'd ever see the light of day again. My brother was quick to take over, and he made it clear that I would not be given a fair trial. In the end, all turned out well, but overall it was the most hellish experience of my life. Still, I would not trade it away for the simple reason that I would not want to lose all that I learned as a result. Would you be interested to know what I learned?"

"Very much, Your Grace," she said.

"First of all, I learned that sometimes life dishes out circumstances that are simply beyond our doing, and beyond our control. Bad things happen to good people, and sometimes bad people are behind them. We can't control what happens, but we can take control of how we handle what we're given. I came to learn that sometimes things just don't work out the way we want them to in this life, and I reached a point where I was willing to accept that, with the faith that justice would be met in the life after this one. And that whatever happened here and now, I had to be at peace with myself. I also learned that pride and fear were the very things that would keep me from finding that peace. Whether I succeeded in my quest or failed, I had to let go of the fear and pride that kept me from looking at who and what I am, and coming to terms with it. Abbi taught me that. Now that's a very brief summary of some grueling experiences, but I felt you should know that. But most of all I came here to give you the most important gift that Abbi gave me."

"What is that?"

"Hope," he said as if it were a magic word. "You must never lose hope, Nadine. Whatever evidence may stand against you, whatever the outcome may be, you must never lose hope . . . in yourself, in the goodness of mankind that *does* exist in spite of the ugliness of this world. And most importantly, you must never lose hope that God is mindful of you and that His will is what prevails in the end. I know that's true, Nadine. I can't tell you how I know. I just know."

Nadine nodded, momentarily too moved to speak. She finally managed to say, "You love Abbi very much."

He sighed deeply, as if the very concept were as overwhelming as the existence of the universe. "I love her beyond life itself. What I share with Abbi is the most perfect and precious aspect of my life. I would wish such love on every good person who walks the earth. There were times when I was such a fool, but she had a way of putting me in my place and always giving me another chance. She never lost hope and faith in me, even when I couldn't find it in myself. She is the backbone of this country, Nadine. Let there be no question about that. She stands behind me and beside me in all that I do. Because of her, I am a better sovereign. Horstberg is strong because of the love and life she breathes into it. Yes, my dear, I love Abbi very much."

Nadine could only smile, so touched by his candor and his tenderness toward his wife. She recalled Lance mentioning more than once of the love that Cameron and Abbi shared, that its strength gave Cameron no reason to fear that Abbi would stray. She also recalled Lance talking of how he honored Abbi, and now Nadine could understand a little more why he felt the way he did.

"Forgive me if I'm out of line," Cameron went on, "but I want to apologize once again on behalf of my brother. I have been confronted with many women who shared your plight in one way or another, and each time I ached for them. But having remained in contact with you, I have been more keenly aware of the damage he has done that will go on for many years beyond his death. I want you to know that I admire the way you have handled your situation. And as long as I'm apologizing, I want you to know how I regret that meeting this morning. What Mr. Hertz said was completely uncalled for, and I was grateful for the way that Lance stood up to him."

"Yes, so was I," she said, looking down. "And you did, as well."

"In spite of my position, it's important for me to let others speak their mind and make their contributions, but I have my limits. I want you to know that there were two kinds of women that Nikolaus consorted with. There were the tawdry, cheap tramps who were as promiscuous as he was. And there were the innocent, guileless, tender-hearted women—like yourself—who were victims, plain and simple. By no stretch of the imagination could you be put into the same category as the first, and I apologize for the inference otherwise. However, I must inform you that . . . as far as gossip goes, Georg informed me later that your association with Nikolaus is already a circulating topic. I fear that servants are very observant and known for speculating on what they hear and see. Apparently your arrival in Horstberg and being brought to my attention drew some curiosity. And many of Nikolaus's past escapades are common knowledge. People suspect. I can only apologize again for my brother putting you into this position, and I'm confident that a woman of your grace and dignity will be able to handle the situation appropriately."

"Your concern is appreciated, Your Grace . . . truly—more than you know. It's not a surprise, and . . . I'll just have to take it on the best I can. I'm grateful for your visit. It was good of you to take the time."

He stood, taking both her hands into his. "Hope, my dear," he said and kissed her cheek.

"Forgive me, but . . . I have to ask," she said, "has anything more come up about . . . the paper I found? I've not breathed a word to anyone."

Cameron sighed and a heaviness came into his eyes. "No, I admit that I've thought about it a great deal, but there has simply been too much weighing on him to bring up something like that now."

"Of course. I understand. I was just wondering." She looked down and added, "Whatever happens, you will look out for him, won't you."

"Of course I will." His voice softened. "He is my brother, and the truest of friends."

He pressed her hand to his lips, bringing her attention once again to the ring he wore. "Forgive my asking, but . . . I was wondering the significance of the red lion . . . on your ring."

"Oh," he glanced at it nonchalantly, "as the story goes, I have an ancestor, many generations back, who conquered and settled this valley. He gained the nickname 'the red lion' because of the red tunic and cloak he wore, as well as his remarkable courage."

"How fascinating," she said. "I was just wondering."

"You take care of yourself, my dear," he said and squeezed her hand.

Long after the duke left her cell, Nadine was struck by the nearly tangible hope he'd left remaining in his wake. Hours passed while she lay back on her bunk, contemplating the things he had said and how they applied to her life. Pride and fear. She certainly had plenty of both. How could she not recall Lance's words to her? *You're scared, plain and simple. And you're using what I did as an excuse to lock your heart away so you don't ever have to worry about getting hurt again.*

She thought of Cameron's reverent words about Abbi and the love that they shared. Certain words repeated over and over in her mind. *I would wish such love on every good person who walks the earth.* Nadine knew she had been blessed enough to have such love, but she had thrown it away for reasons she still had difficulty understanding. In her mind she kept hearing Cameron say, *There were times when I was such a fool, but she had a way of putting me in my place and always giving me another chance.* So, why did Nadine find it so difficult to think of giving her relationship with Lance a second chance? She knew that it was ridiculous to think that any man would never make a mistake. She'd certainly made plenty. But she'd been so hard on him. Just recalling the pain in his eyes threatened to rip her heart out, knowing that it was her doing. Still, how could she ever fix what was wrong between them, especially when he had accused her need for him coming from desperation now that her circumstances had changed? Perhaps he was right—to some degree, at least. And even if she were out of this dreadful place, and no longer desperate, she wondered if she could ever get beyond her own fears enough to trust him the way he deserved to be trusted. She could lower her pride enough to admit that the problem was with her, but she didn't know what to do about it. She finally determined that when she got out of prison, she would work on that. And if she was never able to prove her innocence, it really wouldn't matter. Either way she couldn't help wondering if this estrangement between them was for the best. Not knowing the outcome of her present situation, she felt it was better that their relationship remain as it was. Perhaps, when all was said and done, he would be better off without her—either way.

Chapter Twenty
REVELATION

Two days beyond Nadine's interrogation, Lance had to admit he was exhausted. He'd never been so exhausted in his life. Not sleeping well was the least of it. Through every hour he wasn't in bed, he felt as if he were running like a madman, overseeing the most intense investigation this country had ever endured to find Albert Crider and prove Nadine innocent. His only reprieve was the snatches of time he found with Dulsie. And he avoided going to see Nadine at all. Unable to bear her rejection was as great a motive as knowing that he had no answers to give her any hope. In spite of all the efforts of him and his men, they had nothing to go on. The more time that passed with no new evidence turning up, the more Lance had to face the possibility that Nadine would stand trial for the murders, and if the evidence against her stood as it did now, she would be executed for crimes that she had not committed. And the worst irony for him was the fact that he would be the one to give that order. He just couldn't live with that. He couldn't.

After lunch Lance went to the duke's office for a meeting, but he was relieved to know this was a standard monthly meeting on the state of the country, mostly focusing on the economy. It had nothing to do with the criminal investigation—a topic that made him increasingly weary. He slipped in just as the meeting started, among a group that consisted of Cameron, Georg, and a handful of the duke's advisors and solicitors. The meeting was pleasantly brief, and Lance felt anxious to have a few extra minutes with Dulsie. He stood to leave, but one of the duke's solicitors put a hand on his arm. "A moment please, Captain." He was then distracted by something another man was saying to him. By the time that man finished and left, the office had emptied except for the two of them and Cameron and Georg.

The solicitor turned his attention to Lance, saying, "You recently turned thirty, I believe."

"That's right, in the fall." He noticed Cameron and Georg exchange a confused glance that made it evident they'd overheard, and they were equally baffled over the solicitor's purpose.

"I thought so," he said. "I actually have something for you that was meant to be delivered on your thirtieth birthday, but I was ill in the fall and became terribly behind." He reached into his case and handed Lance a sealed envelope that simply read, *Lance Dukerk* on the outside.

"What is it?" Lance asked, his uneasiness deepening when he noticed Cameron and Georg both looking no longer confused but concerned, perhaps mildly upset.

"Quite truthfully, I don't know, Captain. The duke gave it to me; I'm just acting on his instructions."

Lance looked toward Cameron and chuckled. "The duke?" He might have thought this was one of Cameron's practical jokes, except that his expression was so severe.

"The former duke, His Grace's father, before he died," the solicitor said and closed his case. "I must be on my way." He left the room and closed the door, leaving the three of them in tense silence.

"Strange," Lance finally said and tucked the letter into his pocket. "I think I'll look at it later, and—"

"I think you should look at it now," Cameron said, and Lance noticed Georg nod firmly toward Cameron, as if to confirm that he agreed.

"You know what it is," Lance stated, taking it back out.

"We've got a pretty good idea," Cameron said. "Although, if it's what I think it is, I've only known about it for a matter of days. I was feeling that I needed to tell you, but I wasn't sure how to do it, and then . . . with all that's been happening, it just got brushed aside."

"You're scaring me," Lance said, turning the envelope over in his hands. He became even more afraid when he received no comment in return. If there was no reason for him to be scared, surely they would have said so. "Can't you give me a hint?" he asked, taking a seat.

"I think you should just open it, and if it's not what I think it is, I'm going to tell you what I know anyway." Cameron's voice held a grave quality that Lance had only heard when the severest of difficulties were discussed.

"Get on with it," Georg said.

"I take it *you* know as well."

"I'm afraid I do," Georg said.

Lance took a deep breath and broke the seal. He pulled out two pages and hesitantly unfolded them. He scanned the first page and let out a confused chuckle.

"What does it say?" Cameron asked.

"It's . . . an inheritance. Apparently he wanted me to have some . . . ridiculous amount of money when I turned thirty. I can't imagine why. And I certainly don't want the money; I don't need it." He chuckled again. "I hardly knew the man. I mean . . . I spent a great deal of time here as a youth; you know that. Nik and I were always together, but . . . your father never even acknowledged me that I recall."

"Well, that would be typical," Cameron said. "The only time he ever acknowledged me was to reprimand me, or to tell me that it was a pity I didn't have the backbone to rule a country."

"He said that?" Lance looked up at Cameron, appalled.

"Many times," Cameron said. "I still hear it in my head. It's one of many reasons that Nik felt justified in taking over the country. Father had told him the birthright should have been his, because he was the *strong* one."

"That's ludicrous," Lance said.

"Yes, it is," Cameron agreed. He leaned forward and spoke with fervor. "Let me tell you about my father, Lance. As a political leader, he was a genius. He kept this country safe and strong, but he had a hard edge, a lack of compassion that was difficult to abide. He was unkind to my mother and indifferent toward his children unless they displeased him. I know he had a number of affairs—not the way Nikolaus did. Nik would sleep with any woman he could lure into his trap. My father had serious relationships with a handful of different women . . . as I understand it."

"How do you know all of this?" Lance asked. "Surely he didn't tell his children that—"

"No, he never told us. I suspected. But after he'd died, those who knew him well were the same men training me to be a duke. And they spoke openly of him. I've had some fairly difficult feelings toward my father, Lance. It was Abbi who finally helped me come to terms with those feelings. Of course, they creep up now and again, but she helps me keep perspective." Cameron leaned back in his chair. "No matter what happens, we must always keep perspective."

Cameron was apparently finished, and Lance looked back to the document in his hands, feeling baffled. Then, in the same moment that he recalled Cameron's preamble to his opening the envelope, he recalled that there was another page. He put the first behind the second and glanced up long enough to see that Georg and Cameron were visibly tense. He briefly considered the possible reasons, but when his eyes focused on the paper in front of him, he realized that he never could have conceived such an idea in his wildest imaginings. The first words to jump out came from the center of the brief note. *I cared very much for your mother.* But even then the implication didn't fully sink in until he read the next phrase. *What we shared is manifested in you, my son.* Lance watched the pages in his hand begin to shake before he determined that he was trembling, then the papers floated to the floor.

A noise of disbelief jumped from Lance's throat the same moment his heart began to pound and his chest tightened. His mouth went dry, his eyes blurry, and he felt sick to his stomach. The blood rushed from his head and his surroundings became splotched with black. He dropped his head between his knees and heaved for breath, feeling the world as he knew it come to an end. While he concentrated on allowing the blood back into his brain, the conversation leading up to this moment came back to him. Everything Cameron had said about his father, and his insistence that Lance not be alone to open the envelope. Questions pounded into his mind, but he couldn't bring a single one to his lips while he struggled just to stay coherent. He felt hands on his shoulders and realized Cameron was kneeling beside him. The contact fed strength into him and he demanded, "How long have you known?" He kept his head down and his eyes closed, fearing any other course would start him heaving again.

"Not so many days," Cameron said.

"How . . ." was all he could manage to say.

"Some . . . old records were being . . . reorganized, and it came up. It was brought to my attention. I knew that I needed to tell you. I just didn't know how to do it. The letter from the solicitor was just . . . coincidence."

"Or an answer to prayers," Georg interjected.

Lance groaned. He couldn't even entertain the idea that this had anything to do with God. "I can't believe it," he muttered, finally managing to sit up, but he had to press his hand over the pounding in his forehead. "Please tell me this is one of your sick, practical jokes, Cameron. Please tell me this isn't real."

"I can't tell you that, Lance, because it is real."

"Oh, heaven help me," Lance said as his whirling mind attempted to change the entire perspective of his life. One point stood out strongly, making his stomach smolder. "And what of Gwen? She is my sister, and you were married to her? Are you trying to tell me that your relationship with her was something perverse and wrong because—"

"No, it was not!" Cameron said firmly. "It was an arranged marriage, Lance. We were betrothed from our early youth. My father would not have done such a thing if he'd thought there was the remotest possibility she had his blood. She was older than you. I'm certain he knew she had been born legitimate."

Lance took that in with some relief but had to say, "As opposed to me, who was *not* born legitimate."

Following a miserable length of silence, Cameron said, "I don't know what to say, Lance. Should I regret finding out that such a good man is my brother?"

Lance shot his head up, sharing a gaze with Cameron that provoked a thousand emotions all at once. He felt his chest tightening again, and feared he would crumble right here and now. He erupted to his feet. "I . . . need to be alone. I . . . I . . . can't even think . . . or know what to think and . . ." He lumbered toward the door. "Tell Dulsie I'm not feeling well, and . . . I'll see her . . . I don't know when I'll see her. Tell my men the same. I have to go." Lance took a deep breath and steeled himself to appear normal to whoever he might encounter between here and his apartment. Thankfully he made the brief walk passing no one that took any notice of him. Once inside the door, he locked it and leaned against it until the reality of what he'd just discovered enveloped him with stark abhorrence. He began heaving again. He wrapped his arms up over his head while his back slid down the door and he wilted onto the floor, groaning through clenched teeth. He lost track of time as the anguish racked through him, and he finally ended up laying with the side of his face against the cold, stone floor, wrapped in his cloak.

Motivated by a sudden chill, Lance trudged up the stairs and built a fire in his room. He removed the coat of his uniform and his boots and sat on the floor, staring at the flames, feeling as if he didn't even know who he was. He fell asleep on the rug and woke in the night only to stoke the fire and climb into bed. Sleep eluded him through the remainder of the night, and he was awake when the cleaning lady knocked at the front door. He opened it only a crack to tell her that he was ill and to come back in a few days. A short while later, Lieutenant Kepler came to the door to say that he'd heard he wasn't feeling well.

"Is there anything I can get for you?" he asked through the crack in the door.

"No, thank you, Lieutenant. I just need time and some rest, I'm sure. Just see that everything remains under control, and keep that investigation going."

"Of course, sir," he said and Lance heaved a sigh to see him go.

He wandered the apartment, lost and restless. When the growling of his stomach turned to hunger pangs, he dug into his pantry but found nothing that didn't spur nausea worse than his hunger. Late afternoon a knock came at the door. He remained as he was in the parlor, not wanting to see or talk to anyone. The knocking persisted, then he heard Cameron call, "I know you're in there, and I'm not going away. Just open the door and get it over with!"

Lance knew he meant it and rose reluctantly to let him in.

"You look terrible," Cameron said, closing the door behind him. "Have you been drinking?" he asked.

"No, I haven't been drinking. There's nothing around here to drink anyway. Even if there were, I'm not *that* stupid."

"I didn't know you were stupid at all. Does knowing you have my father's blood suddenly make you stupid? If that's what you're saying, then I'm not certain I like the implication."

Lance recognized his effort to lighten the mood with typical bantering. But he simply wasn't up to it. "There are no implications in regard to you, Your Grace."

Cameron's voice softened. "Nothing has changed, you know."

"*Everything* has changed," Lance said. "Everything." Cameron sighed loudly and Lance added, "I appreciate your visit, and I know you mean well, but . . . I just need to be alone. I need some time."

"Time to do what? To wallow in self-pity?" Lance glared at him but said nothing. "Have you eaten anything? I know you better than to believe that there's anything here that could do more than barely sustain life for about an hour."

"No, I haven't eaten. I'm fine. I just . . . need to be alone."

Cameron sighed again. "Fine. All right. But I'll be back."

"I'm sure you will," Lance said with sarcasm, grateful to close the door and be alone again. But he wasn't terribly surprised to hear another knock less than an hour later. He moved grudgingly to the door and opened it only a crack until he saw that it was Abbi.

"What are you doing here?" he demanded and walked away, leaving the door open.

"My husband suggested that I check on you," she said, closing the door behind her. "He's worried about you."

"No need for that," Lance said, plopping down on the sofa and putting his bare feet up on the coffee table.

"Oh, it would seem to me that there most certainly is a need for that." He noted that she was holding a tray covered with a white cloth, and a basket hooked over her arm. "Sit up," she ordered, nudging his feet off the coffee table with her leg. "I'm going to sit here and watch you eat this."

He moved his feet and she set the tray there and removed the cloth. He had to admit that it looked good, but he found it difficult to find the motivation to do anything about it. "Eat!" she ordered.

"Yes, Your Grace," he said and picked up the fork, forcing himself to take a bite. Once he got started, his hunger responded and he ate with zeal.

"Careful, don't make yourself sick," she said. "I'll be right back."

She left the room and came back just as he cleared away the last bite. She handed him a tall glass of water. "Drink it. If you've gone a long while without eating, it will keep you from getting a headache. I don't know why; it just does."

She sat down across from him. "Now, I've left two rounds of bread, butter, some of the best apples from our cellar, and some jerked meat. If you need to hole up for a while and come to terms with this, fine. But don't stop eating. You need to keep up your health or you'll never get through this."

Just hearing her words settled the reality in a little deeper and he looked away, sighing loudly. "Thank you" was all he could think to say. "It's a good thing somebody is looking out for me."

"Lance," she said gently, "your being upset over this is understandable."

"Upset is a gross understatement, Your Grace. I cannot even begin to fathom that this is real. It feels like a very bad dream, and I keep praying to God that I will wake up and it will be over."

"Well, it's not a dream, Lance, and the sooner you accept the reality for what it is, the sooner you can get on with your life."

Lance gave a scoffing laugh. "Get on with my life? What life? The only woman I've ever loved is languishing in prison while I face the possibility of giving the order for her execution. Before she came along, my life was my work and the reputation I'd worked so hard to gain. What will the people of Horstberg think to discover that their captain is a bastard? My world turned upside down, Abbi, and I fell off. I don't even know which way is up. What I believed to be the foundation of my life has now been pulled out from under me as a myth, a fallacy. How am I supposed to cope with that?"

"I'm not trying to tell you that such an adjustment is, or should be, easy. It's not. But nobody is going to cope with it but you. You're just going to have to exchange the old reality for a new one. In essence, your life will not change, only your perception of it. So, you're just going to have to get used to it. There are people who need you, Captain, and I am one of them. The world will not go on the same without you. You, of all people, should have the honor and integrity to live up to what's expected of you."

"Honor?" he echoed cynically. "What honor? You have no idea what you're talking about."

Without a moment's hesitation Abbi slapped him hard across the face. He turned back to look at her, stunned and betrayed. "We may be friends, and I know you're hurting, but don't you *ever* speak to me like that again. I am still the duchess, and you are still the captain. Don't start *acting* like a bastard, as if this gives you an excuse to be less of a man."

Lance squeezed his eyes shut and blew out a long breath. "Forgive me, Your Grace. It won't happen again."

"I'm certain it won't," she said. He opened his eyes to look at her and became briefly distracted from his misery as he considered the woman before him. He had seen her evolve from a defiant girl in calico to a reluctant duchess, timid and afraid of her own position. And now she had no qualms about putting him in his place, hard and fast. And rightfully so. It was no wonder that everywhere she went, people were in awe of her. She was as kind as she was powerful, which manifested itself when she went on in a tone of gentle compassion, as if the prior incident had not occurred. "I'll tell you *what* honor, Lance. The honor you've earned in the way you have lived your life. That is who and what you are, and that is what people see in you. So stop feeling sorry for yourself and take hold of reality. You're just going to have to learn to be comfortable with what you have learned."

"I don't know if that's possible," he said, but he said it kindly.

He almost wondered if she had read his thoughts a moment ago when she said, "I woke up one day faced with a new reality, and I was terrified. I had no idea that I would be the Duchess of Horstberg. But it was my destiny, Lance. I know beyond any doubt that God knew from the beginning of my life that this is where I must be, and I simply had to relearn how I perceived myself. You helped teach me how to be a duchess, Lance, which is one of many reasons that I love you the way I do. And now I'm going to teach you something. You might not have known before who your father was, but God knew. He's laid out a good life for you, and perhaps he knew that becoming established as an adult before you knew the truth would keep the stigma from distorting your perception of yourself. You are still the same man you were last week. Same knowledge and wisdom, same integrity and honor, same face, same hair, same heart and soul. Same blood flowing in your veins. Only your perception has changed, not you. So, you're going to have to practice being the illegitimate son of

Ferdinand du Woernig." Lance closed his eyes, unable to even hear it without cringing. "Say it."

"I can't," he said. "I can't even think it without feeling sick to my stomach."

"Say it, Captain. That's an order," she said. Again he was stunned, especially when he realized she was serious. When he hesitated she added, "Do you know what they do to officers who disobey my orders, Captain?"

"Six days in the keep, Your Grace," he said, only barely terse. "But at least I would be in good company. Perhaps she would open her heart to me again if we were both considered criminals."

"Perhaps," she said, "except they would never put you anywhere near her. So just say it and get it over with."

"I don't think I realized what a hard woman you had become."

"I am when I have to be," she said. "Say it."

Lance drew courage and forced it through his lips with difficulty. "I am . . . the illegitimate son of . . . Ferdinand du Woernig."

"There now," she said. "That didn't hurt too much."

"It hurts like hell . . . Your Grace."

Abbi pressed a gentle hand to his face, and he saw his friend come back into her countenance. "It will heal, Lance. Just give it time. And in the meantime, you must come back among the living. You must. Your country needs you. I need you."

"I need some time," he said. "You're right, Abbi, I need to come to terms with it, but . . . right now I just feel like I don't even know who I am." He repeated softly, "I need time. And since you've brought me food, I promise to take care of myself."

"Very well," she said.

"How is Nadine?" he asked.

"Fine, as far as I know. I keep sending work to her, and she sends it back beautifully done."

"At least she's keeping busy. Heaven help me, my heart aches for her. I cannot even imagine how she must be feeling. And now with this . . . on top of that . . . I just . . ." Tears rose into his eyes and he couldn't go on.

"It's all right," Abbi said, touching his face, and the next thing he knew he was crying in her arms.

When he'd finally gained some composure, he muttered

sheepishly, "Some captain I am, sworn to defend and protect you and regularly cry like a baby in your lap."

"You are one of my dearest friends, Lance, and what you are up against warrants a good cry now and then. I would rather have you crying to me than all by yourself."

"I've been doing plenty of that, as well."

Abbi talked with him a while longer, telling him what Dulsie had been doing and distracting him from his heartache. When she finally left, he had to admit that her visit had soothed him, but he soon felt the emptiness surround him again, and his thoughts went to Nadine. Through the next twenty-four hours, he continued to pore over this revelation that had been thrust upon him and the ramifications of what he had learned. Interspersed with his grief over that, his heart was continually heavy with concern for Nadine. And at the root of everything was the reality that even in the absence of all else, Nadine had shut him out of her life. And in a way, that was the most difficult of all.

Lance was grateful for the food Abbi had left, not wanting to even give his hunger a second thought with all else that was on his mind. He slept intermittently through the day, and night found him restless, feeling empty and alone. His thoughts naturally gravitated to Nadine. He thought of how she had soothed him and offered perspective after the funeral and execution. He longed to just be with her and drink in her presence but feared she would turn him away. Recalling that the last time they'd talked and she had asked him to stay the night with her, he found that his desire to be with her overpowered his fear.

Lance didn't bother checking his appearance before he pulled on his boots and grabbed his cloak and headed across the courtyard. He had no idea of the time; he only knew it was the middle of the night. The officer on duty at the door of the keep came immediately to attention, looking startled to see him.

"Give me the keys," he demanded and the officer handed them over. "I will be in Mrs. Rader's cell. Don't interrupt, and don't go starting any nasty rumors. I assure you it will be a chaste encounter."

"Of course, sir," he said seeming embarrassed, and Lance ambled down the long hall.

Nadine came out of a fitful sleep, hearing the key turn noisily in the lock. She sat up as the door opened and light shed from the hallway, guiding a dark, cloaked figure into the room. She managed to focus just as the door closed, then it became evident who her visitor was. As he hung the lantern on the hook near the door and tossed his cloak onto the chair, something tightened inside of her. She'd never imagined such despair in his eyes; she'd never seen him look so unkempt. His hair was mussed, his face unshaven, his eyes hollow. He wore a blousy white shirt, not the close-fitting kind he wore with his uniform. It was unbuttoned halfway down his chest, and his braces hung down around his hips.

"What's happened?" she asked, but he said nothing. He only stared at her, his expression somewhere between anger and despondency. "Is it the trial? Is it over for me? Will they—"

"No, it's not that," he said and turned the chair around before he sat on it, stretching out one leg and putting the other booted foot flat on the floor. "I don't know why I'm here, really. I guess you could say it would be the same reason I ended up at the inn when I was troubled. It was like this . . . inexplicable homing instinct in me . . . that brought me to you . . . when I was . . ."

"Hurting?" she guessed. He only hung his head.

"You're not still pining over me, are you?" she asked as if doing so would be a crime.

"*Still* pining over you?" he echoed belligerently. "How long has it been, Nadine, since you threw my heart on the floor and trampled on it? A matter of days? Has losing me been so easy for you that you would accuse me of *still* pining over you?"

"No, it's not easy for me," she said. "But it's the way it has to be."

"Of course," he said. "Well, don't bother telling me why it's the way it has to be. What I am dealing with now has absolutely nothing to do with you. Although the timing is incredible. Do you think God sees a man that's barely managing to stay on his feet and decides to just pull the rug out from under him completely? Or is it Lucifer who does such things? I only know I'm not very impressed with the timing. A week ago I thought I was facing the most difficult thing in my life—ever—when you kicked me out. Then you were arrested and I thought it couldn't possibly get any worse. And now, I feel as if the world is no longer round, but flat and colorless, and I have been kicked off the edge."

Nadine's palms began to sweat as she realized that she knew what was coming. Cameron had told him about his paternity. Forcing a steady voice, she said, "I'm listening."

Lance suddenly couldn't think of anything to say. He was so distracted by just being with her that he couldn't put his words together. Memories of the good times they'd shared flitted through his mind, and he longed to just go back to those early days of their relationship before all these layers of hurt and fear and crime had intruded upon their lives. But in spite of all that, looking at her now made one thing very clear in his mind. He loved her. He loved her with all his heart and soul. He just didn't know what to do about it.

Chapter Twenty-One
THE INTRUDER

"So talk to me," she said. "At the very least, we ought to be civil enough to be friends."

"At the very least," he echoed with sarcasm, then he sighed, hating this bitter, cynical side that had come out in him.

"So, are you going to tell me why you feel as if you've been kicked off the edge of the world? Or did you just come to talk about the weather? Still cold, isn't it?"

Lance looked at her hard. "Yes, it's still cold," he said, unable to avoid a double meaning. How he missed her warmth!

"Talk to me," she said with just enough of that warmth showing through to soften him.

"I have recently learned . . ." he began, but he found it difficult to go on. "Uh . . ." He cleared his throat, recalling how Abbi had made him say it. He had to accept it. He had to adjust. He had to *say* it! "I have learned," he began again, "that . . . in reality . . . I am," he cleared his throat again, "the illegitimate son of . . . Ferdinand du Woernig."

He watched her and waited for some kind of shock, for her to be appalled and disgusted, but her expression didn't change. "An illegitimate child with royal blood," she said, "just like Dulsie."

Lance took a sharp breath. In all his pondering and stewing over this, the connection had never occurred to him. And how could he forget Dulsie once telling him that they were the same? An innocent statement with more depth behind it than he ever could have known at the time.

"Yes," he said, "like Dulsie. At least I can hope it's like Dulsie."

"What do you mean?"

"I can hope that my mother truly loved the duke, as opposed to being some tramp. I *do* know, however, that she was married to my father, when . . ." He stopped and cursed under his breath before he corrected himself. "She was married to Jacob Dukerk, the man I *thought* was my father, at the time. So, the tramp theory seems to carry more weight."

"You know absolutely nothing about that relationship, Lance," she said firmly. "No, it wasn't right, but that doesn't automatically mean it was cheap and ugly. And even if it were, that doesn't make your existence the same."

"Then why do I suddenly feel that it is?" he said sadly.

"What?"

"That my existence is cheap and ugly."

"You're obviously very upset over this."

He chuckled with no humor. "Upset? Oh, Nadine . . . upset is the least of it." He looked at her hard and commented on what had felt incongruent since he'd mentioned it. "You're apparently not . . . upset, I mean. At the very least, I thought you would be . . . surprised. Or shocked."

"I was," she said, praying he would take this well, knowing she couldn't deceive him, "when I initially learned of it."

Lance's heart quickened painfully. "What are you saying?"

"I already knew."

Lance erupted from his chair and resisted the urge to kick it across the floor. "Who told you? What business did they have to discuss something like this without—"

"Why don't you calm down and listen to what I have to say."

"And should I follow your example on how to do that?" he asked, his voice acrid.

Nadine looked down and sighed, reminding herself that he had just cause to feel about her the way he did. "No," she said, forcibly calm, "you should have more character than that."

Lance sat down. "I'm listening."

"Nobody told me," she said. "I found it . . . among the files when . . . " She saw his eyes widen with enlightenment. "I didn't know what to do. I was wishing I'd never seen it. I felt sure it would be better left buried forever. But once I knew, I couldn't pretend that I didn't. Still, it wasn't my place to tell you. So . . . I took it to

Cameron, and I put the matter in his hands. He's probably wishing I'd never found it, either. I assume it was he who told you."

Lance absorbed what he had just heard and how the scene of his discovery had played out. He felt an almost tangible heat penetrate his heart as he recalled Georg saying that the way the discovery had been made was an answer to prayers. At the time, Lance had felt so shocked and angry that he couldn't imagine such a concept. But what he'd just heard put an entirely new light on the situation. What if Cameron hadn't known? He never would have insisted Lance open the letter there in his office. What if the solicitor hadn't been ill last fall and the letter had been delivered under different circumstances at a different time? He knew he had a long road to come to terms with this, but what he felt in that moment put a glimmer of hope in the midst of an otherwise black sky. He instinctively felt God's hand in this, and for the first since he'd discovered the truth, he felt that it might actually be *possible* to come to terms with it.

"Lance," Nadine said, breaking into his thoughts, "I said that I assume it was Cameron who told you."

"Uh . . . no," he looked directly at her, but his mind still felt distracted, "a . . . solicitor . . . gave me a letter. He handed it to me after a meeting; said it was to have been delivered on my thirtieth birthday . . . last fall, but he'd been ill and had gotten behind. He said it was from the duke—Cameron's father. Cameron heard what he said and . . . well, I was going to open it later, but he insisted I open it there . . . with him, and . . . I'm grateful I did. He . . . kept me together, and . . . I shudder to think what I would have done alone, and I . . . don't know if I ever could have told him if it hadn't worked out that way, and . . . I'm just so glad he already knew."

Nadine became silently teary. Her troubled heart felt soothed over knowing that her discovery had made a positive difference and had turned out to be a blessing rather than a hindrance. "I'm so glad," she said. "I've worried about it terribly."

"Perhaps God is looking out for us, after all."

"Yes, I believe He is."

Following minutes of silence, Nadine said gently, "Tell me why this is so difficult for you." He looked hesitant and she added, "When we were practically strangers, you told me how you'd had to kill

Nikolaus and why that was so difficult. Surely you can talk to me about this now."

Lance appreciated the theory, but he had to point out, "When we were practically strangers there were no hurtful words between us, no lack of trust, no misunderstanding. Should I trust you enough to bare my soul after all that's happened?"

Nadine looked away, taking his point but hating it. "That's up to you. I'm offering to listen. That's all I can do."

Lance watched her for a long moment and realized that before him was an opportunity to show her that he *was* willing to trust again, in spite of being hurt. And perhaps, one day, she might be able to draw from his example and give him a second chance, as he was giving her.

Nadine waited for him to get up and leave with some bitter remark, but he said softly, "I told you of the stability I grew up with." She met his eyes. "My mother died when I was very young; I barely remember her. My father was stern, not necessarily warm, but a good man. Forgive me if I'm repeating myself. I know you've heard this before but . . . in spite of the lack of warmth between us, my father was a pillar in my life. He was my sense of constancy. He had a military career and he didn't force the same on me, but his example of serving his country with pride made me want to do the same. He was honest, intelligent, and respectful. I loved him. I honored him, both in my career and in the way I lived my life. When choices were difficult, I always asked myself what my father would have me do. He was a man of honor and integrity. It was easy to know which path he would have followed and would have had me follow." Lance sighed and pushed his hands through his hair. "And now," his voice became shaky, "now I discover that he wasn't my father at all. And I wonder . . . did he know? Did he know that his wife had been sleeping with the duke? Did he know I was not his son?" He gave a dubious laugh. "He was one of the duke's friends. I mean . . . I don't know that they were close as far as . . . talking about personal things, the way Cameron and I do, but . . . they socialized privately. Could he have done that, knowing of the affair going on? There are just . . . so many unanswered questions—questions that haunt me. And I feel so . . . disoriented. What does a man do when what he's believed all his life suddenly turns out to be false? I don't know how to keep going, Nadine. I don't feel like I know who I am anymore."

"And what if you had just learned that you'd been adopted, as opposed to being born illegitimate? Would that make a difference in your perception?"

"I don't know," he admitted.

"Does the stigma of illegitimacy bother you?"

He knew the answer without thinking about it, but he found it difficult to admit. "Yes."

"It's not your fault. You had no control over the circumstances under which you were born."

"No more than any other person in this country born illegitimate. But that doesn't change the way they are looked down upon, the way they are treated badly." He thought of the recent suicide he had dealt with and the irony tightened his nerves further.

"Which is one of many reasons that I'm grateful people believe I was married. Well, *most* people. I guess there's no secret from the committee of national security."

Lance groaned. "When I think of what he said to you, I still want to belt him in the jaw."

Nadine felt warmed by his vehemence but said, "Better that you don't. They'd have you serving time for assault."

His voice was soft as he said, "That wouldn't be so bad, if I could be in here with you."

She met his eyes. "I doubt that's the standard protocol."

"No," he looked down, "I'm afraid it isn't."

The silence grew long again until he said, "I should go . . . and let you get some sleep."

"I can sleep just about any time," she said.

"Still," he said, then no words followed.

Lance felt hesitant to leave but didn't know what else to say. Then a thought occurred to him that he found disturbing, and he knew he had to ask or he'd always wonder. "Nadine, if you already knew, then . . . please don't tell me that your knowing I was a bastard had anything to do with our separation."

Her astonished expression was proof enough that it didn't, but he was still glad to hear her say, "I could no more denounce you for that reason than I could denounce my own daughter. I can assure you there was no connection." Her voice softened. "In truth, I knew before you asked me to marry you."

Lance felt taken aback, not only by her knowing that long, but to hear the evidence that they had once been betrothed—and now they were not. Her comparison between him and Dulsie made him wonder if she was admitting she loved them both. He believed she *did* love him, but apparently love wasn't enough. He stood and moved toward the door.

"Lance," she said and he turned back to face her, "are you going to be all right?"

"Eventually," he said.

"You have to find a way to come to terms with this and not allow it to change who and what you are."

"That may be easier said than done."

"Perhaps," she said. "But you once told me that Nikolaus's circumstances changed, and he allowed his circumstances to change him. Will you do the same? Will this change in your life change who you are?"

He heaved a deep sigh, taking her point with some trepidation. "Thank you for listening," he said and unlocked the door.

"Any time," she said. "You know where to find me."

"Yes," he said and opened the door. "Get some sleep."

Nadine stared after the closed door long after the key had turned in the lock, and the sound of his boots had dissipated down the length of the hall. Oh, how she loved him! How her heart ached for him! If only her wounded heart could fully take him in and give him the love he deserved. But that would take a miracle, and right now she was in need of several. Getting even just one seemed impossible.

Lance returned to his apartment with a great deal to think about, but still close to despair. He went straight to bed and did nothing but sleep and eat and ponder the situation through the following day and into the night. As memories of different things he'd been told came back to him, he drew one firm conclusion: he *did* have to keep living. It wasn't in him to let something like this undo him. He knew he would never be the same, but he could come up with the guts to scrape himself off the ground and get back to his life—however defiled it seemed to be.

Through the day Nadine's thoughts were even more preoccupied than usual with Lance. She wondered how he was adjusting and kept a prayer in her heart for him. She finished up all of the invitations and had them sent to Abbi. A message came back that they would all be delivered the following day, and she was given what she needed now to work on place cards to be set out on the tables. She couldn't fathom what she would do without this work to keep her occupied.

That night she was again awakened in the middle of the night by a key turning in the lock. She rolled over and attempted to adjust her eyes to the light of the lantern being hung on the hook by the door, next to the one that had been extinguished for the night. Just as the door was slammed and locked, she realized that this was not Lance, and never before had any officer come to her room in the middle of the night for any purpose. Her instincts told her this was not good, and she steeled herself to be firm and strong.

"What are you doing here?" she demanded, sitting up. "It's the middle of the night."

"Indeed it is, madame. Any other time of day would draw too much attention."

Nadine's pulse quickened as her sense of danger blossomed. His lack of subtlety was evidenced more when he added, "I'll tell you what, pretty lady, you give me what I want, and I'll get you and your daughter out of the country before this trial ever happens."

"I seriously doubt you would be capable of such a thing," she said with indifference, as if his implication of what he was after had not left her with heart-pounding fear. "And even if you were, I'm not interested. Now get out."

"I wouldn't be so quick to toss me out," he said, stepping closer. She recognized his face as an officer she had seen coming and going, but she couldn't begin to know his name. "I have more influence here than you might believe. A woman denied of common necessaries in a place like this could be awfully miserable."

Nadine sized up her situation as he stepped closer. Through

years on her own, working in pubs and the like, she'd learned something about keeping a man in place. But she'd never been confronted with such a situation, alone in a locked room with thick walls. She held her breath and waited until he put a hand on the wall above the bed and leaned over her, then she scraped her fingernails across his face with one hand and hit him hard across the bridge of his nose with the other. He groaned and cursed while she jumped to her feet and moved away. He took a moment to get his bearings while she contemplated getting the pistol out of his belt. She was taken off guard when he backhanded her across the face with such force that she fell to the floor, and by the time she could see straight, he was on his knees, leaning over her. She uttered a prayer for strength and lifted her knee into his groin with all the force she possessed. He howled with pain and rolled onto his back, curling into a ball. Nadine sighed with relief. Even if he came to his senses, he'd not be having his way with any woman until long after her breakfast arrived. While he was preoccupied with the pain, she removed the pistol from his belt and pointed it at him.

"Get out!" she growled. "I don't care if you have to crawl. Get out of here before I give you a bullet right where I gave you my knee."

He groaned again and struggled to his feet, but he couldn't begin to stand up straight.

"If you breathe a word to anyone about his," he growled, "I will kill you."

"Get in line," she said and actually laughed. She'd been hiding from a serial killer, and now she was facing the possibility of a firing squad.

Nadine kept the pistol poised until he'd left and locked the door. Only after he'd gone did it occur to her that she had a weapon in her possession. She just tossed it on her bed and let out a relieved chuckle. She doubted it was standard protocol, but then, being assaulted in the middle of the night likely wasn't either.

Lance forced himself to rise at dawn and face the day. He bathed and got dressed and left some extra money and a note for the housekeeper. The apartment was in worse shape than it had been since he'd moved in. Crossing the courtyard, he had to admit that it felt good to be out and seeing to his normal routine, but he didn't feel like himself. He simply had to keep going with the hope that eventually his heart would catch up with what his head had learned.

Lance went to the private nursery, knowing that Cameron and Abbi would still be there with the children. He barely had the door open when Dulsie ran into his arms, giggling with delight. He laughed as well and held her close to him, relishing how tightly she held to him.

"Oh, I missed you, my little darling," he said.

"I missed you too," she said. "Are you feeling better? Erich's mama said you were feeling sick."

"Yes, I was, but I am feeling better now."

He set her down and she took hold of his hand, pulling him into the room.

"Good morning," Cameron and Abbi said together, both pleased to see him.

"Good morning," he replied.

"You're looking much better," Abbi said. "How are you feeling?"

"I'll be all right," he said without enthusiasm, but it was the best he could come up with.

He sat with Dulsie on his lap to read her a storybook before the children were left in care of the nanny.

"Would you join us for breakfast?" Cameron asked.

"I'd like that, actually," he said. "Thank you."

Lance was grateful to have the breakfast room void of any people beyond him and Georg and Cameron and Abbi. Except for when the servants came in to bring something, he was able to talk freely about what he was feeling and his determination to accept it. They offered compassion and support, and he was grateful for the circle of friendship he had there, which meant more to him now than it ever had.

As the meal was winding down, Cameron said to him, "When you're finished, Captain, there is something I wanted to talk with you about for a few minutes before we begin our day."

"Of course," Lance said, setting aside his napkin. "I'm finished."

They both stood at the same time. Cameron kissed Abbi's lips, and Lance kissed her cheek before they left her visiting with Georg. Lance followed Cameron to the ducal office where they both entered and he closed the door. He wondered if this had anything to do with Nadine and if it was business or personal. Lance took his usual chair. Cameron leaned against the edge of the desk, rather than sitting down.

"Lance," he said, an indication that this would be more personal. His heart pounded as he wondered if in his absence there had been negative developments in Nadine's case. But Cameron sighed and went on to say, "Since this discovery has been made . . . of your paternity, I've given the matter a great deal of thought, and there's something I need to say." Lance wondered for a moment if Cameron would feel it necessary to make clear that his illegitimacy gave him no rights or privileges in regard to the royal family. Lance knew that and he would not have assumed otherwise, but he felt disheartened to think of Cameron feeling the need to clarify such a thing.

"Yes," Lance said when he hesitated too long. "Just say what you have to say."

Cameron sighed. "I don't have to tell you that Nikolaus was a difficult person. Growing up beside him was a challenge, even in the best of times. It was as if he'd come into this world angry and selfish."

"No, you don't have to tell me that. I grew up with him, too."

"You were closer to his age," Cameron said, "and my mother often said that you had a gift for being able to draw out the good in Nikolaus and keep him in line."

"I didn't know that," Lance said. "Your mother was a good woman." A thought occurred to him and he had to ask, "Do you think she knew that I was . . ."

"I don't know," Cameron said. "She knew her husband was unfaithful, but we may never know the full extent of what she did and didn't know." Lance nodded and Cameron went on. "What I'm trying to say is that . . . in spite of difficult circumstances, I consider it an honor and a privilege . . . to be your brother."

Lance was momentarily too stunned to speak. Cameron took advantage of the silence and added, "Nikolaus was never a brother to me, Lance, but as I look back over the years—especially these last few years—I realize that in many ways, you always were. I would not be where I am now without you. I just wanted you to know that."

It still took Lance a moment to gather his words. "I'm . . . over-whelmed," he said. "I . . . just assumed that this would be a . . . stigma to you; that it would put a strain between us."

"No," Cameron shook his head. "If I thought that people would not make the worst of it, I would gladly shout it from the rooftops. I'm proud to have you share my blood, Lance. I only hope that you can come to terms with this. And I want you to know that I'm here for you. I'm certain it will take time to fully accept what we've learned, but perhaps we can work it through together."

"Thank you," Lance said, actually feeling choked up. "I can't tell you what that means to me." His mind wandered through a length of silence, then he saw Cameron holding out a piece of paper. "What is this?" he asked, taking it from him.

"It's your inheritance," Cameron said the same moment Lance realized it was a bank note.

"I don't want this, Cameron," he said. "I just . . . can't take it. If I needed it, I might feel differently and be able to consider it a blessing, but I just . . ."

"Lance," he said, "our father wanted you to have this. Perhaps money was the only way he knew how to compensate for the strug-gles he knew you would face as a result of this. It doesn't matter whether or not you need it, you can find something better to do with it than having it sit in my accounts. Donate it to charity, build a hostile, start a fund for something that has meaning for you. Use it for good, and then you will have tangible evidence that something good has come out of this."

Lance looked at the note again and had to admit, "Well, if you put it that way . . . I think I like that idea."

"Good. It was Abbi's idea."

"Of course," Lance said and they both chuckled.

Lance folded the note and tucked it into an inside pocket of his uniform, where it would be safest. While the opportunity was before him, he had to ask, "I need to know . . . were there others like me? Children of your father's affairs?"

"Funny you should ask. I looked into that very thing after this came up initially. I couldn't help wondering, myself. Apparently, in spite of our father's weaknesses, his affairs were serious and careful, and he took responsibility for the children that resulted—unlike

Nikolaus." He paused and added, "There were two others. One passed away of illness several years ago; he had never married and had no remaining family. The other left the country with her mother more than twenty years ago, and there are no leads to find them."

Lance took in the information with mixed feelings. In a way he was relieved to know that searching out half-siblings wasn't feasible, but a part of him couldn't help wondering about them and the lives they'd lived. "Thank you," he said. "Now I can quit thinking about *that.*" He stood and held out a hand toward Cameron. "Thank you, Your Grace. In spite of the difficulty of this for me, I too am honored . . . to have you as a brother. We've been through much together."

"Yes, we have." Cameron smiled and took his forearm into a firm grip that held fast as they shared a long, brotherly embrace. "You'd better get that in the bank," Cameron said.

"I will, thank you."

"We're praying for Nadine . . . and for you."

"Thank you," Lance said and left the room. There were no words to describe what Cameron's words meant to him, and he couldn't deny that his attitude helped. But as he returned to his office and heard the reports of all that had happened in his absence, the full reality descended upon him and it took great self-discipline not to return to his apartment and crawl back into bed. He felt impatient and foul-tempered with his men, when he knew his mood had nothing to do with them. He had been dealt too many blows in too short a time, and he was finding it difficult to even be civil. His hiding away to deal with his own personal struggles had kept his concern for Nadine at bay. Now he had to face, once again, the cold reality that time was running out for her. All he could do was pray, but under the circumstances, that was likely the best thing that could be done. Nothing short of a miracle would ever undo this mess.

When Nadine's breakfast was brought in, she said to the officer, "I need to see the captain, as soon as possible."

"Is there something I can help you with, madame? As of last night, he was indisposed."

She thought about that for a moment and added, "No, I need to speak with him personally concerning an especially sensitive matter. Just see that he gets the message."

Less than an hour later, her cell door opened. The officer stepped in to take her breakfast tray, saying, "The captain is apparently back to work this morning and I will give him the message as soon as he comes out of the meeting he is in."

"Thank you," Nadine said.

Ten minutes later, she heard the door being unlocked. Her heart quickened as Lance entered the room and closed the door. His effect on her hadn't lessened in the slightest. He had returned to his typical well-groomed appearance, but there was no missing the pain in his eyes. She reminded herself of the circumstances and focused on her purpose.

"Is this business or personal?" he asked skeptically, removing his gloves.

"I wonder, Captain," she said tersely, making it evident she was all business, "how many female prisoners you get in here."

"Not many, but some. Why?" he asked.

"And is it standard procedure for such women to be threatened with their virtue in order to attain common necessaries?"

"What happened?" he demanded angrily. Nadine turned toward him, and the lantern hanging near the door illuminated the right side of her face. "Who did this to you?" he asked, his anger deepening.

"How should I know? He was wearing a uniform and he had the keys to my cell. He's the one with scratches on his face." She lifted a hand. "I drew blood."

Lance crossed the room and took her shoulders into his hands. "Tell me what happened. All of it!"

"Is that an order, Captain? Is your interest business or personal?"

"It's both, dammit. Just tell me."

"He came here in the middle of the night. At first he was sweet-talking me, telling me he could get me and my daughter out of the country if I gave him what he wanted. When I made it clear I wasn't interested, he tried to force himself upon me."

"Tried?"

"Tried. He did not succeed, if that's what you want to know. I kicked him hard enough that he won't be having his way with *any* woman for days yet. He threatened to see that I was denied common necessaries, and he even threatened to kill me if I said a word to anybody."

"You must not have believed him," Lance said, "or you wouldn't be telling me."

"I've got too many people trying to kill me to let that be a concern. I knew he was just trying to bully me into silence. I knew if *you* knew, you'd have his head on a platter. Not literally, I hope."

"Not quite, but close," he snarled. "I can assure you, Mrs. Rader, that the culprit *will* be found and severely punished."

"Thank you," she said and he moved toward the door. "One more thing." He turned back and she held out the pistol toward him by holding the barrel. "I should return this," she said.

Lance took it from her, unable to hide his astonishment. "You've had a pistol in your possession?"

"Since I took it off the man who tried to assault me early this morning," she said. "And yes, it's loaded."

"Why didn't you just use it to get his keys and get out of here?" he asked.

"Because that would have been dishonest, Captain," she said and he wished the committee of national security could be here to see this. If he told them, they'd never believe it.

"Thank you," he said. "I'll return it to its proper owner after I shoot him with it."

"Not really, I hope."

Lance shrugged. "Depends on how bad my mood gets before I find out who it belongs to."

Chapter Twenty-Two

RESIGNED

It didn't take Lance very long to find out who had been on the night shift, and of the two men on duty, their history told him everything he needed to know. There was only one possibility of who might have been in Nadine's cell in the night: Lieutenant Wurtzur. Lance told himself he shouldn't be presumptuous and jump to conclusions, just because he hated the man. But he knew Wurtzur had stood by Nikolaus, as his right-hand man, through many atrocious endeavors. Wurtzur was the man that Nikolaus could bribe into doing the dirty deeds that Lance would not do. When Cameron had been in prison, Wurtzur had beaten him on Nikolaus's orders. Cameron had kept him on the force with the stipulation that he work in the keep, and that he would be watched very closely. Well, today Lance would be watching very closely to see if the man's face bore any evidence of last night's escapade. He told the officers on duty in the keep that he wanted to see Wurtzur the moment he arrived late afternoon to begin his shift. "I don't care where I am," he said, "you tell him to find me before he does anything else."

Near the end of Lance's work day, he was in the principal library of the castle looking over some charts spread across a table with Cameron and two lieutenants when a knock came at the door.

"Come," Cameron called and Lance looked up to see Wurtzur enter the room—his face clearly scratched.

"You wanted to see me, sir," he said to Lance, and all of his anger over several issues in his life came lurching out. He belted Wurtzur in the jaw with one fist, and in the belly with the other, then he slammed him against the wall, muttering hotly, "You filthy scum. How many before her actually let you get away with it?" He slammed him again and Wurtzur groaned.

"Whoa," Cameron said, appearing at Lance's side. He looked at both of them, then said to Lance, "I assume the crime warrants the punishment."

"It does indeed, Your Grace," Lance snarled.

"And you have proof of this crime?" Cameron asked.

"You see those scratches on his face."

"I see them," Cameron said. "Cat get you, Wurtzur?"

"Mrs. Rader did that," Lance said, "in the middle of the night while he was attempting to have his way with her, making numerous threats."

Cameron glared at Wurtzur while Lance unmistakably caught the frightened, cornered look in the lieutenant's eyes. "Is this true?" Cameron asked, close to Wurtzur's face. "And don't lie to me. I can always tell when you're lying to me."

"And what if it is true?" Wurtzur growled. "She's a criminal and she—"

Cameron didn't wait for him to finish before *he* landed a fist in Wurtzur's middle, then he pressed a hand to the back of his neck and forced him to his knees. "That's one mistake too many, Wurtzur," Cameron said. "You will never serve on this force again. But then, by the time you get out of the keep, you will be far too old to care." Cameron stepped back and motioned toward the officers standing close by.

"Lock him up," Lance said, "and notify his family."

"Make certain they have what they need," Cameron added.

"Yes, Your Grace, Captain," one of them said as they took Wurtzur firmly and led him from the room.

The moment they were alone, Cameron said to Lance, "Is she all right?"

"Relatively speaking. I thank heaven she knows something about defending herself, or she wouldn't be. The very idea makes me sick. And does this mean he has raped other female prisoners who were too afraid to speak up?"

"I shudder to think," Cameron said and blew out a burdened sigh.

"Are we done here, then?" Lance asked.

"Yes, it can wait," Cameron said and Lance turned to leave, still fuming more than he cared to admit.

"Lance," Cameron said, putting a hand to his arm, "maybe you should take some time off."

"I've already taken time off," he said. "I need to find a way to prove her innocence, and I've already wasted too much time as it is."

"Lance," Cameron sighed, "what I'm trying to say is . . . if her innocence cannot be proven, I think you should take some time off, leave the country."

Lance teetered slightly and reached for the back of a chair to steady himself. He knew well what Cameron meant. If it came to Nadine going before a firing squad, Cameron wanted him out of the country so that he wouldn't have to give the order and see it happen.

"You need some time off," Cameron said. "Heaven knows you've earned it. I don't think you've taken a vacation day since I came back over three years ago."

Lance quickly found his equilibrium and stood up straight. "Thank you for the offer, Your Grace, but I'm fine. I have work to do."

Lance hurried away, wondering if his deepest fears on Nadine's behalf would become imminent.

Lance finally crawled into bed when he was so thoroughly exhausted he couldn't remain upright another minute. He slept quickly but woke with a gasp in the darkest part of the night. It took him a moment to recall the content of his dream, and when he did he couldn't breathe. He heaved for breath and groaned in anguish as his worst memories merged with the present, consuming him with an unfathomable fear. Unable to calm down as the images played over and over, he dropped to his knees beside the bed and stayed there until his back ached and his knees felt like they'd become a part of the floor. Over and over he prayed for peace and courage and the ability to know what he needed to do. And he prayed for a miracle.

Barely past dawn, Lance hurried into the castle and knocked at

Cameron and Abbi's bedroom door. "One moment," Cameron called only a second before he pulled open the door, buttoning his shirt.

"Did I wake you?" Lance asked.

"No, Abbi's having trouble sleeping. I've been reading to her. Come in."

"Thank you," Lance said and entered the elaborate ducal bedroom to see Abbi leaning against many pillows at one side of the huge bed. "I'm sorry to bother you so early," he added.

Cameron sat on top of the covers beside Abbi, putting his arm around her. "Sit down, Captain. I assume you need to talk."

"What makes you think so?" he asked, not completely serious.

"You just have that look on your face."

Lance scooted a chair closest to Abbi's side of the bed, since it was the side on which he was standing. "First of all," he said, "I just want to tell you how much I appreciate your friendship—both of you. I would be so completely lost without you."

"It's not something selfless and marvelous we're doing, Lance," Cameron said. "You have made many sacrifices on our behalf. Being a friend to you comes very naturally, I can assure you."

"Amen," Abbi said. "When I think where we might have ended up without your help during the reclamation, I can't even begin to imagine."

"Well . . . anyway . . . thank you."

"What's troubling you?" Abbi asked, reaching for his hand. The moment he took it her eyes showed alarm. "You're shaking! What's happened?"

"Nothing's happened . . . really. I just . . ." He looked deeply at her and had to ask, "Have you had any more dreams, Abbi? About the murders? Or anything else that could . . . have to do with this?"

"No," she said, "nothing." Lance sighed and hung his head with relief.

"Why?" Cameron asked.

"I had a dream—a horrible dream. And I'm not even implying that it's something that could literally come to pass, because it couldn't, but . . . I can't help wondering if it could be symbolic, or . . . oh, heaven help me." He retracted his hand from Abbi's and stood up, pacing frantically. "I don't know how I can get through this. I . . . I . . ."

"Tell us about the dream," Cameron urged gently.

Lance stopped walking but he didn't sit down. "It was . . . a memory. It felt as if I were really there all over again, and the two of you were there . . . just as it happened."

"What?" Cameron asked.

Abbi said with definitiveness, "Nikolaus's death."

"That's right," Lance said. "How do you do that? I would swear you *are* psychic sometimes."

"I am not," she insisted. "I know how difficult that was for you and how it's troubled you. It was a guess. Was that it? The dream was a memory?"

"It was all exactly the same until . . . I heard myself say that . . . the execution was complete and then as . . ." He started gasping for breath and squeezed his eyes closed. "I . . . I . . . pushed that knife . . . into his heart and . . . I could see the blood on my hand and then . . . he looked up at me with that hurt, betrayed look in his eyes that I will never forget, but as I lowered the body to the ground, it . . ." he gasped again, ". . . it wasn't Nikolaus. It was *her*. It was Nadine!"

"Good heavens," Cameron muttered.

"What do you think it means?" he asked, looking at Abbi.

"Maybe it doesn't mean anything," she said. "It could be nothing more than . . . anxiety manifesting itself in your sleep. As I understand it, most dreams are just kind of like . . . dumping the trash from our brains."

"Or maybe," Lance said, "it means that Nadine is going to die, and I'm going to be expected to give the order for the execution."

Abbi was visibly startled. "It can't come to that," she said. "It just can't." But Cameron met his eyes with a gaze that he understood clearly. They both knew that any other option wasn't looking good. And there was nothing that either of them could do about it.

Lance did his best to force the images from his dream out of his mind and get through the day. Later that morning as he sat in a meeting with the committee of national security, the reality of the dream's implication began to settle in with an unfathomable dread. He wanted to scream and break something as he endured another long oration from Mr. Fruberg concerning his ongoing fascination with serial killers. He mentioned a case he'd recalled learning about at university where there was a pattern of female victims being raped and beaten. When the culprit was finally apprehended and studied, it was discovered that he had a severely abusive mother, and the crimes were his attempt to lash out and project his hatred toward his mother on women who resembled her. Lance was hoping the committee could see that this theory did not coincide with their belief that Mrs. Rader would be killing other women, but he kept his mouth shut. He was relieved when Georg said that it seemed they were overlooking the obvious, that the man stalking Mrs. Rader was the one committing the crimes with a pattern of women who fit the same profile as Mrs. Rader. But the majority of the committee seemed to believe that they had their killer, and Lance wondered how much of their motive in that belief was the desire to simply be done with the case and not have to discuss it any further. Those who held to the belief that Mrs. Rader was innocent could offer no valid proof to counteract the evidence, and it seemed as though a trial was imminent. And Lance knew what that meant. The evidence would be officially held against her, and that would be the end.

As the meeting progressed and the evidence was recounted once again, Lance felt skeptical glances coming at him from some men and compassionate ones from others. It was easy to see where the division lay. He felt sick to hear details of the crimes again and to think of the victims and their families and of Nadine being stalked and lured into this horrible trap. Instinctively he knew that eventually another murder would occur, but he had a difficult time with the idea that another woman getting killed could prove Nadine's innocence. The point was brought up that more days had passed since the second murder than there had been between the first two, which some felt implicated Mrs. Rader further. Lance saw no significance there in light of the crimes committed by this man in the past. There had been no specific intervals of time, and he was grateful when Mr. Fruberg brought up that very point, adding that eventually another crime would be committed, if indeed, Mrs. Rader was innocent. But no one wanted to entertain the thought that had already plagued Lance—that it would take another death to prove her innocent. Thinking of the women who had died, it occurred to Lance that he had missed the funeral of the second victim while he had been wallowing in his grief. He felt bad, but there was little to be done about it now.

Lance was grateful to hear Cameron say, "And what if you execute this woman and the crimes continue?"

Georg quickly followed with the comment, "Why would Mrs. Rader even do such a thing? What motive could she possibly have?"

While Lance appreciated the question, he was in no mood to have Mr. Fruberg answer it. He launched a boring analogy of the possible mental illnesses that prefaced violent crimes. The issue resurfaced of what Mr. Hertz had brought up during the interrogation concerning Nadine's possible hatred and jealousy toward women who had been involved with Nikolaus. But an officer quickly brought forward his findings on the first victim having had no connection with Nikolaus du Woernig, since she had not even lived in Horstberg until after his death. Lance took a breath of relief on that one. Then Mr. Fruberg went on with ridiculous speculations about Mrs. Rader having some form of self-hatred that spurred her to lash out at women who were like herself. He finished by commenting that, "Her self-hatred could possibly stem from her betrayal and abandonment by Nikolaus du Woernig."

Once again Lance sighed and wanted to slither into the upholstery of his chair. He was grateful when the meeting finally adjourned— except for the feeling of helplessness and hopelessness that remained with him, clouding his heart and soul with a deep dread that was growing deeper. He was grateful for a supper invitation from Abbi, even though no amount of distraction could pull this weight from his mind and heart. After the meal he sat with Cameron and Abbi and Georg while their children played together on the rug. His mind was wandering when he looked up to see Abbi standing in front of him, holding out her hand. "Walk with me, Captain," she said.

Lance stood and took her hand as she said to Cameron, "We'll return shortly."

"Take your time," Cameron said with a warm smile.

"Tell me what's on your mind," she said as they ambled down a dimly lit hallway.

"I fear it's coming to an end," he said, "and I don't know if I can live with that."

"You mean Nadine."

"Yes, I mean Nadine."

"You mean . . . your relationship with Nadine?"

"No, Abbi. I'm talking about her life," he said.

She gasped and stopped walking. "Is it really that bad?"

"It really is. There is no evidence in this case at all in her favor except for her testimony, which is in direct contradiction to the evidence against her. The committee is impatient to have this over with. My hands are tied."

"I can't believe it," Abbi said, continuing to walk, wiping her face with her hand as silent tears fell.

"Neither can I," Lance said. "Cameron thinks I should leave the country, so I don't have to be involved. It will probably go to trial in the next few days, and once the trial is over . . ."

Abbi stopped again and pressed a hand over her mouth, her eyes widened in horror. She pulled her hand reluctantly away in order to say, "So you don't have to be involved? Is he talking about . . . I can't even say it."

"Well, let me say it, Abbi. He's talking about an execution. He didn't say it in so many words, but I'm sure he doesn't want me to have to stand in the courtyard and give the order for her to be killed. I couldn't do it. I couldn't. And I think he knows that. So, what do you think, Abbi? Give me some perspective."

"I . . . don't know what to say," she muttered, overcome with emotion.

"Well, I don't know what to say either," he walked on, urging her beside him. "I've prayed and pondered and done everything I can think of to scour this country and find that man. And I come up empty. I have no more ideas, Abbi, and I'm weary; I'm exhausted."

Her voice was compassionate as she said, "Maybe it's time to let go. Maybe we just have to accept that it *will* come to this."

Lance swallowed the knot in his throat, but his voice still cracked when he admitted, "That's what I've been thinking, but I couldn't bring myself to say it aloud. I think I just . . . need to . . ." He stopped walking and hung his head as tears stung his eyes and burned his throat.

"To what?" she asked, putting a hand on his shoulder.

A stifled sob accompanied his words into the open. "I need

to . . . tell her goodbye and just . . . leave the country until it's over. I don't know what else to do."

"You have to be sure, Lance," she said, crying herself. "You have to know in your heart that there really is nothing more you could do."

"Yes, I know, but I don't have much time."

"Whether or not this is the end for her is not in our hands, Lance. It's up to God whether or not she will end up dying for this, and if there is anything you can do, He is the only one who can inspire your mind to do it. And if there is nothing more you can do, then He can help you find peace over this and let go. Whatever happens, you have to come to terms with this. You must find a way to be at peace."

"I know," he said, sobbing again. "I just don't know if . . . I can."

Abbi wrapped her arms around him and let him cry before they walked slowly back to where they'd left the others, talking through the situation more carefully. Lance stayed long enough to read Dulsie a bedtime story and tuck her in, then he wandered to the castle chapel where he spent most of the night on his knees. He returned to his apartment to get a few hours of sleep before facing the day. In his heart he knew what he had to do. He could only pray that he would have the courage to do it.

Lance sat in his office, gazing at the wall, listening to the clock tick while he rehearsed what he needed to say. He didn't want Nadine to know how bleak the situation was, or perhaps it was more accurate that he didn't want her to hear it from him. Still, he had to be honest, and he prepared himself to find an appropriate balance. Glancing at the clock, he knew he couldn't wait any longer.

"Bring Mrs. Rader to my office," Lance barked at the officer near the door. "Right now."

"Yes, sir," he said and left to see to it.

Lance hung his head and pressed his hands into his hair. He wondered if anything in his life had ever been as difficult as this. Even learning of his illegitimacy paled in comparison. He became so thoroughly absorbed in the horror of his thoughts that he was startled when the officer appeared in the door. "Mrs. Rader, sir."

"Thank you," Lance said and stood as she was escorted into the room, her hands bound in front of her. "Leave us alone, please," he added and the door was closed.

For a long moment they shared a familiar gaze that made him want to kiss her, or better yet, just bodily carry her away from here, someplace far away where they could begin a new life together and never be found. But he couldn't. He couldn't live a lie. And he couldn't run. It simply wasn't in him to do such a thing.

"You wanted to see me, Captain," she said, breaking the spell between them.

"Yes," he said so gravely that Nadine's heart sunk.

"Have they set a trial then?" she asked, attempting to show some courage and dignity.

"No," he looked away. "Please . . . sit down." She took a chair and he sat on the edge of the desk. "First of all, I want you to know that the man who tried to assault you is behind bars and has been expelled from the force. He has a long history of being less than . . . ethical. I'm only grateful nothing worse happened."

Nadine nodded, but the expectancy in her eyes brought him back to her question. "They haven't set a trial yet, but . . . it doesn't look good. I don't know what to do, Nadine. I've prayed and prayed, and I've had the entire force working double time, tearing this country apart, trying to find the answers, trying to find this man. And we just come up . . . empty. I'm still holding out for a miracle, but even while hoping for the best, I believe we must be prepared for the worst."

"I see," she said. "And what is that, exactly?" He only looked away and she saw the muscles in his face tighten. "A firing squad then," she said and he squeezed his eyes closed, grimacing visibly. But the knots inside of her melted into despair when she saw a single tear fall from beneath his closed eyelid, splashing unheeded down his face. Her compassion for him made it suddenly easier to gather the courage she needed. "Well," she added, "at least I hear it's quick and painless. I trust you've trained these men to aim well. Right through the heart and it's over in an instant." Her voice softened as she asked, "Will you be giving the order then? That is how it works, isn't it?"

He finally opened his eyes and looked at her. "Yes, that's how it works. And no, I will not be giving the order. If it comes to that, Nadine, I will be leaving the country until it is long over." He hung his head and she was surprised to hear him groan with anguish.

Nadine stood and moved toward him, lifting his chin to find his face streaked with tears. "No need to cry for me, Captain," she said, wiping at his tears the best she could with her bound hands.

"I love you, Nadine," he said and pushed his arms around her, pressing his face into the folds of her dress. "Whatever estrangements have come between us, I love you. I feel so . . . powerless. How can I just stand by and watch this happen to you?"

"What choice do you have?" she asked and he sobbed with his face pressed tightly against her.

Nadine wanted to fall to her knees and beg him to steal her away from here. She wanted to beg his forgiveness for the awful things she'd said to him, and tell him how very much she loved him. But a part of her wondered if this wasn't for the best. Perhaps if she were dead it would be easier for him to get beyond his feelings for her, and she would never have to face the deep recesses of her heart that found it so difficult to trust him completely.

When he'd calmed down somewhat, she knelt before him and again wiped at his tears. "It will be all right," she said gently. "You'll go on. You must go on."

"No," he insisted, pressing his face closer to her hands, "my life will never be the same. Never."

A noise in the hallway beyond the closed door startled Lance to his senses, reminding him of who and where he was. "We mustn't let them find us like this," he said, taking her arms to urge her to her feet as he stood. Still holding to her he said, "I don't know if I'll see you again."

Nadine felt a defined panic rush to her heart, but she fought to keep a brave face, for his benefit, if not her own. "When I'm certain there is nothing more I can do, I'm leaving. It's the only way I can hope to get through this and remain standing at all."

Nadine quickly pondered what might be left undone, what she might need his help with if this truly was the end. "Dulsie," she said. "I must know that Dulsie is cared for in the best possible way. How can I be sure she won't end up in some horrible orphanage or—"

Lance wanted to promise her that he would never allow that. He wanted to tell her that he would personally see to her upbringing and consider it a privilege. But the alienation between them came back to him. She didn't trust him with her own heart. Would she trust him with her daughter? Forcing himself to a point where he could get through this and not fall apart again, he said systematically, "You need a will. Then your wishes will be carried out and the government will back you."

He opened a drawer and pulled out a sheet of paper with typed printing on it, laying it on the desk. "What is this?" she asked.

"A standard will. Just fill in the blanks and sign your name."

"I see," she said. "You've done this often, apparently."

"No," he said and she looked as if she would accuse him of lying. "I have helped many criminals prepare to face their deaths appropriately. I have never had a hand in sending someone innocent to a firing squad. Just my luck the first time would be a woman—the woman I love, no less."

"I'm sorry for everything I've put you through."

Lance met her eyes and saw her meaning. They both knew that these criminal charges were not of her doing and beyond their control. But he knew that her apology was more personal. And he couldn't come up with a single word to respond. He finally cleared his throat and said, "It's in the past. Just fill out the paper."

Nadine held up her bound hands and Lance unlocked the cuffs without hardly looking at them. Once free she stretched her hands and sat down at the desk. As she read over the will he said, "Her Grace told me she would gladly take responsibility for Dulsie, if it came to that. No one could raise her better, I'm sure."

"She told me the same," Nadine said while she was writing.

Before she signed her name, he said, "Hold on a minute." He opened the door and said, "Lieutenant, would you come in here for a moment please." The officer appeared and Lance added, "Would you please witness Mrs. Rader signing her will."

"Of course, sir," he said as if he'd done it many times. He watched Nadine sign, then he signed his own name as a witness, and watched Lance sign his name as the second witness.

"Thank you, Lieutenant. That will be all. Give us a few more minutes, please."

After he left, Nadine stood to face Lance. "So this is goodbye," she said, startlingly calm. It was as if the reality of what lay before her was being held back by a great dam that was threatening to burst, but as of yet was still intact. She prayed it would stay intact until she was alone in her cell.

"Perhaps," he said and took her chin into his fingers before he pressed his mouth over hers. His kiss began meekly, but it quickly became filled with all the passion and desperation they were both feeling. She wrapped her arms around him, and felt him do the same. When their lips broke contact, they both had tears on their faces. "In another time," he whispered, "another place . . ." He sighed and pressed a kiss to her brow. "I will love you forever, Nadine."

He stepped back abruptly and cleared his throat, wiping his face on his sleeve before he picked up the handcuffs from the desk and nodded toward her hands. She lifted them obediently and watched his hands gently and efficiently bind her wrists together. "I love you too," she said. He paused a long moment to gaze at her, then he opened the door and took hold of her arm to escort her back to her cell. She could feel his hand trembling where he held her, and while she wondered what farewells they might exchange once they arrived in her cell, he stopped beside an officer in the long hallway and said, "Escort Mrs. Rader back to her quarters."

"Yes, sir," the man said and took her other arm in the same moment that Lance let go. Without a word spoken, he turned and walked away while she was led the other direction. She'd only been alone a minute before the full torrent of grief overtook her and she sobbed helplessly, huddled in the corner of her bunk until long after night had fallen.

Lance returned to his office, praying he could hold himself together until he was able to be alone. He couldn't even allow his mind to think of what was taking place, or he would end up throwing a fit here and now, and likely be committed for insanity. Once he saw to a few minor matters, he could go home and start packing. His eye was drawn to Nadine's will on the desk, and he held his breath as he reached out to pick it up. He thought of what a blessing it would be to have Abbi responsible for Dulsie. At least he would be able to see her regularly and be a part of her life. He'd grown to love her as his own, and he had to consider her a blessing that would help get him through this. He could almost imagine having a purpose to go on living, if he could have any part in Dulsie's life.

Lance turned the paper around and focused on the words she had written there. He took a sharp breath as he read his own name written next to the printed words, *I will guardianship of my child/children to.* Something warm and tragic filled him as he considered that Nadine would entrust her daughter to his care. His purpose for living blossomed as he considered the changes he would make in his life to be the best possible father to Dulsie.

Lance found Cameron and Georg in the office, grateful that they were generally easy to find and often together. He handed Cameron two papers and a sealed envelope.

"What is this?" Cameron asked and made no effort to put on his glasses. He seemed to prefer an explanation over looking for himself.

"The first is an official request for a leave of absence, beginning now. The second is Mrs. Rader's will, in which you will note that guardianship of the child has been willed to me. I'm asking for your permission to take the child out of the country as soon as we can be packed. I would be most grateful if Her Grace could arrange for Dulsie to visit her mother and . . . say goodbye." Cameron sighed and Lance went on. "Although, I think it would be best if Dulsie not be told what's happening. I can talk to her about it after we're gone. I don't want her to upset her mother. I want their time together to be positive." Cameron nodded. "Thank you, sir."

"And what is this?" Cameron asked, holding up the envelope.

"A letter that I would like you to deliver to Mrs. Rader, only after the trial is over, and only if she is convicted."

"In other words, only if she is within hours of dying."

"That's right," Lance said.

Cameron sighed loudly and pressed a hand through his hair. "I can't believe this is happening."

"Nor can I, Your Grace. The point is that it *is* happening, and I can't stay here and watch it happen any longer."

"I understand," Cameron said. "I'll speak with Abbi and arrange for a visit with the child. You are free to go." Lance turned to leave and Cameron added, "Take good care of your niece."

Lance turned back, startled by an idea he'd not considered in quite that way before.

"My niece, too," Cameron added. "Bring her back safely."

"I will, of course," Lance said and hurried out of the office. He rushed home and proceeded to pack while he forced himself not to even consider the reality. He could fall apart later.

Chapter Twenty-Three
THE INTERRUPTION

Nadine was pleasantly surprised to be informed that she would have a chance to visit with her daughter. She was taken to one of the interrogation rooms and informed that four officers would be outside the door, but she was allowed to have her hands free. While she was waiting there, it occurred to her that perhaps this visit was another indication that the end was near. She forced such thoughts out of her head, determined to enjoy this time with Dulsie.

Abbi brought Dulsie into the room, and it was so good to see both of them that she couldn't keep from crying. They were allowed to be together for an entire hour while Nadine kept the conversation with her daughter focused on the fun the child had been having and her friends at the castle. She was obviously comfortable and happy, in spite of her mother's absence, and Nadine was grateful. Dulsie intermittently asked questions about Nadine's situation and when she was going to come home. She tried to evade the questions, but Dulsie was imperative. Nadine finally took encouragement from a firm nod that Abbi gave her and did her best to explain.

"I don't know what's going to happen, Dulsie. There are some people who believe I did something bad—something very bad. I didn't do that bad thing, but there is no way to prove that I didn't. I don't know if I'll ever be able to come home, Dulsie." The child looked astonished and tears rose in her eyes. "But whatever happens, I want you to know that you are the best thing that ever came into my life. I love you with all my heart and soul." Nadine couldn't hold back tears, as well. "I want you to be a brave girl, and always be good and do what you know is right, and you will be happy. Her Grace will take care of you and—"

"Can I stay with Lance when he's not working?" she asked eagerly. "I want him to be my father, like we talked about before you were mad at him. Can I?"

"Yes, Dulsie, you can stay with him always, except when he is working. He *is* going to be your father from now on, so no matter what happens, he will see that you're happy and safe."

The child seemed comforted by this, but she still cried through the remainder of their visit and didn't want to leave. Abbi finally took her into her arms and Dulsie hugged her tightly, practically sitting on top of the mound created by the baby inside of her. "I will see you again," Abbi said as she carried the crying child from the room. Nadine sat down and sobbed until the officers came to take her to her cell. Then she sobbed again until she slept.

Early the next morning she asked to see the captain, not knowing what she would say to him, but feeling a desperation to just be with him. She was informed that he had left the country. Nadine knew then that it was over, and she wasn't surprised to be told later in the day that the trial would begin the following morning. Her frame of mind took a dramatic shift as she was confronted with preparing herself to die. Her greatest fear became not death itself but the condition of her soul according to her instinctive belief that she would soon be facing God in His heaven, and she was determined to face him with a clear conscience. For that reason and many others, she was grateful to have the Bible with her, and she hoped that Lance knew how grateful she was for this gift he'd given her.

It was well past midnight before Lance had everything packed and arranged for his journey. He'd told Abbi goodbye before she went to bed, but Cameron stayed up and walked with him as he scooped a sleeping Dulsie up out of her bed, keeping her wrapped in a blanket. They walked together out to the waiting carriage where Lance laid the child on one of the seats before he turned to exchange his fare-wells with Cameron. They shared a firm embrace but said nothing beyond Cameron muttering, "Godspeed, my brother. Our prayers are with you."

Once the carriage pulled away with Dulsie still sleeping soundly on the opposite seat, Lance let the full torrent of his emotions come pouring out. He sat at one end of the seat and pressed his face to the other, crying like a child, praying with all his heart and soul that he could find peace with this, that Dulsie would do the same, and that Nadine would be comforted and strengthened through whatever she might have to face. He hated himself for abandoning her to face this on her own, but the option that faced him in staying was too horrible to consider. He couldn't give that order to fire weapons aimed at her heart and watch her fall. He just couldn't.

Lance cried until he became numb with exhaustion. He fell asleep praying and woke up doing the same. While the carriage still moved at a swift pace, Lance felt both relieved and heartsick to ponder the miles between him and Horstberg. He found comfort in watching Dulsie sleep in the early morning light. An idea occurred to him, seemingly out of nowhere, that showed the situation in a different light. If Nadine had not come to Horstberg, Albert Crider would still have eventually caught up with her, and then what would have happened to Dulsie? If Nadine's time on this earth was simply done, according to some vast divine plan far beyond the earthly comprehension of any human being, then perhaps Lance coming into their lives had been for the purpose of giving Dulsie a bright future. Lance would never know if the thought was some kind of inspiration or simply his own idea, but he found peace in the concept. And peace was something he could use a lot more of.

Lance and Dulsie spent the majority of the day in a quaint village filled with unique shops and good food. The carriage driver, who was an acquaintance of Lance's, spent the day sleeping at the inn where they would stay that night. Lance and Dulsie walked together holding hands, talking and even laughing, while Lance prayed in his heart that he could keep her distracted from thoughts of her mother until he had no choice but to tell her the truth. And then he prayed that she would take the news with the faith of a child. Still, in the deepest part of Lance's heart, he continued to pray for a miracle. He had told Nadine he would hope for the best and prepare for the worst. And he'd tried to do that. He just couldn't stop hoping for a miracle, even if he wasn't there to see it unfold.

They ate supper at the inn with the driver who had finally caught up on his sleep from driving all night. He would likely head back to Horstberg within the hour, and tomorrow Lance and Dulsie would find other means of transportation to continue their journey—even though he wasn't quite sure yet where they were headed.

Once they were settled into their room, Dulsie climbed into her bed that had been made on a little sofa, so much like where she had slept at the inn where she'd lived with her mother. He read to her from a new storybook they had purchased that day, and afterward Dulsie asked if he would rub her hands. He forced a smile and told her he would, but his mind wandered as he rubbed her tiny hand in his. He thought of all that had happened between him and Nadine, independent of the horrors that had come into their lives through these crimes. He missed her so badly that he felt a tangible pain in the center of his chest. While he rubbed Dulsie's other hand, his mind went systematically through the course of events that had eventually landed Nadine in prison. Then a thought occurred to him, once again, seemingly out of nowhere.

"Good heavens," he muttered, sitting forward abruptly. An image appeared in his mind as clearly as if he were recalling something that had happened five minutes ago. Except that this wasn't a memory. It was more like . . . a vision.

"What's wrong, Lance?" Dulsie asked with concern.

He looked into her little face and said firmly, "We have to go back, Dulsie. There's something I have to do."

"Is it something that will help Mama?" she asked eagerly.

"I hope so, Dulsie," he said, erupting to his feet. "You wait here for just a minute. I'm hoping our carriage hasn't left yet. I'll be right back."

Lance ran down the stairs and outside, and literally stopped the driver as he was settling onto the box seat with the reins in his hands. "We're coming with you," Lance shouted. "Just give us five minutes."

The driver nodded and Lance ran back upstairs to find Dulsie stuffing their belongings into the bags they'd brought with them. Within minutes they were on their way back to Horstberg while Lance's mind ran wild with the idea surging through him. It was a miracle, he thought over and over, praying that they would get back before the trial was over—or worse. But then, he concluded, if this idea truly had been inspired, it would not have come to him too late to do anything about it.

Dulsie quickly fell asleep with her head in his lap, and he wondered why he had felt so strongly about leaving Horstberg, only to turn around and go back. Then he recalled something Cameron had once told him. He vaguely remembered the idea, but he couldn't quite place the story. He made a mental note to ask Cameron about it at the first opportunity.

Lance eventually moved to the other seat, carefully adjusting Dulsie's head. He thought through every aspect of what he felt should be done, and he could only hope that God would see him through the necessary steps to make it happen. He couldn't determine the outcome, but he did know what he had to do. He had to try. He just had to.

Nadine woke on her little bunk and realized that this was the day her case would go to trial. And if she was convicted, she would likely be executed at sunrise tomorrow. Less than twenty-four hours to live, she thought, and felt surprisingly calm. She didn't know if that meant she would emerge from this all right in the end, or if she was simply prepared to die. She had written many letters, some longer than others, to say everything that she felt needed to be said. She had prayed more than she ever had in her life, and she felt as much at peace with God as she ever had. She could only hope that a miracle might yet intercede on her behalf.

Soon after breakfast Nadine was taken down the long hall of the keep, across the castle foyer she had passed through once before, and into the courtroom. She couldn't help thinking what a beautiful room it was, in spite of it being filled to the brim with people, all casting curious eyes upon her. She was glad to have been able to get cleaned up and have fresh clothes this morning, but she knew that her many days in prison couldn't look good on her. She'd not had a glimpse in a mirror since she'd come here. In fact, she'd not had a glimpse of sunlight in as many days, which drew her eyes to the high windows of the courtroom, with the sun shining brilliantly in a blue sky. As she was seated with an officer on either side of her, Nadine was freshly struck with the enormity of what was facing her, and she couldn't help wishing that Lance was here. She understood why he'd had to leave, and she couldn't blame him. But she knew she would feel better just to have him in the same room. She wondered about Dulsie. Where was she? What was she doing? And then a loud voice asked all present to rise for the judge to enter. Nadine gasped to see that it was Cameron, wearing judicial robes. She couldn't decide if that was good or not, but she didn't miss the subtle compassionate glance he tossed in her direction as he was seated.

Through the morning many different testimonies were heard, including the officers who had escorted Nadine to the places where the murders had occurred, and people who had seen her visiting the homes of several different women previously. She wasn't sure what all of this was meant to establish. It all seemed like a dreadful waste of time to her. They adjourned for lunch and reconvened to hear the testimony of Mr. Fruberg who rambled on about theories of serial killers, and his speculations on the motive that Nadine might have for killing women like herself. She was pleased and amazed to hear that Nikolaus du Woernig didn't come up, and she couldn't help thinking that Cameron had something to do with that. His threats to the committee on that count during the interrogation came to mind. While Mr. Fruberg's lengthy answers were tedious to endure, she did appreciate his endorsement of the theory that the man stalking Nadine had committed the crimes and had set her up. His testimony ended up offering more speculation than anything, but at least it was unbiased speculation.

Nadine was appalled to have to listen to detailed descriptions of the murders, as described by those who had found the bodies and the officers who had come first to the scene. She feared that this would never end, and then she was called to the witness stand. And then she feared it *would* end, and so would her life.

Lance finally arrived at Castle Horstberg, six hours behind schedule, due to a broken wheel and a lame horse. He'd never been so frustrated in his life, and he could only hope his prayers were being heard. When they came into the courtyard, it was crowded with parked vehicles and tethered horses. He knew what that meant. *A trial.* Only great social events and trials would bring this many people here.

Lance pulled Dulsie into his arms and literally ran to the courtroom. He wasn't surprised by the crowds gathered, even in the foyer. He only hoped a verdict had not yet been given. He squeezed into the back of the room and realized that Nadine was in the process of giving her testimony. She would be the last one called to the stand. He heaved a sigh then wondered how he could follow through on what he felt he needed to do if a verdict was given first. While he was praying in his mind and pondering, Dulsie caught sight of her mother and waved at her. Nadine stopped mid-sentence as she apparently caught the movement and recognized them. He saw her try to keep a straight face, but he recognized the glimmer of pleasure in her eyes to see them. He was so glad he'd come back!

Nadine completely lost her words as she took in Lance and Dulsie at the back of the courtroom. He was dressed in ordinary traveling clothes, and just seeing him made her heart quicken. Then she realized he was trying to tell her something. She saw him mouthing words, but she couldn't quite grasp what they were. She kept stammering to make it appear to the court that she was attempting to gather her thoughts while she focused more on Lance. He pulled out his pocket watch and pointed to it while he mouthed words again, and this time she got them. *We need more time.* Nadine thought quickly and decided that she could use her distraction and stammering to her advantage.

"Your Grace," she said, turning to Cameron, "I'm suddenly feeling rather ill. Is it possible to have a break?"

"I was just wishing for the same," he said. He then added more loudly, "This court will reconvene tomorrow morning at ten o'clock."

Nadine let out a weighted sigh, and she could see Lance's visible relief. She had been hoping for an hour, but tomorrow was even better. She had at least one more day to live. Back in her cell, Nadine hoped that Lance would come to see her, to offer some kind of explanation for his leaving, his return, and his need for time. But she went to bed without seeing him, praying that his call for more time would come to something. At least it gave her some hope. How well she recalled Cameron's admonition to never give up hope. It was all she had left.

Lance hurried out of the courtroom before the crowds hardly had a chance to move. He went through a back hallway, knowing where Cameron and members of the committee would be exiting. He was waiting for Cameron when he emerged.

"What are you doing here?" he asked.

"We need to talk," Lance said. "All of us."

"Who is all of us?"

"The committee. I have an idea. I just ask that you hear me out. I don't want you to say anything. Just . . . leave it to me. Is that possible?"

"Of course," Cameron said. "We're meeting anyway in half an hour to discuss the trial so far. We'll see you then."

"Thank you," Lance said and hurried away to take Dulsie to the nursery before he returned to his apartment to change into his uniform. He noticed all his luggage and packages had been brought there, as well as Dulsie's.

Lance arrived at the meeting just as the men were being seated. He listened quietly as opinions and speculations were batted back and forth, and the entire trial was recounted in pathetic detail. When he could bear no more, Lance finally leaned forward and said, "If I may speak, Your Grace."

"Of course," Cameron said.

"I know that you are all aware of my personal involvement with Mrs. Rader, and I am doing my best to overlook those feelings and stick to the facts. It's occurred to me that if there is a pattern that's likely to continue, then it's likely to happen again, and if the killer is ultimately after Mrs. Rader, then we could catch him by using Mrs. Rader as bait."

"And let her out of that cell?" Mr. Hertz said in a tone that implied his belief that Lance was fishing for excuses to get her out of prison. "I don't think so, Captain."

Lance resisted the urge to reach across the table and belt him in the jaw. He turned more to Cameron and silently thanked God for putting the answers into his mind. "What I suggest is that Mrs. Rader be kept in her cell and an officer be placed outside her door every minute, so there is no question that she remains there. Then we take a woman who can appear to be Mrs. Rader and make it look as though she has been set free. We watch the woman closely, as Mrs. Rader was watched before her arrest, and we may just have our killer turn up. If he turns up, then Mrs. Rader's innocence is proven, and we have our man."

Lance could feel retorts and rebuttals forming among a number of the men in the room, but Cameron quickly said, "I think it's a marvelous idea." Lance smiled, appreciating the dynamics of a monarchy that allowed Cameron's voice to supersede all else, so long as it was legal. It worked especially well with the monarch being his ally. He recalled times when Nikolaus was the monarch that it hadn't worked well at all. And he could feel miracles falling into place when Lieutenant Kepler piped up, saying, "I know a woman who might be perfect for the job."

"Tell us about her," Georg said eagerly.

"She is a friend of my sister's. And quite honestly, the first time I saw Mrs. Rader from behind, I thought it was this woman. She's been terribly upset and nervous over the killings because she fits the same physical description as the victims. But she's spunky. I think she'd be willing to do it. I'm certain the standard financial incentive that comes with such undercover assignments would help a great deal. She's supporting an ailing mother and could certainly use the money."

"Sounds good," Cameron said. "Tell her there's a generous bonus if she can be ready tomorrow."

"I'll do that," Kepler said. "Thank you, Your Grace."

"Wait a minute," Mr. Fruberg said, "if the killer is indeed on the loose, as the captain is suggesting, how do we know he hasn't already spotted this woman? He would know if she wasn't Mrs. Rader."

"Well," Kepler said, "she works as a seamstress and doesn't go out much, which makes it less likely that he's spotted her, as opposed to the other women who both worked in public places."

"And how exactly do we go about replacing Mrs. Rader with this . . . imposter?" Mr. Hertz asked skeptically.

Lance just smiled, grateful for the ideas that had poured into his mind through his journey back to Horstberg and how easily they were meshing with what had just been presented. "You see," he said, "we have Lieutenant Kepler take an officer's uniform into her home in a bag, as if he's taking her a sewing job. This woman comes out looking like an officer. She gets into a carriage with him and is brought here, where she meets Mrs. Rader and puts on some of her clothes. We put out a proclamation that states Mrs. Rader is being let go on newfound evidence, still pending a later trial, which implies that there is still possible guilt, so if our killer reads it, he believes she could still be implicated. Then our imposter leaves the keep and goes to the inn, where she mostly holes up in her room, except for an occasional nighttime walk where it's difficult to see her face, and the officer escorting her appears distracted and puts too much distance between them. We establish the pattern for a few days, and see if our killer doesn't make a move."

"Marvelous plan," Georg said. "I wish I would have thought of it myself."

Lance just leaned back in his chair as the meeting went on and fine details of the plan were discussed. Lieutenant Kepler agreed to make a visit to this woman as soon as the meeting adjourned, and he rehearsed the plan back very carefully, so that all possible cogs were talked through.

When the meeting was finished, Lance waited for everyone to leave except Cameron and Georg. "Were you inspired, my good man, or what?" Cameron asked with a little laugh.

"No doubt about it," Lance said. "I only hope it works. If it doesn't, Hertz will probably have *me* executed."

"Ah, he's just a bag of wind," Georg said. "Unfortunately he's got a good head on his shoulders and we need him."

"It's good to have you back," Cameron said, "and to see hope in your eyes."

"Well, it's good to have hope," Lance said. "Which reminds me . . . I had this feeling when the idea came to me that . . . well, I was wondering why I'd felt so strongly about leaving when I didn't get very far and knew I had to come back. And I'd remembered your sharing a similar feeling with me about some experience in your life, but I couldn't recall exactly. Do you have any idea what I'm talking about?"

Cameron sighed. "I do, actually. When I was trying to prove my innocence and take back the throne from Nikolaus, I honestly didn't know if it would be possible. And then I realized that if I was married to Abbi and she had conceived a child, then there would be a way for the throne to be taken from Nikolaus eventually, whether I lived or not. In essence, I reached a point where I was determined to live, but willing to die for my country if that's what it would take to save it. As soon as I resigned myself to that and put the matter into God's hands, everything seemed to come together. After I had come back into society, the bishop gave a sermon one Sunday about Abraham and Isaac. He talked about each of us being willing to lay our sacrifices upon the altar, and that sacrifices come in many different forms. And there are times when the miracle only comes when we are willing to completely put our lives into God's hands and accept His will—as Abraham did in being willing to offer his son."

"Incredible," Lance said, noticing Georg's smile. Lance knew what they had gone through together in order to get Cameron through his years of exile and to restore him to the throne. All of it had contributed to a bond between them that was immeasurable.

Lance considered how Cameron's story applied to his own recent experience. He had done all that he could and he had done his best to put it into God's hands with the hope that he could find peace no matter what happened. And then the miracle had come. "Well," Lance said, "we can pray that this miracle comes through in the end."

"We can and we will," Georg said, and Lance felt the hope within him deepen.

Nadine woke out of a fitful sleep, hearing a key turn in the lock. Half asleep, she reminded herself that the man who had tried to hurt her before was behind bars, but she couldn't help wondering if there were others who would try the same thing, perhaps with more determination and alternate methods of keeping her quiet and submissive. A lantern was hung by the door, but the wick was low and the glow dim. She could only see a cloaked figure as he locked the door behind him and approached the bed.

"Don't hurt me," she muttered, retracting into the corner.

"Shhh," she heard and felt familiar hands take hold of hers. "It's me," Lance said.

"Oh," she cried softly, "you came back."

"I did," he muttered, pulling her into his arms.

"*Why* did you come back?" she asked as he let go of her.

"Apparently I had some unfinished business," he said as he removed his cloak and tossed it over the foot of the bed.

He started unfastening the coat of his uniform and she asked, "What are you doing?"

"I'm making myself comfortable," he said, hanging the coat over the back of the chair, "unless you have a problem with that."

"No, but . . ."

He sat on the edge of the narrow bed and pulled off his boots. "Move over," he added and slipped beneath the blanket, easing close to her.

"What are you doing?" she asked again, sounding more pleased than alarmed.

"I'm going to hold you," he said, "all night."

"But . . . won't they think I'm a tramp?" she asked, recalling what he'd once said. "Won't they believe that we're—"

"I told them to keep their mouths shut and to consider my reputation if they have any question about what's going on."

"I see," she said, settling her head against his shoulder. She relished his nearness and held to him tightly. "Why are you doing this?"

"Because I love you, Nadine, and it doesn't matter what the future holds, or whether or not you believe in me. I believe in you, Nadine, and I was wrong to let my anger keep me from being there for you when you needed me. I'm not expecting this to change anything between us. But I'm here now, and I'm staying until breakfast."

"You are?"

"I am. I told them to bring mine here."

"Oh!" She let out a joyful cry and held to him more tightly. "You came back," she repeated, unable to express what that meant to her. Feeling his strength and comfort filter into her, fresh emotion rushed forward, first in silent tears, and then in quiet sobbing as she held to him and kept her face pressed to his chest, crying out her every fear.

"I've tried to be brave," she cried, "but I'm not. I've fought so hard to be dignified and handle this graciously, but . . ." she was so upset she could hardly speak, "I don't want to die. I don't want to be here. I miss my little Dulsie. I want to live."

"I know," he muttered, pressing a kiss into her hair as she cried on. "It's all right. You don't have to be brave for me. Heaven knows I've done more than my share of crying over this. You have good cause to cry, Nadine. Just go ahead and cry."

His permission spurred more emotion into the open, and she cried until she slept in his arms.

Lance basked in just being able to hold her, even as she wept, and then to have her sleeping soundly—and safe for the moment—in his arms. He longed to tell her of their plan, and of course she would have to know to some degree since this woman would be borrowing her clothes. Besides that, the remainder of the trial would be postponed. But a part of him feared building up her hope only to have it dashed. Still, hope was what they needed. And he was determined to see this miracle through. Nadine deserved to live, and he was going to do everything in his power to make that happen. And with any luck, when all was said and done, she would choose to live her life with him.

Chapter Twenty-Four

THE IMPOSTER

Nadine came awake feeling disoriented. When her eyes adjusted, she realized the lamp had been left burning with a dim glow. She was laying on her side, facing the wall. She shifted slightly and recalled that she was not alone. She let out a contented sigh as she became aware of Lance's arm around her waist and his even breathing against the back of her neck. She turned carefully, with some difficulty in the narrow space left from two sharing a bed so small. He stirred in response to her movement, opened his eyes for only a second, and smiled. He made a pleasurable noise, eased her closer and went back to sleep. But Nadine chose to keep her eyes open, reasoning that she could sleep any time. This was an experience to be savored, and she couldn't help reveling in the love that she knew he had for her. While he slept on, she contemplated the mistrust she had felt, and she knew in her heart that her fears had blown the situation very much out of proportion. She wanted more than anything to just tell him that she'd been wrong, to beg his forgiveness, to make a fresh start. But she didn't want to renew their relationship in a prison cell, leaving him forever to wonder if her change of heart had come from the desperation of her changed circumstances. While she held onto the hope that a miracle might yet free her from this doom, she had to accept the possibility that she might not survive this escapade. For all she knew, she could only be seeing one more sunrise beyond the one that would meet her execution. And perhaps it was better for him to remain detached to some degree. She had written him a lengthy letter, pouring out her deepest feelings. If it came to that, he would know how she felt. But in the meantime, she simply believed it was better to keep their relationship as it was. Still, how could she not be grateful for his willingness to spend this time with her? Just having him near was like a balm to her soul. She eased her arms more tightly around him, being careful not to disturb him, but a moment later he asked softly, "Are you all right?"

"For the moment," she said. "And you?"

"Right now," he opened his eyes and smiled, "everything is perfect. Well," he chuckled, "the accommodations could use a little refining."

She laughed softly. "Perhaps you could talk to the man in charge about that."

He groaned. "He would just have to consult the committee."

"Then I guess it will have to do," she said and couldn't resist touching his face. She held her breath when he did the same, exploring her features with his fingertips as if she were a rare work of art. And how relieved she was when he kissed her! He kissed her over and over in a slow, savoring way that seemed to tell her they had forever to be this way together. He touched her hair, her throat, her face again, illustrating a depth of intimacy she'd never experienced before. She was left in awe of the way he could kiss her and touch her and look into her eyes, as if they had been lovers forever, and yet they remained completely chaste. She marveled that his kiss could hold such passion, yet he could lie beside her and not leave her feeling the need to defend her virtue.

Lance held her close as the distant sounds of morning came to their ears. No words were spoken between them until Nadine felt the need to say, "I thought I was going to be dead by now."

Lance looked into her eyes and felt compelled to tell her the truth. "You probably would have been if . . ."

"If what?" she asked. He didn't answer and she guessed with relative certainty, "If you hadn't come back and interrupted my testimony?"

"Something like that," he said.

"But the court will reconvene today," she said, "and we both know what the verdict will be."

"No, Nadine," he said, leaning up on one elbow, "the trial has been postponed."

"Why?" she asked breathlessly.

"Because I came up with an idea, and with Cameron's help the committee agreed to give it a chance. We can't possibly predict the outcome, but it will give us some time, and God willing, it could very well lead us to the culprit."

"That's why you came back?" she asked, touching his face.

"Yes," he said, kissing her brow. "This idea seemed to just come out of nowhere, with such clarity, and . . . I knew I had to get back. I had to at least try." His voice softened as he brushed her hair back off her face with his fingertips. "My wish was not to abandon you, Nadine."

"You had to go. I understand why."

"Why?" he tested.

"Because you couldn't be the one to give the order, and I wouldn't want you to be. I understand."

Lance felt some relief in that, but he had to admit, "I took Dulsie with me."

"I know."

"You do? Did Abbi tell you?"

"No, I just . . . had a feeling. And I was grateful. Of course, I saw her with you when you came into the courtroom. She looked so happy. She loves you, you know."

"And I love her," he said, "as I love you."

"I love you too, Lance. I do."

"I know you do, Nadine. Perhaps when this is all over we—"

"Perhaps," she said, pressing her fingers over his lips. "Don't talk of that for now. Just kiss me."

He did as she asked and she savored the sensation, wondering when it might be possible for them to be alone again. She doubted he could get away with spending *every* night in here.

"Will you tell me your idea?" she asked.

"Later," he said and kissed her again. "They'll be bringing breakfast in shortly."

"Does that mean I'll get to see you again soon?"

"That's likely, but it will be business. I mustn't press my luck with pushing the rules."

"Of course," she said. "I'm glad you got away with this much."

"So am I," he smiled and kissed her again and again until the key turned in the lock and he hurried to pull on his boots. He was standing with his coat in his hands when the door came open.

"Good morning, Captain," Lieutenant Kepler said.

"What are you doing here, Lieutenant? Have you been demoted?"

"No, sir," he chuckled. "You mentioned that you would be here should I need anything. I thought that perhaps my handling the delivery of your breakfast personally would allow for more discretion."

"Thank you, Lieutenant. Any progress on what we discussed yesterday?"

"Yes, sir. Exactly as we had hoped. As soon as you're finished here, we'll go over the details."

"Thank you," Lance said and the lieutenant left, locking the door behind him.

Lance and Nadine sat together on the bed with the breakfast tray in between them, feeding each other as they talked intermittently. Nadine hated to see him go, but he held her close and kissed her long and tender before he finally slipped away. And even in his absence she felt the warmth he had left behind. With all her heart she longed for a miracle that would free her from this hell and allow her a chance to make up where she had wronged him. If God would only grant her that, she could ask for no more.

Lance was pleased to hear that the woman who resembled Nadine had been eager to take the assignment. A uniform had been delivered to her the previous evening—the smallest one they could find. And being a seamstress, this woman had been confident she could make some minor adjustments and be ready later today. Another officer had discreetly spoken with Drew and Gerda at the inn, and they were well prepared to have Nadine's look-alike stay in her room. Some of the woman's belongings would be picked up by Drew through the course of his usual shopping for supplies.

Other points of the plan were gone over in fine detail until it was time for lunch. Lance ate with Dulsie in the nursery, as many parents did, then he returned to his office only minutes before one of the ducal coaches pulled into the courtyard and three officers stepped out. They walked into the keep and Lance was actually surprised when they approached him to see that one of them was a woman. Only when she was face-to-face could he tell the difference.

"Captain Dukerk, this is Gretchen Hegel," Lieutenant Kepler said proudly.

"A pleasure, Miss Hegel," he said. "I will refrain from my usual way of greeting a lady, for the sake of appearances."

"Very wise, Captain," she said with a little smirk. "Although, I do believe we've met before."

"I'm sorry," Lance said graciously, "I'm afraid I don't remember. My memory skills are very poor in some instances." What he didn't tell her was that he made no effort to remember the countless simpering women who had vied for his attention in one way or another through the years, just because he wore a uniform that represented a prestigious position. He caught the subtle disappointment in her eyes, and the way she covered it with a coy smile.

Ignoring her antics he said, "Come along, Officer Hegel. I want you to meet the woman you are about to become."

Nadine heard footsteps in the hall and the key turning in the lock. The door came open and a young officer stepped into the room, followed by Lieutenant Kepler and the captain, who closed the door.

"Mrs. Rader," Lance said, "I would like you to meet the new Mrs. Rader, also known as Miss Gretchen Hegel."

Nadine gazed at Lance, baffled to say the least. She looked closely at the officer's face and realized it was a woman only a moment before she removed the typical officer's hat to reveal that her curly, dark blond hair was pinned close to her head.

"I don't understand," Nadine said to Lance.

Lieutenant Kepler explained, "As far as the people of Horstberg know—according to a proclamation that is being posted as we speak—Nadine Rader is being released this afternoon due to the discovery of new evidence, but pending a possible trial. Mrs. Rader's child is being kept in protective custody until the matter is settled. Miss Hegel here will pose as you and return to the inn in your stead, keeping a low profile but going out for late evening walks with officers tailing her, but not too closely. This will hopefully attract Mr. Crider, and give us an opportunity to snag him."

Nadine glanced at Miss Hegel. "But that's so dangerous," Nadine protested.

"Nah," Gretchen said, "they'll watch out for me, and I'm not so bad at holding my own when I have to."

Nadine looked at Lance with protest in her eyes. "I don't know if I like this. If he's killing women that look like me, then . . ." She couldn't go on.

"Nadine," Lance put his hands to her shoulders, "your concern is appreciated, but it's the only option we've got. If not this, then the trial goes forward."

"Well . . . perhaps that would be better than having more innocent women in harm's way."

"He's still out there, Nadine. Even if you die for these crimes—innocent of them, mind you—he will still be out there if we don't find a way to lure him out of hiding. Are you hearing me?"

Nadine nodded reluctantly and Lance kissed her brow. As she turned to look again at Miss Hegel, she saw something close to jealousy in her eyes. Had this woman considered Lance's personal attention some kind of affront? Of course, she was well aware that women everywhere were vying for his attention, but seeing it here, and so blatantly, was a little unnerving.

Nadine was ready to pass it off when Miss Hegel said, "It's too bad you don't remember our previous meeting, Captain. As I recall we had a glorious time."

"Forgive me, Miss Hegel," Lance said.

Kepler cleared his throat as if he sensed the tension rising. "Mrs. Rader," he said, "we would like Miss Hegel to leave the keep wearing the dress you wore in court yesterday, and with her hair done the way that you usually do yours. We'll leave the two of you to take care of the change and to discuss any habits or pertinent information that might make this go more smoothly."

"Of course," Nadine said.

The men moved toward the door as Lance said, "Lieutenant Kepler will be back in a while for you, Miss Hegel, and he'll tell you everything you need to know. We appreciate what you're doing and ask that you be extremely careful."

"Of course," she said. "Anything for the protection of womankind."

Lance stepped into the hall and waited for the lieutenant to lock the door. "I'm sorry about that, Captain," he said as they walked down the hall together.

"What?" Lance asked, baffled.

"I did recommend her for the job, and I really believe she'll do well, but she *is* a flirt, and she does enjoy getting male attention."

"It didn't bother *me,*" Lance said. "I'm getting pretty good at brushing off women who only see a uniform."

"You have that problem too, huh?" The lieutenant chuckled.

"Indeed," Lance said. "Let's just hope that Miss Hegel shows some promise in getting Albert Crider's attention."

"Let's hope," Kepler echoed.

Nadine turned again to look at this woman now that they were alone, but Miss Hegel was looking at the closed door as if to imply some meaning toward the men who had just left the room. She sighed loudly and said, "Men are all alike, aren't they? They'll take what they want when the opportunity presents itself, but a day or two later and their memory has magically faded."

"You know the captain?" Nadine asked, unable to hold her curiosity. She couldn't help wondering if her comment had been directly related to Lance, or men in general.

"Oh, yes," she drawled as if they'd been the best of friends, yet Nadine had seen Lance's obvious indifference toward her. "Of course, it has been a long time since I've seen him, but considering our association, he must have some memory of it. Or maybe," she giggled, "his lack of memory is a result of too much to drink. Oh, the parties we used to have when he and Nikolaus du Woernig would come around."

"Truly?" Nadine said, finding it increasingly difficult to brush this aside.

"Oh, what a pair he and Nikolaus made. Two of a kind, they were."

"Funny," Nadine said, "I don't see much similarity at all."

"Well, perhaps you didn't know them the way I did—back then."

"Perhaps not," Nadine said and tossed the dress at her. She was able to turn the conversation to the assignment they'd been given, but Nadine couldn't deny the uneasiness rising in her. A part of her wanted to be convinced that this was just a simple-headed female grappling for the captain's attention and jealous because Nadine had gotten it. But there was no denying that sensitive place deep in her heart that still felt hesitant to truly believe Lance was everything he put on to be, in spite of her strong feelings for him. She reminded herself that loving a man did not automatically make him worth loving. Was it possible that being in a futile situation *had* altered her perspective? Had she chosen to let go of what her instincts were telling her in regard to Lance, simply because of her loneliness and desperation? Or were her instincts simply so battered that she couldn't feel them at all?

Nadine was relieved when Lieutenant Kepler came back for Miss Hegel. The woman got on her nerves. She always managed to bring the conversation back to her observations of men, some in particular. Nadine was grateful for what this woman was willing to do, but she didn't want to hear her ramble on further about the carousing of Nikolaus du Woernig and the Captain of the Guard. Once the lieutenant had taken her away, she was actually grateful to be alone— until her mind started spinning. Again she tried to convince herself that this woman's opinion had no bearing, and even *if* Lance had once been as she had implied, he deserved to be forgiven and have it put behind. Still, she recalled Lance telling her that he was innocent, that she'd been the first to be so close to him, to draw his attention that way. And the images simply didn't fit with Gretchen Hegel's descriptions of him. Nadine cursed herself for being so mistrusting, but she didn't know what to do about it.

Fearing she would go mad, Nadine forced her thoughts instead to the intrigue that was now underway on her behalf. Annoying qualities aside, Nadine prayed that Miss Hegel would be kept safe, and that the plan would indeed work and free her from this prison hell of wondering how many days she might have left to live.

Forty-eight hours after Miss Hegel walked out of the keep and was returned to the inn, reports came to Lance that her habits were being established and all was going well. Drew and Gerda were receiving many comments from customers about how good it was to see Mrs. Rader coming and going, although no one had gotten close enough to see that it wasn't her.

A new piece of evidence came up as the result of deeper investigation into Albert Crider's past. For Lance, it was a tangible morsel of hope, but he decided to hold onto it until a time when it might have more bearing—or perhaps when the situation became desperate enough that he needed an extra ace.

He finally managed to find a few minutes to visit Nadine, but when he entered her cell, he immediately knew something was wrong. The warmth he'd felt from her the last time he'd been here was completely absent.

"What's the matter?" he asked, locking the door.

"It might be better if I said 'nothing' and leave it at that."

"Not if something's bothering you," he said.

"I really don't want to talk about it," she said with a glare that he recognized.

"You're upset with *me,*" he said. "I was under the impression that things were better between us."

"You told me you weren't expecting the time we spent together to change anything between us."

"Yes, I said that, didn't I. But I couldn't help hoping." He let out a disgusted sigh, unable to hold back the cynicism as he added, "What despicable thing did I do now?" She said nothing and he added, "Will you give me a chance to defend myself this time, or is a fair trial out of the question?"

Nadine felt her heart pricked by his comparison. She reminded herself that she had regretted her lack of fairness in the past, and he *did* have a right to defend himself. "Very well," she said, taking a deep breath before she repeated the things that Miss Hegel had said.

Lance listened to the oration attempting to keep a straight face. When she said the woman had implied that he'd been too drunk to remember their encounters, he actually laughed but stopped abruptly. Nadine obviously didn't think it was funny.

"Nadine, listen to me," Lance said. "Lieutenant Kepler knows this woman. He admitted to me that she's right for the job, but she's a flirt and goes to a lot of trouble to get men's attention. Gretchen Hegel is like a thousand other women out there who are only interested in me for one reason: money and prestige."

"That's two," she corrected.

"Fine, two. This is far from the first time a woman has claimed to have association with me that never happened. You see, with Nikolaus, that kind of thing worked. If a woman led him to believe that he'd spent time with her in the past, he might actually spend time with her. And because he *did* drink too much and couldn't remember half of his nights out, sometimes it worked. Yes, there was a time when I followed Nikolaus around to the pubs and to a few parties. My biggest reason for being there was to see that he didn't get into too much trouble and that he got home safely. After a while, I stopped caring. And I have *never* been drunk enough that I couldn't remember."

Lance watched Nadine's eyes and felt his more recent hopes crash around him. She didn't believe him. Recalling her warmth toward him the last time they were together, he wondered who this imposter was that occasionally took the place of his sweet Nadine. "You know what, Nadine?" he said. "You've got a choice. You can either believe me or Miss Hegel. And if we are going to share any kind of relationship in the future at all—even if that is to be nothing more than friends—you are going to come across many Miss Hegels. So, what's it going to be? Am I what I say I am? Or am I what Miss Hegel says I am?"

"That's what I'd like to know," she said, only slightly terse.

Lance felt such an intense rush of anger that he had to turn his back and count to ten. Then twenty. When he still felt angry he moved toward the door, fumbling to find the right key.

"Where are you going?"

"I have spilt my heart's blood one too many times for you, Mrs. Rader." He unlocked the door and looked over his shoulder. "As much as I have come to love you, my dear, I cannot and will not live with this issue between us. I have given you *no* reason to mistrust me. I deserve better than this."

"Well," she countered, "perhaps I will end up going before a firing squad, and you won't even have to worry about it."

Lance's anger only multiplied. He turned abruptly to face her. "There is a bitter and ugly side to you, Nadine, and it has a way of bringing out the worst in me. I pray to God you can come to terms with it before you *do* face a firing squad. I don't care what Nikolaus du Woernig or anyone else did to you, it doesn't give you the right to pass it on. Good night, Mrs. Rader. Perhaps we will meet again at the next interrogation. But will it be you or me on trial? Perhaps they'll arrest me for impersonating a decent human being."

He left the room and slammed the door, which didn't begin to release the anger that he knew was only the sentinel guarding his hurt and frustration. "Damn her!" he muttered under his breath as he stepped out into the courtyard, grateful to be alone. Three minutes later he walked into Abbi's sitting room. She looked at him over the top of the book she was reading but didn't even get a greeting out before he said, "I know you must be sick to death of me whining to you all the time, but who else am I going to whine to?"

"Whine away," she said, putting the book face down over her belly. "I was lonely anyway." He paced the room while he attempted to gather his words and she commented, "Oh my, you are *angry*. I don't think I've ever seen you so angry."

"That would be accurate," he snarled, continuing to pace.

"Now let's see," she said, "if you were angry with one of your men, you would either smack him in the jaw or put him on report. Must be Nadine." He glared at her and she added, "And don't call me psychic. Nothing but a woman could make a man act like this. Tell me what happened."

Lance repeated the conversation while he continued to pace. When he had nothing more to say, he slumped into a chair and groaned. "You did the right thing," Abbi said. "There was a time when I knew in my heart that Cameron and I were supposed to be together, but his pride and fear were destroying both of us. I had to accept that, in spite of what I might want, he could very well choose to never get beyond those fears. And if that had been the case, I would have had no choice but to move on with my life, and . . . well, I probably would have married you." She laughed as she said it and he couldn't help but smile, mostly because he knew there was the tiniest bit of seriousness in her statement. "Gratefully," she went on, "when I gave him an ultimatum, he came around. His love for me was stronger than his fears. If it's the other way around, there's nothing you can do about it, and you'll only spend your life with these same kind of battles coming up over and over."

"How did you get to be so wise, Your Grace?"

"Wise, no," she laughed softly. "I just . . . observe life and try to learn."

"I'm grateful that you do," he said. "I pray that Nadine will choose me above her fears, and I pray that she will be given the chance to live long enough to make a choice."

"My prayers are with her, as well," Abbi said. A few minutes later, she asked, "How is Dulsie settling in? She was certainly insistent that she needed to live with you now."

"Yes, she was," he said. "I think she's doing well, and I like needing to be done with my work, knowing that somebody is waiting for me. She likes her new room. She picked the one with the flowers on the draperies."

"Of course," Abbi said with a smile.

Lance chuckled, thinking of Dulsie and the light she'd brought into his life, then a frequently nagging thought came forward and he felt his countenance darken.

"What is it?" Abbi asked.

"I am praying continually that Nadine will be released, that the charges will be dropped. But when that happens, what becomes of Dulsie? If Nadine chooses not to be with me, then Dulsie is caught in the middle."

"You can only do the best that you can, Lance. Nadine is her mother. She loves her, and you have to respect her wishes."

"I know that, and I will. I just . . . wish that . . ."

"I understand," Abbi said and he met her eyes, grateful to know that she did. What would he ever do without her?

Lance took the rest of the day off to take Dulsie shopping, and over the next couple of days, he became especially impatient for something to happen related to the case. But he kept busy dealing with other matters of business that had to be seen to, often longing for that vacation Cameron had offered—although he'd prefer to have Nadine with him. He spent time with Dulsie, and was grateful to actually have her sleeping at his house, rather than at the castle. He was glad to have her with him, but he felt the need to ask one evening as he tucked her into bed, "Why did you want to come and live with me instead of with your friend, Erich?"

"Because Mama said that no matter what happened, from now

on you would be my father." Lance was momentarily too stunned to speak, and grateful when she went on. "I think it would be better if I keep calling you Lance so people won't wonder if you really are my father because Mama said that would be scandalous." Lance chuckled, hearing her use such a word. "Since she said you would be my father, I'm supposed to live with you now."

She threw her arms around his neck and Lance squeezed his eyes shut. Oh, how he loved the child! "Well, I'm glad I get to be your father now," he said, but he couldn't help wondering what might happen if Nadine was released and chose to hold onto her mistrust toward him. He prayed that whatever happened, a viable solution could be found for Dulsie.

Chapter Twenty-Five

ABDUCTED

Lance was just about to go to bed when he heard a loud knocking at the front door. He opened it to see a young officer. "Lieutenant Kepler needs to see you," he said. "He sent me to sit with your daughter while you come."

"Thank you," he said and showed him in. "Make yourself at home," he said and hurried to pull on his boots and coat. In the midst of wondering what this might be about, the officer's statement gave him a little burst of pleasure. *His daughter.* In spite of what Dulsie had said about the inference being scandalous, Lance quite liked the sound of it. Everyone who knew him knew she was not literally his daughter, but most were well aware of the situation, and the fact that Nadine had given him legal custody in the event of her death—or at the very least, while she remained in prison.

"What is it?" Lance asked as Kepler met him halfway across the courtyard.

"Drew was given this to give to Mrs. Rader," he said, handing Lance a little piece of paper. It was too dark to read what it said, but it had an overall familiarity, and he knew the implication. "We had Miss Hegel go to the address written here, just as Mrs. Rader had done before, but seeing that Mrs. Rader had arrived both times to find no one there, we sent an officer in ahead of her. He's there now."

Lance found his horse saddled, and he rode with Kepler to the location written on the piece of paper. Lance said as they were riding, "Isn't this guy a fool to think that Mrs. Rader would fall again for that after the trouble it got her into?"

"Either that, or he was testing her to see what she would do. Since she apparently *did* fall for it, maybe he thinks she *is* a fool."

They arrived and tethered their horses. Kepler barely tapped on the door before an officer pulled it open from inside. Lance stepped into the house, hearing the officer say, "This is Captain Dukerk, madame." A woman rose from a chair to greet him, taking his breath away. She fit the profile of the victims—and Nadine—perfectly. But she was *alive!*

"Madame," he said with all the fervor he felt, "it is a pleasure to see you alive and well, even though I've not previously made your acquaintance." He took her hand and found it trembling.

"No one is more pleased on that count than I am," she said, then glanced over her shoulder. "Well, my husband, who is out of the country at the moment, and our two children, who are sleeping in the other room, will be pleased to know that I'm alive, I'm sure."

"Can you tell me what happened?" Lance asked, guiding her back to her chair, and taking one close by.

"I was just about to go to bed when I heard some strange noises, and the dog across the street started barking. I went to check all of the windows, wondering if the wind was blowing, and one of them had come loose. I walked into the back room, the one that my husband uses to keep his books when he isn't working away from home, and there was a man standing there, the window open behind him. He was wearing a hooded cloak. I couldn't see his face at all, but he had a white scarf in one hand." She became upset and paused to gain her composure. "Just as he stepped toward me, a loud pounding came at the front door, and he stepped back. I screamed for help and ran toward the door just as this officer," she motioned to the one standing close by, "shot the lock and came in."

Her emotion overtook her and Lance turned to the officer. "Good work, young man. Can you tell me what happened after you came in?"

"She told me an intruder was in the back room. I came in the room just in time to see him leaving; he'd obviously gone back out the window. I followed but he was nowhere to be seen."

Lance looked at him severely and said, "You saved a life tonight."

"Any man would have done as much," the officer said humbly. "I was just in the right place at the right time."

"For which we are deeply grateful," Lance said. Then he turned to the woman. "Do you have family or friends you can stay with until your husband comes home?"

"Uh . . . yes, I do, actually. I have an aunt on the south side."

"Would you like us to help you take the children there tonight, or would you prefer that an officer stay here with you and make the move in the morning?"

"I think I'd like to go tonight," she said.

"See to that, Lieutenant," Lance said to Kepler.

"Of course, sir."

"Take the standard precautions," Lance added. "One more question," Lance said to the woman. "Do you work outside of your home at all?"

"Yes, I fill a few shifts a week at a pub on Herger Street."

Lance nodded. "Thank you. You've been very helpful." He spoke a few more minutes with the woman before he returned to the castle, frustrated at having the culprit elude them but wondering if this woman's testimony would be enough to free Nadine. He imagined the committee hearing the report and their possible responses. No actual crime had been committed beyond breaking and entering. Perhaps the woman imagined the scarf. Perhaps it was only an intended robbery. There was no evidence that the phantom briefly seen in this woman's home was their killer, and the incident certainly gave them no just cause to relinquish the charges against Nadine. He reminded himself that a victim had been spared and he was grateful. And this was also a clear indication that the culprit did believe Nadine was out of prison, and he was baiting her again. Would he use the note with the address on it once more now that it had failed him?

Lance sat in his office, pondering the situation while he filled out an official report. He knew he'd never be able to sleep and figured the officer looking out for Dulsie was probably more comfortable there than any other place he might be assigned on the night shift. He was nearly finished with the report when a frantic officer ran into the room, breathless and wide-eyed. "It's happened again, sir."

"What?" Lance demanded, his heart pounding as he feared the worst.

And then the worst was verified. "Another murder, sir—just like the others."

On his way to the scene, Lance heard the report from the officer as he rode with him. The victim had been found in the park near the market square by an officer doing a standard patrolling of the area. Blood in the snow indicated that she had likely been killed elsewhere and the body moved to that location as if the killer had wanted it to be found quickly. Before dawn it was determined that the woman worked at a nearby pub; she was also well known as a prostitute. She had no family connections. Lance had no desire to be judgmental, but he couldn't help feeling some relief that the woman with a husband and two children had been spared. And in spite of the horror, his greatest relief was on behalf of Nadine.

The sun was barely up when Lance knocked at the duke's bedroom door. Cameron pulled it open and asked, "More bad dreams?"

"I'm afraid I never went to sleep to have a chance to dream."

"What's happened?" Cameron asked gravely, motioning him into the room. Abbi was sitting up in bed, expectant. She'd obviously overheard.

"Would you like the good news first?" Lance asked.

"Yes," Abbi said.

"A woman with a husband and two children was saved tonight from being another victim." He went on to tell them the details briefly.

"Then the killer is on the prowl again," Cameron said. "He believes Nadine is out of prison."

"Oh, he's most definitely on the prowl," Lance said, "which brings me to the other good news."

"What?" Cameron asked, obviously confused by the statement in contrast to Lance's expression.

"The charges against Nadine will be officially dropped as soon as the committee convenes this morning."

Abbi put a hand over her mouth. Cameron sighed and hung his head, saying gravely, "Which brings us to the bad news."

He briefly told them all he knew and they talked for just a few minutes. "I need to be there when Dulsie wakes up," he said. "An officer has been with her all night. I'll see you both later."

Lance hurried home and excused the officer who was sitting in a chair outside Dulsie's room, reading a newspaper. He sat by Dulsie and watched her sleeping, grateful for her peace and safety. He felt overwhelmed with unspeakable relief to know that Nadine would be free and at least that portion of the nightmare was over. But now he had to face the reality that she would be out of prison, where Albert Crider could have access to her. And what of Dulsie? She belonged with her mother, but Lance knew how her mother was feeling toward him right now, and the idea of once again dealing with the estrangement between them broke his heart.

Lance had breakfast with Dulsie and took her to the nursery before the committee meeting began. He was glad to have Cameron immediately turn the time over to him, and he stood to say what he had to say, well aware that every man in the room had been informed of last night's events. "Our killer has been duped," he growled, tossing the official report onto the table. "Nadine Rader is locked tightly in her cell. Another woman is dead, and still another came very close. Evidence is not always what it seems." Lance paused and looked over the faces of the committee. Those who had stood by him met his eyes with pleasant confidence. The other faces wore varying degrees of sheepishness and contempt.

"Lieutenant," Lance motioned toward Kepler, "will you tell the committee what you told me a few days ago that came up in the report you received from the legal authorities in Albert Crider's hometown."

"Yes, of course," Kepler said. "It seems that Mr. Crider's crimes began with a series of incidents regarding document forgery."

"Document forgery, gentlemen," Lance said with a bite. "If a man can forge signatures, how difficult do you think it would be for him to steal a woman's journal and duplicate her handwriting enough to implicate her? If she spurned him and he hated her for it, would it not be the ultimate revenge to see her die for the crimes he had committed as a projection of his feelings for her?"

"And I would also suggest," Georg said, "that if this villain was watching Mrs. Rader closely enough to know that she *owned* a white silk scarf, he would know exactly who was receiving her affection. Perhaps part of his motive in framing her for the crimes was to put the other suitor, if you will, in a horrible position. The ultimate revenge."

Lance swallowed carefully as he heard some of his deepest heartache over this drama clearly voiced. He forced back his emotion and leaned his hands onto the table, looking directly at each of the men who had been eager to put Nadine in front of a firing squad. "Do you think, gentlemen, that a woman being stalked and framed for a violent crime was enough to endure without being subjected to degrading interrogations and some senseless rush to have her killed and be done with it? I suggest that in the future we take more care in considering reasonable doubt and pay a little more attention to our gut instincts as opposed to our impatience and discomfort over a difficult issue."

"Hear, hear," one of the advisors said, followed by another.

"I rest my case," Lance said and moved toward the door.

"Where are you going?" Mr. Hertz demanded. "This meeting is not over yet, Captain."

"It is for me. I am going to unlock Mrs. Rader's cell. And God willing, we will catch up with this killer before he catches up with her. Good day, gentlemen."

Lance quickly saw to some arrangements, then he went to Nadine's cell, tormented by memories of his last visit there and the ugly argument that had taken place. He reminded himself that he had come with good news, but even that was tainted by the tangible fear he felt in exposing her once again to Albert Crider. He unlocked the door and stepped inside, and unlike standard protocol, he didn't lock it behind him.

Nadine watched Lance enter the dimly lit room and knew immediately that something was wrong. His expression clearly matched the heartsickness in his eyes.

"What's happened?" she asked. "Please don't tell me that something happened to her. If she—"

"Not to her," he said. "But to someone else. There's been another killing. Exactly the same."

Nadine put one hand to her heart and the other over her mouth, weeping immediately. "I can't believe it," she muttered through her tears. "How could someone be so completely evil? It's got to stop. It just . . ." She hesitated when it became evident by his expression that he needed to say something else. "What?" she demanded.

"Do you realize what this means?"

She looked baffled until he motioned toward the door. She caught her breath and held it as the implication settled in.

"You're free to go," he said. "A carriage is waiting for you in the courtyard to take you back to the inn. Her Grace would prefer that you stay at the castle, for your own protection."

"Her Grace or you?" she asked, her voice only slightly sour.

"I see your needs have changed now, Mrs. Rader. At the very least, Her Grace requests that you return to work tomorrow. And I need to know what course you will be taking with Dulsie. She's not been informed of your release. She needs some time to have her things gathered and—"

"I want her to stay with you," she said. "I told her that you would be a father to her now, no matter what happened. I can't back down on that. And of course, she would be safer with you until all of this is settled. I'll come to see her."

"And what of you?" he asked. "What of your safety?"

"I'll be all right," she insisted, but he felt sure it was more pride talking than any form of practicality.

"I'm reinstating the usual precautions. Two officers will be on duty around the clock at the inn. You'll not go anywhere without one of them at your side."

"Of course," she said. "Thank you, Captain."

They remained in tense silence for a full minute before he said, "Gather your things. Don't keep the carriage waiting."

Nadine watched him walk away, leaving the door wide open. For a moment she just stared at it, feeling as if it must be some kind of trick. The reality settled in and she quickly gathered her belongings in the basket that Abbi had brought them in. While her heart ached for the woman who had lost her life to make this possible, and for her loved ones as well, she couldn't help being grateful for her own freedom and to know that she would not end up dying for someone else's crimes.

Stepping into the courtyard, the sun hurt her eyes. Shading them with her hand, she just stood and looked around herself, barely managing to keep from crying, just to see the world and be able to be a part of it again. An officer motioned her to the waiting carriage and helped her inside. The moment it rolled forward, her tears surged into the open and she cried helplessly until the carriage halted at the inn and she frantically wiped her face dry. *She was free!* But as she lay in her bed at the inn that night, the harsh reality occurred to her that free as she was, she could very well end up dying anyway. If Albert

Crider was truly after *her*, she could only hope that the law was more clever than this despicable, evil man.

Lance felt grateful and relieved to know that Nadine would allow Dulsie to stay with him—at least for the time being. After supper he explained to her that the charges had been dropped against her mother and she had been set free, but they felt it was better that Dulsie stay with him. She seemed pleased that she could stay, and especially pleased when he suggested that her mother would likely visit her tomorrow when she came to work.

The following morning Lance arrived in his office to be informed that the usual proclamation had been distributed that morning to inform the people that the charges had been officially dropped against Mrs. Rader, with a minimal explanation. It was standard protocol, and Lance listened with a certain indifference until something struck him with a burst of fear.

"It's already been posted?" he asked.

"Yes, sir."

"Damn," he muttered under his breath.

"What is it, sir?" the officer questioned, seeming panicked.

Lance thought quickly, trying to discern if he was overreacting. Concluding that he would rather be safe than sorry, he ordered, "I want another man posted at the inn every minute Mrs. Rader is there. One of them will shadow her every footstep."

"Yes, sir. I'll see to it now."

Lance leaned back in his chair and sighed. By announcing Nadine's innocence, they had practically informed Albert Crider that he had been duped. With a little thought, the man would realize how they had tricked him and that the *real* Mrs. Rader was now out of prison. Gut instinct told him that this man's sick desire to get his hands on Nadine would probably magnify immensely once he read that proclamation.

Nadine thoroughly enjoyed sharing lunch with Dulsie at the castle, and just the feeling of being free. Their time together went well until they were walking back to the nursery and Dulsie asked, "Why won't you come and live with me and Lance?"

Nadine said carefully, "Because a man and a woman should not live together if they are not married."

"Then you should get married. You were going to get married. Why don't you get married now?"

"I don't know if I can marry Lance," she said. "It's very complicated and—"

"You're just making excuses," Dulsie said angrily. "You're just being stupid."

She ran ahead before Nadine could stop her. She felt tempted to follow and reprimand her for talking that way to her mother, but Dulsie went through the nursery door and Nadine felt no motivation to continue the conversation. Maybe she *was* being stupid, but she didn't know how to get past feeling this way.

For two days Lance kept to his business, grateful to be with Dulsie in the evenings and well aware that her mother was visiting her during the day and they were sharing lunch together. For Dulsie's sake, he was grateful to have such an arrangement. But personally, he hated it. The three of them should have been spending every spare minute together just enjoying life and anticipating a wedding. As it was, they could only be aware of the other's existence from a distance. And he *hated* it!

Nadine came awake with a start, certain she'd heard a strange noise but not certain what it had been. As she lay in her bed listening to the silence and looking into the darkness, she was reminded of the feeling she'd had when an officer had come into her cell with the intent of doing her harm. The hair at the back of her neck bristled, but she credited it to the derisive memory. Then she heard the subtlest noise and was struck with the impression that she was not alone. Before she had a chance to contemplate the possibility, a gloved hand clamped over her mouth. Her wildest fears became reality as Albert Crider's voice whispered behind her ear, "At last the time has come for us to be together again, my love."

Nadine squirmed and struggled as she was dragged from her bed, while her most prominent thought was being grateful to know that Dulsie was safe in Lance's care. She wondered what had happened to the officers who had been assigned to protect her and felt horrified to contemplate what their fate might have been. Her instincts demanded that she use every ounce of strength, every grain of knowledge to protect herself. She twisted in an attempt to scratch his face, but she was barely aware of a sharp blow to the back of her head before everything went black.

Lance rose early and felt unexplainably restless. He was actually grateful to know he had an early-morning meeting with some of his officers, if only so that he could be occupied. He carried Dulsie as she slept into the room she had used when she'd been staying with Cameron and Abbi. They knew she would be there, due to his meeting, and they would see that she had breakfast and got to the nursery.

Lance arrived at the keep a few minutes early, and he felt compelled to the cell where Nadine had spent many days. He stood in the center of the little room, contemplating how cold and dark it was without her. Alone there, he was able to capture, if only to the tiniest degree, how it might have been for her. He thought how pathetic it was to come here, of all places, to feel close to the woman he loved. And he wondered how he might have felt coming here if she had been executed. A cold chill barraged him as he pondered the horror, and he was grateful to at least have that behind them.

As Lance returned to his office, that horrible feeling remained with him. At first he felt certain it was solely due to the negative course of his thoughts, but as the inclination persisted, he interrupted the meeting only ten minutes into it.

"Forgive me, gentlemen, but I just . . . feel that I need to check on something. Proceed without me and give me a full report."

He hurried from the room, ignoring the baffled expressions of his men and quickly rode down the hill and toward the inn. He was startled to pass an officer galloping at a speed that indicated panic. He paused and turned back to see the officer halt and turn around.

"Captain," he said, approaching quickly. "Good, it's you. I was just coming to get you."

"What is it?" he demanded, so tangibly afraid that his insides threatened to explode.

"She's missing, sir," he said with a compassion that made it evident who he was talking about.

"Missing?" Lance breathed in response, and his heart stopped beating.

Unable to put together an intelligible question, he was grateful for the officer's thorough explanation. "The three officers on duty at the inn were all wounded and left unconscious, but they're alive. The doctor has been summoned. Drew and Gerda awoke at the usual time to find one of them at the foot of the stairs. Drew ran looking for help and I was just around the corner on my usual patrol. I found two other men and came for you. They're scouting the area now. With your permission, sir, I'll ride on to the castle and arrange for the entire force to be called out and for the usual search procedures to be deployed."

"Yes, of course," Lance said, trying to tell himself they were talking about somebody else. Some other woman missing, some other victim. "Thank you," he managed to add before the officer nodded and rode on up the hill. Lance sat as he was for a long minute, waiting for the reality to penetrate his clouded brain. When it didn't, he spurred the stallion beneath him to a gallop, thinking perhaps it was better that he *couldn't* feel, couldn't believe it, couldn't *accept* it. Was Albert Crider hurting her? Was she dead? Or suffering? For the moment, he told himself he needed to be the Captain of the Guard; he needed to find her. Later, he could react. For now he had to believe she was still alive, and he had to find her. He just had to!

The reality came a little closer to penetrating him when he arrived at the inn to find Drew visibly shaken and Gerda crying beyond control. The ailing officers had been moved to rooms upstairs and the doctor was with them. The officers that had been called in reported having done a thorough initial search of the inn and its surrounding area with no distinct evidence. Of course, they knew that it took much more manpower to conduct the necessary search, but they had done their duty well and he was grateful. One of them followed him up the stairs where he took a deep breath before entering *the victim's* room. His heart thudded painfully as memories assaulted him. He pretended not to be affected as he scanned the room for clues, knowing a more thorough investigation would be done within the hour. But the main facts were easy to assess. Her cloak and shoes remained. Her bed showed indication of struggle. She'd been dragged from her sleep and taken as she was. The lock on the door was broken in a way he had never seen before, the same as the main door to the inn, he'd been told. There was blood on the floor in the hall, which he was informed belonged to the officer who had been guarding the door.

Feeling tangibly ill, Lance went to each of the rooms where the wounded men had been taken. They were in pain but conscious. They each had been hit over the head to be knocked out and had received a deep stab wound to the right upper thigh, apparently to render them immobile. The doctor assured Lance that they would need some time to recover, but they would be fine. Lance uttered a silent prayer of gratitude. The culprit could have easily stabbed these men through the heart as opposed to the leg. Apparently he didn't kill casually. They had not been objects of his obsession, only an impedance to getting what he wanted.

When there was nothing more Lance could do for the moment beyond tear the entire country apart with his own two hands, the reality began to settle into him. Perhaps knowing that his men would search quickly and thoroughly and do everything he could, but multiplied by hundreds, he found it possible to allow himself to feel what was happening. An accumulative exhaustion saturated his entire being. If he hadn't been able to find this man before, what made him think he could find him now? And what reason did he have to even believe that Nadine was still alive? His mind recounted all else that had happened in his life in the midst of this nightmare. This estrangement with Nadine had had only a brief reprieve, and he'd been informed of his illegitimate birth, a fact that had shaken his entire being. Just thinking of it still left him disturbed and upset. And now, with this new development, Lance didn't feel capable of going on. He was weary and exhausted to the depths of his soul.

He waited with one of the wounded officers until his family

came with a carriage to take him home where he could be cared for. After he was gone, Lance sat in the empty room, staring at the blood on the bedsheets, stunned by the horror.

Lance was startled to notice someone standing in the doorway when he hadn't heard footsteps in the hall. "Your Grace," he said, coming to his feet. "What are you doing here?"

Cameron closed the door slowly, saying, "I thought you could use some company."

Lance felt briefly disoriented, unable to recall Cameron ever appearing at the scene of a crime, even though he was kept well informed. In wondering over his appearance now, Lance was struck with panic. Had they found her? Dead? And they'd told Cameron instead of him because they thought the news should come from a friend?

Unable to wonder even another second, he quickly said, "If you've come here to tell me something they don't want to tell me, get it over with and—"

Cameron looked alarmed. "No." He shook his head. "No, of course not. They're still looking. Hundreds of volunteers have rallied and joined the search. It's one of those times when you realize that in spite of the ugliness of the world, the majority of people are good and caring and they band together when needs arise."

Lance nodded and sank back into his chair, unable to stand another second. Cameron scooted a chair close to him and sat down. He put a hand on Lance's shoulder and spoke gently. "I can't promise you they'll find her alive and well, Lance. I can't promise that this will turn out the way we're all hoping and praying. I can only tell you that whatever happens, I will be at your side, every minute of every night and day for as long as you need me, if that's what you need to keep going."

Lance looked into his eyes. "Why?" he asked breathlessly. "Why would you be willing to give so much for me? You're the Duke of Horstberg, Cameron. You can't just—"

"Let me tell you what I can do as the Duke of Horstberg, Lance, and why I can do it. I can do whatever I have to do within the parameters of the law to keep this country safe and strong. And I am in a position to do that because of a series of miracles, not the least of which is you."

"Me?" he gave a scoffing laugh.

"Yes, Lance, you. To begin with, your interest in Abbi during my absence may, to some, be considered coincidence, but I believe differently. At the very time when I needed a public forum to make my reclamation, you were not only in a position to create that forum, but you were willing to do it. You were willing to take on a woman who was already married, not knowing for certain if her husband was alive or dead, and raise her child as your own. No questions asked. And then when you figured out it was me and I was intent on causing trouble, you risked your very life to continue with the ruse of marrying Abbi, and you stood behind me—even if you wouldn't admit it at the time.

"Now, let me tell you something that you probably weren't aware of. There were many times when I doubted I would live to reclaim my country—and my wife. But I knew if I didn't, my wife would have been in the best possible hands. I knew that you would care for her, honor her, and protect her with your very life, simply because I knew you were that kind of man. You always had been. But there's more to it than that. I've hinted at this before, but I want you to really stop and think about the full depth of that situation from my perspective. What I knew that Abbi didn't know was that the child she carried would be heir to the throne, with precedence over Nikolaus. The documentation had all been put into place, Lance. It was completely official. If I had died and you had married Abbi, the moment Erich was born, he would have been the Duke of Horstberg, and *you,* as his stepfather and legal guardian, with your experience in political matters, your military expertise, and your lifetime association with the royal family, would have been the duke regent until he came of age."

Again Lance gave a scoffing laugh, certain this was some attempt to distract him and appease his heartache. But Cameron tightened his hand on Lance's shoulder and his eyes became as intense as Lance had ever seen them. "I'm not joking, Lance. It was not happenstance that you were in that position. God put you there, the same way He sent Abbi to me. And I don't know if God knew the outcome at the beginning; I believe He did. I don't know if He provided a backup plan for the sake of circumstances that could have evolved differently. Either way, I know He gave *me* a backup plan; one that was completely foolproof, because He knew I could not put my life at risk with any peace of mind unless that plan was in place, and I could not have reclaimed my country without putting my life at risk. And that plan was foolproof only because I knew you were a man of such honor that you would have laid your very life down before you would have let anything happen to Abbi or that baby. You would have found a way to see that Nikolaus never brought harm to them. And my theory was proven twice through that period of time."

Lance waited for him to explain, unable to even make a sound. "First of all," Cameron said, "you deliberately deceived your men to lead their attention away from Abbi, and from me—even though you were technically breaking the law to do so. Of course, there were many factors involved, but I believe you allowed your instincts to override the technicality of the law."

"Yes, I suppose I did."

"And I've seen you do the same many times since, with great success. That's one of the characteristics of a great leader, Lance, and one of many reasons that I insisted you keep this position when you wanted to resign. One of the others had to do with the second incident that let me know you would have done anything to keep Abbi safe."

"What is that?" he asked, overwhelmed and in awe of all he was hearing.

"You killed for her," Cameron said and Lance squeezed his eyes shut, caught off guard. "I wasn't in a position to do anything about it, and you were. And you did what had to be done. But maybe what you don't realize is that you not only saved Abbi's life that night, you saved the very heart and soul of Horstberg."

Lance tightened his gaze on Cameron as he continued. "You see, she is the backbone of this country. She stands behind me and beside me in all that I do. Because of her I am a better sovereign. Horstberg is strong because of the love and life she breathes into it. Without her I would be so much less than I am, and it's impossible to believe that such a loss would not affect the way I rule this country. When I ask you to look out for Abbi, to some it might seem a trivial duty that any officer could see to. But I'm telling you, Captain, if I ever feel the slightest uneasy about letting her go somewhere or do something, I want you at her side because you are protecting the heart and soul of Horstberg. And I *know* you would die for her."

"Yes, I would," Lance said with no hesitation.

"Not only that," Cameron said, "the friendship you share with her adds to her happiness. I would be a fool to think that I could fill every emotional need that Abbi has, even if I had the time to be with her every minute I want to be. I understand that women need friends, but she's a beautiful and passionate woman, and I will tell you beyond any doubt that I would not be having her alone with *any* other man beyond bare minimum duty. It's not that I don't trust Abbi; it's the *men* I don't trust. But with you I know that her happiness and virtue are as important as her life, and I don't have to wonder."

Lance attempted to absorb everything he'd just been told, wondering what point there might have been to his lengthy oration. Cameron succinctly made his point when he eased back in his chair and said, "*That* is why."

"Why what?" Lance asked, disoriented.

"You asked why I would be willing to give so much for you. I was answering the question. The brief version is that I consider it an honor to be your friend, your ally, and to serve with you in a common cause. I only wish that I could retire from being the duke the way you can retire from being the captain. I have to do this until I die. I would prefer that we retire together, because I can't imagine doing my job with anyone else in your position."

"The feeling is mutual," Lance said, while a deep comfort surrounded his aching heart. Just when he had believed he could never go another step, Cameron had come and let him know that he wasn't walking this path alone.

Chapter Twenty-Six

UNDER THE BED

Nadine felt herself slipping into consciousness with the sensation of being dragged upward from a crouched position. She groaned and opened her eyes enough to gather that the room was dark beyond the dim glow of a lamp. It was some kind of cellar, but she had no idea where. It only took slight movement to realize that her wrists and ankles were bound, and there was a scarf tied around her head and through her mouth to keep her silent. She felt terribly cold, especially her feet since they were bare. While she now slumped over the strong arm crushing her waist, barely able to hold onto consciousness, she realized that she had been inside of a large barrel a short time before. The aroma surrounding her now made sense. Baking flour. An empty barrel that had once held baking flour. She saw the lid being put back onto the barrel before she was lifted and carried into another room and a door was closed behind her. She was laid on a bed in a room that was equally dark and damp, and a blanket was tucked around her. She was grateful at least for that. With the bed beneath her, Nadine longed to slip back into the oblivion of unconsciousness where she didn't have to consider the reality of what was happening to her. She felt herself relaxing in spite of the pain at the back of her head, until she was startled by a cold hand against her face.

"Oh, my sweet Nadine," she heard. The voice was sickeningly familiar. It had haunted her memory and consumed her fears. And now her worst nightmare was coming to pass. She attempted to retract from his touch but he held her head with his other hand and caressed her face with his fingertips as if he had a right to do so. His touch alone felt evil and repulsive. She wanted to scream at him and demand that he let her go and leave her in peace, but she was completely helpless. "We are together at last," he murmured and pressed a kiss to the side of her face. She choked on the bile that rose in her throat and attempted to turn away, whimpering into the wet fabric filling her mouth.

Minutes felt like hours and the hours eternal as he lay close beside her, whispering to her continually in a way that turned her stomach and made her sick. She was grateful when his touching her never crossed inappropriate boundaries, but his words certainly did, and she felt certain it was only a matter of time before he took full advantage of her. He seemed to be savoring some kind of sick anticipation as he told her details of all that he planned to do with her.

"And then," he murmured, close to her face with foul breath, "once you are mine completely, I will free you from the boundaries of this world, my love. Once that dagger goes through your heart, you will be mine forever, and no man will ever have you again. You will be mine, all mine."

The hours crept on while he told her gruesome details of the women he'd killed and how each of them had led him a step closer to her through some kind of perverse obsession that Nadine couldn't begin to understand. She cried and whimpered as everything inside of her wanted to scream in protest. He finally untied her only long enough to give her a few minutes of much-needed privacy, although he threatened her severely and remained close by. And then she was bound again. Hunger growled in her stomach long before he left and returned with food. Before he removed the scarf from her mouth so that she could eat, he threatened her hotly with remaining silent, making it clear that she would starve if she didn't keep quiet long enough to eat. He kept her hands bound and fed her one bite at a time. Her need to eat overruled her repulsion of having him touch her food. When she'd had her fill and been given water to drink, she expected him to put the scarf back into her mouth. Instead he pressed his lips over hers in a way that by no means resembled a kiss. She struggled against the hands that held her head from moving, and when he eased back, smiling triumphantly, she spit in his face. He immediately slapped her, calling her horrible names as he put the scarf back into her mouth, making it clear that eventually she would kiss him and like it, or she would suffer unspeakable things.

With the meal taken care of, Albert Crider began again what seemed to be a lengthy, memorized oration of his plans for her. When that was finished, he repeated the gruesome details of the murders he committed and how he would eventually do the same to her. She began to wish that he would just kill her and get it over with rather than subjecting her to his horrifying discourse. Many hours passed while he talked on and on. They ate again and she kept waiting for him to let her sleep, but he didn't. Each time she'd start to drift off, he would slap her face and tell her to sit up and listen to what he had to say. The cold dampness of the cellar crept deeply into her since he only kept the blanket over her once in a while, and her feet began to feel numb.

Nadine came awake and realized that he'd actually let her drift to sleep, but she knew it hadn't been for long. She steeled herself to hear him begin his oration again. Instead, his words took a different turn. "I think you'd be amazed, my dear, to realize what I know about you. It wasn't very difficult to get a good look at that marriage certificate of yours. Nikolaus du Woernig of Horstberg. It didn't take much effort to find this country where you were married, and to find out a great deal about this man who pretended to love you. You see, it became quickly evident what kind of person he was, and it was easy to find people like him, people who knew him, who had grieved his death. And you can't imagine how fascinated I was to learn that your sweet Nikolaus was well affiliated with your father. But what fascinated me most of all was to learn that your father's treasonous activities had flowed over into *you*, my dear. I wonder what the Captain of the Guard would think to realize that the woman he loves is guilty of treason. Eventually I'm certain he *will* find out. People know. People told me. And when he finds out what you did, however well meaning it might have been, I believe he'll be grateful that you died when you did. Oh, the taint such scandal would have put into his life, his career, his glorious reputation."

Nadine listened with growing horror as Albert Crider repeated details of an incident that she had believed no one knew about beyond Nikolaus, her father, and his business partner—who were all dead. He spoke of the ill that had occurred due to what she had been involved with, and she couldn't deny the truth in what he was saying. She *had* committed treason. And a part of her was grateful to know that she would never have to face Lance Dukerk again.

The search for Nadine continued through that day and into the night. At Cameron's insistence, Lance took time off work as any employee of the government would do when facing a family crisis. He let his force do the work they were trained to do and spent the time being with Dulsie or in heartfelt prayer. There was hope only in the fact that all of the murder victims had been found quickly. Mr. Fruberg, the criminal analyst, made a private visit to tell Lance that he truly believed with the killer's pattern that if Nadine were dead, he would want her to be found. Lance prayed that he was right. The negative side of that point was in wondering *what* he might be doing to her if she was alive. Lance couldn't think about that at all. He just had to pray that she would be spared, that she would be found, and that she would be able to recover from this and be happy.

While Lance doubted he could sleep, Cameron insisted that he go to bed as usual. Every officer of the Guard and countless volunteers were resting in shifts and continuing their zealous search. And Lance knew that his pacing or panicking would not help them find her any more quickly. His sleep was fitful and littered with disturbing images in his dreams, but he did get some rest. He knew he'd been asleep when he heard a loud pounding at the front door of his apartment.

"Heaven help me," he muttered, practically sliding down the stairs. Had they found her? Was she alive? Dead? Had she been hurt? Violated? The emotion surrounding the questions threatened to kill him. He pulled open the door to see Cameron, looking disheveled. His thoughts in regard to yesterday's visit came back to hm. Had they sent him to be the bearer of bad news?

"Tell me," Lance insisted.

"I have nothing to tell you . . . at least as far as the search goes. Nothing has turned up."

Lance motioned him inside and closed the door. "What *do* you have to tell me? It's not even dawn yet."

Cameron turned to look at him, his eyes severe. "Abbi had a dream."

Lance moved unsteadily into a chair, already shaken. And he didn't even know yet what the dream was about. Cameron sat across from him and leaned forward. "She apologized for not coming herself. She said that you can go and talk to her about it if you need to, but . . . she's not feeling well. The pregnancy is getting increasingly difficult and . . ."

He hesitated and Lance guessed, "She's upset? The dream upset her?"

"Yes, it did," Cameron said carefully.

"Tell me. Get it over with. Is she dead?"

"Not in the dream, she wasn't. She was very much alive."

Lance absorbed that with heart-pounding relief. "Tell me," he said again.

"She repeated it to me three times and made me say it back so that I would get it right. She said that she could see Nadine, her hands and feet bound, her mouth gagged." Lance sighed and closed his eyes against the image, but it only became more clear. He squirmed in his seat as Cameron went on. "Her feet were bare. She was wearing a nightgown, wrapped in a blanket."

"But where?" Lance asked. "Does she know where?"

"This is the strange part," Cameron said. "Abbi kept saying it was dark and cold, and it was under the bed."

"Under the bed?" Lance repeated, certain he'd heard it wrong.

"That's what she said. She was under the bed."

"What bed?" Lance demanded. "I hate to state the obvious, but we looked under all the beds at the inn. So what bed? Everybody in Horstberg has a bed."

"I don't know, Lance."

Lance stood up and started pacing, hoping his thoughts would be inspired with the missing pieces. When nothing came to him, he said, "I need to ask Abbi one question. Give me a minute to finish getting dressed."

"Not a problem," Cameron said.

Lance got dressed and scooped Dulsie up to carry her to the castle. Leaving her settled into the bed that she often used there, Lance went with Cameron to his bedroom where a lamp had been left burning low. Lance could immediately hear Abbi crying. Cameron sat on the bed and took her into his arms. "Lance is here," he said gently. "He wants to ask you a question."

She turned toward him and held out a hand. Lance knelt beside the bed and took it. "You dreamed that she is alive," Lance said, if only to verify that fact.

Abbi nodded. "But to see her in such circumstances . . ." She became increasingly upset then forced her composure enough to say, "I know what it's like to be . . . so helpless . . . so powerless . . . at the mercy of a *sick* man."

Lance took a ragged breath and saw Cameron grimace while he held Abbi closer. He'd forgotten that Abbi had once been taken hostage by Nikolaus du Woernig. Lance didn't know the full extent of what he'd done to her, but he knew Nikolaus's crimes against Abbi had been deplorable, and her spirit had struggled to recover. But she *had* recovered. If nothing else, *that* gave him some measure of hope.

"Oh, Lance, you have to find her," Abbi said.

"I'm going to, Abbi. I have to believe that I'm meant to, or you wouldn't be given such a vision. There's one thing I need to know. You said that she's under the bed. Whose bed? What bed? Do you know?"

Abbi said, as if it were obvious, *"Her* bed."

Lance took a deep breath. "Thank you, Abbi," he said, pressing a kiss to her brow, "that's all I need to know." He moved toward the door. "I'll keep you informed."

"Be careful," Abbi called.

Lance arrived at the inn and went to the kitchen door to find Drew and Gerda working to prepare breakfast. Their solemnity matched his own, but they were eager to help.

"On a hunch," he said, "I want to check around again. Drew, would you have a few minutes to come with me?"

"Of course," he said with enthusiasm.

"I can manage here just fine," Gerda said. "Take your time."

Lance went first to Nadine's room, saying immediately, "Would you help me move the bed."

"Sure," Drew said, baffled. Lance hadn't expected to find anything, but he had to check and be absolutely certain that there wasn't some kind of clue left here. There was absolutely nothing beneath the bed except a lot of dust. He felt the floorboards and found them all tight and solid.

Lance then went down to the dining room and walked the perimeter of the room, looking above him. "Her room would be . . . where?" he asked, pointing at the ceiling.

Drew said easily, "Her north wall starts at that beam. I helped build the place. The walls of the rooms upstairs coincide with those ceiling beams."

Lance looked around the room, silently praying for guidance, feeling nothing. "I'm going to look outside," he said on a hunch and went out the kitchen door, slowly walking the perimeter of the building with Drew close behind him. He said nothing. He felt nothing. Until they came to a set of heavy wooden doors that were raised off the ground by only a few inches, jutting out from the side of the inn. "What is this?" Lance asked, glancing toward the kitchen door that wasn't far away. "A cellar, I assume."

"That's right," Drew said.

"Do you keep it locked?" he asked, noting there was a latch, but no lock.

"No. I'm in and out of it all the time. Only once did I have some food stolen out of there, but it didn't amount to much and I figured whoever took it must have needed it. I've never felt a need to lock it."

"I assume my men searched down there."

"They did," Drew said firmly. "I opened the doors for them myself. They were down there a good long while."

Lance looked at the cellar doors again and noted how there was absolutely no snow between the kitchen door and the cellar door. Drew had likely cleared a path following the last storm, which had been many weeks. Beyond that path, there were countless footprints in the packed snow from people coming and going. Horses were often tethered and vehicles parked back here for customers. Seeing nothing out of the ordinary, Lance started to walk away. Then he stopped and turned back as a thought consumed his mind. *Under the bed. Beneath the place where she sleeps.* "May I?" he asked Drew, his heart pounding.

"Of course, Captain."

Drew opened the doors and walked down the stone steps just

ahead of him, lighting a lantern that hung on the wall. He handed
it to Lance and lit another one that he carried himself. Lance lifted
the light high, illuminating a well-organized room of well-stocked
shelves, and rows of kegs. Large barrels lined one wall. "What do
you keep in there?" Lance asked, pointing at the barrels.

"Flour for baking," he said.

"May I see?" Lance asked, and Drew opened the barrel closest
to the door. It was more than half full of flour. The next two were
completely full. The last one was empty.

"When three are empty I load them up and go to the mill for
more," Drew explained.

Lance crossed the room and paid special attention to two doors.
"Where do these go?" he asked.

"One to the root cellar, the other to a storage room. We keep
supplies in there where me and Gerda could stay if there was an
emergency."

Lance knew what he meant. Most people had some place they
could go in the event of war or horrible storms where they could
hide and be safe. "Are you sure my men checked both these rooms?"
he asked.

"I wasn't with them, but I told them to, and they said they had."

"Of course," Lance said, knowing his men would be very thorough. "May we look again?" he asked.

"You go right ahead," Drew said. "I just remembered something
I need to check in the kitchen that Gerda might not think of. I'll be
back in a few minutes. Just do whatever you need to."

"Thank you," Lance said and first went into the root cellar. It was
little more than a large hole in the dirt, where fruits and vegetables
were stored. Nothing out of the ordinary there. He closed that door
and went into the other room, surprised by its size. The glow of his
lantern didn't reach the far end of the room. There were a couple of
beds and many shelves filled with blankets, bottles of water, lanterns,
fuel, and food. And then he heard it. A noise, barely distinguishable,
but undeniable. The room was too clean and tidy to have rats. Lance's
heart quickened and his mouth went dry. He stepped further into
the room and the glow of the lamp hit the back wall. He actually felt
disappointed to see nothing, then he heard another noise, a subtle
shuffling, behind him. Maybe it was Drew coming back. Maybe it

wasn't. Before he could turn to see, he heard an unfamiliar voice speak clearly, and with malice.

"Go ahead and turn around, Captain, and you can *watch* me kill her."

Lance took a sharp breath and told himself to stay composed, stay calm. *Don't let your emotions get her killed,* he cautioned himself. He heard a soft, female whimper, muffled, in a tone of protest. He steeled himself not to respond, but to focus on the man talking to him. Going with his instincts, he decided that what he needed was to catch him off guard. In a tone of complete indifference, he asked, "Kill who?"

"The woman you're looking for," that voice said.

"Dead or alive," Lance said, "once this is over I can go home and get some sleep." He turned to face him and tried not to show surprise in seeing only a man, holding a pistol that was pointed directly at Lance. *But where was Nadine?* Another whimper. *She was under the bed!* He kept his focus on the man he was facing, startled at how accurately he fit the description Nadine had given, words that he'd read over and over. So this was Albert Crider. But there was definitely a flicker of confusion in his eyes.

"I thought you were in love with her, Captain."

"Not that it did me any good," Lance said, amazed at his own calmness and his ability to act this out. But then, he'd had some practice with these angry feelings. "She spurned me like she spurned you, and she wasn't any too nice about it. So, maybe I should just buy you a drink and we can commiserate." As he said the last, Lance stepped forward abruptly, taking advantage of Crider's confusion. He knocked the pistol to the floor with one hand and belted him in the jaw with the other. Crider reeled backward into the other room. He appeared to be outdone, but Lance approached him with caution. Still, he was caught off guard with the way Crider lunged for him, knocking him to the floor where Lance received a blow to his middle and one to his face before he was able to gain some advantage and deliver a deep slug into Crider's belly.

The tables turned again, and for a moment Lance feared this fiend would actually outdo him. He heard Nadine's muffled whimpering from the other room, and it fed his determination. He would die before he'd let this monster anywhere near her again. But he couldn't die. He couldn't even allow himself to be outdone. For Nadine, his dominance in this fight could mean her life. He reminded himself that this was a fight for good against evil, and he was on the right side. He turned his heart to prayer while he kept his mind focused on Crider's next move. His prayers were apparently heard when he rolled and got Crider face down on the floor. With a knee in his back, Lance yanked his arms up behind him, ignoring his groans of protest. When a string of vulgarities flew out of his mouth, Lance slapped him across the back of the head. He realized how intense the brawl had been when his breathlessness made him barely able to say, "Shut up, you degenerate scum."

That very moment two officers came down the steps into the cellar. He didn't know where they'd come from, but he was grateful. "Just in time," Lance said, waiting to stand until they each had hold of one of Crider's arms.

Drew appeared close behind the officers, saying, "I heard the ruckus and went for help. I was afraid from the sound of things that you were going to get the worst of it."

Lance just nodded in agreement and said to the officers, "Take him to the keep. If he so much as squirms or utters a word, shoot him."

"Yes, Captain," they both said. They knew him enough to know he wasn't completely serious. But Crider seemed to believe that he was.

Free of Crider, Lance's attention turned to Nadine, who was still whimpering loudly in the other room. "Drew, you get Dr. Furhelm, quickly," Lance ordered and hurried to get Nadine. He dropped to his chest on the floor and could see only enough to know that she was facing the wall. He took hold of her shoulders with both hands to ease her toward him. Her whimpering increased with a tone of unbridled terror that struck his heart.

"Nadine, it's me," he muttered but she didn't hear him. She thrashed and moaned as he brought her out and turned her over. Her hands and bare feet were bound; she had a scarf tied around her head that went through her mouth. Her face was swollen and discolored, but he couldn't tell if that was due to any injury or just dirt and crying. But she was *alive!* And it was over.

He knelt beside her while she continued to protest, clearly

believing that he was Crider. But she kept her eyes squeezed closed as if she couldn't bear to open them. "Nadine!" he said loudly to be heard above her whimpering. He pulled the scarf out of her mouth, wondering how long it had been there by the marks left on her face. "It's me," he said. "He's gone. You're all right."

She stopped squirming and became silent beyond her strained breathing. "It's all right," he said, untying her hands. "It's over. I'm here."

She opened her eyes to look at him just as he pulled the rope off and tossed it. Her crying took on a completely different tone as she reached for him and he scooped her into his arms, cradling her against him. She felt cold and he yanked a blanket from the bed, wrapping her in it. She sobbed and shook and clung to him while he murmured words of comfort and felt tears streak his own face.

"I thought he would kill you," she finally managed to say. "He said he would kill you if . . . you tried to take me away from him. I . . . heard your voice and then . . . the fighting and . . . I thought he would kill you and then he would . . ."

Her sobbing took over again just as Lieutenant Kepler appeared beside him. "Captain!" he said, astonished. "You found her!"

"I did," he said. "Call off the search. Spread the word that she's alive and safe. I want a hearing this afternoon. See that it's arranged. Then meet me upstairs."

"Yes, sir," he said with enthusiasm and hurried away.

Lance tightened his arms around her and forced himself to ask the question that had haunted him since her disappearance. "Did he hurt you, Nadine? Did he do . . . *anything* to hurt you?"

She shook her head against his shoulder. "No," she said firmly. "He . . . slapped me a few times, but . . . that was all. But . . ." She became upset again. "He . . . he . . . said such awful things to me. He . . . talked about the women he'd killed. And he . . . talked about what he was going to . . . do to me before he killed . . . me. He said that . . ." Her crying took over and she had to calm down before she added, "He said that . . . after he . . . made me his, he would kill me. And then he would know . . . that I was his forever, and no man could ever have me again."

With that in the open, she sobbed even harder. Lance pushed away the horror with his knowledge that she was safe and Crider was in custody. He spoke close to her ear. "I'm going to take you back to your room now. The doctor is going to make certain you're all right."

"That's not necessary," she said more calmly. "He didn't hurt me."

"It's mandatory for the crime report, Nadine. And . . . I'm sorry, but . . . they'll have to ask you details of what happened for the same reason. That's why I asked Lieutenant Kepler to come back. I know you're upset but . . ."

"It's all right," she said as he came to his feet, still holding her in his arms. "Will you stay with me?"

"Of course," he said and moved toward the stairs.

"Where are we?" she asked and he realized she had no idea how close she was to home.

"In the cellar of the inn," he said and she moaned.

"How did you find me?" she asked as they emerged into the daylight and her eyes squinted against the sun.

In a voice that cracked he simply said, "Abbi had a dream. I'll tell you about it later."

Lance carried her through the kitchen door. Gerda turned from her work and gasped. "Oh my!" she said. "I knew Drew had gone for the doctor, but I thought it was for you, Captain, and . . ." She followed him into the dining room and toward the stairs. "What can I do, Captain?"

"She's freezing and dirty," he said. "If you could prepare a hot bath to be ready as soon as the doctor has seen her and we've had a chance to ask her some questions."

"Of course," she said and slipped past him to open the door to Nadine's room. She hurried to turn down the covers and watched him lay her on the bed. "Oh, you're all right," she said tearfully to Nadine, who glanced toward her. "I'm so grateful." Nadine reached out a hand and Gerda took it. "I'm so grateful," she repeated then wiped her face with her apron. "I'll get that water on to heat. Breakfast will have to wait."

"Thank you, Gerda," Lance said as he untied the cords from around Nadine's feet, noting how her ankles were red and swollen, similar to her wrists. Her feet were freezing.

Nadine looked around the room as Lance tucked another blanket around her. Her weeping took over again, but he couldn't tell if she was relieved to be home or still upset over the ordeal. Likely both, he concluded.

Gerda returned holding a bed warmer filled with hot coals, which she slid beneath the covers near Nadine's feet. "That should help," she said with a tearful smile.

"Thank you," Lance said and she left the room while Nadine remained too upset to respond. When minutes passed and he couldn't get her to calm down, he noticed her jar of hand cream and grabbed it. Sitting beside her, he took out a generous amount and starting rubbing it into one of her hands while he whispered soothing words and reminded her repeatedly that Albert Crider was behind bars. She was safe. It was over. The hand massage worked and she gradually calmed down. While he did the second hand, she lay with her eyes closed. He wondered if she was asleep until she said, "Is this standard protocol for recovered hostages, Captain?"

"Only the one that I love," he said. She opened her eyes to look at him, but her expression was unreadable. He honestly had no idea where he stood with her. But at the moment, it didn't matter.

The doctor arrived, apologizing for taking so long. He'd been in the middle of delivering a baby.

"That's fine," Lance said. "It's not an emergency." He whispered to the doctor on his way out of the room, "We need a full report."

"I understand," the doctor replied and Lance closed the door, knowing Dr. Furhelm would be gentle and compassionate.

Lance felt immediately restless, left alone in the hall. He wondered if there was some other business he should be about, but he knew his orders would be carried through, and Nadine was in good hands. He could hear a great deal of noise from the dining room below and knew the breakfast rush was well underway. He hoped Drew and Gerda were not too overwhelmed by this morning's events.

Lance began to pace the hall, praying the doctor's report would coincide with what Nadine had told him. To find her alive was an answer to many prayers. To think that this fiend who had stalked and abducted her had refrained from violating her was nothing short of a miracle. Hearing footsteps on the stairs, he turned to see who might be coming. A woman and a man, he determined from the different sounds. Drew and Gerda with bath water, he guessed. Then Lance felt his eyes fill with hot mist before he'd barely had a chance to absorb what it meant to have Cameron and Abbi come here now. Before the mist cleared from his eyes, he felt Abbi's arms go around him, holding him as close as it was possible with her huge belly. He blinked and the tears spilled down his face while his hands were pressed to her back. She eased away and wiped the tears from his cheeks while he focused enough to see that she too was crying.

"You're hurt," she said, touching bruises on his face that he'd forgotten about until her touch reminded him they were tender.

"I'm fine," he said. "It's nothing."

"She's safe. You found her," she added.

"Thanks to your gift of dreams, my lady," he said.

"Where is she now?" Cameron asked.

"Doctor Furhelm is with her," he said, nodding to the door of her room.

"Oh, he's wonderful," Abbi said. "He treated me so well through getting Erich here."

"Where did you find her? How?" Cameron asked. "They told us nothing except that she had been found."

Lance guided them through an open door into the room next to Nadine's. He left the door open as they each took a chair. He noticed Abbi moving with difficulty and said, "You should not have come all the way down here in your condition, Your Grace."

"I'm just fine," she protested. "It was a simple carriage ride. Now stop fussing and tell us what happened."

Lance shook his head and let out a disbelieving chuckle. "She was under the bed," he said, "literally and figuratively." At their confusion he took a deep breath and clarified. "I just . . . started looking around the place. When you said it was *her* bed, I knew there had to be a clue here. I think I expected to find just that: a clue. I didn't expect to literally find her here because I couldn't imagine how that was possible. My men are very thorough when they search."

"They've been trained well," Cameron said.

"You can't give me all the credit for that," Lance said. "You were overseeing their training long before I ever became the captain." Cameron motioned for him to go on. "Well," Lance said, "when I was outside, I saw the door to the cellar." Abbi gasped. Lance went on. "And the idea came to me that under the bed meant beneath the place she sleeps. I don't know where they were when the initial search was done, but they were down there when I went into the cellar. Crider and I had it out, and thankfully I got the better of him. And there's a couple of beds down there. She was under one of them, bound and gagged, just like you said she was." Lance squeezed his eyes closed as the horror struck him all over again.

"Oh, I'm so grateful," Abbi said.

"So am I," Lance added, "more than you can possibly imagine."

Cameron took Abbi's hand into his. "Oh, I think I can imagine."

"Yes, I suppose you can."

Lance heard footsteps on the stairs and stepped into the hall just as Gerda came up with two buckets of steaming water. "There's more heating," she said as Lance hurried to take them from her.

"Thank you," Lance said, setting them at the edge of the hall. "I hope all of this hasn't made your morning too difficult," he said. "I can't thank you enough for all that you've done for her."

Gerda smiled. "She's a good woman, Captain. We're just glad she's safe. And we're doing great down there. Business is booming; we're rather popular all of a sudden. People are celebrating. And there's all kinds of folks volunteering to help serve and helping in the kitchen too. Don't you worry about us. And since we've got so much help downstairs, that will leave me free to help Nadine with her bath. Then I'll see that she gets something to eat and has everything she needs."

Lance smiled. And it felt good to smile. "Thank you, Gerda," he said again and she hurried down the stairs.

"Celebrating?" Cameron said as Lance came back into the room. "As they should be."

Abbi added, "The entire country has struggled with this—having such a criminal in their midst. Now that he's been apprehended, Nadine's safety represents a triumph to them."

Lance said nothing, fearing he would start crying again. He doubted Abbi and Cameron were impressed with the amount of tears being shed these days by their captain. He had barely sat down again when he heard a door open and stepped into the hall to meet Dr. Furhelm, who pulled Nadine's door closed and asked, "Is there a place we can sit for a—"

"Here," Lance motioned to the room he'd just left. "Their Graces are here, and need to hear the report anyway."

"Of course," the doctor said and followed him into the room.

Cameron rose to greet him with a firm handshake, then Dr. Furhelm turned to Abbi and took her hand, "And how are you, Your Grace? Still feeling all right?"

"Just big and tired," she said.

"All very normal," the doctor commented and sat down. "Well," he said, "she's in fairly good shape, all things considered. She's got some minor bruising on her face and some rope burns on her wrists and ankles. And there is a nasty bump on her head that had some minimal bleeding from being hit on the head. Beyond that I see no physical evidence of abuse." He paused and added, "I know you're wondering so I'll tell you straight out. She was not sexually violated. I'm absolutely certain." They all took a deep breath simultaneously. "Emotionally she seems all right, albeit somewhat shaken, which is understandable. Knowing the culprit is behind bars should help her get over it more quickly. But it could take time. Such things vary with different people."

A wan smile toward Abbi, then Cameron, needed no further explanation. Dr. Furhelm had been well aware of the adjustment Abbi had struggled with following what Nikolaus had done to her.

"Of course," Lance said. "Thank you."

"I'll fill out the usual paperwork and see that it's submitted right away," the doctor said, standing to leave. "Now, if you'll excuse me, I'm certain I have patients waiting."

"Thank you again," Lance said.

The doctor smiled. "A pleasure to be able to give such a favorable report in such an unfavorable situation."

"Indeed," Cameron said.

"I would like to stay here with Nadine for a while," Abbi said after the doctor was gone. "I can't do much to help her, but Gerda can do that, and I can be company."

Lance felt some relief. Perhaps her personal experience with such matters could help more than anything else. "I'm sure she'd like that," he said, "and I would be relieved to know that you're with her." He sighed and added, "I fear in spite of all that's happened, the estrangement between us still exists. Once the drama is over, she will likely keep me at a distance."

Neither Cameron nor Abbi said anything. There was nothing to be said.

"What will you be doing now?" Cameron asked a moment later.

"When Lieutenant Kepler returns, we have to officially question her, and then there will be a hearing this afternoon."

"Well then," Cameron said, "I think I'll just sit with my wife while you finish your business here, then you and I can return to the castle together. I think I should like to be with you when you visit Mr. Crider to inform him of what will transpire in what little will be left of his life."

"I'd like that very much," Lance said. Perhaps Cameron could keep him from killing Crider on the spot. "Thank you, my friend," Lance said, gripping Cameron's forearm firmly.

Cameron smiled and said, "A pleasure . . . my brother."

Lance could only turn and leave the room. He wasn't up to giving his raw emotions any further invitation to come to the surface.

Chapter Twenty-Seven
Cleaning Up

Lance knocked lightly at Nadine's door and heard her call, "Come in." He stepped into the room to see her leaning against pillows that were propped against the headboard. She barely made eye contact with him before she glanced away, absently smoothing the bed covers.

"How are you?" he asked and left the door open.

"I am very well, Captain, thank you. I am no longer at the mercy of that . . . *pervert*. On top of that, he's behind bars, and I'm actually beginning to believe that I don't have to be afraid of him anymore."

"That's right. You don't," he said, sitting in a chair near the bed. "He will be executed tomorrow at dawn."

"And you will be giving the order," she said.

"With pleasure."

She turned to look at him and her eyes narrowed on his face. "You're hurt," she said.

Lance absently touched the side of his face that was the most tender. He'd not even bothered to look in a mirror and assess the damages. "It's nothing," he said.

"You said you'd tell me later," she said.

"What?"

"About Abbi's dream."

"Maybe she should tell you herself. She's here, actually. She'll be in to see you as soon as we talk with the Lieutenant. He should be here any time."

"Why don't *you* tell me," she said. "You're the one who found me."

Lance found it difficult to come up with the words. He sought for the simplest means to explain. "Uh . . . she had a dream that you were bound and gagged, and it was dark and cold. And she said you were under the bed."

"Incredible," she said breathlessly. "But how did that lead you to—"

"She said you were under *your* bed. When I saw the cellar doors it occurred to me that it could mean beneath the place where you sleep. I knew it had been thoroughly searched right after your disappearance, and I don't know where you were at the time, but . . . you were there today."

"I think I was in a barrel," she said.

"You *think?*" he asked.

"Well, he . . ." She hesitated as a knock sounded at the open door.

"Lieutenant," Lance said. "Come in. Have a seat."

The lieutenant first approached Nadine and took her hand. "It is an inexplicable pleasure to see you alive and well, Mrs. Rader."

"Thank you," she said.

"Lieutenant Kepler has put countless hours in on your behalf," Lance said. "He has overseen the entire investigation and has done a marvelous job."

"Then I owe you my deepest appreciation," Nadine said.

"All in the line of duty," he said humbly.

"Mrs. Rader was about to tell me what happened from her perspective. Your timing is good, Lieutenant. Under the circumstances, I want you to hear everything firsthand from her so that my *personal bias* will not interfere with the matter."

"Of course," the lieutenant said and took a small notebook and pencil out of his pocket.

"First, I have a question," Nadine said. "I have to know what happened to the officers who were patrolling the inn. Please don't tell me they were—"

"They're fine," Kepler said. "They were each knocked unconscious and suffered a knife wound to the leg. They're home recovering with their families and they will be just fine."

"Oh, I'm so relieved," Nadine said. "I worried and worried. I knew he wouldn't have gotten in here without doing them harm, and I feared the worst."

"He also broke the locks in a way we've never seen before," the lieutenant said. "He's a master criminal, this man. We'll keep piecing the evidence together. We have officers thoroughly combing the cellar again as we speak."

"He was living down there," Nadine said. "From the time the description of him was posted, he went into hiding down there. There were beds and lanterns and plenty to eat. During the days he would tidy everything perfectly and hide in case someone came into that room, but he said no one ever came in except right after I'd been taken, and he'd been expecting that."

"How do you know all of this?" Kepler asked.

"He talked almost constantly," she said. "He bragged and bragged about how brilliant he'd been in eluding the law, not only in one country but two. And he . . ." her voice broke, "he bragged about the women he'd killed, telling me horrific details and . . ." She squeezed her eyes shut and shook visibly.

"You don't need to talk about that right now," Lance said gently. "Tell us what you were about to say when the lieutenant came in . . . about the barrel."

She became more steady as the subject became easier. "He dragged me out of my bed and knocked me on the back of the head. When I woke up, I was being pulled out of a barrel, and I smelled like baking flour."

"So," Lance said more to the lieutenant, "he knocked her out, put her in the barrel and went elsewhere while he knew the initial search was taking place. Do you suppose they looked in all the barrels?"

"Probably one or two, and when they saw the contents, they may have moved on if the lids on the others were nailed down."

"And I thought they were thorough," Lance said with an edge of disgust. Although he had to admit it was an understandable oversight.

Lance listened for more than an hour as she answered the lieutenant's questions and her ordeal came more fully to light. Albert Crider had teased and tormented her, talking to her in crude and vulgar language as he reiterated over and over the fantasies he'd had about her and how he intended to make them come to pass before he killed her. Lance could only be grateful that Abbi's dream had come in time to prevent such a heinous atrocity.

Lieutenant Kepler finally stood, saying, "Thank you. I think that's everything we'll need. I know you have a hot bath waiting for you whenever you're ready."

"Are you hungry?" Lance asked her.

"A little," she said, "but I'd rather bathe first, thank you."

Kepler left the room, eager to get the report filled out before the hearing. Lance stood as well, reluctant to leave, even though he had business to attend to.

"I need to see Dulsie," she said without looking at him. "Will you bring her to see me, when it's convenient?"

"Of course," he said. "This evening." He swallowed carefully and asked what he knew he needed to. "Would you like me to bring her things so she can stay here with you now that—"

"No," Nadine said abruptly. "Tell her I'm not feeling well and I need some time to . . . well, just tell her I need some time. I know you can explain it to her better than I can." She sighed. "Surely you can understand that I need some time."

"Of course," he said. And while he desperately wanted Dulsie to be a part of his life, and he *did* understand that she needed time, he felt uneasy. He sensed there was something more, something deeper in her desire to leave Dulsie with him. He wanted to ask but didn't know how and feared opening an argument. The last thing they needed on such a day was an argument. "I'll bring her by this evening for a visit," he added gently.

"Thank you," she said.

"Is there anything else you need?" he asked. "Gerda will help you get a bath and something to eat. And as I said, Abbi is here."

"I'll be fine, thank you," she said and he moved toward the door.

"Captain," she said and he hated the formal tone of her voice that clearly indicated the state of their relationship.

"Yes, Mrs. Rader." He turned back, unable to help feeling angry—even while he recognized the hurt and frustration at the root of his anger.

"I can't thank you enough . . . for everything. I'm only sorry that I brought such trouble to Horstberg."

"It is my duty to serve, madame," he said with the same formality she had used with him. "May I speak on behalf of the ducal committee in saying that we are pleased to have the matter put to rest and to see that you are safe and exonerated of all charges. Good day, Mrs. Rader." He walked away then glanced over his shoulder long enough to add, "If we can be of further service, you know where to find me."

Lance took a moment in the hall to compose himself before he realized Cameron and Abbi were not in the room where he'd left them. He went downstairs and informed Gerda that Nadine was finally ready for a bath. He found Cameron and Abbi in the dining room. Abbi was just finishing an early lunch.

"Join us," Cameron said. "In fact, I was waiting to eat with you, if only to make sure that you eat. I bet you've had nothing today."

"I hadn't thought about it," Lance said. "But you're right."

"How is she?" Abbi asked.

"She seems all right, but she's not talking—not to me, anyway. Perhaps you can better assess how she *really* is. She wants me to bring Dulsie for a visit this evening, but she wants her to stay with me for the time being. I'm not complaining; I'm glad to have her. But it doesn't make sense."

"Well," Abbi said, "I'm done here. I think I'll go up and see what I can do."

Cameron rose to help her with her chair and they exchanged a kiss. He said to her, "I'm taking one of the officer's horses to go back with Lance. The officer will stay and see that you have what you need." He motioned toward a man in uniform across the room, who smiled at them. "And he'll ride back in the carriage with you when you're ready."

"Thank you, my dear," she said. "You think of everything."

Abbi kissed Lance's cheek and went up the stairs.

Nadine watched Lance leave the room, wishing she knew how to make him understand that their relationship was better this way. She only wished they could at least be friends, without this horrible tension between them.

She was immeasurably grateful for a hot bath, and she tried

to imagine it washing away the entire incident with Albert Crider, although she knew it would take a great deal more time and effort to be completely free of the experience and the impression it had left on her mind. While she was soaking in steamy scented water, Gerda changed her bed linens. Once Nadine was back in bed wearing clean nightclothes, Abbi visited with her for a long while. Abbi confessed some details Nadine had never heard regarding the time when Nikolaus had threatened her life. Nadine was appalled and disgusted to learn how cruel Nikolaus had been and the abuse Abbi had endured. Abbi had struggled in her efforts to come to terms with the event, but it had been impacted by other challenges in her life at the time. While their situations varied in many ways, there were more than enough similarities to give them a common bond that was almost eerie. Abbi truly understood how Nadine felt, and Abbi's example and wisdom settled deeply into Nadine. Talking the details through with Abbi left Nadine tangibly hopeful that she could come to terms with her anger toward Albert Crider. But Lance didn't come up at all, and she felt it was better that way. She simply wasn't ready to address what she felt was best in regard to him. For now, she simply focused on her gratitude at being alive and well and for being surrounded by people who took such good care of her and of Dulsie. For now, nothing else mattered.

Lance and Cameron sat together and ate their meal, then Lance looked at his watch and said, "We have a hearing in less than half an hour, Your Grace. And it's my responsibility to inform the prisoner of his rights."

"Does he have any?" Cameron asked, coming to his feet.

"Beyond food and water, no."

They rode quickly to the castle and went immediately into Albert Crider's cell. Two officers waited at the door as Cameron and Lance went inside.

"Ah, Captain," Mr. Crider said as if it were a social call, "how good to see you again."

"I seriously doubt it," Lance said.

"And who is this?" Crider asked, glaring at Cameron.

"This is the Duke of Horstberg," Lance said, "and you will address him appropriately or not at all."

"Ah, so I am being honored with royalty."

"I wanted to see what kind of man would cause such an uproar in my country," Cameron said. "The picture becomes very clear now that I see you."

"What picture is that . . . Your Grace?" he added snidely.

"A man who isn't man enough to win a woman suitably has to kill to get her attention and hold her bound and gagged to get her affection."

Crider's eyes turned dark before he rose his hand to strike Cameron. But Cameron intercepted the blow and grabbed Crider's wrist, twisting it up behind his back until Crider went to his knees, moaning in response to the pain. "You're nothing but a sniveling little rat," Cameron said and let go, taking a step back. Crider scrambled to his feet, glancing skeptically at Cameron.

"I am here to inform you of your rights," Lance said. "It won't take long because you don't have many. You will be given food and water and common necessaries for the length of time you are in our care, which will be until you go before a firing squad."

"I demand a trial."

"What you get is a hearing," Lance said. "I'm doing you a favor in that regard. If the public were allowed to hear of your crimes, they would be so set on getting to you that it would take my entire force to protect you. And you're not worth the time or the trouble. I can assure you that getting shot through the heart will be much quicker and painless than being stoned to death by an angry mob. The hearing will convene in a matter of minutes. You will be polite and respectful to the committee, as you will be to those who work in this keep who will see to your needs. If there is so much as a sniffle out of line, you will be experiencing hell before you even get there. Do I make myself clear?"

"Quite clear, Captain," he said, then he went on in a tone that seemed an attempt at testing the threat he'd just been given. "You know, Captain, I've come to know you quite well through this experience. People around here talk about you as if you're some kind of a god, but I know better. You weren't man enough to do what had to be done. You turned and left the country right when she needed you most."

Lance clenched a fist unwillingly and heard Cameron whisper, "Stay calm. Hurting him now won't do any good."

"Even you, Captain, with your reputation of honor and glory were not capable of making her happy. She tossed you out just like she tossed me out, but if you ever do get into her bed, remember that with the conversations she and I shared, a part of her mind will always be with me."

"All right," Cameron whispered, "now you can let him have it."

Lance threw a hard fist into Crider's jaw and watched him reel backward. Before he'd gained his footing, Lance took him by the collar and slammed him against the wall. "You filthy, degenerate scum," Lance snarled. "You are going to die tomorrow at sunrise, and you are going straight to hell."

Crider lifted an arm as if he intended to strike back, but he'd barely moved before Cameron had pulled the pistol from Lance's belt and had it pressed to Crider's temple. Lance lifted a knee into Crider's stomach and allowed him to slide to his knees as he stepped back. Crider looked up at him with evil glistening in his eyes. "Isn't there some rule about the treatment of prisoners?" he snarled.

"Yes, actually, but it has exceptions in cases like yours. You can file a report and we'll see if we can get to it next week." Lance turned to leave, saying, "You've got five minutes before the hearing. Try to look presentable."

Lance and Cameron left the cell and went to Lance's office where Kepler was waiting. "I thought you might be interested in seeing these," Kepler said and led them to a room where several items were spread over a table. There were daggers and white scarves that implied a number of possible victims. Lance wondered if he would have stopped after he'd killed Nadine. He doubted it. There were also some pieces of women's clothing, including underclothing. "Mrs. Rader's size," he said. Lance opened one of three well-worn books to see that it was a journal. "The journals she had stolen from her, presumably," Kepler said. "These things were all found in the cellar beneath the inn. They were in a box on one of the shelves, appearing to be among the other storage. Some of his own personal effects were there as well. We also found that one of the barrels had some strands of Mrs. Rader's hair in it and evidence that the top had once been nailed shut, unlike any of the others."

Lance looked over the materials but said nothing. He only exchanged a deep gaze with Cameron before all three men walked to the committee interrogation room. Lance hadn't been here since the day Nadine had been interrogated. He felt incredibly grateful for the way the tables had turned to see justice met.

The hearing played out quickly and with no surprises. Crider confessed his crimes with a boastful attitude that made Lance sick. But then, looking at the other men in the room, he realized that in this they were unanimous. They all looked sick. The verdict was given, and an execution at sunrise was ordered. Crider was returned to his cell, escorted by four officers.

"And now what?" Cameron asked Lance, but Lance didn't have an answer. "Why don't you take the rest of the day off? You'll have an early day tomorrow. Get some rest. Spend time with Dulsie. It's almost over. You can relax now."

"Yes, I suppose I can," Lance said.

Cameron walked with Lance into the castle, and they parted at the staircase where Lance would go up to get Dulsie from the nursery. "I'll see you very early tomorrow," Cameron said and walked on down the hall.

"Your Grace," Lance called and Cameron turned back. "Thank you."

Cameron nodded and smiled and moved on.

Once inside the nursery door, Dulsie came running into his arms. She hugged him tightly then said, "You found my mother?"

"I did," he said. "She's fine and she wants you to come and visit her this evening."

"Does she need me to stay with her and take care of her?" Dulsie asked like an adult.

Lance sensed that as much as she had enjoyed staying with him, she missed her mother and wanted to be with her. And in spite of his own personal bias, he knew that was the best thing. But he acted on Nadine's request and said, "What she went through was very hard on her, and she needs some time to feel better before you go and stay with her, all right?" Dulsie nodded. "But for today, I don't have to work anymore. I was thinking we could go read some books and do a puzzle, and then we could go to the inn for supper and you can see your mother. What do you think?"

Dulsie nodded eagerly and they walked together back to the apartment. They were crossing the courtyard when Dulsie said, "I heard some of the kitchen ladies talking about me today. They didn't know I was listening."

"How do you know they were talking about you?" he asked.

"They were talking about Mama first. They said it was horrible what had happened to her and they were happy that she'd been found. They talked about you, too. They said it was . . . romantic that you had found her, because you're going to marry her." Lance swallowed and reminded himself that the country was not aware of the estrangement between him and Nadine. He'd not officially called off the wedding, hoping for some miracle to intervene. Either way, he wasn't terribly happy at the thought of the entire country discussing his personal life. Dulsie distracted him when she asked, "What's romantic?"

"Uh . . . it's like nice things that happen when a man and a woman love each other." Recalling where this conversation had begun, he asked, "So, what did they say about you?"

"They said they were glad my mother was all right, since I already had enough to deal with because I'm a royal bastard."

Lance stopped walking and looked down into her innocent face. He wanted to hunt down the women who had said this and have them reprimanded. But he couldn't track down every gossip monger in Horstberg. Dulsie looked concerned as she asked, "Lance, what's a royal—"

"I'm not exactly certain," he said, walking on, attempting to be nonchalant. "I'll have to look it up in the dictionary." He was grateful for an excuse that would give him some time to think of an appropriate answer. He couldn't protect her from the gossip and the way people might see her. But he could teach her what it meant in a way that would help her be stronger in handling it. However, he hated his own uneasiness over the topic that flowed into more personal territory. He too was a royal bastard. He'd just been so busy trying to keep Nadine alive that he'd pushed that reality out of his mind each time he'd thought about it.

Through the afternoon the subject didn't come up again. He enjoyed the time he spent with Dulsie but felt decidedly nervous about taking her to see her mother. He didn't have to wonder why.

His relationship with Nadine was anything but how he wanted it and seeing her only brought the reality home more starkly. His gratitude to have her alive and well was beyond description. But his worry for her had relented and allowed plenty of space in his mind for thoughts regarding the other challenges in his life that had been brushed aside.

At the inn Gerda told them that Nadine had just finished her supper. She insisted that they get something to eat before Dulsie saw her mother, since Nadine had been resting when Gerda had gone up to get the supper tray. Lance and Dulsie shared their meal while she told him about her friends in the nursery and the silly games they would play. He loved to hear her laugh, and the way she could make him laugh as well, even when he felt so burdened.

When their meal was finished, Dulsie ran up the stairs and he had to hurry to keep up with her. "You must knock," he said quietly. "She might be changing her clothes or something."

Dulsie nodded and knocked at the door. Nadine called, "Come in," and Dulsie burst through the door, laughing as she ran into the room and bounded onto the bed. Lance hovered in the doorway, watching the reunion, grateful to hear Nadine laugh as well. She was sitting up against the pillows, the bed covers around her waist. She wore a different nightgown and looked much better. Now that the dirt had been cleaned away, he could see some subtle bruising on her face, but it was minimal. And he was grateful. He looked around the room, surprised to see more than a dozen bouquets of flowers in vases on the bureau and table and opened gifts scattered on the floor.

"My, you've been busy," he said, drawing their attention to him.

Dulsie jumped down to look at the flowers. Nadine said, "People have been sending flowers from the hothouse—people I don't even know. And gifts and cards, wishing me well. There have been books to read while I'm recovering, and a lovely shawl, and a couple of quilts, and . . . oh, I don't remember. It's been so overwhelming."

"So, I see," Lance said and smiled at her. "People have been worried about you. The whole country was searching . . . praying."

"So, I keep hearing," she said. "I thought people would be angry with me. I'm the one who led him here."

Lance was so grateful to have her talking to him that a degree of relief bathed over him. "Your innocence in this is readily evident, Nadine. I'm just grateful that it's over."

"Yes, so am I," she said with a heaviness to her voice. He suspected it would take time for her to be free of the emotional effects of what had happened, but considering how recent her ordeal had been, she seemed to be doing well.

"So, how are you feeling?" he asked.

"I'm much better, thank you," she said. "I thought my feet would never be warm again, but a hot bath did wonders, and I'm happy to say that they are."

"That's good then," he said.

"The doctor suggested I rest for a few days, but I really am feeling fine. I told Abbi I would be back to work on Monday. There is much to do for Christmas, and not much time to do it in."

"Of course," Lance said. They were supposed to be married before Christmas. He *hated* this!

While Dulsie was busy examining the contents of the unwrapped packages on the floor, Nadine asked, "So what have you been up to, Captain?"

He felt startled by the question and it took him a moment to reply. "Just . . . cleaning up."

"Cleaning up?"

"Oh, that's what we say in reference to finalizing a case—all the little details to finish it up and see it closed. Just . . . cleaning up."

"When will the trial be?" she asked.

"It's over," he said and she looked astonished. "There was no need for an actual trial. There was a hearing. The evidence was staggering and undeniable, but he confessed to everything."

"So now what?" she asked, her voice unsteady. Was she counting the minutes as he was until Albert Crider would no longer be breathing and therefore could pose no threat—ever again?

"He will be executed at sunrise," he said and saw her breathe in relief.

Silence descended while Dulsie smelled all the different flowers. Lance forced himself to remember where he stood. "I'll just . . . go and let you have some time with Dulsie. When do you want me to come back for her?"

Nadine looked mildly distressed. "Oh . . . I don't know. I . . . where will you go? Back to the castle, or . . ."

"Probably not. I'll just . . ."

"Why don't you just stay here?" she said. "You could . . . read one of those books, or . . . just relax. It's up to you. But you're welcome to stay."

Lance debated only a moment before he decided that passing up such an opportunity would be stupid. "Thank you," he said and closed the door. He wanted to just sit and watch the two of them interact. He wanted to just stare at Nadine and absorb the reality that she was alive and well and the nightmare of having her life threatened was over. Not wanting to be that obvious, he looked through the books she'd been given and found one that held some minimal appeal. He sat on the little sofa and made himself comfortable while Dulsie climbed on the bed and sat close to her mother. Lance pretended to read while he listened to Nadine ask her daughter endless questions about what she'd been doing. Dulsie asked Nadine questions about what had happened to her, and Nadine answered them honestly and calmly.

There was a lull in their conversation just before Dulsie asked, "Mama, what's a royal bastard?" Lance shot his head up to see Nadine looking at her daughter in astonishment. He knew Dulsie must have realized the term was unfavorable simply by getting the same reaction from her mother that she'd gotten from him earlier. Dulsie went on to say, "Lance said he had to look it up in the dictionary."

Nadine turned toward him. The pleading in her eyes made him feel as if they were allies. At least in regard to Dulsie, they were. And that was good. Lance set the book aside and moved to a chair near the bed, grateful he'd had some time to think about it.

"Well, I did look it up, Dulsie, and now I think I know what those ladies meant when you overheard them say that." He tossed a cautious glance to Nadine.

"What ladies?" Nadine asked with a kindness in her voice that didn't match the alarm in her eyes.

"The kitchen ladies," Dulsie said. "They help serve us our lunch, and they were talking, and they didn't know I was close by, but I knew they were talking about me because they were talking about you and the bad man that took you and then they said I was a—"

"Let me explain this to you, Dulsie," Lance said, taking her hand. "A bastard is a person who is born when the father is not married to the mother." Deep concentration overtook her little face while he wondered if she understood what he meant. He caught a glance from Nadine that seemed to say he was doing all right so far. "Dulsie," he said, "do you understand what I'm saying?" She said nothing and he added, "When a man and a woman love each other and they sleep in the same bed together, that's when they have a baby together. If they aren't married, then sleeping in the same bed is not a good thing. That's why people call the baby a bastard."

Dulsie immediately said, "But my father and my mother were married. My father died."

Lance saw Nadine hang her head. She pressed a hand over her mouth to hide the fact that she was crying. "Dulsie," Lance said, hoping to distract her attention away from her mother, "I want you to listen very closely to what I have to tell you. You're getting more grown up now, and it's important for you to know what happened. Your father was not a very nice man. Your mother loved him, but he didn't love her. He tricked her into believing they were married, when they really weren't. Your mother didn't know the marriage wasn't real until she came to Horstberg, and she was very sad. Now this is the important part. It's all right that your father wasn't a nice man. Do you know why? Because your mother loves you so much that she makes up for how he lied to her. And I know, because your mother told me, that even though he lied to her and wasn't very nice, she is still glad that she thought she was married to him, because she has you. And you are more precious and important to her than anything else in this world."

Dulsie seemed to take all of that in then asked matter-of-factly, "What does royal mean?"

"Royal is a certain kind of person; it's a person who belongs to a very special family, the kind of family that rules over countries and kingdoms."

"Like Erich's family?" she asked.

"That's right," he said. "Erich's mother and father are the rulers of Horstberg. They are royal."

"Was my father royal?" she asked.

"Yes, Dulsie, he was."

"Is he really dead, or was that a lie to keep from hurting my feelings?"

"It wasn't a lie, Dulsie. Your mother never lied to you. There were some things she didn't tell you because she thought you should be older so that you could understand better. When she told you she was married to your father, she believed that she was. Do you understand?" She nodded. "Your father really is dead, Dulsie. I knew your father. He was a friend of mine. And I was there when he died."

"Was he a bad man like the man that took Mama and killed those women?"

Lance's first impulse was to tell her no. Then it occurred to him that Nikolaus du Woernig had murdered a woman and had abducted another and done deplorable things to her. The comparison was suddenly startling. He met Nadine's eyes and found unmistakable approval to tell her the truth.

"Yes, Dulsie, he was. And for that reason we are glad that he didn't really marry your mother, because we would not have wanted him to be involved in your lives. Sometimes good things come out of bad things. And that's what happened with you. You are a very good thing that came out of a difficult situation."

Dulsie turned to her mother and said, "Don't cry, Mama. It's all right." She then turned to Lance and added, "Do you think we could go have our pie now?" She said to Nadine, "Gerda said we could have pie when the dining room wasn't so crowded."

Nadine smiled through her tears and Lance said, "Why don't you go down and ask Gerda if it's all right. Maybe we could bring pie up here and eat it with your mother."

"I'll ask Gerda," she said and hurried out of the room.

"Thank you," Nadine said. "I'm afraid I would have turned it into a horrible drama." She shook her head. "I suppose I was a fool to hope that she could grow up never knowing the truth."

"I'm not sure that would be a good thing," he said. "Eventually she would find out."

"You mean the way *you* found out," she said and Lance was startled at how difficult it was to hear the topic shift to him.

He went to his feet and hurried from the room, saying, "I'd better see what Dulsie is up to." He wanted to think that Nadine hadn't noticed his reaction. But he felt sure she knew him better than that. He only wished that she knew him well enough to know that she could trust him.

Chapter Twenty-Eight

BARRIERS

Nadine watched Lance leave the room while a tangible heart-ache filled her on his behalf. She knew he was struggling and wished he would talk to her about his feelings. But just wanting him to do so made her feel like a hypocrite. His angry words catapulted through her mind. *I have spilt my heart's blood one too many times for you.* Looking back to the beginning of their relationship, she knew that right from the start he had opened himself to her, confessing his deepest feelings and heartache when they were practically strangers. Now, through her repeated mistrust of him, she had put him into a position he felt he could no longer trust *her*. He had told her that he deserved better, and he was right, which was one of many reasons that she had to wonder if it would be better for *him* if she were to let him go now—while the ties between them were already partially severed.

Facing death—not once, but twice—had given Nadine great cause for reflection. She knew in her heart that Lance had been abso-lutely right when he'd said that he'd given her no reason not to trust him. The very fact that she allowed such incidents to affect her so deeply made her wonder if she simply wasn't the right woman for him. Perhaps she had jumped into her relationship with him too fast, only thinking of what *she* wanted and not giving any consideration to what might be best for him. But then, in spite of all that had happened, she sensed that Lance truly loved her and wanted to be with her. Of course, he'd told her that he would not live with the issue of mistrust between them. Most of all, Nadine felt confused. And while memories of her experience with Albert Crider were still so close, her mind felt even more clouded. Still, one fact stood out above all else. Albert had stirred up memories that she had believed were dead and forgotten. If he knew what she'd done, then someone else knew as well. And it was only a matter of time before Lance found out that she was guilty of treason. She had already put him and Dulsie through the hell of seeing her go to prison and face the possibility of going before a firing squad. It was better that they were both in a position now to make this as easy as possible—for all of them.

Nadine became so lost in her thoughts that she was startled when Lance and Dulsie came back into the room. The three of them shared Gerda's apple-raisin pie, covered with cream, then Lance took the dishes back to the kitchen while Dulsie had a few more minutes with her mother. When he returned, Nadine said, "You go on downstairs, Dulsie, and say good night to Drew and Gerda. I need to talk to Lance for a minute." She kissed her mother and took up her coat and gloves and left the room.

"What is it?" he asked, wondering if this conversation would give him hope or leave him devastated. Her expression urged him more toward the latter.

Nadine took a deep breath and told herself to just come straight to the point. "I just want to be certain that you're all right with keeping Dulsie. You were willing to take her on completely if I had died, so I assume it's all right if she stays with you now."

"Of course it's all right," he said. "When you get feeling better just let me know and I'll bring her things back and—"

"No, Lance," she said, "I'm talking about a permanent arrangement."

He was so stunned that it took him a moment to respond. "Why would you want such a thing, Nadine?"

"I just . . . think it would be better . . . for all of us."

"*You* think? Maybe you should ask her what *she* thinks."

"It's evident she loves being with you, and you do so well with her. She's too young to understand what's best for her."

"Nadine," he emitted a humorless chuckle, "I can't believe you're saying this. Don't you think people will wonder why you're not raising your own daughter?"

"I was under the impression you didn't care what people thought. Why should I? It's none of their business."

"I don't give a damn what people think, Nadine, except for the way it will affect you."

"People will believe this experience was simply too traumatic for me, and I never recovered enough to be a good mother. It was, after all, rather devastating. Being stalked. Going to prison. Being abducted. Most women would be scarred for life."

"You're not most women, Nadine. You're stronger than that, and I know it."

"Well, maybe you don't know me as well as you think you do," she snapped. "You have no idea what I went through in prison . . . and in that cellar."

"All right, I concede there. But it's not even been a day. How can you say that you won't take care of your own daughter?"

"Because it has a lot more to it than that. I'm willing to let people believe that my abduction was the reason, but . . . I simply believe she's better off with you. You are capable of giving her so much more than I ever could. The stigma of her birth will be overcome much more easily through your connections, your position. She loves you, and I know you love her and you'll be a good father to her."

Lance sighed and resisted the urge to scream. In a voice of forced calm, he said, "Nadine, I *do* love Dulsie, and I want to be a father to her, but not like this. She should be in a home with two parents. Surely we can overcome our differences enough to give her that."

"This is much more complicated than our differences, Lance."

"How is that?" he demanded.

"I . . . really don't want to talk about it right now."

"Well, when do you want to talk about it?"

"I don't know. I don't know if there's anything to say. I just want to be able to see my daughter whenever it's possible. Surely that's not so difficult for you to understand."

"I understand your wanting to see her, but what you're asking me to do surely warrants some kind of explanation."

"If you don't want her," she snapped, "just say so."

"I *do* want her. Now that she's been in my home, I don't want to ever be without her, but you're her mother. I don't understand how you can—"

He stopped, hearing a child's footsteps running up the hall. "Are you coming, Lance?" Dulsie asked, peeking her head into the open doorway.

"Yes darling, I'm coming." To Nadine he said, "We'll talk about this later. Come along," he said, taking Dulsie's hand. "Let's go home."

Lance fought to push the conversation with Nadine out of his head. He was so stunned and confused he couldn't even think straight. Once they were home, he sent Dulsie to get ready for bed while he stoked up the fires, then he read a story to her and tucked her in.

He had difficulty sleeping and was forced to rise far too early the next morning. Before the sun peered over the east horizon, he was standing in his appointed position in the courtyard, adjacent to the twelve officers lined up at attention, their rifles positioned at their sides. Cameron and Georg stood on the balcony above him, and the prisoner was brought into the courtyard. Just seeing him urged an unfathomable anger to the surface in Lance, and he felt a certain pleasure as he called loudly, "Ready!"

The regiment systematically set their booted feet together and flipped their rifles to their shoulders, all in perfect unison. "Aim!" he called and they simultaneously dropped their weapons, all pointed directly at Albert Crider's chest. Crider's cockiness from the previous day was completely absent. He showed no dignity or courage, but rather a complete lack of it. Cameron had been right. Crider was nothing but a sniveling little rat.

"Fire!" Lance said and the twelve rifles fired at exactly the same moment, although only one had been loaded with a ball on top of the powder. And no one knew which man had been holding the lethal weapon.

Lance watched Crider fall then turned toward Cameron and called, "The execution is complete, Your Grace."

"Thank you, Captain," Cameron called back while their gaze exchanged a deep, silent understanding. Lance's most prominent thought was a deep gratitude that such a moment had not come to pass for Nadine. He prayed that in the years ahead as he continued to serve his country, that he was never again faced with the possibility of putting an innocent person in front of a firing squad.

In the hours following the execution, Lance wasn't surprised at the memories being stirred of his killing Nikolaus. But now something stirred the memories closer than they'd ever been. What he felt now reminded him so much of his feelings surrounding Nikolaus's death that it almost frightened him. He was *angry*. And with that anger came a certain degree of pleasure in watching a man die. Was that why killing Nikolaus had haunted him the way it had, because he'd actually found some tiny bit of pleasure in it? The thought made him sick now just as he'd felt sick right after he'd done it. Whatever pleasure there might have been had quickly given way to the reality that he'd killed a man, however justified it might have been. And in Nikolaus's case, it had been a man that Lance had cared for deeply through most of his life. And now Lance couldn't deny that he'd felt a certain amount of pleasure in watching Albert Crider die. The common bond this man shared with Nikolaus was his ability to destroy people's lives with no apparent remorse. And the very idea that a human being could be so depraved just made Lance angry.

That afternoon Lance saw to a matter of business that, as the captain, he would have seen to regarding any such case. He paid one final call upon the victim. He knocked at the door to Nadine's room and heard her call for him to come in. He opened the door to find her in bed with a book, and while he'd expected her to look a little better today than she had last night, she actually looked worse. Apparently the reality of what had happened was sinking in now that the relief of having it over had settled. Her countenance looked tired and worn, and he wanted to just take her in his arms and soothe the heartache away—for both of them. But barriers stood between them that he didn't know how to break past.

Nadine's heart quickened to see Lance enter the room and close the door behind him, holding a box under one arm. "This is business," he said tersely. "I have come to inform you that Albert Crider is dead and buried." Nadine absorbed the news with a relief that bathed her every nerve. "I am also returning what I assume to be a number of your belongings. They are no longer needed as evidence."

He set the box on the bed beside her. She gave him an inquisitive glance before she opened it to see some familiar articles of clothing and her journals that had been stolen. She picked up one of the journals and thumbed through it, then the others. But she couldn't bring herself to touch the clothes. "Thank you," she said. "I don't want the clothes. I'd be most grateful if you'd just . . . burn them."

Lance tossed the contents of the box into the fire. "The case is officially closed, Mrs. Rader. Officials from the other countries that aided us in this investigation have been notified of the outcome. We are done."

"Thank you," she said, "for everything."

"All in the line of duty," he said. "Now, in a more personal vein, I want to know if you're absolutely certain about my taking official guardianship of Dulsie. Because I won't have her tossed back and forth according to your whims. Either she lives with me, or she doesn't. You can see her as much as you like, but she lives with me. Is that the way you want it?"

Nadine swallowed carefully and looked at him with firm eyes. "Yes, that's what I want."

"Are you going to tell me why?" he asked.

She looked away and her face tightened. "I already did. She's better off with you."

"It makes no sense to me, Nadine. Are you just going to spend the rest of your life completely alone?"

"Possibly."

"Possibly?" he echoed with cynicism. "Do you think that some magic solution to whatever you're struggling with is just going to jump out of a blue sky and bite you? If you can't take what I'm offering you now, what makes you think a better offer is going to come along?"

"I was under the impression that your offer was null and void, Captain. You told me that you would not live with this issue between us. And I don't know that it's possible to get rid of the issue."

"You're fooling yourself if you think that's true. We are capable of doing anything we set our minds to. If you choose to let the issue between us rule your life, then you are making the choice to be alone. But I wish you could see this situation from the outside for just a moment and gain some comprehension of what an absolute fool you are being. I love you, Nadine, and I know you love me. Anything else is workable, but only if you choose to work it out."

"I just don't know if that's possible," she said, looking away.

Lance felt a familiar frustration rise to a point where anger was creeping into him. His instincts were firm on knowing there was more to this than she was letting on. He just didn't know how to get her to talk about it. "I need to go," he said. "If you need anything, you know where to find me." He left the room before she could say another word. He was amazed at how he could love her so much and want to physically shake some sense into her at the same time.

Lance was grateful to have the following day be Sunday. He enjoyed a leisurely morning with Dulsie since church in the castle chapel didn't begin until noon. The bishop oversaw the meeting after doing an earlier one at the cathedral, which warranted the later time. He was about to shave and get ready to go when he heard a knock at the front door. It was so unlike the usual hard pounding he got when an officer was summoning him. Still, he wasn't prepared to open it and see Nadine.

"Good morning," she said with a bright smile that seemed somewhat forced.

"Good morning," he repeated, stunned. Why did she have to be so beautiful?

Nadine briefly took in his appearance and the confusion it stirred in her. The top few buttons of his shirt were unfastened and his braces hung around his hips. His face was unusually stubbled and his hair slightly mussed. She'd rarely seen him when he wasn't meticulously dressed and groomed, and she found the contrast intriguing. Seeing him now, she wondered how she could ever resign herself to live without him. But it was for the best. She would far prefer to preserve in her memory the tender moments they had shared, rather than adding more ugliness to the situation until it outweighed the good completely.

"I . . . thought I might go to church with the two of you . . . if that's all right."

"Of course," he said and motioned her inside.

"I know I'm early, but . . . I didn't want to miss you and . . . perhaps I could do Dulsie's hair."

"That would be good," he said. "I can brush it well enough, but I have to let Abbi or the nannies do anything more." He motioned toward the stairs. "She's upstairs in her room. Make yourself at home while I finish getting ready."

"Thank you," she said in a voice that was friendly and polite, but it was a voice she would use with any person of acquaintance.

While Lance shaved and got into his dress uniform, he could hear Nadine and Dulsie talking and laughing in the other room. *This is the way it should be all the time,* he thought and tried to ignore his heartache in wondering if it ever would be. Oh, how he missed her! Not just being with her, but the warmth they had shared, the tender conversation, the affection. How he longed to just take her in his arms and kiss her! But he had to wonder if their affection of the past was all they would ever share.

When he was ready, he appeared in the doorway to Dulsie's room to see them sitting on the edge of the bed, looking at a picture book. Dulsie's hair was in two long braids that hung over her shoulders.

"Shall we go?" he asked.

"Don't you look nice," Nadine said with a smile. He was grateful for the lack of animosity between them, but the arrangement just felt so wrong.

They each held one of Dulsie's hands as they crossed the courtyard and entered the castle chapel. Nadine was greeted by many who expressed their gratitude at seeing her alive and well. She accepted their wishes graciously, but Lance sensed something in her countenance that seemed disbelieving, perhaps ashamed. It was almost as if she didn't agree with them. But how could she possibly *not* wish to be alive and well? He was left with an uneasiness that made him wonder what else Albert Crider might have done—or said—that she hadn't told him. Something had changed in her since the abduction. He simply didn't know how to find out what it was, or what he might do about it.

Dulsie sat between them through the service. Afterward they were approached by Abbi and Cameron, who was holding little Erich. "You must come and have dinner with us," Abbi said.

"Oh, thank you," Nadine said, "but I'm really not feeling up to it. I should go. But I'll see you in the morning." She quickly told Dulsie goodbye and said nothing to Lance before she hurried away.

"Well," Abbi said, looking after her as she departed, "I'm certain she needs some time to adjust after such an ordeal."

"I'm certain she does," Lance said and avoided any further comment.

"But *you* will join us for dinner, won't you, Captain?" Abbi went on. "Georg and Han will be there too, of course."

"We'd love to," he said, lifting Dulsie into his arms. The child said nothing, but he noted her confused expression, certain she was as baffled as he by her mother's behavior.

The remainder of the day was relatively pleasant, barring Georg's usual somber mood with Elsa's absence and Lance's constant wondering over Nadine's behavior. That evening he was tempted to go and visit her, but he simply didn't have the fortitude. He knew he'd get no more understanding than he already had. And he'd likely end up arguing with her. So, he spent the time with Dulsie, praying that he could somehow compensate for the way she was losing her mother.

Nadine was grateful for the books she'd been given by a number of people she didn't even know. Reading every waking minute kept her thoughts distracted from the horror of her experience with Albert Crider, and the reality of what her future would be like from now on.

The following morning she arrived at the castle early, knowing there was much work to be done in order to follow through on the Christmas charity projects and to be ready for the socials. She'd lost a great deal of time through her ordeal and was determined to make up for it. Working hard would keep her as distracted as reading did in her free time. There was only one matter of concern that she had to deal with, and she figured the sooner she got it out of the way the better. She wanted to tell Abbi about the decision she'd come to before Lance did—if he hadn't already. Either way, Abbi had been a good friend to Nadine, and she felt that Abbi should hear it from her.

As they set to work, Abbi asked how she was doing and their conversation progressed with no mention of Lance. When the moment seemed right, Nadine just came out and said, "I'm giving Lance custody of Dulsie."

"What in the name of heaven for?" Abbi countered, so completely astonished that it took Nadine off guard. At least she didn't have to wonder if Lance had told her. He'd obviously said nothing.

Nadine answered calmly. "I just feel that she's better off with him. They're happy together. I don't want to uproot her again."

"Nadine," Abbi said in the same dumbfounded tone that Lance had used when she'd told him what she wanted. "I don't understand. Dulsie is your daughter."

"I know, Abbi. I know it sounds strange, but . . . it's difficult to explain. It's complicated. I just believe it's better this way. I wonder if my feelings for Lance were simply for some bigger purpose; that maybe it was about Dulsie all along so that she would have the opportunity to be raised in a better situation."

"I don't believe that for a minute," Abbi said, almost angry. "I know how you feel for him, and him for you. Surely you can overcome your differences enough to—"

"This is not just about our differences, Abbi. I don't expect you to understand. I just wanted you to know the decision I've come to. I need your support in helping with—"

"Well, I *don't* understand, Nadine. And how can I support you if I don't understand? Why, Nadine? You're not making any sense. Give me an answer that makes sense, and I will stand by you, whether I agree with you or not. But you are not the same woman you were before that fiend abducted you. And I think you need to talk about what happened. I sense a heavy burden, and you're a fool if you believe that any human being can carry such a burden alone and not completely destroy their own life. And everyone who loves you will be affected. Now, please tell me." Nadine said nothing and she added firmly, "I'm not going anywhere until you do."

Nadine searched the intensity of Abbi's eyes and felt certain she meant it. In moments such as this it was easy for Nadine to see why this woman was the Duchess of Horstberg. And in a way, Nadine felt some relief at Abbi's insistence. In the deepest part of herself, she ached to share her burden, but her fear of the repercussions had been stronger than her desire to talk about it. Abbi's coercion took the decision out of her hands.

Nadine sighed and searched for the right words to begin. "When Albert Crider first set his sights on me, I was polite. He was kind. He bought me a meal. We talked. I told him I was married and waiting for my husband to send for me. He offered to keep me company as a friend in the meantime. Then his attention became far too friendly, and I had to become assertive and tell him I wasn't interested. When time passed and Nikolaus didn't send for me, he became a nuisance, pestering me and insisting that I couldn't possibly be married; no man would go so long without sending for his wife. I told him there were extenuating circumstances that he didn't understand." She took a deep breath. "When I was . . . with him . . . last week, he . . . well, it's clear to me now that he actually . . . broke into my rooms and apparently he found my marriage certificate. It seems he actually came to Horstberg, searching out Nikolaus du Woernig, because his name and the location of the marriage were on the certificate."

"Good heavens," Abbi said, her alarm apparent. "So, he knew a whole lot more about the situation than we ever imagined."

"Precisely. As far as I can figure, he was very good at digging up information. Of course, anyone in Horstberg would know the name Nikolaus du Woernig. And Albert told me that when he realized Nikolaus was dead, he knew I would be a very rich widow, which apparently added to his incentive. Of course, I didn't know Nikolaus was dead, and neither of us knew the marriage wasn't valid. I also doubt it would be difficult to find out that Nikolaus wasn't well liked. And Albert said that he knows how to find the right kind of people to tell him the right kind of information." She shuddered as she recalled his telling her these things. "Knowing Nikolaus was attracted to a certain kind of people, Albert said that he went to a certain kind of pub and searched out those kind of people."

"Darkness is attracted to darkness," Abbi said. "And of course, we're well aware that there are some who remain quietly loyal to Nikolaus, who have some distorted belief that if he had lived and remained on the throne, life would somehow be more in their favor. They are likely the people that Nikolaus bought drinks for and with whom he shared his vulgar lifestyle."

"No doubt," Nadine said.

"So Mr. Crider searched out these kinds of people, asked questions, and came in contact with people who had known Nikolaus."

"That's how it seems," Nadine said.

"And he told you all of this?" Abbi asked, astonished.

"In explicit detail," she said. "He talked almost constantly. If I started drifting to sleep, he would slap me."

"I can't even imagine how horrible it must have been," Abbi said, taking her hand. "Please go on."

"Well," Nadine looked down, "this is where it becomes difficult. You see . . . he discovered something that happened . . . years ago. Something that I thought only Nikolaus and my father and my father's partner knew about. And they are all dead. I never imagined that it would come to the surface again, and . . ." Her voice broke. "I never imagined the horrible repercussions of what I had done. But he knew all about it, in horrifying detail."

"What, Nadine?" Abbi asked gently. "What did he know?"

Tears came abruptly as Nadine arrived at the heart of the problem. She looked deeply at Abbi and tightened her grip. "I committed treason, Abbi. And he knew. Albert Crider knew. And if he knew, then somebody else out there knows, and it's only a matter of time before it comes to light and—"

"Wait," Abbi interrupted. "Nadine, what are you talking about? Slow down and tell me what you mean."

Nadine forced herself to breathe deeply. "It was something that happened with my father," she said. "I suspected at the time that the situation was not what it appeared to be, but I did what I felt I had to do in order to protect my father. I had no idea what the outcome would be. And now, all these years later, Albert Crider knew about it. He knew such details, and things that I hadn't known but I knew they were true because it made so much sense with what I *did* know."

Abbi remained calm in spite of a defined alarm in her eyes. "Maybe you should tell me exactly what it is you did, Nadine."

A horrible thought occurred to Nadine and she had to express it. "Perhaps it would be better if I didn't. What if your knowing caused trouble for you? You're the duchess. You wanted to know why I felt it would be better if Dulsie stayed with Lance. Well, that's the reason. I committed treason and it's only a matter of time before it comes to light. Can you imagine what that would do to Lance? To his career? His reputation? And it's better for Dulsie to be settled with him so that she won't have to go through losing me again."

Abbi remained thoughtful for more than a minute before she said, "Nadine, you can't carry a burden like this. You can't spend your life fearing that it will catch up with you."

"You're not going to tell Cameron, are you?"

"Not if you don't want me to," she said. "But I think *you* should. Come clean with it, Nadine. Surely it can't be that serious."

"Serious is relative," Nadine insisted. "What I did might not be such a big thing, but I did it knowingly defying authority, and the results were horrible."

"How do you know?" Abbi asked. "Are you taking Albert Crider's word for it?" Nadine couldn't answer, knowing how absurd such a concept sounded. But how could she explain the power his words had over her? "Listen to me, Nadine." Abbi leaned closer. "Think of Cameron and Georg and Lance as your friends. We'll sit down. We'll talk to them in complete confidentiality. They can advise you on what to do."

"And if what I did was illegal, are they not bound by the law to see that justice is met? How can I give them such information and not expect to go to prison?"

Abbi sighed. "If they really feel that way, I swear to you that I will personally see that you are allowed to leave the country and make a fresh start elsewhere and the matter will be dropped. If it's already been years, there's a good chance that the crime will be considered minimal and such drastic measures will not be necessary."

Nadine sighed. "Well, perhaps leaving the country would be the best thing, anyway."

"Talk to them first," Abbi pleaded. "I've grown accustomed to your friendship, Nadine. I don't want you to leave. Please. I will arrange it. I'll go with you."

Nadine sighed again. "I'll think about it," she said and Abbi nodded.

Silence fell between them and Nadine was relieved that lunchtime had arrived. She went to the nursery to have lunch with Dulsie, grateful that Lance didn't show up to do the same. After they had eaten and Dulsie had returned to her playing, Nadine took a stroll through long castle hallways, needing to let Abbi's plea settle into her. She wondered if following her advice would truly be the best thing. If she came clean and confessed, at least she would have nothing to fear. And then Lance would understand her reasons for doing what she had to do. Then, perhaps, they could each just get on with their lives.

Chapter Twenty-Nine
RELATIVE TREASON

*L*ance found his mind wandering to concern for Nadine as the meeting in the duke's office droned on. A knock at the door was a pleasant reprieve to the boring speech of one of the duke's advisors, and even more pleasant when he heard Abbi's voice say, "I'm in need of some assistance and wondered if I might have the captain accompany me for a short errand."

"Of course, my dear," Cameron said eagerly. Then to Lance, "I'll catch you up later, Captain."

"Thank you, Your Grace," Lance said, coming to his feet. "If you will excuse me, gentlemen."

Lance stepped out into the hall and closed the door. Once they were past earshot of the officers at the door, he said to Abbi, "I owe you a favor for that one. I thought he'd never stop talking."

Abbi laughed slightly. "Glad to help. But you might prefer such a boring speech when I tell you what I *really* need."

"What?" he asked, mildly alarmed.

"I need to talk to you about Nadine," she said, "privately."

Lance motioned toward an open doorway to one of the parlors along the main hall. They slipped inside and he closed the door.

"The servants will think we're having an affair," he said.

"They've got to have something to talk about," she replied nonchalantly.

Lance stoked up the coals in the grate and added some wood to the fire before he sat down across from Abbi, who already had her feet up on the sofa where she sat.

"This is confidential," she said. "I don't want Nadine to know I told you, but honestly, I feel that you need to know. I'm going with my instincts on this."

"I've always trusted your instincts, my dear," he said. "I'll not say a word. Go on."

"I believe I understand why Nadine wants you to raise Dulsie."

"How did you know she did?"

"She told me, of course."

"All right, why?" he asked sharply.

"It's likely the same reason she feels it would be better if she didn't become your wife."

"Why?" he asked, his voice deep and impatient.

"She committed treason."

"What?" he asked with a breathy laugh.

"She doesn't want her crimes of the past to creep up and ruin your life, your reputation, your career. And she doesn't want Dulsie subjected once again to being taken from her mother when she's arrested and tried and possibly executed. I truly doubt that it's as serious as all that, but it is the reason behind her behavior."

"That's absurd," he insisted. "Treason? Nadine?"

"That's what she tells me."

"And what exactly did she do?" he demanded.

"She was vague on that, but she seems to believe it was rather serious."

"So, what are you saying? That all along she knew she was guilty of treason and . . . what? Did she just expect it to magically go away?"

"No, Lance. But tell me, what *does* a Captain of the Guard do if he discovers that the woman he loves is guilty of treason? What if she were his wife? Do you think perhaps her concerns are valid? She's had some fairly accurate experience in regard to the fact that you have to abide by the law no matter what your personal relationships might entail. How would such a thing affect your life? Your career?"

Lance met Abbi's eyes. He had nothing to say. He simply didn't have any answers. Unable to believe what he was hearing, Lance said, "Surely there must be some mistake, some reasonable explanation."

"From what she told me and a little intuition," Abbi said, "I think that whatever she did, she did in innocence. Or she simply didn't understand that what she was doing actually fell under the category of treason. *Or,* perhaps she did it to protect someone she loved."

"Who?" he asked more quietly.

"I'm just guessing, but . . . she did say something about her father." Abbi's eyes softened on him as she added, "You once told me that you'd realized a person would do just about anything to protect someone they love. At the time, you were talking about protecting me."

Lance sighed and looked down. "Yes, I believe I was."

"And at the time, *I* was guilty of treason." He snapped his head up and she added, "Was I not?" He said nothing. "I was aiding and harboring an exiled criminal. And *you* lied to military personnel in order to protect me."

"Yes, I did," he said, his voice tinged with anger. "So, what's your point?"

"My point is that treason is a relative crime. You know this already, but let me remind you. Treason is a matter of timing. One day Cameron and Georg were revolutionary rebels, seeking to over-throw the crown and overtake the country. The next day they were in charge. One day anyone who was caught supporting them would have been shot, the next, they were celebrated as heroes. According to the duke, treason is determined according to a person's intent and actions based upon the betterment of the country."

"So do you think that whatever Nadine did was for the better-ment of the country?"

"I have no idea," Abbi said. "I'm simply trying to help you see some perspective before this gets all misconstrued and magnified."

Lance sighed. "And what brought this up all of a sudden? Do you think this has been an underlying part of her reluctance to marry me all along?"

"No," she said and Lance's eyes widened. "According to what she tells me, Albert Crider brought this up."

"What?" Lance practically shouted, but Abbi remained calm.

"She told me that something happened many years ago, and she thought that no one knew about it who was still living. But Mr. Crider told her that he'd seen her marriage certificate and went searching for Nikolaus du Woernig of Horstberg. Apparently he knew a lot more about Nadine and the situation here than we had ever realized. And while he was digging for information about Nikolaus, someone told him about this incident. I get the impression that he expounded on repercussions of what she did. She believes that if *he* found out, someone else will find out eventually, and it will end up hurting you and Dulsie. She's trying to protect the two of you." She paused and added, "A person would do just about anything to protect someone they love."

Lance squeezed his eyes closed and sighed. *Treason.* After all they had gone through, all that had come between them, all they had survived, how could something so ugly as treason be thrown into the mixture? Still, one point stood out to him. "If Albert Crider stirred this up, I'm going to guess that it's not nearly as bad as she seems to think it is."

Abbi smiled. "My thoughts exactly. I encouraged her to come clean. I told her I would arrange for her to discuss the incident with Cameron and Georg—and you. That the discussion would be as friends, completely confidential, and that the three of you could advise her on what to do. I told her if you truly deemed that it was severe and punishable, that I would help her leave the country."

"That sounds reasonable," he said while the thought of her leaving tore his heart out. But then, she was absent emotionally anyway—at least to him. "What did she say?"

"She's going to think about it. And like I said, I don't want her to know we talked—not yet at least. But I thought you should be prepared and that you should have some time to think about it."

"I appreciate that . . . Your Grace." He sighed and added, "You know, I was supposed to be getting married later this week."

"I know," she said with sadness. "Personally, I'm still holding out for a miracle."

Lance just sighed again and said, "I think I've been given my fair share of miracles already."

"You mustn't give up hope, Lance," she said gently. "Even if the marriage doesn't occur when you wanted it to, there's still a chance that the two of you will have a future together." She smiled, albeit sadly, and said again, "You mustn't give up hope."

He wanted to believe there was reason to have hope, and in his heart he'd never stopped praying that they might end up together.

But at the moment he felt just plain weary. And now, after everything else, he had to contend with treason. It was such an ugly word.

Lance went to his office and attempted to focus enough to accomplish what needed his attention. Early afternoon he received a message that the duke wanted to see him. He entered Cameron's office to find only him and Georg there.

"Thank you for coming, Captain," Cameron said. "Apparently Mrs. Rader wants to speak with us about something. She should be here any minute."

"I see," Lance said, pretending ignorance.

"I assume it has something to do with her recent ordeal," Cameron added.

"Perhaps," Lance said and took his usual seat just as the door came open and Nadine entered with Abbi at her side. The men all stood until the ladies were seated and typical greetings were exchanged, then they sat back down.

"So," Cameron said to Nadine, "what can we do for you?"

Lance noticed the way she wrung her hands. She was visibly nervous. Considering what he knew, he could well imagine. "This is . . . difficult for me," she said. "I ask for your patience."

"Of course," Cameron said.

"Take your time," Georg added and she offered a forced smile.

"Uh . . ." she began and cleared her throat, "I've committed treason, Your Grace . . . some years ago."

Nadine checked the expressions of the men in the room and found them unreadable. She was surprised to hear Cameron chuckle and say, "Well, perhaps those of us here should start a club or something."

Nadine's confusion buffered her alarm. "I don't understand."

Cameron went on lightly. "Abbi, you could be the president. Let's see, what was it you did exactly?"

"Aiding and harboring an exiled criminal," she said. "A criminal who was most definitely very busy with treasonous activities."

"That would be me," Cameron said proudly. "Although, Georg was very busy helping me with those treasonous activities. What would you say our crimes were, Georg?"

"Oh, the list is awfully long," Georg said. "I don't think we have time. But my favorite is gathering a revolutionary force to overthrow the crown."

"That's my favorite, too," Cameron said. "And what about you, Captain?"

Lance resisted breaking into a broad grin. He couldn't begin to express his appreciation to Cameron for putting some perspective on this matter, straight up front. He eagerly went along, admitting readily, "I deliberately misled military personnel to lure them away from the treasonous actions of the woman who was guilty of aiding and harboring an exiled criminal. And then I was definitely in on overthrowing the crown."

"You definitely were," Georg said, as if it was a matter of great pride.

"This is all very amusing," Nadine said, "but I fail to see how it relates to what I have to say."

"Well, we won't know until you tell us exactly what you did, Mrs. Rader," Cameron said. "The point I'm trying to make is that treason is relative. This is a conversation we've had amongst ourselves many times. I personally weigh an act of treason greatly on the intent. Was the act for the betterment of the country or was it otherwise? Treason becomes a tricky word when you have a selfish tyrant at the helm of a country. But in *my* country, the definition of treason is very clear. So, why don't you tell us exactly what you did, Mrs. Rader, and we can talk about it."

"Very well," she said. "Years ago, during the time when I was . . . I mean when I believed I was married to Nikolaus, an incident occurred that caused me great concern at the time. As with many things in life, my concern over it dissipated with time, and I had assumed that it was over and forgotten. I had believed that the only people who were aware of it were dead. But I have recently realized that's not the case. I wish to bring the matter to your attention now before it comes to your ears through other sources."

"May I ask," Georg said, "what happened recently to bring this back up?"

"Albert Crider was aware of it," she said straightly. Georg looked surprised and exchanged a concerned glance with Cameron. "And if someone was aware of it enough to tell him, then that someone is still out there, and it's only a matter of time before it comes out. Abbi suggested that it would be better for me to tell you myself, rather than fear having it come forward by other means."

"Go on," Cameron said.

Nadine repeated what she had told Abbi about Crider coming to Horstberg, looking for information regarding Nikolaus, and how he had learned that there had been a connection to her father. She explained that her father had been very good to her, and their relationship had been positive for the most part, but that she had suspected he was not completely ethical in his business dealings.

"And what business was your father in?" Georg asked.

"He ran a lumber mill, along with his partner, a Mr. Brunsen. I kept books for the company for a couple of years before my father died. I was eighteen when my father became friendly with Nikolaus. I believe they met at a pub and started drinking together, something they were both very good at. You know about my relationship with Nikolaus, so I will avoid that topic. During this time my father told me that he was concerned about some things that Mr. Brunsen was involved with—things that hinted at treason. I'd never really liked Mr. Brunsen, but I couldn't fathom him being involved with political matters. It just didn't seem like something that would interest him. I didn't give it much thought beyond that. One day, out of the blue, Nikolaus and my father sat me down and explained that there was someone high up in the government who worked closely with Nikolaus who was involved in many treasonous activities and causing a great deal of trouble for Nikolaus. They said this man was shrewd and clever and always managed to avoid being implicated, and if Nikolaus was to succeed as a ruler, he needed to find a way to be rid of this man and see justice met. Of course, at the time I had no idea what kind of ruler Nikolaus was. I was naive and gullible. I believed everything he told me. He could be very convincing."

"That he could," Abbi said and the men made noises of agreement.

"Nikolaus told me that he had papers in his possession that would provide valid evidence against this man, but if the papers came from him, it would appear too suspicious. He asked me to claim that the papers had been inadvertently left at the mill by a customer, that I wasn't sure who the customer was, but I thought the authorities should see them, and so I was turning them in. I should say that I had barely glanced at them and felt that I should do my patriotic duty. I agreed to do it, albeit reluctantly. I didn't feel good about it, but I wanted to please Nikolaus, and my father was backing him so eagerly that I knew if I didn't do it, he would be displeased."

"So you delivered the papers?" Cameron asked. "Is this what you are considering treason? Oh, my dear Nadine. You can hardly—"

"You don't understand," Nadine interrupted. "I *didn't* deliver them. I just couldn't feel good about it. So I hid them instead, and I told Nikolaus I had given them to an officer, but I didn't know his name. I figured that he would believe the officer had lost or destroyed them, and that's why nothing ever came of it. He wouldn't know which officer to blame and it would end there. But Mr. Crider told me that it was because of my not getting the papers into the right hands that the—"

"Wait," Cameron said, "how would anyone have known that you didn't turn them in?"

"I don't know. Maybe I was followed enough to know that I never made contact with an officer. I only know that Mr. Crider knew the papers had never made it to their intended destination and that someone out there who is a loyal follower of Nikolaus du Woernig knows that. He said that because of my neglect in doing so, Mr. Brunsen's death, as well as my father's, were directly related, and that Nikolaus's eventual fall occurred because I had willfully disobeyed the duke's orders, and that was considered treason."

Nadine's heart beat painfully hard while she looked into Cameron's eyes, waiting for a response. He finally sighed loudly and turned to look at Georg, then Lance. "Well, he's good, don't you think, gentlemen?"

"Indeed," Georg said and Lance made a noise of disgust.

"I don't understand," Nadine said.

"Albert Crider was manipulating you, Nadine. He was playing with your mind, trying to twist your thoughts and beliefs."

"But . . . why?" Nadine asked.

Georg said, "We know he didn't intend to let you go, but perhaps he had somewhat of a back-up plan in case that happened. If, by chance, you got away from him, he would still have some power over your life if he led you to believe that certain things were true. May I ask what else he said in relation to this supposed treason you committed? Did he say something about how it might affect your life?"

"He did, actually," Nadine said and her heart quickened. "He said that . . ." She glanced hesitantly at Lance but he gave her a subtle nod of encouragement and she felt it was just as well that he heard it here, which would save her from having to explain later. "He talked about how . . . it would be for the Captain of the Guard to . . . discover that the woman he was going to marry was guilty of treason and what it would do to his reputation and his career."

Lance snarled quietly, "Forgive me for saying that I am glad to know this man is rotting in hell right now. And did he also imply that you would go back to prison? Go before a firing squad?"

Nadine nodded as pieces of the picture settled into her, though some of it was still puzzling. As if the duke sensed her confusion, he said gently, "Allow me to tell you how I see this. I don't know what Mr. Brunsen or your father did or what happened to them. You can tell me that in a minute. I do know that refusing to deliver something for the duke can in no stretch of the imagination be deemed as treason. If you were a military officer serving under the duke and you refused to follow through on his orders, you could serve some time in the keep or be expelled from the force, but it would not constitute treason by any means, no matter what the results might have been. Do you hear what I'm saying?"

A quiet sob jumped out of Nadine's throat before she could hold it back. Lance let out a deep sigh of relief and exchanged a discreet glance with Abbi.

"Unless you have something else to confess, Nadine, then this is not an issue. I don't know how or where Mr. Crider got his information, but I'd say he very cleverly made a mountain out of a molehill. For the sake of clarification, I would like to hear whatever you know concerning your father and Mr. Brunsen. If gossip ever does come to my ears concerning the matter, I will already have heard your side of the story."

"Well," Nadine said, feeling more relaxed now, "all I know is that Mr. Brunsen was convicted of treason. I have no idea of what or how. He was executed and all of his property confiscated. I felt especially concerned when my father suddenly ended up with extra money soon thereafter, but not many days later he was robbed on his way home from town one night and shot in the process. After his death, evidence came forward that he too was guilty of treason, and his property was confiscated as well, which left me with nothing. But Nikolaus assured me that he would take care of me. That was about the time I discovered that I was pregnant, and he sent me away. You know the rest of the story."

"Indeed we do," Cameron said. "Now let me explain something else to you. When I took back my country, one of the many messes I had to clean up was the result of circumstances like you just described. It was apparently one of Nikolaus's games to frame people for treason, have them executed, confiscate their property for his own gain, and leave the families homeless."

"That's horrible," Nadine said, vaguely recalling that Lance had mentioned something to that effect when she'd first told him about her father.

"Yes, it is. Once I took over, one of our first matters of business was to see that these people had their needs met and were given an opportunity to get back what they had lost. Unfortunately, we could not bring back the people who had been needlessly killed. But it seems that Mr. Brunsen could have been a victim of this very thing. And while it appears that your father may have been consorting with Nikolaus on this and received some compensation, obviously he was a victim in the end as well."

"It would seem so," Nadine said, continually appalled at the kind of man Nikolaus was.

"Considering Nikolaus's history," Cameron said, "and all that was going on in Horstberg at the time, I would strongly suspect that whatever Nikolaus asked you to deliver was not valid. He was likely trying to implicate someone innocent who was making it difficult for him to pursue his vulgar lifestyle. Therefore, your not delivering the papers was for the betterment of the country. The case rests."

"Nadine," Georg said, leaning forward in his chair, "you said you hid the papers you were given to deliver. Did you ever go back for them?"

"No."

"Were they well hidden?"

"I believe so," she said.

"What I'm wondering is . . . if they might still be where you left them. Can you perhaps remember well enough to tell some officers who could try and retrieve them for us?" He leaned back again. "I can't help being curious as to who Nikolaus was trying to implicate and exactly how he was intending to go about it. Most of our advisory committee was in place under him and gladly made the change when Cameron took over. If papers are out there that could be falsely incriminating, it would be better to find and destroy them."

"Agreed," Cameron said.

Georg brought in the officers outside the door and Nadine told them about a place in the basement of the house next to the mill her father had owned, which mill was now under new ownership. They were given a search warrant signed by the duke and were quickly off.

Lance came to his feet the moment they were gone and held out a hand toward Nadine. "Would you walk with me for a few minutes while we're waiting?" he asked.

She looked at him with hesitance then slipped her hand into his and came to her feet. They stepped out into the hall and moved in the direction of the main entrance at a slow pace. He pressed her hand over his arm and held it there, but nothing was said for several minutes.

"So that's it," he finally said. "You were going to resign yourself to these contrived charges of treason, give your daughter to me, sentence yourself to living alone and sentence me to life without you. And you weren't even going to tell me why?"

Nadine couldn't find any valid argument. She simply said, "You must forgive me on that count. He was very convincing."

"I'm certain he was. Having you tied up and believing he would kill you surely added to his charisma." His voice was subtly sarcastic. "Still, I would hope that, in spite of the challenges between us, you could trust me enough to tell me what the problem was. Or is trust still one of the challenges between us?"

Nadine looked up at him, marveling at the overt evidence in his expression that he still loved her. After all she had put him through, his love was readily evident. Even so, she knew that challenges existed between them, and in spite of certain misunderstandings having been cleared up, she needed time to fully consider where she stood and what was best for all of them. The only answer she could give him was, "I'm not certain, Lance. I need some time."

He nodded but said nothing, and they walked on in silence. Reaching the end of what Nadine considered a ridiculously long hall, they turned and walked back while she forced some conversation regarding Dulsie's comical antics, if only to fill the silence. They returned to the duke's office to find Abbi sitting with her bare feet in Cameron's lap while he rubbed them for her. Georg was looking over some paperwork at one end of Cameron's huge desk.

"I was thinking," Georg said, "it's perhaps too bad we hadn't known about this before Crider was executed. I have a few unanswered questions that I wonder if he might have been able to answer."

"He likely wouldn't have, even if he knew," Nadine said scornfully.

"What unanswered questions?" Cameron asked.

"Like who exactly told him all of this. Is there really someone out there who knows details of Nikolaus's antics? Is Crider's involvement really what he led Nadine to believe it was? Or is there more to it than that?"

"We will likely never know," Cameron said.

"Mrs. Brunsen might know something," Nadine suggested, "if she is still living."

"So she might," Georg said, seeming to like the idea. Before any more could be said, the officers returned. A large, thick, very dirty envelope was placed on the desk as one of them reported, "Right where Mrs. Rader said it would be, under the stone in the corner of the basement floor."

"Thank you," Lance said. "Good work."

The officers left the room and closed the door.

"Captain, would you do the honor?" Cameron said, as if the matter were amusing.

"Of course," Lance said and leaned forward to pick up the envelope. He leaned back in his chair and crossed his ankle over his knee. He broke the seal and found another envelope inside that already had the seal broken. "Presumably," he said, "this was to appear that Nadine had broken the seal, looked at what was inside, and put it into a new envelope and resealed it."

"That's right," Nadine said.

Lance pulled out several sheets of paper that were folded in half together. He unfolded them to see that they were upside down, and turned them around, reminded of the moment he'd opened the envelope that had changed his life with the realization that his birth had not been what he'd believed it to be. It was a moment he'd never forget, and it had happened in this very room; he'd been sitting in this very chair. Initially, he credited the memory for making his heart quicken. Then his eyes focused on what he was looking at, and he felt a little queasy. He lifted the first page to look at the next, and the next, and a tangible sickness began to smolder inside of him. He couldn't believe it.

Nadine watched Lance closely, waiting for a reaction. She wasn't certain what she'd expected, but she felt decidedly alarmed when his hands began to shake.

"What is it?" Cameron asked with an alarm that made it clear he'd noticed Lance's reaction.

Lance looked up at Cameron, his eyes expressing shock and horror. "It's me," he murmured.

"I don't understand," Abbi said.

Lance flipped through the pages almost frantically. "My name is all over this. Letters, documents with my signature, in my hand-writing. But I didn't write these; I've never seen them before in my life."

"Good heavens," Abbi said breathlessly. Nadine said nothing. As the implication began to settle in, she felt rather shaky herself.

Lance's voice picked up an angry edge as he said to Cameron, "The fiend was trying to get me executed a couple of years before you came back. When I think of all the times he stood beside me and called me his friend, of the way he played on that friendship to talk me into things that I didn't agree with, how he talked about loyalty and allegiance. Was there no limit to the depths of evil this man would go to?"

Cameron stood long enough to reach over and grab the papers from Lance's hand. He put on his glasses and looked over them quickly, then he tossed them into the fire. "There," he said firmly. "Let's be grateful we found and destroyed them."

"Oh, I think I'm feeling rather queasy," Abbi said, putting a hand over her belly.

"It must be contagious," Georg said. "When I think of the chain

of events that could have played out so differently if Lance had not been here . . . I can't even think about it without feeling sick."

"My thoughts exactly," Cameron said with a severity that caught Nadine's attention more fully. She realized there were deeper ramifications here than simply the fact that Lance could have lost his life many years ago. "If Lance had not been affiliated with Abbi, he would not have been there to protect her from the Guard when they connected her to me. She very well could have faced charges of treason for that alone."

"And," Georg interjected, "if Lance had not been there to marry Abbi, there would have been no forum for your reclamation. And he purposely misled the Guard's attention so that it could all come together."

"No back-up plan," Cameron said, giving Lance a long gaze that seemed to imply some secret they shared. And Lance's eyes made it clear that he understood. "And it was Lance that kept an eye on Nikolaus after the reclamation."

"And it was Lance who saved my life that night," Abbi said, her eyes turning to Nadine. She watched tears spill down the duchess's face as she said, "It would seem you saved Horstberg, my dear, long before any of us knew the events that would free her of Nikolaus's tyranny."

"I can't believe it," Lance muttered, shaking his head. "I feel as if . . . I've just found out that I'm not really supposed to be alive, that I should have died several years ago. I can't believe he would do that to me."

"Why do you suppose he didn't keep trying after his first attempt failed?" Georg asked.

Lance thought about that for a minute. "I remember reaching a point where I . . . well, I think I instinctively knew that he would do whatever he pleased regardless of anything I said or did, and if I kept my mouth shut I could quietly accomplish more good by remaining in my position. Perhaps that shift in attitude saved me." He shook his head again. "I just can't believe he would do that."

"Let's be grateful that his plan was foiled," Abbi said.

"Amazing, though," Georg said. "If Nadine had not been abducted, would the matter have ever come to light? What if someone had inadvertently come across those papers? I always find it fascinating how God pieces the puzzles of our lives together."

Lance glanced around the room and suddenly felt as if the walls would close in on him. He felt angry and stunned and unable to think. "I need to go," he said, erupting to his feet.

"Where are you going?" Cameron asked, sounding concerned.

"I don't know. I just . . . need to be alone; I need some time." He hurried out of the room before he could be questioned any further.

Chapter Thirty

RECONCILIATION

With each hurried footstep, Lance felt the anger tightening in his chest. He found himself in the castle chapel and slumped onto a pew, pressing his head to the back of the pew in front of him, grateful to be alone. Thoughts of Nikolaus consumed him, threatening to eat him alive from the inside out. And mingled into them were thoughts of Albert Crider. Sporadic memories jumped in and out of his mind, adding to his confusion and anger. But the strongest memories were those of killing Nikolaus and giving the order for Albert Crider to die. The feelings associated with both were the same. He had felt so consumed with anger that there had been momentary pleasure in seeing them die. He wondered what kind of man he had become to feel that way, and while he longed to be rid of such feelings and put both episodes behind him, the bitterness possessing him now was too intense to allow him to believe that it could ever relent and leave him in peace.

Lance heard the door open behind him and booted feet on the stone floor. He kept his eyes closed as if in prayer, wanting to remain obscure to whoever else might have come here seeking solitude. When he heard someone sit directly next to him, he opened his eyes to see Cameron at his side.

"I know you said you wanted to be alone, but I had a feeling that you didn't really mean it."

"What? Are you psychic now too? You spend far too much time with that wife of yours."

Cameron chuckled. "No, actually, I do not spend nearly enough time with that wife of mine. And I could never hope to gain even half of the insight and intuition that she possesses. I simply thought you might do better to talk it through, as opposed to letting it stew and simmer inside of you. Trust me when I tell you that having no one to talk to can most definitely distort the problem." He sighed. "Three years of complete solitude made me appreciate the simple gift of a listening ear."

"I imagine it would," Lance said.

"So, I'm listening."

Lance said nothing and Cameron added, "You're obviously angry and upset."

"Obviously," Lance said with subtle sarcasm. "Your brother's lack of moral fiber continually amazes me. I find it difficult to believe that any human being could be so ruthless and unfeeling."

"I find it difficult to believe, myself," Cameron said. "But I'm not going to let you forget that he's *your* brother, too." Lance groaned and was amazed to hear Cameron chuckle. "Oh, to share such a burden!" he said dramatically. "To not be the only man who has to claim Nikolaus du Woernig as my brother!" He chuckled again then added, "Seriously, Lance, whether or not we shared the same blood, there is no other man who could fully understand the deep hurt and betrayal that Nikolaus inflicted. He took my birthright, my country, my father's affection, and he twisted it all into a tangled mess. And he killed my wife, who was also your sister. If I'd not escaped from prison, Lance, I would have faced a firing squad innocently. And what would have become of Horstberg? When I look at what happened to her in four years' time, I can't even imagine the destruction that could have taken place had his reign gone on and on. God's hand is readily evident in putting all the pieces back together, but I want you to know that putting the pieces together on the inside have not been so easy."

"I'm listening," Lance said when he hesitated.

"*I* was supposed to be listening," Cameron said, mimicking a spoiled child. They both chuckled before Cameron became serious again. "You are well aware of the hard work that's gone into getting this country back on its feet. I've used the analogy many times, and it applies, that it's as if a horrible storm swept through our country, leaving great devastation in its wake. I don't have to tell you that there were people homeless and starving while Nikolaus freely spent the money that he had often taken directly away from them. It's been a long and grueling job to give these people back the security he stole. And then there are the women with broken hearts, betrayed and left to fend for themselves. Women like Nadine. And children like Dulsie. We'll probably never know how many there really are. I know you knew all of that. You've been at my side through much of what's needed to be done. But I don't know if I ever told you how difficult it is for me to look into the eyes of such people and know that my own brother did this to them. He shares my name, my blood, and he crushed the people of Horstberg beneath the heel of his boot, laughing as he did so. He killed my wife and framed me for the crime, made it clear I would not get a fair trial, and left me to be beaten by one of his thugs. And there is Abbi. My sweet Abbi. You were there. You know how he dragged her out of her bed, defiled and abused her, threatened her life—and threatened to finish what he'd started and complete his violation of her. And on top of all that, I know in my heart that our father favored him above me. And he was not subtle in his preferences. I can't begin to tell you how many times I have stopped to think about it, and I have *boiled* inside. Even after his death—or perhaps especially after his death—when I had realized the full extent of what he'd done, it would consume my thoughts until I would practically make myself sick. It was Abbi who finally helped me understand that it was up to *me* to forgive Nikolaus. It was me carrying the burden, and I would carry it as long as I allowed myself to. So . . . it took some time, but not as long as I thought it would. And I just . . . gave that burden to God."

Lance felt a little stunned. "And you don't feel angry with him anymore?"

"Well," Cameron chuckled, "I have moments. Sometimes when something new comes up, or something reminds me of an old issue, I'll feel some anger creeping in. But I just stop and remind myself that I have forgiven him. It's in the past. I already gave that burden away, and the feelings relent." Cameron leaned closer and his voice lowered intently. "He was an indecent, deplorable human being, and I refuse to give him any power over me by allowing the hurt he inflicted to keep hurting me."

Lance felt a brisk chill rush over his back in response to Cameron's words, combined with the conviction in his eyes. Was that the answer for him? Was that why he'd continued to struggle with his memories and the feelings associated with them? In the midst of his thoughts, Cameron added, "You need to forgive him, Lance, and let go. And you also need to forgive yourself for killing him. You did the right thing. You did what I would have done if I had been in a position to do it."

"I know that," he said. "In my heart I know that, but there are moments when something inside of me isn't so sure. He would have gone before a firing squad within hours, and I wish sometimes that it would have worked out that way."

"He had a gun at Abbi's head, Lance. We've talked this through many times. You just have to forgive him—and yourself—and let it go."

Lance inhaled Cameron's words and had to admit, "I'm sure you're right. And I guess that means I need to forgive Albert Crider, too."

"Yes, you do. And I'm not going to tell you that such a thing is easy. It might take some time. But justice has been met, both with him and with Nikolaus. Undoing the damage takes longer, but they have both given their lives for their crimes. The rest is in God's hands. And you must reconcile this with Him, and within yourself. You will be able to help Nadine heal more effectively if *you* are not harboring anger toward the man who caused her so much grief."

"Both of them," Lance said.

"Yes, both of them."

Lance sighed. "I'm not sure Nadine is going to allow me to help her do anything. Now that she knows she's not guilty of treason, I believe she'll take Dulsie—as she should, but . . ."

"She's still holding onto that lack of trust?" Cameron's concern was evident.

"To be quite honest, I don't know. I only know there is a barrier between us, and I don't know how to be rid of it. A barrier put there initially by Nikolaus, I might add. Even in death he comes between me and the woman I love."

"Well," Cameron said, "I don't have all the answers, but I firmly believe if you can let go of your own hard feelings for Nikolaus, it could very well go a long way toward healing the rift between you and Nadine. It certainly can't hurt any."

"No, I'm certain it can't."

"Is there anything else you want to talk about?" Cameron asked and Lance felt freshly amazed at the depth of commitment he'd received from him through many aspects of this ordeal.

"No . . . thank you, Cameron. Your friendship is appreciated more than you could possibly know."

"Well, I'd like to say that I'm quite stunned by the ironies of what we discovered today."

Lance blew out a harsh breath. "Yes, I am as well." He shook his head. "I can't even imagine where we would all be if . . . well, I would be dead."

"And where any of the rest of us would be is equally horrible—too horrible too ponder. It's just one more piece of evidence that God has been with us, and He will continue to be with us, Lance, as we strive for the common good of our people."

"I'm sure you're right," Lance said.

"You know where to find me," Cameron stood, "anytime . . . night or day."

"Thank you," Lance said. "I think I just need some time alone . . . here."

"Would you like me to see to Dulsie?"

"Would you, please? If you could just let Abbi . . . or Nadine . . . know that I . . ."

"She'll be fine. Take your time."

"Thank you," Lance said and watched Cameron walk away before he turned his mind to prayer, longing with all his heart and soul to find reconciliation with these feelings that had plagued him far too long already.

Hours slipped by as Lance remained in the chapel, grateful to be completely alone. Much of the time he spent on his knees, feeling a deep appreciation to have been raised with an understanding of God and the principles that bound Him to man—principles of right and wrong, good and evil—and the faith to believe that right and good would prevail if sought after earnestly. Lance felt some perspective on the struggles of his life, especially those of the past several weeks, as he considered the blessing of simply knowing in his heart that God was with him and with those he loved. All else seemed less ominous and more subject to hope with such knowledge.

Lance prayed and prayed for his own weaknesses to be forgiven, especially in harboring such feelings. And he prayed to be able to forgive those who had wounded him and the people he loved, and to be able to let go of the burden. He felt no instantaneous, miraculous change occur in him, but he had to acknowledge that he left the chapel feeling markedly different than when he'd arrived. There was a lessening of his burden, and a lightening of the load he carried. He couldn't say that a complete reconciliation had occurred within himself, but some steps had been taken in the right direction.

Walking the hallway that led away from the chapel, he turned a corner and almost bumped into Cameron, who chuckled and said, "I was just coming to make sure you were all right before I go to bed."

"I'm fine," Lance said. "But thank you, anyway."

"I also wanted to tell you that Nadine took Dulsie to your apartment to put her to bed, and she said she would stay there until you came home."

"Thank you," Lance said. "I'm on my way there now."

Lance moved past him then stopped when Cameron asked, "Are you feeling any better?"

"Yes, actually, I believe I am."

"Good," Cameron said. "I'll see you tomorrow." He hesitated then added, "You know, it's likely irrelevant, but it occurred to me that we never solved the mystery of the woman who was apparently an accomplice to Albert Crider."

"I'd thought about that myself," Lance said. "We'll probably never know."

"Good night, then," Cameron said and hurried away.

Lance returned quickly to his apartment where he found a lamp burning low in Dulsie's room. Dulsie and Nadine were both sound asleep in the bed that was normally far too big for a little girl. He couldn't resist just watching them sleep, mother and daughter, both so beautiful and fine. He relished the peace of having them both safely beneath his roof. Although, he concluded as he doused the lamp and went to his own room, he would far prefer to have Nadine sleeping in *his* bed. It took a long while for him to fall asleep, but he further pondered the thoughts and feelings that had been with him in the chapel. He felt a definite hope in being able to let go of the feelings related to killing Nikolaus that had plagued him. He found it was more difficult to do the same with his feelings toward Albert Crider. But then, the wounds he'd inflicted on this country—most specifically Nadine—were still fresh and raw. Perhaps he just needed to give the matter some time in order to heal.

Lance awoke to a glimmer of daylight and the smell of coffee. He hurried to freshen up and get dressed and went quietly into Dulsie's room. The child was still sleeping, but Nadine was gone. He feared she had slipped away early in order to avoid any difficult conversation with him. But, oh how he ached to just be with her! He went downstairs, fully expecting to find that she'd left coffee brewing but had escaped while she had a chance. His heart quickened when he entered the kitchen to find her seated at the table, a cup of coffee wrapped in her hands. She looked so beautiful it took his breath away.

"Good morning," he said, trying not to sound overly pleased, although he did add, "What a fine way to start a day."

"How is that?" she asked.

"To see you here," he said and caught the barest hint of a smile.

"Let me get your coffee," she said, pouring some into a cup that she'd left within her reach.

"Thank you," he said, sitting across from her as she slid the cup toward him, followed by cream and sugar. "I was just thinking of a conversation we had very early in our relationship. We were practically strangers at the time, but I found myself spilling my heart to you . . . about my difficult feelings concerning . . . some memories that had plagued me."

"I remember," she said.

"It seems a lifetime ago," he said, "but it's only been a matter of weeks." He chuckled, but it was more sad than humorous. "Funny how I can't seem to recall what life might have been like before I met you."

"I know what you mean," she said, but she wouldn't look at him.

Lance wanted to get down on his knees and beg her to be a part of his life, to set aside their trivial issues and misunderstandings and make a fresh start. In his mind he could see himself pleading and crying. But his dignity was one of the few things that had remained through all that had occurred, and even that could be considered hanging by a thread in light of all the tears he'd shed and the way he'd thrown his heart at her feet. He simply cleared his throat and said,

"As I was saying, I've been thinking about that conversation between us, because I said then that I hoped I could figure out a way to be free of such difficult feelings, because I didn't want to have them keep coming up to haunt me over and over."

"I remember," she said again.

"And you said if I figured it out to let you know, because you struggled with the same thing."

"So, did you?" she asked. "Figure it out?"

"I think so," he said. "I'm still working on it, but . . . well, I must confess that what happened yesterday was . . . upsetting."

"Which is understandable," she said. "I'm sorry about that."

"Sorry? What have you got to be sorry for?"

"It just seems that, without even trying, I tend to bring a great deal of . . . disturbance into your life."

"The *disturbance* of yesterday likely saved someone else from finding those papers eventually. And when I think of your having them in your possession . . . years ago, and the decision you made, I just . . ." His voice picked up a definite tremor. "You saved my life, Nadine."

"Now we're even," she said, her voice tender.

A silent tension fell between them until Lance cleared his throat and said, "And as for the other disturbances that have come up, the results have been good . . . for the most part. I'm certainly grateful that Cameron knew about . . . my paternity, before the solicitor delivered those papers." He took a deep breath and hoped he wouldn't regret it when he added, "You are a blessing to me, Nadine, in spite of certain . . . issues."

She looked surprised, then looked away. The tension between them thickened until she felt compelled to say, "And how are you doing with that? The discovery of your paternity, I mean."

Lance sighed loudly. "Truthfully, I just try not to think about it. Every time it comes up, I feel sick. I know I should come to terms with it, but . . . I don't know if that's possible."

Nadine felt tempted to press him on that, certain he *needed* to come to terms with it eventually. But she only said, "You were telling me what you'd learned about being free of difficult feelings."

Lance wondered momentarily if the concept of forgiveness he was exploring also applied to his difficult feelings regarding his illegitimacy, but he had too much on his mind to contemplate that right now. One step at a time, he reminded himself and focused on the topic at hand.

"So I was," he said. "Cameron found me yesterday . . . in the chapel. I was feeling terribly angry . . . especially toward Nikolaus. I am continually amazed at the damage that keeps popping up in my life as a result of his conniving. Cameron reminded me that he knows well how I feel. The hurt and betrayal for him has been deep, especially considering Cameron's commitment and responsibility to Horstberg. But he's dealt with those difficult feelings toward his brother."

"How?" she asked, genuinely intrigued.

Lance's voice lowered almost to a whisper. "He forgave him. And while I spent hours pondering all I was feeling, I knew in my heart that I had to do the same thing if I ever wanted to be free of what he did to my life."

"And did you?" she asked.

"I can't say all those difficult feelings are magically gone . . . but close, perhaps. I do feel that I made some progress, and I'm determined to keep working on it." She looked intrigued, but perhaps skeptical. He leaned closer and said, "I gave the burden to God, Nadine. He will see justice met. It's not our burden to carry."

Nadine watched his eyes and felt a little startled to realize that she could see a marked difference. He'd always been a good man, and his eyes had reflected the depth of his integrity. But they had also reflected the difficulty of his feelings whenever Nikolaus had come up. And she knew well how he felt. But something had changed in him. She could see it and she longed to emulate it, but she wasn't certain if she had it in her to be as noble as he.

Lance broke the silence by saying, "And Nikolaus is not the only one I'm having difficult feelings toward." Nadine watched him expectantly, wondering if he meant her. She was relieved when he said, "Albert Crider has created a great deal of anger in me. And those feelings are still very close. I admit that it may still take some time."

"That certainly gives us something in common," she admitted. "Funny, that you and I would both feel such anger toward the same two people."

"Ironic, isn't it," he said. "Or maybe it's . . . destiny."

"Maybe," she admitted, meeting his eyes.

"There have been far too many coincidences . . . ironies . . . whatever you might call them, for me to believe otherwise. It *was* destiny for us to come together, Nadine. Surely you can see that."

"Yes, I can see that," she said, filling him with a bright ray of hope that was quickly dashed when she added, "but for what purpose? You've been a great blessing to our lives, Lance. But that doesn't necessarily mean we're meant to be together forever."

He said nothing but Nadine noticed the muscles in his face tightening. She knew that pressing the matter further would only provoke him, but she felt compelled to address the problem head on. "Apparently you don't agree," she said.

He snapped his eyes toward hers. His gaze intensified and his voice took on that commanding quality of the Captain of the Guard. "I believe with all my heart and soul that you and I *are* meant to be together forever, Nadine, but it's evident that this equation is not solely up to me. You seem content to be friends, which I would certainly say is better than nothing at all, but it's a far cry from what it *should* be. And that's the one place where my anger toward Nikolaus is having difficulty being reconciled. He came between you and me, and we allowed him to do it. Even from the grave he holds this jaded power over us, and I *hate* him for it."

"Maybe it's not him," she said in a voice that should have calmed him, but it only made him more angry to see how calm she could be when he felt as if he were being eaten alive inside. The depths of this anger that had just taken hold so quickly made him realize he had a long way to go in coming to terms with his feelings. "Maybe it's me," she added. "Maybe it's me you should be angry with; maybe it's me you should hate."

"Maybe it is," he said, realizing he needed to get out of there before he came to a point of losing his temper. He marveled at how he had been such a calm and controlled person before she had come into his life. Now, he often felt as if he were losing his mind. "But you know what, Nadine?" He came to his feet. "I'm willing to forgive you and let it go. I'm willing to open my heart, in spite of the way it's been wounded, and give what we have another chance." He slid his chair under the table abruptly and she winced. "I only wish you might be willing to do the same." He headed toward the door. "I have to get to work. Would you please see that Dulsie gets to the nursery?"

"Of course," she said quietly, with regret tinging her voice. But was it enough for her to reach beyond this ridiculous barrier and correct the problem?

"Let me know when you're feeling up to taking her back, and I'll see that her things are moved." He left before she could respond, and he had to pause outside to breathe in the cold air and calm down. He was amazed at how she could set him off without even trying. But then, it wasn't so much that she was quarrelsome; she was just so *stubborn*. And her stubbornness was depriving him of what he wanted most in his life. He wanted *her*.

Nadine sat as she was for a long while after Lance left, wondering what was wrong with her. Why did she find it so difficult to just reach out and take the life this man was offering her? What was it that kept her from believing it was right for them to be together? She put her thoughts on hold when Dulsie woke up, and did her best to enjoy the time with her daughter. But once Dulsie was happily engaged in the nursery with her little playmates, Nadine was glad to know that she would have time with Abbi. She needed the sound wisdom of this woman who had become such a dear friend. But Nadine arrived at Abbi's office to find a note waiting for her. The duchess wasn't feeling well and was lying down. There was a list of a few things that Nadine could do, and Abbi would be available after lunch to go over their final lists and see that all was in order.

Nadine put her focus on doing what Abbi had asked her to do, finishing up just before lunch. She went to the nursery and ate with Dulsie, then she returned to the duchess's rooms to find her propped up in bed with pillows.

"Are you not feeling well?" Nadine asked.

"Oh, nothing that giving birth won't cure," she said. "Some days are just worse than others."

"I understand," Nadine said. "Tell me what I can do to help get you through."

"First of all, you can bring those lists in here and we'll go over them and see if we're ready."

Nadine left and returned a minute later with the lists. She sat on the edge of the bed at Abbi's request, and they went over checklists for each of the Christmas parties and for the charity projects. Abbi was pleased to note that everything had either been completed or delegated—except for the delivery of a number of baskets of charitable goods. From her involvement in the preparations, Nadine knew that there were a number of different qualifications that would warrant an individual or a family receiving such goods at Christmastime. Anyone on the government's list of having received assistance in the past year would receive something extra, according to their needs. The delivery of these goods was mostly overseen through a church network and divided among the different areas of the country, according to the districts where they lived. And then there was the elite group of Horstberg's residents whose names had appeared on what Abbi called the "special needs list." These were people who had been struck with severe hardship or tragedy in the past year. The list included the family of the officer who had been killed in the line of duty right after Nadine's arrival, as well as the families of the murder victims, among others. At Nadine's suggestion, it also included the family of the thief who had been executed for killing the officer. She had pointed out to Abbi that the family was not responsible for his behavior and was likely struggling as much as the officer's family. Abbi agreed and proposed that she would make a habit of considering such situations in the future.

"Now, there is only one problem," Abbi said. "I am simply not feeling up to making these deliveries tomorrow. Therefore, I shall send you in my place."

"Me?" Nadine was stunned. At Abbi's surprised expression she softened her voice. "I mean I would do whatever you want me to do, but . . . I make a poor substitute for the duchess. Perhaps we could—"

"You'll do just fine. The carriage driver will know exactly where you need to go, and everything will be loaded for you. All you have to do is knock on doors and be gracious. That shouldn't be too difficult."

"I'm certain I can manage," Nadine said. "Will I be going alone, then?"

"No, of course not. Considering the nature of the situations these families are in, I have traditionally been escorted by the Captain of the Guard. He will go with you."

"I see," Nadine said, wishing it hadn't sounded so downhearted.

"Is there a problem?" Abbi asked, sounding very much like a duchess.

"No, of course not. I just . . . can't help wondering if this errand you're sending me on is somewhat contrived."

"I can assure you that it's not," Abbi said, "but perhaps I *should* contrive something more. Do you need spending time with him to be contrived?"

"Perhaps," Nadine admitted.

"Most women would give all they own for such a privilege as being on assignment with the captain."

"I am not most women."

"No, you certainly are not, which is one of many reasons that he loves you."

Nadine had no response to that. But she wasn't surprised when the duchess pressed the subject. "Now that you know you're not guilty of treason, is there some purpose for your hesitance in renewing your relationship with Lance?"

The question spurred unexpected emotion, and Nadine realized it was something she'd been fighting to avoid even thinking about. "I don't know," she admitted tearfully. "Most of all I just feel so . . . . confused. And I wonder if . . . if . . ." Her tears overtook her and Abbi motioned her closer.

"If what?" she urged gently.

"I wonder sometimes if . . . it would be better if . . . I just . . . went away. Maybe it would be better . . . for all of us." Her words fell into the open on a string of sobs and she ended up crying with her face pressed into the bedcovers at Abbi's side, while Abbi gently rubbed her shoulder and whispered soothing words.

When her crying finally quieted, Abbi asked gently, "Why would you feel that way, Nadine? Talk to me. Help me understand."

"How can I help you understand, when I don't understand it myself?" Nadine said, still lying close beside Abbi.

"Then perhaps talking about it will help you understand," Abbi said.

"Perhaps," Nadine said and sniffled loudly. "But I don't know if—"

She was interrupted by a knock on the open door between the

bedroom and sitting room. Nadine sat up abruptly and wiped at her tears, but it was evident that Lance had seen her crying from the open doorway.

"Forgive me, ladies," he said. "You weren't in your office and . . . the doors were open."

"It's all right," Abbi said, but Nadine wanted to yell that it *wasn't* all right. Just what she needed, to have him see her like this and speculating on what the problem might be. She wondered what he might have overheard. "What can we do for you?" Abbi asked as Nadine moved to look out the window, keeping her back turned.

"I was simply wondering," he said, "if it will be tomorrow that you'll need me to escort you on your deliveries." Nadine knew what was coming.

"Yes, it's tomorrow," Abbi said, "but I'm afraid that I won't be going personally. I'm just not feeling up to it. Nadine will be taking my place."

She heard a long pause and could well imagine them exchanging some kind of skeptical glance. "I see," he finally said. "How delightful," he added in a voice that indicated it wouldn't be. "So, we'll plan on leaving at ten in the morning, Mrs. Rader?" he asked.

"That would be fine," she said without turning around.

"Very well then," he said. "I'll just be off and—"

"No need for you to hurry away, Captain," Nadine said. "I must be going anyway." She quickly said to Abbi, "Since everything is under control, I'll check with you in the morning before we set out." Abbi nodded and Nadine hurried and left the room, fearing she might start crying again otherwise.

Chapter Thirty-One

FORGIVENESS

"What was that about?" Lance asked once Nadine had left the room through the main door, closing it behind her.

"She's confused . . . and upset."

"I gathered that," he said. "So I take it my timing wasn't very good."

"Not really, but it will be all right."

"How is that, Your Grace?" he asked, hearing a terseness in his own voice that he hated.

"You'll be seeing her tomorrow," she said as if that were great news.

"I wish I could share your enthusiasm. Quite frankly, being with her does little but frustrate the hell out of me."

"My, aren't we testy," she said curtly.

"Forgive me, Abbi. I . . . well, yes . . . I *am* testy. According to the calendar, I'm supposed to be married in four days. I've kept telling myself that a miracle could still happen, but I'm beginning to wonder."

"Maybe you won't be married in four days, Lance, but that doesn't mean there's no hope. Just give her some time. I really believe she loves you and wants to be with you, but most women don't endure being stalked, imprisoned, and abducted through the process of falling in love. It's not the typical courting scenario."

Lance couldn't help but chuckle. "No, it certainly isn't. What would be a typical courting scenario?" he asked and sat down, putting his booted feet up on another chair.

"How should I know?" she asked. "I wasn't courted. I was

snowed in with a very stubborn and ornery man who wouldn't even tell me his name. Looking back, I should have known he was a sovereign, just by his arrogance."

Lance smiled. "Oh, do tell."

"Oh, he said things like . . ." Abbi lowered her voice to mimic Cameron. "'What do you think you're doing? This is my house. Don't get too uppity, girl.' And my favorite was . . . 'I see you're missing that ladies' maid again.' At first he didn't even want to know my name, and he was none too kind about letting me know."

Lance laughed again. "Surely you're joking. I cannot even imagine him speaking to you that way."

"Oh, I am quite serious," she said and he could see by her expression that she was. "He was so wrapped up in pride and fear that he wouldn't let me anywhere near his heart."

"Obviously, he got over it," Lance said.

"Yes, he got over it. I told him he could just rot in the hole he'd carved for himself, unloved and unremembered."

"Now *that* I can imagine. Feisty little Abbi telling the Duke of Horstberg to rot."

"I didn't know he was the Duke of Horstberg," she countered.

"Would it have made a difference?"

"Not likely."

"I'd never really stopped to think how difficult those months were for the two of you. I knew you had been together, and I knew the results were good, but . . . I'd just never thought about how it came to that."

Abbi's eyes became distant. "I think one of the most difficult things for me was . . ." She looked at him intently. "I've never told anyone this before."

"You don't have to tell me if you don't want to," he said.

"No, I think that . . . maybe I *should* tell you. I'm not sure why, but . . . I feel like I should."

"All right," he said eagerly. "Tell me. I could use a bedtime story."

"It's the middle of the afternoon."

"I'll think about it when I'm going to sleep," he said.

"We had reached a point where we . . . I guess you could say we'd become friends. We'd grown comfortable with each other, but each time anything started to open up between us, he would back off and become distant and cold. Of course, I didn't realize who or what he was. He feared for my safety. He knew if we became involved I could be convicted of treason. But I didn't know that. And I believe it was more complicated than even that. Anyway, one night I had a dream and it shook me up terribly. I didn't dare discuss it with him, but I was upset over it for days. He finally forced me to tell him what I had dreamed, and when I did he . . . yelled at me and told me it was madness, that the very idea was absurd. I'd never seen him so angry. Later he mocked me and told me I saw senseless visions. I'll never forget him saying to me . . ." Again she lowered her voice and her eyes became distant, almost sad. "'I wonder if you've ever thought to question the source of your inspiration. As far as I see it, your presence here is nothing but torment. You are a thorn in my side, Abbi girl.'"

Lance listened, stunned. He had to admit, "I once knew Cameron to be somewhat difficult. But . . . I just can't believe he would treat you that way."

"It's in the past, and now it's easy for me to see the perspective. At the time I loved him deeply and I believed in my heart that we were meant to be together. Now that we are where we are, those difficulties seem almost insignificant." He was startled when she added, "That's why you need to keep perspective, Lance. These weeks have been a very small portion of your life, and they have been filled with a great deal of drama. Cameron was worth waiting for; perhaps Nadine is too. Perhaps it's not as bad as it seems."

"Perhaps it's not," he said, realizing her analogy had helped. If Cameron and Abbi had endured such blatant difficulties in their relationship and now shared such a fine marriage and a good life together, perhaps there *was* hope for him and Nadine. He thought about that for a long minute, then said, "May I ask what you dreamed that made him so angry?"

"Of course," she said. "I dreamed of a child on a hobbyhorse."

"That's it?" he asked and she laughed.

"That's exactly what Cameron said when I first told him."

"There must have been more to it than that."

"He said that too." She chuckled. "I saw a child with Cameron's face, riding a hobbyhorse, the color of wood, with a red lion painted where the brand would be. And the child's hair was red. That's the part that really got to him."

Lance took a moment to absorb what she'd told him. "Erich," he said. "And the horse that now sits in the nursery."

"That's right," she said. "Actually, that horse has been in the nursery for years. Cameron himself played with it as a child. But I didn't know that."

Lance let out an amazed chuckle. "You dreamed of Erich before you and Cameron even considered marriage?"

"That's right," she said.

"Why do you suppose he got so angry?"

"I believe he'd become so comfortable in his hiding that he simply couldn't fathom ever getting beyond it. There was a great deal of guilt and regret in regard to his country, and also a great deal of helplessness in fearing that any effort to return and rectify the situation would only land him in prison or dead. He went through an enormous amount of soul searching before he was able to come to terms with all of that and be willing to do what was necessary to take the country back."

Lance looked at her deeply, saying, "And he did it for you. He risked his life to take back his country so that he could be at peace and have a life with you."

"That's what he tells me."

"It's a beautiful story," he said. "People talk about it and speculate, you know. To them it's practically legend."

"I just . . . followed my heart, Lance. And that's what you must do. You too have a beautiful story; it just needs a little work. But already what the two of you have shared is more than most people would endure in a lifetime. You mustn't give up hope."

Lance inhaled the hope that she breathed into him. "I love her, Abbi. I could never give up completely."

She smiled and said, "I have a confession to make."

"What's that?"

"Years ago . . . when you asked me to marry you, I had some opinions of you that I know now were completely wrong."

"Really?" He was intrigued.

"When you proposed to me, I remember thinking that you had no idea what real love was like. I know now that I was looking more at my feelings for Cameron, as opposed to my feelings for you. I know now that you *did* really love me, even then. It was simply a different kind of love. When I think of what you were willing to do, what you actually *did* for me, I am in awe." She smiled again. "I just wanted you to know that. I apologize for my misconceptions."

"No, you were right, Abbi. I *didn't* know the kind of love that should exist between a man and a woman. I was intrigued with you; I enjoyed your company. But I had no idea of the intensity and passion that should have been there. I got my first clue when I saw the way you and Cameron looked at each other. After that it was actually easier to let you go, because I had to admit that I had never looked at you that way, and I honestly had no idea what kind of feelings would spur such a gaze."

"But you know now," Abbi said gently.

"Yes, I know now." His voice turned sad.

"And it will be all right. You'll see."

"Did you have a dream, Abbi? Did you foresee my happiness?"

"I don't need to have a dream, Lance. I know you well enough to know that you *deserve* to be happy. And surely you will be. You simply have to trust in God's timing, as well as His plan for you."

Through the remainder of the day, Lance did his best to keep the hope Abbi had given him close to his heart, but lying in his bed alone that night, he had difficulty grasping anything but discouragement. The following morning he went to his office to see to some matters of business before setting out with Nadine to do the duchess's deliveries. He wished that he could feel any anticipation or enthusiasm whatsoever, but the prospect only filled him with dread. He hated being with her when everything between them was all wrong.

Lance had only been seated at his desk a short time when Georg walked through the open door and tossed a file onto his desk.

"What is this?" Lance asked, picking it up.

"The Brunsen case," he said. "Mr. Brunsen, the business partner to Nadine's father. He was tried and executed for treason and his property confiscated by the government. When Cameron was reinstated, his widow was one of the first in line to declare that her land had been taken illegally. The government reinstated the property willed to her by her husband, and he was exonerated of all charges. Fat lot of good it did him, seeing that he was already dead. But it gave the family some peace over the matter, if nothing else. At last report, Mrs. Brunsen was doing well. She has a married son and his wife living in the family home with her. They see to her needs. Nadine suggested that Mrs. Brunsen might be able to shed some light on what actually happened. Perhaps if you took Nadine along it might help, since Mrs. Brunsen might remember her. It's just a thought."

"Thank you," Lance said, opening the file enough to see the address of the Brunsen home. "I just might do that."

"Enjoy your deliveries," Georg said with a little smirk.

"I'll certainly try," Lance said. "You know, you seem awfully perky. You haven't been perky since—"

"Since Elsa left, I know. Well, she's coming home in three days. There is reason to go on living."

"Indeed," Lance said and watched him leave the office. How could he not think that he was supposed to have been married on the day that Elsa was scheduled to return? He recalled Georg saying that she would likely be home that morning and would be able to attend the ceremony. He forced his mind from wandering into unpleasant territory and focused on his work until it was time to meet Nadine. An officer informed him that the carriage had been loaded, and he was provided with a list of where they would be delivering the goods. A few minutes later he found Nadine waiting in the courtyard near the carriage.

"Good morning, Mrs. Rader," he said, trying not to be distracted by how beautiful she looked in the morning sun.

"Good morning, Captain," she replied.

"Shall we go?" he asked, opening the carriage door for her.

"Oh, it's awfully crowded," she said, noting how the seats and floor were covered with gift baskets.

"It's all right," he said, actually feeling some relief. "I'll ride on the box seat."

He helped her in and made certain she was comfortable before he closed the door and climbed up beside the driver, far preferring the cold air to being in close quarters with Nadine and feeling as if a stone wall existed between them.

Nadine sat among the beautiful baskets, filled with abundance, and tried not to feel the distance between her and Lance. She told herself that his choosing to ride with the driver was merely a matter of practicality. But she knew it was more. She sensed his aggravation with her, and while she certainly couldn't blame him, she feared that it would never be possible to bridge the gap between them.

At each stop he helped her out of the carriage before they went together to the door. She was freshly amazed at his genuine diplomacy with the people who were presented with gifts, and she longed for the times gone by when she had been his and he had been hers, and there had been no ugliness or mistrust between them. She knew she was mostly to blame for the problem, but she wasn't sure it could be fixed. It certainly didn't *feel* fixable.

After a third recipient commented on their forthcoming marriage, Nadine said to Lance on their way back to the carriage, "People still believe we're getting married." She couldn't deny her deepest hope that he would beg her to reconsider and go forward with the wedding.

Instead he said, slightly curt, "Forgive me. I didn't take the time to post a proclamation declaring your aversion to marrying me. I was rather busy trying to keep you alive."

Nadine was unable to respond due to sudden emotion, even though she couldn't be exactly certain what she was feeling. The remainder of their deliveries went smoothly. But even when most of the baskets were gone and the carriage was nearly empty, Lance continued to ride with the driver. The very idea tempted tears into her eyes, but she fought them back, determined to get through this without making a fool of herself. After the last basket was delivered, she expected to return to the castle, but the carriage went the opposite direction for quite some time before it stopped. When Lance opened the door and held out a hand for her, she asked, "Where are we?"

"We are at the Brunsen home," he said. "I'm hoping you won't mind accompanying me on a little visit. I'd like to see if I can put together some missing pieces."

"I don't mind," she said, feeling as if she were lying. She had barely known Mrs. Brunsen and her memories were of a kind, gentle woman, but the subject was sensitive and the memories difficult.

She felt nervous as Lance knocked at the door, but the woman who answered looked familiar.

"Mrs. Brunsen?" Nadine asked.

"Yes," she said.

"I don't know if you will remember me. I'm Nadine Rader. My father and your husband were—"

"Oh, of course," Mrs. Brunsen said. "Do come in." She opened the door wide and they stepped into the moderate entry hall.

"Thank you," Lance said as she closed the door.

"You must forgive the mess," she said with a little laugh. "My son and his wife have been away on holiday mixed with business; they've been gone since October. Should be back for Christmas any day now. But I've not been feeling well in their absence and just haven't kept things up."

"Oh, you mustn't worry about that," Nadine said.

Mrs. Brunsen smiled. "And who might this gentlemen be?"

"This is Captain Dukerk. He is—"

"Ah," her face lit up, "the well-known Captain of the Guard. Everyone in Horstberg knows that name. What a pleasure it is to meet you, Captain."

"And you, Mrs. Brunsen," he said as if her fame exceeded his own.

"Come in. Sit down," she said, guiding them to a little parlor.

"Thank you," Lance said again and they were all seated.

"What a pleasant surprise this is," she said to Nadine, "but I can't help wondering what this might be about. We never knew each other well enough for this to be a social call."

"I confess," Nadine said, "we were hoping you might be able to help us understand more what happened concerning my father and your husband and . . . Nikolaus du Woernig."

"Oh, I see," she said, more disgusted than uncomfortable. "I knew His Grace had an interest in you, my dear, which was something that concerned me, but I didn't feel it was my place to say anything. And I shouldn't call him that, should I. His brother has that title now, and rightfully so. Nikolaus du Woernig never deserved the title. Never did any of us a lick of good."

"No, he certainly didn't," Lance said. "I wonder, Mrs. Brunsen, if you might be able to shed some light on the situation with your husband. We've had some things come up in relation to Mr. Rader's death and his involvement with Nikolaus du Woernig. Was Nikolaus with your husband very much?"

"Yes, actually. The first time he walked into my home, I was rather struck with awe. But it soon became evident he had an arrogance that didn't necessarily make him pleasant company. He made an investment in the mill and took an interest in other investments with my husband and Mr. Rader, which I now believe were just a scheme. I told my husband I didn't feel good about what he was doing, so he just stopped telling me about it. Well, not that he told me much to begin with. I can't say I knew anything exactly of what was going on. Next thing I know, papers show up that incriminate my husband in treasonous activities and he's being arrested, and we lost everything. Thankfully we got it all back. God bless His Grace; Cameron du Woernig is a good man."

"Yes, he is," Lance said. "It's a privilege to work with him."

"And you worked with his brother too, I warrant."

"Yes, I did, Mrs. Brunsen. Something that I am still attempting to recover from."

"Oh, you poor dear," she said as if he were a child who had skinned his knee.

"So," Lance said, "Nikolaus du Woernig started consorting with your husband and Mr. Rader, there was talk of some business investments, then your husband was accused of treason. Do you think Mr. Rader's involvement had anything to do with his death?"

"I'd bet money it did," she said. "Of course, I don't know any details, so I couldn't tell you what happened. But the timing was just a little too suspicious. I wonder what Nikolaus du Woernig would have done to keep somebody from exposing his evil ways. Well, isn't that why he killed the duchess? That's what I heard anyway."

"I believe that had something to do with it," Lance said with a tightness in his voice that evoked Nadine's compassion for him. She doubted that Mrs. Brunsen had any idea the duchess had been Lance's sister.

"After your father died," Mrs. Brunsen said to Nadine, "I was actually relieved that you were going away. Nikolaus told me he thought it would be better for you to live elsewhere after losing your father that way."

"Did he?" Nadine asked, trying to be nonchalant. Obviously Mrs. Brunsen didn't have a clue regarding her relationship with Nikolaus and the fact that her being pregnant had given him great motivation to send her away.

"Occasionally he seemed to come up with some concern. He did seem pleased that you would be taking his suggestion to move to . . . I don't remember the place, but . . . it was where his friend was from, and he would be able to look after you. Do you remember his friend? What was his name?"

Nadine shook her head. "I'm sorry. I don't know who you mean. I don't recall anyone else ever being with him when he was around."

"Well, this man did kind of just sneak in and out. Real quiet he was. He was helping with the bookkeeping for a while, and he came and went with Nikolaus. Of course, they mostly met here at the house, so you wouldn't have been around. Oh, what was his name? Albert somebody."

Nadine gasped and was grateful for Lance saying in a straight voice, "Would that be Albert Crider?"

"That's it!" she said, pointing at him. "Do you know him?"

Lance stole a concerned glance at Nadine then he carefully repeated the physical description that had been distributed through the valley. "Yes, that sounds like him," she said firmly.

"Mrs. Brunsen," Lance said, "that name and description were posted on a proclamation. Did you not see it?"

"As I said, I've been rather ill. My neighbor brings in groceries and such, but she's not much for talking about anything beyond her children and grandchildren, and when it comes to them, she never shuts up."

"Of course," Lance said and Nadine fought to keep her expression steady while the implication constricted her chest and strangled her heart.

"Why was his description on a proclamation?" Mrs. Brunsen asked.

"He was recently executed, Mrs. Brunsen. He readily confessed to murdering several women."

"Good heavens!" she gasped. "Well, that would be the type to run with the likes of Nikolaus du Woernig, it would seem. Oh, how they must have been up to no good!"

"Indeed," Lance said, well aware that Nadine wasn't doing well, in spite of her efforts to cover her alarm. "Apparently Mr. Crider was also very good at document forgery. I can't help thinking that Nikolaus's interest in him may have had to do with his ability to produce the papers that incriminated your husband and others like him."

"Well, that certainly makes sense, doesn't it," Mrs. Brunsen said, seeming aghast as she took in all she was learning that had deeply impacted her life as well.

Lance realized now what all of this meant in regard to the papers that could have incriminated *him*. He felt prone to joining Nadine in barely maintaining composure. He quickly stood, holding to her arm to urge her to her feet beside him. "Thank you for your time, Mrs. Brunsen. You've been most helpful. I only regret the loss of your husband."

"It was difficult," she said, "but not for the reasons you might think. Just between you and me, he really wasn't easy to live with. It all turned out well in the end, thanks to His Grace for helping set things right."

"I'm glad that's the case," Lance said and graciously made an exit, with Nadine barely managing to tell the woman good bye.

"Just keep walking," Lance whispered to Nadine once the door was closed.

He heard her gasping for breath as they moved toward the carriage. He helped her step inside and sat beside her. Once the door was closed, she spurted, "I can't believe it." She heaved to catch her breath as the carriage rolled forward.

"Calm down, Nadine," he said. "Take a deep breath before you pass out."

Nadine fought to slow her breathing until she said more calmly, "I can't believe it. That filthy wretch put me right into Albert Crider's path, like tossing a bone from the dinner table to some ravenous dog."

"It sure sounds that way," Lance said and she groaned. "And I would bet a month's wages that Albert Crider forged the records that would have seen me executed, had you delivered them."

Nadine groaned again. "So, Nikolaus was consorting with a master forger. I wonder what kind of deal they had worked up to incriminate innocent people so that Nikolaus could take all they had. Maybe I was part of that deal. Once Nikolaus was done with me, he just sent me to Albert Crider's hometown. Oh," she moaned and doubled over, "will we never stop discovering things that man did to us?"

"I don't know, Nadine," Lance said, realizing he felt relatively calm. Perhaps his hours in the chapel had touched him more deeply than he'd believed. "But we've got to let it go."

Nadine looked at him deeply. "You mean we have to forgive him."

"That's right."

"Do you really believe that's possible?"

"Yes, Nadine, I do. If Cameron can let go of what Nikolaus did to *him,* surely we can let go of what he did to each of us."

"Have you forgiven him?" Nadine asked intently.

"I'm working on it. I feel a whole lot better now than I did yesterday."

Nadine sighed loudly. "I've been thinking about what you said yesterday . . . about this very thing. I know you're right, Lance. I'm just . . ."

"What?" he pressed.

"Nothing," she said, looking down.

"You're lying to me," he said with an edge of anger that startled her. Looking into his eyes, she wondered if she was the cause of his anger. He had good cause to be angry with her; she knew that. But the reality was still difficult to swallow. He added in a voice that was not much gentler, "You're the one who told me that the only way to truly find reprieve from one's difficult thoughts is to be free of them. Talking or writing is the only way to do that. Isn't that what you said?"

"Perhaps I did," she said, "but I don't think I'm in a position to do either at the moment."

His voice became sad and distant as he looked toward the window and asked, "Why won't you talk to me, Nadine? Has the trust between us been so completely defiled that you won't talk to me?"

"It's not that," she said.

"Then what is it?" he demanded.

"I . . . don't know. I'm just . . . confused. More than anything, I'm confused."

"Well, you're not going to get any less confused by holding it all inside."

Nothing more was said before the carriage halted in the castle courtyard. Lance stepped out and held up a hand to help Nadine do the same. Before letting go he said, "I'm bringing Dulsie back with her things tomorrow evening. She needs to be with her mother."

He walked away before she could respond, leaving Nadine so flooded with emotion that she could only hurry into the castle, hoping to find a quiet place to be alone before the dam broke on her tears and they flooded all over the place. Just inside the door, a maid said to her, "Her Grace asked that you join her for lunch in her sitting room as soon as you returned. She is waiting."

"Thank you," Nadine said and pushed her emotions down while she traversed the long castle halls and climbed the huge staircase to the duchess's rooms. Her efforts felt futile as her insides roiled with unshed tears of confusion and heartache. But Lance's words came back to her. Perhaps she *did* need to talk about it. But she could hardly talk to Lance when he was the biggest source of her confusion. In that respect, perhaps the duchess's lunch invitation was an answer to prayers she'd never thought to utter. If she'd ever needed a friend, it was now.

Chapter Thirty-Two
PROPERLY PLACED

Nadine found Abbi sitting at the table, looking through a catalog. "Hello," she said. "I didn't wait for you. It was cold food to begin with, so it should still taste fine. Go ahead and eat while I . . ." She looked at Nadine more closely and set her catalog aside. "What's wrong?"

"I don't know," Nadine said. "I just . . . I can't eat right now. I need to talk, but . . . I don't know where to start and . . ."

Abbi stood and put her arms around Nadine with perfect acceptance. "Come sit down," she said, guiding her to one of the small sofas in the room. The moment Nadine was seated, her face fell against Abbi's shoulder and she cried without restraint. Long after her tears were spent, they sat together in peaceable silence, as if Abbi would give her all the time she needed.

"I don't know what to do," Nadine finally said.

"About what?" she asked gently.

"I love him, Abbi, I do," she said firmly, "but I wonder if it would be better for him if I just . . ."

"What?" Abbi asked, easing back enough to look into her eyes. "If you left him with a broken heart? Tell me what kind of thinking would make you believe that he would be better off without you." Nadine felt stunned to hear it put that way. "I have to ask: what else did Albert Crider say to make you doubt yourself?"

"It's not just what he said," Nadine insisted. "It's . . ."

"What?" Abbi asked but Nadine couldn't give her an answer. "I have a feeling that whatever may have been wrong before he got his hands on you was fueled greatly by what he had to say to you."

While Nadine's thoughts were tumbling in chaos, Abbi added, "May I share a thought with you?"

"Of course."

"Albert Crider was obviously a genius at playing games with people's minds. The way he eluded the law, the way he incriminated you for his deeds, and the way he twisted the truth to make you believe you'd committed treason. And I wonder if some portion of his quest was simply to have power over you, Nadine. And maybe, even when he had you in his possession and he was threatening to kill you, he considered the possibility that you might be rescued before that happened. But if he convinced you that you and the captain were better off apart, he would still have power over your life by coming between the two of you."

Nadine gasped as the idea sank into her heart.

"So, why don't you tell me what he said?" Abbi asked.

She had to think about it for a minute. "He said that . . ." Tears fell as she admitted, "He said that Nikolaus du Woernig had made a whore out of me, and I was a fool to believe that any man with any decency and honor would want anything to do with me. He said that a man like the captain might marry me, but he would soon see me for what I really am, and his interest would wander and . . ." Nadine gasped again as she heard the words come back to her.

"Do you hear what you're saying, Nadine? Can you honestly tell me there is any truth to that in relation to Lance's feelings for you? Does that ring true at all in regard to Lance's character?" Nadine shook her head vehemently, grateful when Abbi clarified, "But when a man has your life in his hands, his words can leave a deep impression."

Nadine said through her tears, "And do you know what we found out today? We visited Mrs. Brunsen and . . . Nikolaus knew Albert Crider . . . years ago. Lance believes he was using Albert to forge the documents that framed people for treason."

"That's incredible!" Abbi said breathlessly.

"I was so sure that he couldn't have followed me to Horstberg; I'd been so careful. But he didn't have to follow me. He knew where I was going. And Mrs. Brunsen said that Nikolaus had told her he was sending me away to the place where Albert lived so that he could look after me. So, does that mean I was part of some . . . sick deal they made? Nikolaus was through with me so he just . . . tossed me to the dogs to let them do what they would. And Albert knew. He knew all along that I was pregnant with Nikolaus's child. Nobody told him about the papers I didn't deliver. He already knew, because he was in business with Nikolaus long before I left Horstberg."

"It's unbelievable," Abbi said, her expression as stunned as her voice. After taking some time to absorb what had been said, she added, "But now you know that Albert Crider truly was baiting you, Nadine. He was playing a game with you. And anything he said to you was simply talk. He was lying to you as surely as the devil himself, who would deceive you straight down to hell. It's going to take some time, but you've got to find a way to separate the things that man told you from the truth. Are you hearing me?"

"Yes," Nadine admitted, "I know you're right."

"So, in that light, let's talk about how you *really* feel about Lance."

"Oh, I love him, Abbi. I do. But I know he's angry with me, and I don't know what to do. I'm the one who created this horrible rift between us. I know I was wrong. I know my mistrust was completely out of line. But . . . what if it's too late? What if he . . ."

Abbi actually laughed. While Nadine was considering a way to tell the Duchess of Horstberg that her humor was misplaced, Abbi said gently, "Oh, Nadine, my dear. When you love someone as much as he loves you, it's never too late."

Nadine thought about that and had to admit, "Perhaps I'm just being stubborn, but . . . I really find it difficult to imagine myself as his wife, and I have to wonder if it's simply not meant to be."

"Did you feel that way before you were abducted?"

"In a way, yes."

"But you were willing to marry him anyway. Why?"

"Well . . . because I love him, and I wanted to be with him, but . . . perhaps truly loving someone is being realistic enough to accept that being together would only be . . . a burden, or an embarrassment. I'm not certain I have what it takes to be the wife of such a man. He's nearly as well known as *your* husband, and I know there are certain social responsibilities that would go along with being his wife, and I just don't know if it's in me."

"You once believed you were married to the Duke of Horstberg."

"Yes, and it was all just like a fantasy in my head that never felt completely comfortable. I'm truly grateful that it didn't work out, because I couldn't have done it."

"Nadine," Abbi took her hand, "let me tell you something about myself. Never in a million years would I have foreseen myself in this position. And when I woke up and realized that I was actually the Duchess of Horstberg, I panicked. Cameron helped me get through that, but I couldn't seem to get over believing that it just wasn't right for me. I wanted to be Cameron's wife, but I did not want to be the duchess. Obviously the two cannot be separated. After Erich was born, I slipped into a horrible depression, and then I came to some startling realizations. One of them occurred when my father came to see me, and he told me something that changed my life. I had been imagining that any woman could have been guided into Cameron's life, won him over, and supported him in his role. But my father had known Cameron many years, and he told me that Cameron du Woernig was not a man to be trifled with. He asked me if some senseless tomboy would have been able to come into his life and knock him on his ear. He told me that Cameron was a man who knew his power and that his first wife had never been able to toy with him. He said that I had tamed a lion. But more important than his words, Nadine, was the way they made me feel. The truth of what he was saying pierced my heart, and I knew that not only was I capable of being the duchess, it was my destiny. God had led me into Cameron's life. It was no accident or coincidence."

Abbi sighed and tightened her grip on Nadine's hand, leaning a little closer. "Now let me tell you about Lance Dukerk, my dear. He has a tender heart and a sensitive spirit. He's not afraid to cry or admit to fear or misgiving. But I have seen him stand up to cocky officers and difficult citizens and put them in their place quicker than you can snap your fingers. I have seen him deal with the basest of criminals in a way that has left me breathless." Her voice lowered to a quavering whisper. "I have seen him kill a man, Nadine, and he did it to save my life. He is a man among men. He will not tolerate insubordination from his men any more than he would tolerate shallow pretenses from the countless women who were batting their eyes at him. I have watched him attend dozens of socials where women were falling all over themselves to get his attention, and he had no use for such women. But you, Nadine, you found your way into his heart. You turned his life upside down and his heart inside out simply by allowing him to love you. You *are* capable of being the wife he needs you to be simply because of who and what you are. There's no mandate for how you fill that role. The important thing is that the two of you are happy. But think of all the good you could do in such a position. Not that such a reason should be your purpose in marrying a man, but it's something to consider. You, with your struggles and experiences, could do so much for the women of this country. And remember that Lance loves you. He loves *you*. And such an amazing man would not feel the way he does for just anybody. He is not a man to be trifled with, Nadine, any more than Cameron would be. They both have a natural power that can't be explained. Lance is tough when he needs to be, and if you sense that he's angry, I suspect that he likely doesn't know where he stands. If you have responsibility in the problem, then it's up to you to do everything you can to bridge that chasm and make it right."

Nadine allowed Abbi's words to settle into her, but she had to say, "I . . . need some time . . . to think."

"Of course," Abbi said.

A minute later Nadine added, "Maybe you should talk to him first. If you could find out where his heart really is, then maybe . . ."

"And maybe you should just tell him how you feel so that you can both get on with your lives."

Nadine sighed. "Maybe," was all she said, then Abbi insisted that she eat her lunch.

Lance was sitting in his office getting little done while he contemplated following through on what he'd told Nadine about returning Dulsie to her mother tomorrow. The very idea threatened to break his heart, but if Nadine did not want to be a part of his life, he could do nothing about it. And Dulsie needed to be with her mother.

He was startled by an officer entering the room. "A message for you, sir."

"Thank you," Lance said and opened it to read in Abbi's hand, *I'm far too fat to be moving furniture on my own, and the library is beginning to bore me. I need your help as soon as your schedule will allow.*

Lance chuckled then heaved a deep sigh. Hurrying to the library, he felt grateful for an opportunity to talk with Abbi. She seemed to have a sixth sense about when he needed her advice. Nothing had changed, and he wasn't certain Abbi could tell him anything that he didn't already know, but she had a way of putting perspective on his struggles. He opened the door and stepped inside, then he took a sharp breath when the woman sitting on the sofa didn't have the red hair he'd expected. It was blond. His heart raced as Nadine turned to look at him. He closed the door and leaned against it, wondering what her motives might be.

"Forgive me," she said, "I know you were expecting Her Grace. Other things came up and she felt certain that I could take her place in seeing that the furniture was properly placed."

Lance took a deep breath and told himself not to jump to any conclusions. "And did Her Grace also tell you that her requests to rearrange the furniture are little more than a ploy to get me to do her bidding? I think she gets a perverse pleasure out of seeing me do menial tasks. She's probably trying to keep me humble."

"That shouldn't be too difficult," Nadine said and Lance's heart quickened further. She actually seemed to mean it. "Of course, Her Grace also told me that we should probably just keep the furniture where it is, and we can say we moved it and put it back. She said that in most cases it's likely best to put things back the way they were . . . the way that worked best."

Lance sauntered toward her. "Was she talking about furniture?"

"Not likely."

"She's a very wise woman, Her Grace."

"Yes, she is. And I understand you almost married her."

"Yes, I did," he said proudly and plopped down on the opposite end of the long sofa where Nadine was sitting. "And I almost married another woman. She too was very wise . . . and beautiful. But she left me."

"Is it true what they say then?" she asked. "That the Captain of the Guard has a broken heart?"

Nadine's emotion swept close to the surface as she heard his voice break. "The captain's heart is so broken that at moments he wonders why he is even living. As I understand it, he would do anything to get her back, if only he knew what to do." She could hardly believe what she was hearing. Had her way of thinking become so distorted that she had missed the meaning behind his behavior? Her heart quickened almost painfully as he went on. "Perhaps you might have some advice for him. How does a man win back the only woman he's ever truly loved, when a seemingly simple misunderstanding becomes blown into a huge complicated mess? How does a man convince such a woman that, in spite of his imperfections, his heart was always sincere?"

Nadine swallowed her emotion in order to play along in a firm voice. "Well," she said, "it sounds like this woman needs a huge dose of her own medicine. I wonder how she would like it if she were accused of something she wasn't guilty of, and in spite of her every effort to tell the truth and set the record straight, she was still condemned and put away. Perhaps some time languishing in prison and nearly losing her life would help her see what a fool she was being. Most women don't require such drastic measures, but she sounds pretty stubborn."

Lance didn't know whether to laugh or cry as her words leaked into his wounded heart, healing the cracks and crevices and giving him a hope that far surpassed the inexplicable pain he'd been enduring. "Perhaps," he said, his voice barely steady, "she too has a broken heart, and she has good cause to be stubborn."

"Perhaps," she said, "but then, she should learn that all men are not alike, and if she would only get past her foolish pride, she would see that you are the most . . ." tears crept into her throat, "honorable man in the country."

"Did you go door to door?" he asked, his tone lightening the mood.

She smiled and teased, "Yes, actually, I did. And I found one person who insisted you would make a more imposing captain if you were to wear a beard."

Lance laughed. "And what do you think?"

"Oh, I think you're perfect. I wouldn't change a thing . . . except perhaps how far away you're sitting."

Nadine met his eyes and saw that familiar sparkle mingled with a hint of hesitancy. She reached her hand toward him, saying gently, "I'm asking you to forgive me, Lance. You were right, and I was terribly unfair. If you could find it in your heart to give me another chance, perhaps we could . . ." Her voice slipped into the tears that refused to be held back any longer.

Lance reached out a hand to take hers and her weeping increased. In one agile movement, he slid across the sofa and took her into his arms. She clutched onto him with a desperation that was comparative to her behavior in prison, sobbing against his chest while he held her close and cried silent tears, grateful beyond words to have her back in his arms and in his life. He hated the doubts that crept into him, but he determined immediately that he had to address them.

"Nadine," he said, easing back to look into her eyes, "I'm grateful for what you're saying, but . . . I have to know . . . beyond any doubt that this is for real. I couldn't bear to take you into my heart again only to have something come between us. I have to know, Nadine, that there will be complete trust between us. That whatever challenge might come up, that we will work it out—together—and not let *anything* come between us. Promise me."

"Oh, I promise, Lance. I do. I need you to know that I've thought about what you said, and I realized that not only did I need to forgive Nikolaus, I need to forgive myself. And I'm working on that. But . . . in trying to let go of my hard feelings for Nikolaus, I realized that by forgiving him I *could* let myself be more trusting, I could open my heart more fully. And I also want you to know that there were some things Albert Crider said that made me believe it would be better for you if I stayed out of your life." He looked astonished and she quickly clarified. "I know now that he was just playing games with my mind, but under the circumstances, it was difficult to keep perspective and . . . I believe that with time I'll be able to put all of that behind me, completely. I've also realized that I have a choice. I was thinking just a while ago about the women I met who had also been betrayed by Nikolaus. There was such a stark contrast between them, and I know it's up to me how I let what he did affect me. I can either hold onto that bitterness and become bitter, or I can put it behind me and make the kind of life for myself that I deserve. And you're a part of that life, Lance. I want you to know that I will devote my life, my heart, my soul, to being a good wife to you." She became emotional again and he held her close while she cried.

Lance could feel the sincerity radiating from her, and he silently thanked God for this miracle. He'd kept hoping for a miracle, but doubt and discouragement had plagued him, and he found it difficult to believe that it had happened.

"There's something I have to ask you," she said when her emotion had calmed somewhat. She sat up straight, not giving him time to check his emotion, and she smiled as she wiped away his tears. "Oh, I'm so sorry."

"For what? For seeing the Captain of the Guard cry?"

"No," she laughed softly, "I consider that a privilege. I'm sorry for what I've put you through. I wouldn't blame you if you never wanted to see me again or—"

"Hush," he said, pressing his fingers over her lips. "It's in the past. It's forgiven. I'm just grateful to have it behind us. Now, what were you going to ask me?"

"I just have to know—after what I said this morning—if you sent out a proclamation or something, declaring your fiancée unfit and calling off the wedding."

"No," he said, touching her face, "the original proclamation still stands."

"It does?" Her surprise touched him deeply. "You mean . . . everyone still thinks we're getting married in two days?"

"I kept hoping that a miracle would bring you back to me. I just couldn't bring myself to call it off. So, unless there's some reason *you* want to call it off, I propose that you marry the Captain of the Guard the day after tomorrow. And this time, it would be nice if he left the cathedral actually *married.*"

"Oh!" She laughed and threw her arms around his neck. "You've made me the happiest woman in the world."

He laughed with her and kissed her long and hard. "Oh, Nadine," he muttered and kissed her again, urged on by a response from her that let him know she had ached for him as he'd ached for her. He finally forced himself to stand and urged her to her feet, but he had to kiss her again before he said, "Come along, my love. We've got to make certain that everything is under control. We're getting married."

They found Cameron and Abbi and Georg just going into the dining room for supper.

"Oh, you must join us," Abbi insisted, grinning as she glanced toward their clasped hands. "Dulsie's eating with the other children and you must give her time to finish."

"Very well," Lance said. "You talked us into it."

"I take it everything's all right now," Cameron said.

"We're getting married the day after tomorrow, if that's what you mean," Lance said. Abbi laughed and hugged Nadine. Cameron and Georg each slapped Lance on the shoulder and chuckled.

"So," Abbi said as they were all seated, "did you get the furniture in the library rearranged?"

"Oh, not again!" Cameron quipped.

"We moved it then put it back," Nadine said quite seriously.

"We decided," Lance added, "that we liked the arrangement exactly the way it was before."

He met Abbi's eyes across the table and they exchanged a knowing smile, then he turned to Nadine and absorbed the glow in her eyes as he kissed her hand. He'd never dreamed that he could be so happy.

When supper was over, Lance and Nadine went together to get Dulsie. Walking down a long, deserted hallway, Lance had to stop three times just to kiss Nadine, as if doing so might convince him that they were really together. And they were getting married the day after tomorrow.

"Oh, how I love you," he muttered and pressed her back against the wall. "How I missed you!" He kissed her again and felt her hand at the back of his neck, then in his hair.

"I was such a fool," she said and kissed him again, urging him closer.

"Yes, you were," he said and they both laughed.

"We must get Dulsie," she said. "I know she loves to play with her friends, but . . . it's almost her bedtime."

"Yes, of course," he said, dragging himself away from her.

When they entered the nursery together, holding hands, Dulsie's surprise quickly turned to a trill of laughter as she ran and jumped into Lance's arms. "You're together," she said. "And you're smiling. I haven't seen you smile very much for a long time."

Lance laughed and relinquished Dulsie so that she could hug her mother. "Come along," Nadine said, "we must get some rest. We've got a busy day tomorrow, and an even busier day the next."

"What are we doing?" Dulsie asked as they left the nursery, each holding one of her hands.

"We're going to have a wedding," Nadine said and Dulsie laughed and jumped up and down in the hall.

"Does that mean I get to stay with Lance forever?" the child asked. "And you'll stay there, too?"

"That's what it means," Nadine said, and they both laughed at Dulsie's excitement.

Back at Lance's apartment, they couldn't get Dulsie to calm down enough to go to sleep. Nadine finally sat on her bed and rubbed her hands while Lance read a story to her. After two more stories, she eventually slept.

"Is it my turn now?" Lance asked, tucking the covers tightly around Dulsie.

"With pleasure," she said. "I think I'm way behind."

"Oh, you are," he said. "It might take you a lifetime to catch up."

Nadine laughed softly and they went to the sitting room and sat close together on the sofa while she massaged his hands. They talked through more of their feelings on the issues that had come between them and their resolve to never let such turbulence come into their relationship again. Lance took a turn rubbing Nadine's hands as well, while they talked on about the process of forgiveness they were both working on and the dreams for the future they shared—without any fear of Nikolaus du Woernig or Albert Crider ever interfering in their lives again.

When they both became too tired to talk any further, Lance said, "Won't you stay here tonight? I know I could get an officer to stay with Dulsie—or to escort you home, but . . . I'd prefer that you stay."

She smiled coyly, saying, "We'll be married soon. I would think you could wait to—"

"And I *will* wait," he said with a smirk, knowing well that she was teasing. She knew him better than that. "You can sleep with Dulsie, like you did before. Or there is another vacant room that—"

"I would love to stay, thank you. I suppose we're past caring what people might think."

"Indeed we are," he said and kissed her.

He made certain she had what she needed before they shared a long, lingering kiss in the hall and went their separate ways. But Lance went to bed with a deep, abiding peace that he'd not felt in weeks. Soon, he would begin a new life with his new little family. And loneliness would never again be his trial.

The following morning Lance barely had time to wake Nadine with a kiss before he hurried to the keep for an early meeting with his officers.

"So, you're getting married in the morning," Lieutenant Kepler said.

Lance was grateful to be able to smile and say, "Yes, I am." He knew that a few of his closest officers were vaguely aware of the strain between him and Nadine, but he'd never said anything to anyone but Cameron, Abbi, and Georg about their estrangement. He was glad now that he didn't have to tell them the wedding had been called off. *It was a miracle.*

"And then," Lance added, "I'm taking a very long honeymoon, so you and the rest of these gentlemen can earn your living for a change." The men in the room laughed. They all worked hard and they knew that Lance appreciated the fact. And they all knew that Lance was the one who never took his allotted vacation time, and he had a great deal accumulated. "I'm certain you can manage without me for a few weeks."

"I'm certain we will," Kepler said, then he prompted the next order of business, which would be the military escort for the wedding procession. The reality provoked a swarm of butterflies in Lance's stomach, and he found himself chuckling occasionally for no apparent reason. His men just smirked and made jokes about him becoming a married man. And Lance just soaked it all in. He was counting the hours.

Chapter Thirty-Three
TO PERFECT HAPPINESS

Nadine arrived at Abbi's office near the usual time, grateful to have all of the Christmas festivities and projects under control when Abbi eagerly insisted she help make certain that all was in order for the wedding. They went over a checklist and sent for Nadine's wedding gown to be delivered to the castle.

"You must get ready here," Abbi said, "since the wedding procession will start here and go to the cathedral."

"Procession?" Nadine echoed. "What in the world does my wedding have to do with—"

"The Captain of the Guard is getting married, my dear. And there *will* be a procession. Only a royal wedding would be more grand than this, but not by much. Everything is arranged. All you have to do is sit in the open coach and look beautiful, which will not be a problem. I've arranged for Bruna to do your hair, and you will stay here tonight so that we can have you and Dulsie ready, bright and early."

"Good heavens," Nadine said, pressing a hand over her quickened heart, and another over her quavering stomach, "I'm getting married tomorrow . . . to the Captain of the Guard."

"Yes, you are, my dear friend. And it is going to be the most delightful event this country has seen since the day I married Cameron."

"You mean the day you almost married Lance," Nadine said.

"That too," Abbi said and laughed.

The remainder of the day flew by while Nadine felt busier than she ever had in her life. Abbi mostly sat with her feet up, but she helped Nadine keep a level head and was very good at seeing that everything got written down so that nothing would be forgotten. Late in the day, Nadine realized that she hadn't gotten anything for Lance for Christmas—not to mention a wedding gift. And she also needed shoes to be married in. She took Dulsie into town to do some shopping and found great pleasure in just being able to freely walk the streets of Horstberg and not wonder if she was being watched or followed by someone with evil motives. They also went to the inn and cleared out all of their belongings since Nadine would be staying at the castle that night. Drew and Gerda were thrilled to hear that all was well, and they promised to be at the wedding as well as the festivities at the castle later in the day. Nadine gave them an early Christmas gift and thanked them for all they'd done for her. They exchanged embraces and Nadine and Dulsie returned to the castle where all of their packages and Nadine's belongings were taken into Lance's apartment. She was grateful for the help of a couple of eager officers who seemed to have nothing better to do for the moment.

That evening they again shared supper with Cameron and Abbi. And Georg, who could hardly stop talking about Elsa's return the following day. Word had come that she would not be making it in time for the wedding, but she would be there for the combined Christmas-wedding festivities that would begin in the afternoon. When supper was over, they all went to one of the winter parlors for coffee. Dulsie, Erich, and Han were brought there, and the adults enjoyed watching the antics of the children as they pretended to be horses, neighing and whinnying at each other and galloping about the room. The conversation covered many topics, but every few minutes Nadine felt Lance catch her eye, and his smile would melt her from the inside out, while everything else in the room faded into the distance.

Talk of the wedding helped the prospect of getting married feel more real, and it served as a distraction from the constant tremor inside of her. She enjoyed hearing Georg reminisce about his court-ship and marriage to Elsa, then Cameron said, "I was married four times, but three of them were to Abbi."

Georg and Lance laughed heartily, and Nadine appreciated Abbi explaining, "We exchanged private vows when we were snowed in together, then the marriage was made official with the bishop, and then we were married publicly."

"That's the one I remember," Lance said, "but it won't be as memorable as tomorrow's wedding."

"That's a matter of opinion, I suppose," Cameron said.

It was difficult for Nadine to say good night to Lance, and once alone in a guest bedroom in the castle, Nadine found it practically impossible to sleep. In the deepest part of the night, negative voices began to fill her head, telling her that she was not capable of making a man like Lance Dukerk happy, that she would disappoint him and he was better off without her. Nadine closed her eyes tightly and prayed with all her heart and soul to be free of such horrible thoughts, and gradually she felt them dissipate behind a brighter picture of her future and a positive belief that she *could* make him happy. And she would!

Lance crawled into bed and heard himself laugh out loud as the happiness just seemed to burst out of him. He was getting married in the morning, which was nothing short of a miracle. Recounting all that had happened since Nadine had arrived in Horstberg, he was left stunned and in awe of the drama they'd endured and the string of miracles that had made it possible for them to both come through unscathed and prepared to embark on a bright future together.

Attempting to quiet his mind and get some sleep, Lance felt startled to find disturbing thoughts trickling into his head. And his efforts to force them away only seemed to make them more stubborn and relentless. Through his concerns for Nadine's life and then his heartache over their estrangement, he had managed to keep the issue of his illegitimate birth at bay. But now that all else was settled, there were no other worries or pressures to fill his mind, and his difficult feelings over his mother's affair with the duke completely took over. He'd had thoughts concerning the matter creep into his mind regularly, but he'd always been able to push them away with more pressing concerns. But now, the matter was front and center. While he longed to be able to just put the issue away and not let it bother him, a part of him believed that he'd never be free of the uneasiness of knowing the truth about his paternity. Considering the forgiveness he'd worked so hard at in relation to Nikolaus, and even Albert Crider, he wondered if he was feeling angry with his parents for having an affair. Truthfully, he wasn't quite sure how he felt toward them. And even more disconcerting, he wasn't quite sure how he felt about himself. He was deeply grateful for Nadine's acceptance. In spite of all their challenges, she'd never been anything less than accepting of him in relation to this, and he was grateful. He felt equally grateful for the unquestionable acceptance of Cameron and Abbi, and even Georg. If the discovery had created tension between them, he couldn't even imagine how he would have coped. As it stood now—even in spite of their acceptance—he doubted that he could ever feel completely good again about who and what he was.

When sleep continued to elude him, Lance found himself searching for the answers. His mind was drawn to his sister's promiscuity. He felt certain now that it likely had a great deal to do with their mother being the same. Pondering memories of his mother, he wondered if his struggle was mostly due to his misconceptions of her. His memories of her had always been positive. She'd been warm and sweet, and now he could only imagine her as some kind of harlot. And he wondered what his mother's perception of *him* might have been. Had she seen him as an inconvenience that had occurred by mistake? And what of Jacob Dukerk, the man who had raised him as a son? Had he known the truth? As the questions circled in his head, he had to admit that his perception of himself had been shaken by not understanding his parents' perception of his existence. And perhaps he never would.

When the same thoughts began running over and over, Lance got up and read from the Bible until he got sleepy. Only then was he able to get some rest, keeping the thought foremost in his mind that within hours he would be married, and if he had his way, he would never sleep alone again.

Nadine finally slept until Bruna woke her to say, "Her Grace would like you to join her for breakfast in her sitting room before you begin dressing for the wedding."

Nadine wrapped herself in a dressing gown that had been delivered with the new clothes that she'd ordered along with her wedding dress. She hurried to Abbi's sitting room and sat across from her where breakfast was waiting. Abbi gave her an almost mischievous smile and Nadine couldn't hold back a little giggle. "I'm getting married today," Nadine said.

"Yes, you are," she said.

"How are you feeling?" Nadine asked, pouring out coffee for both of them.

"I've certainly felt better, but I'm not missing this for the world. I'll rest this afternoon. There will be plenty of time for that between the wedding and the festivities."

"That's good, because I certainly didn't get enough sleep last night."

Abbi smirked and said, "Oh, I don't know that *you* will have time to get any rest."

It took Nadine a moment to figure what she meant, then she felt herself turn warm while Abbi let out a girlish laugh.

"What's so funny?" Cameron asked, appearing in the doorway.

"Oh, nothing," Abbi insisted.

"What you really mean," he said, sauntering toward them, "is that it's one of those feminine secrets you won't share with me."

"That's what I mean," Abbi said and laughed again.

Nadine watched him bend over to kiss his wife, briefly resting a hand on the mound created by the baby inside of her. She recalled what Lance had said about once envying the way they felt about each other, but now he simply understood those feelings. And so did she.

"What are you doing here?" Abbi asked. "I thought you had important business to see to this morning."

"Oh, I do," he said, "and some of it concerns the soon-to-be Mrs. Dukerk."

"Me?" Nadine said, surprised.

"Yes, you," he said, taking an empty chair between her and Abbi. "It occurred to me that you have no father or brother to give the bride away. Were you planning to walk up the aisle alone, then?"

"I hadn't really thought about it," she said. "Dulsie will be walking ahead of me. Is there a problem? Walking alone is all right, isn't it?"

"It is if that's what you want to do," he said, "but in the event that you would prefer *not* to walk alone, I would be most privileged if you would allow *me* to give the bride away."

Nadine gasped, but she could think of nothing to say. Abbi finally filled the silence. "If you would prefer to walk alone, Nadine, it's all right. He is simply offering."

"That's right," Cameron added.

"Oh, it's not that I prefer to walk alone. It would be such an honor to have you walk with me, but . . . I'm just surprised by your offer. And . . . I thought you were standing up with Lance."

"I am, of course," he said. "But I can do both. Georg did the same when Abbi and I were married. Today, he has the singular privilege of staying at Abbi's side and being certain that she is well. So, what do you say, Nadine?"

"It would be an honor, Your Grace," she said, "but I'm still wondering . . . why. Did Lance ask you to do this or—"

"No, this was my idea," Cameron said. "Occasionally I come up with an idea or two on my own." He exchanged a comical glance with Abbi, then his eyes deepened on Nadine. "In some small way," he said, "I would hope that this gesture might further your healing from the turmoil put into your life by my brother. Of course, there are many women who have suffered your fate, and I cannot personally ease their burdens. But you have, in many ways, come to represent those women to me. I don't know how much gossip about your situation might have spread in regard to your recent ordeal, but my hope is that my appearing in public with you this way will be somewhat of a silent declaration that I respect and honor you as a lady in every respect. And of course, Lance has become one of my dearest and closest friends." He lowered his voice to a whisper. "And he is my brother. It would be a singular honor if you would allow me to place the hand of his bride into his."

Nadine was so touched she found it difficult to speak. Instead she threw her arms around his neck, hoping it wasn't inappropriate for her to casually hug the Duke of Horstberg. When he chuckled and returned the embrace, she figured she wasn't too far out of line.

"Does that mean yes?" he asked when she eased away.

"Yes, of course," she said. "It is I who would be honored, Your Grace. Thank you."

"You're welcome," he said, "and you're practically family. Unless we are in public, Cameron would be fine."

Nadine smiled at him as he stood. He kissed Abbi once more, then took Nadine's hand and kissed it as well. "I will see you ladies very soon. I think it's time we all started getting ready for this wedding."

He hurried from the room and Nadine said to Abbi, "He's a wonderful man, your husband."

"Yes, he is," Abbi said with pride in her voice. "As your husband will be."

They exchanged a smile and hurried to finish their breakfast. As soon as they'd eaten, Bruna came to help them both with their hair and into their gowns. Nadine examined her reflection in a long mirror while Abbi fastened the long row of tiny buttons down her back. She'd never felt so beautiful, so loved, so perfectly happy. The picture was completed when she put on the diamond jewelry that Lance had given her. Seeing how the gems sparkled in the light, she felt a tangible reminder of the love he had for her.

"Oh, you look divine," Abbi declared once Bruna had put the veil into place in her carefully arranged hair.

Nadine gave Abbi a careful embrace, saying tearfully, "I cannot ever thank you enough for all that you've done for me—for standing by me even when I was being such a fool. I've never had such a friend as you, and I'm truly grateful."

"We will be friends forever, my dear," Abbi said. "Now come along. They're waiting."

"They are?" Nadine asked, panicked.

"Just have a look," Abbi said, motioning toward the window. Then to Bruna, "Would you please fetch my velvet cloak? The dark blue one? It will keep her warm and elegant."

"Yes, Your Grace," Bruna said and left the room just as Nadine approached the window and looked down to the courtyard below. She caught her breath to see a stationary version of the funeral procession she had seen pass through the center of Horstberg soon after her arrival. But instead of a hearse and a funeral coach, there was the ducal coach and a beautiful white and gold open coach, draped with white streamers and bows, harnessed to four white caparisoned horses. The officers were all waiting at ease, as well as the standard bearers and drummers. Those who would be riding horses were standing beside their mounts, some visiting casually. The procession itself wound into a spiral in the courtyard, and she could well imagine how it would smoothly unwind as it eased out the castle gate and down the hill. The very idea was so perfectly ethereal that she found it difficult to believe the beautiful coach was waiting for *her*.

"It's incredible," Nadine said as Abbi appeared beside her.

"Yes, it is," Abbi said, putting the velvet cloak around Nadine's shoulders. "A wedding fit for a queen. Come along, my friend."

Just before they left the window, Nadine saw Lance and Cameron appear from a doorway at the opposite side of the courtyard and approach the officers who were holding their horses for them. Cameron wore the red robe of his position, which flowed out from his shoulders as he walked. Lance wore a finer version of his military cloak, black trimmed with red and gold, and it too flowed around him.

Nadine and Abbi arrived in the main hall to find Dulsie waiting there with one of the nannies. She was wearing her new dress, with her hair styled like the finest of ladies and her face beamed with pleasure, brightening even further when she saw her mother. The ladies waited just inside the door until the procession started out the gate to the beat of a lively drum cadence that carried a different mood entirely from the funeral procession that Nadine had witnessed. Once Cameron and Lance were beyond the gate, officers escorted the ladies into the courtyard so that the groom would not see the bride before the wedding. Nadine and Dulsie were helped into the open coach, and Georg rode with Abbi in the ducal coach.

As the procession wound down the hillside, Nadine marveled at the reality of what was happening. Dulsie sat beside her, all aglow, looking happier than she ever had. Moving through town, Nadine was amazed at the amount of people gathered along the street, waving and cheering as if this day were glorious for them all. She concluded that Lance Dukerk was a highly respected and well-known man, and the people were pleased to see him getting married. She felt tempted to pinch herself to be certain that she was indeed the woman he would marry.

The coach finally stopped in front of the cathedral, and Nadine and Dulsie were helped down by officers of the Guard who escorted them inside. They were taken into a room where Cameron and Abbi were both waiting, and Nadine removed her cloak. Abbi smiled as she adjusted Nadine's veil and smoothed her hair. "You look perfect," she said and stepped aside for Cameron to approach her. As he did, she realized he was wearing the simple crown that she had seen him wear previously.

Cameron took both her hands into his and pressed a kiss to her brow. "May this day be among the happiest of your life," he said. "You could not be marrying a finer man."

"I know," she said and he carefully lifted the top portion of her veil and draped it over her face.

"It's time," Abbi said and the three of them stepped out of the room and stood near the huge doors at the rear of the cathedral. Georg was waiting to escort Abbi to her seat.

"Just like my wedding," she said, putting her hand over Georg's arm. "Georg gave the bride away and . . . well, look at that—same groom at the other end of the cathedral." She laughed softly.

"Go sit down," Cameron said, lightly scolding. "I showed up, didn't I."

"Indeed, you did," she said and kissed Cameron quickly before she and Georg moved away.

The music took a dramatic shift and Nadine urged Dulsie to begin her slow walk toward the front of the cathedral. "Just like we practiced," Nadine said softly and Dulsie moved forward with confidence.

Cameron whispered, "We're off, my dear." He held his arm suspended and set her hand over his before they started down the aisle. She quickly matched her step to his and again felt as if she should pinch herself. She was being escorted down the center of this huge, magnificent cathedral on the arm of the Duke of Horstberg. And there, in the closing distance, near the altar, was a man equally fine, looking magnificent in his formal uniform.

Suddenly nervous, Nadine whispered to Cameron, grateful for the music that would prevent them from being overheard. "So, I hear when you *did* show up to the wedding, you were on a horse, with military escort."

He chuckled softly. "Well, I wasn't only getting married, I was reclaiming my country. This cathedral is also used for political cere-monies, and it was more that than a wedding." He chuckled again. "Actually, we'd been married for quite some time, and she was signifi-cantly pregnant."

"I'm glad it all worked out."

"Yes, so am I," he said softly. "If it hadn't, I'd be dead and you wouldn't be marrying the captain, because he'd already be married."

"For that and many other reasons," she smiled toward him, "I'm *really* glad it all worked out."

He smiled in return and they pressed forward. Nadine was now close enough to see, even through her veil, the expectancy in Lance's countenance and the undeniable adoration in his eyes as he watched her approach. When they finally reached the altar, Dulsie was waiting like a perfect lady beside Lance. Cameron kissed Nadine's hand and set it into Lance's before he stepped back, urging Dulsie to stand beside him as Lance escorted Nadine to the altar where they both knelt before the bishop.

The ceremony was perfect, and Nadine only thought for a moment of the contrast between this moment and the mock marriage that Nikolaus had lured her into. Beyond that, her mind, her heart, and her soul were all focused on this moment and the reality that she was among the most blessed women in the world. As Lance lifted the veil to kiss her, she felt as if she could hear angels singing.

Once they were declared husband and wife, Lance escorted her from the cathedral. At the door, they were both helped into their cloaks before they stepped into the open coach where he sat beside her for the return to Castle Horstberg. Nadine knew that Dulsie would be riding back with Abbi, who would see that she was looked after her until the festivities began this afternoon.

"I love you dearly, Mrs. Dukerk," Lance said and kissed her the moment they were seated.

Nadine laughed at the sound of her new name and urged him to kiss her again. How grateful she was to be alive, to be free, and to be married to the finest man she had ever known.

The return trek to the castle felt completely dreamlike with Lance's arm around her and his ring on her finger. It was like something out of a fairy tale. Of course, they had been through much, and she was not naive enough to believe that life would be free of challenges. But in her heart she knew that, together, with the love and commitment they shared, they could overcome anything.

As the coach started up the castle hill, matching the pace of the officers on foot, Lance whispered close to her ear, "Did you have plans for the rest of the day, my dear?"

"Nothing beyond getting to that party later. I did help plan it, you know, and it's been adjusted to be in our honor."

"Yes," he smiled, "but that's hours away."

Nadine looked into his eyes and said, "I was thinking I'd just try to adjust to believing that I'm your wife."

"Sounds delightful," he said and kissed her. Now that they had traveled beyond the crowded streets, she realized that no one could see them, given that the officers ahead were facing the opposite direction. He kissed her and kissed her, over and over, with a passion that she'd never felt come through in his affection before. Her respect for him deepened as she felt the evidence of how he had carefully kept his passion in check until now. And now he was her husband. The prospect of what that meant filled her with jittery excitement.

"I love you . . . Captain," she said, pressing a hand over his face while he gazed into her eyes with an intensity that let her know he shared her anticipation.

When they finally arrived at the castle, Lance helped her down from the coach and they walked hand in hand across the courtyard and down the exterior corridor that led to his apartment. He opened the door then lifted her into his arms to carry her over the threshold, laughing as he did. He kicked the door closed then set her down long enough to lock it before he picked her up again and headed up the stairs. She held to him tightly and laughed at the weightlessness she felt. In the bedroom he kicked that door closed, as well.

"We're all alone," he muttered, letting her feet slide to the floor.

"Yes, we are," she said, looking into his eyes.

"And we're married," he added as if he found it as difficult to believe as she did.

"Yes, we are," she said again.

He bent to kiss her with a passion that even exceeded what she had felt from his kisses in the coach. He drew her completely into his arms, but she found herself confronted with the numerous medals across the front of his uniform. Without hesitating a moment, she unfastened the hooks down the front of the beautiful red coat and pushed it off of his shoulders. He hung it over the back of a chair and closed the drapes while she turned down the bed and stood to face the mirror in order to remove the veil that was clipped into her hair. As she laid it over the top of the bureau, he set his hands on her shoulders and pressed a kiss to the back of her neck. He teased at her earlobe with his lips and pressed his hands down her arms and back up again before he began unfastening the long row of buttons down her back. The heavy dress fell in a circle around her as he pushed it forward, over her shoulders and down her arms. She stepped out of the circle and into his embrace where he met her with a kiss that quickly turned warm and moist. She pushed his braces over his shoulders and tugged at the buttons of his shirt while he kissed her, on and on, slowly savoring each moment of the experience. Feeling her every nerve respond, an unexpected surge of tears overwhelmed her. When a quiet sob interrupted his kiss, he drew back abruptly. "What is it?" he asked in quiet alarm.

"I don't know," she muttered. "I just . . ." She looked into his eyes. "Oh, Lance. I thought I was going to die, first in prison, and then when . . . he had me, and . . . even when I tried to hope that I would make it through alive, I just couldn't bring myself to believe that there would ever be another chance for us. I'd been such a fool, and I . . . just thought you deserved better than me . . ." Her crying increased. "But here we are. You stood by me in spite of myself. You saved my life, not once, but twice. And here we are. I just . . . feel so blessed, so completely lucky to be the woman who won your heart, and . . . oh, I love you, Lance."

He laughed softly and wiped at her tears. "I love you too, Nadine—with all my heart and soul." He lifted her into his arms and carried her to the bed where he lay close beside her, kissing her tears away as surely as his love erased all that she had ever suffered in her life. Never had she imagined such perfect bliss and contentment, and she marveled at the realization seeping into her heart that the joy of sharing her life with him would not be short lived, but he would be hers for as long as there was air to breathe.

Lance leaned his head into his hand and watched Nadine emerge from what seemed a perfect, celestial dream, although he knew she'd not been sleeping. He gently pressed her hair back off her face, in awe of what they had just shared. The crass descriptions he'd spent years hearing in pubs and among his fellow officers were so far removed from all that he had experienced in the last hour. She opened her eyes to look at him and smiled as if they now shared some deep secret. And they did. He knew in his heart that no matter what struggles came into their lives, they would always have this perfect, sacred part of their relationship that no one or nothing could intrude upon.

"Where are your thoughts, my love?" she asked, pressing her fingertips over his face.

"There are no words," he muttered and kissed her brow. "I never imagined that it could be so completely . . . magnificent."

"Nor did I," she said with a glisten of moisture appearing in the corners of her eyes. "It was never like this . . . before. I would have never believed it could be so . . . emotionally filling, even spiritual. I had believed he loved me. Now I know he had no comprehension of love."

"No, I don't believe he did," Lance said and kissed her. "But he gave you Dulsie, and for that I am grateful."

"Yes, so am I," she said and kissed him. She wrapped her arms around his neck without severing her lips from his, and it took little urging for him to make love to her again.

Nadine slept in his arms and woke to the sound of his voice close to her face. "Wake up, Mrs. Dukerk, or we'll be late for the party." He chuckled. "I'm afraid our tardiness would be starkly noticed, and I would never live it down with those scoundrels I have to work with."

"Are your men scoundrels?"

"Yes, but I was talking about Cameron and Georg," he said and she laughed as she stretched herself awake.

She slipped into her underclothing then looked in the mirror and gasped. "Oh, my hair is horrible. And I can't very well run across the courtyard and hunt down Bruna to fix it again for me."

Lance came behind her. "Just . . . brush it down," he said. "Abbi wore her hair down for her wedding festivities. Between the two of you, it could start a new trend."

"I wouldn't embarrass you?" she asked, feeling for pins in her hair.

"That is simply not possible," he said with a grin and helped her search for the pins. When they were finally all out, he took up the hairbrush and smoothed her hair down the length of her back.

"Are you enjoying yourself?" she asked.

"Yes, actually," he admitted.

"Well, I think it's sufficiently smooth. If we don't hurry, you'll never live it down. Remember?"

"Of course," he said, setting the brush aside. "I will look forward to continuing this later."

"Indeed," she said and stepped into her dress. Lance fastened the buttons for her before she pinned the veil in place while Lance put on the coat of his uniform.

"Are we ready?" he asked, holding out his arm.

"Not quite," she said and kissed him in a way that betrayed the intimacy they had shared. He pulled her into his arms while their kiss went on and on. She finally eased her lips from his and murmured, "Now I'm ready."

Lance sighed loudly. "With any luck this party won't last too long."

"If it does, we'll just . . . disappear."

"An excellent plan, Mrs. Dukerk," he said and guided her down the stairs.

They went together to Cameron and Abbi's rooms where they found Abbi all ready, with her feet up, and Cameron's valet clipping the robe to his shoulders.

"Good, you're here," Cameron said, tossing an unmistakable smirk toward Lance. "We can't make our grand entrance without you, since you are the guests of honor."

"In a way," Lance said as the valet left the room. "It's still a Christmas party, so let's not forget what we're *really* celebrating. I can assure you that without God's help, *I* would have little worth celebrating at all."

"As it is," Abbi said, "Lance is the happiest man alive. Have you ever seen him look so happy, Cameron?"

Cameron smirked again. "Never," he said. "But I dispute his being the happiest man alive." He bent to kiss Abbi. "I thought it was me."

"Of course," Abbi said as Cameron tenderly helped her to her feet. "Shall we go?"

"Are you up to this?" Cameron asked.

"I'll make my entrance and have something to eat," she said, "then I'm going to bed early."

"That sounds reasonable," Cameron said. "I don't want you overdoing it."

"Yes, Your Grace," she said and they moved into the hall.

Lance and Nadine followed them to the head of the grand staircase that descended into the ballroom. They could hear laughter and chattering and knew that the celebrations were well underway. Cameron and Abbi stepped out onto the landing and the music soon came to a halt. A loud voice bellowed, "Their Graces, the Duke and Duchess of Horstberg." They descended while Lance kissed Nadine, then he cleared his throat and chuckled before they stepped onto the landing just in time to see Cameron and Abbi reach the bottom of the stairs. That voice then said just as loudly, "Captain and Mrs. Dukerk."

A cheer and applause came up from the crowd and Nadine whispered, "I've never felt so conspicuous in my whole life."

"Just be glad you don't have to do this at *every* party, as Cameron and Abbi do."

"Oh, I am glad for that," she said. "Although," she smiled at him, "being conspicuous on your arm isn't so bad. With you beside me, I think I could endure just about anything."

He laughed as they reached the ballroom floor, and a servant guided them to where they would receive guests who wished to congratulate them on their marriage. Nadine enjoyed meeting people for the most part, and she was amazed at how many people Lance knew and how well he could remember their names. The only people who came that *she* knew were Drew and Gerda and the girls who worked at the inn, which apparently had been closed for this event.

Nadine was relieved to have supper finally served, since they had foregone lunch.

"I'm starving," Lance muttered near her ear as they walked into the huge dining room that was beautifully decorated for the holiday.

"You missed lunch," she said and he chuckled.

"Did I? I don't think I noticed."

Near the end of the meal, Cameron stood and tapped the side of his goblet to get everyone's attention. "I would like to propose a toast," he said, raising his glass, "to the Captain of the Guard, a man among men, whose honor and integrity and courage have greatly contributed to the strength of our dear Horstberg, and whose friendship has made me a better man. The kind of man that I would choose for a brother, if the choice were given me."

Lance felt briefly startled until he realized that the way he had worded it had been completely hypothetical. The entire crowd came to their feet and raised their glasses, declaring, "Hear, hear!" before they drank.

"And," Cameron went on, "to the new Mrs. Dukerk, a woman who has shown remarkable strength and courage in overcoming recent challenges that would have broken most women."

Nadine met his eyes and felt near tears. She'd never looked at it that way before; she'd only been able to see how she'd been so emotional and confused. But here, in a matter of days from when she'd been abducted and threatened with her life, she felt free and whole. And Cameron had apparently noticed.

"But that's not really a surprise," Cameron added, "given that she is the woman who won the heart of a man who is highly reputed for being the fussiest bachelor in Horstberg." There was laughter before they all drank and were seated to finish their meal. Lance turned to look at Nadine and smiled as he raised his glass, saying quietly, "To perfect happiness."

"Hear, hear," she said, clicking her glass to his.

Chapter Thirty-Four

THE STORM

*F*ollowing supper there was dancing and games and then a reverent enactment of the Nativity, followed by more dancing. Dulsie occasionally reported to Lance and Nadine some bit of excitement, but she seemed to prefer hovering with one of her nursery friends who was there with her family. Abbi had long since retired to her rooms, but Cameron hovered among their guests and was often near Lance and Nadine, as if he simply preferred their company. A thought occurred to Lance and he asked, "Where's Georg? I've not seen him since this morning."

"Pacing the halls and cursing, presumably," Cameron said. "He got word just after lunch that Elsa's carriage would be delayed. Apparently the friend who went with her was ill and unable to travel for a day, which set them behind. She's fine and they're on their way, but Georg is fit to be tied. I pray she never leaves us again. He's managed to be tolerable, but he's not been himself."

"I can well imagine," Lance said, reaching for Nadine's hand.

"Yes, so can I," Cameron said. He then smirked and added, "The two of you are looking awfully tired. Perhaps you should call it a day."

"What an excellent idea," Nadine said. "I confess that I didn't sleep well at all last night."

"Dulsie is happy and busy at the moment," Cameron said. "We'll watch out for her tonight, just as we planned. No need to worry about her."

"Make our excuses," Lance said to Cameron, then he held out a hand. "Thank you . . . for everything."

"A pleasure," Cameron said, shaking his hand firmly. "It's good to see you so happy."

"It's good to be happy," Lance said and he rushed Nadine discreetly from the ballroom and into the hall. He gave her a long, warm kiss before they hurried back to their apartment.

"Tomorrow is Christmas Eve," Lance said as he locked the door and Nadine was lighting a lamp.

"Yes, I know," she said, "and never has the prospect of Christmas been so appealing."

"Amen," he said and followed her up the stairs.

"And then," she said, "the day after Christmas we get to leave for a very long honeymoon. Usually the day after Christmas is such a letdown, but not this year."

"Amen," he said again with more enthusiasm and she laughed softly.

Nadine set the lamp down and Lance started undoing the buttons on her gown. "All of your dresses don't take this long to get in and out of, do they?"

"No, of course not," she said. "And most of them I can get in and out of all by myself."

"I'm terribly glad to hear it," he said, "because I believe our time would be better spent on other things."

"Indeed," she said and they both laughed.

Nadine thoroughly savored preparing a late breakfast in the kitchen that was now hers. She was glad she'd had the insight to pick up some groceries when she'd gone to town with Dulsie, and she felt a perfect contentment doing something she enjoyed for someone she loved. She frequently paused to look out the window, surprised at the dark, heavy sky. She'd hardly seen a cloud in all the weeks she'd been in Horstberg, and now it looked as if the sky would open up with torrents of snow at any moment. She was startled to feel Lance's arms come around her from behind. He laughed close to her ear and kissed her throat before she turned to face him and look him up and down with a noise of approval. "How very common you look without your uniform, Captain."

"Exactly as a man should look who is on holiday," he said. "I'm not going back to work until after the honeymoon."

"What a delightful thought," she said.

"You're cooking."

"I am."

"You really don't have to do that," he said. "In fact, I've been thinking that perhaps we should hire someone full time to help with the house and such. The woman who comes in to do some cleaning has other full-time work, but I'm sure we could find someone you'd be comfortable with."

"I'm not certain that's necessary," she said, handing him a cup of coffee.

"I'm sure you could manage," he said, "but I want you to be able to spend your time doing . . . well, whatever you want. Abbi's always got her fingers into one goodwill project or another. I'm sure she'd appreciate your help, and the two of you would have a marvelous time at it."

"That does sound appealing," she said. "I don't know. I'll have to give it some thought. We'll worry about that after the honeymoon."

"Of course," he said and kissed her warmly.

"Are you helping Abbi today?" he asked, knowing that she was concerned about Abbi not feeling well and trying to do too much, especially since Elsa hadn't returned when she'd been scheduled to.

"No, *we* are helping Abbi today," she said.

"Of course," he chuckled. "It doesn't involve moving furniture, does it?"

"I wouldn't think so."

They shared a leisurely breakfast, and he raved about her cooking. Together they cleaned the dishes, kissing so much in between that Nadine felt certain they would end up back in the bedroom. But her concern for Abbi forced her to keep her reason. "Come along, Captain," she said, urging him toward the door, "we'll have plenty of time for such things after Christmas."

As the stepped out into the courtyard, an officer who had apparently been loitering nearby approached them with obvious hesitance. Nadine recognized him as Lieutenant Kepler.

"Forgive me, Captain," he said. "I know this is your day off, and I'm well aware that I could handle the situation enough to get by until you return from your honeymoon, but I just felt that you would want to know that the woman who was an accomplice to Albert Crider has come forward."

"Really?" Lance said, sounding more intrigued than concerned. "She just . . . walked in and confessed?"

"Yes, actually. She's forty-four years old, never been married, has no family connections. She works as a household servant and he picked her up at the café where she eats lunch on her days off."

Lance made a noise of interest and said, "I think that warrants taking a break from my vacation. I'll be there shortly."

"Very good, Captain," Kepler said and hurried away.

Lance turned to Nadine. "You go along and see what Abbi needs. I'll hurry. I'm sure she'll understand."

"Yes, she'll understand why I need to go with you," Nadine said firmly, almost expecting him to argue with her. While he just looked at her, seeming dazed, she asked, "Is it against standard protocol for the captain's wife to accompany him when interrogating a woman?"

"No," Lance said, his voice gentle. "I'm just wondering if you're really up to this. It hasn't been all that long; it was traumatic for you. I have no idea what to expect."

Nadine thought about that for a moment. "I appreciate your concern, but . . . I feel like I should be there. If it gets difficult, I'll leave."

"Agreed," he said. "Come along then."

Nadine felt more relief than anything when they entered the keep. She was a free woman and her difficult memories of this place were counteracted by her present happiness. They walked down a hallway, following Lieutenant Kepler past Lance's office to a room that she recognized. This was where she and Dulsie had waited to speak with the captain the first day she'd come to Horstberg. Oh, if she'd only known then what she knew now! Here she was, less than two months later, his wife. And what adventures they'd gone through to come to this day!

"Miss Schmidt," Kepler said, "this is Captain Dukerk and his wife. Captain, Wilhelmina Schmidt."

The woman came to her feet, nervously wringing her hands as Kepler closed the door and leaned against it. Nadine knew well that feeling of having an officer guard every avenue for retreat. Wilhelmina

Schmidt was a tall, wiry woman, rather plain, with dark brown hair pulled into a tight knot at the back of her head. Nadine took one glance at her fearful eyes and felt nothing for her but compassion. She whispered to Lance, "This is no accomplice; she's a victim." He turned to look at her, startled, then he cleared his throat and put his attention to the woman in question.

"Miss Schmidt," Lance said in that tone Nadine recognized well. He was the captain now, and even dressed as he was without his uniform, he was no less imposing. "So, you were acquainted with Albert Crider."

"I was, yes," she said in a shaky voice.

"Please, sit down," he said, motioning her toward the chair she'd just risen from. Nadine sat as well. Lance leaned against the edge of the table in the center of the room. "Now, could you please tell us what possessed you to become involved with a man like Albert Crider? Did he bribe you? Threaten you?"

"Well . . . no," Miss Schmidt looked flustered and frightened and close to tears. "Not at first. No. He . . . well, he . . . he just . . . he . . ."

After she'd stammered for another couple of minutes, Nadine moved to sit closer to this woman. Taking the woman's hand, she looked into her eyes and said gently, "Where exactly did you meet him, Wilhelmina? May I call you Wilhelmina?"

"Of course," she said, already more relaxed. "Actually, I go by Mina. I was eating lunch where I always do on my day off, and he just . . . approached me and asked if he could join me. I don't get much attention from men. I never have. At first I was flattered, but before I knew it, he was actually sleeping in my home, eating my food, and manipulating me into doing his bidding."

Lance listened to Nadine converse with this woman for nearly an hour, amazed at the way his wife was managing to pull every little detail of the story out of her, while Mina remained completely comfortable. She talked of buying the white scarves, delivering messages to the inn where Nadine worked, and other deeds he had threatened her into doing. He felt the conversation winding down, but there was one question he still needed answered. It was always the most difficult to ask regarding female victims, but it had to be done. He was about to interject that he needed to say something when Nadine leaned closer to this woman and asked in a tender voice, "Did he hurt you, Mina? Did he ever do *anything* to physically hurt you?"

"He slapped me a couple of times," she said, turning her eyes downward.

Nadine glanced at Lance and he nodded subtly, hoping she understood that there was more they needed to know. Nadine cleared her throat gently and asked, "Did he ever attempt anything sexual, Mina?"

She looked startled before she blushed visibly and glanced at the men in the room as if she couldn't believe that such a word would even be spoken in mixed company. "It's all right," Nadine said. "Unfortunately, these men have dealt with such issues many times in the past. Whatever you tell them will be completely confidential."

"No," Mina said, "he never *did* anything, but he talked and talked about it, saying horrible things." She started to cry. "It was just so . . . horrible."

Nadine put an arm around her and said quietly to Lance, "I think she's told us all there is to tell."

"Yes, thank you, Nadine," he replied and Mina shot her head up.

"Nadine?" she said, looking at her with wide eyes, then she turned to Lance with the same stunned expression. "The captain? You're married?"

"We are," Lance said.

"You're the one," Mina said to Nadine. "You're the one he was talking about, the woman he was stalking."

"That's right," Nadine said.

"And you're all right," she said, even more astonished.

"I am."

"And you're married."

"I am," Nadine said again.

"Oh, forgive me," Mina said. "I just . . . well, I knew you had gotten away from him before he was arrested. Everybody knew that, but . . . he played such games with a person's mind, and he told me over and over that even if he didn't succeed in making you his, he would be sure that your head was too messed up to ever be any good to any other man. But you look so . . . happy."

"I am," Nadine said still again, this time with a little laugh. "It's all right, Mina. It took me a while to figure it out, but I will not let that man have power over me or my life. I let my anger and bitterness toward him go, and I have put the episode in the past. You must do the same."

"Do you have everything you need?" Lance asked gently.

Mina looked startled. "I don't understand."

"You have a place to live? Plenty to eat?"

"Yes, of course," she said.

"Could we provide you with transportation home?" he asked and the confusion on her face deepened.

"But . . . I thought you would arrest me. Was I not an accomplice to this man's crimes? Didn't I—"

"Miss Schmidt," Lance said, tossing a brief appreciative glance to Nadine, "you are a victim of Albert Crider's manipulation. We are only grateful that you have lived to tell of your experiences. We appreciate your time and hope that you have a merry Christmas. Lieutenant Kepler will arrange for you to be taken home."

"Oh, thank you," she said with fresh tears and followed Kepler from the room. She turned back long enough to say, "And merry Christmas to you. I wish you both the best."

"And you," Nadine said.

When they were alone, Lance turned to Nadine and said, "Do you have any idea how amazing you are?" She only looked baffled. "In spite of a great deal of practice, I have never been able to question a woman and get that much information with so little trauma. I think I need to give you a job."

Nadine just gave a flippant laugh and walked out of the room, knowing he would follow. They stepped outside to find it snowing significantly. "Oh my," Nadine said and Lance threw his cloak over her before they ran to the main entrance of the castle.

"Can you believe that?" Nadine asked once they were inside.

"What?"

"Poor woman, coming here on Christmas Eve, believing she would be arrested simply because she had been manipulated and threatened into helping the . . . fiend. I'm glad that you're a *good* captain."

"I certainly try," he said. "But I think *you* should be the captain from now on. I'll just do whatever you tell me."

"Really? Anything?"

"Anything," he said.

"Then kiss me," she insisted and he did.

Through the next few hours, Horstberg became submerged beneath a heavy blanket of white. And it looked as if the clouds were not about to let up anytime soon. Nadine stayed close to Abbi, who readily admitted that she was worn out from the previous day and simply didn't feel up to getting out of bed. Abbi relaxed once she was assured that the Christmas celebrations for that day were completely delegated and under control. A grand party would begin midday for everyone remotely connected to Castle Horstberg and its military personnel who had not been involved in the previous day's festivities. The royal family and close friends, which included Georg and Elsa, and Lance and Nadine, would be having a more intimate Christmas celebration with their children later in the evening.

Long after lunch when Abbi became restless and had mentioned several times that she was concerned over the fact that Elsa had not yet arrived, they went together down the stairs to the ducal office where they found Cameron, Georg, and Lance. Abbi quickly went to a chair and put her feet up in another one, but once she was settled it became evident that the mood in the office was not agreeable. Georg was pacing the floor. Lance and Cameron were silently tense.

"I'm certain she's fine, Georg," Abbi said.

"Well, then why do I feel certain that she's not?" he growled and Nadine couldn't ever recall seeing Georg be anything but calm and cool. "She should have been here nearly three hours ago. The inn where they stayed last night is only half a day's ride from here, and they were leaving at dawn."

Nadine expected Abbi to reassure him and calm him down, but she asked intently, "Do you really feel that way?"

"I really do," he said.

"Then what are you going to do about it?" she asked.

Georg gazed at her for a long moment before he said, "I'm going to go find her."

Cameron and Lance jumped out of their seats as if they'd suddenly become hot. "I'm going with you," Cameron said. Then to Lance, "You look out for Abbi and—"

"I'm looking out for *you*," Lance insisted. "Nadine will look out for Abbi. Won't you, my dear?"

"Of course," she said easily. "Please be careful."

"Of course," he repeated in the same tone.

Lance and Cameron each kissed their wives and hurried to catch up with Georg.

"Now, I suppose you'll have to help me back up those stairs," Abbi said and Nadine held to her arm while Abbi came carefully to her feet. "I really feel terrible," she said. "I don't know that I want to feel this way for another few weeks. I'm really praying that she comes early."

"She?" Nadine asked, helping Abbi up the stairs.

"I just feel like it's a girl. I was right last time. I guess we'll see."

"Well," Nadine said, "I hope *she* comes when she is strong enough to make it on her own."

"Amen," Abbi said.

Once in the bedroom, Abbi plopped onto the bed and declared, "I think I'm staying in this room until the baby comes. I can't go up and down those stairs anymore."

"You're the duchess. I'd say you can stay anywhere you want. We'll arrange for your every need to be brought to your bedside."

"Ah, there are advantages to being married to royalty," Abbi said with a little laugh. "But then, all those tedious receptions and such— that's the down side. Still, it's worth it."

"Only because you love him. I suspect that you would be just as happy if he were a farmer or a shopkeeper."

"Indeed I would," Abbi said, "and I've told him as much."

"Would you like me to rub your feet?" Nadine asked. "I'm very good with a hand massage, and I can do that as well if you like. But your feet are so swollen. I remember mine being that way. Perhaps a good rubbing would help them feel better."

"Oh, it sounds wonderful," Abbi said and Nadine sat on the bed to remove Abbi's slippers and stockings. "And while you're at it, tell me what you were going to earlier . . . about the woman who came to the keep today."

Nadine repeated the details of what Mina Schmidt had said and how it had made her feel. She was surprised to hear Abbi say, "It's evident that you have a gift, my dear. And you certainly have more experience than the average woman on how it feels to struggle and be in frightening circumstances. Perhaps you could find some true purpose for yourself, Nadine. And you can do it at your husband's side."

Nadine could think of nothing to say. Lance had joked about giving her a job; he'd said she'd been amazing. She hadn't felt amazing. She'd just connected on an emotional level with a woman in a difficult situation. She thought of how she'd searched out the women who had been victims of Nikolaus's betrayal. And while she doubted she'd done any good in that particular endeavor, she couldn't deny the feelings that had spurred her to do it. Letting the notion settle into her, she was surprised to note how comfortable she felt with the idea of simply being a support for the women her husband came in contact with through his work. Whether they were criminals or victims, they were women and they needed to be dealt with differently. She finally said, "Maybe you're right."

Abbi just smiled and said, "So, it would seem you are the perfect wife for Captain Dukerk after all."

Lance rode carefully through the thick snowfall with Cameron at his side, barely able to see Georg riding just ahead of them. He was grateful at least that they still had some significant daylight left and grateful for the two officers riding behind them who had volunteered to go along. The wind wasn't horrible, but it was significant. They rode for more than an hour and saw nothing, following the road that led out of the country in the direction that Elsa would have been returning. Lance moved ahead a little to ride beside Georg.

"Does this bring back any memories?" he asked.

Georg turned to look at him. "You read my mind. I really thought Abbi was dead that night."

"I did too," Lance said. "But she wasn't. We were blessed with a miracle. Surely we'll be blessed with another."

"I pray you're right," Georg said and they plodded on through the storm.

Abbi became so relaxed with Nadine rubbing her feet that she nearly fell asleep. She made a pleasurable noise that let Nadine know she was awake, then a moment later, Abbi gasped and her eyes flew open.

"What?" Nadine asked, wondering if the baby had kicked her. She'd seen such reactions before from that very thing, and had even experienced it herself when she'd been pregnant with Dulsie. Abbi didn't respond and Nadine asked, "Is something wrong?"

Abbi sat up from her reclined position and grimaced. "Yes," she said breathlessly. "My water just broke."

Nadine gasped as well. "Good heavens! It's too soon, isn't it?"

"Yes, but . . . I don't think that matters."

Nadine realized that Abbi was calm and she was panicking. She reminded herself to be levelheaded enough to be able to help her through this. And the men were all gone, and heaven only knew how long they would be. Of all the lousy timing! She took a deep breath and said in a voice that was only a little bit shaky, "I'm going to send someone for the doctor. What else do you need me to do?"

Before Abbi could answer she grimaced and moaned. "That was a pain, wasn't it," Nadine said.

"It most definitely was," Abbi said, sounding less calm. She blew her breath out slowly and said, "Have one of the maids get Mrs. Norberg who works in the kitchen. She has midwife experience. She can help me until the doctor gets here and . . ."

Abbi grimaced again and Nadine felt panic tighten her stomach. "That was another pain!" Nadine said. "And it's only been a minute or so."

"Yes, it was," Abbi said, panic evident in her own voice. "Hurry . . . get help. Hurry back. I need you."

Nadine rushed into the hall and down the stairs. She found a maid who literally ran to get Mrs. Norberg and an officer near the main door who went to get Dr. Furhelm. On her way back up the stairs, Nadine forced herself to calm down and be composed. Abbi needed somebody to assuage her concerns, not add to them.

She took a deep breath and entered the duchess's room to find her squirming and gripping the bedspread with clenched fists.

"Oh," Abbi cried, "it didn't come on this quickly before."

"It will be all right," Nadine said, sitting on the edge of the bed. She held Abbi's hand and smoothed her hair back off her face. "I'll stay with you every minute if that's what you want."

"Oh, yes. I need you." She endured another pain then asked, "Is Cameron . . ."

"They're not back yet," she said.

"I need Cameron," Abbi cried. "Last time he was gone when it started, but he got back in time."

"Then we'll pray that he gets back in time," Nadine said. She knew from Abbi telling her the story that Cameron had been present during the birth of their first child. Even though it wasn't customary for the father to be in the room during childbirth, she had long ago stopped expecting Cameron and Abbi to be typical people.

Abbi grimaced through more pain then said breathlessly, "I nearly died last time, Nadine."

"It will be all right," Nadine said again, praying with all her heart that it would be.

Through the blinding snow, Lance and Georg both saw something unusual coming toward them. It took several seconds for them to realize it was a rider approaching from the other direction. If nothing else, Lance thought they could ask if this person had passed anything unusual, but the rider bolted past at a dangerous speed for such conditions. Lance saw Georg halt abruptly and turn to look as the cloaked figure disappeared into the snow, but a moment later the rider came back, slowing down as he approached them. Georg pushed back the hood of his cloak, as if it might allow him to get a better look at the man, then a woman's voice cried out, "Georg! It's you."

The woman pushed back the hood of her cloak as she dismounted and ran toward him.

Not a man at all.

"Elsa!" Georg muttered and slid from his mount, pulling her into his arms with enormous zeal. "Oh, Elsa," he murmured, kissing her face, her lips, her face again, while Lance and Cameron exchanged a smile. Then it occurred to Lance that something wasn't right. Elsa hadn't been traveling alone. "How I missed you! I've been so worried. Are you—"

"I was coming for help," she said, apparently brought back to her purpose now that she'd properly greeted her husband.

"And we were coming to find you," Georg said.

"Good. That will save us time," Elsa said. "The carriage overturned; it slid off the road." She became upset but managed to state the problem clearly. "The driver is unconscious, and I think the lieutenant has a broken leg. We had to shoot one of the horses, and—"

Lance interrupted her to ask, "Do you think the carriage is functional, or do we need to send back for another?"

"I think it's all right, if we can get it upright. From what I could see, the wheels appear to be intact."

"Let's go and see what we've got to work with," Lance said, not wanting to waste any more time or daylight. Elsa mounted and led them for another ten minutes before the carriage appeared at the edge of the road, lying on its side. Horses were tethered in the trees on the opposite side of the road. The one that had been shot was covered with snow. Opening the carriage door that was now facing upward, they found Elsa's friend Gertie, Lieutenant Joerger with his leg splinted, and the driver who was gaining consciousness. They were cold but shielded from the snow. The two officers carefully helped them out, and within minutes the men were able to get the carriage back on its wheels and it was declared fully functional. The three remaining horses were found to be uninjured and another was added to the harness by the officer who would drive the carriage home. The injured men were helped back into the carriage with Gertie, who would look after them through the journey. Elsa chose to ride with Georg, and Lance noted that Georg kept his arm tightly around her as they set out.

The snow worsened somewhat and they had to move slowly. It was nearly dark before the castle finally came into view, lit up for the Christmas festivities. Like a guiding star it loomed before them, beckoning them home through the storm.

Chapter Thirty-Five

DELIVERANCE

Abbi's labor progressed quickly, while Nadine held tightly to her hand and continually offered reassurance. Memories of her own experience giving birth came back to her, and she couldn't decide if it was harder to be in labor or to helplessly watch someone you cared for enduring so much pain.

Mrs. Norberg was calm and seemed to know what she was doing, but when she declared that this baby was coming soon and the doctor had not yet arrived, Abbi panicked. Mrs. Norberg gently assured Abbi that all was well with her and the baby, and she could safely deliver it. Then the doctor could make certain all was well when he arrived. Abbi seemed reassured, and her focus turned to the absence of her husband. "I need Cameron," she muttered over and over.

Dr. Furhelm was ushered into the room and Mrs. Norberg said, "Good, you're here. I'm certain she'll be more comfortable with your expertise."

While he was thoroughly washing his hands, he said, "After what happened last time, I'm certain she has cause to be nervous."

"Of course she does," Mrs. Norberg said with perfect compassion.

"All will be well, Your Grace," the doctor said close to Abbi's face while he dried his hands on a clean towel. "Forgive me for being so slow to come; that storm is getting dreadful."

Abbi nodded and said, "I need Cameron."

"I understand he's not returned. Right now we'll concentrate on getting this baby here. I'm certain your husband will be with you soon enough."

Nadine felt a little more relaxed with the doctor present. His confident manner helped, but minutes after his arrival Abbi reached that point of labor where the pain would not relent and Nadine felt helpless in spite of her every effort to encourage her and keep her calm. She prayed that this would be over soon whether Cameron arrived for the birth or not. And she refused to even wonder if the men were all right in the face of this dreadful weather. They just had to be.

The moment Lance rode through the castle gate with Cameron at his side and the carriage coming behind, an officer ran toward them, shouting, "Is that you, Your Grace?"

"It is, yes," Cameron called.

"You must hurry inside, sir. It's Her Grace . . . the baby . . . the doctor is with her."

Cameron dismounted and bolted toward the castle door. Lance exchanged a concerned glance with Georg even though they could barely see each other's faces. "I'll see to this," he said to Georg, who nodded and thanked him before he quickly ushered Elsa inside. Elsa had been with Abbi when Erich was born; surely Abbi would be more at ease with her there.

"Give me two or three good, strong pushes, and this baby will be here," the doctor said. Abbi groaned and he added, "Everything is all right. It will be over soon."

Abbi bore down and groaned, digging her fingernails into Nadine's arms. Abbi screamed as the pain consumed her, and in the midst of it, the door flew open and Cameron rushed into the room, tossing his cloak and gloves onto a chair. Nadine was so relieved, she couldn't hold back tears as she watched Cameron fall to his knees beside the bed, taking Abbi's hand into his.

"I'm here," he muttered, pressing her hand to his lips.

"Oh," Abbi cried, touching his face. "You're here. You're so cold. Oh . . ." Her relief trailed into evidence of more pain, but Nadine eased back as Cameron wrapped Abbi in his arms and she held to him tightly while she bore down.

The door came open again and a woman Nadine had never seen before entered. Her red face and damp hair made it evident she'd been out in the storm. "Abbi, my darling," she said, easing close to her.

"Elsa!" Abbi exclaimed just before the pain overtook her again. Nadine couldn't help feeling a little displaced. She had done Elsa's job in her absence, and she had sat with Abbi through this labor because everyone else had been gone. But now they were here, and she was simply observing from what suddenly felt like a great distance.

Lance hated the tension that filled his every nerve. How could he not recall the difficulties Abbi had endured the last time she'd done this? He felt sure Cameron and Georg's thoughts were in the same vein. He quickly gave orders to see that the injured men would be cared for and the carriage unloaded. He was told that Mrs. Dukerk was with the duchess, and the moment he knew everything was under control, he hurried inside and up to the ducal bedroom. He found Georg alone, pacing the hall. And then he heard Abbi scream and the two men exchanged a horrified glance.

At Abbi's scream, Nadine felt Cameron's eyes move briefly toward her with some kind of silent pleading. She had no idea what he wanted of her. All she could do was helplessly stand by and pray that it would be over soon.

"It's coming," the doctor said. "One more push. Just one more."

Abbi responded to the hope that this would soon be over and groaned with her final effort. Nadine held her breath as she saw the baby slide into the doctor's hands. The doctor chuckled while he worked quickly to tie off the cord. "Curly, red hair," he said just before the baby's cry broke the air. "It's a girl," he added. "She's tiny, but she looks perfect."

Abbi wept in Cameron's arms. Nadine stood back and watched in awe as this tiny little princess was wrapped in a little blanket and given to Abbi. Tears showed in Cameron's eyes as he pressed a kiss into Abbi's hair and watched her with the baby.

"What will you call her?" Mrs. Norberg asked, standing close to the doctor.

"MagdaLena," Abbi said tenderly.

"MagdaLena Amelia LeeAnna du Woernig," Cameron said.

"But we shall call her Maggie," Abbi added and Nadine slipped quietly into the hall, grateful to have been a part of such an experience at all and to have had these weeks with the privilege of being close to the duchess. Now Elsa had come back and Nadine was grateful to be leaving on her honeymoon. She had her own life to focus on.

Closing the door behind her, she was startled to look up and find Lance and Georg standing there, both staring at her expectantly. Their nerves were evident and she knew they both cared deeply for Abbi.

"It's a girl," she said. "She's tiny, but everything's all right."

Lance and Georg both slumped with visible relief before Lance took Nadine into his arms and held her tightly. He took her shoulders into his hands and looked into her eyes. "And how are you?"

Nadine couldn't answer any more than she could hold back the tears.

"Come along," Lance said. "Let's get Dulsie and go home. It's Christmas Eve, and I think that dinner with the du Woernigs will be postponed. Right now, I just want to be with *my* family."

Nadine laughed softly and walked within his grasp, overwhelmed by the miracle of life she had just witnessed and the mixture of emotions churning inside of her. But with Lance at her side, she knew that all would be well. It was Christmas, the people they cared about were safe, and they were together. Nothing could be better than that.

Dulsie bubbled with excitement as she helped decorate the Christmas tree that Lance had ordered to be delivered along with some fine decorations he'd ordered from a shop in town. "I've never had a tree in my home since I've been on my own," he said, "but that's going to change now."

As excited as Dulsie was about Christmas, it was very late before she finally went to sleep. Only then were Lance and Nadine able to share their feelings of the day's events. Lying close together in bed, they talked about the appearance of Wilhelmina Schmidt, which led to Nadine talking about the idea Abbi had put into her head that she could perhaps help women that Lance came in contact with. Lance was not only pleased with the idea, he was eager for her to follow through and offered his full support.

They talked about his adventure in helping Elsa and those traveling with her to return home safely, and she spoke with emotion of how difficult it had been to be with Abbi through her labor. But the miracle of birth had touched her deeply. Lance told her how he'd been with Abbi when she'd gone into labor with Erich and it had taken some time for Cameron to appear. He had deep empathy for the frustration of seeing a loved one suffer that way.

Nadine admitted that having Elsa return felt a bit disorienting, knowing that she would no longer be working with Abbi. "Not literally," Lance said, "but the two of you are friends now, and you are going to love Elsa as you love Abbi, once you get to know her. And the other way around." He pressed a kiss to her brow and looked into her eyes. "You are an amazing woman, Nadine Dukerk, and all who know you will be blessed by your presence."

"I don't know about that," she said, "but as long as I am blessed by your presence, I will be happy."

He kissed her then chuckled. "What's funny?" she asked.

"I just realized something that makes me deliriously happy. We're having a pillow chat."

"So we are," she said. "But why does—"

"Abbi told me once how she and Cameron would lay in bed at the end of the day and talk; she called it a pillow chat. And I longed for someone to share such a delightful ritual with. And now we're having a pillow chat."

"We shall have to make a habit of it," Nadine said and kissed him, feeling deliriously happy herself.

Far past midnight, they finally slept, and Dulsie woke them early, excited to open her gifts. Nadine's happiness deepened observing her daughter. She'd never seen Dulsie so content and full of life. Nadine declared more than once that Lance had spoiled her terribly with all the gifts he'd gotten for her, but she couldn't deny how good it felt to see her little daughter spoiled after all she had been through in her young life. When Dulsie had opened her gifts and was preoccupied putting her new dolly into its blue velvet dress, Lance and Nadine exchanged their gifts for each other, and Nadine felt every bit as spoiled as her daughter. He clearly enjoyed the gifts she had given him as well. He especially liked the leather-bound journal, and he promised to start using it regularly, as he knew that both Cameron and Abbi kept journals. The last gift she gave him was a little tin box. He looked confused as he pulled away the paper to reveal it, then more confused when he opened it to see nothing but a small amount of ashes.

"I don't understand," he said with a little laugh.

She smiled serenely as she said, "I am giving you the gift of putting the past behind us, completely and forever. The box holds all that remains of my mock marriage certificate." Her smile broadened. "I have a new, valid one to replace it. I think I'll have that one framed."

"What an excellent idea," he said and laughed as he kissed her. "Thank you," he said, then he hurried up the stairs.

"Where are you going?" she asked, following behind him.

He went directly to the sitting room and opened the window that faced toward the mountains, and he tossed the ashes into the continuing snowfall, laughing again. "There," he said, then he set the open box on the mantle. "To remind us of how far we have come," he added and kissed her again.

They returned together to the parlor where Dulsie was still playing. A few minutes later, a knock came at the door and Lance rose to open it. He was surprised to see Cameron, brushing the snow out of his dark hair. "Still snowing," he said. "It'll take us a week to dig out if this keeps up."

"Come in," Lance said, opening the door wider.

"I'm sorry to disturb you, but—"

"You're not disturbing us," he said. "How are the mother and baby this morning?"

"Doing well, I'm glad to say," Cameron said. "Maggie has a healthy set of lungs," he chuckled, "and Abbi is feeling well beyond being sore and tired."

"I'm glad to hear it," Lance said. "Come in. Sit down."

Cameron hung his cloak on a rack near the door before they entered the parlor to find Nadine helping Dulsie gather her new things to take them up to her room. "Good morning, Cameron," Nadine said and quickly kissed his cheek. "Merry Christmas."

"It is, actually," he said.

"Amen," Lance muttered.

"I'll be right back," she said, following Dulsie out of the room. "Make yourself at home."

Lance and Cameron sat down on opposite ends of one of the sofas. "I'm supposed to tell you," Cameron said, "that last night's dinner and . . . whatever else we do . . . will be this evening, and it will all take place in my bedroom for Abbi's benefit."

"Sounds delightful," Lance chuckled. "Good thing you have a big bedroom."

"Yes, it is," Cameron said.

"So, to what do I owe this pleasure? Did you just need some fresh air, or was no one else available to deliver the message? Not that I'm complaining," he added lightly.

"Actually, I wanted to show you something," he said, "and I thought this would be an appropriate day."

"Very well," Lance said, leaning his forearms onto his thighs. Cameron scooted a little bit closer and pulled a small black box from a pocket inside his jacket. He opened it to reveal a ring very much like the one he wore on his little finger, gold with a red lion. "It's like the one you wear," he commented.

"Yes, it is," Cameron said, "which my parents had made for me when I came of age. *This* one," he pointed to the one in the box, "was actually worn by our father." Lance tossed him a startled glance and Cameron added, "You still seem disconcerted over that."

"What?" Lance feigned innocence.

"The fact that he is your father as much as he is mine."

"No, Cameron. He was married to *your* mother. There is no equality in the comparison whatsoever."

"Would you prefer to have the name du Woernig? It has brought more grief than joy into my life, I can assure you."

"No, I do not wish to be a du Woernig. Never have I coveted your name, your wealth, your position—never. What I wish is to be what I had always believed myself to be: a Dukerk."

"And you are," Cameron said. "It's my opinion that a man is what he is raised to be, far more than what he is born to be."

"Except in cases of royalty and bastards, who have no choice but to be what they were born to be."

"I did not come here to upset you, Lance," Cameron said gently. "My hope is that you will find peace in being both what you were born to be and what you were raised to be. But most of all to understand that you are what you have made of your life. And the man you are makes me proud to call you brother. I did not feel that way about Nikolaus. But I want you to know that in spite of the difficulty of this discovery—especially for you—I have found a deep peace and gratitude in sharing this bond with you. I would only hope that you might eventually feel the same way."

Lance wanted to say that it was entirely different for Cameron. There was no scandal or shame related to his birth. But he said nothing. He couldn't deny his gratitude for Cameron's acceptance. To fill the silence he finally said, "Your attitude about this is appreciated, Cameron . . . truly. It's just difficult for me to accept."

"Some things simply take time," Cameron said. "And perhaps one day you will gain some new level of understanding that will bring it together for you." He set the little box in Lance's hand. "I want you to have this. Merry Christmas."

"What?" Lance was stunned. "You can't give this to me!"

"I can! I just did."

"It belonged to your father, and—"

"*Our* father, Lance. I want you to wear this." He took it out of the box and slid it onto the little finger of Lance's right hand, just as Cameron wore his. "It even fits. You won't have to get it sized."

Lance looked at the ring on his finger, too stunned to speak. He knew the symbolism of this ring. And he knew that the people of Horstberg were well aware of that symbolism. No man outside of the royal family would dare wear the symbol of the red lion. It would simply be considered inappropriate. For Cameron to ask him to wear it was far too bold a move to be considered a passive gesture. Wondering over his motives, Lance said, "People will notice if I wear this. And they'll gossip. What are you trying to do? Shout from the rooftops that we are brothers?"

Cameron shrugged his shoulders. "If I had died and you had become the duke regent, you would have worn the symbol."

"But you didn't die."

"People know of our friendship. Let them speculate on the gift as a designated brotherhood."

"And they know of your friendship with Georg. Would they believe that in terms of friendship Georg is any less your confidant, your colleague, than I? No, I don't think so. The closeness you share with Georg is beyond compare, Cameron. If I wear this ring, the implication will be very clear. You're asking me to publicly declare that I am a bastard."

Cameron leaned a little closer and spoke in a firm, quiet voice. "Try, for just a moment, Lance, to think of this as a bond between you and me, a symbol of something that the sharing of blood only strengthens. Think of this as a declaration to yourself, and to anyone who would care to notice, that you are who you are and that what anyone might think or speculate is simply irrelevant. You are my brother, Lance, and I find no shame in that. Whatever wrong was committed, whatever shame there may have been, it belongs to a generation now dead and gone."

Again Lance felt as if Cameron could never understand. The situation from his perspective was completely different. Almost feeling angry, he hurried to say, "Thank you for the ring, Cameron. It's a beautiful gift, and I appreciate the sentiment. I need to give some thought as to whether or not I can wear it. I can only ask you to understand."

"Of course," Cameron said. "I do understand. I'll leave you to enjoy your holiday, and we'll see you this evening."

They both stood at the same time, and Cameron put an arm around Lance, giving him a firm, brotherly embrace. "Merry Christmas," Cameron said.

"And to you," Lance said. "Thank you again."

After Cameron left, Lance sank onto the sofa again with a deep sigh. He opened the little box and put the ring back into its velvet lining. "Is something wrong?" Nadine asked, startling him.

"Cameron gave me a gift," he said, holding the box out toward her. While she was gazing at the ring he added, "He thinks I should wear it."

"And what do you think?" she asked, her tone careful.

Lance blew out a long, slow breath. "I don't know what to think." He took the box and rose to set it on the mantle. "I know that we're supposed to have lunch with my stepmother, and we'd better hurry. Even in the sleigh it will take longer than usual to get there with the snow."

"I'll be ready in a few minutes," she said, "but don't think you're going to get out of talking about this, Captain." She kissed him to stop any protest and hurried from the room.

Dulsie did most of the talking through the trip to Ramona's house, and Lance was grateful. His conversation with Cameron weighed heavily on him, and he wasn't certain why. Why did the issue trouble him so deeply? He'd gotten past the shock of the revelation, but still he felt so uneasy about it. He wondered if it would ever be possible to feel completely comfortable with himself again. Arriving at his stepmother's house, he was grateful for the distraction of Christmas celebrations with her and her sister, Salina. They shared a wonderful meal and exchanged gifts, while the ladies made a ridiculous fuss over Dulsie, spoiling her even further. Ramona and Salina took Dulsie upstairs to show her something, giving Lance and Nadine a moment alone.

"You know," Nadine said, "it just occurred to me that perhaps Ramona might know something about the very thing that's troubling you." Lance wanted to pretend that nothing was troubling him, but he was well aware that Nadine knew him better than that. "She's your stepmother, Lance; surely she must know something. Surely her husband confided in her."

Lance was so startled by the possibility that he felt breathless and had to sit down. His relationship with Ramona had never been deep or terribly tender, but it was secure and stable. To think that she might be aware of this situation that caused him such grief was unsettling. But he couldn't help being intrigued with Nadine's idea. Maybe Ramona did know something. But he had to say, "And if she doesn't know about it, I certainly don't want to tell her. I'd prefer that she not see me any differently than she always has."

"Surely there's a way to bring it up without saying anything you don't want said, and at least you could get an idea of whether or not she knows. If you . . ."

Ramona entered the room and interrupted their conversation. Nadine tossed him a glance that seemed to say, "Now's your chance."

"They're having a wonderful time looking at Salina's doll

collection. Yes, they're having a wonderful time. I dare say they'll be a while. But that will give us a chance to chat, since they'll probably be a while."

Lance and Nadine exchanged a subtle smile. Ramona was known for repeating herself, and everyone was well aware of it but her. They chatted for a few minutes about trivial matters. A brief lull prompted Lance's heart to pound. His instincts told him he should ask her, and he could only pray that the conversation didn't end up being a disaster.

"Ramona," he said, "may I ask you something . . . about my father?"

"Of course," she said eagerly.

He struggled for the right words then hurried to say them before he changed his mind. "Were you aware of the . . . unusual circumstances of . . . my birth?"

She looked surprised, and perhaps concerned. "Yes, I'm aware," she said, "but I had no idea that you were. I had no idea."

Lance sighed and took that in. Now he could only hope they were talking about the same thing, and that there weren't *more* unusual circumstances that he wasn't aware of.

"Well, I didn't have any idea until not so many weeks ago," he said. "I received a letter that was delivered through the duke's solicitor." He watched her eyes closely. "It was from Ferdinand du Woernig."

"Oh, I see," she said and he had no doubt that she was well aware of the connection. "Come to think of it, you did turn thirty last fall, didn't you. I'd forgotten the significance of that."

Lance exchanged an apprehensive glance with Nadine before he focused more fully on Ramona. "If there is anything you know that could help me shed some light on this," he said, "I would be most grateful to hear it. It's been difficult to learn something about myself that was contrary to what I'd been raised to believe."

"I imagine it would be," Ramona said. "Yes, I would imagine."

"If you knew then . . . surely you must know more than I do."

Ramona stood and moved to sit right next to Lance on the sofa, taking his hand into hers. "Oh, my dear boy," she said gently. "I knew this day would come eventually, and you would have to know the truth about who your father really was, and I have prayed that the truth would not upset you too badly. Yes, I have prayed a great deal. Your father—my husband—I'm going to call him your father because in every respect but one, he *was* your father. He loved you dearly, my boy. You were the delight of his life. Oh, he wasn't one for showing his emotions, but he spoke openly to me. He didn't seem to care one bit that you were not his blood. At first, when he found out your mother was pregnant, he was deeply hurt. Of course, I only met him years after your mother had passed on, but he did tell me the whole story. Yes, he told me the whole story—more than once."

Ramona cleared her throat gently and went on. "You see, Ferdinand and your father agreed that it would be best for you to only be made aware of the truth once you were well established as an adult."

"Wait a minute," Lance said, putting up a hand. "They *agreed?*"

"Well, yes," she said as if such a thing should be expected. "They were friends, Lance. As I said, your father was deeply hurt when he learned of Katarina's affair with Ferdinand. Apparently it had been going on for quite some time, but it was only when she got pregnant that your father found out about it. Yes, he was deeply hurt."

Lance willed himself to ask a question that he'd wondered over many times. "How could they be absolutely certain that the baby was Ferdinand's?"

Ramona was matter-of-fact as she stated, "Because there had been no intimacy, whatsoever, in the marriage for years." Lance was stunned speechless, and grateful when she went on to say, "We're all adults and I'm not going to be embarrassed about discussing such things with you. I think you need to know the truth, my boy. Yes, I think you need to know. Your father was a good man, Lance. During the four years I was married to him before his death, he was kind and good to me, and we dearly enjoyed each other's companionship. But he was not a passionate man—quite the opposite in truth. In fact, he had somewhat of an aversion to marital intimacy, and he readily admitted it. He spoke to me about the problem before we were ever married. He told me that I should be aware and fairly warned. He admitted that he had a problem, although he didn't understand its source. But he felt certain it had been the reason he'd lost Katarina. She loved your father, and he loved her. But she was young and passionate and she simply was not content with the lack of affection and intimacy in their marriage. The one and only time they had shared a bed was their wedding night, when Gwendolyn was conceived. And it never happened again. No, it never happened again."

"That's astonishing," Lance said. "I had no idea."

"No, of course you wouldn't. In every other respect, he was a good husband and father. When Katarina told him of her pregnancy, he was deeply hurt but not entirely surprised. He took some accountability in the situation. Her loneliness did not make adultery right, but it certainly made the affair understandable. And she admitted that. I know that Katarina blamed herself for Gwen's promiscuousness, believing she had been a bad example. But your father felt certain Gwen didn't know about the affair and that her choices had been her own. She was simply one of those people who came into this world determined to be difficult. But Ferdinand loved her as well, simply because she was Katarina's daughter. I suppose that might have something to do with his arranging her marriage to Cameron. And as I said, Ferdinand and your father were friends; they'd worked together for years. Ferdinand was arrogant and he knew his place as the ruler of this country, but he shared a mutual respect with your father and had certain regrets regarding the affair. As I understand it, he'd had at least one mistress before Katarina, and another one after she died. But he treated them well and took responsibility for his actions, which is a far cry above the behavior of his son, Nikolaus. But then, I don't have to tell you about that."

"No, you don't," Lance said, glancing toward Nadine, who gave him a wan smile.

Ramona talked on about the admirable traits of her husband, and how he had revered Katarina in spite of the challenges between them. Lance enjoyed listening to her talk without being required to comment very often, which allowed the perspective he was hearing to settle deeply into him. And he felt better. It was as Ramona had said—his mother's loneliness did not make the wrong suddenly right, but it did help him understand. His perception of his mother now rang true with his memories of her from his early childhood. He felt suddenly lighter, as if he could breathe more easily than he'd been able to since the news of his birth had turned his world upside down. He felt as if he'd been delivered from some ugly monster that had distorted his entire perception of himself and his life. He felt free.

On the way home, Dulsie quickly fell asleep with her head in Lance's lap. Nadine commented, "You feel better, don't you."

"I do," he said. "I don't know why it makes a difference, but it does."

"Well, I'm glad." She smiled. "However, I want you to consider that even if your mother had simply been promiscuous and irresponsible, that would not make you a bad person. Dulsie is a shining example of that. She's kind and good in spite of what her father may have been."

Lance sighed and brushed Dulsie's hair back from her face. He looked at Nadine intently and said, "*I am Dulsie's father*—in every respect but one. And that one just doesn't matter."

"No, it doesn't matter," Nadine smiled. "Except that . . . you actually share her blood. And when it comes right down to it, that's a nice thought. Just as you share Cameron's blood; you are brothers in every sense."

"Yes," Lance said, "that's a nice thought." He chuckled and added, "I'm beginning to sound like Ramona."

Chapter Thirty-Six

EVERYDAY LIFE IN HORSTBERG

Later that evening, after sharing a fine meal with the people that Lance cared for most in this world, they all sat casually around the ducal bedroom, chatting and laughing while Abbi leaned against the headboard, holding her infant daughter against her shoulder. Once she'd gotten a good burp out of the baby, which provoked deep laughter throughout the room, Elsa rose to take her, fussing over her red curly hair and making silly noises. After holding her for a few minutes, she set her into Nadine's arms, saying, "You'll have your own before long. And I do hope you'll let me help with your children, as well. I do so love babies."

Nadine exchanged a smile with Elsa, already liking her immensely. Her concerns of feeling displaced now that Elsa had returned were quickly vanishing.

While Nadine cuddled the baby, Lance put his arm around her shoulders and they exchanged a smile. The prospect of having his children filled her with more joy and peace than she'd ever thought possible.

Lance pressed his free hand gently over the baby's wispy hair, and Elsa commented, "Oh, what a beautiful ring. I've never noticed it before." Cameron turned abruptly to meet Lance's eyes just as she added, "It's like Cameron's."

"Yes," Cameron said, "his father gave it to him. We recently discovered that our fathers were very close."

"Very close indeed," Lance said.

"So," Elsa sat back down beside her husband, "Lance got married while I was gone, and I missed it. We've been so busy with the baby that I haven't heard any of the news. Did anything else exciting happen while I was away? Or was it just the usual everyday life in Horstberg?"

Following a long moment of silence, everyone in the room burst into unified laughter, while Elsa looked pleasantly baffled. Lance couldn't help thinking how grateful he felt to be able to laugh about all that had happened since Elsa's departure. They truly had come far in not so many weeks.

"I'll tell you about it later, Elsa," Georg said with a chuckle. "In fact, I'll tell you tomorrow. It could take all day."

Cameron leaned back in his chair and put his hands behind his head. "I'm looking forward to a nice long stretch of everyday life in Horstberg."

"Amen," Lance said and smiled at Nadine.

Eleven Months Later

Lance came into the door of the apartment and flung his cloak on the rack near the door while he brushed the snow out of his hair. The smell of coffee lured him to the kitchen where he found Mina just pulling some hot cinnamon buns out of the oven.

"Good morning, Captain," she said. "An early meeting today?"

"Yes, and I'm glad it's over." He made a pleasurable noise as he inhaled the aroma rising from the baking sheet. "Have I ever told you that you're not only the best housekeeper in Horstberg, but you are by far the best cook?"

"Quite often, Captain," she said with a little laugh.

"Well, I wouldn't want you to feel unappreciated."

"That shouldn't be a problem," she said. "Give me a minute and I'll dish you up some to have with your coffee."

"Has Nadine eaten?" he asked.

"Mrs. Dukerk is just getting out of the bath and hasn't eaten yet. Little Dulsie walked with her friend across the way to school, and I'm happy to say she actually left on time this morning and did much better with not dawdling over her breakfast."

"Very good," he said with a chuckle. "You're a good influence."

Dulsie was doing well in school, which she attended with the other children in the castle. The teachers were some of the best, and Dulsie had many friends there and was happy.

"I'll eat with Nadine whenever she's ready," he added. Mina just smiled and Lance hurried from the room and up the stairs. He couldn't help pondering what a blessing Mina had been to their family through the months she'd been working for them. Nadine's pregnancy had started out with a great deal of illness, and even though she was feeling much better, Lance liked having someone here to look after her and to see to the busy work, allowing Nadine to do whatever she wished with her time.

Lance entered the bedroom just as Nadine was buttoning a dress over the front of her well-rounded belly. "Good morning, my love," he said, pressing a hand over where their baby grew while he pressed his lips over hers.

"Good morning," she said with a smile that warmed him through. "It's snowing," she said, touching his damp hair. "I can tell even though I haven't opened the drapes yet. How was your meeting?"

"Business as usual."

"That's good then," she said. "A lack of drama is a good thing."

"Yes, it is," he eagerly agreed. "However, we had a female prisoner brought in late last night. Her crimes are minimal, but she'll be there a while. Do you want to go see her, or should I have Mina see to it?"

"I can do it," she said. "I'll be going out anyway."

"Where are you going?" he asked, sounding slightly panicked. "Doctor Furhelm said the baby could come any day. I don't think you should be out and about when—"

"I'm going to my meeting," she interrupted gently. "Abbi and Elsa are going with me, and half the women there know how to deliver babies. I'll not stay long, and I'll be just fine."

"Let me know when you get back so I can stop worrying about you."

"I'll do that," she said and kissed him again.

They shared breakfast and walked together across the courtyard where Lance went to his office to continue his work and Nadine approached the officer on duty in charge of the prisoners.

"I understand a woman was brought in last night," she said. "I have some things for her."

"She's a prostitute and a thief," the lieutenant stated, as if that made it difficult for him to understand why Nadine would want to see her at all.

"I don't care what she's done, she's still a woman. God created women differently and they have different needs, and I'm going to see that she survives this place with those needs met."

"You're a good woman, Mrs. Dukerk."

"Now you're flattering me, Lieutenant," she teased. "Hoping to get me to bribe Mina to bring some of her baked goods this way, I'd wager."

The lieutenant chuckled. "No one can bake like your Mina," he said and turned the key in the lock for her.

Nadine entered the cell to see a woman in her early twenties with an angry countenance and fire in her eyes. Nadine had come to know the type well. The woman had been in trouble so many times through her life that she'd passed beyond being afraid—she just didn't want to be here.

"Good morning," Nadine said as the door was closed and locked behind her. "I'm Mrs. Dukerk, but you may call me Nadine. I've brought you a few things that might make your stay here a little more comfortable and meet your feminine needs." She set a basket on the table. "I think it's all rather self-explanatory, so I'll just leave it and let you look it over later. There are a couple of books to read. Do you read?" The woman gave a scoffing laugh and Nadine hurried to add, "If you'd like I can arrange for a woman to come in every day and read with you, and she can even teach you to read and write if you would like."

The woman looked suspicious and disbelieving, which Nadine had expected. After looking Nadine up and down thoroughly, she asked, "Why are you doing this?"

"I spent some time in here myself once," Nadine said.

"You?" she said as if she didn't believe it. "Such a lady? In here?"

"Yes," Nadine said, "and I've come to believe that for whatever reason a woman ends up in a place like this, she deserves to know that somebody actually cares what happens to her. No woman ever sets out to end up in prison. Whether it's bad luck or the result of bad upbringing, I would like to think that every woman has the right to choose whether or not she'll ever end up back here again. Change is always possible when someone can believe in you and give you a chance. I'm here to give you a chance . . . if you're interested."

The woman said nothing, but her eyes clearly indicated her interest, so Nadine kept talking. She told this woman about the organization she had founded with the backing of the duchess to help displaced women get back on their feet. "We meet once a week to assess the needs of our members and other women in our social circles. We simply share experiences on how we have conquered our struggles, and once we have risen above them, we do what we can to help those who are still struggling. When a woman's needs are met and she can work to provide for herself respectably, great things can happen." She paused and added, "Now, would you like someone to come in and read with you every day or not? I can arrange it if you're interested."

"I'm interested," the woman said. "I always wanted to read. Would she really teach me to read?"

"She really would," Nadine said.

"So, who pays for this stuff?" She nodded toward the basket. "And who pays to help women start over that way?"

Nadine smiled. The question came up often and she was eager to answer it. "The women who serve volunteer their time; some make donations. Most of the funding comes from an inheritance my husband received from his late father. Now, if you need something or feel like there's a problem while you're serving your time, you can leave a message with one of the officers and they will be sure I get it. My husband greatly frowns on his men neglecting to give me my messages."

"Your husband?"

"The Captain of the Guard," she said and the woman nodded.

Nadine talked with the woman for a while longer before her time was up and the door was unlocked for her to leave. "Thank you," the woman said before the door was closed again.

"I'm glad to help," Nadine said and left the keep.

At the meeting, she repeated the situation of their new prisoner, who had been violated at an early age and had felt so poorly about herself that she'd turned to a life of crime and prostitution. It was a story they'd heard before, and there was a great deal of compassion as ways were discussed on how she could be helped in changing her life. Four different women volunteered to visit her in the prison and help her learn to read.

After a light luncheon was served, Nadine rode home in the carriage with Abbi and Elsa. The three of them talked and laughed in a typical way, and the moment they returned, Nadine went to Lance's office. She entered the open door and said, "You can stop worrying about me now."

He smiled and tossed his pen on the desktop. "I wasn't really worried," he said. "Not much, anyway. I just wanted an excuse to see you." He sighed ridiculously loud. "What did I ever do to deserve having such a beautiful wife? And so capable, too. People are talking about you, you know. They say you're doing marvelous things with my father's money."

Nadine smirked. "And are they talking about who your father was?"

"I don't know. I don't care. I just listen to what they say about *you,* and if you . . ." He stopped when Nadine grimaced and took hold of the edge of the desk. "Are you all right?"

"No, I don't think I am," she said and he rushed around the desk to take hold of her shoulders.

"The baby?" he asked.

"That would be a logical conclusion," she said. "Whether or not that was a labor pain, I couldn't say for sure, but I think I'm going to go home and lie down."

Lance helped her to their apartment and into bed, grateful that they'd made the decision to live here so that his work would rarely take him very far from his family. He stayed with her, feeling far more nervous than he cared to admit. An hour after he'd tucked her into bed, it became clearly evident that she was in labor. Mina sent for the doctor and went personally to find Abbi and Elsa, who were quickly at Nadine's side.

The next few hours were likely the most difficult Lance had ever endured—and he knew he'd endured some pretty tough experiences. Never had he imagined that childbirth entailed such pain. Abbi kept telling him that the labor was moving quickly and Nadine was doing well, but it seemed very slow and horrible to him. He stayed close by her side, doing his best to encourage her and stay calm, while inside he felt tempted to start screaming right along with her. He was in the midst of making a silent oath that he would never put her through this again when the baby emerged into the world and alerted them to its presence with a healthy cry.

"It's a boy," the doctor announced with a chuckle. "He's big and strong."

Lance watched as the baby was laid into Nadine's arms. The tears in her eyes and the joy in his heart made him want to do this again and again—given some time in between. He'd never imagined such perfect bliss.

A few minutes later, Abbi whispered to him, "Why don't you go spread the news while we get her cleaned up and let her rest. The doctor will stay long enough to be sure that all is well."

"Of course," Lance said and quickly kissed her brow. "Thank you, my lady."

Abbi smiled and touched his face. "It is truly a pleasure to see you as a father, my dear friend."

Lance kissed Nadine and murmured close to her face, "Oh, how I love you! You just keep making me happier every day."

"I thought it was the other way around," she said, her voice weak and tired.

"Get some rest," he said, kissing her again. "I'll come back soon."

She nodded and he hurried from the room, going directly to the ducal office where a long advisory meeting was just adjourning. Thankfully he'd not been required at this one, therefore his presence wouldn't have been missed.

"Hello, gentlemen," he said, entering the office once everyone had left except Georg and Cameron. "Would you have any idea where your wives are?"

They looked at each other and back at Lance. "Are they spending money again?" Cameron asked in mock anger.

Lance laughed. "No," he drawled, "they would be fussing over my new son."

Cameron and Georg broke into laughter and came to their feet, each shaking Lance's hand, slapping him on the shoulder, and ultimately embracing him tightly.

"And what will you call him?" Georg asked.

"Oh, that's easy," Lance said. "Jacob Ferdinand Dukerk . . . after my fathers."

Cameron smiled and hugged him again.

That evening Cameron and Georg came to see the new baby; their wives were still with Nadine, taking care of her and the baby with great expertise. While they were all sitting around the bedroom, talking and laughing, Cameron leaned back in his chair and put his hands behind his head. "Life doesn't get any better than this," he said.

"Oh, I don't know," Lance said, "it seems to me that it just keeps getting better and better." He caught Nadine's eye and saw her smile. Oh, how he loved her!

ℰlizabeth D. Michaels began writing at the age of sixteen, immersing herself ever since in the lives created by her vivid imagination. Beyond her devotion to family and friends, writing has been her passion for nearly three decades. While she has more than fifty published novels under the name Anita Stansfield and is the recipient of many awards, she boldly declares *The Horstberg Saga* as the story she was born to write, with many volumes in the works. She is best known for her keen ability to explore the psychological depths of human nature, bringing her characters to life through the timeless struggles they face in the midst of exquisite dramas. For more information, please visit her author page on WhiteStarPress.com.

Made in the USA
San Bernardino, CA
03 December 2014